A TEXT BOOK OF

ENGINEERING PHYSICS

FOR

SEMESTER – I

FIRST YEAR DEGREE COURSES IN ENGINEERING

Strictly According to New Revised Credit System Syllabus
of Savitribai Phule Pune University
(Effective from Academic Year – June 2015)

COMMON FOR ALL DEGREE ENGINEERING BRANCHES

I. A. SHAIKH

M.Sc.
Assistant Professor, Physics Deptt.,,
Bharati Vidyapeeth Deemed University
College of Engineering,
Dhankawadi, Pune.

Dr. H. R. KULKARNI

M.Sc., Ph.D., F.A.Z.I., M.B.S.,
Asso. Prof., & Head, Engg. Science Deptt.
KJEI's Purandar College of Engineering
and Mgt. Research,
Pisoli, Pune.

Dr. U. P. MOHRIL

M.Sc., Ph.D.
Asso. Prof. & Head, Engg. Science Deptt.,
Marathwada Mitramandal's
Institute of Technology,
Lohgaon, Pune 47.

S. F. KHAIRNAR

M. Sc. M.Phil, B.Ec., LMISTE
Dattakala Group's, Faculty of Engg.,
Swami Chincholi (Bhigwan), Pune.
Formerly, Asst. Prof. & Head, Physics Deptt.,
SCOE Vadgaon, (Bk), Pune.

Dr. S. P. JAGTAP

M.Sc., Ph.D., B. Ed. (Maths, Science)
Head, First Year Degree Engineering.
RMD Sinhgad School of Engineering,
Warje, Pune 58.

N2752

ENGINEERING PHYSICS (FE)   **ISBN 978-93-80725-30-7**

Third Edition   :   June 2017
©   :   Authors

Published By :   Polyplate
NIRALI PRAKASHAN
Abhyudaya Pragati, 1312, Shivaji Nagar,
Off J.M. Road, Pune – 411005
Tel - (020) 25512336/37/39, Fax - (020) 25511379
Email : niralipune@pragationline.com

☞ DISTRIBUTION CENTRES

PUNE

Nirali Prakashan : 119, Budhwar Peth, Jogeshwari Mandir Lane, Pune 411002, Maharashtra
Tel : (020) 2445 2044, 66022708, Fax : (020) 2445 1538
Email : bookorder@pragationline.com, niralilocal@pragationline.com

Nirali Prakashan : S. No. 28/27, Dhyari, Near Pari Company, Pune 411041
Tel : (020) 24690204 Fax : (020) 24690316
Email : dhyari@pragationline.com, bookorder@pragationline.com

MUMBAI

Nirali Prakashan : 385, S.V.P. Road, Rasdhara Co-op. Hsg. Society Ltd.,
Girgaum, Mumbai 400004, Maharashtra
Tel : (022) 2385 6339 / 2386 9976, Fax : (022) 2386 9976
Email : niralimumbai@pragationline.com

☞ DISTRIBUTION BRANCHES

JALGAON

Nirali Prakashan : 34, V. V. Golani Market, Navi Peth, Jalgaon 425001,
Maharashtra, Tel : (0257) 222 0395, Mob : 94234 91860

KOLHAPUR

Nirali Prakashan : New Mahadvar Road, Kedar Plaza, 1st Floor Opp. IDBI Bank
Kolhapur 416 012, Maharashtra. Mob : 9850046155

NAGPUR

Pratibha Book Distributors : Above Maratha Mandir, Shop No. 3, First Floor,
Rani Jhanshi Square, Sitabuldi, Nagpur 440012, Maharashtra
Tel : (0712) 254 7129

DELHI

Nirali Prakashan : 4593/21, Basement, Aggarwal Lane 15, Ansari Road, Daryaganj
Near Times of India Building, New Delhi 110002
Mob : 08505972553

BENGALURU

Pragati Book House : House No. 1, Sanjeevappa Lane, Avenue Road Cross,
Opp. Rice Church, Bengaluru – 560002.
Tel : (080) 64513344, 64513355,Mob : 9880582331, 9845021552
Email:bharatsavla@yahoo.com

CHENNAI

Pragati Books : 9/1, Montieth Road, Behind Taas Mahal, Egmore,
Chennai 600008 Tamil Nadu, Tel : (044) 6518 3535,
Mob : 94440 01782 / 98450 21552 / 98805 82331,
Email : bharatsavla@yahoo.com

niralipune@pragationline.com | www.pragationline.com

Also find us on 🇫 www.facebook.com/niralibooks

Dedicated to ...

Our Budding Engineers

(All FE Students)

...Authors

PREFACE TO THE THIRD EDITION

We are glad and excited to announce that the Second Edition of this book received an overwhelming response from the engineering student community, compelling us to release its **Third Edition** within a very short period of time.

This thoroughly revised **Third Edition** has been **updated** with **additional matter**, many solved problems, including **all University Examination Papers** and Numerous Exercises for practice.

Special care has been taken to maintain high degree of accuracy in the theory and numericals throughout the book.

We take this opportunity to express our sincere thanks to Dineshbhai Furia of Nirali Prakashan, a reputed and pioneer in the field of publication. Our special thanks to Jignesh Furia for their effective cooperation and great care in bringing out this revised edition. We also appreciate the efforts of M. P. Munde and the entire staff of Engineering Books Deptt. of Nirali Prakashan namely Mrs. Deepali Lachake (Co-ordinator) and Mrs. Shilpa Kale for bringing this book to the students in a timely manner.

We sincerely hope that this "**Third Edition**" will also be warmly received by all concerned as in the past.

Valuable suggestions from our esteemed readers to improve the book are most welcome and highly appreciated.

Pune   **–Authors**

PREFACE TO THE FIRST EDITION

It gives us great pleasure in publishing this text book on **"Engineering Physics"** for the Students of First Year Degree Courses in Engineering. This book is strictly written According to New Revised Credit System Syllabus of Savitribai Phule Pune University (2015 Pattern).

As per the policy of the University, Engineering Syllabi is revised every five years. Last revision was in the year 2012. New revision is coming little earlier, as university has introduced **Online** system of examination from year 2012.

In New Credit System, there will be two online examinations conducted at the end of first and second month in every semester. The first online (Phase I – 25 Marks) examination will be based on units I and II and the second online (Phase II – 25 Marks) examination will be based on units III and IV. Both the online examinations will be based on Multiple Choice Questions. End Semester Examination (Theory - 50 Marks) will be based on all six units and will be descriptive type and theory course will have 4 credits.

We have given Free Separate book of Multiple Choice Questions (MCQ's) which will be very useful to the students, especially for Online Examinations.

The subject matter is presented in a lucid, fluent and comprehensive manner. All efforts have been taken to present the text matter in Simple & Lucid Language, Illustrative Figures, University Question Papers and Solved Problems with Answers have been added. **Also, University Question Papers (New Pattern) have given (Dec. 12 to Nov. 16) at the end of the Book, and it will help student to understand nature of questions that could be asked in the final examination.**

We take this opportunity to express our sincere thanks to Shri. Dineshbhai Furia, Shri. Jignesh Furia, Mrs. Nirali Verma and Shri. M. P. Munde and entire team of Nirali Prakashan namely Mrs. Deepali Lachake (Co-ordinator) who really have taken keen interest and untiring efforts in publishing this text.

Finally, we express our gratitude to our family members for their continuous support and encouragement, thanks to all.

We have no doubt that like our earlier texts, student's community will respond favourably to this new venture.

The advice and suggestions of our esteemed readers to improve the text are most welcomed, and will be highly appreciated.

July 2016   **Authors**

Pune.

SYLLABUS

Unit – I : Interference : Diffraction and its Engineering Applications   (8 Hrs.)

Interference : Introduction, Concept of thin film, Interference due to thin films of uniform thickness (with derivation), Interference due to wedge shaped thin films (qualitative), fringe width (with derivation), Formation of colours in thin films, Newton's rings, its applications (i) for the determination of wavelength of incident light or radius of curvature of a given plano-convex lens, (ii) for the determination of refractive index of a given liquid. Applications of interference (i) Testing of optical flatness of surfaces, (ii) Thickness of thin film, (ii) Antireflection coating. **Diffraction :** Diffraction of waves, Classes of diffraction, Fraunhofer diffraction at a single slit (Geometrical method), Condition for maxima and minima, Intensity pattern due to a single slit, Diffraction at circular aperture, Plane diffraction grating (Qualitative only), Conditions for maxima and minima, Intensity pattern, Scattering of light as an application of diffraction (Qualitative only).

Unit – II : Sound Engineering   (8 Hrs.)

Definitions : Velocity, Frequency, Wavelength, Intensity, Loudness (expression), Timbre of sound, Reflection of Sound, Echo, Reverberation, Reverberation time, Sabine's formula (Qualitative only), Remedies over reverberation. Absorption of sound, Absorbent materials, Conditions for Good Acoustics of the Building, Noise, its effects and remedies - Production of ultrasonics by piezo-electric and magnetostriction oscillator. Detection of ultrasonics, Engineering Applications of Ultrasonic (Non-destructive testing, Cavitation, Measurement of gauge).

Unit – III : Polarization and Laser   (8 Hrs.)

Polarization : Introduction, Polarization of waves, Polarization of light, Representation of PPL, UPL and Partially polarized light, Production of PPL by (i) Reflection, (ii) Refraction (pile of plates), (iii) Selective absorption (Dichroism), (iv) Double refraction, Law of Malus, Huygen's theory of double refraction, Cases of double refraction of crystal cut with the optic axis lying in the plane of incidence and (i) Parallel to the surface, (ii) Perpendicular to the surface, (iii) Inclined to the surface, Retardation plates, QWP, HWP, Optical activity, Specific rotation (Qualitative only), Optically active materials, LCD (as an example of polarization).
Laser : Absorption, Spontaneous emission, Requirement for lasing action (Stimulated emission, Population inversion, Metastable state, Active medium, Resonant cavity, Pumping), Characteristics of laser : Monochromaticity, Coherence, Directionality, Brightness. Various levels of laser systems with examples (i) Two level laser system - Semiconductor laser, (ii) Three level laser system - Ruby laser, (iii) Four level laser system - He-Ne laser. Applications in Industry (drilling, welding, micromachining etc.), Medicine (as surgical tool), Communication (principle and advantages only), Information technology (Holography - Recording and reconstruction).

Unit – IV : Solid State Physics   (8 Hrs.)

Solid State Physics : Band theory in solids, free electron theory (Qualitative), Electrical conductivity in conductor and semiconductor, Influence of external factors on conductivity (temperature, light and impurity), Fermi energy, Density state (Qualitative), Concept of effective mass, electrons and holes, Fermi-Dirac probability distribution function (effect of temperature on Fermi level with graph), Position of Fermi level in intrinsic semiconductor (with derivation) and extrinsic semiconductor, Dependence of Fermi level on temperature and doping concentration (Qualitative), Diffusion and drift current (Qualitative), Band structure of PN junction diode under (i) Zero bias, (ii) Forward bias, (iii) Reverse bias, Working of transistor (NPN only) on the basis of band diagram, Hall effect (with derivation), Photovoltaic effect. Working of solar cell on the basis of band diagram and its applications.

Unit – V : Wave Mechanics   (8 Hrs.)

Wave Mechanics : Wave particle duality of radiation and matter, De Broglie's concept of matter waves, Expressing De Broglie wavelength in terms of kinetic energy and potential, Concept and derivation of group and phase velocity, group and phase velocity of matter waves, Heisenberg's uncertainty principle, Illustration of it by electron diffraction at a single slit, Why an electron cannot exist in the nucleus, Concept of wave function ψ and probability interpretation of $|\psi|^2$, Schroedinger's time independent and dependent wave equations, Applications of Schroedinger's time independent wave equation (i) Particle in 1-D rigid box (infinite potential well), Comparison of quantum mechanical and classical mechanical predictions, (ii) Particle in 1-D non-rigid box (finite potential well-qualitative, results only), Tunneling effect, Example of tunneling effect in tunnel diode and scanning tunneling microscope.

Unit – VI : Superconductivity and Physics of Nanoparticles   (8 Hrs.)

Superconductivity : Introduction to superconductivity, Properties of superconductors (Zero resistance, Meissner effect, Critical fields, Persistent currents), Isotope effect, BCS theory, Type-I and Type-II superconductors, Applications (superconducting magnets, transmission lines etc.), DC and AC Josephson effect. **Physics of Nanoparticles :** Introduction, Nanoparticles, Properties of nanoparticles : Optical, Electrical (quantum dots, quantum wires), Magnetic, Structural, Mechanical, Brief introduction to different methods of synthesis of nanoparticles such as Physical, Chemical, Biological, Mechanical. Synthesis of colloids, Growth of nanoparticles, Synthesis of metal nanoparticles by colloidal route, Application of nanotechnology - Electronics, Energy, Automobiles, Space and Defense, Medical, Environmental, Textile, Cosmetics.

CONTENTS

UNIT - V : WAVE MECHANICS

✠ ✠ ✠

CHAPTER 1
INTERFERENCE

1.1 INTRODUCTION

- The most common type of radiation which we come across in day to day life is electromagnetic wave or photon (the light quanta). Some of the electromagnetic waves can stimulate retina and some cannot. The part of the electromagnetic wave which can stimulate the retina is called **'light'**.

- The branch of physics which deals with light is called **'optics'**. Further, optics can be broadly classified as (a) **'geometrical optics'**, (b) **'physical or wave optics'** and (c) **'quantum optics'** depending upon the basic behaviour of light assumed for explaining the optical phenomena. In the current course our main focus will be on physical optics, where we assume the wave nature of light.

- From basic optical phenomena such as interference and diffraction, we can conclude that the light has a wave nature. In this unit, we will be studying these two basic properties of light.

- But these properties fail to explain the type of oscillations involved i.e. polarisation. The polarisation of light will be studied in later part of the text.

- The wave theory of light was proposed by Chritian Huygen in 1679 but interference was demonstrated by Thomas Young only in 1802. There are several examples of interference that can be observed in everyday life. Basically, oil is colourless but a film of oil floating on water shows bright colours and also keeps on changing co our Similarly a soap bubble, a compact disc, a thin sheet of mica or cellophane appear coloured. All this is due to interference of light.

- In engineering too, interference has wide applications such as measurement of thickness and stress, testing flatness of a surface, anti-reflecting coating etc.

1.1.1 Interference of Waves

- If two waves of same frequency travel in same direction with a constant phase difference with time, they combine so that their energy is not uniformly distributed in space, but is maximum at certain points and minimum (or zero) at other points. This phenomenon is called **interference**.

- In interference, energy is neither created (at maxima) nor destroyed (at minima) but is redistributed so that there is more energy at certain points (maxima) and less energy at other points (minima). Even after interference the total energy of the system remains constant.

- Thus, interference is the redistribution of energy due to superposition of two or more waves.

Principle of Superposition

'The principle of superposition states that when two or more waves are superposed in space or a medium, the waves travel independently, through each other and the resultant displacement of each position is the algebraic/vector sum of the displacements due to each wave'. Fig. 1.1 shows superposition of two waves.

- In Fig. 1.1 (a), two crests, with amplitude a_1 and a_2, are approaching each other and the point where they meet the resultant amplitude $(a_1 + a_2)$ is more than the individual amplitudes. After this, they pass through each other as though they have not interfered at all. Similarly, in Fig. 1.1 (b), one crest and one trough, with amplitude a_1 and $-a_2$, are approaching each other. At the point where they meet the resultant amplitude $(a_1 - a_2)$ is less than the individual amplitudes.

- The first case is called **'constructive interference'** and the second case is called **'destructive interference'**.

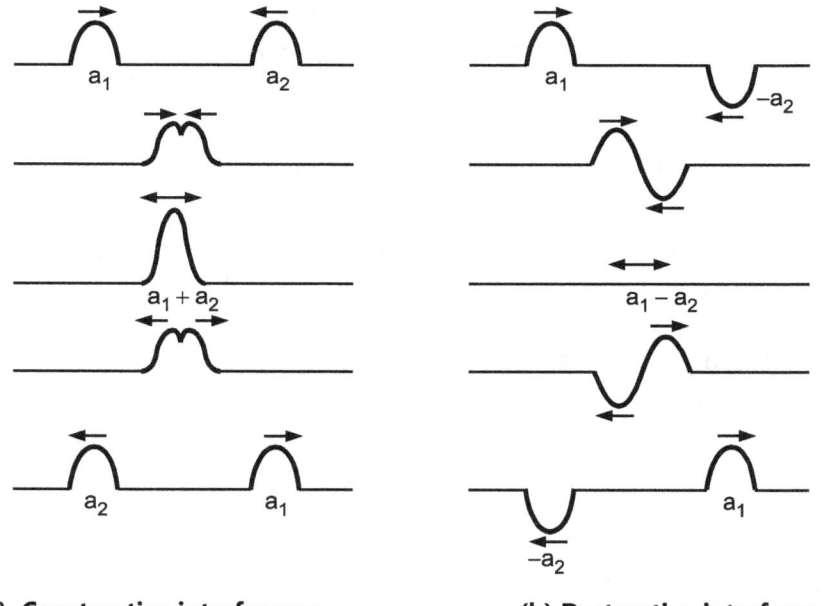

| (a) **Constructive interference** | (b) **Destructive interference** |

Fig. 1.1: Superposition

(1) Constructive Interference

- When the crest of one wave overlaps the crest of the other or the trough of one overlaps with the trough of the other, the displacement is maximum. This is called as **'constructive interference'**.

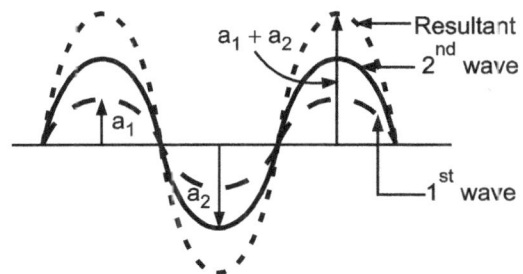

Fig. 1.2: Constructive interference

- In this case, the waves are in phase and the resultant amplitude equals the sum of the two component amplitudes.

  i.e. $A = a_1 + a_2$ ... (1)

  If $a_1 = a_2 = a$

  then $A = 2a$ ... (2)

  The resultant intensity will be $I = A^2 = 4a^2$ ... (3)

- Here the path difference between two waves is 0. Constructive interference will also take place when the path difference is λ or 2λ. In general, condition for constructive interference is,

  Path difference, $\Delta = n\lambda$ ... (4)

  where $n = 0, 1, 2, \dots n$.

  In terms of phase difference,

  Phase difference, $\delta = k\Delta$, where $k = \dfrac{2\pi}{\lambda}$

  $\therefore$ $\delta = \dfrac{2\pi}{\lambda} \cdot n\lambda$

  $\delta = 2n\pi$ ... (5)

(2) Destructive Interference

- In the other case, when the crest of one wave overlaps the trough of other or vice-versa, the displacement is minimum. This is called as **'destructive interference'**.

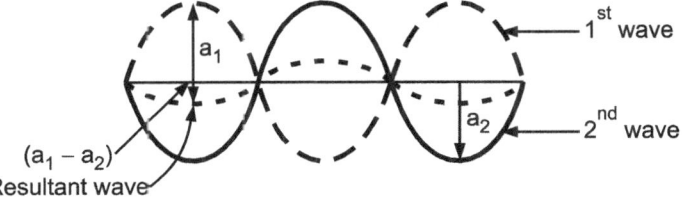

Fig. 1.3: Destructive interference

- In this case, the waves are 180° out of phase and the resultant amplitude is the difference of the two component amplitudes.

  i.e. $\qquad\qquad\qquad\qquad\qquad A = a_1 - a_2$ $\qquad\qquad\qquad\qquad$ ... (6)

  If $\qquad\qquad\qquad\qquad\qquad a_1 = a_2 = a$

  then $\qquad\qquad\qquad\qquad\qquad A = 0$ $\qquad\qquad\qquad\qquad\qquad$ ... (7)

  The resultant intensity, $\qquad\quad I = A^2 = 0$ $\qquad\qquad\qquad\qquad$ ... (8)

- Here the path difference between two waves is $\lambda/2$. The same thing will happen when the path difference is $3\lambda/2$ or $5\lambda/2$. In general, destructive interference will occur when

$$\text{Path difference, } \Delta = \left(n + \frac{1}{2}\right)\lambda \qquad\qquad\qquad ...(9)$$

  where $\qquad\qquad\qquad\qquad\qquad n = 0, 1, 2, ..., n.$

  or $\qquad\quad$ Phase difference, $\delta = k \cdot \Delta$ where $k = \dfrac{2\pi}{\lambda}$

$$\delta = \frac{2\pi}{\lambda}\left(n + \frac{1}{2}\right)\lambda$$

$$\delta = (2n + 1)\,\pi \qquad\qquad\qquad ...(10)$$

(3) Conditions Necessary for Stable Interference

- ➢ The two interfering waves should emit light of **same wavelength or frequency**.
- ➢ The two interfering waves must be **coherent**.
- ➢ The interfering waves must have **equal amplitudes**.
- ➢ The two interfering waves must be propagated along **the same line**.
- ➢ The **separation between the two sources must be as small as possible** so that the path difference between the two interfering waves, reaching a particular point, is not very large.
- ➢ The source of two interfering wave must be **narrow**, as a broad source will be equivalent to many fine sources.

(4) Intensity Distribution in the Fringe System

- If the amplitude of interfering waves are a_1 and a_2, and the phase difference is δ, then the vector sum of these two amplitude vectors will be A, as shown in Fig. 1.4.

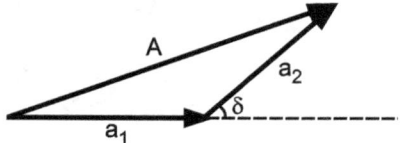

Fig. 1.4: Addition of waves

- The resultant amplitude A will depend upon the phase difference δ.

- For maxima, the angle δ is zero and the component amplitudes a_1 and a_2 will be parallel. So the resultant amplitude will be A = 2a (if $a_1 = a_2 = a$).

- For minima, a_1 and a_2 are in opposite directions (antiparallel) as the phase difference is 180°. The resultant amplitude is zero (if $a_1 = a_2 = a$).

- Thus, the intensity at a point will depend on the cosine of the angle made by two interfering waves.

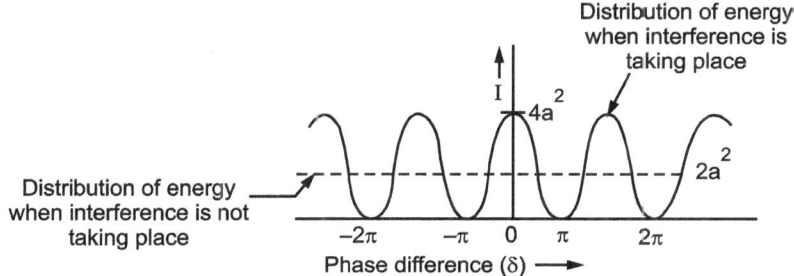

Fig. 1.5: Intensity distribution

- The energy which apparently disappears in minima is present in the maxima, where the intensity is greater than the intensity produced by two waves acting separately.

- In other words, the energy is not destroyed but redistributed in the interference pattern. The average intensity on the screen is exactly the same as what it would be in absence of interference.

- In interference pattern, the intensity varies between $4a^2$ and zero, whereas in absence of interference, we would have an uniform intensity of $2a^2$, as shown in Fig. 1.5.

1.1.2 Analytical Treatment of Interference

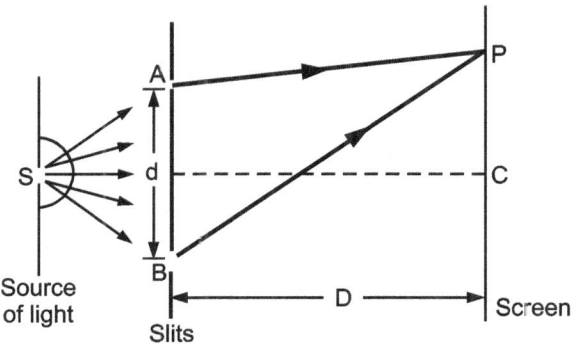

Fig. 1.6

- Consider a monochromatic source S emitting light of wavelength λ. Points A and B are equidistant from S, acting as two virtual coherent sources separated by a distance d.

- Let 'a' be the amplitude of the emitted waves from each slit. The screen is at a distance D from the virtual source.
- Consider a point P on the screen where interference takes place. If δ is the phase difference between the two rays AP and BP reaching point P.

  Then,
  $$y_1 = a \sin \omega t$$
  $$y_2 = a \sin (\omega t + \delta)$$

- According to the principle of superposition the resultant displacement y will be sum of individual displacements y_1 and y_2.

$$y = y_1 + y_2$$
$$y = a \sin \omega t + a \sin (\omega t + \delta)$$
$$y = a \sin \omega t + a (\sin \omega t \cos \delta + \cos \omega t \sin \delta)$$
$$y = a \sin \omega t (1 + \cos \delta) + a \cos \omega t \sin \delta$$

Let, $a (1 + \cos \delta) = A \cos \theta$ ... (1)

and $a \sin \delta = A \sin \theta$ ... (2)

∴ $y = A \sin \omega t \cos \theta + A \cos \omega t \sin \theta$

             $y = A \sin (\omega t + \theta)$ ... (3)

This represents the equation of a simple harmonic vibration of amplitude A.

Squaring and adding (1) and (2),

$$A^2 \sin^2 \theta + A^2 \cos^2 \theta = a^2 \sin^2 \delta + a^2 (1 + \cos \delta)^2$$
$$A^2 = a^2 \sin^2 \delta + a^2 + a^2 \cos^2 \delta + 2a^2 \cos \delta$$
$$A^2 = 2a^2 + 2a^2 \cos \delta$$

∴ $A^2 = 2a^2 (1 + \cos \delta)$

$$A^2 = 2a^2 \left(\sin^2 \frac{\delta}{2} + \cos^2 \frac{\delta}{2} + \cos^2 \frac{\delta}{2} - \sin^2 \frac{\delta}{2} \right)$$

$$A^2 = 4a^2 \cos^2 \frac{\delta}{2}$$

As the intensity at any point is proportional to the square of the amplitude,

$$I = A^2 \text{ (constant of proportionality is taken as unity)}$$

∴ $I = 4a^2 \cos^2 \delta/2$

Condition for Maximum and Minimum

1. **Constructive Interference:** When the phase difference $\delta = 0, 2\pi, 2(2\pi) \dots n(2\pi)$ or path difference $\Delta = 0, \lambda, 2\lambda \dots n\lambda$ then, $I = 4a^2$.

   i.e., intensity is maximum when phase difference is a whole number multiple of 2π or the path difference is a whole number multiple of λ.

2. **Destructive Interference:** When the phase difference δ = $\pi, 3\pi, ... (2n + 1)\, \pi$

   or the path difference $\Delta = \dfrac{\lambda}{2}, \dfrac{3\lambda}{2}, ... (2n + 1)\, \dfrac{\lambda}{2}$ then, $I = 0$.

   i.e. intensity is minimum when phase difference is an odd integer multiple of π or the path difference is an odd integer multiple of $\lambda/2$.

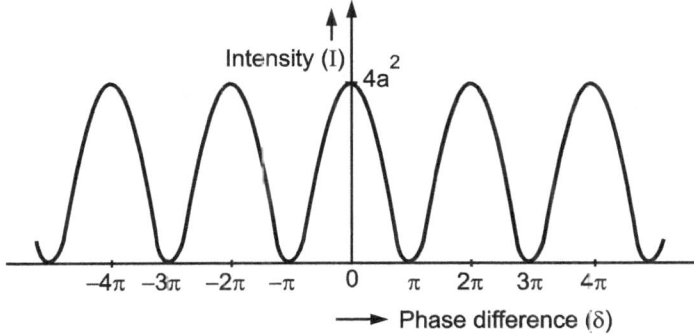

Fig. 1.7: Energy distribution curve

1.2 CONCEPT OF THIN FILM

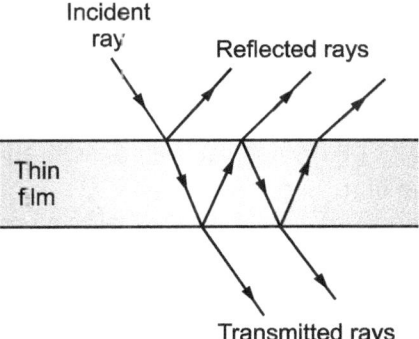

Fig. 1.8: Multiple reflections in a transpaarent thin film

- A film is said to be '***thin***' when its thickness is of the order of wavelength of visible light (taken to be 5500 A°, which is the centre of the visible spectrum).

- If the thickness of the film is about 10 μm to 50 μm, it is considered to be a thick film.

- A thin film may be a thin sheet of transparent material like glass, mica or an air film enclosed between two transparent sheets or a soap bubble.

- A light ray incident on a thin transparent film undergo reflection from the upper and lower surfaces of the film. They travel along different paths and may be reunited to produce '***interference***'.

- In a thin film, a small portion gets reflected from the upper surface while a major portion is transmitted into the film. The lower surface reflects a small portion, of the transmitted

- component, back into the film while the rest of it emerges out of the film from other side.
- Hence, a small portion of light gets partially reflected in succession several times within the film (as shown in Fig. 1.8). In a transparent thin film, the two surfaces strongly transmit and weakly reflect the incident light. In such cases, only the first few reflection at the top surface and the first few reflection at the bottom surface will be of appreciable strength. Hence, only the first two rays will be considered in the discussion.
- At each reflection, the incident amplitude is divided into a reflected and transmitted component' Therefore, interference in thin films is called *'interference by division of amplitude'*. This phenomenon was first observed by Newton and Robert Hooke but was correctly explained by Thomas Young.
- **In the Ongoing Discussion, Following Facts are Assumed**
  1. When a ray of light gets *'reflected'* from a *'denser medium'* into a *'rarer medium'*, it undergoes a *'phase change of π'* or a *'path change of $\lambda/2$'*.
  2. A *distance 't'* traversed by light in a medium of *refractive index 'μ'* has an equivalent *optical path 'μt'*.

1.3 INTERFERENCE DUE TO THIN FILMS OF UNIFORM THICKNESS   [May 14, 15]

- Consider a thin film of uniform thickness 't' and refractive index 'μ'. Let XY and X'Y' be the faces of this parallel sided film. The film is surrounded by air on both the sides.
- A plane monochromatic light ray, which can be considered as a parallel beam, is incident on the upper surface of the film.

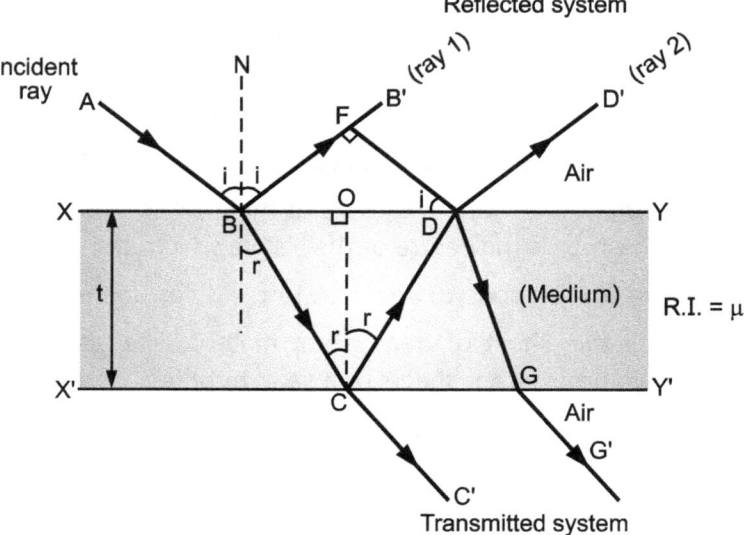

Fig. 1.9: Reflection of light from a parallel thin film

- Let AB represent one of the incident rays. The light ray travelling along AB is incident at an angle 'i' on the upper surface of the film. A part of the incident light is reflected at the upper face along BB' and a part is refracted at an angle 'r' along BC.

- At C, it is partly reflected back into the film along CD, while a major portion is transmitted along CC'. The ray along CD emerges along DD' parallel to BB .

- Both rays BB' (ray 1) and DD' (ray 2) are obtained from the same incident ray. They are, therefore, coherent and can produce interference. The condition of interference depends on the optical path difference between rays 1 and 2.

- To compute the optical path difference between the reflected ray BB' (ray 1) and the refracted ray DD' (ray 2), draw a normal DF from ray DD' on line BB'. Beyond points F and D, both rays travel equal distances.

- While ray BB' has covered a distance BF in air, the ray DD' has covered a distance BCD in the film of refractive index μ.

- The geometric **'path difference'** between ray 1 and ray 2 is, BC + CD − BF.

$\therefore$ Optical path difference is, $\Delta = \mu (BC + CD) - BF$ ... (1)

(Since, distances BC and CD are travelled in medium of R.I. = μ)

From Δ BCO and Δ DCO, $\cos r = \dfrac{CO}{BC}$ and $\cos r = \dfrac{CO}{CD}$

$\therefore$ $\qquad\qquad\qquad\qquad\qquad \cos r = \dfrac{t}{BC}$ and $\cos r = \dfrac{t}{CD}$ $\qquad\qquad\qquad$ ($\because$ CO = t)

$\therefore$ $\qquad\qquad\qquad\qquad\qquad$ BC = CD $= \dfrac{t}{\cos r}$ $\qquad\qquad\qquad\qquad\qquad$ ... (2)

and $\qquad\qquad\qquad\qquad\qquad$ BF = BD sin i $\qquad\qquad\qquad\qquad\qquad$ (from Δ BFD)

But $\qquad\qquad\qquad\qquad\qquad$ BO = OD = BC sin r $\qquad\qquad\qquad$ (from Δ BCO and Δ DCO)

$\therefore$ $\qquad\qquad\qquad\qquad\qquad$ BF = 2 BC sin r sin i $\qquad\qquad\qquad\qquad$ as BD = BO + OD

From equation (2), $\qquad\qquad$ BF $= \dfrac{2t}{\cos r}$ sin r sin i

Dividing and multiplying by sin r,

$\qquad\qquad\qquad\qquad\qquad$ BF $= \dfrac{2t}{\cos r} \sin^2 r \dfrac{\sin i}{\sin r}$

$\qquad\qquad\qquad\qquad\qquad$ BF $= \dfrac{2\mu t}{\cos r} \sin^2 r$ $\qquad\qquad\qquad \left(\because \dfrac{\sin i}{\sin r} = \mu \right)$ ... (3)

Substituting equations (2) and (3) in equation (1),

$$\Delta = \mu \left(\frac{t}{\cos r} + \frac{t}{\cos r} \right) - \frac{2\mu t}{\cos r} \sin^2 r$$

$$\Delta = \frac{2\mu t}{\cos r} - \frac{2\mu t}{\cos r} \sin^2 r$$

$$\Delta = (1 - \sin^2 r) \frac{2\mu t}{\cos r}$$

$$\Delta = \frac{2\mu t}{\cos r} \cos^2 r \qquad\qquad (\because \ \sin^2 r + \cos^2 r = 1)$$

$$\Delta = 2\mu t \cos r \qquad\qquad\qquad \text{... (4)}$$

1.3.1 In Reflected System   [May 15]

- The path difference given by (4) is not the true optical path difference between rays 1 and 2. The phase change due to reflection is to be taken into account.
- At B, the reflection is in a rarer medium. So, a path change of $\lambda/2$ occurs in the reflected ray BB'. At C, reflection is in a denser medium, therefore no path change occurs in ray 2.

  $\therefore$ Total path difference between rays 1 and 2 is given by,

    Total path difference = Path difference due to thin film + Path difference

                                                            due to reflections

$$\Delta = 2\mu t \cos r \pm \frac{\lambda}{2} \qquad\qquad\qquad \text{... (5)}$$

(i) Condition for Constructive Interference

- If the total path difference is equal to an integral multiple of λ then rays 1 and 2 meet in phase and undergo constructive interference.

  i.e., $\Delta = n\lambda$

  $\therefore$ $2\mu t \cos r \pm \lambda/2 = n\lambda$

                          $2\mu t \cos r = (2n \pm 1)\, \lambda/2$ where n = 0, 1, 2, 3 ...   ... (6)

(ii) Condition for Destructive Interference

- If the optical path difference is equal to an odd integral multiple of $\lambda/2$, then rays 1 and 2 meet in opposite phase and undergo destructive interference.

  i.e. $\Delta = (2n \pm 1) \dfrac{\lambda}{2}$

  $\therefore$ $2\mu t \cos r \pm \dfrac{\lambda}{2} = (2n \pm 1) \dfrac{\lambda}{2}$

                          $2\mu t \cos r = n\lambda$ where n = 0, 1, 2 ... and is called order of
                                                            interference   ... (7)

- The rays incident on the film at the same angle are divided into two rays which become parallel on reflection from the surfaces of the film. Parallel rays do not intersect at finite distances, hence fringes are not observed at finite distances.

- The rays are to be condensed by a lens and interference is observed in its focal plane. Else, it can be observed by the unaided eye focused at infinity. Therefore, these interference fringes are said to be *localized at infinity*.

(iii) Important Cases

- If the film is extremely thin .e. t << λ or t → 0 then the path difference, Δ ≈ λ/2. The film will appear dark in reflected light.

- When monochromatic light is incident normal to the film then cos r = 1.

$$2\mu t = (2n + 1)\frac{\lambda}{2} \text{ for brightness}$$

and $$2\mu t = n\lambda \text{ for darkness.}$$

This implies that the film will appear bright in reflected light if the film has thickness of $t = \dfrac{\lambda}{4\mu}, \dfrac{3\lambda}{4\mu},$ .... and it will appear dark for a thickness of t $= \dfrac{\lambda}{2\mu}, \dfrac{2\lambda}{2\mu}, \dfrac{3\lambda}{2\mu}$ ......

- If the incident monochromatic light is parallel, the whole film will be uniformly bright or dark as film thickness 't' and angle of refraction 'r' are constant. For a given incident wavelength (say green) the condition of constructive interference causes the incident colour to intensify (intense green).

- A change in the angle of incidence of the rays causes a change in the path difference. The optical path difference decreases with increase in angle of incidence. Hence, as inclination of the film is changed, it will appear alternately dark and bright for incident monochromatic light.

- If white light is incident on the film, the optical path difference will vary from one colour to the other as λ is different. Hence, the film will appear coloured, the colour being that of the rays which interfered constructively. Further, as the inclination of the film is changed, the film will appear coloured.

- If the incident white light is not parallel, the optical path difference will change due to change in the incident angle. Hence, the film will show different colours when viewed from different directions.

1.3.2 In Transmitted System

- When the film is observed in transmitted light, it can be shown that the path difference between rays CC' and GG' (Fig. 1.9) is equal to 2µt cos r. Reflections at C and D are in a denser medium. So, no additional path change will occur due to reflection.

$$\text{Total path difference} = \text{Path difference due to thin film}$$
$$+ \text{Path difference due to reflections}$$

$$\therefore \qquad \Delta = 2\mu t \cos r + 0 \qquad \qquad \text{... (8)}$$

(i) Condition for Constructive Interference

- For constructive interference the total phase difference should be an integral multiple of λ.

  i.e. $\qquad\qquad\qquad\qquad \Delta = n\lambda$

  $\therefore \qquad\qquad\qquad 2\mu t \cos r = n\lambda \qquad\qquad\qquad \text{... (9)}$

(ii) Condition for Destructive Interference

- For destructive interference the total phase difference should be an odd integral multiple of $\lambda/2$.

  i.e. $\qquad\qquad\qquad\qquad \Delta = (2n \pm 1)\dfrac{\lambda}{2}$

  $\therefore \qquad\qquad\qquad 2\mu t \cos r = (2n \pm 1)\dfrac{\lambda}{2} \qquad\qquad \text{... (10)}$

As is evident, the condition for brightness on reflection becomes the condition for darkness on transmission and vice versa.

1.4 INTERFERENCE IN FILMS OF NON-UNIFORM THICKNESS (WEDGE SHAPED FILM)

- A **wedge** is a plate or film of varying thickness, having zero thickness at one end and progressively increasing to a particular thickness at the other end.

- Consider two plane surfaces XY and X'Y' inclined at an angle α. The thickness of the film increases linearly from X to Y.

- When the wedge is illuminated by a parallel beam of monochromatic light, the rays reflected from its two surfaces will not be parallel. They appear to diverge from a point S near the film.

- When the film is viewed with reflected monochromatic light, **equidistant interference fringes** are observed which are parallel to the line of intersection of the two surfaces. The fringes are alternately bright and dark and are localised at the surface of the film.

- On illuminating the film with monochromatic light, one system of rays is reflected from the front surface XY and the other system of rays is obtained by transmission at the back surface X'Y' (not shown in Fig. 1.10) and consequent reflections at the front surface. As both rays are obtained from a single source, they are coherent and produce interference.

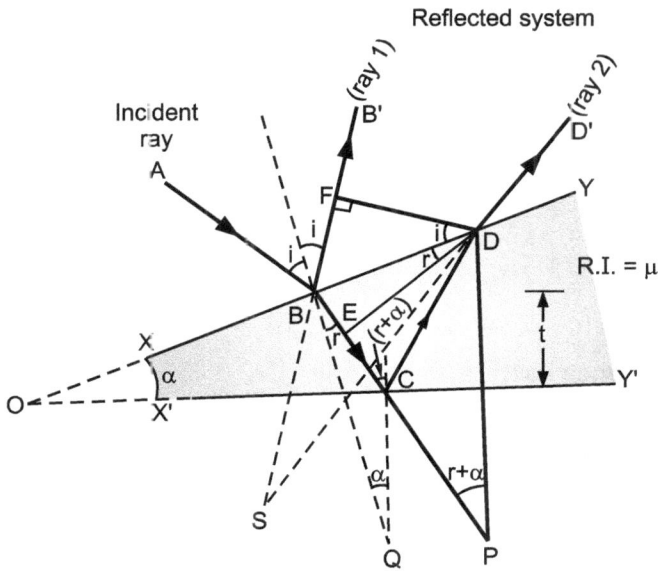

Fig. 1.10: Wedge-shaped film

- The optical path difference between them is given by,

$$\Delta = 2\mu t \cos (r + \alpha)$$

[**Note:** Derivation not expected.]

(i) In Reflected System

- Due to reflection, an additional path change is introduced in the reflected system at point B.

∴   Total path difference = Path difference due to thin film

+ Path difference due to reflections

$$\Delta = 2\mu t \cos (r + \alpha) \pm \frac{\lambda}{2} \qquad \qquad \dots (1)$$

Condition for Constructive Interference

For constructive interference the total phase difference should be an integral multiple of λ.

∴ $$\Delta = n\lambda$$

i.e. $$2\mu t \cos (r + \alpha) \pm \frac{\lambda}{2} = n\lambda$$

∴ $$2\mu t \cos (r + \alpha) = (2n \pm 1)\frac{\lambda}{2} \qquad \qquad \dots (2)$$

Condition for Destructive Interference

For destructive interference the total phase difference should be an odd integral multiple of $\lambda/2$.

$$\Delta = (2n \pm 1)\frac{\lambda}{2}$$

i.e. $2\mu t \cos(r + \alpha) \pm \dfrac{\lambda}{2} = (2n \pm 1)\dfrac{\lambda}{2}$

$\therefore$ $2\mu t \cos(r + \alpha) = n\lambda$ ... (3)

(ii) Nature of Interference Pattern

- If the film is illuminated by parallel light, then 'i' is constant everywhere and so is 'r', the angle of refraction. In addition, if monochromatic light is used, the path change will occur only due to 't'. In this case, the fringes will be of **'equal thickness'**.

- For a wedge shaped film, 't' remains constant only in a direction parallel to the thin edge of the wedge. So, straight fringes parallel to the edge of the wedge are obtained. The fringes are alternately bright or dark for monochromatic light.

- For white light, coloured fringes are obtained.

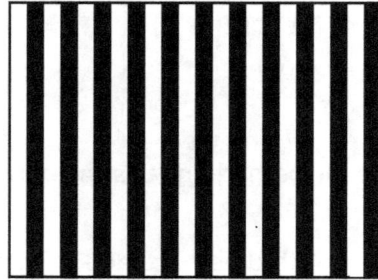

Fig. 1.11: Interference pattern in wedge-shaped film

Alternately bright and dark bands are parallel

[**Note:** In transmitted system we will get exactly opposite of reflected system]

1.5 FRINGE WIDTH (β)   [Dec. 12]

- When a wedge film is illuminated by monochromatic light of wavelength λ, it gives fringes of equal thickness. Fringe width can be calculated by knowing the position of consecutive minima or maxima. Here, for mathematical simplicity, we will consider minima.

For n^{th} minimum, we have

$2\mu t \cos(r + \alpha) = n\lambda$

For normal incidence, $r = 0$

$\therefore$ $2t\mu \cos \alpha = n\lambda$ ... (1)

Let this n^{th} dark band be formed at a distance x_n from the thin edge.

∴ $t = x_n \tan \alpha$ (from Fig. 1.12) ... (2)

From equations (1) and (2),

$2\mu x_n \tan \alpha \cos \alpha = n\lambda$

or $2\mu x_n \sin \alpha = n\lambda$ ... (3)

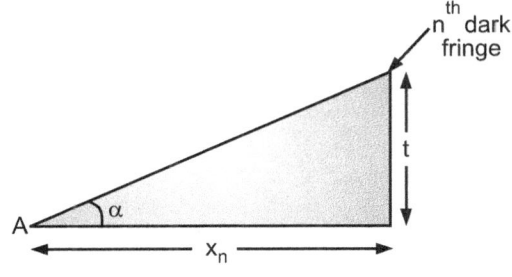

Fig. 1.12

- Similarly, if the $(n + 1)^{th}$ minimum is obtained at a distance x_{n+1} from the thin edge, then

$$2\mu\, x_{n+1} \sin \alpha = (n + 1)\, \lambda$$ ... (4)

- Subtracting equation (6) from equation (7), we get fringe width of a bright fringe.

$$2\mu\, (x_{n+1} - x_n) \sin \alpha = \lambda$$

∴   Fringe width, $\beta = x_{n+1} - x_n = \dfrac{\lambda}{2\mu \sin \alpha}$

$\beta = \dfrac{\lambda}{2\mu \sin \alpha} \cong \dfrac{\lambda}{2\mu\alpha}$ (for small α and in radians)   ... (5)

- For an air film ($\mu = 1$), fringe width,

$\beta = \dfrac{\lambda}{2 \sin \alpha} \approx \dfrac{\lambda}{2\alpha}$ (for small α)   ... (6)

- Similarly, it can be shown that the fringe width for dark fringes is given by.

$\beta = \dfrac{\lambda}{2\mu \sin \alpha}$ ... (7)

which is the same as that of a bright fringe.

- The width of a dark or bright fringe is however equal to half the fringe width.
- In equation (5), as all quantities on the right side are constant, β is constant for a given wedge angle α. It means that the **interference fringes** are **equidistant** from each other.
- According to relation (6), as angle α increases, the fringes move closer. At $\alpha = 1°$, the interference pattern vanishes. If α is gradually decreased, the fringe separation increases and ultimately the fringes disappear as the faces of the film become parallel ($\alpha = 0°$).

1.6 FORMATION OF COLOURS IN THIN FILMS

- From article 1.3 (equations 6, 7, 9, 10) it is clear that the conditions of interference are complementary i.e. the conditions of interference in the case of reflected and transmitted systems are opposite. For a given path difference if a bright fringe is observed in reflected system, a dark fringe will be observed in the transmitted system.

- The condition for maxima in reflected system is $2\mu t \cos r = (n \pm 1/2)\lambda$. If white light is incident on the film the wavelength satisfying above relation will be present in reflected system and corresponding colour will be seen.

- The colour appearing on the film will change if μ, t and r are changed. So different colours in reflected (or transmitted) rays are seen if, one of the three parameters μ, t and r is changed.

- When oil is dropped on water surface, it spreads slowly and a thin film is formed. The film itself is although **colourless** but **appears colourful** and keeps on changing colour, **due to interference**.

- The thin film keeps on changing colour as the oil film changes the thickness. The thickness changes as the oil spreads on the water surface and due to waves present in the water surface.

- A soap bubble is water film which is basically colourless but appears colourful due to interference and the colour also keeps on changing. The colour changes due to change in the thickness of the bubble which is caused by the gravitational force.

- When the soap bubble is about to burst the thickness is negligible and total path difference is just $\lambda/2$. Due to which the waves interfere destructively and bubble becomes black.

- A soap bubble floating in air also changes the colour as the angle of incidence and hence angle of refraction r changes.

SOLVED PROBLEMS

Problem 1.1: *In a certain region of interference we get 490th order maximum for sodium 5890 A° line. What will be the order of interference maximum at the same plane for sodium 5896 A° ?*

Data: $n = 490$, $\lambda = 5890$ A°

Formula: $\Delta = n\lambda$

Solution: Path difference for n^{th} order maximum, $\Delta = n\lambda$

∴   Path difference for 490th order maximum when λ is 5890 A°

$$\Delta = 490 \times 5890 \times 10^{-8}$$

$$\Delta = 2.89 \times 10^{-2} \text{ cm}$$

For sodium light of wavelength λ_1 = 5896 A°, the order of interference is n_1. Then the

$$\text{Path difference} = n_1 \lambda_1 = 2.89 \times 10^{-2}$$

$$\therefore \qquad n_1 = \frac{2.89 \times 10^{-2}}{\lambda_1}$$

$$\therefore \qquad n_1 = \frac{2.89 \times 10^{-2}}{5896 \times 10^{-8}} = 489.5$$

$\therefore$ The order of interference maximum = $\boxed{489}$

Problem 1.2: *Fringes are produced with monochromatic light of λ = 5450 A°. A thin glass plate of μ = 1.5 is then placed normally in the path of one of the interferring beams and the central band of the fringe system is found to move into the position previously occupied by the third bright band from the centre. Calculate the thickness of the glass plate.*

Data: λ = 5450 A° , μ = 1.5, n = 3

Formula: $\qquad\qquad t(\mu - 1) = n\lambda$

Solution: $\qquad\qquad t = n\dfrac{\lambda}{(\mu - 1)}$

Substituting, $\qquad\qquad t = \dfrac{3 \times 5450 \times 10^{-8}}{1.5 - 1}$

$$\boxed{t = 0.000327 \text{ cm}}$$

Problem 1.3: *When light falls normally on a soap film, whose thickness is 5×10^{-5} cm and whose refractive index is 1.33; which wavelength in the visible region will be reflected most strongly ?*

Data: t = 5×10^{-5} cm, μ = 1.33

Formula: $\qquad\qquad 2\mu t \cos r = (2n + 1)\lambda/2$ where   n = 0, 1, 2, 3, ... etc.

Solution: For normal incidence,

$$\cos r = 1$$

$$\therefore \qquad 2\mu t = (2n + 1)\frac{\lambda}{2}$$

$$\therefore \qquad \lambda = \frac{2 \times 2\mu t}{2n + 1}$$

$$\lambda = \frac{4 \times 1.33 \times 5 \times 10^{-5}}{(2n + 1)}$$

For n = 0, $\qquad\qquad \lambda = \dfrac{4 \times 1.33 \times 5 \times 10^{-5}}{1} = 2.66 \times 10^{-4} \text{ cm}$

$$\boxed{\lambda = 26,600 \text{ A°}}$$

For n = 1,

$$\lambda = \frac{4 \times 1.33 \times 5 \times 10^{-5}}{3} = 8.866 \times 10^{-5} \text{ cm}$$

$$\boxed{\lambda = 8866 \text{ A}^\circ}$$

For n = 2,

$$\lambda = \frac{4 \times 1.33 \times 5 \times 10^{-5}}{5} = 5.32 \times 10^{-5} \text{ cm}$$

$$\boxed{\lambda = 5320 \text{ A}^\circ}$$

For n = 3,

$$\lambda = \frac{4 \times 1.33 \times 5 \times 10^{-5}}{7} = 3.8 \times 10^{-5} \text{ cm}$$

$$\boxed{\lambda = 3800 \text{ A}^\circ}$$

The wavelength 5320 A° will be most strongly reflected in the visible region.

Problem 1.4: *A parallel beam of sodium light λ = 5890 A° strikes a film of oil floating on water. When viewed at an angle of 30° from the normal, 8ᵗʰ dark band is seen. Determine the thickness of the film if refractive index of oil = 1.5*

Data: $\lambda = 5890$ A°, $\angle i = 30°$, $\mu = 1.5$, $n = 8$

Formulae: (i) $2\mu t \cos r = n\lambda$ or $t = \dfrac{n\lambda}{2\mu \cos r}$ ... (1)

(ii) $\mu = \dfrac{\sin i}{\sin r}$

Solution: $\sin r = \dfrac{\sin i}{\mu}$

$\cos r = \sqrt{1 - \sin^2 r}$

∴ $\cos r = \sqrt{1 - \dfrac{\sin^2 i}{\mu^2}}$

∴ $\cos r = \sqrt{1 - \dfrac{\sin^2 30}{(1.5)^2}}$

$\cos r = 0.943$

Substituting in (1),

∴ $t = \dfrac{8 \times 5890 \times 10^{-8}}{2 \times 1.5 \times 0.943}$

$= \boxed{1.6302 \times 10^{-4} \text{ cm}}$

Problem 1.5: *Two glass plates enclose a wedge-shaped air film, touching at one edge and are separated by a wire of 0.03 mm diameter at a distance of 15 cm from the edge. Monochromatic light of λ = 6000 A° from a broad source falls normally on the film. Calculate the fringe width of the fringes thus formed.*

Data: $\lambda = 6000 \times 10^{-8}$ cm; For air film, $\mu = 1$

Diameter $= 0.03$ mm $= 0.003$ cm

Distance of fringe from the edge $= 15$ cm

Formula: Fringe width,

$$\beta = \frac{\lambda}{2\mu \sin \alpha} \approx \frac{\lambda}{2\mu \tan \alpha}$$

Solution:

$$\beta = \frac{6000 \times 10^{-8}}{2 \times 1 \times \dfrac{0.003}{15}} = \boxed{0.15 \text{ cm}}$$

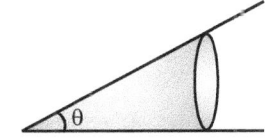

Fig. 1.13

Problem 1.6: *Interference fringes are produced by monochromatic light falling normally on a wedge-shaped film of cellophane whose refractive index is 1.4. The angle of the wedge is 20 sec of an arc and the distance between the successive fringes is 0.25 cm. Calculate the wavelength of light.*

Data: $\beta = 0.25$ cm, $\mu = 1.4$, $\theta = 20$ sec $= \dfrac{20}{60 \times 60} \times \dfrac{\pi}{180} = \dfrac{1}{180} \times \dfrac{\pi}{180}$ radians

Formula: $\qquad\qquad\qquad\qquad \beta = \dfrac{\lambda}{2\,\mu\,\alpha}$

∴ $\qquad\qquad\qquad\qquad\qquad \lambda = 2\mu\,\alpha \cdot \beta$

Solution: $\qquad\qquad\qquad \lambda = 2 \times 1.4 \times \dfrac{\pi}{180 \times 180} \times 0.25$

$$\boxed{\lambda = 6.79 \times 10^{-5} \text{ cm}}$$

Problem 1.7: *Two plane rectangular pieces of glass are in contact at one edge and separated by a hair at opposite edge, so that a wedge is formed. When light of wavelength 6000 A° falls normally on the wedge, nine interference fringes are observed. What is the thickness of the hair ?*

Data: $\lambda = 6000 \times 10^{-8}$ cm, $n = 9$, $r = 0$ for normal incidence

Formula: $\qquad 2\mu t \cos (r + \alpha) = n\lambda$

Solution: If the fringes are seen normally and the angle of wedge is very small, then $r = 0$, so that

$$\cos (r + \alpha) = \cos \alpha = 1$$

For air film, $\mu = 1$

$\therefore$
$$2\,\mu\, t = n\,\lambda$$
$$2 \times 1 \times t = 9 \times 6000 \times 10^{-8}$$

$\therefore$
$$t = \frac{9 \times 6000 \times 10^{-8}}{2} = \boxed{27 \times 10^{-5} \text{ cm}}$$

Problem 1.8: *A square piece of cellophane film with index of refraction 1.5 has a wedge-shaped section, so that its thickness at two opposite sides is t_1 and t_2. If with light of $\lambda = 6000$ A°, the number of fringes appearing on the film is 10, calculate the difference $t_2 - t_1$.*

Data: $\lambda = 6000 \times 10^{-8}$ cm, $\mu = 1.5$

Formula:
$$2\,\mu\, t_1 \cos(r + \alpha) = n\,\lambda \qquad \ldots (1)$$

Solution: For $(n + 10)^{th}$ dark fringe,
$$2\,\mu\, t_2 \cos(r + \alpha) = (n + 10)\,\lambda \quad \ldots (2)$$

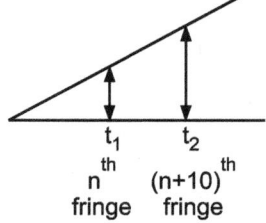

Fig. 1.14

For normal incidence, $r = 0$ and if the angle of wedge is small,
$$\cos(r + \alpha) = \cos \alpha = 1$$

$\therefore$ Equations (1) and (2) become
$$2\,\mu\, t_1 = n\,\lambda \qquad \ldots (3)$$
$$2\,\mu\, t_2 = (n + 10)\,\lambda \qquad \ldots (4)$$

$\therefore$ Subtracting equation (3) from equation (4), we get
$$2\,\mu\,(t_2 - t_1) = 10\,\lambda$$

$\therefore$
$$t_2 - t_1 = \frac{10\,\lambda}{2\,\mu} = \frac{10 \times 6000 \times 10^{-8}}{2 \times 1.5}$$

i.e.
$$\boxed{t_2 - t_1 = 2 \times 10^{-4} \text{ cm}}$$

Problem 1.9: *A parallel beam of light of wavelength 5890 A° is incident on a thin film of refractive index 1.5, such that the angle of refraction into the film is 60°. Calculate the smallest thickness of the film which will make it appear dark by reflection.*

Data: $\lambda = 5890$ A°, $r = 60°$, $\mu = 1.5$

Formula: For darkness,
$$2\mu t \cos r = n\lambda. \quad \text{Let} \quad n = 1$$

Solution:
$$t = \frac{\lambda}{2\mu \cos r} = \frac{5890 \times 10^{-8}}{2 \times 1.5 \times \cos 60}$$

$$\boxed{t = 3.926 \times 10^{-5} \text{ cm}}$$

Problem 1.10: *The optical path difference between two sets of similar waves from the same source arriving at a point on the screen is 199.5 λ. Is the point dark or bright ? If the path difference is 0.012 cm, find the wavelength of the light used.*

Data: $\Delta_1 = 199.5\ \lambda,\quad \Delta_2 = 0.12$ cm

Formula: For 199.5 λ it is odd path difference, therefore point is a dark fringe and for darkness,

$$\Delta = (2n - 1)\frac{\lambda}{2} \qquad\qquad \left(\because \left(\frac{2n-1}{2}\right) = 199.5\right)$$

Solution: $0.012 = 199.5\ \lambda$

$$\lambda = \frac{0.012}{199.5}$$

$$\lambda = 6.015 \times 10^{-8}\ \text{cm}$$

$$\boxed{\lambda = 6015\ \text{A}^\circ}$$

Problem 1.11: *Two pieces of plane glass are placed together with a piece of paper between the two at one edge. Find the angle in seconds of the wedge shaped air film between the plate, if on viewing the film normally with monochromatic light of wavelength 4800 A°, there are 18 bands per cm.*

Solution: 18 bands per cm

∴   Band width, $\beta = \dfrac{1}{18}$

$\beta = 0.0556$ cm

We know, $\beta = \dfrac{\lambda}{2\alpha}$

$$\alpha = \frac{\lambda}{2\beta} = \frac{4800 \times 10^{-8}}{2 \times 0.0556}$$

$$\alpha = 4.3165 \times 10^{-4}\ \text{rad}$$

Note conversion of radians into seconds.

$$\alpha = 4.3165 \times 10^{-4} \times \frac{180}{\pi} \times 60 \times 60$$

$$\boxed{\alpha = 89.02\ \text{seconds}}$$

Problem 1.12: *Two optically plane glass strips of length 10 cm are placed one over the other. A thin foil of thickness 0.010 mm is introduced between the plates at one end to form an air film. If the light used has wavelength 5900 A°, find the separation between consecutive bright fringes.*

Solution: $\tan \alpha = \dfrac{t}{x}$

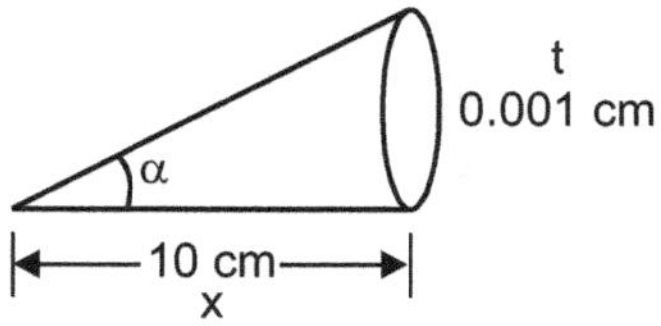

Fig. 1.15

As α is very small, $\tan \alpha = \alpha$

$$\alpha = \frac{t}{x} = \frac{0.001}{10}$$

$$\alpha = 0.0001 \text{ rad}$$

$$\beta = \frac{\lambda}{2\alpha} = \frac{5.9 \times 10^{-5}}{2 \times 0.0001}$$

$$\boxed{\beta = 0.295 \text{ cm}}$$

Note while using α in calculation it must be all the time in radians. If it is given in seconds then convert it in rad.

Problem 1.13: *Find the thickness of a wedge-shaped film at a point where fourth bright fringe is situated. λ for sodium light is 5893 A°.*

Data: n = 4, λ = 5893 A°

Formula: For bright band and wedge-shaped film,

$$2\mu t \cos (r + \alpha) = (2n - 1)\frac{\lambda}{2}$$

Let normal incidence, r = 0 and α is very small $\therefore$ $\cos (r + \alpha) = 1, \mu = 1$

$\therefore$ $\qquad\qquad 2t = (2n - 1)\dfrac{\lambda}{2}$

Solution: $\qquad 2t = \dfrac{(2 \times 4 - 1)\, \lambda}{2}$

$$t = \frac{7}{4} \times 5893 \times 10^{-8}$$

$$\boxed{t = 1.031275 \times 10^{-4} \text{ cm}}$$

Problem 1.14: *Monochromatic light emitted by a broad source of light of wavelength 6×10^{-5} cm falls normally on two glass plates which enclose a thin wedge-shaped film of air. The plates touch at one end and are separated at a point 15 cm from the end by a wire 0.5 mm in diameter. Find the width between any two consecutive bright fringes.*

Solution:

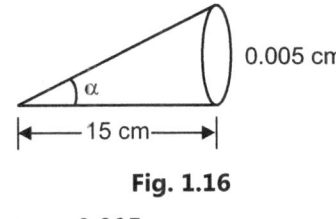

Fig. 1.16

$$\alpha = \frac{t}{x} = \frac{0.005}{15} = 3.333 \times 10^{-4} \text{ rad}$$

$$\text{Bandwidth, } \beta = \frac{\lambda}{2\alpha}$$

$$\beta = \frac{6 \times 10^{-5}}{2 \times 3.333 \times 10^{-4}}$$

$$\boxed{\beta = 0.09 \text{ cm}}$$

1.7 NEWTON'S RINGS   [Dec. 12, 14, Nov. 13, 15, May 13, 15]

- When a **plano-convex lens** of large focal length with its convex surface is placed in contact with a **plane glass plate**, an air film of gradually increasing thickness is formed between them. The thickness of the film at the point of contact is zero and increases gradually outwards.

- If monochromatic light is allowed to fall normally, and the film is viewed in reflected light, alternate **bright and dark rings** are observed. These rings are concentric around the point of contact between the lens and the glass plate. These fringes are called as **Newton's rings** as they were discovered by Newton. [See Fig. 1.17 (a)]

(i) Experimental Arrangement

- A plano-convex lens L of large radius of curvature is placed on a plane glass plate P. The point of contact between them is O. The light from an extended monochromatic source (sodium lamp) falls on a glass plate G held at an angle of 45° with the vertical.

- The glass plate G reflects normally a part of the incident light towards the air film between the lens L and the glass plate P. A part of the incident light is reflected by the curved surface of the lens L and a part is transmitted which is reflected back from the plane surface of plate P (i.e. rays are reflected from the top and bottom surfaces of the air film). These two reflected rays interfere and produce an **interference pattern** in the form of **circular rings**.

- These rings are *localised* in the air film and can be seen with a microscope focused on the film.

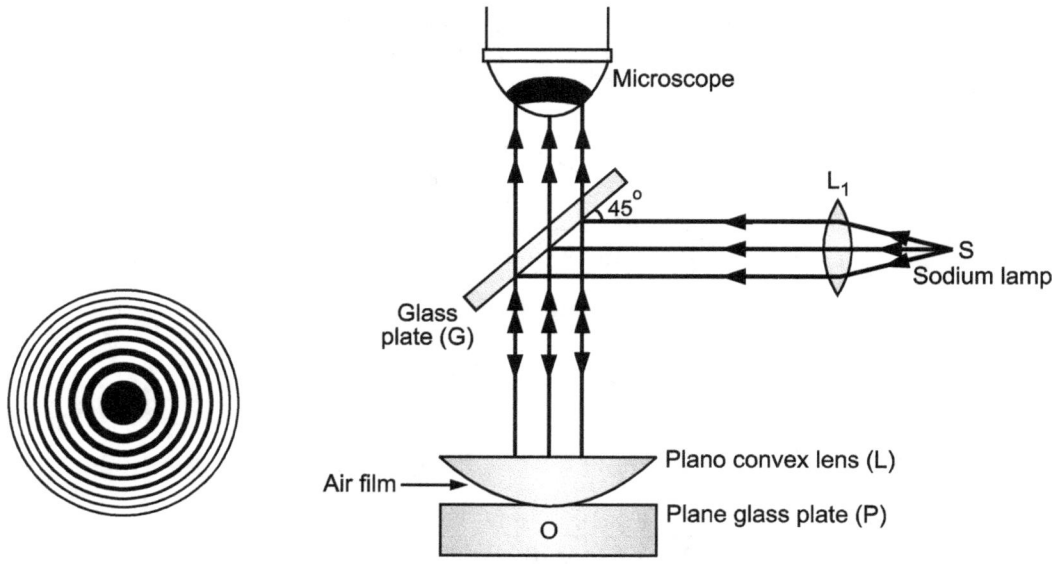

(a) Typical Newton's rings pattern observed in reflected light

(b) Experimental arrangement for observing Newton's rings

Fig. 1.17

(ii) Explanation of the Formation of Newton's Rings

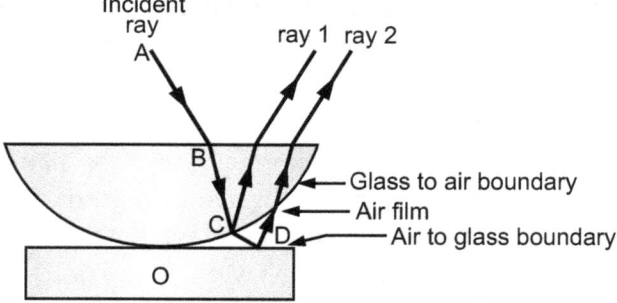

Fig. 1.18: Formation of Newton's rings

- When a monochromatic ray of light AB, is incident on the system, it gets partially reflected at C, the bottom of curved surface of the lens (glass-air boundary). This goes out in the form of ray 1 without any phase reversal. The other part is refracted along CD.
- At D, the top surface of the plane glass plate, it gets partially reflected to form ray 2. This ray has, a phase reversal as it is reflected from air to glass boundary.
- As the rays 1 and 2 are derived from the same source and are coherent, so they interfere to form fringes. Interference does not take place between rays reflected from the surfaces of lens and glass plate due to their thickness which is much larger than wavelength of light.

(iii) Derivation

- The radius of curvature of plano-convex lens is very large and the small section of the air film trapped between lens and the glass plate will be similar to a wedged air film. Therefore, the optical path difference will be same as that of wedged air fim.

The optical path difference for wedge film is,

$$\Delta = 2\mu t \cos (r + \alpha) \qquad \ldots (1)$$

For air film, $\mu = 1$, for normal incidence $\cos r = 1$ and $\alpha \approx 0$

$$\therefore \qquad \Delta = 2t \qquad \ldots (2)$$

In Reflected System

Total optical path difference = Path difference due to thin film

+ Path difference due to reflections

$$\therefore \qquad \Delta = 2t \pm \frac{\lambda}{2} \qquad \ldots (3)$$

Condition for Constructive Interference

For constructive interference the total phase difference should be an integral multiple of λ.

$$\Delta = n\lambda$$

$$\therefore \qquad 2t \pm \frac{\lambda}{2} = n\lambda$$

$$2t = \left(n \pm \frac{1}{2}\right)\lambda \qquad \ldots (4)$$

Condition for Destructive Interference

For destructive interference the total phase difference should be an odd integral multiple of $\lambda/2$.

$$\Delta = (2n \pm 1)\frac{\lambda}{2}$$

$$\therefore \qquad 2t \pm \frac{\lambda}{2} = (2n \pm 1)\frac{\lambda}{2}$$

$$2t = n\lambda \qquad \ldots (5)$$

Radii of Bright Rings

- The plano-convex lens LOL' is placed on a glass plate AB. The point C is the centre of the sphere of which LOL' is a part. Let R be the radius of curvature of the lens and r_n be the radius of the nth Newton's rings corresponding to the constant film thickness 't'.

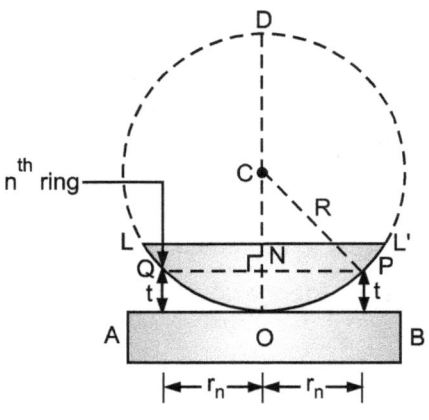

Fig. 1.19

- By the property of circle (theorem of intersecting chords),

$$NP \times NQ = NO \times ND$$

i.e. $$r_n \times r_n = t(2R - t) = 2Rt - t^2 \approx 2Rt \ \text{(as } t^2 \text{ is very small)}$$

∴ $$r_n^2 = 2Rt \qquad \qquad \text{... (6)}$$

or $$t = \frac{r_n^2}{2R} = \frac{D_n^2}{8R} \qquad (D_n \text{ being diameter of } n^{th} \text{ bright ring)}$$

$$\text{... (7)}$$

From equations (7) and (4), $$\frac{2r_n^2}{2R} = (2n \pm 1)\frac{\lambda}{2}$$

$$2 \cdot \frac{D_n^2}{8R} = (2n \pm 1)\frac{\lambda}{2}$$

$$D_n^2 = (2n \pm 1) \cdot 2\lambda R$$

$$D_n = \sqrt{2\lambda R} \cdot \sqrt{2n \pm 1} \qquad \text{i.e. } D_n \propto \sqrt{2n \pm 1} \ \text{... (9)}$$

Equation (9) shows that diameter of a bright ring is proportional to the square root of odd natural numbers.

Radii of Dark Rings

The condition for formation of dark Newton's ring is,

$$2t = n\lambda \qquad \qquad \text{... (10)}$$

Substituting for t from (8), $$2 \cdot \frac{D_n^2}{8R} = n\lambda$$

$$D_n^2 = 4n \lambda R \qquad \qquad \ldots (11)$$

$$D_n = 2\sqrt{n\lambda R} \ \text{ i.e. } \ D_n \propto \sqrt{n} \qquad \qquad \ldots (12)$$

Thus, the diameter of a dark ring is proportional to the square root of a natural number.

1.7.1 Properties of Newton's Rings

- **Rings get Closer Away from the Centre:** Consider equation (12) giving the diameter of a dark ring. We have

$$D_n \propto \sqrt{n} \ \text{ and } \ D_{n+1} \propto \sqrt{n+1}$$

$$\therefore \qquad \qquad D_{n+1} - D_n \propto (\sqrt{n+1} - \sqrt{n})$$

If constant of proportionality is taken as 1, then

$$D_{n+1} - D_n = \sqrt{n+1} - \sqrt{n}$$

$$\therefore \qquad \qquad D_2 - D_1 = \sqrt{2} - \sqrt{1} = 0.414$$

$$D_3 - D_2 = \sqrt{3} - \sqrt{2} = 0.317$$

Therefore, the *fringe width decreases* with the order of the fringe and the fringes get closer as the order increases. This can be shown for bright rings too.

This can also be explained in another way. The angle of the wedge increases as one moves away from the centre. From the equation for fringe spacing $\beta = \dfrac{\lambda}{2\mu\alpha}$, the fringe separation decreases as the wedge angle α increases. Hence, the rings come closer with increase in their radii.

- **Dark Central Spot:** At the point of contact of the lens with the glass plate, the thickness of the air film t = 0. From equation (3), it can be seen that the path difference between rays reflected from the top and bottom surfaces of the film is $\lambda/2$. Hence the interfering waves at the centre are opposite in phase and interfere destructively. Thus, a *dark spot* is produced at the centre.

- **Fringes of Equal Thickness:** It can be seen from equations (4) and (5) that *maxima and minima occur alternately* due to variation in the thickness 't' of the film. Each maxima or minima is, therefore, a locus of constant film thickness. Hence the fringes are called fringes of equal thickness.

- **Circular Fringes:** The circular wedge of air film may be regarded as having an axis passing through the point of contact O. This film bulges from the point of contact to outward with gradually increasing thickness of air film. The locus of points having the same thickness falls on a circle having its centre at the point of contact. Thus the thickness of the air film is the same at all points on any circle having O as the centre. The fringes are therefore circular. If the thickness satisfies the condition for constructive interference, the **circular fringe** is bright; otherwise it is dark.

- **Localised Fringes:** When the system is illuminated with a parallel light beam, the reflected rays are not parallel. They interfere near to the top surface of the film. When viewed from the top, the rays appear to diverge. As the fringes are seen at the upper surface of the film, they are said to be localised in the film.

- **White Light:** With white light, few **coloured fringes** are seen at centre. Away from centre they overlap.

1.8 APPLICATIONS OF NEWTON'S RINGS

1.8.1 Determination of Wavelength of Incident Light or Radius of Curvature of Plano-convex Lens

- The experimental arrangement is shown in Fig. 1.17 (b). Let R be the radius of curvature of the lens and λ the wavelength of the light used. If D_n is the diameter of the nth dark rings, then

$$D_n^2 = 4 n \lambda R \qquad \qquad \dots (1)$$

Similarly, for $(n + p)^{th}$ dark rings,

$$D_{n+p}^2 = 4 (n + p) \lambda R \qquad \qquad \dots (2)$$

Subtracting (1) from (2), we get,

$$D_{n+p}^2 - D_n^2 = 4 p \lambda R$$

$$\therefore \qquad \lambda = \frac{D_{n+p}^2 - D_n^2}{4 p R} \qquad \qquad \dots (3)$$

- The microscope is adjusted to obtain Newton's rings. The centre of the cross wire is made to coincide with the central dark fringe. Counting the central fringe as n = 0, the cross wire is moved to n^{th} and $(n + p)^{th}$ dark fringe to the left and position of microscope is noted on micrometer screw gauge.

- In the same way position of nth and $(n + p)^{th}$ fringe is noted on right. Subtracting position on left and right for n^{th} and $(n + p)^{th}$ fringe gives diameter of nth and $(n + p)^{th}$ fringe respectively.

- Radius of curvature 'R' is found using a spherometer.

- The wavelength λ of monochromatic source of light is found using relation (3). If λ is known, then same relation may be used to find R.

1.8.2 Determination of Refractive Index of a Liquid

- Firstly, perform the experiment when there is an air film between the class plate and plano-convex lens. The system is placed in a metal container. The diameter of nth and $(n + p)^{th}$ dark rings are determined using a travelling microscope.

  For air,
  $$D_{n+p}^2 - D_n^2 = 4 p \lambda R \qquad \qquad \dots (1)$$

- Pour the liquid, whose refractive index is to be determined, in the container without disturbing the arrangement. The air film between the lower surface of the lens and the upper surface of the plate is replaced by the liquid. Now, measure the diameter of the nth and $(n + p)^{th}$ dark rings.

- For liquid, we have $2\mu t \cos (r + \alpha) = n\lambda$ as the condition for darkness.

  For normal incidence, $r = 0$ and $\alpha = 0$.

  $\therefore$
  $$2\mu t = n\lambda \qquad \qquad \dots (2)$$

  But
  $$t = \frac{r_n'^2}{2R} = \frac{D_n'^2}{8R} \qquad \qquad \dots (3)$$

  From (2) and (3),
  $$2\mu \cdot \frac{D_n^2}{8R} = n\lambda$$

  $$D_n^2 = \frac{4n \lambda R}{\mu} \qquad \qquad \dots (4)$$

- If $D_n'^2$ and $D_{n+p}'^2$ are the diameters of nth and $(n + p)^{th}$ dark rings in liquid, then

  $$D_n'^2 = \frac{4 n \lambda R}{\mu} \qquad \qquad \dots (5)$$

  $$D_{n+p}'^2 = \frac{4 (n + p) \lambda R}{\mu} \qquad \qquad \dots (6)$$

  Subtracting (5) from (6), we get

  $$D_{n+p}'^2 - D_n'^2 = \frac{4 p \lambda R}{\mu} \qquad \qquad \dots (7)$$

  From equations (1) and (7),
  $$\mu = \frac{D_{n+p}^2 - D_n^2}{D_{n+p}'^2 - D_n'^2} \qquad \qquad \dots (8)$$

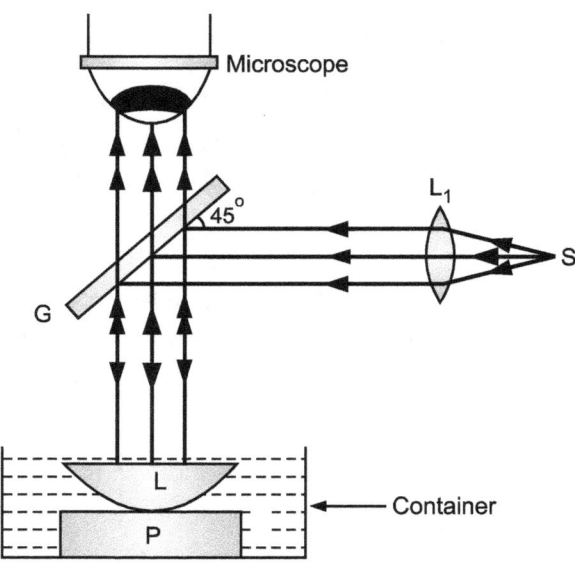

Fig. 1.20: Experimental arrangement for measurement of R.I. of liquid

SOLVED PROBLEMS

Problem 1.15: *A convex lens is placed on a plane glass slab and is illuminated by a monochromatic light. The diameter of the 10th dark ring is measured and is found to be 0.433 cm. The radius of curvature of the lower surface of the lens is 70 cm. Find the wavelength of the light used.*

Data: R = 70 cm, n = 10, D_n = 0.433 cm

Formula: $D_n^2 = 4\,n\,R\,\lambda$

Solution: $(0.433)^2 = 4 \times 10 \times 70 \times \lambda$

∴ $\lambda = \dfrac{(0.433)^2}{4 \times 10 \times 70}$

$\lambda = 6.696 \times 10^{-5}$ cm = $\boxed{6696\ A^\circ}$

Problem 1.16: *In a Newton's rings experiment, the diameter of the 15th dark ring was found to be 0.590 cm and that of the 5th dark ring was 0.336 cm. If the radius of the plano-convex lens is 100 cm, calculate the wavelength of the light used.*

Data: D_{15} = 0.590 cm, D_5 = 0.336 cm, R = 100 cm, m = 10

Formula: $\lambda = \dfrac{(D_{n+m})^2 - (D_n)^2}{4mR}$

Solution: $\lambda = \dfrac{D_{15}^2 - D_5^2}{4 \times 10 \times R} = \dfrac{(0.590)^2 - (0.336)^2}{4 \times 10 \times 100}$

$\lambda = 5.880 \times 10^{-5}$ cm

$\boxed{\lambda = 5880\ A^\circ}$

Problem 1.17: *The diameter of a dark ring in Newton's rings experiment decreases from 1.4 cm to 1.2 cm when air is replaced by a liquid as medium between lens and flat surface. Calculate the refractive index of the liquid.*

Data: D_{air} = 1.4 cm, D_{liquid} = 1.2 cm

Formula:
$$\mu = \frac{D_{air}^2}{D_{liquid}^2}$$

Solution:
$$\mu = \frac{(1.4)^2}{(1.2)^2}$$

$$\boxed{\mu = 1.36}$$

Problem 1.18: *The diameter of the tenth dark ring in Newton's rings experiment is 0.5 cm. Calculate the radius of curvature of the lens and the air thickness at the position of the ring. The wavelength of light used is 5000 A°.*

Data: D_{10} = 0.5 cm, n = 10, λ = 5000 × 10^{-8} cm

Formulae: (i) $D_n^2 = 4nR\lambda$, (ii) $t = \dfrac{D_n^2}{8R}$

Solution: (i)
$$R = \frac{D_n^2}{4n\lambda} = \frac{0.5^2}{4 \times 10 \times 5000 \times 10^{-8}}$$

$$\boxed{R = 125 \text{ cm}}$$

(ii) Thickness is given by

$$t = \frac{D_n^2}{8R} = \frac{0.5^2}{8 \times 125} = \boxed{2.5 \times 10^{-4} \text{ cm}}$$

Problem 1.19: *In a Newton's ring experiment, find the radius of curvature of the lens surface in contact with the glass plate when with a light of wavelength 5890 A°, the diameter of the third dark ring is 0.32 cm. The light is incident normally.*

Data: λ = 5890 A°, D_3 = 0.32 cm, n = 3

Formula: $D_n^2 = 4Rn\lambda$

Solution: $R = \dfrac{D_n^2}{4n\lambda}$

$$R = \frac{(0.32)^2}{4 \times 3 \times 5890 \times 10^{-8}}$$

$$\boxed{R = 144.87 \text{ cm}}$$

Problem 1.20: *In Newton's rings, the diameter of a certain bright ring is 0.65 and that of tenth ring beyond it is 0.95 cm. If λ = 6000 A°, calculate the radius of curvature of a convex lens surface in contact with the glass plate.*

Data: $D_n = 0.65$ cm, $D_{n+p} = 0.95$ cm, $\lambda = 6 \times 10^{-5}$ cm

Formula: $\dfrac{(D_{n+p})^2 - D_n^2}{4m\lambda}$

Solution: $R = \dfrac{(0.95)^2 - (0.65)^2}{4 \times 10 \times 6 \times 10^{-5}}$

$$\boxed{R = 200 \text{ cm}}$$

Problem 1.21: *In a Newton's ring experiment, a drop of water $\left(\mu = \dfrac{4}{3}\right)$ is placed between the lens and the plate. In this case, the diameter of the 10th ring was found to be 0.6 cm. Calculate the radius of curvature of the face of the lens in contact with the plate. Given: λ = 6000 A°.*

Data: $\mu = 1.3333$, $D_{10} = 0.6$ cm, $\lambda = 6 \times 10^{-5}$ cm, $n = 10$

Formula: $D_n^2 = \dfrac{4n\lambda R}{\mu}$

Solution: $R = \dfrac{D_n^2 \times \mu}{4n\lambda} = \dfrac{(0.6)^2 \times 1.3333}{4 \times 10 \times 6 \times 10^{-5}}$

$$\boxed{R = 200 \text{ cm}}$$

Problem 1.22: *Newton's rings are observed in reflected length of λ = 5900 A°. The diameter of the 5th dark ring is 0.4 cm. Find the radius of curvature of the lens and thickness of the air film.*

Data: $\lambda = 5.9 \times 10^{-5}$ cm, $n = 5$, $D_5 = 0.4$ cm, $\therefore r = 0.2$ cm

Formula: $D_n^2 = 4nR\lambda$

Solution: $R = \dfrac{(0.4)^2}{4 \times 5 \times 5.9 \times 10^{-5}}$

$R = 135.59$ cm

$t = \dfrac{r^2}{2R} = \dfrac{(0.2)^2}{2 \times 135.59}$

$$\boxed{t = 1.475 \times 10^{-4} \text{ cm}}$$

Problem 1.23: *In a Newton's ring experiment, the diameters of 4th and 12th dark rings are 0.4 cm and 0.7 cm respectively. Calculate the diameter of 20th dark ring.*

Data: $m = 12$, $n = 4$, $D_m = 0.7$ cm, $D_n = 0.4$ cm.

Formulae: (i) $\qquad R = \dfrac{D_{n+m}^2 - D_n^2}{4\,(m-n)\,\lambda}$

(ii) $\qquad D_n^2 = 4nR\lambda$

$\therefore \qquad D_n^2 = 4n\left(\dfrac{D_{n+m}^2 - D_n^2}{4\,(m-n)\,\lambda}\right) \cdot \lambda$

$\qquad D_n^2 = \dfrac{4n\,(D_{n-m}^2 - D_n^2)}{4m}$

Solution: $\qquad D_{20}^2 = 4 \times \dfrac{(0.7)^2 - (0.4)^2}{4\,(8)} \times 20 = \boxed{0.908 \text{ cm}}$

Problem 1.24: *If the diameter of nth dark ring in a Newton's ring experiment changes from 0.3 cm to 0.25 cm, as liquid is placed between the lens and the plate, calculate the value of μ of the liquid.*

Data: $\qquad D_{air} = 0.3$ cm. $\quad D_{liquid} = 0.25$ cm

Formula: $\qquad \mu = \dfrac{(D_n)_{air}^2}{(D_n)_{liquid}^2}$

Solution: $\qquad \mu = \dfrac{(0.3)^2}{(0.25)^2} = \boxed{1.44}$

1.9 APPLICATIONS OF INTERFERENCE

1.9.1 Testing of Optical Flatness of Surfaces

- Interference is now widely used for testing the quality of a surface finish. Even after machining, machine components retain certain surface irregularities. These act as sources of stress, leading to cracks thereby limiting the suitability of the components to certain applications. Therefore, the surfaces of components, which will be subjected to high stresses, are required to have a high surface finish. There are two ways in which the optical flatness or smoothness of a surface may be tested.

- The specimen surface is placed over the optically plane surface. If the surface is optically plane, no interference fringes will be observed. Because there will be no a r film enclosed between the two planes and the path difference between the reflected pairs will be $\lambda/2$, which is the condition for destructive interference. If the given surface is not optically flat but has some imperfections, fringe pattern will be observed.

- If the specimen to be tested is placed inclined to an optically flat surface, a **wedge shaped air film** will be enclosed between them. The air wedge produces **straight** and **equidistant fringes** if the surface of the component is **smooth**. These fringes are parallel to the line of intersection of two surfaces. The fringes or bands are of equal thickness as each fringe is the locus of the points at which the thickness of the film has a constant value. If the fringes are curved towards the contact edge, the surface is concave and if the fringes curve away, it is convex.

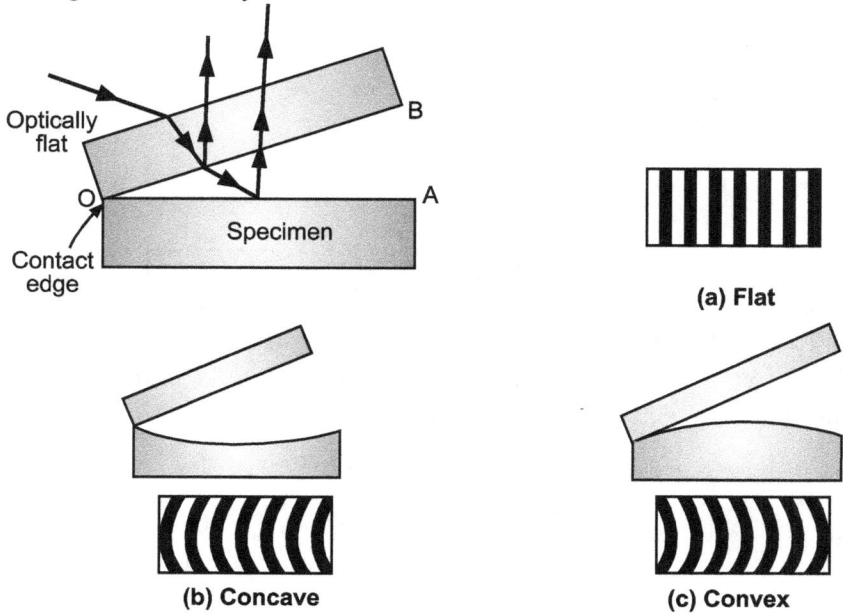

Fig. 1.21: Testing of surfaces for optical flatness

1.9.2 Thickness of Thin Film

- For increasing efficiency and effectiveness, some surfaces are coated with the films of uniform thickness. The effectiveness of the film depends on the thickness along with other parameters involved. So measuring the thickness of a film is necessary. The thickness of such film can be done by using the principle of thin film interference.

- A partially coated substrate is used for determination of film. The surfaces of the substrate and the thin film on it are coated with transparent metallic film. A glass plate is also coated on one of its surfaces with the transparent metallic film, when the substrate and the glass plate are placed in contact and examined with the monochromatic light. A fringe system as shown in Fig. 1.22 (b) is seen.

- A shift occurs in the fringes from the region occupied by thin film to the region where the film is absent there is displacement of fringes. The amount of displacement is given by

$$s = 2t$$

where t is the thickness and s is the displacement.

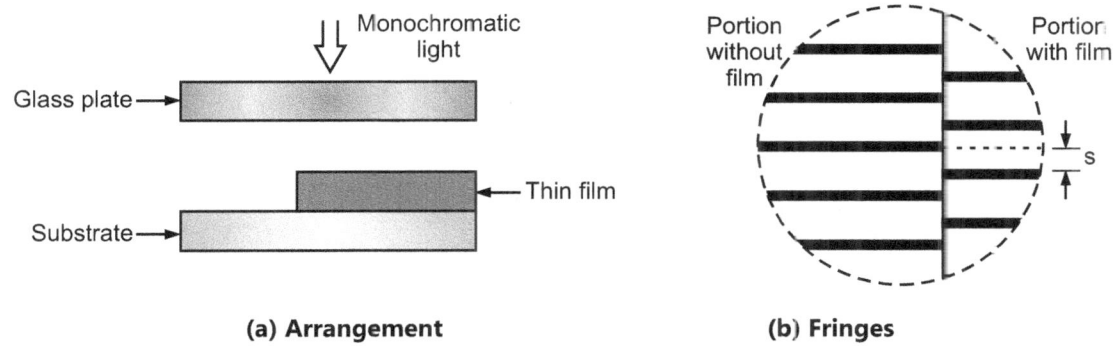

(a) Arrangement   **(b) Fringes**

Fig. 1.22: Thin film thickness

1.9.3 Antireflection or Non-Reflecting Coatings   [May 13, 16]

- Optical instruments like telescopes, cameras, etc. use multicomponent glass lenses. When light is incident on these lenses, part of the light is reflected. Hence, the transmitted component has reduced intensity. When the number of reflections are large, the quality of the image produced will be poor.

- It was in 1935 that Alexander Smakula discovered that the phenomenon of interference could be used to reduce reflections from a surface by coating it with a thin transparent film. Such a film coated to reduce reflections is called **an antireflection film (AR coating) or non-reflecting film**.

- A thin film can act as an AR coating if the waves reflected from its top and bottom surfaces are exactly 180° out of phase and the waves have equal amplitudes To achieve this, surfaces of lenses, prisms, etc. are coated with a thin layer cr fi m of hard transparent material with refractive index intermediate between that of air and glass (less than that of glass).

- Light is reflected, from both surfaces of the layer, from a medium of greater refractive index than that in which it is travelling. So, the same phase change occurs in both reflections.

- If the film thickness is a quarter of the wavelength in the film, the total path difference is a half wavelength. Light reflected from the first surface is out of phase with light reflected from the second surface leading to destructive interference.

- The path difference due to non-reflecting film,

    Δ = path difference due to film + Path difference due to reflections.

$$\therefore \ \Delta = 2\mu t \cos r + 0 \qquad \qquad ...(1)$$

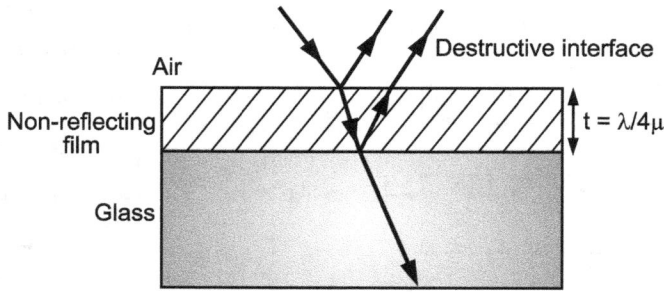

Fig. 1.23: Anti-reflection film

Considering normal incidence, the condition for destructive interference is,

$$2\mu t = (2n \pm 1)\frac{\lambda}{2}$$

For n = 0, $$2\mu t = \frac{\lambda}{2}$$

or $$t = \frac{\lambda}{4\mu}$$ ... (2)

- This means that the optical thickness, μt, of the material that has to be coated for reducing reflections is a quarter of the wavelength.

- For glass ($\mu = 1.5$), the materials having refractive index nearer to this value are magnesium fluoride ($\mu = 1.38$) and cryolite ($\mu = 1.36$) are usually used. In addition, the materials should adhere well, should be durable, scratch proof and insoluble in ordinary solvents. The coating is obtained by evaporating magnesium fluoride on the surface in vacuum.

- It is seen that condition (2) is satisfied only at a particular wavelength. This is usually chosen in the central yellow-green portion of the spectrum ($\lambda = 5500$ A°), where the eye is most sensitive. This leads to more reflection at both longer (red) and shorter (blue) wavelengths. The reflected light will therefore have a *'purple hue'*.

- The overall reflection from a lens or a prism surface can be reduced, in this manner, from about 5% to 1%. This helps in increasing transmitted light. The same principle is used to minimize reflections from silicon photovoltaic cells (solar cells) by using a thin layer of silicon monoxide. This helps in increasing the amount of light actually reaching the solar cell.

Problem 1.25: *MgF$_2$ of refractive index 1.38 is coated on a glass plate in order to reduce the reflection from the glass surface using interference. How thick is the coating needed to produce a minimum reflection at the centre of visible spectrum (5500 A°) ?*

Data: $\mu = 1.38$, $\lambda = 5500 \times 10^{-8}$ cm

Considering normal incidence, $\cos r = 1$.

Formula: $2 \mu t = \dfrac{\lambda}{2}$

∴   Thickness of coating, $t = \dfrac{\lambda}{4 \mu}$

Solution: $t = \dfrac{5500 \times 10^{-8}}{4 \times 1.38}$

$$\boxed{t = 996.37 \times 10^{-8} \text{ cm}}$$

UNIVERSITY SOLVED PROBLEMS

Problem 1.26: *Fringes of equal thickness are observed in a thin glass wedge of refractive index 1.52. The fringe spacing is 1 mm and the wavelength of light is 5893 A°. Calculate the angle of wedge in seconds of an arc.*   **(04) (Dec. 03, May 07)**

Data: $\mu = 1.52$

$\lambda = 5893 \ A°$

$\beta = 1 \text{ mm}$

Formula: Fringe width is,

$$\beta = \dfrac{\lambda}{2 \alpha}$$

Solution: $1 \times 10^{-1} = \dfrac{5893 \times 10^{-8}}{2 \alpha}$

∴ $\alpha = \dfrac{5893 \times 10^{-8}}{2 \times 1 \times 10^{-1}}$

$\alpha = 2.9 \times 10^{-4}$ radian

or $\alpha = \dfrac{2.9 \times 10^{-4} \times 180 \times 60 \times 60}{3.14}$ of an arc = $\boxed{59.8 \text{ sec.}}$

Problem 1.27: *A parallel beam of sodium light strikes a film of oil floating on water. When viewed at an angle 30° from the normal, in the reflected light, eighth dark band is seen. Determine the thickness of the film. Refractive index of oil is 1.46 and $\lambda = 5890 \ A°$.*

(04) (May 04)

Data: $i = 30°$

$\mu = 1.46$

$\lambda = 5890 \ A°$

Formulae: (i) By Snell's law,

$$\dfrac{\sin i}{\sin r} = \mu$$

     (ii) $2\mu t \cos r = n\lambda$

Solution: (i) $\dfrac{\sin 30}{\sin r} = 1.46$

$$\sin r = \frac{0.5}{1.46} = 0.34247$$

∴ $\boxed{r = 20°}$

(ii)   The thickness is given by relation (condition for minima)

$$2\,\mu t \cos r = n\,\lambda$$

$$t = \frac{8 \times 5890 \times 10^{-8}}{2 \times 1.46 \times \cos 20°}$$

$$\boxed{t = 1.7 \times 10^{-4} \text{ cm}}$$

Problem 1.28: *In a Newton's rings experiment, the diameter of the 5th ring was 0.336 cm and that of 15th ring was 0.59 cm. Find the radius of curvature of the plano-convex lens, if the wavelength of light used is 5890 A°.* **(03) (Jan. 05)**

Data: $D_{15} = 0.59$ cm

                       $D_5 = 0.336$ cm

                       $\lambda = 5890$ A°

                       $m = 10$

Formula: $R = \dfrac{D_{n+m}^{2} - D_n^{2}}{4\,m\,\lambda}$

Solution: $R = \dfrac{D_{15}^{2} - D_5^{2}}{4 \times 10 \times \lambda}$

$$R = \frac{(0.59)^2 - (0.336)^2}{4 \times 10 \times 5890 \times 10^{-8}}$$

$$\boxed{R = 99.83 \text{ cm}}$$

Problem 1.29: *A soap film of refractive index 4/3 and thickness 1.5×10^{-4} cm is illuminated by white light incident at an angle of 45°. The light reflected by it is examined by a spectroscope in which is found a dark and corresponding to wavelength of 5×10^{-5} cm. Calculate the order of interference band.* **(04) (Nov/Dec. 05)**

Data: $\mu = 4/3 = 1.33$

                      $t = 1.5 \times 10^{-4}$ cm

$$i = 45°$$

$$\lambda = 5 \times 10^{-5} \text{ cm}$$

Formulae: (i) By Snell's law,

$$\frac{\sin i}{\sin r} = \mu$$

(ii) $\quad 2\mu t \cos r = n\lambda$

Solution: (i) $\quad \dfrac{\sin 45°}{\sin r} = 1.33$

$$\sin r = \frac{0.707}{1.33}$$

$$\sin r = 0.53038$$

or $\qquad \boxed{r = 32°}$

(ii) The order of interference will be given by (condition for dark band)

$$2\,\mu t \cos r = n\,\lambda$$

$$n = \frac{2 \times 1.33 \times 1.5 \times 10^{-4} \times \cos 32°}{5 \times 10^{-5}}$$

$$\boxed{n = 6.78}$$

The order of interference,

$$n = 6$$

Problem 1.30: *A wedge shaped air film having an angle of 40 seconds is illuminated by monochromatic light and fringes in reflected system are observed through a microscope. The distance between the consecutive bright fringes was measured as 0.12 cm. Calculate the wavelength of light used.* **(04) (May 06)**

Data: $\qquad\qquad \alpha = 40 \text{ sec.}$

$$\beta = 0.12 \text{ cm}$$

$$\alpha = 40 \text{ sec}$$

$$\alpha = \frac{40 \times \pi}{60 \times 60 \times 180} \text{ radian}$$

Formula: $\qquad \alpha = 1.9 \times 10^{-4} \text{ rad.}$

The fringe width is given by,

$$\beta = \frac{\lambda}{2\,\alpha}$$

$$\lambda = 2\,\beta\alpha$$

Solution:
$$\lambda = 2 \times 0.12 \times 1.9 \times 10^{-4}$$

$$\lambda = 5 \times 10^{-5}\ cm$$

$$\boxed{\lambda = 5000\ A°}$$

Problem 1.31: *In Newton's rings experiment the diameters of nth and $(n + 8)^{th}$ bright rings are 4.2 mm and 7.00 mm respectively. Radius of curvature of the lower surface of the lens is 2.00 m. Determine the wavelength of the light.* **(04) (Dec. 06)**

Data:
$$D_n = 4.2\ mm$$

$$D_{n+8} = 7\ mm$$

$$R = 2\ m$$

Formula:
$$\lambda = \frac{D_{n+m}^2 - D_n^2}{4\ m\ R}$$

Solution:
$$\lambda = \frac{D_{n+8}^2 - D_n^2}{4\ (n + 8 - n)\ R}$$

$$\lambda = \frac{0.7^2 - 0.42^2}{4 \times 8 \times 200}$$

$$\lambda = 5 \times 10^{-5}\ cm$$

$$\boxed{\lambda = 5000\ A°}$$

Problem 1.32: *Newton's rings are formed by light reflected normally from a plano-convex lens and a plane glass plate with a liquid between them. The diameter of nth ring is 2.18 mm and that of $(n + 10)^{th}$ ring is 4.51 mm. Calculate the refractive index of the liquid, given that the radius of curvature of the lens is 90 cm and wavelength of light is 5893 A°.*

(04) (May 07)

Data:
$$D'_n = 2.18\ mm$$

$$D'_{n+10} = 4.5\ mm$$

$$R = 90\ cm$$

$$\lambda = 5893\ A°$$

Formula:
$$R = \frac{\mu\,(D'^2_{n+m} - D'^2_n)}{4m\lambda}$$

$$\mu = \frac{4\, m\, \lambda\, R}{D_{n+m}^{'2} - D_n^{'2}}$$

Solution:

$$\mu = \frac{4 \times 10 \times 5893 \times 10^{-8} \times 90}{0.45^2 - 0.218^2}$$

$$\boxed{\mu = 1.368}$$

Problem 1.33: *A parallel beam of monochromatic light of wavelength λ = 5890 A° is incident on a thin film of μ = 1.5 such that the angle of refraction is 60°. Find the maximum thickness of the film so that it appears dark for normal incidence, what is the thickness required ?*   **(04) (May 08)**

Data: λ = 5890 A°

                   r = 60°

                   μ = 1.5

Formula: For dark band,

          2 $\mu t \cos r$ = $n\lambda$

          $t = \dfrac{n\lambda}{2\,\mu t \cos r}$

Solution: For maximum thickness, n = 1

          $t = \dfrac{1 \times 5890 \times 10^{-8}}{2 \times 1.5 \times \cos 60}$

          t = 4 × 10⁻⁵ cm

For normal incidence, r = 0 and hence cos r = 1.

∴ $t = \dfrac{1 \times 5890 \times 10^{-8}}{2 \times 1.5 \times \cos 0}$

          $\boxed{t = 2 \times 10^{-5}\ cm}$

Problem 1.34: *An oil drop of volume 0.2 cc is dropped on the surface of a water tank of area 1 sq. m. The thin film spreads uniformly over the whole surface and white light reflected normally is observed through a spectrometer. The spectrum is seen to contain a first dark band whose centre has a wavelength of 5.5 ×10⁻⁵ cm. Find the refractive index of oil.*   **(04) (Dec. 08)**

Data: V = 0.2 cc

                   A = 1 sq. m.

                   n = 1

                   λ = 5.5 × 10⁻⁵ cm

Formulae: (i) Volume = Area × thickness (ii) $2\mu t \cos r = n\lambda$

Solution: (i)

$$0.2 = 1 \times 10^4 \times t$$
$$t = 2 \times 10^{-5}\,cm$$

(ii) For minima,

$$2\mu t \cos r = n\lambda$$

Let,

$$r = 0$$
$$\mu = \frac{n\lambda}{2t}$$
$$\mu = \frac{1 \times 5.5 \times 10^{-5}}{2 \times 2 \times 10^{-5}}$$
$$\boxed{\mu = 1.375}$$

Problem 1.35: *A beam of monochromatic light of wavelength 5.82 × 10⁻⁷ m falls normally on a glass wedge of wedge angle of 20 seconds of an arc. If the refractive index of glass is 1.5, find the number of dark interference fringes per cm of the wedge length.*

(04) (Dec. 08)

Data:

$$\lambda = 5.82 \times 10^{-7}\,m$$
$$\theta = 20\ seconds$$
$$\mu = 1.5$$

The angle in degrees,

$$\theta = \frac{20}{60 \times 60} \times \frac{\pi}{180}$$
$$\theta = 9.69 \times 10^{-5}$$

Formula:

The fringe width, $\beta = \dfrac{\lambda}{2\mu\theta}$

Solution:

$$\beta = \frac{5.82 \times 10^{-7}}{2 \times 1.5 \times 9.69 \times 10^{-5}}$$

∴ $\beta = 0.2 \times 10^{-2}\,m = 0.2\,cm$

∴ Number of dark fringes/cm

$$= \frac{1}{\beta} = \frac{1}{0.2} = \boxed{5}$$

Problem 1.36: *A parallel beam of sodium light of wavelength 5890×10^{-8} cm is incident on a thin glass plate of refractive index 1.5, such that the angle of refration into the plate is 60°. Calculate the smallest thickness of the plate which will make it appear dark by reflection.*

(04) (May 09)

Data:
$$\lambda = 5890 \times 10^{-8} \text{ cm}$$
$$\mu = 1.5$$
$$r = 60°$$

Formula: The condition for dark fringe in reflected system is
$$2\mu t \cos r = n\lambda$$

Solution: Taking $n = 1$
$$2 \times 1.5 \times t \times \cos 60 = 5890 \times 10^{-8}$$

$\therefore$
$$t = 3.926 \times 10^{-3} \text{ cm} = \boxed{3.926 \times 10^{-5} \text{cm}}$$

SUMMARY

- The superposition of two waves of equal amplitude, frequency and a constant phase difference is called as interference. The result is alternate cark and bright fringes.

  Conditions on path difference (x):

  (a) Constructive interference or bright fringe – Whole number multiple of λ.

  (b) Destructive interference or dark fringe – Odd integer multiple of $\dfrac{\lambda}{2}$.

- A film is said to be thin if its thickness is of the order of a few wavelengths.

- In a thin film of uniform thickness in reflected system, condition for

  (a) constructive interference: $2\mu t \cos r = (2n + 1)\dfrac{\lambda}{2}$

  (b) destructive interference: $2\mu t \cos r = n\lambda$

  (c) in transmitted system, the conditions reverse.

- In a wedge-shaped film, the condition for

  (a) constructive interference: $2\mu t \cos (r + \alpha) = (2n + 1)\dfrac{\lambda}{2}$

  (b) destructive interference: $2\mu t \cos (r + \alpha) = n\lambda$

  (c) fringe width: $\beta \approx \dfrac{\lambda}{2\mu\alpha}$

  (d) fringes obtained are: equal in thickness, straight, parallel and equidistant.

- Newton's rings are: circular in shape, centre is dark for reflected light.

- Radius for

  (a) Bright ring (reflected light) $D_n^2 = (2n \pm 1) \cdot 2\lambda R$

  (b) Dark ring (reflected light) $D_n^2 = 4n\lambda R$

- Wavelength of monochromatic source of light $\lambda = \dfrac{D_{n+p}^2 - D_n^2}{4pR}$

- Refractive index of liquid $\mu = \dfrac{D_{n+p}'^2 - D_n'^2}{D_{n+p}^2 - D_n^2}$

- Michelson's interferometer uses monochromatic light and is used for high precision measurement of wavelengths.

  (a) Wavelength of monochromatic source $\lambda = \dfrac{2x}{N}$

  (b) Resolution of two spectral lines $\Delta\lambda = \lambda_1 - \lambda_2$

  $$= \dfrac{\lambda_{avg}^2}{2x}$$

  (c) Refractive index of material $\mu = \dfrac{x}{t} + 1$

  (d) Thickness of plate $t = \dfrac{x}{\mu - 1}$

- Interference is used to test optical flatness of a surface.

- Antireflection coatings are thin transparent coatings of quarter wave thickness

  $$\mu t = \dfrac{\lambda}{4}$$

IMPORTANT FORMULAE

- Constructive interference, $x = n\lambda$, $n = 0, 1, 2 \ldots$

- Destructive interference, $x = (2n + 1)\dfrac{\lambda}{2}$, $n = 0, 1, 2 \ldots$

- $2\mu t \cos r = (2n \pm 1)\dfrac{\lambda}{2}$, $n = 0, 1, 2 \ldots$

- $2\mu t \cos r = n\lambda, \quad n = 0, 1, 2 \dots$

- $2\mu t \cos (r + \alpha) = (2n \pm 1) \dfrac{\lambda}{2}, \quad n = 0, 1, 2 \dots$

- $2\mu t \cos (r + \alpha) = n\lambda, \quad n = 0, 1, 2 \dots$

- $\beta = \dfrac{\lambda}{2\mu \sin \alpha}$

- $D_n^2 = \sqrt{2\lambda R} \cdot \sqrt{2n \pm 1}$ (bright)

- $D_n^2 = 4n\lambda R$

- $\lambda = \dfrac{D_{n+p}^2 - D_n^2}{4pR}$

- $\mu = \dfrac{D_{n+p}^{'2} - D_n^{'2}}{D_{n+p}^2 - D_n^2}$

- $t = \dfrac{\lambda}{4\mu}$

EXERCISE

1. Explain the phenomena of interference.

2. What is constructive and destructive interference ?

3. Derive the conditions for constructive and destructive interference.

4. Explain the phenomenon of interference in thin films in reflected light.

5. What are Newton's rings ? Explain how they are formed.

6. Explain the formation of colours in thin films.

7. Explain the phenomenon of interference in thin film in transmitted light.

8. How can Newton's rings be obtained in the laboratory ? How will you use them to measure the wavelength of sodium light ?

9. Explain the theory and the experimental arrangement of Newton's rings experiment.

10. What have you understood by non-reflecting films ? Explain.

11. Explain how the phenomenon of interference is utilized in testing the planeness of a surface.

12. In Newton's rings, show that the radii of dark rings are proportional to the square root of natural numbers.

13. When seen by reflected light, why does an excessively thin film appear to be perfectly black when illuminated by a white light ?

14. Explain, why colours are not observed in the case of a thick film when illuminated by a white light.

15. How can Newton's rings be used to determine the refractive index of a liquid ? Derive the formula used.

16. Prove that in reflected light Newton's rings, the diameters of bright rings are proportional to the square root of the odd natural numbers.

17. How can Newton's rings be obtained in the laboratory ? Prove that for Newton's rings in reflected light, the diameters of dark rings are proportional to the square root of natural numbers.

18. Explain how the principle of thin film interference can be used for measurement of thickness of thin film.

UNSOLVED PROBLEMS

1. A parallel beam of light of wavelength 5890 A° is incident on a thin film of refractive index 1.5, such that the angle of refraction into the film is 60°. Calculate the smallest thickness of the film which will make it appear dark by reflection.

   (Ans. 3.926×10^{-5} cm**)**

2. Two pin holes separated by a distance of 0.5 mm are illuminated by a monochromatic light of wavelength 6000 A°. An interference pattern is obtained on a screen placed at a distance of 100 cm from the pin holes. Find the distance on the screen between the fifth and tenth dark fringes.   **(Ans.** 0.6 cm**)**

3. An oil drop of volume 0.2 cc is dropped on the surface of a tank of water of area 1 sq. meter. The film spreads uniformly over the whole surface and white light reflected normally is observed through a spectrometer. The spectrum is seen to contain first dark band whose centre has wavelength of 5.5×10^{-5} cm. Find the refractive index of oil.

   (Ans. 1.375**)**

4. A soap film of refractive index $\frac{4}{3}$ and of thickness 1.5×10^{-4} cm is illuminated by white light incident at an angle of $60°$. The light reflected by it is examined by a spectroscope in which is found a dark band corresponding to a wavelength of 5×10^{-5} cm. Calculate the order of interference of the dark band.   **(Ans.** $n = 6$)

5. The optical path difference between two sets of similar waves from the same source arriving at a point on the screen is $199.5\ \lambda$. Is the point dark or bright ? If the path difference is 0.012 cm, find the wavelength of the light used.   **(Ans.** Dark, 6015 A°)

6. In a Newton's rings experiment, the diameter of the 5th ring is 0.336 cm and the diameter of the 15th ring is 0.590 cm. Find the radius of curvature of the plano convex lens, if the wavelength of light used is 5890 A°.   **(Ans.** 99.82 cm)

7. In a Newton's rings experiment, find the radius of curvature of the lens surface in contact with the glass plate when with a light of wavelength 5890 A°, the diameter of the third dark ring is 0.32 cm. The light is incident normally.   **(Ans.** 144.9 cm)

8. In Newton's rings, the diameter of a certain bright ring is 0.65 cm and that of tenth ring beyond it is 0.95 cm. If $\lambda = 6000$ A°, calculate the radius of curvature of a convex lens surface in contact with the glass plate.   **(Ans.** 200 cm)

9. In a Newton's rings experiment, a drop of water $\left(\mu = \frac{4}{3}\right)$ is placed between the lens and the plate. In that case, the diameter of the 10th ring was found to be 0.6 cm. Calculate the radius of curvature of the face of the lens in contact with the plate, given $\lambda = 6000$ A°.   **(Ans.** 200 cm)

10. Newton's rings are observed in reflected light of $\lambda = 5900$ A°. The diameter of the 5th dark ring is 0.4 cm. Find the radius of curvature of the lens and the thickness of the air film.   **(Ans.** 35.59 cms   0.000295 cm)

11. In a Newton's ring experiment, the diameters of 4th and 12th dark rings are 0.4 cm and 0.7 cm respectively. Calculate the diameter of 20th dark ring.   **(Ans.** 0.894 cm)

12. In a Newton's rings experiment, the source emits two wavelengths $\lambda_1 = 6000$ A° and $\lambda_2 = 4500$ A°. It is found that n^{th} dark ring due to λ_1 coincides with $(n + 1)^{th}$ dark ring due to λ_2. If the radius of curvature of the curved surface is 90 cm, find the diameter of nth dark ring for λ_1.   **(Ans.** 0.2538 cm)

13. If the diameter of nth dark ring in a Newton's ring experiment changes from 0.3 cm to 0.25 cm, as a liquid is placed between the lens and the plate, calculate the value of μ of the liquid. **(Ans.** μ = 1.44)

14. A wedge-shaped air film, having an angle of 45 seconds, is illuminated by monochromatic light and fringes are observed vertically through a microscope. The distance measured between the consecutive fringes is 0.12 cm, calculate the wavelength of light used. **(Ans.** 5233 A°)

15. Two pieces of plane glass are placed together with a piece of paper between the two at one edge. Find the angle in seconds, of the wedge shaped air film between the plates, if on viewing the film normally with monochromatic light of wavelength 4800 A°, there are 18 bands per cm. **(Ans.** 89.1 seconds)

16. Two rectangular pieces of a plane glass are laid one upon the other and a thin wire is placed between them, so that a thin wedge shaped air film is formed between them. The plates are illuminated with sodium light of λ = 5893 A° at normal incidence. Bright and dark bands are formed, there being 10 of each per cm length of the wedge measured normal to the edge in contact. Find the angle of the wedge.

(Ans. 2.94 × 10^{-4} radians)

17. Two optically plane glass strips of length 10 cm are placed one over the other. A thin foil of thickness 0.010 mm is introduced between the plates at one end to form an air film. If the light used has wavelength 5900 A°, find the separation between consecutive bright fringes. **(Ans.** 0.295 cm)

18. Find the thickness of a wedge-shaped film at a point where fourth bright fringe is situated. λ for sodium light is 5893 A°. **(Ans.** 1.03 × 10^{-4} cm)

SOLVED UNIVERSITY QUESTIONS

DECEMBER 2012

1. Define fringe width for wedge shaped film, obtain an expression for it. **[3]**

Ans. Please Refer to Article 1.5 on Page No. 1.14.

2. Prove that in Newton's Rings by reflected light the diameter of bright ring are proportional to the square root of the odd natural number. **[6]**

Ans. Please Refer to Article 1.7 on Page No. 1.23.

MAY 2013

1. Explain the formation Newton's ring with diagram and drive the diameter of bright ring. **[6]**

Ans. Please Refer to Article No 1.7 on Page No. 1.23.

2. Explain with diagram how interference Principle is used to design anti reflection coating. **[3]**

Ans. Please Refer to Article No 1.9.3 on Page No. 1.35.

NOVEMBER 2013

1. What are Newton's rings ? Draw the experimental set-up to obtain Newton's rings in the laboratory. Show that diameters of Newton's dark rings are proportional to the square root of natural numbers. **[6]**

Ans. Please Refer to Article 1.7 on Page No. 1.23.

2. Interference fringes are produced with monochromatic light falling normally on a wedge shaped film of refractive index 1.4. The angle of wedge is 10 sec of an arc and the distance between successive fringes is 0.5 cm. What is the wavelength of light used ? **[3]**

Ans. Data: $\mu = 1.4$

$\alpha = 10 \sec = \dfrac{10}{3600} \times \dfrac{\pi}{180}$ radian , $\beta = 0.5$ cm

Formula: $\beta = \dfrac{\lambda}{2\mu\alpha}$

$\lambda = \dfrac{2 \times 1.4 \times 10 \times 3.14 \times 0.5 \times 10^{-2}}{3600 \times 180}$

$\therefore$ $\lambda = 0.6783 \times 10^{-6}$ cm

or $\lambda = 6783$ A°

MAY 2014

1. Derive the equation of path difference between reflected rays when monochromatic light of wavelength 'λ' falls with angle of incidence 'I' on the uniform thickness film of refractive index 'μ'. Write the conditions of maxima and minima. **[6]**

Ans. Please Refer to Article 1.3 on Page No. 1.8.

DECEMBER 2014

1. Prove that in Newton's ring by reflected light the diameter of bright ring is proportional to square root of the odd natural numbers. **[6]**

Ans. Please Refer to Article 1.7 on Page No. 1.23.

2. A monochromatic beam of light of wavelength 5893 A° is incident normally on the top of a glass which is coated by transparent material MgF_2 having R.I. 1.38. Calculate smallest thickness of the MgF_2 layer which will act as a non reflecting surface. **[3]**

Ans. Similar Problem 1.25 on Page No. 1.37.

MAY 2015

1. Derive an equation for path difference in reflected light when monochromatic light falls on the uniform thickness film and hence state the conditions for maxima and minima. **[6]**

Ans. Please Refer to Article 1.3 and 1.3.1, Page No. 1.8 to 1.10.

2. Explain the formation of Newton's rings in the laboratory. **[3]**

Ans. Please Refer to Article 1.7 on Page No. 1.23 to 1.27.

   (Note: Derivation is not expected).

NOVEMBER 2015

1. Prove that in Newton's rings by reflected light the diameter of dark ring is proportional to square root of a natural number. **[6]**

Ans. Please refer to Article 1.7 on Page No. 1.23.

2. A soap film having refractive index 1.33, and thickness 5×10^{-5} cm is viewed at an angle of 35° to the normal. Find the wavelengths of light in the visible spectrum which will be absent from the reflected light. **[3]**

Ans.

Data:
$$\mu = 1.33$$
$$t = 5 \times 10^{-5} \text{ cm}$$
$$Q = 35°$$

Formula: (i) By Snell's Law $\dfrac{\sin i}{\sin r} = \mu$

(ii) $2 \mu t \cos r = n\lambda$

Solution:

(i) $\dfrac{\sin 35}{\sin r} = 1.33$

∴ $\sin r = 0.431$

∴ $r = 25.53°$

(ii) $\lambda = \dfrac{2 \times 1.33 \times 5 \times 10^{-5} \times \cos 25.53}{n}$

                      $\lambda = \dfrac{12000}{n}$ A°

for $n = 1$

                      $\lambda = 12000$ A°   (not is visible region)

for $n = 2$

                      $\lambda = \dfrac{12000}{2} = 6000$A°   (In visble region)

for $n = 3$

                      $\lambda = \dfrac{12000}{3} = 4000$A°   (Ir visble region)

for $n = 4$

                      $\lambda = \dfrac{12000}{4} = 3000$A°   (not ir visible region)

∴   Wavelengths absent from visible region are 6000A° and 4000A°.

MAY 2016

1. Explain with suitable diagram how interference is used to design anti-reflection coating.   [3]

Ans. Please Refer to Article 1.9.3 on Page No. 1.35.

2. A parallel beam of light 622 nm incident on a glass plate of refractive index 1.5 such that angle of refraction into the plate is 60°. Calculate the smallest thickness of the plate which will appear dark by reflection.   [3]

Ans. Data : $\lambda = 622$ nm, $\mu = 1.5$, $r = 60$, $n = 1$

Formula : $2\mu t \cos r = n\lambda$, **Solution:** $2 \times 1.5 \times t \times \cos 60 = 622 \times 10^{-9}$

$$t = \left[\frac{6.22 \times 10^{-9}}{2 \times 1.5 \times \cos 60°}\right]$$

$$t = \frac{622 \times 10^{-9} \text{ m}}{3 \times \frac{1}{2}}$$

$$t = \frac{622 \times 2 \times 10^{-9}}{3}$$

$$t = \frac{1244}{3} = 414.3 \times 10^{-9}$$

REFERENCES

For better understanding of interference patterns from thin films:

http://dev.physicslab.org/Document.aspx?doctype=3&filename=PhysicalOptics ThinFilmInterference.xml.

Animations of thin film interference patterns:

http://www.wellesley.edu/Physics/Yhu/Animations/tfi.html

To understand physics behind antireflection coatings:

http://mysite.verizon.net/vzeoacw1/thinfilm.html

Photographs of Newton's Rings pattern:

http://www.fas.harvard.edu/~scdiroff/1ds/LightOptics/NewtonsRings/NewtonsRings.html

More information about Michelson's interferometer and photographs of fringes:

http://www.phy.davidson.edu/StuHome/cabell_f/diffractionfinal/pages/Michelson.html.

✠ ✠ ✠

CHAPTER 2
DIFFRACTION

2.1 INTRODUCTION   [Nov. 13, May 14]

- Along with interference, diffraction is another phenomenon which supports the wave theory of light. Diffraction is responsible for the appearance of brilliant colours in a wide variety of natural phenomena. Diffraction with white light results into a beautiful rainbow like pattern.
- The flamboyant colours in the feathers of a peacock, the irridescent colours on the neck of pigeons, on the skins of snakes and on the back of beetles are due to diffraction of light.
- In practical applications, the diffraction affects the resolution of optical instruments such as microscopes and telescopes. Thus diffraction decides the usefulness of these devices.
- Diffraction of X-rays from the crystals is used in understanding the crystal structure. In engineering, diffraction is used for measurement of dimensions, stress, pressure etc.

Definition

- Diffraction is **bending of light** due to presence of an obstacle in the path of light. A diffraction pattern results from the interference of waves, diffracted by an obstacle, coming from the same source of light.
- For visible diffraction pattern,
  (a) The size of obstacle should be **comparable to the wavelength** of light.
  (b) The source of light must be a **point source**.
- Diffraction is also defined as the encroachment of light in the region of geometrical shadow.
- According to Huygen's wave theory, each progressive wave produces secondary waves, the envelope of which produces the secondary wavefront.

OR

- Every point of a wavefront may be considered as a source of secondary wavelets that spread out in all directions with a speed equal to the speed of propagation of waves.

Huygen's Theory

- In Fig. 2.1 (a), 'S' is a monochromatic source of light, MN is a small aperture, M'N' is the screen and AB is the illuminated portion on the screen in the absence of the aperture.
- Above A and below B, it is supposed to be a geometrically shadow region. But practically, the shadows formed are not sharp and light encroaches in the geometrical shadow region.

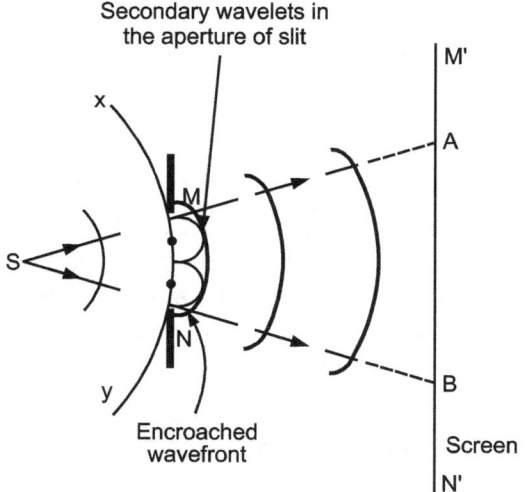

Fig. 2.1 (a)

- This is because when the primary wavefront XY is incident on the aperture MN, every point within the aperture can be viewed as creating secondary waves which propagate outward from the aperture. The envelope of all these secondary waves gives a new circular wavefront, thus slit works as a new source of light.

- The centre of the wave has more intensity and it fades out at the edges in the geometrical shadow region. Thus light through the aperture does not create a perfect image of the aperture and the diffraction observed can be explained.

- Similarly, if an opaque obstacle MN is placed in the path of light [See Fig. 2.1 (b)], the geometrical shadow region 'AB' is not sharp.

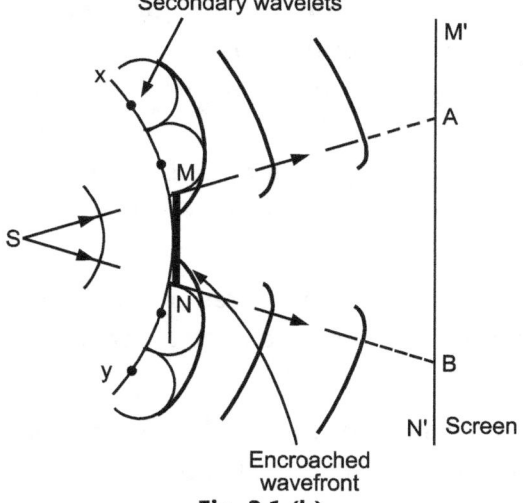

Fig. 2.1 (b)

- This is because when the primary wavefront XY is incident on the aperture MN, it develops a secondary wavefront. The envelope of this secondary wavefront encroaches in the geometrical shadow region.

2.2 DIFFRACTION OF WAVES   [Dec. 14]

- In general, a diffraction situation requires a source of light, an obstacle and a screen to form the diffraction pattern as shown in Fig. 2.2.

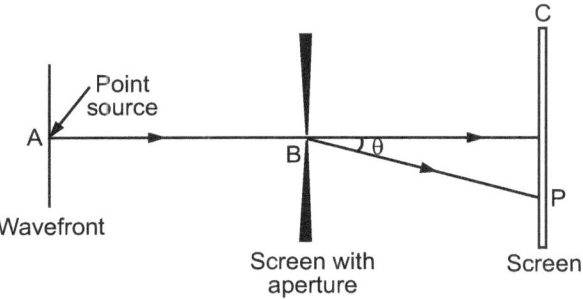

Fig. 2.2: General diffraction situation

- A plane wavefront A falls on an opaque screen B containing an aperture of arbitrary shape. The screen C receives the light that passes through this aperture.
- The light intensity pattern on the screen can be calculated by subdividing the wavefront into elementary areas **ds**, each of which becomes a source of expanding Huygen's wavelets. The light intensity at an arbitrary point P is found by superposing the wave disturbances caused by the wavelets reaching P, from all these elementary radiators.
- The wave disturbances reaching P differ in amplitude and phase because (i) the elementary radiators are at varying distances from P, (ii) areas of the radiators are different, and (iii) the light leaves the radiators at different angles to the normal to the wavefront.
- Diffraction patterns are not often observed in everyday life. This is because, ordinary light sources are not monochromatic and are not point sources.
- If an ordinary light bulb is used instead of a point source, each wavelength of light, from every point of the bulb, forms its own diffraction pattern. These patterns overlap and no individual pattern is observed.
- There is no fundamental difference between interference and diffraction. The term interference is used for effects involving waves from two sources. Diffraction involves a continuous distribution of secondary waves from a large number of sources or aperture. But, both phenomena are governed by the same basic superposition and Huygen's principle.

2.3 CLASSES OF DIFFRACTION   [Dec. 14]

- The diffraction involves a source, an obstacle and a screen. Depending upon the distances between source to obstacle and obstacle to the screen, diffraction is classified into two classes:
  - ➢ Fraunhofer's diffraction.
  - ➢ Fresnel's diffraction.

Fraunhofer's Diffraction	Fresnel's Diffraction
1. It is also called **far field** diffraction.	1. It is also called **near field** diffraction.
2. The source and screen are at **large distance** (infinite) from the obstacle.	2. The source and/or screen are at **small distance (finite)** from the obstacle.
3. The wavefronts incident on the obstacle and screen is a **plane wavefront** i.e. the rays are parallel.	3. The wavefronts incident on the obstacle are **spherical or cylindrical** i.e. rays are diverging.
4. The diffraction pattern is **not sensitive** to the distance.	4. The diffraction pattern is **sensitive** to the distance. (If distance is increased to large value it will be converted to Fraunhofer's diffraction.)
5. A **pair of convex lenses** are used for making the rays parallel.	5. The wavefront is directly allowed to fall on an obstacle or the screen.
6. 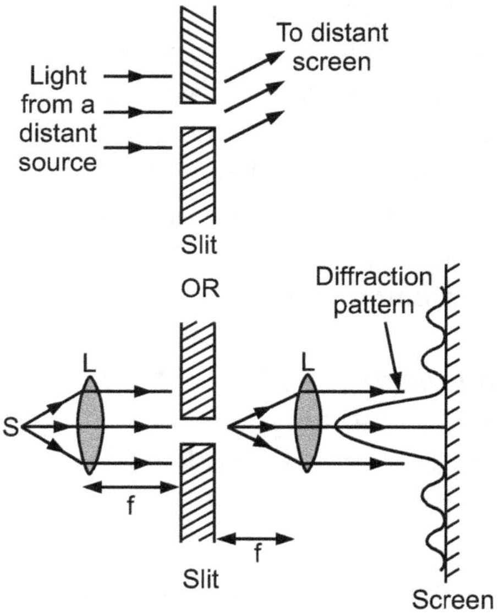 **Fig. 2.3 (a)**	6. 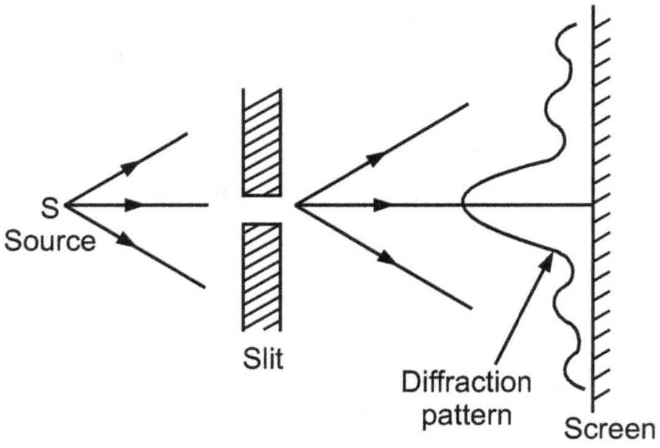 **Fig. 2.3 (b)**
7. The maximums and minimums are **well defined**. 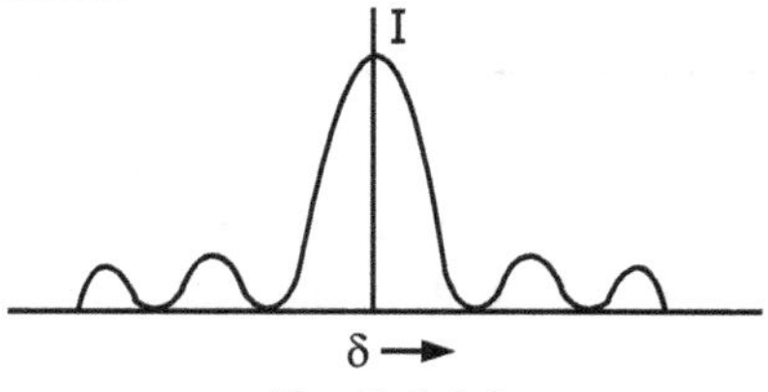 **Fig. 2.4 (a)**	7. The maximums and minimums are **not well defined**. 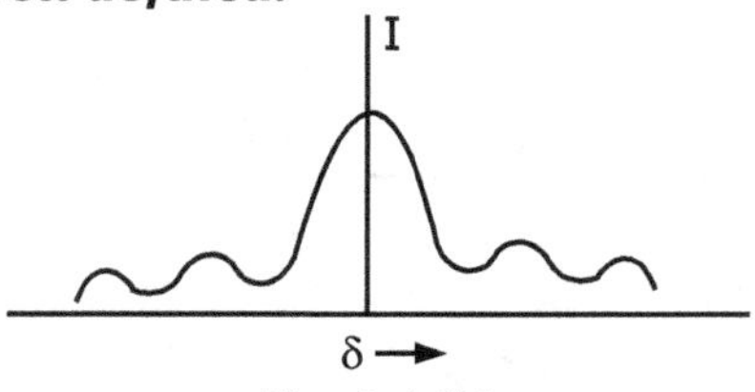 **Fig. 2.4 (b)**
8. Mathematical treatment is **simple**.	8. Mathematical treatment is **complicated**.

2.4   FRAUNHOFER'S DIFFRACTION AT SINGLE SLIT (GEOMETRICAL METHOD)

- For obtaining a Fraunhofer's diffraction pattern, the incident wavefront must be plane. Thus, **the source of light should either be at a large distance from the slit or a collimating lens must be used**.

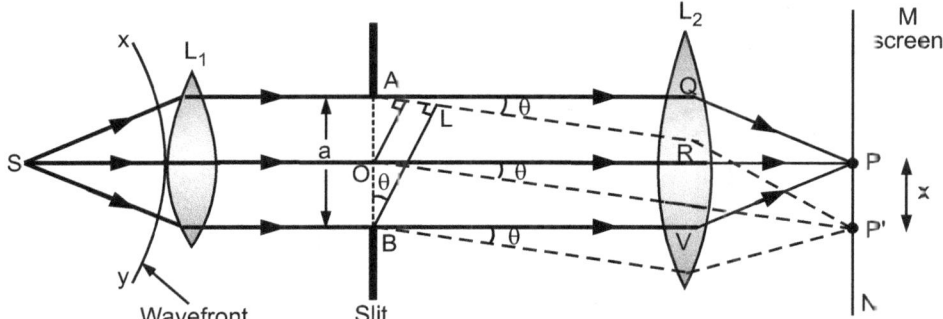

Fig. 2.5

- In Fig. 2.5, 'S' is a narrow slit perpendicular to the plane of the paper and lluminated by a monochromatic light to act as a source of light. The wave coming from source S is made parallel by the collimating lens L_1.

- A plane wavefront is incident on the slit AB and each point on this wavefront is a source of the secondary wavefront. The secondary waves from points equidistart from O and situated in the upper and lower halves OA and OB of the wavefront, travel the same distance to reach P and hence the path difference is zero. The secondary waves interfere with one another and P will be a point of **maximum intensity**.

- Now, consider that the secondary waves are travelling in the direction AR, inclined at an angle θ to the direction OP. All the secondary waves travelling in this direction reach the point P' on the screen.

- The point P' will be of **maximum** or **minimum intensity** depending on the path difference between the secondary waves originating from the corresponding points of the wavefront.

Phasor Method

- The diffraction pattern for a single slit can be found out by the phasor method. Our approach is as follows.

- We divide the slit into a large number of narrow **pseudoslits N** of equal width, $\Delta x = \dfrac{a}{N}$, where 'a' is the width of the slit. The contribution of each pseudoslit will be represented by a phasor. To find the resultant wave amplitude, we add the N phasors.

- For convenience in drawing, the slit of width 'a' in Fig. 2.6 (a) has been split into six pseudoslits. If we call the phase difference between the first and the last phasor as ϕ, it will be the angle labelled as ϕ in Fig. 2.6 (b).

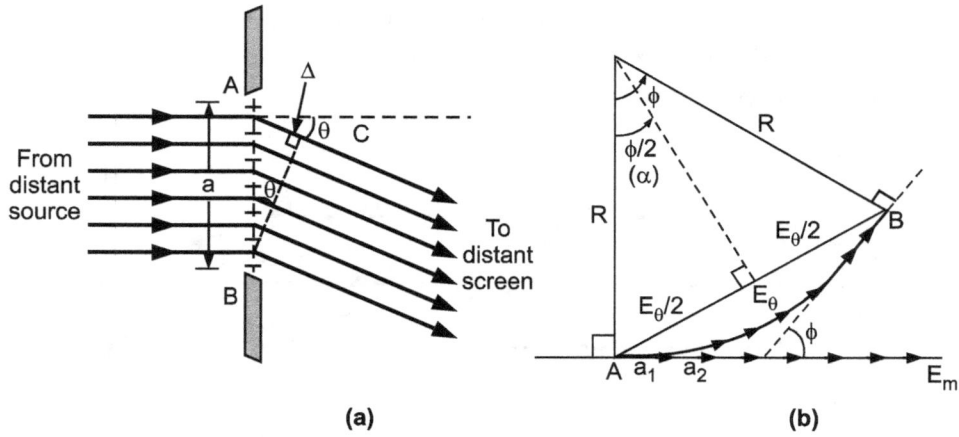

(a)   (b)

Fig. 2.6: (a) Diffraction from singe slit
(b) Phasor diagram

- The path difference between first and last wave is

$$\Delta = AC$$

$$\Delta = a \sin \theta \quad \text{[From Fig. 2.6 (a)]} \qquad \ldots (1)$$

$\therefore$ Phase difference,

$$\phi = k \cdot \Delta, \text{ where } k = \frac{2\pi}{\lambda}$$

$\therefore$

$$\phi = \frac{2\pi}{\lambda} \cdot \Delta = \frac{2\pi}{\lambda} (a \sin \theta) \qquad \ldots (2)$$

For simplicity we will define angle α, such that,

$$\alpha = \frac{\phi}{2} = \frac{\pi}{\lambda} (a \sin \theta) \qquad \ldots (3)$$

The phase difference between the waves reaching at the point from adjacent slit is

$$\Delta\phi = \frac{2\pi}{\lambda} (\Delta x \sin \theta) \qquad \ldots (4)$$

- The amplitude a_n contributed at a point on the screen by any one of the pseudoslit will be the same, since they are of equal width. But the phases of these amplitudes will be different at different points.

- Let δ be the phase difference between two adjacent amplitudes which is constant. So each amplitude is inclined at an angle δ with the preceding one and their vector sum E_θ is the resultant amplitude.

- If the wavefront is divided into large or infinite number of equal elements, the vector a_n will become shorter and δ will decrease by the same proportion. In this way, the vector diagram will approach **an arc of a circle**. The resultant amplitude E_θ is still the same and equal to **the length of the chord of arc**.

- The length of arc is just the amplitude E_m obtained when all of the amplitudes are in phase i.e. slit is not there and diffraction is absent. The radius of arc is R and a perpendicular has been dropped from the centre on the chord E_m. This will divide the apex angle and chord into two equal halves ($E_\theta/2$ and $E_\theta/2$)

- In Fig. 2.6 (b), from the right triangle with apex angle $\phi/2$, we see that

$$\frac{E_\theta}{2} = R \sin \phi/2 \qquad \ldots (5)$$

$$\therefore \quad E_\theta = 2R \sin \alpha \qquad \left(\because \alpha = \frac{\phi}{2} \right)$$

Also,
$$\phi = \frac{\text{length of arc}}{\text{radius}} = \frac{E_m}{R}$$

This gives
$$E_m = R\phi \quad \text{or} \quad E_m = 2R\alpha \qquad \ldots (6)$$

Dividing (5) by (6)

$$\frac{E_\theta}{E_m} = \frac{2R \sin \alpha}{2R\alpha}$$

$$\therefore \quad E_\theta = E_m \frac{\sin \alpha}{\alpha} \qquad \ldots (7)$$

Equation (7) gives the amplitude for the single slit diffraction pattern at any angle θ.

The intensity I_θ is proportional to the square of the amplitude.

$$\therefore \quad I_\theta = I_m \left(\frac{\sin \alpha}{\alpha} \right)^2 \qquad \ldots (8)$$

where $I_m = E_m^2$ is the maximum amplitude.

2.5 CONDITIONS FOR MAXIMA AND MINIMA

(i) Principal Maximum

- The resultant amplitude in diffraction pattern of a single slit is given by,

$$E_\theta = E_m \frac{\sin \alpha}{\alpha} = \frac{E_m}{\alpha} \left[\alpha - \frac{\alpha^3}{3!} + \frac{\alpha^5}{5!} - \frac{\alpha^7}{7!} + \ldots \right]$$

when $\sin \alpha$ is written in ascending powers of α, where $\alpha = \frac{\pi}{\lambda} a \sin \theta$.

$$\therefore \quad E_\theta = E_m \left[1 - \frac{\alpha^2}{3!} + \frac{\alpha^4}{5!} - \frac{\alpha^6}{7!} + \ldots \right]$$

For E_θ to be maximum, the negative terms in the bracket must vanish. This is possible only when $\alpha = 0$ i.e. $\alpha = \dfrac{\pi}{\lambda}$ a sin $\theta = 0$ or sin $\theta = 0$ or $\theta = 0$.

- Thus, the maximum value of E_θ is E_m and the principal maximum is formed at $\theta = 0$. The condition $\theta = 0$ simply means that this maximum is formed by parts of the secondary wavelets which travel normally to the slit. The position of principal maximum is directly opposite to the slit and it is bordered symmetrically by dark and bright bands.

(ii) Minimum Intensity Positions (Minima)

- The intensity $I_\theta = I_m \left(\dfrac{\sin \alpha}{\alpha}\right)^2$ will be zero in the diffraction pattern if,

$$\sin \alpha = 0 \text{ and } \alpha \neq 0.$$

The values of α which satisfy this condition are

$$\alpha = m\pi \qquad\qquad \text{where } m = \pm 1, \pm 2, \pm 3, \dots\dots$$

$$\therefore \qquad\qquad \alpha = \dfrac{\pi}{\lambda} \text{ a sin } \theta = m\pi$$

Thus, the condition for minima is

$$a \sin \theta = m\lambda \qquad\qquad\qquad\qquad \dots (1)$$

where $m = 0$ is not possible, because then θ becomes zero, which corresponds to the principal maximum.

Equation (1) gives the positions of minima on either side of the principal maximum in the diffraction pattern of a single slit.

(iii) Secondary Maxima

- Analysis shows that the secondary maxima lie approximately half way between the two minima. They are found from

$$\alpha = \pm\left(m + \dfrac{1}{2}\right)\pi, \qquad\qquad m = 1, 2, 3, \dots\dots$$

$$\text{or} \qquad a \sin \theta = (2m + 1)\cdot\lambda/2$$

Substituting this value of α in $I_\theta = I_m \left(\dfrac{\sin \alpha}{\alpha}\right)^2$, we get

$$\dfrac{I_\theta}{I_m} = \left\{\dfrac{\sin\left(m + \dfrac{1}{2}\right)\pi}{\left(m + \dfrac{1}{2}\right)\pi}\right\}^2 = \dfrac{1}{\left(m + \dfrac{1}{2}\right)^2 \cdot \pi^2}$$

For $m = 1, 2, 3, \dots\dots$

$$\dfrac{I_\theta}{I_m} = 0.045, \ 0.016, \ 0.0083 \ \dots\dots$$

2.6   INTENSITY PATTERN DUE TO A SINGLE SLIT   [May 14]

- Consider monochromatic plane waves incident on a single slit of width 'a'. When aperture is very small, only one secondary wavelet comes through and the wavefront is spherical. Suppose the slit width is such that several secondary wavelets pass through the slit. At the distance screen, these secondary wavelets superpose giving a rippled intensity distribution which is called **the single-slit diffraction pattern** as shown in Fig. 2.7.

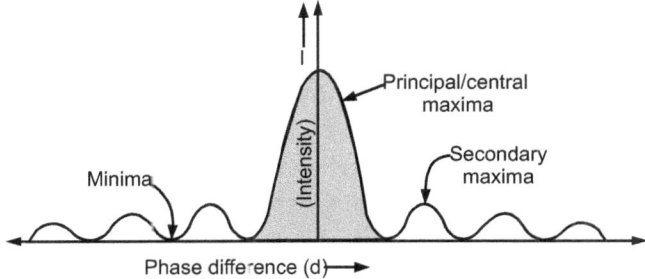

Fig. 2.7: Intensity distribution

- The intensity in the pattern has a central maximum and then falls to zero (the first minimum), past the first minimum the intensity rises to a relatively small secondary maximum before again dropping to zero (the second minimum). The rippling continues with each secondary maximum having less magnitude than the previous secondary maximum.

Dependence of Spectrum on Width and Wavelength

- The position of the minimum is given by, $a \sin \theta = m\lambda$. Therefore, the angular width of the spectrum will depend upon the slit width a, wavelength λ and order of interference m.
- The width of spectrum inversely depends upon the slit width, hence **smaller the slit width, wider will be the spectrum**. Fig. 2.8 shows spectrum width for different slit width.

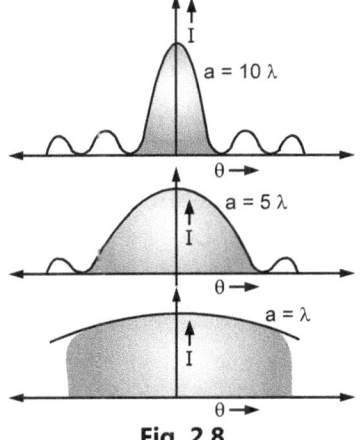

Fig. 2.8

- Fig. 2.8 shows the variation of single slit diffraction pattern as the slit width varies. Decreasing the aperture size from 10λ to 5λ causes the diffraction pattern to spread out about twice as far.

- The wavelength directly decides the spectrum width. If the slit is illuminated by white light, the light of different wavelengths will form a spectrum of different angular width. All this will overlap giving a colourful spectrum.

- The spectrum width directly depends on the order 'm'. But for higher order, the intensity decreases.

2.7 DIFFRACTION AT CIRCULAR APERTURE

- The diffraction pattern formed by a plane wave from a point source passing through a circular aperture is of considerable importance as it is applied to the resolving power of optical instruments such as telescopes, microscopes etc.

- The geometric optics assumes that the image of a point source will be a point. The geometrical optics does not consider the wave nature of light and hence diffraction at the edges of aperture of the instrument is neglected.

- But in practice the image is not a point image but a diffraction pattern formed by circular aperture. The diffraction pattern consists of a bright central maxima, corresponding to the image in geometrical optics, surrounded by fainter secondary maxima and minima.

- Fig. 2.9 shows diffraction pattern at a single slit.

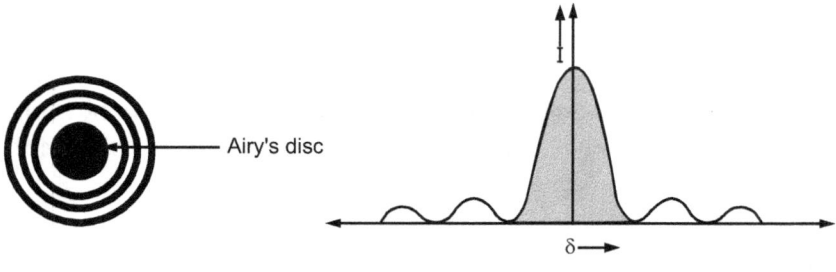

(a) Intensity pattern   (b) Intensity distribution

Fig. 2.9: Diffraction pattern

- The diffraction pattern consists of a bright central disc, known as **Airy's disc**, surrounded by a number of fainter rings. Neither the disc nor rings are sharply limited but shade off gradually at the edges, being separated by circle of zero intensity (minima).

- The condition for minima for a single slit is given by

$$a \sin \theta = m\lambda \quad \text{where } m = 0, 1, 2 \ldots \qquad \ldots \text{(I)}$$

In case of circular aperture, m is not an integer but can have fractional values such as m = 0, 1.22, 1.635 … .

The value $\theta = 0$ gives principal maxima while m = 1.22 gives first minima.

- The position of first minima decides the diameter of principal maxima, hence the resolving power of the instrument.

  Therefore, equation for first minima becomes

  $$a \sin \theta = 1.22\lambda \qquad \qquad \dots \text{(II)}$$

  If d is the diameter of circular aperture then,

  $$d \sin \theta = 1.22\lambda \qquad \qquad \dots \text{(III)}$$

  For small values of θ, $\qquad \sin \theta \approx \theta$.

  $$\therefore \qquad \qquad \theta = \frac{1.22\lambda}{d} \qquad \qquad \dots \text{(IV)}$$

2.8 PLANE DIFFRACTION GRATING

- **Grating:** An arrangement consisting of a *large number of parallel* slits of the same width and separated by equal opaque spaces is known as *diffraction grating*.

- A grating is prepared by ruling equidistant parallel lines on a plane glass plate with the help of a diamond point. The lines act as opaque spaces and the incident light cannot pass through them. The space between any two lines acts as a slit and is transparent to light.

- A plane transmission grating generally contains 15,000 to 20,000 lines per inch. It was first constructed by Fraunhofer.

- If the lines are drawn on a silvered surface, it acts as a *reflection grating*.

Theory of Plane Diffraction Grating

- Consider the diffraction pattern of N parallel slits each of width 'a' and separated by equal opaque spaces 'b'. The distance between the centres of adjacent slits is d = (a + b) and it is called the *grating element*.

- The grating element is defined as the reciprocal of number of lines per cm i.e.

  $$(a + b) = \frac{1}{N} \text{ , where N is lines per cm}$$

  or (a + b) = 2.54/N where N is lines per inch.

- Let a plane wavefront of wavelength λ be incident normally on the slits. According to Huygen's principle every point in the slit is regarded as the origin of secondary wavelets which spread out in all directions. Therefore, rays are diffracted from each slit in all directions.

- The resultant amplitude of light from a single slit of width 'a' in a direction making angle θ with the normal is given by

  $$E_N = E_m \left(\frac{\sin \alpha}{\alpha} \right) \qquad \qquad \dots \text{(1)}$$

where $\qquad \alpha = \dfrac{\pi}{\lambda} a \sin \theta$ $\qquad$ ... (2)

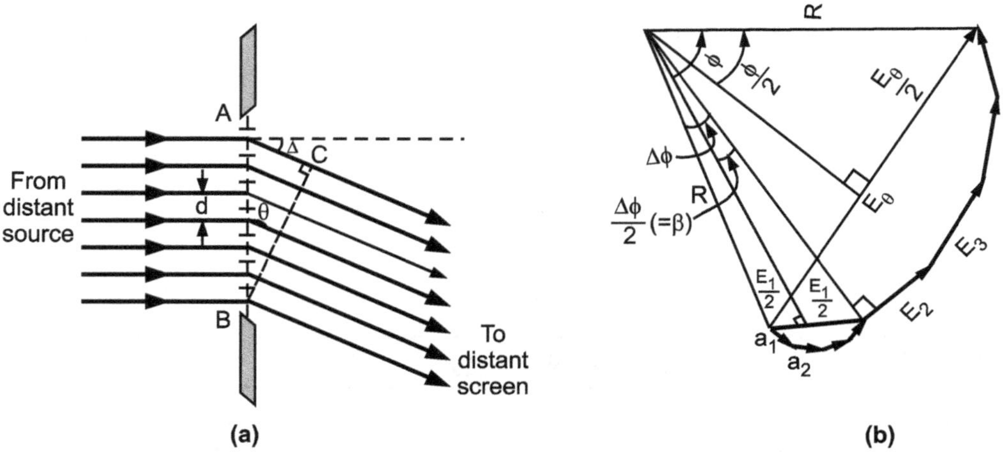

Fig. 2.10: (a) Diffraction at N slits, (b) Phasor diagram

- We can replace all the secondary wavelets in each slit by a single wave of amplitude $E_m \dfrac{\sin \alpha}{\alpha}$, starting from its mid-point and travelling at an angle θ with the normal.

- We need, therefore, find only the N-slit interference pattern and multiply it by $E_m \dfrac{\sin \alpha}{\alpha}$ to obtain the complete pattern.

- To find the interference pattern for N slits, we make use of phasors. Assuming each phasor to have amplitude E_N and at an angle $\Delta\phi$ the phasor diagram is as shown in Fig. 2.10 (b).

- The phase angle $\Delta\phi$ is the phase difference between the waves coming from adjacent slits and is given by

$$\Delta\phi = k \cdot \text{(path difference between consecutive slits)}$$

$$\Delta\phi = \frac{2\pi}{\lambda} (a + b) \sin \theta$$

$$\Delta\phi = \frac{2\pi}{\lambda} d \sin \theta \qquad \text{... (3)}$$

- We will define angle β such that

$$\beta = \frac{\Delta\phi}{2} = \frac{\pi}{\lambda} (a + b) \sin \theta \qquad \text{... (4)}$$

- The total phase difference between first and last wave will simply be sum of the phase differences added by each slit individually.

$\therefore \qquad\qquad\qquad \phi = N\Delta\phi$

$$\phi = N \frac{2\pi}{\lambda} (a + b) \sin \theta \qquad \text{... (5)}$$

or $\qquad\qquad\qquad \phi = 2N\beta \qquad\qquad \text{[from equation (4)] ... (6)}$

- As the slits of a grating are of equal width, the amplitude of light diffracted from each slit will be same. The amplitude of diffracted wave will be,

$$E_1 = E_2 = \dots\dots = E_N = E_m \left(\frac{\sin \alpha}{\alpha}\right) \qquad \dots (7)$$

- Mathematically, it can be proved that the resultant amplitude is,

$$E_\theta = E_m \frac{\sin \alpha}{\alpha} \cdot \frac{\sin N\beta}{\sin \beta} \qquad \dots (3)$$

Intensity is square of the amplitude.

$$\therefore \qquad I_\theta = I_m \left(\frac{\sin \alpha}{\alpha}\right)^2 \cdot \frac{\sin^2 N\beta}{\sin^2 \beta} \qquad \dots (9)$$

- The first factor $\left(\frac{\sin \alpha}{\alpha}\right)^2$ in equation (9) gives the intensity distribution in the **diffraction pattern due to a single slit**. The second factor $\frac{\sin^2 N\beta}{\sin^2 \beta}$ may be said to give the interference pattern for N slits.

- Thus, we can say that each of the N slits gives rise to a diffracted beam in which the intensity distribution depends on the width of the slit. These diffracted beams then interfere with one another to produce the final diffraction pattern.

2.9 CONDITIONS FOR MAXIMA AND MINIMA   [May 16]

(i) Principal Maxima

- The condition for principal maxima is that, the path difference between the waves from adjacent slits must be an integer multiple of λ. Therefore, the condition for principal maxima is

$$(a + b) \sin \theta = m\lambda, \text{ where, } m = 0, 1, 2, 3, \dots\dots m \qquad \dots (1)$$

Here m is called the **order of interference**.

This is equivalent to saying that,

$$\beta = \frac{\pi}{\lambda} (a + b) \sin \theta$$

$$\beta = \frac{\pi}{\lambda} (m\lambda) = m\pi \qquad \dots (2)$$

For these values of β, $\frac{\sin N\beta}{\sin \beta}$ becomes indeterminate.

But by L'Hospital's rule,

$$\underset{\beta \to m\pi}{\text{Lim}} \frac{\sin N\beta}{\sin \beta} = \underset{\beta \to m\pi}{\text{Lim}} \frac{N \cos N\beta}{\cos \beta} = \frac{N \cos Nm\pi}{\cos m\pi} = \pm N$$

$\therefore$ The intensity of the principal maxima is given as

$$I_\theta = N^2 \left(I_m \frac{\sin^2 \alpha}{\alpha^2} \right) \qquad \qquad \dots (3)$$

Thus, the intensity of principal maxima increases with increasing N. The intensity of the principal maximum is greatest while on either side of it, the intensities of other maxima go on decreasing.

(ii) Minima

- The intensity is given by, $I_\theta = \left(I_m \frac{\sin \alpha}{\alpha} \right)^2 \cdot \frac{\sin^2 N \beta}{\sin^2 \beta}$

For minima, $\sin N\beta = 0$ but $\sin \beta \neq 0$. i.e. $N\beta = m\pi$, where m has any integral value except N, 2N, 3N .... etc., because for these values of m, $\beta = 0, \pi, 2\pi....$ etc. and these correspond to principal maxima.

Thus, for minima, $N\beta = m\pi$

or $\beta = \dfrac{m\pi}{N}$ But $\beta = \dfrac{\pi}{\lambda} (a + b) \sin \theta$

$\therefore$ The condition for minima becomes

$$\frac{\pi}{\lambda} (a + b) \sin \theta = \frac{m\pi}{N}$$

or $(a + b) \sin \theta = \dfrac{m}{N} \lambda$, but $m \neq nN$ $\dots (4)$

where n = 0, 1, 2, 3, ...

Hence, the positions of minima are given by

$$(a + b) \sin \theta = \frac{\lambda}{N}, \frac{2\lambda}{N}, \frac{3\lambda}{N} \dots\dots \qquad \dots (5)$$

There are (N – 1) minima between any two consecutive principal maxima.

(iii) Secondary Maxima

- As there are (N – 1) minima between two consecutive principal maxima, there must be (N – 2) other maxima coming alternatively with the minima between two consecutive principal maxima. These maxima are called the secondary maxima. The positions of secondary maxima are obtained by differentiating the expression for intensity with respect to β and equating to zero.

2.10 INTENSITY PATTERN

- A diffraction pattern due to diffraction grating consists of m principal maximum, one each for integer value of m. But the intensity of the principal maxima goes on decreasing with order.
- In between any two principal maxima there are minima and secondary. The intensity of secondary maxima is negligible in comparison with the intensity of principal maxima.

The intensity from maxima to minima or minima to maxima changes gradually as a function of sine.

- The number of minima and secondary maxima in between principal maxima is not fixed but depends upon the number of slits in grating.
- If the number of slits in grating are N, then the number of minima will be (N − 1) and secondary maxima will be (N − 2).
- Fig. 2.11 shows diffraction pattern for N = 5, which has (N − 1 = 4) minima and (N − 2 = 3) secondary maxima.

Diffraction pattern for N = 5

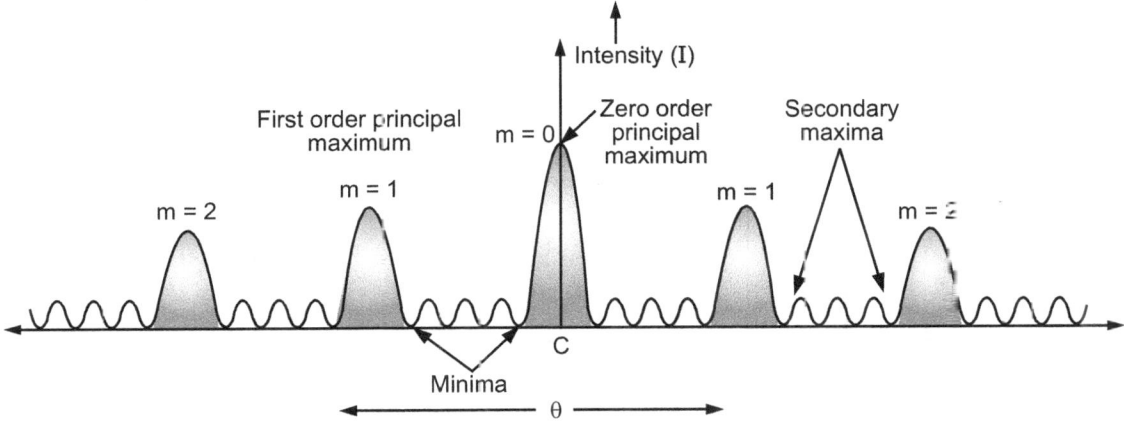

Fig. 2.11: Diffraction pattern for a grating

2.11 SCATTERING OF LIGHT AS AN APPLICATION OF DIFFRACTION (QUALITATIVE ONLY)

- When light of intensity I_o enters a long glass cylinder filled with smoke, the intensity of the beam emerging from the other end will be less than the original intensity and will depend on the length of the tube.
- If d is the length of the tube then the intensity of the emerging beam I will be

$$I = I_o\, e^{-\alpha d} \qquad \qquad \dots \text{(I)}$$

where α is the extinction coefficient.

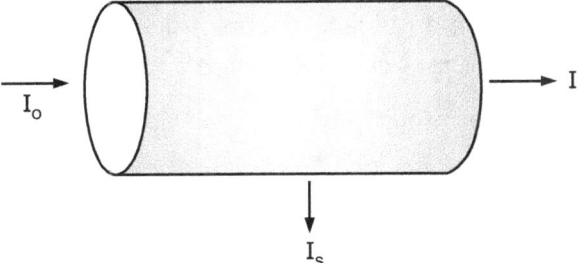

Fig. 2.12: Scattering of light

- The extinction coefficient consists of two parts, α_a due to absorption and α_s due to scattering.

$\therefore$
$$I = I_o \, e^{-(\alpha_a + \alpha_s) \, d}$$
... (II)

- In most of the cases, one may be negligible with respect to other, but in some cases both may be present significantly.

- The scattering of light is due to smoke particles in the tube and can be seen from the sides of the tube.

Scattering

- When a beam of light strikes the obstacle and size of obstacle is greater than the wavelength of light, the light coming from the reflector will be short segments of plane wavefront, not sharply bound at their edges but spreads slightly due to diffraction. Fig. 2.13 shows the reflection/diffraction for light waves.

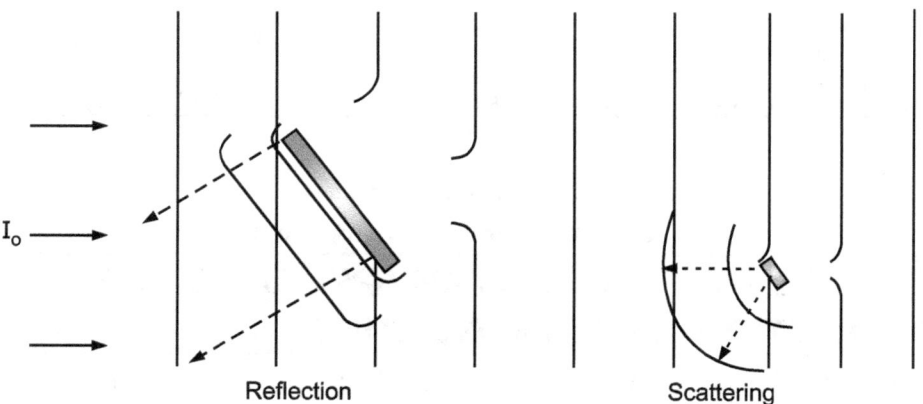

Reflection   Scattering

Fig. 2.13: Reflection/Diffraction of light

- When the obstacle is much smaller than the wavelength, the spreading is so much that the reflected waves differ very little from uniform spherical waves. In this case the light is said to be **scattered** rather than reflected, thus scattering is a special case of diffraction.

- When light is scattered from an object much smaller than the wavelength of light the wavefront will be spherical. This is called **Rayleigh's scattering**.

- In Rayleigh's scattering the intensity of scattered light is proportional to the incident intensity and wavelength.

i.e.
$$I_s = K \cdot \frac{I}{\lambda^4}$$
... (III)

where K is a constant.

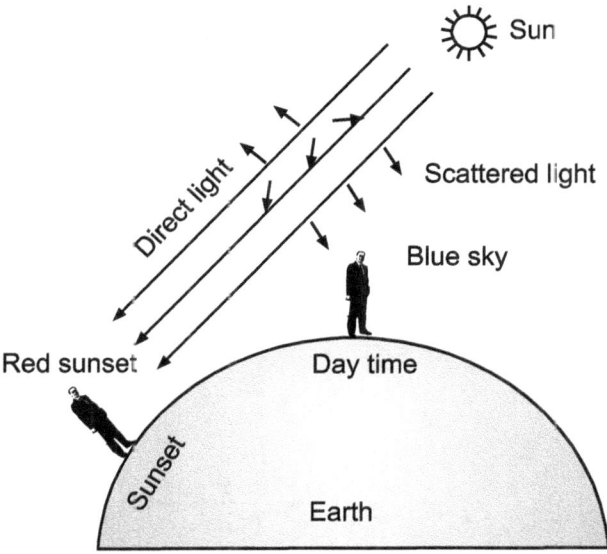

Fig. 2.14: Rayleigh's scattering

- From the equation it is clear that for given size of the particle, longer wavelengths would be less effective scattered than the short one. Therefore scattering of blue colour will be more than red colour.

- In day time an observer receives scattered light from the molecules of atmospheric gas, therefore, sky appears to be blue.

- But at the time of sunrise or sunset as the light travels larger distance in atmosphere, so by the time it reaches the observer it lacks in blue colour because of scattering and has becomes rich in red colour. Therefore, sunrise or sunset is red.

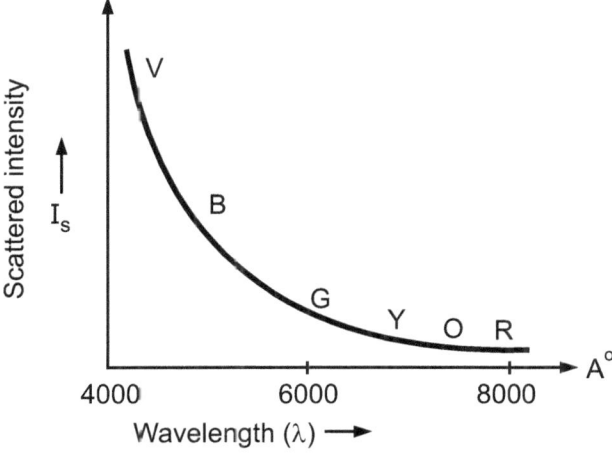

Fig. 2.15: Variation of scattered intensity with wavelength

SOLVED PROBLEMS

Problem 2.1: *A slit of width 0.16 mm is illuminated by a light of wavelength 5600 A°. Find the half angular width of the central maximum.*

Data: $a = 0.016$ cm, $\lambda = 5600 \times 10^{-8}$ cm, $n = 1$.

Formula: $a \sin \theta = n\lambda$.

Solution:

$$a \sin \theta = n \lambda$$
$$\text{but} \quad n = 1$$

$\therefore$

$$\sin \theta = \frac{\lambda}{a}$$

$$\theta = \sin^{-1} \frac{\lambda}{a}$$

Substituting,

$$\theta = \sin^{-1} \left(\frac{5600 \times 10^{-8}}{0.016} \right)$$

$\therefore$

$$\boxed{\theta = 12'}$$

Problem 2.2: *A slit of variable width is illuminated by red light of $\lambda = 6500$ A°. At what width of the slit, the first minimum will fall at $\theta = 30°$?*

Data: $\lambda = 6500 \times 10^{-8}$ cm, $\theta = 30°$, $n = 1$

Formula: $a \sin \theta = n\lambda$.

Solution:

$$a \sin \theta = n \lambda$$
$$\text{but} \quad n = 1$$

$$a = \frac{\lambda}{\sin \theta}$$

Substituting,

$$a = \frac{6500 \times 10^{-8}}{\sin 30}$$

$\therefore$

$$\boxed{a = 0.13 \times 10^{-3} \text{ cm}}$$

Problem 2.3: *A light of $\lambda = 6000$ A° falls on a screen at a distance of 200 cm from a narrow slit. Find the width of the slit, if the first minimum lies 5 mm on either side of the central maximum.*

Data: $\lambda = 6000 \times 10^{-8}$ cm, $f = 200$ cm, $x = 0.5$ cm, $n = 1$.

Formula: $a \sin \theta = n\lambda$, $\tan \theta = \frac{x}{f} \approx \sin \theta$

Solution:

$$\sin \theta = \frac{\lambda}{a} = \frac{x}{f} \qquad \because n = 1$$

$$\frac{\lambda}{a} = \frac{x}{f}$$

$$a = \frac{\lambda f}{x}$$

Substituting,

$$a = \frac{6000 \times 10^{-8} \times 200}{0.5}$$

$$\boxed{a = 0.024 \text{ cm}}$$

Problem 2.4: *A lens whose focal length is 40 cm forms a Fraunhofer diffraction pattern of a slit 0.3 mm wide. Calculate the distance of the first dark band and of the next bright band from the axis. Given $\lambda = 5890 \text{ A}^\circ$.*

Data: $\lambda = 5890 \times 10^{-8}$ cm, $f = 40$ cm, $a = 0.03$ cm

Formula: $a \sin \theta = n\lambda$

$$\sin \theta = \frac{x}{f}$$

$$a \sin \theta = (2n + 1) \frac{\lambda}{2}$$

Solution:

For $n = 1$,

$$\sin \theta = \frac{\lambda}{a}$$

For first dark band,

$$\sin \theta = \frac{x}{f}$$

∴

$$\frac{\lambda}{a} = \frac{x}{f}$$

∴

$$x = \frac{\lambda f}{a}$$

Substituting,

$$x = \frac{5890 \times 10^{-8} \times 40}{0.03}$$

∴

$$\boxed{x = 0.0785 \text{ cm}}$$

For bright band, $n = 1$

$$a \sin \theta = (2n + 1) \frac{\lambda}{2} \qquad \dots (1)$$

$$\sin \theta = \frac{x_1}{f} \qquad \dots (2)$$

From (1) and (2),

$$\frac{x_1}{f} = (2n + 1) \frac{\lambda}{2a}$$

$$x_1 = \frac{3}{2} \frac{\lambda}{a} f$$

Substituting,

$$x_1 = \frac{3}{2} \frac{5890 \times 10^{-8}}{0.03} \times 40$$

$$\boxed{x_1 = 0.11775 \text{ cm}}$$

Problem 2.5: *A lens of focal length 100 cm forms Fraunhofer's diffraction pattern of a single slit of width 0.04 cm in its focal plane. The incident light contains two wavelengths λ_1 and λ_2. It is found that, fourth minimum corresponding to λ_1 and the fifth minimum corresponding to λ_2 occur at the same point 0.5 cm from the central maximum. Calculate λ_1 and λ_2.*

Data: $f = 100$ cm, $a = 0.04$ cm, $x = 0.5$ cm

Formula: $a \sin \theta = n\lambda$, $\sin \theta = \dfrac{x}{f}$.

Solution: Condition for fourth minimum

$$a \sin \theta_1 = 4 \lambda_1$$

$\therefore$ $\qquad\qquad\qquad\qquad \sin \theta_1 = \dfrac{4 \lambda_1}{a}$ $\qquad\qquad\qquad$ ... (1)

Also, $\qquad\qquad\qquad\qquad \sin \theta_1 = \dfrac{x}{f}$ $\qquad\qquad\qquad\qquad$ ... (2)

From (1) and (2), $\qquad\qquad \dfrac{x}{f} = 4 \dfrac{\lambda_1}{a}$

$\therefore$ $\qquad\qquad\qquad\qquad \lambda_1 = \dfrac{x}{f} \cdot \dfrac{a}{4}$

$$\lambda_1 = \dfrac{0.5}{100} \times \dfrac{0.04}{4}$$

$$\boxed{\lambda_1 = 5 \times 10^{-5} \text{ cm}}$$

It is given that fourth minimum of λ_1 coincides with fifth minimum of λ_2. In that case, $\theta_1 = \theta_2 = \theta$, where θ_1 and θ_2 are the angular deviations for the fourth and fifth minimum respectively, then

$$a \sin \theta_1 = 4 \lambda_1 = 5 \lambda_2$$

or $\qquad\qquad\qquad\qquad 5 \lambda_2 = 4 \lambda_1$

$$\lambda_2 = \dfrac{4}{5} \lambda_1$$

$\therefore$ $\qquad\qquad\qquad\qquad \lambda_2 = \dfrac{4}{5} \times 5 \times 10^{-5}$

$$\boxed{\lambda_2 = 4 \times 10^{-5} \text{ cm}}$$

Problem 2.6: *In Fraunhofer's diffraction pattern due to a single slit, the screen is at a distance of 100 cm from the slit and the slit is illuminated by a monochromatic light of wavelength 5893 A°. The width of the slit is 0.1 mm. Calculate the separation between the central maximum and the first minimum.*

Data: f = 100 cm, λ = 5893 × 10⁻⁸ cm, a = 0.1 mm = 0.01 cm

Formula: $a \sin \theta = n\lambda$, $\tan \theta = \dfrac{x}{f} \approx \sin \theta$

Solution:

$$x = f\frac{\lambda}{a}$$

$$x = \frac{100 \times 5893 \times 10^{-8}}{0.01}$$

$$\boxed{x = 0.5893 \text{ cm}}$$

Problem 2.7: *Calculate the angular position of the first minimum in Fraunhofer's diffraction pattern of a slit 10⁻⁴ cm wide, if it is illuminated by light of wavelength 5000 A°.*

Data: λ = 5000 A°, a = 10⁻⁴ cm, n = 1

Formula: $a \sin \theta = n\lambda$.

Solution:

$$a \sin \theta = n\lambda$$

$$\sin \theta = \frac{n\lambda}{a}$$

$$\theta = \sin^{-1}\left(\frac{n\lambda}{a}\right)$$

$$\theta = \sin^{-1}\left(\frac{1 \times 5000 \times 10^{-8}}{10^{-4}}\right)$$

$$\boxed{\theta = 30°}$$

Problem 2.8: *A light of wavelength 5 × 10⁻⁵ cm is incident normally on the plane transmission grating of width 3 cm and having 15000 lines. Find the angle of diffraction in the first order.*

Data: λ = 5 × 10⁻⁵ cm, $(a + b) = \dfrac{3}{15000}$, n = 1

Formula: $(a + b) \sin \theta = n\lambda$.

Solution:

$$(a + b) \sin \theta = n\lambda$$

$$\sin \theta = \frac{n\lambda}{a + b}$$

$$\theta = \sin^{-1}\left(\frac{\lambda}{a + b}\right)$$

Substituting, $$\theta = \sin^{-1}\left(\frac{5 \times 10^{-5}}{3} \times 15000\right)$$

$$\boxed{\theta = 14° \ 29'}$$

Problem 2.9: *The limits of a visible spectrum are approximately 400×10^{-7} cm to 700×10^{-7} cm. Find the angular width of the first order visible spectrum produced by a plane grating having 15000 lines/inch when light is incident normally on the grating.*

Data: $\lambda_1 = 400 \times 10^{-7}$ cm, $\lambda_2 = 700 \times 10^{-7}$ cm, $a + b = \dfrac{1}{\dfrac{15000}{2.54}} = \dfrac{2.54}{15000}$ cm

Formula: $(a + b) \sin \theta = n\lambda$.

Solution: Let θ_1 and θ_2 be the angles corresponding to λ_1 and λ_2.

Here, $$n = 1$$

$\therefore$ $$\sin \theta_1 = \frac{\lambda}{a + b}$$

or $$\theta_1 = \sin^{-1}\frac{\lambda_1}{(a + b)}$$

$$\sin \theta_2 = \frac{\lambda_2}{a + b}$$

$$\theta_2 = \sin^{-1}\left(\frac{\lambda_2}{(a + b)}\right)$$

$\therefore$ Angular width of first order visible spectrum will be $\theta_2 - \theta_1$.

Substituting, $$\theta_1 = \sin^{-1}\left(\frac{400 \times 10^{-7} \times 15000}{2.54}\right)$$

$$\theta_1 = 13° \ 40'$$

$$\theta_2 = \sin^{-1}\frac{700 \times 10^{-7} \times 15000}{2.54}$$

$$\theta_2 = 24° \ 30'$$

$\therefore$ $$\theta_2 - \theta_1 = 24° \ 30' - 13° \ 40'$$

$$= \boxed{10° \ 50'}$$

Problem 2.10: *A parallel beam of sodium light is allowed to be incident normally on a plane grating having 4250 lines per cm and a second order spectral line is observed to be deviated through 30°. Calculate the wavelength of the spectral line.*

Data: $\theta = 30°$, $a + b = \dfrac{1}{4250}$, $n = 2$.

Formula: $(a + b) \sin \theta = n\lambda$.

Solution:

$$(a + b) \sin \theta = n \lambda$$

$$\text{but} \quad n = 2$$

$$\therefore \qquad \lambda = \frac{(a + b)}{2} \sin \theta$$

$$\text{Substituting,} \qquad \lambda = \frac{1}{4250} \times \frac{1}{2 \times 2}$$

$$\lambda = 5.880 \times 10^{-5} \text{cm} = \boxed{5880 \, A°}$$

Problem 2.11: *How many orders will be visible, if the wavelength of the incident radiation is 5000 A° and the number of lines on the grating is 2620 in one inch ?*

Data: $\lambda = 5000 \times 10^{-8}$ cm, $(a + b) = \dfrac{2.54}{2620}$ cm

Formula: $(a + b) \sin \theta = n\lambda$.

Solution: $(a + b) \sin \theta = n \lambda$

To have maximum order, the maximum possible value of $\sin \theta = 1$

$$\therefore \qquad n = \frac{(a + b)}{\lambda}$$

$$\text{Substituting,} \qquad n = \frac{2.54}{2620} \times \frac{1}{5 \times 10^{-5}}$$

$$\therefore \qquad \boxed{n = 19.38}$$

Hence, the highest order of the spectrum which can be seen is 19.

Problem 2.12: *In a plane transmission grating, the angle of diffraction for the second order principal maximum for the wavelength 5×10^{-5} cm is 30°. Calculate the number of lines in one cm of the grating surface.*

Data: $\lambda = 5 \times 10^{-5}$ cm, $\theta = 30°$, $r = 2$.

Formula: $(a + b) \sin \theta = n\lambda$.

Solution: $(a + b) \sin \theta = n \lambda$

$$\text{but,} \quad n = 2$$

$$\therefore \qquad (a + b) = \frac{n\lambda}{\sin \theta}$$

Substituting, $\qquad (a + b) = \frac{2 \times 5 \times 10^{-5}}{1/2}$

$\therefore \qquad (a + b) = 20 \times 10^{-5}$ cm

But $\qquad (a + b) = \frac{1}{\text{no. of lines/cm}}$

$\therefore \qquad$ No. of lines/cm $= \frac{1}{a + b} = \frac{1}{20 \times 10^{-5}} = \boxed{5000 \text{ lines/cm}}$

Problem 2.13: *Monochromatic light of wavelength 6×10^{-5} cm falls normally on a slit of width 0.001 cm. Calculate the angular width of the central bright maximum.*

Data: $\lambda = 6 \times 10^{-5}$ cm, $a = 0.001$ cm

Formula: $a \sin \theta = n\lambda$.

Solution: $\qquad a \sin \theta = n\lambda$

$\qquad$ but, $n = 1$

$\therefore \qquad \sin \theta = \frac{\lambda}{a}$

$\qquad \theta = \sin^{-1} \frac{\lambda}{a}$

$\qquad \theta = \sin^{-1} \frac{6 \times 10^{-5}}{0.001} = 3° \ 26'$

$\therefore$ The angular width of the central bright maximum $= 2\theta = \boxed{6° \ 52}'$

Problem 2.14: *Monochromatic light of wavelength 6.56×10^{-5} cm falls normally on a grating 2 cm wide. The first order spectrum is produced at an angle of $18° \ 14'$ from the normal. What is the total number of lines on the grating ?*

Data: $\lambda = 6.56 \times 10^{-5}$ cm, $\theta = 18° \ 14'$, $n = 1$.

$\qquad$ Total width of the grating $= 2$ cm

Formula: $(a + b) \sin \theta = n\lambda$.

Solution: $\qquad (a + b) \sin \theta = n\lambda$

As $\qquad n = 1$

$\therefore \qquad (a + b) = \frac{\lambda}{\sin \theta}$

Substituting, $\qquad (a + b) = \frac{6.56 \times 10^{-5}}{\sin 18° \ 14'} = \frac{6.56 \times 10^{-5}}{0.3123}$

$$(a + b) = 21.005 \times 10^{-5} \text{ cm}$$

But $$(a + b) = \frac{1}{\text{No. of lines/cm}}$$

$$21.005 \times 10^{-5} = \frac{1}{\text{No. of lines/cm}}$$

∴ $$\text{No. of lines/cm} = \frac{1}{21.005 \times 10^{-5}}$$

$$= \boxed{4761 \text{ lines/cm}}$$

Since, the grating has 2 cm width, total number of lines on the grating is 4761 × 2 = $\boxed{9,522}$

Problem 2.15: *A grating has 6000 lines/cm. Find the angular separation of two yellow lines of mercury of wavelengths 5770 A° and 5791 A° in the second order.* **(May 99)**

Data: $a + b = \dfrac{1}{6000}$ cm. $\lambda_1 = 5770 \times 10^{-8}$ cm

$$\lambda_2 = 5791 \times 10^{-8} \text{ cm}$$

$$n = 2$$

Formula: $(a + b) \sin \theta = n\lambda$.

Solution: $(a + b) \sin \theta_n = n\lambda$

For λ_1, $(a + b) \sin \theta_2 = n\,\lambda_1$

$$\sin \theta_2 = \frac{n\,\lambda_1}{(a + b)} = 2 \times 5770 \times 10^{-8} \times 6000 = 0.6924$$

$$\theta_2 = 43.82°$$

For λ_2, $(a + b) \sin \theta_2 = n\,\lambda_2$

$$\sin \theta_2 = \frac{n\,\lambda_2}{(a + b)} = 2 \times 5791 \times 10^{-8} \times 6000 = 0.6949$$

$$\theta_2 = 44.02°$$

Angular separation between the two yellow lines $= \theta_2' - \theta_2$

$$= 44.02 - 43.82 = \boxed{0.2° \text{ or } 12'}$$

Problem 2.16: *Calculate the angles at which the first dark band and the next bright band are formed in Fraunhofer's diffraction pattern of a slit of 0.2 mm wide. Given $\lambda = 5890$ A°.*

Data: $a = 0.2$ mm, $\lambda = 5890$ A°.

Formulae: (i) $a \sin \theta = n\lambda$ (ii) $a \sin \theta' = \left(n + \dfrac{1}{2}\right)\lambda$

Solution:

(i) For n = 1 $\Rightarrow$ $\sin\theta = \dfrac{n\lambda}{a} = \dfrac{5890 \times 10^{-10}}{0.2 \times 10^{-3}} = 2.945 \times 10^{-3}$

$\theta = \sin^{-1}(2.945 \times 10^{-3}) = 0.1687° = \boxed{10.12°}$

(ii) For n = 2 $\Rightarrow$ $a \sin\theta' = \left(n + \dfrac{1}{2}\right)\lambda$; $\sin\theta' = \left(n + \dfrac{1}{2}\right)\dfrac{\lambda}{a} = \dfrac{3\lambda}{2a}$

$\sin\theta' = 4.4175 \times 10^{-3}$; $\theta' = 0.2531° = \boxed{15.18°}$

Problem 2.17: *Examine if two spectral lines of wavelengths 5890 A° and 5896 A° can be clearly resolved in the (i) first order and (ii) second order by a diffraction grating 2 cm wide and having 425 lines per cm.*

Data: $\lambda_1 = 5890$ A°, $\lambda_2 = 5896$ A°, w = 2 cm, N = 425 lines/cm

Formula: $(a + b)\sin\theta = m\lambda$

Solution: $(a + b) = \dfrac{2}{425} = 4.7 \times 10^{-3}$ cm , n = 1

In first order:

$$\sin\theta_1 = \frac{n\lambda_1}{a + b} = \frac{1 \times 5890 \times 10^{-8}}{4.7 \times 10^{-3}}$$

$$\sin\theta_1 = 0.0125$$

$$\theta_1 = 0.71°$$

$$\sin\theta_1 = \frac{n\lambda_2}{a + b} = \frac{1 \times 5896 \times 10^{-8}}{4.7 \times 10^{-3}}$$

$$\sin\theta_1 = 0.01254$$

$$\boxed{\theta_1 = 0.71°}$$

In second order: $\sin\theta_2 = \dfrac{n\lambda_1}{a + b} = \dfrac{2 \times 5890 \times 10^{-8}}{4.7 \times 10^{-3}}$

$$\sin\theta_2 = 0.02506$$

$$\sin\theta_2 = 1.44°$$

$$\sin\theta_2 = 0.02508$$

$$\boxed{\theta_2 = 1.4376}$$

θ_2 both values slightly differ means slightly resolved.

Problem 2.18: *Calculate the wavelength of light whose diffraction maximum in the diffraction pattern due to a single slit falls at θ = 30° and coincides with the first minimum for red light of wavelength 6500 A°.*

Data: $\theta = 30°$, $\lambda = 6500$ A°

Formulae: (i) $a \sin \theta = n\lambda_1$, (ii) $a \sin \theta = \left(n + \dfrac{1}{2}\right)\lambda_2$ for bright band

'a' is constant, θ is constant order.

Solution: (i) $n\lambda_1 = \left(n + \dfrac{1}{2}\right)\lambda_2$ here n = 1

(ii) $\lambda_2 = \dfrac{n\lambda_1}{\left(n + \dfrac{1}{2}\right)} = \dfrac{\lambda_1}{3/2} = \boxed{4333.33 \text{ A}°}$

Problem 2.19: *Monochromatic light of wavelength λ = 6560 A° falls normally on a grating. The spectral line is diffracted at an angle of 19°9' from the normal in the first order. Find the grating element.*

Data: $\lambda = 6560$ A°, $\theta = 19° 9'$, n = 1

Formula: $(a + b) \sin \theta = m\lambda$

Solution: $(a + b) = \dfrac{m\lambda}{\sin \theta} = \dfrac{1 \times 6560 \times 10^{-8}}{\sin (19° 9')}$

$= \dfrac{6560 \times 10^{-8}}{0.340} = 1.9 \times 10^{-4} = \boxed{2 \times 10^{-4} \text{ cm}}$

Problem 2.20: *Light is incident normally on a grating 0.5 cm wide with 2500 lines. Find the angles of diffraction for the principal maxima of the two sodium lines in the first order spectrum $\lambda_1 = 5890$ A° and $\lambda_2 = 5896$ A°.*

Data: w = 0.5 cm, Total lines = 2500 lines, $\lambda_1 = 5890$ A°, $\lambda_2 = 5896$ A°.

Solution: In 1 cm = 2500 × 2 = 5000 lines ∴ $(a + b) = \dfrac{1}{5000} = 2 \times 10^{-4}$ cm, order n = 1.

For wavelength $\lambda_1 = 5890$,

$\sin \theta_1 = \dfrac{n\lambda_1}{a + b} = \dfrac{1 \times 5890 \times 10^{-8}}{2 \times 10^{-4}}$

$\sin \theta_1 = 0.2945$

$\boxed{\theta_1 = 17.12°}$

$\sin \theta_2 = \dfrac{n\lambda_2}{a + b} = \dfrac{1 \times 5896 \times 10^{-8}}{2 \times 10^{-4}}$

$\sin \theta_2 = 0.2948$

$\boxed{\theta_2 = 17.2°}$

Problem 2.21: *What is the highest order spectrum that is visible with light of wavelength 6000 A° by means of a grating having 5000 lines per cm ?*

Data: λ = 6000 A°

N = 5000 lines per cm, $a + b$ = $\dfrac{1}{5000}$ cm

Formula: $(a + b) \sin \theta = n \lambda$

Solution: Take, $\sin \theta = 1$

$\therefore$ $a + b = n\lambda$

$\dfrac{1}{5000} = n \times 6000 \times 10^{-8}$

$\boxed{n = 3.3}$

The highest order is n = 3.

UNIVERSITY SOLVED PROBLEMS

Problem 2.22: *Light of wavelength 5460 A° falls on a diffraction grating normal to its surface. The grating is ruled with 7500 lines per cm. What is the angle corresponding to the first bright fringe produced by the grating ?*   **(04) (Jan. 05)**

Data: λ = 5460 A°

N = 7500 lines per cm

n = 1

$a + b$ = $\dfrac{1}{7500}$ cm

Formula: $(a + b) \sin \theta = n \lambda$

Solution: $\dfrac{1}{7500} \sin \theta = 1 \times 5460 \times 10^{-8}$

$\sin \theta = 0.4095$

$\boxed{\theta = 24.17°}$

Problem 2.23: *Calculate the angular separation between the first order minima on either side of the central bright maxima when slit is 6×10^{-4} cm wide and λ = 6000 A°.* **(04) (Jan. 05)**

Data: $a = 6 \times 10^{-4}$ cm

λ = 6000 A°

Formula: $a \sin \alpha = n \lambda$

Solution: Take n = 1

$$\sin \theta = \frac{1 \times 6000 \times 10^{-8}}{6 \times 10^{-4}}$$

$$\sin \theta = 0.1$$

$$\theta = 5.739° = \boxed{5° \ 44'}$$

Problem 2.24: How many orders will be visible if the wavelength of the incident light is 6000 A° and the number of lines on the grating is 5.0 × 10³ lines per cm ? *(03) (Nov./Dec. 05)*

Data: $\lambda = 6000 \ A°$

$N = 5.0 \times 10^3$ lines per cm

Solution: $(a + b) \sin \theta = n\lambda$

take $\sin \theta = 1$

$$\frac{1}{N} = n\lambda$$

$$n = \frac{1}{5 \times 10^3 \times 6000 \times 10^{-8}}$$

$$\boxed{n = 3.33}$$

The number of order, $n = 3$

Problem 2.25: A slit of width 'a' is illuminated by white light. For what value of 'a' will the first minimum for red light fall at an angle 30°? Wavelength for red light is 6500 A°.

(03) (May 06)

Solution: See Problem 2.2, page 2.20.

Problem 2.26: Monochromatic light of wavelength 6.56 × 10⁻⁵ cm falls normally on a grating 2 cm wide. The first order spectrum is produced at an angle of 18° 14' from the normal. What is the total number of lines on the grating. *(04) (Dec. 06)*

Solution: See Problem 2.14, page 2.27.

Problem 2.27: What is the longest wavelength that can be observed in the third order for a transmission grating having 7000 lines per cm ? Assume normal incidence. *(03) (May 07)*

Data: $n = 3$

$N = 7000$ lines per cm, $(a + b) = \frac{1}{7000}$ cm

Formula: $(a + b) \sin \theta = n\lambda$

Solution: Take $\sin \theta = 1$

$$\frac{1}{N} = n\lambda$$

$$\lambda = \frac{1}{7000 \times 3}$$

$$\lambda = 4.761 \times 10^{-5} \, cm$$

$$\boxed{\lambda = 4761 \, A°}$$

Problem 2.28: *What is the highest order of spectrum which may be seen with the light of wavlength 6328 A° by means of a grating with 3000 lines km ?*   **(03) (May 08)**

Data: N = 3000 lines /cm

$$\lambda = 6328 \, A°, \quad (a + b) = \frac{1}{3000} \, cm$$

Formula: $(a + b) \sin \theta = n \lambda$

Solution: Take $\sin \theta = 1$

$$\frac{1}{N} = n \lambda$$

$$n = \frac{1}{3000 \times 6328 \times 10^{-8}}$$

$$\boxed{n = 5.26}$$

The highest order, n = 5

Problem 2.29: *A grating has 6000 lines per cm. How many orders of light of wavelength 4500 A° can be seen ?*   **(03) (Dec. 08)**

Data: N = 6000 lines per cm

$$\lambda = 4500 \, A°, \quad (a + b) = \frac{1}{6000} \, cm$$

Formulae: (i) $(a + b) = \frac{1}{N} \, cm$ (ii) $(a + b) \sin \theta = m\lambda$

Solution: (i) $(a + b) = \frac{1}{6000} = 1.666 \times 10^{-4} \, cm$

(ii) $(a + b) \sin \theta = m\lambda$

Take $\sin \theta = 1$

$$m = \frac{1.666 \times 10^{-4}}{4500 \times 10^{-8}}$$

∴ $\boxed{m = 3.7}$

Hence, highest order visible = 3

Problem 2.30: *A single slit diffraction pattern is formed using white light. For what wavelength of light does the second minimum coincide with the third minimum for the wavelength 4000 A° ?* **(04) (Dec. 08)**

Data: $\qquad\qquad\qquad \lambda_1 = 4000 \text{ A}°$

$\qquad\qquad\qquad\qquad n_1 = 3$

$\qquad\qquad\qquad\qquad n_2 = 2$

Formula: For single slit minima,

$\qquad\qquad\qquad a \sin \theta = n\lambda$

Solution: $\qquad a \sin \theta = 2 \times \lambda_2$

and $\qquad\qquad a \sin \theta = 3\lambda_1$

$\therefore \qquad\qquad\qquad 2\lambda_2 = 3\lambda_1$

$\therefore \qquad\qquad 2 \times \lambda_2 = 3 \times 4000 \text{ A}°$

$\therefore \qquad\qquad\qquad \boxed{\lambda_2 = 6000 \text{ A}°}$

Problem 2.31: *A light of wavelength 5.8×10^{-7} m is incident on a slit having a width of 0.3×10^{-3} m. The viewing screen is 2.00 m from the slit. Find the position of the first dark fringes and the width of the central bright fringe. What happens to the diffraction pattern if the slit width is increased ?* **(05) (May 09)**

Data: $\qquad\qquad\qquad \lambda = 5.8 \times 10^{-7} \text{ m}$

$\qquad\qquad\qquad\qquad a = 0.3 \times 10^{-3} \text{ m}$

$\qquad\qquad\qquad\qquad D = 2.00 \text{ m}$

$\qquad\qquad\qquad\qquad n = 1$

Formulae: (i) For single slit,

$\qquad\qquad\qquad a \sin \theta = n\lambda$

(ii) From Fig. 2.16, $\sin \theta \approx \dfrac{d}{D}$ (for large D)

Solution: From (1) and (2),

$\therefore \qquad\qquad\qquad a\dfrac{d}{D} = \lambda$

$\therefore \qquad\qquad\qquad d = \dfrac{D\lambda}{a}$

$\qquad\qquad\qquad d = 3.87 \times 10^{-3} \text{ m}$

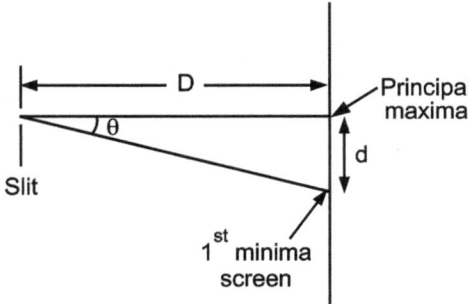

Fig. 2.16

The width of central bright fringe

$$= 2d$$

$$= \boxed{7.74 \times 10^{-3} \text{ m}}$$

If the slit width is increased, width of principal maxima decreases.

Problem 2.32: *A monochromatic light from a helium-neon laser (λ = 623.8 nm) is incident normally on a diffraction grating containing 6000 lines/cm. Find the angles at which the first and second order maxima are obtained.* **(04) (May 09)**

Data: $\lambda = 623.8$ nm $= 623.8 \times 10^{-7}$ cm

$$N = 6000 \text{ lines/cm}, \quad (a + b) = \frac{1}{6000} \text{ cm}$$

Formulae: (i) $(a + b) = \frac{1}{N}$ cm,   (ii) $(a + b) \sin \theta = n\lambda$

Solution: (i) $(a + b) = \frac{1}{6000} = 1.66 \times 10^{-4}$ cm

(ii) $(a + b) \sin \theta = n\lambda$

For n = 1, $\theta_1 = \sin^{-1}\left(\dfrac{1 \times 623.8 \times 10^{-7}}{1.66 \times 10^{-4}}\right) = \boxed{22.31°}$

For n = 2, $\theta_2 = \sin^{-1}\left(\dfrac{2 \times 623.8 \times 10^{-7}}{1.66 \times 10^{-4}}\right) = \boxed{49.39°}$

Problem 2.33: *Find the half angular width of the central maxima in the fraunhofer diffraction pattern of slit having width 10 × 10−5 cm. When illuminated by light having wave length 5000 A°.* **(03) (Dec. 12)**

Data: $a = 10 \times 10^{-5}$ cm, $\lambda = 5000$ A° $= 5000 \times 10^{-8}$ cm, n = 1

Formula: $a \sin \theta = n\lambda$

∴ $a \sin \theta = n\lambda$

But $n = 1$

∴ $\sin \theta = \dfrac{\lambda}{a}$

∴ $\theta = \sin^{-1}\left(\dfrac{\lambda}{a}\right)$

∴ Substituting, $\theta = \sin^{-1}\left(\dfrac{5000 \times 10^{-8}}{10 \times 10^{-5}}\right)$

∴ $\theta = \mathbf{30°}$

Problem 2.34: *Monochromatic light from He-Ne laser source ($\lambda=6328 A0$) is incident normally on a diffraction grating having 6000 lines/cm. find the angle at which one would observe second order maximum.*   *(03)(May 13)*

Data: $\lambda = 6328 \ A°$

                                 $N = 6000 \ \text{Lines/cm}$

                                 $\eta = 2$

Formula: (i) $(a + b) = \dfrac{1}{N}$

           (ii) $(a + b) \sin \theta = \eta \lambda$

Solution: (i) $(a + b) = \dfrac{1}{6000}$

                     $(a + b) = 1.6667 \times 10^{-4} \ \text{cm}$

        (ii) $\theta = \sin^{-1}\left(\dfrac{2\times6328\times10^{-8}}{1.6667 \times 10^{-4}}\right)$

                         $\theta = 49.4°$

Problem 2.35: *In a grating, the angle of diffraction for the second order principal maximum for the light of wavelength 5×10^{-5} cm is 30°. Calculate the number of lines per centimetre of the grating surface.*   *(03) (May 14)*

Data: $\lambda = 5 \times 10^{-5} \ \text{cm}$

                                 $a = 30°$

                                 $n = 2$

Formula: (i) $(a + b) \sin \theta = 2\lambda$

        (ii) $N = \dfrac{1}{(a + b)}$

Solution: $\dfrac{1}{N} \sin 30° = 2 \times 5 \times 10^{-5}$

$$N = \dfrac{1}{2 \times 2 \times 5 \times 10^{-5}}$$

$$N = 5000 \text{ Lines per cm}$$

Problem 2.36: *Interference fringes are produced with monochromatic light falling normally on a wedge shaped film of refractive index 1.4. The angle of wedge is 10 sec of an arc and the distance between successive fringes is 0.5 cm. What is the wavelength of light used ?*

(03) (Nov. 13)

Data: $\mu = 1.4$

$$\alpha = 10 \text{ sec} = \dfrac{10}{3600} \times \dfrac{\pi}{180} \text{ radian} , \quad \beta = 0.5 \text{ cm}$$

Formula: $\beta = \dfrac{\lambda}{2\mu\alpha}$

$$\lambda = \dfrac{2 \times 1.4 \times 10 \times 3.14 \times 0.5 \times 10^{-2}}{3600 \times 180}$$

$\therefore$ $\lambda = 0.6783 \times 10^{-6} \text{ cm}$

or $\lambda = 6783 \text{ A}°$

SUMMARY

- The bending of waves around the corners of the obstacle and their encroachment into the region of geometrical shadow is called "diffraction of waves".

- Three elements of diffraction: source, obstacle or aperture and the screen.

- Diffraction phenomenon can be observed only when the size of the obstacle or aperture is comparable to the wavelength of incident waves.

- Fraunhofer's diffraction pattern due to a single rectangular slit consists of a central bright maximum.

- The intensities of the secondary maxima lying on either side of central maxima go on decreasing away from the central maxima.

- The intensity for a single slit diffraction pattern at any angle θ is

$$I_\theta = I_m \dfrac{\sin^2 \alpha}{\alpha^2}$$

- Condition for maxima in the single slit diffraction pattern is

$$\alpha = 0, \quad \theta = 0.$$

- Condition for minima in the single slit diffraction pattern is

$$\alpha = \pm m\pi$$

$$a \sin \theta = m\lambda$$

- Condition for secondary maxima in the single slit diffraction pattern is

$$\alpha = \pm \left(m + \frac{1}{2}\right) \pi$$

$$a \sin \theta = (2m + 1)\frac{\lambda}{2}$$

- A plane diffraction grating is a device having N narrow slits side by side separated by opaque spaces.

- Grating is an application of multiple slit diffraction.

- The intensity for diffraction grating is

$$I_\theta = I_m \frac{\sin^2 \alpha}{\alpha^2} \cdot \frac{\sin^2 N\beta}{\sin^2 \beta}$$

- Condition for principal maxima in the intensity pattern of a grating,

$$(a + b) \sin \theta = m\lambda$$

- Condition for minima,

$$(a + b) \sin \theta = \frac{m}{N} \lambda$$

IMPORTANT FORMULAE

- $a \sin \theta = n\lambda$

- $\sin \theta = \frac{\lambda}{a}$ if $n = 1$

- $\sin \theta = \frac{x}{f}$

- $a \sin \theta = (2n + 1)\frac{\lambda}{2}$

- $(a + b) \sin \theta = n\lambda$

- $(a + b) \sin \theta = \frac{m}{N} \lambda$

- $a + b = \dfrac{1}{N \text{ lines/cm}}$

EXERCISE

1. Distinguish between Fresnel and Fraunhoffer diffraction.

2. Explain the phenomenon of diffraction of light. State its types and distinguish between them.

3. Explain: (i) Diffraction of light (ii) Diffraction grating.

4. Explain the difference between interference and diffraction.

5. Describe the phenomenon observed when a monochromatic light falls on a single slit.

6. Derive an expression for the intensity at a point in the Fraunhofer's type of diffraction produced by a single slit.

7. Explain the formation of spectra by a plane transmission grating.

8. Obtain the conditions for maxima and minima in Fraunhofer diffraction due to a single slit.

9. What is plane transmission grating ? Explain how it can be used for determining the wavelength of given monochromatic light.

10. Give the theory of plane transmission grating.

11. Discuss Fraunhofer's diffraction at a single slit and derive the condition for obtaining secondary minimum intensity positions.

UNSOLVED PROBLEMS

1. Light is incident normally on a grating 0.5 cm wide with 2500 lines. Find the angles of diffraction for the principal maxima of the two sodium lines in the first order spectrum λ_1 = 5890 A° and λ_2 = 5896 A°.   **(Ans.** θ_1 = 17.1°, θ_2 = 17.2°)

2. What is the highest order spectrum which can be seen with monochromatic light of wavelength 6000 A° by means of a diffraction grating with 5000 lines/cm ?   **(Ans.** n = 3)

3. A plane grating has 15000 lines per inch. Find the angle of separation of 5408 A° and 5016 A° lines of helium in the second order spectrum.   **(Ans.** $(\theta_2 - \theta_1)$ = 16')

4. A diffraction grating used at normal incidence gives a line λ_1 = 6000 A° in a certain order superimposed on another line, λ_2 = 4500 A° of the next highest order. If the angle of diffraction is 30°, how many lines are there in a cm in the grating ?   **(Ans.** 2778 lines/cm)

5. What is the highest order spectrum which may be seen with light of wavelength 5000 A° by means of a grating with 3000 lines/cm ?   **(Ans.** n = 6)

6. A plane diffraction grating has the value of grating constant equal to 15×10^{-4} cm. Calculate the position of third order maximum for λ = 2.4×10^{-4} cm.   **(Ans.** θ_3 = 28.7°)

7. Monochromatic light of wavelength λ = 6560 A° falls normally on a grating. The spectral line is diffracted at an angle of 19° 9' from the normal in the first order. Find the grating element.   **(Ans.** 2×10^{-4} cm)

8. A single slit Fraunhofer's diffraction pattern is formed using white light. For what wavelength of light does the second minimum coincide with the third minimum for the wavelength 4000 A° ?   **(Ans.** 6000 A°)

9. In a plane transmission grating with 5000 lines/cm and for wavelength 5000 A°, if the opaque spaces are exactly 2.0 lines the transparent spaces, which order of spectra will be absent ?   **(Ans.** 3rd, 6th, 9th etc. orders)

10. Light of wavelength 6×10^{-5} cm falls on a screen at a distance of 100 cm from a narrow slit. Find the width of the slit if the first minimum has 1 mm on either side of the central maximum.   **(Ans.** 0.06 cm)

11. Calculate the angles at which the first dark band and the next bright band are formed in Fraunhofer diffraction pattern of a slit of 0.3 mm wide, given λ = 5890 A°. **(Ans.** 6.7', 10')

12. Calculate the angular separation between the first order minima on either side of central bright maximum, when slit is 6×10^{-4} cm wide and λ = 6000 A°. **(Ans.** 73° 4')

13. Light of wavelength 5500 A° falls normally on slit of width 22×10^{-5} cm. Calculate the angular position of the first two minima from the central bright maximum.

                                                       (Ans. 14° 29', 30°)

14. Plane waves of λ = 6000 A° fall normally on a single slit of width 0.2 mm. Calculate the total angular width of the central bright maximum and also the linear width as observed on a screen placed 2 m away.   **(Ans.** 20', 1.2 cm)

SOLVED UNIVERSITY QUESTIONS

DECEMBER 2012

1. Find the half angular width of the central maxima in the fraunhofer diffraction pattern of slit having width 10×10^{-5} cm. When illuminated by light having wave length 5000 A°.   [3]

Ans. Data: $a = 10 \times 10^{-5}$ cm, $\lambda = 5000$ A° $= 5000 \times 10^{-8}$ cm, $n = 1$

Formula : $a \sin \theta = n\lambda$

$\therefore$ $a \sin \theta = n\lambda$

But $n = 1$

$\therefore$ $\sin \theta = \dfrac{\lambda}{a}$

$\therefore$ $\theta = \sin^{-1}\left(\dfrac{\lambda}{a}\right)$

$\therefore$ Substituting, $\theta = \sin^{-1}\left(\dfrac{5000 \times 10^{-8}}{10 \times 10^{-5}}\right)$

$\therefore$ $\theta = 30°$

MAY 2013

1. Monochromatic light from He-Ne laser source ($\lambda=6328A^0$) is incident normally on a diffraction grating having 6000 lines/cm. find the angle at which one would observe second order maximum. **[3]**

Ans. Data:

$$\lambda = 6328A^0$$

$$N = 6000 \text{ Lines/cm}$$

$$\eta = 2$$

Formula: (i)

$$(a+b) = \frac{1}{N}$$

(ii)

$$(a+b) \sin\theta = \eta\,\lambda$$

Solution: (i)

$$(a+b) = \frac{1}{6000}$$

$$(a+b) = 1.6667 \times 10^{-4} \text{ cm}$$

(ii)

$$\theta = \sin^{-1}\left(\frac{2 \times 6328 \times 10^{-8}}{1.6667 \times 10^{-4}}\right)$$

$$\theta = 49.4^0$$

2. What is diffraction ? Distinguish between Fresnel and Fraunhofer diffraction (2 points). **[3]**

Ans. Please Refer to Articles 2.1 and 2.3 on Page No. 2.1 and 2.3.

MAY 2014

1. Define diffraction of light. Draw intensity distribution pattern obtained because of diffraction of light at a single slit and label the significant points in the same. **[3]**

Ans. Please Refer to Article 2.1 and 2.6 on Page No. 2.1 and 2.9.

2. In a grating, the angle of diffraction for the second order principal maximum for the light of wavelength 5×10^{-5} cm is 30°. Calculate the number of lines per centimetre of the grating surface. **[3]**

Ans. Data:

$$\lambda = 5 \times 10^{-5} \text{ cm}$$

$$a = 30°$$

$$n = 2$$

Formula: (i)

$$(a + b) \sin\theta = 2\lambda$$

(ii)

$$N = \frac{1}{(a + b)}$$

Solution:

$$\frac{1}{N} \sin 30° = 2 \times 5 \times 10^{-5}$$

$$N = \frac{1}{2 \times 2 \times 5 \times 10^{-5}}$$

$$N = 5000 \text{ Lines per cm}$$

DECEMBER 2014

1. What is diffraction ? What are the types of diffraction ? Distinguish between them (any two point). **[3]**

Ans. Please Refer to Article 2.2 and 2.3 on Page No. 2.3.

MAY 2015

1. A laser light of wavelength 6328 A.U. falls normally on a grating which is 2 cm long. The first order spectrum is observed at an angle of 20°. Find the total number of slits on grating. **[3]**

Ans.

Data:

$$\lambda = 6328 \, A°$$

$$\text{Length of grating} = 2 \text{ cm}$$

$$n = 1$$

$$Q = 20°$$

Formula: (i) $(a + b) \sin \theta = n \lambda$

(ii) $N = \dfrac{1}{a + b}$

Solution: $(a + b) = \dfrac{1 \times 6328 \times 10^{-8}}{\sin 20}$

$$(a + b) = 1.850 \times 10^{-4} \text{ cm}$$

$\therefore$ $N = \dfrac{1}{1.850 \times 10^{-4}}$

$$N = 5404 \text{ lines/cm}$$

Therefore, total lines on grating of length 2 cm = $5404 \times 2 = 10808$ lines.

NOVEMBER 2015

1. The resultant amplitude of a wave when monochromatic light is diffracted from a single slit is $E_\theta = E_m \dfrac{\sin \alpha}{\alpha}$. Then derive the condition of minima. **[3]**

Ans. Please Refer to Article 2.5, Page No. 2.7.

MAY 2016

1. For a plane diffraction grating, starting from the equations of resultant amplitude and intensity, derive conditions for maxima and minima of the diffraction pattern. **[6]**

Ans. Please Refer to Article 2.9 on Page No. 2.13.

The resultant amplitude is $E_Q = E_m \dfrac{\sin \alpha}{\alpha} \cdot \dfrac{\sin N\beta}{\sin \beta}$

REFERENCES

Animation of single slit diffraction pattern:

http://www.walter-fendt.de/ph14e/singleslit/htm

An interactive animation of diffraction pattern with a grating:

http://www.physics.uq.edu.au/people/mcintype/php/laboratories/index.php?e=14.

More information about resolving power:

http://www.astronomynotes.com/telescop/s6.htm

More information about X-ray diffraction:

http://www.eserc.stonybrook.edu/ProjectJava/Bragg/

✠ ✠ ✠

CHAPTER 3
SOUND ENGINEERING

3.1 INTRODUCTION   [Dec. 14]

- The word **acoustics** originated from a Greek word meaning to *hear*. Hence, acoustics is defined as the **Science of Sound**. It deals with the scientific study of sound and sound waves i.e. production, transmission and reception of sound.

- The sound wave is produced when the air in contact with the vibrating body is suddenly compressed. Due to the elastic nature of air, these compressions travel away from the source. Thus, the vibrating body sets up waves of compressions and rarefactions in the medium.

- When these waves come near ear drums, we feel a sensation of hearing.

- When the sound waves are periodic and harmonic, they give a pleasing effect. Such sound is called a **musical sound**. On the other hand, if they are non-periodic and non-harmonic, they give unpleasant effect. Such sound is known as **noise**.

- The musical sound wave is periodic, harmonic and free of irregularities and discontinuities. On the other hand, noise wave is distorted with discontinuities and irregularities. Fig. 3.1 shows waveform of musical sound and noise.

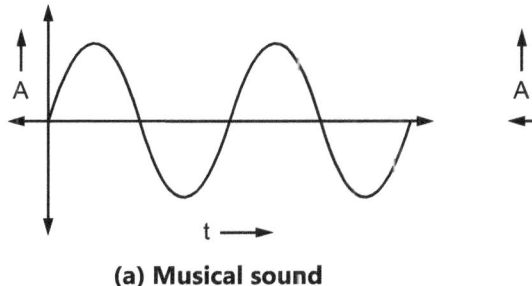
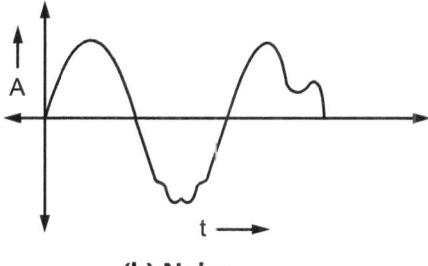

(a) Musical sound   (b) Noise

Fig. 3.1: Sound

- The human ear is sensitive to the waves in the range from 20 Hz to 20 kHz. But the word acoustics is applied to the similar waves with frequencies outside the range of human audibility i.e. ultrasonics and subsonics. Ultrasonics have frequencies above 20 kHz and subsonics below 20 Hz.

- One more parameter which decides the audibility along with frequency is the intensity. The minimum intensity that can be heard by human being is 10^{-12} W/m² and is called **threshold of hearing**. At one particular intensity it starts giving painful effect. The intensity at which this happens is called **threshold of feeling** and the value is 10 W/m².

3.2 DEFINITIONS

3.2.1 Velocity

- The velocity of sound v is defined as the velocity with which a sound wave travels in a given medium. In a particular medium, the velocity of sound remains the same. But when the medium changes, the velocity also changes.

- In fluids i.e. air and liquid the velocity is mainly function of density of medium and temperature. As these features are different for different materials, the velocity of sound is also different. In gases, the velocity is given by

$$v = \sqrt{\frac{\gamma P_o}{\rho_o}} \qquad \qquad \ldots (1)$$

where, γ = Ratio of the specific heat of the gas at constant pressure to that at constant volume

                               P_o = Pressure

                               ρ_o = Density

- For most gases the ratio P_o/ρ_o is nearly independent of pressure i.e. doubling the pressure is accompanied by doubling of the density of gas. If the atmosphere is homogeneous and isothermal the velocity remains independent of altitude.

- In practice, the change in velocity is significant with change in temperature in comparison with the change due to inhomogeneity.

- The relation of change in velocity with the temperature is given by

$$v = v_o + 0.6t \qquad \qquad \ldots (2)$$

where, v_o = 331.6 m/sec = velocity of sound at 0°C

and t = temperature in °C

- The behaviour of velocity of sound in solids is more complicated and is given by the equation

$$v = \sqrt{\frac{\upsilon \, B_T}{\rho_o}} \qquad \qquad \ldots (3)$$

where B_T is the isothermal bulk modulus.

- As all the above parameters depend upon temperature and pressure of liquid, therefore they will decide the velocity of sound in liquid. The empirical formula giving the velocity of sound in distilled water as a function of temperature at a pressure is given by

$$v = 1403 + 5t - 0.06t^2 + 0.0003t^3 \qquad \qquad \ldots (4)$$

where t is in °C.

- The following table gives velocity of sound in different materials at 20°C.

Sr. No.	Medium	Velocity (m/s)
1.	Hydrogen	1305
2.	Air	344
3.	Pure water	1480
4.	Soft wood	3350
5.	Concrete	3400
6.	Mild steel	5050
7.	Glass	5200
8.	Granite	6400

3.2.2 Frequency

- A sound wave is produced by a vibrating body, which sets the medium molecules into vibrations. These oscillating molecules transfer the energy from source to listener. In the process, the molecules maintain their position and only transfer the energy.
- The number of vibrations or cycles completed in second is termed as frequency. Mathematically,

$$\text{frequency} = \frac{1}{\text{period}} \quad \text{Hz or cycles/sec.}$$

i.e. $$f = \frac{1}{T}$$

3.2.3 Wavelength

- A sound wave travels in the form of periodic wave i.e. the wave repeats itself in equal intervals of time.
- For a sinusoidal wave, the wavelength is the spatial period of the wave, the distance over which the wave's shape repeats. The wavelength is determined by considering the distance between consecutive corresponding points of the same phase such as crests, troughs or zero crossings as shown in Fig. 3.2.

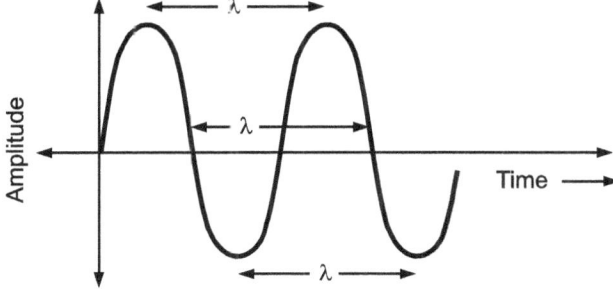

Fig. 3.2: Wavelength of wave

- The wavelength is a characteristic of travelling waves as well as standing waves. The common notation for wavelength is **lambda** (λ).

3.2.4 Intensity [Nov. 15]

- The sound coming from different sources have different loudness, which is decided by the intensity of the sound along with the sensitivity of ears. The difference in loudness gives the information about the sources from which the sound is coming.

- The sound waves transport energy from source to listener and the amount of energy that flows per second across the unit area in the direction of propagation is called the **intensity** of the wave.

i.e.
$$\text{Intensity} = \frac{\text{Energy}}{\text{Area} \times \text{Time}} = \frac{E}{A \times t} \qquad \dots (1)$$

But,
$$\frac{\text{Energy}}{\text{Time}} = \text{Power}$$

∴
$$\text{Intensity} = \frac{\text{Power}}{\text{Area}} = \frac{P}{A} \qquad \dots (2)$$

- The unit used for intensity is W/m^2 or W/cm^2. The lower limit of sound intensity which can be heard by humans is 10^{-12} W/m^2 or 10^{-16} W/cm^2 while the upper limit is 10 W/m^2 or 10^{-4} W/cm^2.

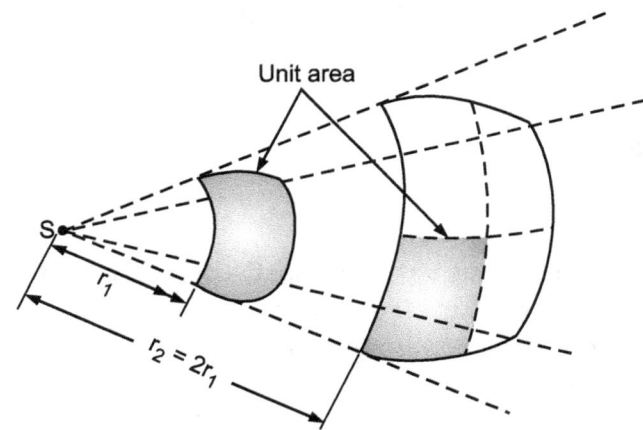

Fig. 3.3: Intensity

- The sound waves produce variation in the pressure of medium as they cause compression and rarefaction as they travel through the medium. Thus the intensity is related to the pressure by the following relation

$$I = \frac{P^2}{2\rho_o v} \qquad \dots (3)$$

where,
P^2 = Square of pressure amplitude
ρ_o = Density of medium
v = Velocity of sound

- A point source in homogeneous medium produces spherical wavefront and the intensity will decrease with the distance from source to listener. For two listeners L_1 and L_2 at distances r_1 and r_2, the intensities received will be I_1 and I_2 respectively.

- The relation between I_1 and I_2 is given by equation

$$\frac{I_1}{I_2} = \frac{r_2^2}{r_1^2} \qquad\qquad \dots (4)$$

3.2.5 Intensity Level

- The sound intensity level is measured on logarithmic scale rather than linear scale.

- One reason for using logarithmic scales is that it compresses the range of numbers required to describe the wide range of sound intensity and pressure. e.g. audible intensities range from 10^{-12} to 10 watts/m².

- Second reason is that human ear judges the relative loudness of two sounds not by direct ratio, but by the logarithms of the ratio of their intensities. i.e. $L \propto \log I$ which was first give by Weber-Frecher and is called Weber-Frecher's law.

- It is customary to describe acoustical intensity and acoustic pressure on a logarithmic scale as logarithm to the base ten of the ratio of two intensities and two pressures in experimental work.

- This is known as **sound intensity level** (denoted by SIL) or **sound pressure level** (denoted by SPL). The unit of sound level or SPL is Bel but the unit deciBel is more frequently used, 1 deciBel (dB) is $\frac{1}{10}^{th}$ of a Bel.

- If I_1 and I_0 represent the intensities of two sounds of a particular frequency, and L_1 and L_o the corresponding measures of loudness, then,

$$L_1 \propto \log_{10} I_1$$
$$L_1 = K \log_{10} I_1$$

Similarly, $\qquad\qquad L_0 = K \log_{10} I_0$

- The difference in loudness of the two is technically known as intensity level I.L.

$$\therefore \qquad\qquad I.L. = L_1 - L_0 = K\ [\log_{10} I_1 - \log_{10} I_0]$$

i.e. $\qquad\qquad I.L. = K \log_{10} \dfrac{I_1}{I_0} \qquad\qquad \dots (1)$

where K is a constant that depends on the units.

- I_0 is the standard reference intensity taken as 10^{-16} watts/cm² or 10^{-12} watts/m². This corresponds to the intensity of sound, which can be just heard at a frequency of about 1000 hertz. This is taken as the **threshold of audibility** of a normal ear.

- In the above equation, when K = 1 (unity), the difference in loudness (intensity level) is expressed in "Bels", a unit named after Alexander Graham Bell, inventor of telephone.

i.e. $$\text{I.L.} = 1 \log_{10} \frac{I_1}{I_0}$$

If $$I_1 = 10 I_0$$

then $$\text{I.L.} = 1 \log_{10} 10 = 1 \text{ Bel}$$

- This unit is rather too large, hence one tenth of it, the deciBel (dB) has become the standard, so that to express the intensity level of a sound of intensity I in deciBels, equation (1) should be written as

$$\text{I.L.} = 10 \log_{10} \frac{I_1}{I_0} \text{ dB}$$

- The following table gives the approximate values of some intensity of sounds measured in deciBels.

Source	Intensity Level in dB
Threshold of hearing	0
Rustle of leaves	10
Whisper	20
Ordinary conversation	60
Heavy traffic	80
Thunder	110
Painful sounds	130 and above

- Now, acoustical intensity and acoustic pressure are related as $I = \dfrac{P_e^2}{\rho c}$, where P_e is the measured effective pressure of the sound wave, ρ is the density of the medium and c is the velocity of sound. Since the intensity is proportional to the square of pressure, the sound pressure level (SPL) or intensity level (I.L.) is given by $\text{SPL} = 20 \log_{10} \left(\dfrac{P_e}{P_o}\right)$ dB. P_o is the reference standard pressure $= 2 \times 10^{-5}$ newton/m^2.

3.2.6 Loudness (Weber and Frechner's Law)

- Loudness is the characteristic of all sound. It is associated with the intensity of sound which is a definite physical quantity. But there is a marked difference between the loudness and the intensity of sound. Loudness of a sound is the ***degree of sensation*** depending on the intensity of sound and the sensitiveness of the ear.

- Loudness does not increase proportionally with intensity but as its logarithm.

  According to Weber and Frechner's law,

$$L \propto \log I \qquad \qquad \dots (1)$$

  where L represents the sensation of loudness and I the intensity of sound.

- Since loudness is the degree of sensation and depends on the ear of the listener, it cannot be measured by physical apparatus. However, greater the intensity of sound, greater is its loudness. Loudness of sound depends on all the factors on which the intensity of sound depends.

- The loudness depends on sensitivity of ears and ears are more sensitive to high frequencies than low frequencies. Therefore, it needs higher intensity at low frequencies than at high frequencies to give the sensation of the same loudness.

- The intensity of 60 dB at 40 Hz and of 0 dB at 1000 Hz gives the same loudness. The loudness of intensity of sound in dB over threshold of hearing as sensed by the ear at 1000 Hz is called **phon**.

- If the intensity of sound at 1000 Hz is 0 dB, it is 0 phon loudness. If it is 40 dB, the loudness is 40 dB. If an intensity of 60 dB at 40 Hz gives the same loudness as 0 dB intensity at 1000 Hz, then loudness at 40 Hz is zero phon, not 60 phon. Thus, loudness in phons at 1000 Hz is always equal to the intensity of sound in dB. But at any other frequency, the level of loudness can be found out only by determining the intensity of sound in 0 dB required at 1000 Hz to give the same loudness.

- While phon is used to compare the loudness level for different frequencies, another unit **sone** is used to determine the increase in loudness. Loudness sensation produced by 1000 Hz sound of 40 dB is called 1 sone.

3.2.7 Timbre of Sound   [Nov. 13]

- The sound waves produced by speech and musical instruments are not pure sine waves, but are complex waves containing the fundamental frequencies and their harmonics. The fundamental frequency is called **tone** and other than the fundamental are called **overtones**.

- The proportion of tones and overtones in a sound form the special characteristics by which a particular sound can be recognised, even if all the sources produce the same fundamental frequency. This quality of sound is called **timbre**.

- This quality of sound helps us to recognise a person even if he is not visible.

3.2.8 Reflection of Sound

- Whenever sound waves are incident on an obstacle whose dimensions are much larger than the wavelength of wave, a part is reflected and a part is absorbed. The reflected wave makes same angle as that of angle of incidence.

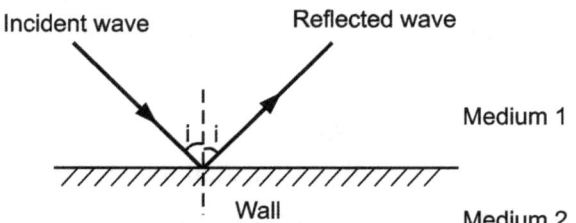

Fig. 3.4: Reflection of sound wave

- The amount of sound energy reflected or absorbed depends upon the nature of the surface while the amount of energy transmitted outside the room depends upon the sound insulation properties of the surface.

- A concave surface leads to the concentration of reflected waves at certain points. Hence concave surfaces may be used to work as a **reflector**. A convex surface tends to spread the reflected waves. Hence, convex surfaces may be used to **spread** the sound throughout the room.

- Fig. 3.5 shows reflection of sound from different types of surfaces. The laws of reflection of sound help in deciding the shape of the room and its surfaces.

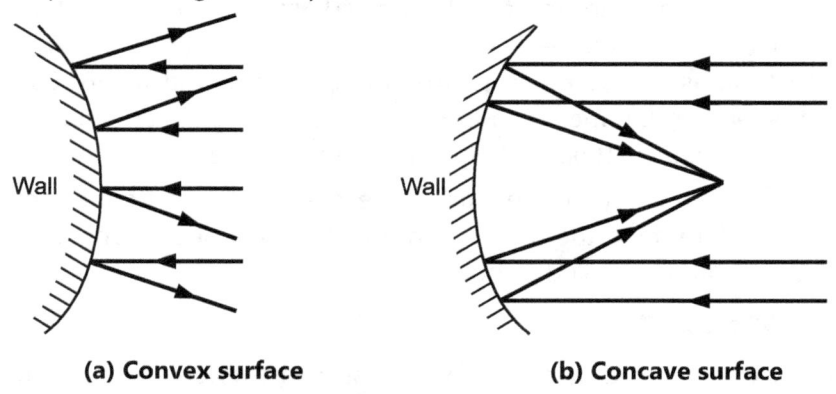

(a) Convex surface   **(b) Concave surface**

Fig. 3.5: Reflection of sound waves

- The behaviour of reflected sound plays an important role in architectural acoustics. The main defects that are caused by reflection of sound are echo, reverberation, focussing and echelon.

3.2.9 Echo

- An echo is produced when the reflected sound waves reach the ear just when the original direct sound from the same source has already been heard. Thus, echo is the repetition of same sound due to reflections from an obstacle.

- The sensation of sound persists on human ear for 0.1 sec after the sound is heard. So, if the reflected sound reaches the listener with delay more than 0.1 sec, the reflected sound (of diminished intensity) is clearly distinguished from the original sound.

- Taking the velocity of sound as 340 m/s the reflected sound must travel a total distance of 340 × 0.1 = 34 m (to and fro) before reaching the listener for a clear echo. If the source and listener are same the distance between the source to obstacle should be 17 m or more for echo. In this case, the distance between the source and the obstacle will be calculated by formula $t = \dfrac{2d}{v}$, where d is the distance between the source and the obstacle.

3.3 REVERBERATION

- Whenever sound is produced in a hall, it lasts for quite sometime. This is because sound waves keep on reaching the listener a number of times. Initially the listener receives sound waves directly from the source. Thereafter he receives the sound reflected from walls, ceilings, floor of the hall, etc. Thus, the sound lingers in the hall even when the source has been stopped or the listener continues to receive series of sound of decreasing energy. But due to reflection, at every stage, some energy is lost.

- Therefore, some interval of time is required for the sound energy to die out completely. The loss of sound energy is brought about by friction between the sound waves and air particles and also between sound waves and the surfaces with which it come in contact. The more the friction, the quicker will be the sound energy loss.

- This gradual process of loss of sound energy over a certain interval of time is known as **reverberation** or reverberation can be defined as **the persistance or prolongation of sound in the hall even after the sound source has been stopped**.

- If the reverberation of a syllable prolongs even after the utterance of another syllable, then a condition of unintelligibility will arise. This may lead to a bad acoustical condition.

3.3.1 Reverberation Time

- The time during which sound persists in the hall is called **reverberation time**. This time is measured from the instant the source stops emitting sound.

- In an auditorium when the sound source is switched on the intensity starts increasing with time. Because at any given instant, the total intensity will be sum of the intensity due to sound source (which is fixed) and due to reflections from the boundary (which increases with the number of reflections and hence with time). But the intensity cannot increase above a critical value as at some instant amount of sound reflected and absorbed will be same.

- When the sound source is switched off, the intensity due to sound source becomes zero and sound due to reflections decays exponentially resulting in reverberation. Fig. 3.6 shows rise and decay of sound in an auditorium.

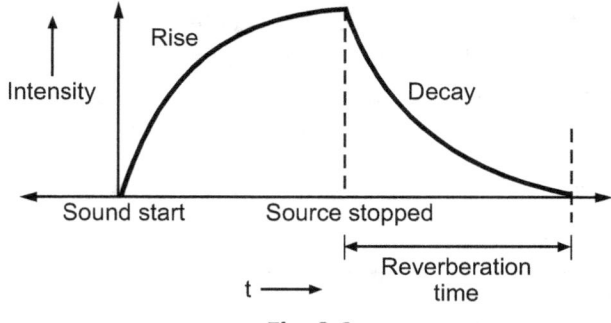

Fig. 3.6

- The time of reverberation is also defined as the time taken for the sound to fall below the minimum audibility measured from the instant when the source stopped sounding.

- Professor Sabine by using an organ pipe of 512 vibrations per second found that its sound became inaudible when its intensity fell to one millionth of its intensity just before stopping the organ pipe. Hence, Sabine defined the standard reverberation time as the time taken by sound to fall to one millionth of its intensity just before the source is cut off. He also found that the time of reverberation depends upon the size of the hall, loudness of sound and the kind of music for which the hall is used.

- There are several *factors which control the reverberation time*.

  ➢ The reverberation depends on the reflecting properties of the walls, floor and ceiling. If they are good reflectors, then sound would take long time to die away. Hence, reverberation time would be large.

  ➢ The reverberation depends on the coefficient of absorption of various surfaces such as carpets, cushions, curtains and furnitures present in the room. Greater the absorption, lesser the time of reverberation.

  ➢ The reverberation time depends on the frequency of the note.

Importance of Reverberation Time

- If a building is to be accoustically good, it is very important that its reverberation time must be optimum. It should neither be too short nor too long.

- A very short reverberation time makes a room sound *dead*. Sensation of speaking in such a room is similar to that experienced when speaking from the top of an isolated building.

- The absorbing powers of materials are different at different frequencies. For higher frequencies, the absorbing power is greater. Hence, the material chosen in a room should be such that, it makes the reverberation time short for high notes and long for short notes. This will make the music sound pleasing.

- A *long reverberation time* is more undesirable than a short one. It causes confusion and renders speech unintelligible and music dissonant.

- The best value for reverberation time depends on the use for which a building is designed. For a listener a time of 0.5 seconds was found to be optimum. For music, the value is between 1 and 2 seconds. The optimum value of reverberation time for auditoriums varies with volume. It varies from 1.1 to 2.3 seconds.

3.3.2 Sabine's Formula

- Prof. W. C. Sabine of Harward University studied the subject of architectural acoustics. He used an organ pipe of frequency 512 Hertz to produce an average audible sound in an empty closed hall. He then measured the time interval for which the audible sound was present in the hall after the source of sound was shut off. This was termed as **reverberation time**. In a similar manner, he found the reverberation time for the hall full of furniture and audience.

- From his experiments carried out in halls of different sizes, he concluded that

  ➢ The reverberation time of a room varies inversely as the effective surface area of different surfaces and directly as the volume of the room,

  ➢ The reverberation time is independent of the position of the source and the listener and the shape of the room.

  Mathematically,
  $$T \propto \frac{V}{A}$$

  i.e.
  $$T = K\frac{V}{A}$$

  where

  A is the total sound energy absorbed by the various sound absorbing materials in the hall.

  V is the volume of the room.

  K is the proportionality constant.

- For auditorium having large number of absorbing materials having different surface area, the total absorption will be the sum of absorptions due to individual absorbing material.

  i.e.
  $$A = \sum_{1}^{n} a\, S = a_1 S_1 + a_2 S_2 + \ldots + a_n S_n$$

  where $a_1, a_2, a_3, \ldots, a_n$ are the coefficients of absorption of materials and $S_1, S_2, \ldots, S_n$ are the surface areas of materials respectively.

  $\therefore$
  $$T = \frac{V}{\sum a_n S_n}$$

- If V is in cubic meters and S is in square meters, K = 0.165. If V is in cubic feet and S is in square feet, K = 0.05.

$$T = 0.165 \frac{V}{A} \text{ in M.K.S. system.}$$

Or

$$T = 0.05 \frac{V}{A} \text{ in British system.}$$

- This equation is called **Sabine's formula** for reverberation time. It is an experimentally found empirical relation.

3.3.3 Remedies over Reverberation

- The reverberation time of an auditorium should be optimum, i.e. neither too less nor too large. The factors which decide the reverberation time are volume of auditorium, absorption coefficient and surface area. But once the auditorium is constructed, the volume cannot be changed easily.

- For reducing the reverberation time, the easiest method is to use sound absorbent materials whose absorption coefficient is large. Depending upon the requirement, sound absorbing material and their surface area (dimensions) can be selected.

- The surface area also can be increased by making pyramid or conical shape on the wall, which helps in increasing the surface area.

- The common absorbent materials used are thick rugs, wooden furniture, thick curtain with folds. Even presence of audiences and windows decreases the reverberation significantly.

- The reverberation can be increased by coating the walls of the auditorium with good reflecting materials. Metals, glasses and polished wooden surfaces are good reflecting surfaces.

3.4 ABSORPTION OF SOUND

- When a sound wave strikes a surface, the total sound energy is distributed in three ways. A part of its energy is transmitted across the surface, a part of its energy is absorbed by friction and the remaining of its energy is reflected back by the surface.

- The property of a material which converts the sound energy into other form of energy is known as **absorption**.

- The sound generated in an auditorium or hall is absorbed in four ways (i) by air (ii) by the audience (iii) by furniture and furnishings and (iv) at the boundary surfaces such as floors, ceilings, walls, etc.

  ➢ **Absorption by Air:** The absorption of sound in air is mainly due to the friction between the oscillating molecules when sound wave travels through it.

> ➤ **Absorption by Audience:** Sound energy is absorbed by the clothing of the audience. Room acoustics change appreciably by the number of audience present. Absorption being more in winter than in summer due to heavy clothing.

> ➤ **Absorption by Furniture and Furnishings:** Furniture, curtains, carpets etc. also absorb sound energy.

> ➤ **Absorption by Boundary Surface:** When sound waves strike the boundary surface such as walls, floors, ceilings, absorption takes place due to the following factors:

>> (a) Penetration of sound into porous materials. This causes resonance within air pockets in the pores until energy is dissipated.

>> (b) Resonant vibration of panel materials.

>> (c) Molecular damping in soft absorbing materials.

>> (d) Transmission through structures.

3.4.1 Absorbent Materials

- Most of the common building materials absorb sound to a small extent. Hence for providing better acoustical requirement, some other materials are to be incorporated on the surface of the room which absorb the sound significantly. Such materials are known as *absorbent materials*.

- A good absorbent material should be water-proof, fire-proof, strong and good in appearance. The absorbent materials are found to be soft and porous.

- They work on the principle that sound waves penetrate into the pores and in this process they are converted into other form of energy by friction. The absorbing capacity of the absorbent materials depends on the thickness of the material, its density and frequency of sound.

- The acoustic properties of the absorbent materials are considerably changed by their modes of fixing.

- Some of the common types of absorbent materials are hairfelt, quilts and mats, acoustic plaster, acoustical tiles, strawboard, pulp boards, perforated plywood, wood particle board etc.

3.4.2 Absorption Coefficient

- When sound energy is incident on a surface, a part of the energy is absorbed by the surface. Different surfaces have different sound absorption capacity. This capacity depends upon the nature of the surface.

- The *coefficient of absorption* of a surface is defined as *the ratio of the sound energy absorbed by it to that of the total sound energy incident on the surface.*

  i.e. Absorption coefficient 'a' $= \dfrac{\text{Sound energy absorbed by the surface}}{\text{Total sound energy incident on the surface}}$

- An open window allows all sound energy incident on it to pass through and it reflects none of the sound energy incident on it. Hence an open window is considered as a perfect sound absorber and an open window of unit area is chosen as the standard for expressing absorption of sound.

- Thus, the absorption coefficient of a material is defined as **the ratio of sound energy absorbed by a certain area of the surface to the sound energy absorbed by the same area of an open window**.

i.e.   Absorption coefficient 'a' = $\dfrac{\text{Sound energy absorbed by a centain area of surface in a given time}}{\text{Sound energy absorbed by same area of an open window in same time}}$

- The unit of absorption coefficient is written as O.W.U. i.e. open window units or Sabines. Total absorption by material = Absorption coefficient × Area of material.

3.5 CONDITIONS FOR GOOD ACOUSTICS OF THE BUILDING

- Basically, acoustics is classified into three branches

   (i) architectural acoustics, (ii) electroacoustics and (iii) musical acoustics.

- In architectural acoustics, we deal with the behaviour of sound in an auditorium. Many times it is found that in an auditorium, sound cannot be heard clearly. Either intensity at some places is not high enough or repeated speeches are heard.

- For making a hall acoustically good, it should have following features.

   ➢ The sound must be **loud enough** in every part of hall.

   ➢ There should not be repeated speeches heard in the hall. i.e. **free of echo**.

   ➢ There should not be overlapping of speeches, i.e. **reverberation time** should have optimum value.

   ➢ **Focussing** of sound should not be there.

   ➢ Should be free of **echelon effect**.

   ➢ Should be **free of resonance**.

   ➢ **External sound** (noise) should be minimum.

3.5.1 Factors which Affect Acoustics of the Building and their Remedy

[May 15, Nov. 15]

An acoustically good hall is the one in which every syllable or musical note reaches the audience is audible and legible and then decays quickly to make space for the next syllable or note. If this aspect is not achieved, the hall is acoustically defective.

The following factors affect the architectural acoustics:

(1) Reverberation

- In a hall, when the reverberation is large, there is overlapping of sound. This will lead to lack of clarity in hearing. If the reverberation is small, there is a deadening effect on sound. As a result, the loudness becomes inadequate.

- Thus the time of reverberation for a hall should neither be too large ror too small. It should have an optimum value.

- This value can be calculated by a formula given by Prof. W. C. Sabine.

$$T \;=\; K\frac{V}{A} \;=\; 0.165\,\frac{V}{A}$$

  where A is the total effective absorption of the hall and V is its volume.

- Reverberation time can be controlled in the following ways:

  ➤ By providing sound absorbing materials on the walls and using carpets on floor.

  ➤ Using curtains and providing acoustic tiles.

  ➤ Providing windows and ventilators.

  ➤ Having furniture and audience.

(2) Echoes

- An echo is heard when reflected waves from the same source reach the listener with a time delay of $1/10^{th}$ of a second. The reflected sound arriving earlier than this helps in raising the loudness while that arriving later produces echoes and causes confusion.

- Echoes can be reduced or avoided by covering long distant walls and high ceilings with absorbent materials like felt, perforated card boards, coarse cloth etc.

(3) Loudness

- The control of reverberation may lead to the reduction in the intensity of sound. Hence the level of intell gible hearing goes down. For satisfactory hearing, sufficient loudness in every part of the hall is very important.

- The loudness can be increased by

  ➤ Providing loud speakers,

  ➤ Providing sounding boards behind the speaker and facing towards the audience,

  ➤ Providing wooden reflectors above the speaker.

(4) Focusing due to Walls and Ceiling

- Focusing surfaces like curved surfaces on the walls or ceiling produce concentration of sound in particular regions, while in some other parts, no sound is heard at all. This leads to poor and uneven sound intensity distribution.

- Uniform sound distribution can be achieved by

  ➤ allowing no curved surfaces or covering the curved surfaces with sound absorbent materials,

  ➤ having low ceiling,

  ➤ providing parabolic reflectors behind the speaker with the speaker at the focus.

  This will help in sending a uniform reflected beam of sound in the hall.

(5) Echelon Effect

- Regular succession of echoes occur when sound is reflected from equally spaced reflecting surfaces like staircase or a set of railings. This effect is known as **Echelon effect**. This makes the original sound confusing or unintelligible.

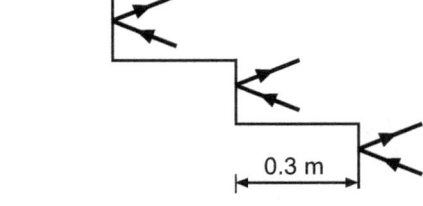

0.3 m

Fig. 3.7

- This effect can be reduced by: (a) Covering the stairs with thick carpets. (b) Breaking the regularity of spacing of the steps.

(6) Resonance

- Sometimes window panes and other parts of the structures which are not rigid are thrown into vibrations and they create other sounds. If some note of the audio frequency and the frequencies of new sounds are the same, then resonance occurs.

- Due to the interference between original sound and the created sound, the original sound is distorted. Thus the intensity of the note is entirely different from the original one. Also enclosed air in the hall causes resonance.

- Such resonant vibrations should be suitably damped.

(7) Seating Arrangement

- The speaker or source of sound should be at the focus of a parabolic reflecting surface. The seats should be arranged such that they are perpendicular to the direction of sound. The seats should be gradually elevated. This arrangement ensures uniform distribution of sound.

(8) Balconies

- The balconies should have shallow depths and high openings. They should have railing bars instead of walls. This allows sound energy to flow readily into space of the balcony.

(9) Noise

- An external noise makes speech or music makes the sound unintelligible. The noise may come to room by air or structure. The noise could be reduced by sound insulations. The noise in the hall should be minimum so that the sound is heard clearly.

3.5.2 Noise - its Effect and Remedies

- Noise can be defined as ***unwanted sound***. As noise is unwanted as, it either reduces the unintelligibility of sound or gives unpleasant effect. Therefore, in good hall, noise should be reduced by blocking the unwanted sound coming from outside as well as generated inside.

- Basically, there are three types of noises:

  (a) Air-borne noise   (b) Structure borne noise and   (c) Inside noise.

- The prevention of the noise inside or outside the hall is known as **sound insulation** or **sound proofing**. The method employed for sound proofing depends on the type of noise to be treated.

(a) Air-Borne Noise

- The noise which reaches the hall from outside through air is called **air-borne noise**. In this the noise is transported by air through open vent, window, door etc. The air-borne noise can be reduced by

  ➢ Avoiding ventilators facing the streets,

  ➢ Placing doors and windows at proper place,

  ➢ Using heavy glass doors, windows and ventilators,

  ➢ Having double wall construction.

(b) Structure-Borne Noise

- The noise which is conveyed through the structure of building is known as **structural noise**. This noise is caused by structural vibrations due to construction activities like hammering, drilling, operating machinery etc. The structure-borne noise can be reduced by

  ➢ Breaking the continuity of the structure,

  ➢ Using double wall,

  ➢ Using anti-vibration mounts like rubber pad.

(c) Inside Noise

- The noise which is produced inside the hall is called inside **noise**. They are produced by equipments and machineries used in the hall itself. This can be reduced by

  ➢ Placing machineries on insulating pods,

  ➢ Covering floor with carpets,

  ➢ Sound absorbing materials should be placed close to noise producing source.

SOLVED PROBLEMS

Problem 3.1: *A loud speaker emits energy equally in all directions at the rate of 1.5 joules/sec. What is the intensity level at a distance of 20 m ? ($I_o = 10^{-6}$ watt/cm²)*

Data: Rate of power = 1.5 J/sec = 1.5 watt, Distance (radius r) = 20 m = 2000 cm

Formula: (i) $SIL = 10\log_{10}\left(\dfrac{I_1}{I_0}\right)$ (ii) $I_1 = \dfrac{Power}{Area} = \dfrac{P}{4\pi r^2}$

Solution: (i)

$$I_1 = \frac{Power}{Area} = \frac{P}{4\pi r^2} = \frac{1.5}{4\pi (2000)^2} \text{ watt/cm}^2$$

$$I_o = 10^{-16} \text{ watt/cm}^2$$

(ii) The intensity level

$$SIL = 10 \log_{10}\left(\frac{I_1}{I_0}\right) = 10 \log_{10} \frac{\frac{1.5}{4\pi (2000)^2}}{10^{-16}}$$

$$SIL = 10 \log_{10} \frac{1.5}{4\pi (2000)^2} \times 10^{-16}$$

$$SIL = 10 \log_{10} \frac{1.5 \times 10^{10}}{16\pi} = \boxed{85 \text{ dB}}$$

Problem 3.2: *A cinema hall has a volume of 7500 m³. It is required to have reverberation time of 1.5 sec. What will be the total absorption in the hall ?*

Data: Volume V $=$ 7500 m³, Reverberation time t $=$ 1.5 sec

Formula: Reverberation time $\quad t = \dfrac{0.165\,V}{A}$

Solution: Substituting $\quad 1.5 = \dfrac{0.165 \times 7500}{A}$

∴ $\qquad A = \dfrac{0.165 \times 7500}{1.5}$

∴ $\qquad \boxed{A = 825 \text{ O.W.U.}}$

Problem 3.3: *The volume of a hall is 3398.4 m³ and its total absorption equals 92.90 m² of open window. Entry of people inside the hall raises the absorption by 185.50 m². Calculate the change in the reverberation time.*

Data: Volume V = 3398.4 m³, Total absorption $A = \sum a\, S = 92.90$ m²,

Total absorption (hall + people) $= \sum a\, S + \sum a_1\, S_1$

Formula: $t = 0.165 \dfrac{V}{\sum a\, S}$ = 185.50 m²

Solution: For hall, reverberation time is

$$t = \frac{0.165\, V}{\sum a\, S} = \frac{0.165 \times 3398.4}{92.90} = 6.04 \text{ sec.}$$

For (hall + people), $t_1 = \dfrac{0.165\, V}{\sum a\, S + \sum a_1\, S_1} = \dfrac{0.165 \times 3398.4}{92.90 + 185.5} = 2.04 \text{ sec.}$

∴   Change in reverberation time $= 6.04 - 2.04 = \boxed{4 \text{ sec.}}$

Problem 3.4: *A hall of volume 5000 m³ has a reverberation time of 3 sec. The surface area of the sound absorbing surface is 3500 m². Calculate the average coefficient of absorption.*

Data: Volume $V = 5000$ m³, Reverberation time $t = 3$ sec., Surface area $S = 3500$ m²

Formula: $t = \dfrac{0.165 \times V}{\sum a\, S}$

Solution: $3 = \dfrac{0.165 \times 5000}{a \times \sum S}$

∴ $a = \dfrac{0.165 \times 5000}{3 \times 3500} = \boxed{0.076 \text{ OWU}}$

Problem 3.5: *A hall of 1500 m³ has a seating capacity for 120 persons. Calculate the reverberation time of the hall when (i) the hall is empty, (ii) the hall is full to its capacity, using the following data:*

Data: Volume V = 1500 m³

Absorption due to plastered walls $= 112 \times 0.03 = 3.36$ OWU

Absorption due to wooden floor $= 130 \times 0.0678 = 7.8$ OWU

Absorption due to wooden ceiling $= 170 \times 0.04 = 6.8$ OWU

Absorption due to wooden floor $= 20 \times 0.06 = 1.2$ OWU

Absorption due to cushioned chairs $= 100 \times 1 = 100$ OWU

∴   Total absorption $= 119.16$ OWU

Average absorption of one human being $= 4.7$ OWU

Formula: $t = 0.165 \dfrac{V}{A}$

Solution: Reverberation time $t = \dfrac{0.165\,V}{A} = \dfrac{0.165 \times 1500}{119.6} = 2.04$ sec.

Absorption due to audience $= 120 \times 4.7 = 564$ OWU

Reverberation time $t = \dfrac{0.165\,V}{A} = \dfrac{0.165 \times 1500}{119.16 + 564} = \dfrac{0.165 \times 1500}{683.16}$

$= \boxed{0.117 \text{ sec.}}$

Problem 3.6: *A window, whose area is 1.4 m^2, opens on a street where the street noise result in an intensity level (at the window) of 80 deciBels. How much acoustic power enters the window via the sound waves ? Given: $I_0 = 10^{-12}$ watt/m^2.*

Data: Area $= 1.4$ m^2, Intensity level $=$ I.L. $= 80$ dB

Formula: $\text{SIL} = 10 \log_{10} \dfrac{I_1}{I_0}$

Solution: Intensity level I.L. $= 10 \log_{10} \dfrac{I_1}{I_0}$

Substituting, $80 = 10 \log_{10} \dfrac{I_1}{10^{-12}}$

$\text{Antilog} \left(\dfrac{80}{10}\right) = \dfrac{I_1}{10^{-12}}$

$\therefore$ $I_1 = 10^{-12} \times 10^8$

$I_1 = 10^{-4}$ watt/m^2

$\therefore$ Power $= I \times$ area $= 10^{-4} \times 1.4$

$\therefore$ $\boxed{\text{Power } = 1.4 \times 10^{-4} \text{ watt.}}$

Problem 3.7: *A lecture hall of 15 $\times$ 12 $\times$ 5 m dimensions has an average absorption coefficient 0.10. Calculate the reverberation time.*

Data: Volume of the hall $V = 15 \times 12 \times 5 = 900$ m^3

Area of inside surfaces $S = 2(15 \times 12 + 12 \times 5 + 5 \times 15) = 630$ m^2

Total absorption $A = 0.1 \times 630 = 63$ OWU

Formula: Reverberation time $t = 0.165 \dfrac{V}{A}$

Solution: $t = \dfrac{0.165 \times 900}{63} = \boxed{2.354 \text{ sec.}}$

Problem 3.8: *A hall of length 20 m, breadth 15 m and height 10 m has average coefficient of absorption 0.10. If 20 micro watt source is used in the hall, calculate the reverberation time and ultimate intensity.*

Data: Volume of the hall $= 20 \times 15 \times 70 = 3000 \text{ m}^3$

Area of inside surfaces $= 2 (20 \times 15 + 15 \times 10 + 10 \times 20) = 1300 \text{ m}^2$

Total absorption $A = 0.1 \times 1300 = 130 \text{ OWU}$

Solution: (i) Reverberation time $t = 0.165 \dfrac{V}{A} = \dfrac{0.165 \times 3000}{130} = \boxed{3.715 \text{ sec.}}$

(ii) Ultimate intensity $I = \dfrac{P}{A} = \dfrac{20}{1300} = \boxed{0.0154 \text{ microwatt/m}^2}$

Problem 3.9: *A hall of volume 5000 m³ has a reverberation time of 2 seconds. If the absorbing surface of the hall has the area 3600 m², calculate the average coefficient of absorption.*

Data: $V = 5000 \text{ m}^3$, $t = 2 \text{ sec}$, $S = 3600 \text{ m}^2$

Formula: $t = \dfrac{0.165 \, V}{\sum a \, S} = \dfrac{0.165 \, V}{a \sum S}$

∴ **Solution:** $a = \dfrac{0.165 \, V}{t \times \sum S} = \dfrac{0.165 \times 5000}{2 \times 3600} = \boxed{0.1118 \text{ OWU}}$

3.6 ULTRASONICS

We all know that sound is due to the **vibrations of particles of the medium**. Human ear can hear the sound waves of frequencies between 20 Hz to 20,000 Hz. This range is known as the **audible range**. The sound waves whose frequencies are greater than 20,000 Hz are known as **ultrasonic waves**. The wavelength of ultrasonic waves is very small as compared to that of audible sound. The sound waves which have frequencies less than the audible range are called as **infrasonic waves**.

The ultrasonic and infrasonic frequencies are inaudible to human beings but they are audible to some birds, dogs and insects. A dog can hear sound of frequencies above 20 kHz. Bats can hear sound waves of frequencies upto 100 kHz. This enables them to move freely even in the dark.

3.7 PRODUCTION OF ULTRASONIC WAVES

- Ultrasonic waves cannot be produced by the ordinary method i.e. by using mechanical vibrations. This is because of the comparatively low natural frequencies of the moving parts. Hence other methods are used for the production of ultrasonic waves. The method chosen depends upon the output power required and the frequency range needed.

- A device which produces ultrasonic waves is called **an ultrasonic transducer**. To generate lower frequencies, a mechanical type device such as Galton's Whistle is used. Magnetostriction method is used when frequencies upto 300 kHz are needed, while piezo-electric generators are used mostly for frequencies above that.

3.7.1 Piezo-electric Effect   [Dec. 12, Nov. 13, 15, May 15]

- When opposite faces of a thin section of certain crystals like tourmaline, quartz etc. are subjected to distortion by applying **pressure or tension**, then **equal and opposite charges** are developed on the faces perpendicular to the faces subjected to distortion. The magnitude of the potential difference developed is proportional to the amount of distortion produced. The polarity of the charges gets reversed when the direction of the force of distortion is reversed. This phenomenon is known as **piezo-electric effect**.

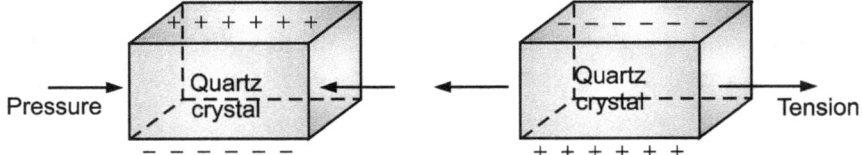

Fig. 3.8: Piezo-electric effect

- The converse of piezo-electric effect is also true i.e. if a potential difference is applied across the two faces of the crystal, it expands or contracts depending on the strength and direction of the applied field.
- Instead of steady voltage if an alternating voltage is applied across the faces of the crystal, then the crystal will expand and contract alternatively. This alternate expansion and contraction will make the crystal vibrate.
- If the frequency of the applied a.c. voltage happens to be equal to one of the modes of vibration of the crystal, resonance occurs and the crystal vibrates with maximum amplitude.

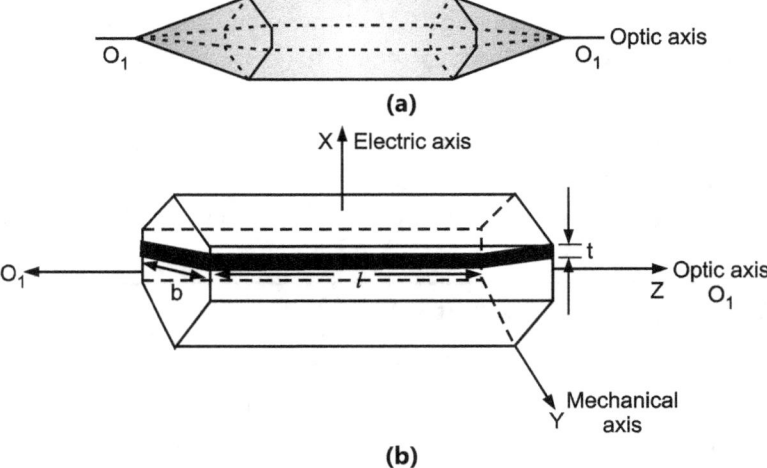

Fig. 3.9: (a) Natural quartz crystal and (b) Transverse Section of Quartz Crystal Cut along a Plane Perpendicular to the Optic Axis

Fig. 3.9 (a) shows a natural quartz crystal and Fig. 3.9 (b) shows a transverse section of the crystal.

- Consider a quartz crystal plate of thickness t and length l (along the optic axis). When an alternating voltage is applied across the faces of this crystal along the electrical axis, then alternating stress and strain is set up both in its thickness and length.
- If the frequency of the alternating voltage coincides with the natural frequency of vibration of the crystal, resonance occurs. The crystal vibrates with large amplitude. On maintaining suitable alternating potential, ultrasonic waves can be generated by this method.

- The frequency of the thickness vibrations, $f = \dfrac{P}{2t}\sqrt{\dfrac{E}{\rho}}$

- The frequency of the length vibrations, $f = \dfrac{P}{2l}\sqrt{\dfrac{E}{\rho}}$

where P = 1, 2, 3, ... etc. for **fundamental**, **first overtone** and **second overtone** respectively, E is the Young's modulus, ρ is the density of the crystal, t is the thickness and l is the length of the crystal.

Piezo-Electric Oscillator

- The experimental set up is as shown in Fig. 3.10.
- The high frequency alternating voltage applied to the crystal is obtained from an oscillatory circuit (inductance L_1 and a variable condenser C_1 in parallel).
- One end of the oscillatory circuit is connected to the plate of valve and the other end to the grid. The quartz crystal is placed in between two metal plates A and B to form a parallel-plate capacitor with the crystal as a dielectric. This is connected in parallel to the variable condenser C_1.
- By adjusting the variable condenser, the frequency of the oscillatory circuit is tuned to the natural frequency of the crystal.
- At this stage, the crystal is set into mechanical vibrations and ultrasonic waves are generated. By this method, ultrasonic waves upto a frequency of 15×10^7 Hz can be obtained.

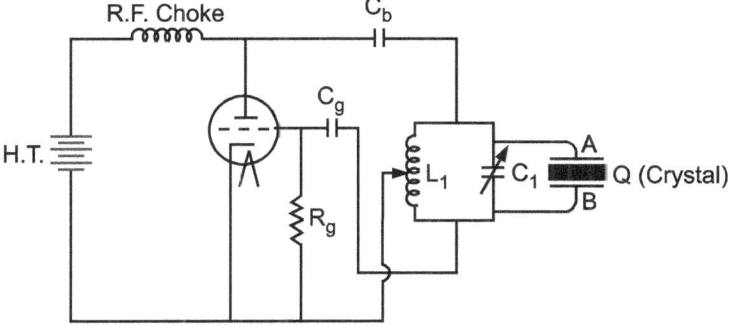

Fig. 3.10: Piezo-electric oscillator

Alternative Method for Piezoelectric Oscillator

Principle

- This oscillator works on the principle of reverse piezoelectric effect. A piezoelectric crystal is placed between the two metal plates. An ac voltage of certain frequency is applied across the two faces of the crystal. There is a change in the dimension of the crystal (contraction or expansion) depending on the direction of the applied voltage. This vibration of crystal produces ultrasonic waves.

Construction

- The piezoelectric oscillator uses basically a Hartley oscillator. The transistor is biased using the resistors R_1, R_2 and R_E. The combination of L_1, L_2 and C_1 works as tuning circuit which is coupled with the transistor with a coupling capacitor C_2. The capacitor C_2 is used to provide positive feedback.

- The resonance frequency of the tank circuit is given by

$$f_r = \frac{1}{2\pi \sqrt{L_r C_1}}, \text{ where } L_r = L_1 + L_2$$

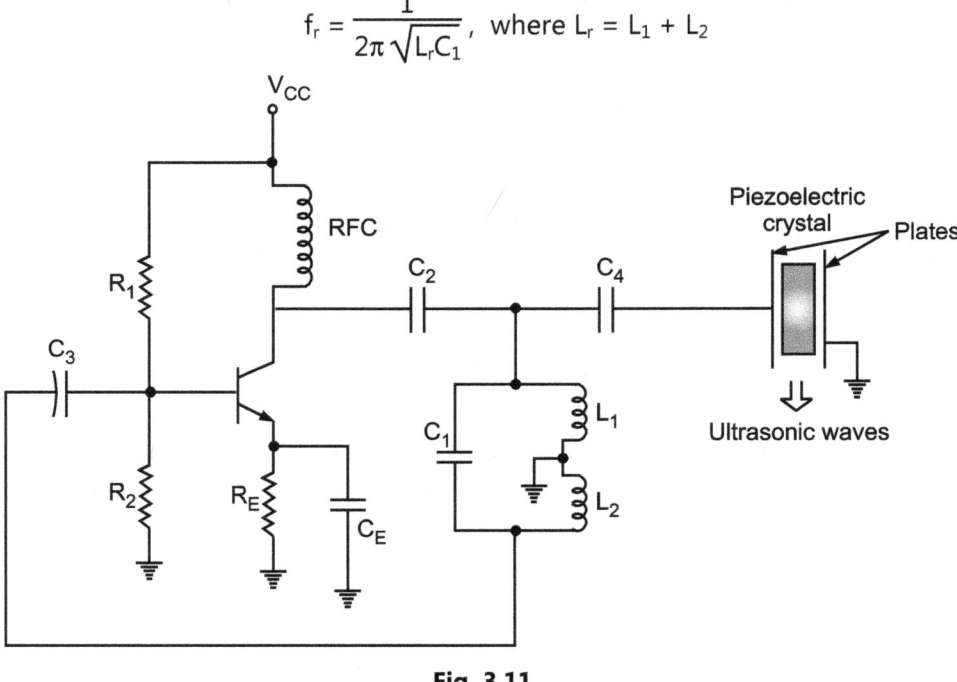

Fig. 3.11

Working

- When the circuit is switched on, oscillating currents are produced in the tuning circuit.

- The oscillating currents generated by the tuning circuit are sustained and the electric signal obtained at the output is applied to the piezoelectric crystal through coupling capacitor C_4.

- When these high frequency electrical signals are applied to the crystal, because of reverse piezoelectric effect, the crystal undergoes alternate contraction and expansion. These vibrations produce ultrasonic waves.

- The frequency of ultrasonic waves can be changed by varying the values of components of the tuning circuit as per the relation $f = \dfrac{1}{2\pi\sqrt{L_T C_1}}$. When frequency of oscillation of the tuning circuit becomes equal to the natural frequency of the crystal $f = \dfrac{P}{2l}\sqrt{\dfrac{E}{F}}$, resonance occurs and crystal oscillates with maximum amplitude and amplitude of ultrasonic waves will be maximum.

- Ultrasonic waves upto frequency of 1.5×10^8 Hz can be produced using piezoelectric oscillator.

3.7.2 Magnetostriction Effect   [May 13, 14, 16, Dec. 14]

- According to this phenomenon, a rod of **ferromagnetic material** such as iron or nickel undergoes a **change in its length** when placed in a magnetic field parallel to its length.

- Instead of a steady field, if an alternating field is used, the rod expands and contracts in length alternately. This sets up a longitudinal vibration in the rod whose frequency is twice the frequency of the alternating magnetic field. If the natural frequency of the rod and the frequency of the alternating field is the same, resonance occurs and the amplitude of vibration of the rod is maximum.

- The range of frequency depends on the dimensions of the magnetostrictive material. The longitudinal vibrations thus produced are exactly like those produced by a rod which is clamped at the mid point but has both ends free.

- The frequency of vibration of such a rod is

$$\boxed{f = \dfrac{1}{2l}\sqrt{\dfrac{E}{\rho}}}$$

where E is the Young's modulus, l is the length of the rod, and ρ is its density of rod.

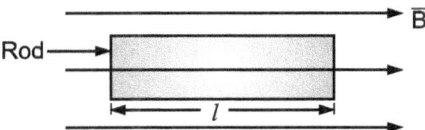

Fig. 3.12: Magnetostriction effect

Magnetostriction Oscillator

- This apparatus generates ultrasonic waves and is based on the principle of magneto-striction.

- When a rod of ferromagnetic material is suddenly magnetised, it undergoes slight change in length. This is known as *magnetostriction*. The change in length depends on the strength of the field and on the type of the material.

- Fig. 3.13 shows the experimental set up of magnetostriction oscillator. It consists of a permanently magnetised nickel or iron rod (magnetised initially by passing direct current in the coil which is wound round it). The rod is clamped at the centre. The two coils L_1 and L_2 are wound over the rod.

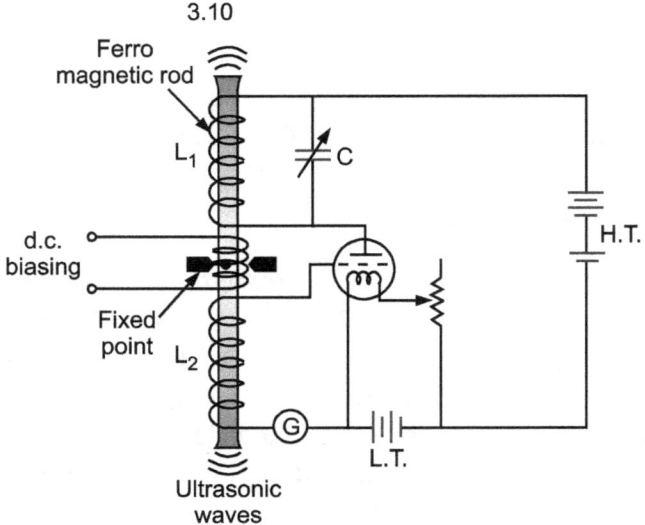

Fig. 3.13: Magnetostriction oscillator

The exciting coil L_1 is connected to the plate circuit of a valve while the coil L_2 is coupled to the plate via the grid circuit.

- By adjusting the variable condenser C, high frequency oscillation currents are set up in the plate circuit. This high frequency current flowing through the coil L_1 produces changes in the length of the rod. Due to this, the rod expands and contracts alternately and a vibration is set up in the rod.

- These vibrations in the length of the rod cause a variation in the magnetic flux through the coil L_2 and an e.m.f. is induced in it. This induced e.m.f. is fed to the grid which produces large variations in the plate current. Thus magnetostrictive effect in the bar is increased.

- When the frequency of the circuit becomes equal to the natural frequency of the rod, resonance occurs and ultrasonic waves of maximum amplitude are produced. By adjusting the length of the rod and condenser capacity, high frequency oscillations of different frequencies can be obtained.

Alternate Method for Magnetostriction Oscillator

Principle

- A ferromagnetic rod is placed in a rapidly varying magnetic field. Eecause of the magnetostriction effect, the ferromagnetic rod expands and contracts alternately with twice the frequency of the applied magnetic field.

- These vibrations of the rod produce ultrasonic waves.

Construction

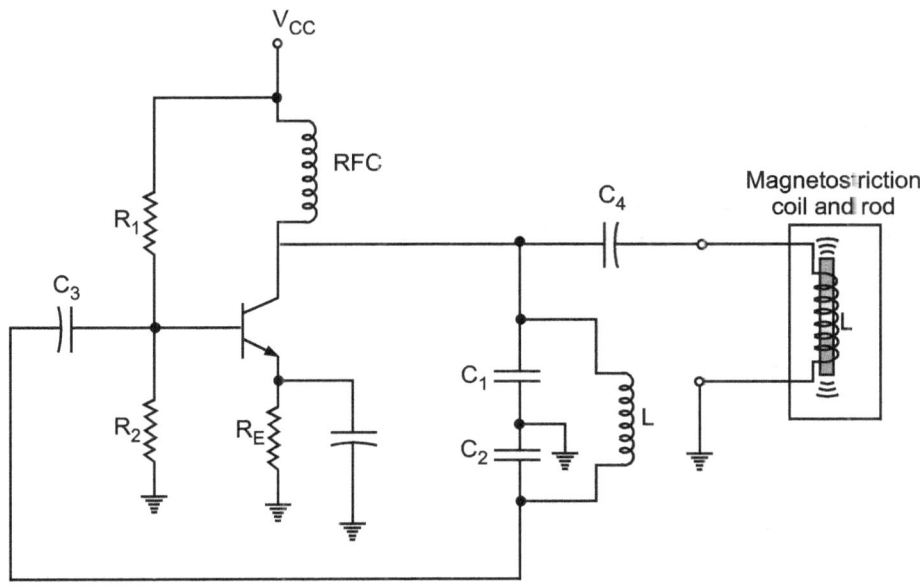

Fig. 3.14

- The magnetostrictive oscillator uses basically a Colpitt's oscillator. The transistor is biased with the help of resistances R_1, R_2 and R_E. The inductance L and capacitors C_1 and C_2 form a tank circuit and C_3 is a feedback capacitor. The tank circuit is used for selecting resonance frequency.

- The appropriate frequencies at the end of the tank circuit are amplified and the oscillations corresponding to them are sustained. The resonance of tank circuit is given by $f_r = \dfrac{1}{2\pi \sqrt{LC_r}}$, where $C_r = \dfrac{C_1 C_2}{C_1 + C_2}$. A ferromagnetic rod is kept surrounding to a coil in the shape of solenoid at the output of the oscillator.

Working

- When the circuit is switched on, oscillating currents are produced in the tuning circuit. The oscillations appearing at output terminal of oscillator circuit are fed to the magnetostriction coil through coupling capacitor C_4. The magnetostriction coil is placed surrounding the ferromagnetic rod.

- The coil produces magnetic field which is alternately changing in opposite directions and is applied around the ferromagnetic rod. Due to magnetostriction effect the changing magnetic field causes rod to contract and expand alternately. These vibrations of the rod travel in surrounding medium in the form of ultrasonic waves.

- The frequency of oscillating current in the tank circuit can be changed by varying the values of the components of the tank circuit.

- The frequency of vibrations of the rod is given by $f = \dfrac{p}{2l} \sqrt{\dfrac{E}{\rho}}$.

  where, p is integer, l is length of the rod, Y is Young's modulus and ρ is density of the rod.

- When frequency of the tuning circuit becomes equal to natural frequency of the rod, the rod vibrates with maximum amplitude and ultrasonic waves with maximum amplitude are obtained.

3.8 PROPERTIES OF ULTRASONIC WAVES

- As the wavelength of the waves is very small, ultrasonic waves suffer least diffraction. They can be *transmitted over longer distances* as a highly directional beam without appreciable loss of energy.
- Ultrasonic waves are *highly energetic* and may have intensities upto 10 kW/m^2.
- On passing through liquids, ultrasonic waves are propagated longitudinally forming nodes and antinodes. This produces *cavitation effect*.
- In solids, ultrasonic waves propagate both longitudinally and transversely. In transverse waves, there exist no nodes or antinodes.
- Velocity of ultrasonic waves depends on the *temperature of the medium* through which it is propagating.
- When ultrasonic waves are passed through a liquid kept in a rectangular vessel, they are reflected from the bottom of the vessel. The directed and reflected rays get superimposed resulting in a stationary wave. Due to the formation of the stationary wave the density of the node is greater than that at the antinode. Now, if a parallel beam of light is passed at right angle to the wave the liquid acts as a diffraction grating. This is called as *acoustical grating*.

3.9 DETECTION OF ULTRASONICS

The ultrasonic waves cannot be heard by human beings, it is not possible to detect them by hearing. Therefore, some instrumental technique has to be employed to detect the ultrasonic waves. Some of the methods are as follows:

1. **Kundt's Tube**

   ➢ Kundt's tube is a glass tube with both ends open and end filled with lycopodium powder in small quantity. When ultrasonic waves are passed through the Kundt's tube, the lycopodium powder collects in the form of heaps at the nodal points and is blown off at the antinodal points as shown in Fig. 3.15.

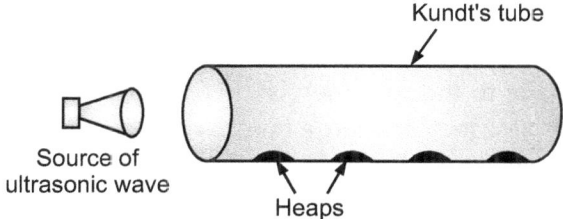

Fig. 3.15: Kundt's tube

2. Thermal Detector

➢ In this method, a thin platinum wire which forms one side of the Wheatstone's bridge is used for detection of ultrasonic waves. When ultrasonic waves pass through the medium, it produces compression and rarefaction. This results in change in temperature of the medium. The temperature is maximum at nodes and minimum at antinodes.

➢ When the platinum wire is moved in the medium where ultrasonic waves are present, the resistance changes due to variation in temperature. The change in resistance will deflect the galvanometer. The deflection changes will be the amplitude of the ultrasonic waves.

3. Piezo-Electric Detector

➢ A quartz crystal can be used for detection of ultrasonic waves. One pair of opposite faces of the crystal is subjected to ultrasonic waves. These waves exert mechanical pressure on the crystal.

➢ As a result, opposite charges are developed on the other pair of faces perpendicular to the one which is facing the ultrasonic waves. These fluctuating charges developed due to compressions and rarefactions on the crystal are amplified and then detected.

3.10 ENGINEERING APPLICATIONS OF ULTRASONIC WAVES
[Dec. 12]

• Ultrasonic waves have a wide range of applications and uses. This is because they are **highly energetic**. They show less diffraction due to their small wavelength and hence cover large distances. Due to these special properties they can travel large distances in air as well as water.

3.10.1 Non-Destructive Testing   [May 13, 16]

• Non-destructive testing is characterized by low intensity of the sound wave used. Here sound wave is not expected to cause any change in the chemical or physical characteristics of the specimen material.

- Such applications are found in testing, inspection and quality control.
- In this case, ultrasonic waves are propagated into the specimen under inspection. When the ultrasonic waves are incident on the defect, reflection of the wave from the interface (between material and defect) in the object takes place. Thus, the defects are located without any real damage to the specimen.
- Ultrasonic waves may be used for a large number of non-destructive testing on different materials. Some of these are
  (i) Ultrasonic flaw detection   (ii) Ultrasonic study of structure of matter.

Flaw Detection
- The strength of components play a significant role in most of the engineering applications. Any kind of defect greatly reduces the strength of materials. These defects can be as large as cracks or as tiny as cavities.
- A high frequency pulse from pulse generator is impressed on a quartz crystal which is placed on the specimen under test. The crystal (transducer) first acts as a transmitter sending out high frequency waves into the specimen.
- Then it acts as a receiver to receive the ultrasonic echo pulses reflected from the flaw and from the far end of the specimen. The received ultrasonic echo pulses are transformed by the transducer into corresponding electric echo pulses of the same frequency. These are then amplified and displayed on the C.R.O. screen as a series of pulses.
- The first pulse corresponds to the transmitted wave, the next pulse corresponds to the reflected wave. i.e. first one from the flaw and the second one from the far end of the specimen. Each reflected pulse is indicated at a particular time after the initial transmitted pulse. The time interval between the transmitted and reflected pulse represents the distance travelled by the wave. From this the exact position of the flaw is located.

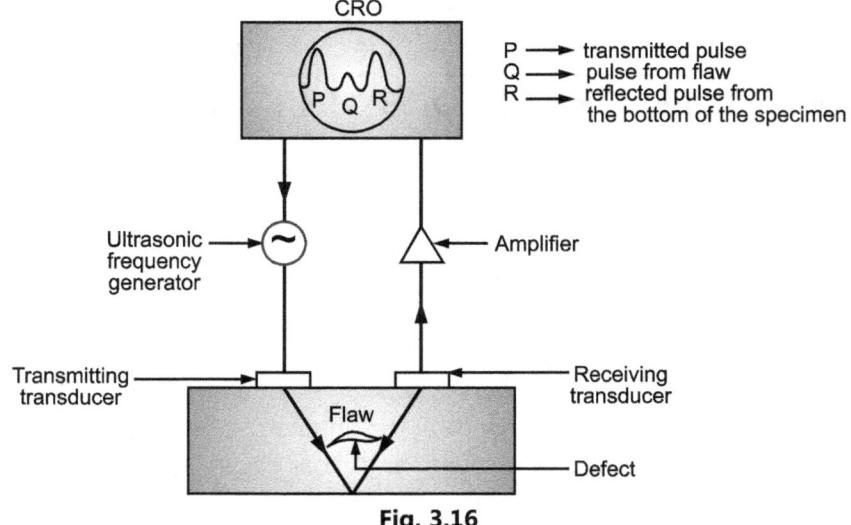

Fig. 3.16

3.10.2 Cavitation   [May 14]

- When an ultrasonic transducer is placed in a liquid, it produces ultrasonic vibrations in it. This results in the development and implosion of bubbles. These bubbles are known as the **cavitation bubbles** and they are formed as follows.

- When a liquid is subjected to a powerful ultrasonic radiation, tension develops at some point in a liquid. The excess stress tears apart the liquid producing a hollow bubble that sucks in dissolved gases and vapours.

- The life time of the bubble is very short, and it collapses very quickly. During the implosion of the bubble, the pressure of the shock wave that is formed near the bubble reaches several hundreds of atmospheres.

- The formation and implosion of bubbles accounts for erosion and pitting of an ultrasonic transducer kept in the liquid. The bubbles have two effects (i) they produce a dense cloud infront of the transducer and block the propagation of ultrasonic waves, (ii) frequent implosion of bubbles destroys the surface of the transducer causing pits.

- Even though cavitation bubbles formed by ultrasonic vibrators in liquids block the wave propagation, it has some successful industrial application like ultrasonic cleaning, ultrasonic emulsification etc

(i) Ultrasonic Cleaning

  ➤ Ultrasonic cleaning is achieved through a combined effect of cavitation and acceleration of the cleaning liquid. Ultrasonic waves in liquid produce cavitation i.e. tiny space in the liquid. The vacuum created in these spaces exerts a strong pull on exposed solid surfaces. This detaches any particles of dust attached to them.

  ➤ The transducer is placed at the bottom of the tank in which the cleaning solution (either a water detergent solution or standard solvents) is taken.

  ➤ For the cleaning of metallic parts, low frequency waves are used while for cleaning fibres, high frequency waves are used. The specimen to be cleaned is kept immersed in the cleaning solution in the tank.

(ii) Ultrasonic Emulsification

  ➤ It has been observed that intense ultrasonic waves can thoroughly mix immiscible liquids like oil and water to form a stable emulsion. The emulsification results because of the cavitation bubbles imploding at the boundary surfaces between a liquid and vibrator, and also between liquid and walls of the container.

  ➤ The two liquids which are to be emulsified are taken in a container. This container is placed in a liquid bath which is subjected to strong ultrasonic vibrations by a transducer. Then emulsification due to gas bubbles takes place at the surface of the container containing the two liquids.

3.10.3 Measurement Gauge

- Ultrasonic thickness measurement is based on the **echo principle**. A piezoelectric transducer attached to the test piece converts the electric pulse into ultrasonic waves. The transducer can be attached to the test piece directly or it can be coupled to the piece by an incompressible medium such as oil or water.

- The ultrasonic waves propagate into the test piece. They travel through the sample and are reflected back from the opposite surface. The same transducer then receives the reflected echo and converts it to an electrical pulse. The time taken for the pulse to travel through the sample is related to the thickness and the velocity in the material. The thickness T can be expressed by the formula,

$$\text{Thickness} = \frac{\text{Velocity of sound in specimen} \times \text{time}}{2}$$

$$T = \frac{vt}{2}$$

where, v is the velocity of the ultrasound in the material and t is the time between the pulse being transmitted and the echo being received.

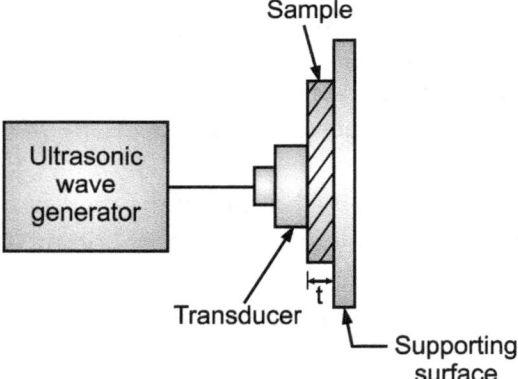

Fig. 3.17

- If the velocity of ultrasonic waves in the material is not known, then the value has to be determined experimentally by using the same material whose thickness is already known. From the known values of T and t, the velocity v of ultrasound in the material can be calculated.

- The advantage of using ultrasonic waves for thickness measurement is that the thickness can be measured from one side of the test piece. There is no need for drilling holes or otherwise inflicting damage to the piece.

SOLVED PROBLEMS

Problem 3.10: *Calculate the natural frequency of the thickness vibrations for quartz plate of thickness 5.5 × 10⁻³ m, given that Young's modulus along X-axis is 8 × 10¹⁰ N/m² and density of crystal is 2.65 × 10³ kg/m³.*

Data: $t = 5.5 \times 10^{-3}$ m, $E = 8 \times 10^{10}$ N/m², $\rho = 2.65 \times 10^3$ kg/m³.

Formula: The fundamental frequency of thickness vibrations is given by

$$n = \frac{1}{2t} \sqrt{\frac{E}{\rho}}$$

Solution:

$$n = \frac{1}{2 \times 5.5 \times 10^{-3}} \sqrt{\frac{8 \times 10^{10}}{2.65 \times 10^3}}$$

$$n = \frac{1}{2 \times 5.5 \times 10^{-3}} \times 5.5 \times 10^3 = 500 \times 10^3 \text{ Hz}$$

$$\boxed{n = 500 \text{ kHz}}$$

Problem 3.11: *Calculate the frequency of the fundamental note emitted by a piezoelectric crystal, using the following data. Vibrating length 3 mm. Young's modulus = 8 × 10¹⁰ N/m² and density of crystal = 2.5 g/cm³.*

Data: $l = 3$ mm, $E = 8 \times 10^{10}$ N/m², $\rho = 2.5$ g/cm³.

Formula: The fundamental frequency of length vibration is given by

$$n = \frac{1}{2l} \sqrt{\frac{E}{\rho}}$$

Solution:

$$n = \frac{1}{2 \times 3 \times 10^{-3}} \sqrt{\frac{8 \times 10^{10}}{2.5 \times 10^3}} = 0.943 \times 10^6 \text{ Hz}$$

$$= \boxed{943 \text{ kHz}}$$

Problem 3.12: *An ultrasonic source of 0.07 MHz sends down a pulse towards the seabed which returns after 0.65 sec. The velocity of sound in sea water is 1700 m/s Calculate the depth of sea and the wavelength of the pulse.*

Data: $f = 0.07$ MHz, $t = 0.65$ sec, $v = 1700$ m/s

Formulae: (i) Depth of sea $= \dfrac{\text{Velocity of sound in sea} \times \text{Time}}{2} = \dfrac{vt}{2}$, (ii) $\lambda = \dfrac{v}{g}$

Solution: (i) $v = \dfrac{1700 \times 0.65}{2} = \boxed{552.5 \text{ m}}$

(ii)   Wavelength of the pulse,

$$\lambda = \frac{v}{f} = \frac{1700}{0.07 \times 10^6 \text{ Hz}} = \boxed{2.4 \text{ cm}}$$

Problem 3.13: *Calculate the natural frequency of 40 mm length of a pure iron rod; given that density of pure iron is 7.25 $\times 10^3$ kg/m^3 and its Young's modulus is 115 $\times 10^3$ N/m^2.*

Data: l = 40 mm, ρ = 7.25 $\times 10^3$ kg/m^3.

Formula: $f = \dfrac{1}{2l} \sqrt{\dfrac{Y}{\rho}}$

Solution: $f = \dfrac{1}{2 \times 40 \times 10^{-3}} \sqrt{\dfrac{115 \times 10^3}{7.25 \times 10^3}} = \boxed{49.75 \text{ kHz}}$

Problem 3.14: *An ultrasonic source of 70 kHz sends down a pulse towards the sea bed which returns after 0.5 sec. The velocity of sound in sea water is 1400 cm/sec.*

  (a) *What is the depth of the sea ?*

  (b) *What is the wavelength of the pulse in water ?*

Data: f = 70 kHz = 70 $\times 10^3$ Hz; t = 0.5 sec, v = 1400 m/sec

Formulae: (i) $\lambda = \dfrac{v}{g}$

  (ii) Depth of sea $= \dfrac{\text{Velocity of water} \times \text{Time}}{2} = \dfrac{vt}{2}$

Solution: (i) $D = \dfrac{1400 \times 0.5}{2} = \boxed{350 \text{ m}}$

  (ii) Wavelength, $\lambda = \dfrac{v}{f} = \dfrac{1400}{70 \times 10^3} = \boxed{20 \times 10^{-3} \text{ m}}$

UNIVERSITY SOLVED PROBLEMS

Problem 3.15: *Calculate the thickness of a quartz plate required to produce ultrasonic waves of frequency 2 MHz.*

  Given: Density of crystal = 2650 kg/m^3

    Young's modulus = 8 $\times 10$ N/m^2   **(03) (Dec. 06)**

Data: F = 2 MHz

          ρ = 2650 kg/m^3

          E = 8 $\times 10^{10}$ N/m^2

Formula: The natural frequency,

          $n = \dfrac{P}{2t} \sqrt{\dfrac{E}{\rho}}$

Solution: Take   P = 1

          $t = \dfrac{1}{2 \times 2 \times 10^6} \sqrt{\dfrac{8 \times 10^{10}}{2650}} = 1.37 \times 10^{-3}$ m

          $\boxed{t = 1.37 \times 10^{-3} \text{ m}}$

Problem 3.16: Calculate the natural frequency of a cast iron rod of 2.6 cm length.

Given: Density of rod = 7.23×10^3 kg/m³

           Young's modulus = 1.16×10^{11} N/m³   **(04) (Dec. 07)**

Data: $l = 2.6$ cm

                          $\rho = 7.23 \times 10^3$ kg/m³

                          $E = 1.16 \times 10^{11}$ N/m²

Formula: $n = \dfrac{1}{2l} \sqrt{\dfrac{E}{\rho}}$

Solution: $n = \dfrac{1}{2 \times 2.6 \times 10^{-2}} \sqrt{\dfrac{1.16 \times 10^{11}}{7.23 \times 10^3}}$

                          $n = 770.29 \times 10^2$ Hz $= \boxed{77.03 \text{ kHz}}$

Problem 3.17: A quartz crystal of thickness 0.001 metre is vibrating at resonance. Calculate the fundamental frequency given that Y for quartz is 7.9×10^{10} N/m² and ρ for quartz is 2650 kg/m³.

Data: t = 0.001 m, $\lambda = 7.9 \times 10^{10}$ N/m², $\rho = 2650$ kg/m³

Solution: $f = \dfrac{1}{2t} \sqrt{\dfrac{\lambda}{\rho}}$

                          $= \dfrac{1}{2 \times 0.001} \sqrt{\dfrac{7.9 \times 10^{10}}{2650}} = 2729.9$ kHz $= \boxed{2730 \text{ kHz}}$

Problem 3.18: The average reverberation time of a hall is 1.5 sec. and the area of the interior surface is 3340 m². If the volume of the hall is 13000 m³. Find the absorption coefficient.   **(03) (Dec 12)**

Data: Volume, $V = 13000$ m³

           Reverberation time, $t = 1.5$ sec.

           Surface area, $S = 3340$ m²

Formula: $t = \dfrac{0.165 \times V}{\Sigma \, a \, S}$

∴ $1.5 = \dfrac{0.165 \times 13000}{a \times \Sigma S}$

∴ $a = \dfrac{0.165 \times 13000}{1.5 \times 3340}$

∴ $a = \mathbf{0.428}$

Problem 3.19: *A auditorium of volume 5500m3 is found to have reverberation time 2.5 secs. The sound absorbing surface of the auditorium has an area of 750m2. Calculate the average absorption coefficient of the auditorium.*   **(03) (May 13)**

Data: $V = 5500m^3$

$T = 2.5 \text{ sec}$

$S = 750m^2$

Formula: $t = \dfrac{0.165V}{\le as}$

Solution: $a = \dfrac{0.165 \times 5500}{750 \times 2.5}$

$\therefore$ $a = 0.484 \text{ OWU}$

Problem 3.20: *Calculate the intensity level of a fighter plane just leaving the runway having a sound intensity of about 100 W/m². Given that threshold intensity = 10^{-12} W/m².*

(03) (May 14)

Data: $I = 100 \text{ w/m}^2$

$I_0 = 10^{-12} \text{ w/m}^2$

Formula: $SIL = 10 \log_{10} \dfrac{I}{I_0} \text{ dB}$

Solution: $SIL = 10 \log_{10} \dfrac{100}{10^{-12}}$

$SIL = 10 \log 10^{14}$

$SIL = 140 \text{ dB}$

SUMMARY

- **Reverberation:** Prolongation or persistance of sound in a closed hall even after sound source has been stopped.

- **Reverberation Time:** Time for which sound persists in a hall.

- **Sabine's Formula:** $T = K\dfrac{V}{A}$.

- **Absorption Coefficient:** The ratio of the sound energy absorbed by any surface to that of the total sound energy incident on the surface.

- **Factors Affecting Architectural Acoustics of a Hall:**

  (a)   Reverberation   (b)   Echo

  (c)   Loudness   (d)   Focussing

(e)   Echelon   (f)   Resonance

(g)   Seating arrangement

(h)   Balconies

- **Ultrasonic Waves:** Sound waves of frequencies greater than 20,000 Hz are called as ultrasonic waves. Sound waves of frequencies less than 20 Hz are called as infrasonics.

- **Piezo-Electric Effect:** When opposite faces of a thin section of certain crystals such as tourmaline, quartz, etc. are subjected to distortion by applying pressure or tension then equal and opposite charges are developed on the faces which are perpendicular to the faces subjected to distortion. This phenomenon is called as piezo-electric effect.

$$f = \frac{P}{2l} \sqrt{\frac{E}{\rho}}$$

- **Magnetostriction Effect:** When a rod of ferromagnetic material such as iron or nickel is subjected to a magnetic field parallel to its length, it undergoes a change in its length. This phenomenon is called magnetostriction.

$$f = \frac{1}{2l} \sqrt{\frac{E}{\rho}}$$

- **Methods of Producing Ultrasonic Waves:**

    (a)   **Magnetostriction Method:** For frequencies upto 300 kHz.

    (b)   **Piezo-Electric Method:** For frequencies beyond 300 kHz.

- **Detection of Ultrasonic Waves:**

    (i)   Kundt's tube

    (ii)   Flame method

    (iii) Thermal detector method

    (iv)   Piezo electric

    (v)   Capacitor microphone.

- **Properties:**

    (i)   The speed of propagation increases with increase in frequency.

    (ii)   Due to very small wavelength, they suffer least diffraction.

    (iii) Due to high frequencies, they are highly energetic.

    (iv)   Propagate longitudinally forming nodes and antinodes in liquids

    (v)   Propagate both longitudinally and transversely in solids.

   (vi)   Velocity depends on temperature through which it is propagated.

   (vii) Forms acoustical grating when passed through a liquid.

- **Applications of Ultrasonics:**

(a) **Scientific:**
   (i)   Echo sounding
   (ii)   Sound signalling
   (iii) Depth sounding
   (iv)   Determining the position of icebergs etc.
   (v)   Cleaning and removing dirt.

(b) **Engineering:**
   (i)   Thickness measurement
   (ii)   Cavitation
   (iii) Ultrasonic cleaning
   (iv)   Ultrasonic emulsification
   (v)   Non-destructive testing
   (vi)   Flaw detection
   (vii) Soldering, drilling and welding.

(c) **Chemical Applications:**
   (i)   Ultrasonic mixing
   (ii)   Coagulation
   (iii) Crystallization
   (iv)   Acceleration of reactions.

(d) **Biological Applications:** To scare away rats and rodents.

(e) **Medical:** Ultrasonography, painless surgery, etc.

IMPORTANT FORMULAE

- $L \propto \log I$

- $SIL = 10 \log_{10} \dfrac{I}{I_o}$

- $T = 0.165 \dfrac{V}{A} = 0.165 \dfrac{V}{\Sigma\, aS}$

- The frequency of the thickness vibrations, $n = \dfrac{P}{2t} \sqrt{\dfrac{E}{\rho}}$.

- The frequency of the length vibrations, $n = \dfrac{P}{2l} \sqrt{\dfrac{E}{\rho}}$.

- Echo principle, $v = \dfrac{2d}{t}$.

EXERCISE

1. Write two points of difference between:

   (a) Echo and reverberation

   (b) Intensity and intensity level.

2. Explain remedies for acoustical planning of a hall.

3. What do you mean by absorption coefficient ? Explain.

4. Explain absorption of sound waves.

5. Define and explain:

   (a) Intensity of sound   (b) Loudness   (c) Intensity level   (d) Echo.

6. Explain limits of audibility.

7. What is reverberation ? Explain.

8. What are the essential features that an acoustically good hall should have ?

9. Give Sabine's formula for standard reverberation time, and give the importance of reverberation time.

10. What are the factors which affect the architectural acoustics ?

11. What are ultrasonic waves ?

12. Give the magnetostriction method of generating ultrasonic waves.

13. Explain piezo-electric effect.

14. Describe how piezo-electric effect can be used for generating ultrasonic waves.

15. Explain any two methods for the detection of ultrasonic waves.

16. Explain any three engineering applications of ultrasonic waves.

17. What is noise ? What are different types of noise ? Give common methods for treating them.

18. Explain how ultrasonic waves are used for:

    (a) flaw detection,

    (b) measurement of thickness.

UNSOLVED PROBLEMS

1. A man shouts standing infront of a mountain, hears an echo after 0.9 seconds later. Calculate the distance between the man and the mountain if the velocity of sound in air is 340 m/sec.   **(Ans.** 153 m)

2. A man standing between two mountain ranges fires a gun and hears the sound of the firing again after a lapse of $1\frac{1}{2}$ secs., $2\frac{1}{2}$ sec and 4 sec. Explain how these repeated echoes are heard.

3. What is the intensity level in deciBels of a sound wave whose intensity is 10^{-10} watt/cm^2 ?   **(Ans.** 60 dB**)**
   Given: $I_o = 10^{-16}$ watt/cm^2.

4. Show that if the reference level of intensity is $I_o = 10^{-16}$ watts/cm^2, the intensity level of sound of intensity I is I.L. $= 160 + 10 \log_{10} I$.

5. A lecture hall with a volume of 4,55,000 cubic feet is found to have a reverberation time of 1.5 seconds. What is the total absorption of the hall ? If the area of the sound absorbing surface is 8000 sq. ft. calculate the average absorption coefficient.

   (Ans. 1500 OWU, 1.90 OWU**)**

6. A hall has a volume of 80,000 cu. ft. It's total absorption is equivalent to 1000 sq. ft. of open window. What will be the effect on the reverberation time if the total absorption increases by another 1000 sq. ft. due to the presence of audience ?

   (Ans. Reverberation time changes from 4 sec. to 2 sec.**)**

7. 10^{-16} and 10^{-10} watts/cm^2 are the sound intensities of two sounds having same frequency. What will be the difference in the intensity levels of these sounds ?

   (Ans. 60 dB**)**

8. An open window whose area is 2 m^2 allows an intensity level of 70 dB to enter. Calculate the acoustic power that has entered through the window.

   (Ans. 2×10^{-5} watt**)**

9. A boy, standing between two parallel high mountains shouts for his mother. He hears his own echo twice one after 3 sec. and the other after 5 sec. If the velocity of sound in air is 340 m/sec., calculate the distance between the two mountains.

   (Ans. 1360 m**)**

10. The volume of a room is 600 m^3. The wall area of room is 220 m^2, the floor area is 120 m^2 and the area of ceiling is 120 m^2. The average absorption coefficient for wall is 0.03, for the floor is 0.06 and for ceiling is 0.8. Calculate the reverberation time.

    (Ans. 0.901 sec.**)**

11. A lecture hall $15 \times 12 \times 10$ m has a reverberation time of 3.0 sec. Calculate the total absorption of its surfaces and the average absorption coefficient.   **(Ans.** 0.11 OWU**)**

12. The dimensions of an auditorium are 17 m long, 13 m wide and 8 m high. The mean absorption coefficient is 0.1. What is the reverberation time ?   **(Ans.** 3.16 secs.**)**

13. A lecture hall has a volume of 1,20,000 m^3. It has reverberation time of 1.5 sec. What is the mean absorption coefficient of the surfaces if the total sound absorbing surface is 25,000 m^2 ?   **(Ans.** 0.528 OWU**)**

14. An ultrasonic source of 70 kHz sends down a pulse towards the sea bed which returns after 0.5 sec. The velocity of sound in sea water is 1400 m/sec.

    (a) What is the depth of the sea ?

    (b) What is the wavelength of the pulse in water ?   **(Ans.** 227.5 m, 20×10^{-6} m)

SOLVED UNIVERSITY QUESTIONS

DECEMBER 2012

1. The average reverberation time of a hall is 1.5 sec. and the area of the interior surface is 3340 m^2. If the volume of the hall is 13000 m^3. Find the absorption coefficient.   [3]

Ans. **Data:**   Volume, V = 13000 m^3

               Reverberation time, t = 1.5 sec.

               Surface area, S = 3340 m^2

Formula : $t = \dfrac{0.165 \times V}{\sum a S}$

∴ $1.5 = \dfrac{0.165 \times 13000}{a \times \sum S}$

∴ $a = \dfrac{0.165 \times 13000}{1.5 \times 3340}$

∴ $a = \mathbf{0.428}$

2. Explain any one application of Ultrasonic Waves.   [3]

Ans. Please Refer to Article 3.10 on Page No. 3.29.

3. Explain how piezoelectric effect can be used for generating Ultrasonic Waves?   [6]

Ans. Please Refer to Article 3.7.1 on Page No. 3.22.

MAY 2013

1. Discuss the use of ultrasonic's for flaw Detection.   [3]

Ans. Please Refer to Article No. 3.10.1 on Page No. 3.29.

2. A auditorium of volume 5500m^3 is found to have reverberation time 2.5 secs. The sound absorbing surface of the auditorium has an area of 750m^2. Calculate the average absorption coefficient of the auditorium.   [3]

Ans. **Data:** V = 5500m^3

               T = 2.5 sec

               S = 750m^2

Formula:
$$t = \frac{0.165V}{\le \text{as}}$$

Solution $a = \dfrac{0.165 \times 5500}{750 \times 2.5}$

∴ $a = 0.484$ OWU

3. Define magnetostriction effect. Explain how magnetostriction oscillator is used to produce ultrasonic waves with the help of neat circuit diagram.   **[6]**

Ans. Please Refer to Article No 3.7.2 on Page No 3.25.

NOVEMBER 2013

1. Define the following terms: **[3]**
   (i) Reverberation.

Ans. Please Refer to Article 3.3 on Page No. 3.9.
   (ii) Intensity of sound.

Ans. Please Refer to Article 3.2.4 on Page No. 3.4.
   (iii) Timbre of sound.

Ans. Please Refer to Article 3.2.7 on Page No. 3.7.

2. Calculate the natural frequency of vibration for X-cut quartz plate of thickness 5.5 mm.   **[3]**

Ans. Note: Incomplete data. For correct problem refer problem no. 3.10.

3. What is piezoelectric effect ? Explain the method to produce ultrasonic waves by using piezoelectric oscillator.   **[6]**

Ans. Please Refer to Article 3.7.1 on Page No. 3.22.

MAY 2014

1. Explain how cavitation technique can be used for cleaning purpose.   **[3]**

Ans. Please Refer to Article 3.10.2 (i) on Page No. 3.31.

2. Calculate the intensity level of a fighter plane just leaving the runway having a sound intensity of about 100 W/m². Given that threshold intensity $= 10^{-12}$ W/m².   **[3]**

Ans. Data: $I = 100 \ w/m^2$

$I_0 = 10^{-12} \ w/m^2$

Formula: $SIL = 10 \log_{10} \dfrac{I}{I_0} \ dB$

Solution: $SIL = 10 \log_{10} \dfrac{100}{10^{-12}}$

$SIL = 10 \log 10^{14}$

$SIL = 140 \ dB$

3. What is magnetostriction effect? With the help of neat circuit diagram, explain the working of magnetostriction oscillator to obtain the ultrasonic waves. **[6]**

Ans. Please Refer to Article 3.7.2 on Page No. 3.25.

Note: Write any one method.

DECEMBER 2014

1. Distinguish between musical sound and noise. **[3]**

Ans. Please Refer to Article 3.1 on Page No. 3.1.

2. Define magnetostriction effect. Explain how magnetostriction oscillator is used to produce ultrasonic waves, with the help of neat ckt. diagram. **[6]**

Ans. Please Refer to Article 3.7.2 on Page No. 3.25.

3. The average reverberation time of a hall is 1.5 sec. and the area of interior surface is 3340 m^2. If the volume of the hall is 13000 m^3. Find the absorption coefficient. **[3]**

Ans. Please Refer to Problem 3.18 on Page No. 3.35.

MAY 2015

1. State any two factors affecting the acoustics of a hall and explain in brief remedies on that. **[3]**

Ans. Please Refer to Article 3.5.1, Page No. 3.14 to 3.17.

2. Calculate the reverberation time of hall with volume of 1500 m^3 and total absorption is equivalent to 100 m^2 Sabine. **[3]**

Ans. Data:

$$V = 1500 \text{ m}^3$$

$$A = 100 \text{ m}^2 \text{ Sabine}$$

Formula:

$$t = \frac{0.165 \, V}{A}$$

Solution:

$$t = \frac{0.165 \times 1500}{100}$$

$$t = 2.475 \text{ sec.}$$

3. What is Piezoelectric effect ? Draw a neat circuit diagram and explain Piezoelectric generator for the production of ultrasonic waves. **[6]**

Ans. Please Refer to Article 3.7.1, Page No. 3.22 to 3.23.

NOVEMBER 2015

1. Explain any two factors affecting the acoustics of a hall and remedies on that. **[3]**

Ans. Please Refer to Article 3.5.1, Page No. 3.14.

2. The classroom has dimension, $20 \times 15 \times 5$ m^3. The reverberation time is 3.5 sec. Calculate the total absorption of its surface and the average absorption. **[3]**

Ans. Data: Volume $V = 20 \times 15 \times 5 m^3$

Reverberation time $t = 3.5$ sec.

Formula: (i) Reverberation time $t = 0.165 \dfrac{V}{A}$

(ii) Total absorption A = a S

Solution:

(i) $\qquad\qquad\qquad 3.5 = 0.165 \times \dfrac{20 \times 15 \times 5}{A}$

$\therefore\qquad$ Total absorption A $= \dfrac{0.165 \times 20 \times 15 \times 5}{3.5}$

$\qquad\qquad\qquad\qquad A = 70.71$ O.W.V.

(ii) $\qquad$ Total surface area S $= 2(20 \times 15 + 15 \times 5 + 5 \times 20)$

$\therefore\qquad\qquad\qquad\qquad S = 9.50$ m^2

$\therefore\qquad$ Average absorption a $= \dfrac{70.71}{950}$

$\therefore\qquad\qquad\qquad\qquad a = 0.0744$

3. Explain piezoelectric effect. Explain how piezoelectric oscillator is used to produce ultrasonic waves, with the help of a neat circuit diagram. **[6]**

Ans. Please Refer to Article 3.7.1 on Page No. 3.22.

MAY 2016

1. Explain how ultrasonic waves are used for detection of flaws in metal. **[3]**

Ans. Please Refer to Article 3.10.1 on Page No. 3.29.

2. A hall of dimensions 20 m × 20 m × 20 m has a reverberation time of 1.2 sec. Find average absorption coefficient. **[3]**

Ans. Data : 20 m × 20 m × 20 m, t = 1.2 sec.

Formula: $\qquad\qquad t = \dfrac{0.165\,V}{as}$

Solution: $\qquad\qquad a = \dfrac{0.165 \times 8000}{6 \times (20 \times 20)} = 0.55$ OWV.

3. What is magnetostriction effect? Explain construction and working of magnetostriction oscillator. **[6]**

Ans. Please Refer to Article 3.7.2 on Page No. 3.25.

REFERENCE

Ultrasonic images
http://www.drgdiaz.com/pat/images.shtml

✠ ✠ ✠

CHAPTER 4
POLARIZATION

4.1 INTRODUCTION

- The phenomenon like interference or diffraction prove the wave nature of light. But it does not tell us whether the light waves are longitudinal or transverse. Because even longitudinal waves, like sound waves, show the phenomena of interference and diffraction.

- The phenomenon of polarization can be explained only by considering the transverse nature of light. And it has been proved by electromagnetic theory that the light is transverse wave.

- In **longitudinal waves**, the particles of the medium vibrate to and fro in the direction of propagation of the wave.

- But in the **transverse waves**, the particles of **the medium vibrate up and down** at right angles to the direction of propagation of the wave.

- The important difference between longitudinal and transverse wave is that the transverse waves can be polarized. Hence the following experiments are considered to explain what polarization is.

4.2 POLARIZATION OF WAVES

- The transverse nature of waves leads to the characteristic phenomenon called **polarization**. The characteristic, polarization is not exhibited by longitudinal waves. Thus only transverse waves could be polarized.

- In a transverse wave, if the directions of all the vibrations at all the points are restricted to one particular plane, then the wave is called **polarized**, more specific plane polarized. A plane polarized wave is the simplest of a transverse wave, which is also termed as linearly polarized wave.

4.3 POLARIZATION OF LIGHT

4.3.1 Mechanical Experiment

- Consider a string AB passing through slits S_1 and S_2. The end B of the string is fixed while the end A is free. The free end A is given up and down motion rapidly such that transverse waves are set up in the string. These transverse waves travel towards the end B. In this case the particles of string vibrate along the direction parallel to S_1 therefore, passes through S_1.

- Since S_2 is parallel to S_1, these transverse vibrations pass through S_2 also, to reach the end B. If the end A is given motion in all possible directions instead of the up and down motion, the particle of the string will vibrate in all directions. When these vibrations reach vertical slit S_1, they are restricted to the vertical plane only. These vertical vibrations will reach the end B if S_2 is parallel to S_1.

- If on the other hand, S_2 is perpendicular to S_1, the vibrations of the string are completely stopped by S_2. This is because the displacement of the particles are now at right angles to the slit S_2. Thus, the string does not vibrate between S_2 and B.

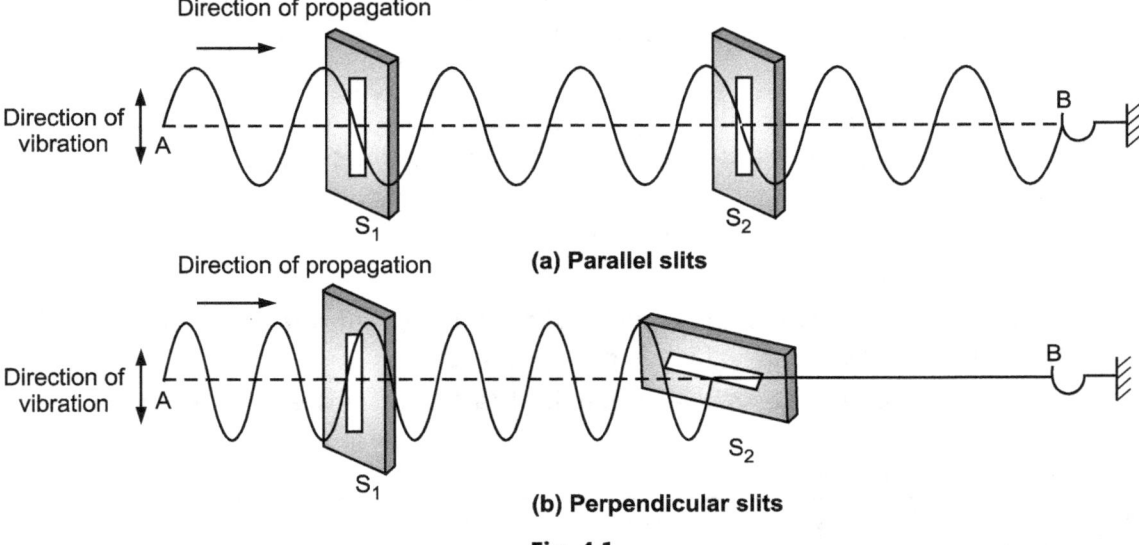

Fig. 4.1

- If longitudinal waves are produced by moving the string forward and backward along it's length, then the waves will freely pass through S_1 and S_2 irrespective of their positions.

4.3.2 Optical Experiment

- Light from a source is allowed to fall normally on the flat surface of a thin plate of tourmaline crystal, cut parallel to it's axis.

- The crystal A is rotated and the intensity of light transmitted through A is noted. No change is observed. Now, another crystal B is placed with it's axis parallel to A. On observing the intensity of the light transmitted through B, no change is observed.

- If now the crystal A is kept fixed and B is gradually rotated, it is seen that the intensity of light emerging out of B decreases. It becomes zero when the axis of B is perpendicular to that of A. If B is further rotated, the intensity increases and becomes maximum when the axes of A and B are again parallel.

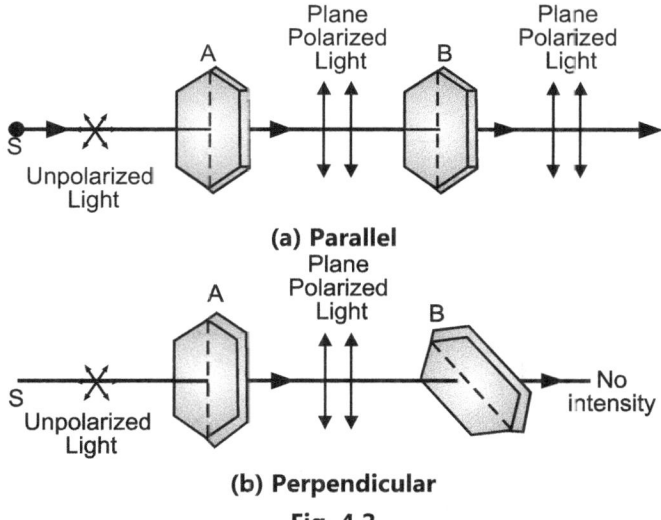

(a) Parallel

(b) Perpendicular

Fig. 4.2

- Thus the intensity of transmitted light is maximum when axes of A and B are parallel, and zero when they are perpendicular.

- From these experiments, it is clear that light waves are transverse If they were longitudinal, then the rotation of crystal B would not have produced any change in the intensity of light.

4.3.3 Polarization

- Thus, light from the source S consists of transverse waves having vibrations in all directions in a plane perpendicular to the direction of propagation of light. When such a beam reaches the crystal A, vibrations parallel to it's axis are only allowed to pass. Thus, the light coming out of crystal A is not symmetrical about the direction of propagation of light.

- It's vibrations are confined only to a single plane, in a plane perpendicular to the direction of propagation.

- Such a light is called a ***plane polarized light***, the crystal A is called ***polarizer*** and crystal B which detects these vibrations is known as ***analyzer***. The phenomenon is called as ***polarization***.

4.4 REPRESENTATION OF PLANE POLARIZED LIGHT (PPL), UNPOLARIZED LIGHT (UPL) AND PARTIALLY POLARIZED LIGHT

- According to the electromagnetic theory, light consists of electric and magnetic vectors vibrating continuously with time in a plane, transverse to the direction of propagation of light and to each other. However, ***in explaining polarization only the vibrations of the electric vector are considered***.

- It does not mean that magnetic field vectors are absent, they are present. But for drawing simplicity they are not shown in the diagram.

4.4.1 Unpolarized Light

- The light having vibrations along all possible directions perpendicular to the direction of propagation of light, is called an **unpolarized light**. It is symmetrical about it's direction of propagation.

Fig. 4.3: Unpolarized light

- It can be considered to consist an infinite number of waves each having its own vibration. Therefore, for any position of the crystal there will be one vibration parallel to its axes, so when such a light is passed through a single tourmaline crystal and is rotated no change in the intensity of the emergent light is observed.

- Since unpolarized light has vibrations along all possible directions, at right angles to the directions of propagation of light, it is represented by a star.

4.4.2 Polarized Light

- The light having vibration only along a single plane perpendicular to the direction of propagation of light is called a **polarized light**. It's vibrations are one sided, therefore it is disymmetrical about the direction of propagation of light.

- When polarized light is passed through a single rotating crystal, a change in the intensity of emergent light is observed.

- The polarized beam of light has vibrations along a single plane. If they are parallel to the plane of the paper, they are represented by arrows [See Fig. 4.4 (a)]. If they are perpendicular to the plane of the paper, they are represented by dots on a ray of light. [See Fig. 4.4 (b)].

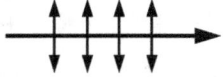

(a) Parallel to plane of paper

(b) Perpendicular to plane of paper

Fig. 4.4: Plane polarized light

4.4.3 Partially Polarized Light

- A partially polarized light is a mixture of plane polarized and unpolarized light. It is represented as shown in Fig. 4.5.

- In partially polarized light the vibrations in the plane of plane polarized light dominate over the vibrations in other directions.

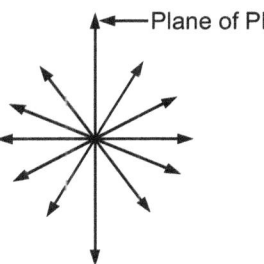
Plane of PPL

Fig. 4.5: Partially polarized light

4.5 PRODUCTION OF PLANE POLARIZED LIGHT (PLL)

- Although polarized light has many applications in science and engineering, but the light available naturally is unpolarized. So different methods have been developed to obtain polarized light artificially.

- Every method uses one or the other optical phenomena like reflection, refraction, scattering, double refraction etc., for getting polarized light.

- Here we will be learning some of the methods for obtaining plane polarized light.

4.5.1 Production of Plane Polarized Light by Reflection

- Polarization of light by reflection from the surface of glass was discovered by Malus in 1808. He found that polarized light is obtained when ordinary light is reflected by a plane sheet of glass.

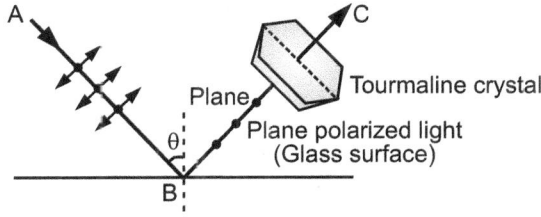

Fig. 4.6

- Consider the light incident along the path AB on the glass surface. A part of light is reflected along BC. In the path of BC, place a tourmaline crystal and rotate it slowly. It is observed that light is completely extinguished only at one particular angle of incidence.

- At any other angle of incidence there is preferential reflection of the components having vibrations perpendicular to the plane of incidence.

- This angle of incidence is equal to 57.5° for a glass surface and is known as the *polarization angle*.

- The vibrations of the incident light can be resolved into components-parallel to the reflecting surface (glass surface) and perpendicular to the reflecting surface. Light due to the components parallel to the reflecting surface is reflected whereas light due to the components perpendicular to the reflecting surface is transmitted i.e. the plane of the vibrations of reflecting rays are at right angles to the plane of incidence and the plane of vibrations of refracted rays are in the plane of incidence. Thus, light reflected by the surface is polarised in the plane of incidence and can be detected by tourmaline crystal.

Note

- If light is polarised perpendicular to the plane of incidence, it means that vibrations are in the plane of incidence.

- If light is polarised in the plane of incidence, it means that vibrations are perpendicular to the plane of incidence.

Polarizing Angle or Angle of Polarization

- It is defined as that angle of incidence on the reflecting surface for which reflected light is completely plane polarized.

- As the refractive index of a substance varies with the wavelength of the incident light, the polarizing angle will be different for light of different wavelength. Therefore, polarising angle will be complete only for light of a particular wavelength at a time i.e. for monochromatic light (for a given surface).

Brewster's Law

- In 1811, Sir David Brewster found that ordinary light is completely polarised in the plane of incidence when it gets itself reflected from a transparent medium at a particular angle known as the *polarizing angle*.

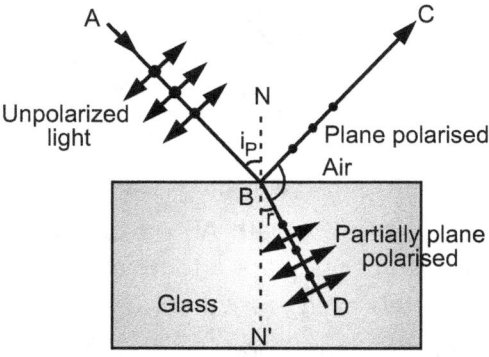

Fig. 4.7

- He was able to prove that, the tangent of the angle of polarisation is numerically equal to the refractive index of the medium. i.e. $\mu = \tan i_p$.

- Consider unpolarised light is incident on the glass surface at the polarising angle. It is reflected along BC and refracted along BD.

From Snell's law,

$$\mu = \frac{\sin i}{\sin r} \qquad \ldots (1)$$

From Brewster's law, $\quad \mu = \tan i_p = \dfrac{\sin i_p}{\cos i_p}$

Comparing equations (1) and (2),

$$\cos i_p = \sin r = \cos\left(\frac{\pi}{2} - r\right)$$

$$\therefore \qquad i_p = \frac{\pi}{2} - r$$

$$i_p + r = \frac{\pi}{2}$$

As $i_p + r = \dfrac{\pi}{2}$, $\quad \angle CBD = \dfrac{\pi}{2}$

Therefore, reflected and refracted rays are at right angles to each other.

4.5.2 Production of Plane Polarized Light by Refraction: Pile of Plates

- When unpolarized light is incident at an polarizing angle on a transparent surface the reflected light is polarized completely whereas refracted light is partially polarized.

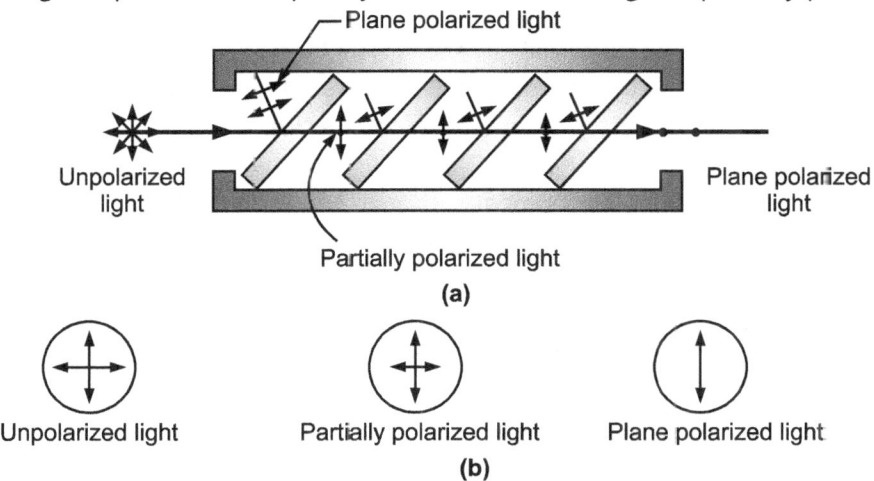

Fig. 4.8: Polarization by refraction

- If more than one refracting surfaces i.e. stack of glass plates are used in place of one, the process is repeated. At every surface, the unpolarized component decreases, thus the polarized component becomes prominent, giving almost plane polarized light in the direction parallel to the pile of plates.

- A pile of plates contains about 15 glass plates placed in a metal tube of suitable size. The plates are kept at 33° with the axis of tube so that the incident unpolarized light is incident at polarizing angle at the first plate.

- The unpolarized light entering in the tube will undergo successive reflection and refraction such that the emerging ray is plane polarized light.

4.5.3 Double Refraction   [Dec. 12, May 13, 14, 16]

Calcite Crystal

- Calcite or Iceland spar is crystallised calcium carbonate ($CaCO_3$). It is found in large quantities in Iceland as a large transparent crystal. It crystallises in many forms and readily breaks into simple rhombohedron.

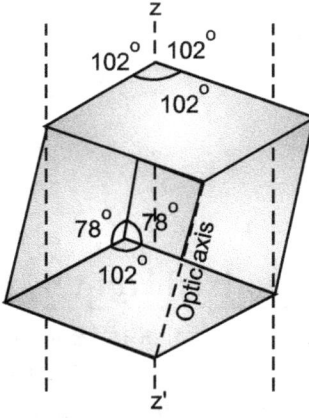

Fig. 4.9: Calcite crystal form

The direction of the optic axis is indicated by broken lines

- For a point in calcite, there are **three principal sections**, one for each pair of opposite faces.

- The principal section does not always suffice in describing the direction of vibrations. Here, we make use of the two other planes, **the principal plane of the ordinary ray**, a plane containing the ordinary ray and the optic axis, and **the principal plane of the extraordinary ray** or a plane containing the E-ray and the optic axis.

- The O-ray always lies in the plane of incidence. This is not generally true for the E-ray. The principal planes of the two refracted rays do not coincide except in special cases. The special cases are those for which the plane of incidence is a principal section as shown in Fig. 4.9. Under these conditions, the plane of incidence, the principal section and the principal planes of the O and E rays all coincide.

Optic Axis

- The **optic axis** is the direction of symmetry of unisotropic media along which doub e refraction does not take place.

- A line drawn through any of the blunt corners making equal angles with each of the three edges gives the direction of the optic axis. In fact any line parallel to this line is also an optic axis. Therefore, optic axis is not a line but **it is a direction** (as shown in Fig. 4.9).

Principal Section

- A plane containing **the optic axis** and **perpendicular to the opposite faces** of the crystal is called the **principal section of the crystal**. The principal section cuts the surfaces of a calcite crystal in a parallelo- gram with angles 109° and 71°.

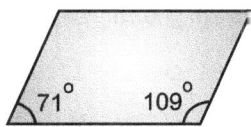

Fig. 4.10: Principal section of calcite crystal

Principal Plane

- The plane containing the optic axis and the ordinary ray is called principal plane of the ordinary ray. Similarly the plane containing the optic axis and the extraordinary ray is called the principal plane of the extraordinary ray.

- Experiments revealed that the vibrations of the ordinary rays are perpendicular to the principal section of the crystal while the vibrations of the extraordinary rays are parallel to the principal section of the crystal. Thus, the two rays are plane polarized, their vibrations being at right ang es to each other.

Double Refraction

- The phenomenon of double refraction was discovered by Erasmus Bartholinus in 1669 during his studies on calcite. When light is incident on a calcite crystal, it is found to produce two refracted rays which are different in properties. The phenomenon of causing **two refracted rays** by a crystal is called **birefringence** or **double refraction**. The crystals are said to be **birefringent**.

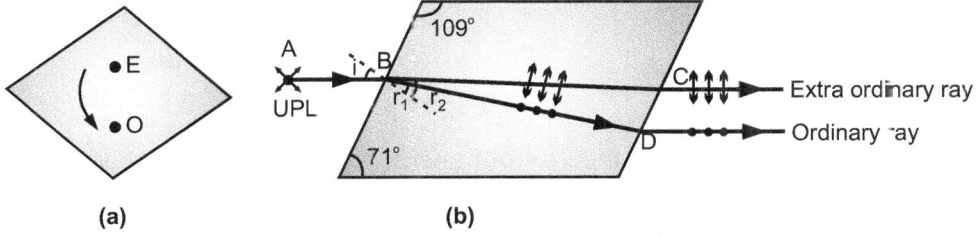

| (a) | (b) |

Fig. 4.11: Double reflection

- All anisotropic materials exhibit double refraction. The two rays formed in double refraction are linearly polarized in mutually perpendicular directions.

- One of the rays **obeys Snell's law** of refraction and hence is called **an ordinary ray or O-ray**. The other ray **does not obey Snell's law** and is called an **extraordinary ray or E-ray.** If one of the rays is eliminated, the light transmitted by the crystal will be a linearly polarized light.

- When a ray of light AB is incident on the calcite crystal making an angle of incidence i, it is refracted along two paths inside the crystal: (i) along BC making an angle of refraction r_2, (ii) along BD making an angle of refraction r_1. These two rays emerge out along DO and CE which are parallel as the crystal faces are parallel.

4.5.4 Polarization by Double Refraction - Nicol Prism

- Nicol prism is an optical device used for producing and analysing plane polarised light.

Principle

- The Nicol prism is made in such a way that it eliminates one of the refracted rays by total internal reflection i.e. O-ray is eliminated and only E-ray is transmitted through the prism.

Construction

- A **calcite crystal** whose length is three times it's breadth is taken. Let ABCD be the principal section of the crystal with $\angle$ BAD = 71°. The end faces of the crystal are cut in such a way that they make angles 68° and 112° in the principal section instead of 71° and 109°.

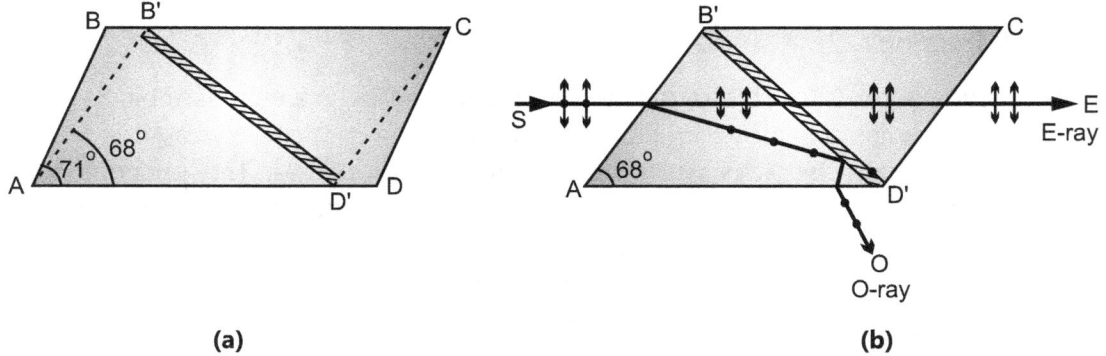

(a)   (b)

Fig. 4.12

- The crystal is then cut into two pieces from one blunt corner to the other along a plane perpendicular to the principal section. The two cut faces are grounded and polished optically flat. It is then cemented together by Canada balsam whose refractive index lies between the refractive indices for the O-ray and E-ray for calcite.

Refractive index of Calcite for O-ray

$$\mu_O = 1.658$$

Refractive index of Canada Balsam

$$\mu_c = 1.55 \quad \text{Using sodium light of } \lambda = 5893 \text{ A}°,$$

Refractive index of Calcite for E-ray

$$\mu_e = 1.486$$

- Canada balsam layer acts as a rarer medium for O-ray and as a denser medium for E-ray. Except the end faces, the sides of the crystal are blackened.

Working

- When a ray of unpolarized light is incident on the prism surface, it splits into O-ray and E-ray. Both the rays are polarized having vibrations at right angles to each other.
- When the O-ray passes from a portion of the crystal into the layer of Canada balsam, it passes from a denser medium to rarer medium. When the angle of incidence is greater than the critical angle, the O-ray is totally internally reflected and is not transmitted.
- When the E-ray passes from calcite to the Canada Balsam layer, it enters in rarer medium. Therefore, the E-ray is not affected and is transmitted through the prism.

Refractive index for O-ray with respect to Canada balsam,

$$\mu = \frac{1.658}{1.55}$$

If C is the critical angle,

$$\therefore \qquad \mu = \frac{1}{\sin C}$$

$$\sin C = \frac{1}{\mu} = \frac{1.55}{1.658}$$

$$C = 69°$$

- As the length of the crystal is large, the angle of incidence at Canada balsam surface for the O-ray is greater than the critical angle. Thus, it suffers total internal reflection while E-ray is transmitted which is plane polarized having vibrations in the principal section.

Special Cases

(a) If the angle of incidence is less than the critical angle for O-ray, it is not reflected and is transmitted through the prism. In this position, both the O-ray and E-ray are transmitted through the prism.

(b) The E-ray also has a limit beyond which it is totally internally reflected by Canada balsam surface. If E-ray travels along the optic axis, its refractive index is the same as that of O-ray i.e. 1.658. But it is 1.486 for all other directions of E-ray. Therefore depending on the direction of propagation of E-ray, μ_e lies between 1.486 and 1.658. Therefore for a particular case, μ_e may be more than 1.55 and the angle of incidence will be more than the critical angle. Then E-ray will also be totally internally reflected.

4.5.5 Production of Plane Polarized Light by Selective Absorption (Dichroism)

- There are certain crystals and minerals which are doubly refracting and have the property of absorbing one of the doubly refracting beams to a greater extent than the other. The crystals showing this property are termed as **dichroic crystals** and the phenomenon is known as **dichroism**.

- This phenomenon of selective absorption is shown by a number of substances but the most notable and outstanding is Tourmaline. Tourmaline absorbs ordinary ray much more strongly than the extraordinary ray.

- When a plate of tourmaline is cut with the face parallel to the optic axis and unpolarized light is allowed to incident on it, the light splits into ordinary and extraordinary rays. Both the rays are plane polarized and travel through the crystal in the same direction.

- When the plate is sufficiently thick, the ordinary ray is almost completely absorbed and the extraordinary ray is partly absorbed and it emerges out. In this way, a plane polarized light with vibrations in the plane of incidence is obtained. Thus, plane polarized light is obtained by the property of selective absorption.

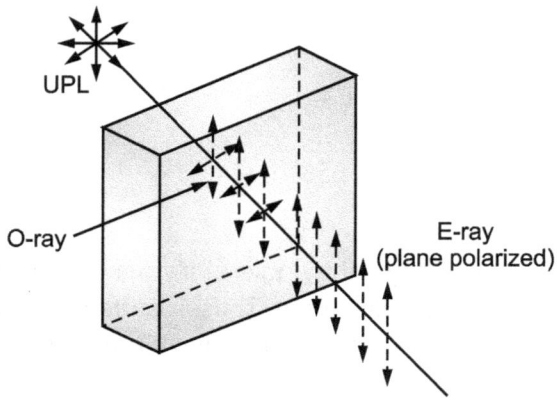

Fig. 4.13

Polaroids

- A polaroid is a polarizing film which produces polarized light from ordinary unpolarized light by the method of selective absorption. Crystals of iodosulphate of Quinine (Heraphite) show dichroism. But individually they are of no use due to their tiny size.

Hence, Land developed a polarizing film in which these crystals are embedded in a volatile viscous medium with their optic axis parallel to each other.

- This is achieved by making a paste of the crystals in nitrocellulose. This is then forced to pass through a narrow slit. On the other side, a ribbon-like film is obtained. The axes of the crystals in the film are parallel, because only those molecules pass through the slit whose axes are parallel to the length of the slit.
- This film enclosed between two glass plates is a polaroid. When ordinary light is incident on such a polaroid, the emergent light will be plane polarized.

Applications of Polaroids

- They are used to produce and analyse plane polarized light.
- They are used in head lights and screens of motor cars.
- They are used in the windows of trains and aeroplanes to control the intensity of light.
- They are used as polarized sun glasses in goggles.

4.6 LAW OF MALUS   [Dec. 14, May 15, Nov. 15]

Statement

- The law states that, the intensity of polarized light emerging from the analyzer is proportional to the **square of the cosine** of the angle between the plane of the transmission for the analyzer and the plane of the polarizer.

Proof

- Let A_o be the amplitude of the incident plane polarized light. Let θ be the angle between the planes of transmissions of the analyzer and the polarizer. The amplitude A_o may be resolved into two components $A_o \cos \theta$ and $A_o \sin \theta$.

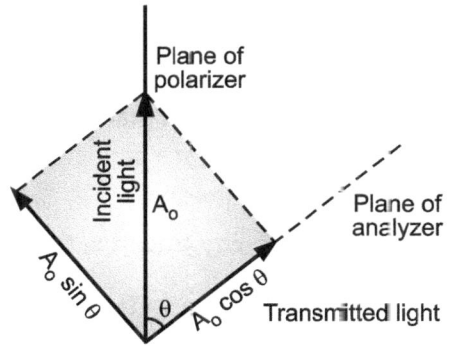

Fig. 4.14

- The vibrations of the former are parallel to the plane of the transmission of the analyzer, while the vibrations of latter are perpendicular to this i.e. $A_o \cos \theta$ is **transmitted** by the analyzer while $A_o \sin \theta$ is **eliminated**.

- The amplitude of the transmitted beam,

$$A = A_o \cos \theta$$

- Therefore, the intensity of the transmitted beam, $I = A^2$ but $A = A_o \cos^2 \theta$

$$\therefore \qquad I = A_o^2 \cos^2 \theta$$

$$I = I_o \cos^2 \theta$$

- As the intensity of incident beam I_o is constant, therefore,

$$I \propto \cos^2 \theta$$

This is called as **law of Malus**.

Note

- In the case of incident unpolarized light, the law of Malus is $I = \frac{1}{2} I_0$. Because unpolarized light vibrates in all possible directions in a plane perpendicular to the direction of propagation. Therefore, the average value of $\cos^2 \theta$ will have to be considered.

Then the intensity of the transmitted light is

$$I = I_0 \cos^2 \theta = \frac{1}{2} I_0$$

Since the average value of $\cos^2 \theta$ over all possible values of θ is $\frac{1}{2} \left(\text{i.e. } \cos^2 \theta = \frac{1}{2} \right)$ i.e. an ideal polarizer will be one which will transmit 50 % of the incident unpolarized light as plane polarized light.

4.7 HUYGEN'S THEORY OF DOUBLE REFRACTION

Huygen explained the phenomenon of double refraction on the basis of the principle of secondary wavelets.

He assumed:

1. When a beam of ordinary unpolarized light strikes a doubly refracting crystal, each point on the surface sends out **two wavefronts**, one for ordinary ray and the other for extraordinary ray.

2. The **ordinary-ray** travels with the **same speed** v_o in all directions and the crystal has a single refractive index $\mu_O = \dfrac{c}{v_o}$ for this wave. Thus, the O-ray has a **spherical wavefront**.

3. The **speed of extra-ordinary ray v_e varies with direction**. So, the refractive index, $\mu_e = \dfrac{c}{v_e}$ also varies with direction for the E-ray. Therefore, the extra-ordinary ray develops a wavefront which is **ellipsoidal**.

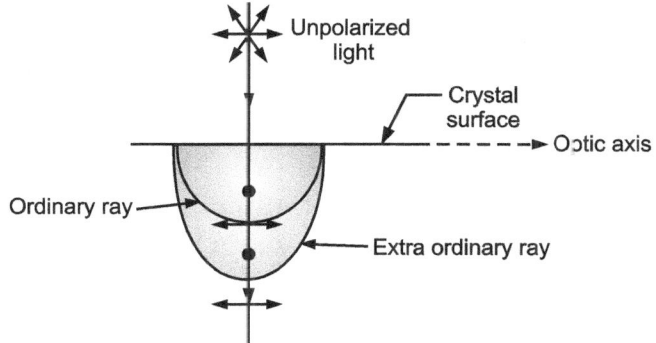

Fig. 4.15: Double refraction

4.   The velocity v_e measured is perpendicular to the optic axis.
5.   The velocities of the O-ray and E-ray are the same along the optic axis
6.   When rays are incident along the optic axis, the spherical and ellipsoidal wavefronts touch each other at points of intersection with the optic axis and double refraction does not take place.
7.   If $v_o > v_e$ or $\mu_o < \mu_e$, the spherical wavefront lies outside the elliptical wavefront. Such crystals are called **positive crystals**. The examples of positive crystal are quartz, ice etc.
8.   If $v_e > v_o$ or $\mu_e < \mu_o$, the elliptical wavefront lies outside the spherical wavefront. Such crystals are called **negative crystals**. The examples of negative crystals are calcite, tourmaline, etc.

4.7.1 Positive and Negative Crystals

Positive Crystals	Negative Crystals
1. For positive crystals, $v_o > v_e$ and $\mu_o < \mu_e$.	1. For negative crystals, $v_o < v_e$ and $\mu_o > \mu_e$.
2. The velocity of O-ray is same in all directions.	2. The velocity of O-ray is same in all directions.
3. The wavefront of O-ray lies outside the wavefront of E-ray.	3. The wavefront of O-ray lies inside the wavefront of E-ray.
4. Examples: Quartz, Ice. X O-ray E-ray S Sphere Y Optic axis **Fig. 4.16 (a)**	4. Examples: Calcite, Tourmaline. X E-ray O-ray S Ellipsoid Y Optic axis **Fig. 4.16 (b)**

4.8 CASES OF DOUBLE REFRACTION OF CRYSTAL CUT WITH OPTIC AXIS LYING IN THE PLANE OF INCIDENCE   [Nov. 13]

4.8.1 Parallel to the Surface   [Dec. 14]

- Fig. 4.17 shows unpolarized plane wavefront AB incident normally on the crystal surface XY. The optic axis lies along XY and is in the plane of incidence.

- At the points A and B, it develops two wavefronts, one spherical for O-ray and one elliptical for E-ray. The envelope of O-ray and E-ray gives the corresponding wavefront which is plane polarized.

- It should be noted that both O-ray and E-ray are plane polarized light. Here both O-ray and E-ray travel along the same direction with different velocities. As O-ray and E-ray travel along the same direction with different velocities, a path difference is introduced between them.

- This principle is used in ***the construction of quarter and half-wave plates***.

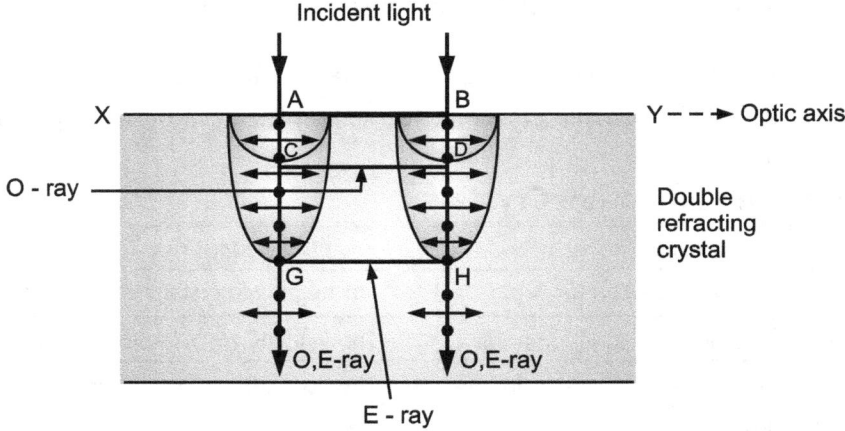

Fig. 4.17

4.8.2 Perpendicular to the Surface

- Fig. 4.18 shows unpolarized plane wavefront AB incident normally on the crystal surface XY. Optic axis lies in the plane of incidence and perpendicular to the crystal surface.

- As the light is incident in the direction of optic axis, O-ray and E-ray travel with the same speed along the optic axis. As a result O-ray and E-ray travel along the same directions with same velocity. Hence the phenomenon of ***double refraction is absent*** in this case. Ordinary and extraordinary wavefronts CD and GH coincide at all instants.

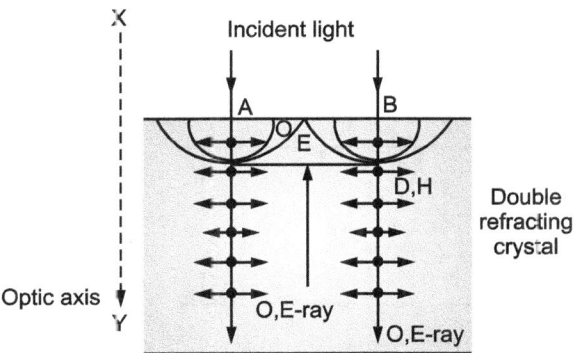

Fig. 4.18

4.8.3 Inclined to the Surface

- Fig. 4.19 shows an unpolarized plane wavefront incident normally on the crystal surface so that the optic axis makes an angle with the crystal surface.

- O-ray and E-ray travel with different velocities in different direction in the crystal. Hence double refraction is seen in this case and both O-ray and E-ray are separated by an angle depending upon the distance travelled in crystal.

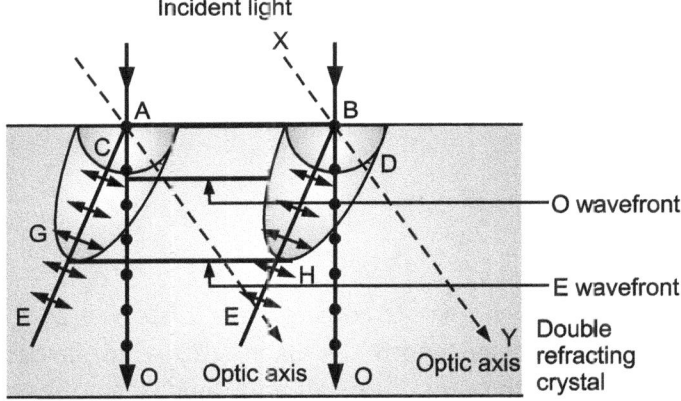

Fig. 4.19

4.9 RETARDATION PLATES

- When an unpolarized light is incident normally on the crystal it develops two wavefronts one spherical and one elliptical. Both the wavefronts travel along the same direction but with different speeds if the optic axis is parallel to the crystal surface.

- In a negative crystal, the sphere lies inside the ellipse. i.e. E-ray travels faster than O-ray. Due to this a path difference is introduced.

- This path difference depends on the thickness of the crystal i.e. the distance which it travels in denser medium, because after coming out of the medium both will travel with the same speed.

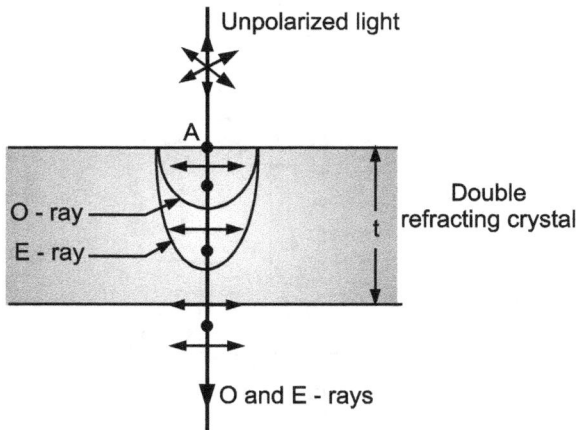

Fig. 4.20: Double refraction

- If the refractive index for O-ray is μ_o and thickness of crystal is t, then optical path will be given by $\mu_o t$. Similarly, for E-ray optical path will be $\mu_e t$.

∴   The optical path difference for negative crystal,

$$\Delta = \mu_o t - \mu_e t$$
$$\Delta = (\mu_o - \mu_e)\, t$$

Or phase difference

$$\delta = k \cdot \Delta = \frac{2\pi}{\lambda}\, (\mu_o - \mu_e)\, t$$

Similarly, for positive crystal,

$$\Delta = (\mu_e - \mu_o)\, t$$

and

$$\delta = \frac{2\pi}{\lambda}\, (\mu_e - \mu_o)\, t$$

- If the thickness t and wavelength λ is constant, the plate will add definite amount of phase difference. Generally, wavelength λ is taken 5893 A° for calculating the thickness. So by using plates of fixed thickness one can add definite amount of phase difference. Such plates are called **retardation plates** and are used for producing and detecting polarized light.

Retardation Plate

- **A plate of proper thickness cut from a double-refracting crystal with its faces, parallel to optic axis so as to produce a desired and definite value of phase difference between O and E-ray of polarized light emerging out of the plate is called a retardation plate.**

- Depending upon the phase difference they add, retardation plates are of two types:
  ➢   Quarter Wave Plate (QWP).
  ➢   Half Wave Plate (HWP).

4.9.1 Quarter Wave Plate (QWP)

- The simplest device for producing and detecting circularly polarized light is a quarter wave ($\lambda/4$) plate. Such plates are made of thin sheet of quartz or calcite cut parallel to the optic axis.

- The thickness is adjusted, so as to introduce a 90° (or $\pi/2$) phase or $\lambda/4$ path difference between O and E-ray. The correct thickness can be calculated by equation of phase difference,

$$\delta = \frac{2\pi}{\lambda} (\mu_o - \mu_e) \, t$$

For QWP, $\delta = \pi/2$

∴. $\frac{\pi}{2} = \frac{2\pi}{\lambda} (\mu_o - \mu_e) \, t$

∴. $t = \frac{\lambda}{4 \, (\mu_o - \mu_e)}$ for negative crystal.

Similarly for positive crystal,

$$t = \frac{\lambda}{4 \, (\mu_e - \mu_o)}$$

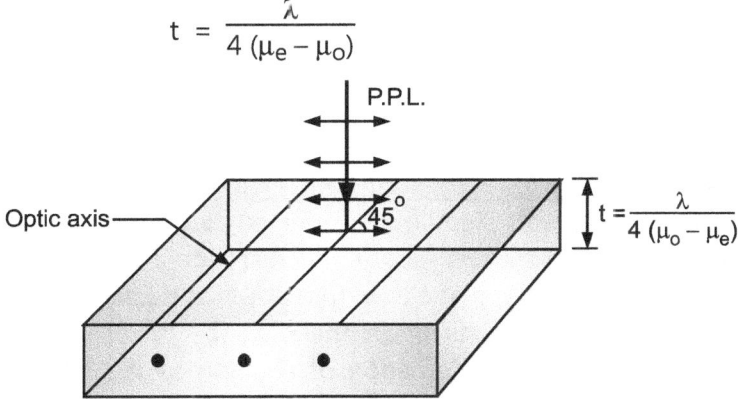

Fig. 4.21: Quarter Wave Plate (QWP)

- When a QWP is oriented at an angle of 45° with the plate of incident plane polarized light as shown in Fig. 4.21, the emerging light is circularly polarized light. For any other angle, other than 0°, 45°, 90°, between 0 to 90° the emerging light is elliptically polarized light.

4.9.2 Half Wave Plate (HWP)

- The thickness of half wave plate is selected such that the O-ray and E-ray have a phase difference π or path difference of $\lambda/2$ on passing through the crystal. The thickness can be calculated by equation of phase difference

$$\delta = \frac{2\pi}{\lambda}(\mu_O - \mu_e)\, t$$

For HWP, $\quad\quad\quad \delta = \pi$

$\therefore \quad\quad\quad\quad \pi = \frac{2\pi}{\lambda}(\mu_O - \mu_e)\, t$

$$t = \frac{\lambda}{2(\mu_O - \mu_e)} \quad \text{for negative crystal.}$$

The equation for positive crystal will be

$$t = \frac{\lambda}{2(\mu_e - \mu_O)}$$

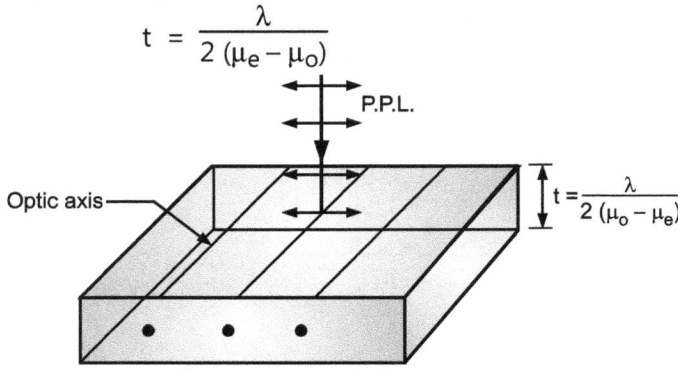

Fig. 4.22

- The half wave plate merely alters the plane of polarization of plane polarized light by an angle 2θ, where θ is the angle between the plane of polarization of incident light and principal section.

4.10 OPTICAL ACTIVITY

- When a beam of a plane polarized light is directed along the optic axis of quartz, the plane of polarization turns steadily about the direction of the beam and the beam emerges vibrating in some other plane than that at which it has entered.
- The amount of rotation depends upon the distance travelled in the medium and wavelength of the light. This phenomenon of rotation of the plane of polarization is called **optical activity**. The substances which show optical activity are sodium chlorate, turpentine, sugar crystal etc. Fig. 4.23 shows optical activity.

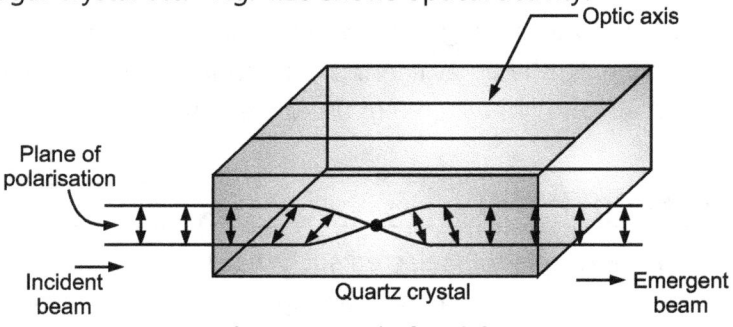

Fig. 4.23: Optical activity

- Some crystals rotate the plane of vibration to the right and some to the left. The substances which rotate to the right are called **right handed or dextro-rotatory** and those which rotate to the left are called **left handed** or **laevo-rotatory**.

4.10.1 Specific Rotation

- A striking feature of optical activity is that different colours are rotated by different amount. This rotation is nearly proportional to the inverse square of the wavelength. This gives a **rotatory dispersion**, violet being rotated nearly four times as much as red light. Fig. 4.24 shows rotatory dispersion.

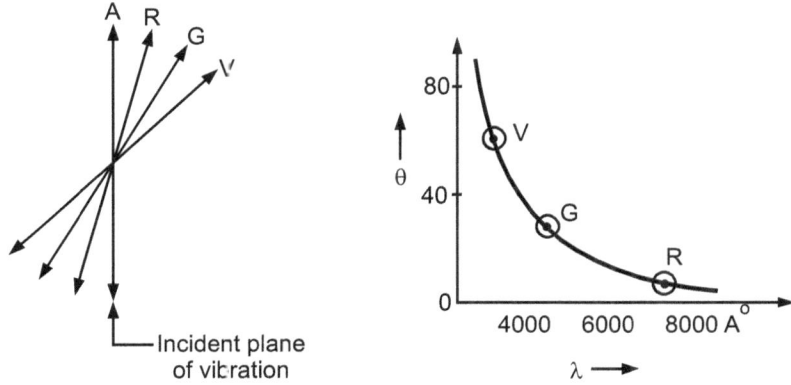

Fig. 4.24: Rotatory dispersion

- The rotation for a 1 mm thick plate is called **the specific rotation**.

4.10.2 Optically Active Materials

- Optical activity is exhibited by organic compounds whose molecular arrangement lacks in symmetry. Therefore, upon entering in the material, the plane polarized light changes the plane of polarization depending upon the molecular arrangement of the material.
- Most of the petroleum exhibits optical activity which are organic in nature. The optical activity is not exhibited by synthetic materials as they are mixture of left handed and right handed molecules in equal quantity, thus giving net zero rotation.

4.11 LCD (AS AN EXAMPLE OF POLARIZATION)

- Liquid Crystal Display (LCD) is a passive device i.e. does not emit light of its own, and works on the principle of polarization. The common applications of LCD are wrist watch calculator, clock and general displays. Recently, LCDs have also replaced Cathode Ray Tube (CRT) in the displays of computers, laptops and TVs.
- A LCD display consists of liquid crystal sandwiched between two thin glass plates with transparent conducting coating on the inner faces. The conducting plate is etched in the form of 7-segment display (to display a digit or alphabet) as shown in Fig. 4 25 (b). The whole assembly is then placed between two polaroid sheets with crossed plane of polarization.

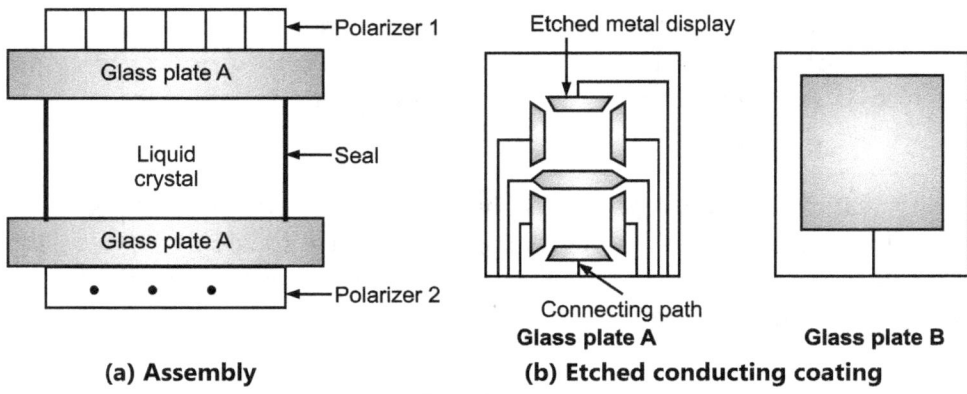

(a) Assembly   (b) Etched conducting coating

Fig. 4.25: LCD

- Basically, liquid crystals are optically active, which rotates the plane of polarization of plane polarized light. Therefore, the thickness of liquid crystal is selected in such a way that it rotates the plane of polarization by 90°.

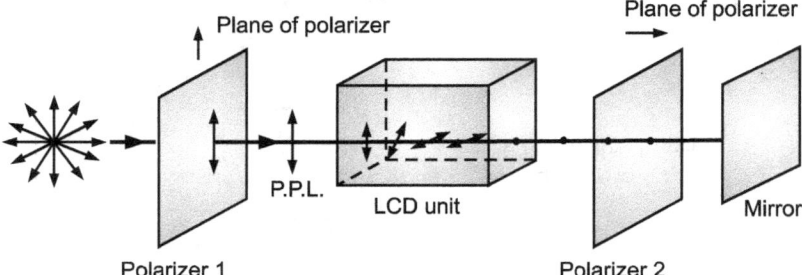

Fig. 4.26: Working of LCD

- Fig. 4.26 shows the schematic working of LCD. When the unpolarized light is incident on polarizer 1, it gets linearly polarized. Upon passing through the liquid crystal it gets rotated by 90° and therefore passes through the polarizer 2 whose transmission axis is perpendicular to that of front polarizer.
- The mirror on back, reflects back the liquid which emerges unobstructed from the front polarizer. This gives impression of uniform illumination.
- When an external voltage is applied the molecules within the electrodes will get aligned in the direction of the field. Therefore, the plane of polarization will not change in this region and will be absorbed by the polarizer. This gives a dark digit or alphabet.

SOLVED PROBLEMS

Problem 4.1: *Two polarizing plates have polarizing directions parallel so as to transmit maximum intensity of light. Through what angle must either plate be turned if the intensity of the transmitted beam is to drop to one third ?*

Data: $\qquad I = \dfrac{I_0}{3}$

Formula:

From Law of Malus, $\qquad I = I_0 \cos^2 \theta$

Solution:

Substituting,
$$\frac{I_0}{3} = I_0 \cos^2 \theta$$

$$\cos^2 \theta = \frac{1}{3}$$

Or
$$\cos \theta = \pm \frac{1}{\sqrt{3}}$$

$$\boxed{\theta = 54° 41' \text{ or } \pm 144° 40'}$$

Problem 4.2: *At a certain temperature, the critical angle of incidence of water for total internal reflection is 48° for a certain wavelength. What is the polarizing angle and the angle of refraction for light incident on the water that gives maximum polarization of the reflected light ?*

Data: Critical angle C = 48°

Formulae: (i) $\mu = \dfrac{1}{\sin C}$,   (ii) $\mu = \tan i_p$

Solution:

(i) Substituting, $\mu = \dfrac{1}{\sin 48°}$

$$\boxed{\mu = 1.345}$$

(ii) From Brewster's law,

$$\mu = \tan i_p$$
$$1.345 = \tan i_p$$
$$i_p = \tan^{-1} (1.345)$$
$$i_p = 53° 22'$$

But $i_p + r = 90°$

∴ $r = 90° - i_p$

$$90° - 53° 22' = r$$

∴ $\boxed{r = 36° 38'}$

Problem 4.3: *Calculate the thickness of a quarter wave plate for which $\mu_0 = 1.544$ and $\mu_e = 1.553$ for light of wavelength 5893 A°.*

Data: $\lambda = 5893 \times 10^{-8}$ cm; $\mu_0 = 1.544$, $\mu_e = 1.553$

Formula:

For quartz, $t = \dfrac{\lambda}{4\,(\mu_e - \mu_o)}$

Solution:

Substituting, $t = \dfrac{5893 \times 10^{-8}}{4\,(0.009)}$

$\therefore$ $\boxed{t = 0.001637 \text{ cm}}$

Problem 4.4: *Two Nicol prisms are oriented with their principal planes making an angle of* 60°*. What percentage of incident unpolarized light will pass through the system ?*

Data: $\theta = 60^\circ$

Formulae: (i) For unpolarized light,

$$I = \frac{I_0}{2}$$

(ii) For plane polarized light,

$$I_T = I \cos^2 \theta = \frac{I_0}{2} \cos^2 \theta$$

Solution: $I_T = \dfrac{I_0}{2} \cos^2 60^\circ$

$$I_T = 0.125\, I_0$$

$\therefore$ The percentage of incident unpolarized light transmitted through the system is

$$\% \, I_T = 0.125 \times 100$$

$\therefore$ $\boxed{\% \, I_T = 12.5\%}$

Problem 4.5: *A polarizer and an analyzer are oriented so that the amount of light transmitted is maximum. How can the analyzer be oriented so that the transmitted light is reduced to (1) 0.75, (2) 0.25 ?*

Data: (1) $I = 0.75 \; I_0$, (2) $I = 0.25 \, I_0$

Formula: $I = I_0 \cos^2 \theta$

Solution:

Substituting $0.75 \; I_0 = I_0 \cos^2 \theta$

$$\frac{3}{4} = \cos^2 \theta$$

$$\pm \frac{\sqrt{3}}{2} = \cos \theta$$

$\therefore$ $\boxed{\theta = \pm 30°, \ \pm 120°}$

$$0.25 \ I_0 = I_0 \cos^2 \theta$$

$$\frac{1}{4} = \cos^2 \theta$$

$$\pm \frac{1}{2} = \cos \theta$$

$\therefore$ $\boxed{\theta = \pm 60°, \pm 150°}$

Problem 4.6: *A quarter wave plate of thickness 2.275×10^{-3} cm is cut with its faces parallel to the optic axis. If the emergent beam of light is elliptically polarized, find the wavelength of monochromatic light made incident normally on the plate. Given that $\mu_o = 1.586$, $\mu_e = 1.592$.* **(May 15)**

Data: $\mu_o = 1.586; \ \mu_e = 1.592; \ t = 2.275 \times 10^{-3}$ cm

Formula: For a QWP, $t = \dfrac{\lambda}{4 (\mu_e - \mu_o)}$

Solution: $\lambda = 4t (\mu_e - \mu_o) = 4 \times 2.275 \times 10^{-3} (1.592 - 1.586)$

$$= 0.0546 \times 10^{-3} \text{ cm}$$

$$= \boxed{5460 \ \text{A}°}$$

Problem 4.7: *Calculate the thickness of mica plate required to make a quarter wave plate and a half wave plate for light of wavelength 5890 A°. The refractive indices for ordinary and extra-ordinary beams are 1.586 and 1.592 respectively.*

Data: $\lambda = 5890$ A°, $\mu_o = 1.586$, $\mu_e = 1.592$

Formulae: (i) $t = \dfrac{\lambda}{4 (\mu_e - \mu_o)}$, (ii) $t = \dfrac{\lambda}{2 (\mu_e - \mu_o)}$

Solution: (i) For QWP: $t = \dfrac{5890 \times 10^{-8}}{4 (1.592 - 1.586)} = \boxed{2.45 \times 10^{-3} \text{ cm}}$

(ii) For HWP: $t = \dfrac{5890 \times 10^{-8}}{2 (1.592 - 1.586)} = \boxed{4.90 \times 10^{-3} \text{ cm}}$

Problem 4.8: *A polarizer and an anlayzer are oriented so that the maximum of light is transmitted. To what fraction of its maximum value and intensity of transmitted light reduced when the analyzer is rotated through (i) 30°, (ii) 45° and (iii) 60°?*

Solution: Law of Malus: $I = I_m \cos^2 \theta$ $\therefore$ $\dfrac{I}{I_m} = \cos^2 \theta$

(i) $\theta = 30°$, $\dfrac{I}{I_m} = (\cos^2 30°) = 0.75$

(ii) $\theta = 45°$; $\dfrac{I}{I_m} = (\cos^2 45°) = 0.50$

(iii) $\theta = 60°$, $\dfrac{I}{I_m} = (\cos^2 60°) = 0.25$

Problem 4.9: *Find the specific rotation of cane sugar solution. If the plane of polarization is turned through 26.4°, the length of the tube containing 20% sugar solution is 20 cm.*

Data: $\theta = 26.4°$, $l = 20$ cm $= 2$ dm; $c = 20\% = \dfrac{20}{100} = 0.20$ gm/cc

Formula: $s = \dfrac{\theta}{l \times c}$

Solution: $s = \dfrac{26.4°}{2 \times 0.20} = \boxed{66° \text{ (as 10 cm = 1 dm)}}$

Problem 4.10: *Plane polarized light is incident on a piece of quartz cut parallel to the axis. Find the least thickness for which the ordinary and extra-ordinary rays combine to form plane polarized light. Given: $\mu_o = 1.5442$, $\mu_e = 1.5633$, $\lambda = 5 \times 10^{-5}$ cm.*

Data: $\mu_o = 1.5442$, $\mu_e = 1.5633$, $\lambda = 5 \times 10^{-5}$ cm.

Formula: The half wave plate combines O and E rays to produce plane polarized light.

$$t = \dfrac{\lambda}{2 (\mu_e - \mu_o)}$$

Solution: $t = \dfrac{5 \times 10^{-5}}{2 (1.5633 - 1.5442)} = \boxed{1.3 \times 10^{-3} \text{ cm}}$

Problem 4.11: *If the plane of vibration of incident beam makes an angle of 30° with the optic axis, compare the intensities of the extra-ordinary and ordinary light.*

[Hint: Amplitude of E-ray = A cos θ, Amplitude of O-ray = A sin θ).

Solution: We know, $I \propto A^2$ and according to law of Malus, $I \propto \cos^2 \theta$

For E-ray: $I_E = A^2 \cos^2 \theta = A^2 \cos^2 30° = 0.75 A^2$

For O-ray: $I_O = A^2 \sin^2 \theta = A^2 \sin^2 30° = 0.25 A^2$

$\therefore$ $\dfrac{I_E}{I_O} = \dfrac{0.75}{0.25} = 3$

$$\boxed{I_E = 3I_O}$$

Problem 4.12: *A beam of linearly polarized light is changed into circularly polarized light by passing it through a slice of crystal 0.003 cm thick. Calculate the difference in the refractive indices of the two rays in the crystal assuming this to be the minimum thickness that produces the effect and that the wavelength is 6×10^{-5} cm.*

Data: $t = 0.003$ cm $= 6 \times 10^{-5}$ cm.

Formula: A circularly polarized light is produced with the help of a QWP.

$\therefore$ For QWP; $t = \dfrac{\lambda}{4 (\mu_o - \mu_e)}$

Solution: $(\mu_o - \mu_e) = \dfrac{\lambda}{4t} = \dfrac{6 \times 10^{-5}}{4 \times 0.003} = \boxed{0.005}$

UNIVERSITY SOLVED PROBLEMS

Problem 4.13: *Polarizer and analyzer are set with their polarizing directions parallel so that the intensity of transmitted light is maximum. Through what angle should either be turned so that the intensity is reduced to (i) 1/2 and (ii) 25% of the maximum intensity ?*

(04) (Dec. 03, 12)

Data: (i) $I = 0.5 I_o$, (ii) $I = 0.25 I_o$

Formula: $I = I_0 \cos^2 \theta$

Solution:

(i) $I = I_o \cos^2 \theta$

                        $0.5 I_o = I_o \cos^2 \theta$

                        $\cos^2 \theta = \dfrac{1}{2}$

                        $\cos \theta = 0.707$

                        $\boxed{\theta = 45°}$

(ii) $0.25 I_o = I_o \cos^2 \theta$

                        $\cos^2 \theta = 0.25$

                        $\cos \theta = 0.5$

                        $\boxed{\theta = 60°}$

Problem 4.14: *A quarter wave plate of thickness 2.275×10^{-3} cm is cut with its faces parallel to the optic axis. The emergent beam is elliptically polarized. Find the wavelength of monochromatic light made incident normally on the plate.* **(04) (May 04)**

Given: $\mu_o = 1.586$, $\mu_e = 1.592$

Data: $t = 2.275 \times 10^{-3}$ cm, $\mu_o = 1.586$, $\mu_e = 1.592$

Formula: $\qquad\qquad\qquad t = \dfrac{\lambda}{4\,(\mu_e - \mu_o)}$ or $\lambda = 4t\,(\mu_e - \mu_0)$

Solution: $\qquad\qquad\quad \lambda = 2.275 \times 10^{-3} \times 4\,(1.592 - 1.586)$

$\therefore \qquad\qquad\qquad\qquad \lambda = 5.46 \times 10^{-5}$ cm $= \boxed{5460\ \text{A}^\circ}$

Problem 4.15: Calculate the thickness of a quarter wave plate and a half wave plate, given that $\mu_e = 1.553$, $\mu_o = 1.544$ and $\lambda = 5000\ \text{A}^\circ$. **(04) (Jan. 05)**

Data: $\qquad\qquad\qquad \mu_e = 1.553$

$\qquad\qquad\qquad\qquad \mu_o = 1.544$

$\qquad\qquad\qquad\qquad \lambda = 5000\ \text{A}^\circ$

Formulae: (i) For QWP, $t = \dfrac{\lambda}{4\,(\mu_e - \mu_o)}$

$\qquad$ (ii) For HWP, $\quad t = \dfrac{\lambda}{2\,(\mu_e - \mu_o)}$

Solution: (i) For QWP, $t = \dfrac{5000 \times 10^{-8}}{4\,(1.553 - 1.544)}$

$\qquad\qquad\qquad\boxed{t = 1.388 \times 10^{-3}\ \text{cm}}$

$\qquad$ (ii) For HWP, $\quad t = \dfrac{5000 \times 10^{-8}}{2\,(1.553 - 1.544)}$

$\qquad\qquad\boxed{t = 2.77 \times 10^{-3}\ \text{cm}}$

Problem 4.16: Calculate the thickness of a half wave plate of quartz for green light of wavelength $5000\ \text{A}^\circ$. Given that $\mu_e = 1.5553$ and $\mu_o = 1.544$. **(04) (May 06)**

Data: $\lambda = 5000\ \text{A}^\circ$, $\mu_e = 1.5553$, $\mu_o = 1.544$

Formula: For HWP, $\quad t = \dfrac{\lambda}{2\,(\mu_e - \mu_o)}$

Solution: $\qquad\qquad\quad t = \dfrac{5000 \times 10^{-8}}{2\,(1.5553 - 1.544)}$

$\qquad\qquad\boxed{t = 2.2 \times 10^{-3}\ \text{cm}}$

Problem 4.17: A polarizer and analyzer are oriented so that the amount of transmitted light is maximum. Through what angle should either be turned so that the intensity of transmitted light is reduced to (i) 0.75 and (ii) 0.25 times the maximum intensity ?

(04) (Dec. 06)

Solution: See problem 4.4, page 4.25.

Problem 4.18: *A 20 cm long tube containing 48 c.c. of sugar solution rotates the plane of polarization by 11°. If the specific rotation of sugar is 66°, calculate the mass of sugar in the solution.* **(04) (Dec. 08)**

Data: l = 20 cm

                              s = 66°

                              θ = 11°

Formula: Specific rotation

$$s = \frac{10\theta}{l \times c}$$

$\therefore$ $$c = \frac{10\theta}{l \times s}$$

Solution: $$c = \frac{10 \times 11}{20 \times 66} = \frac{1}{12} \text{ gm/cc}$$

$\therefore$ 1 c.c. of sugar solution contains 1/12 gm of sugar.

$\therefore$ 48 c.c. of sugar solution will contain,

$$\frac{1}{12} \times 48 = \boxed{4 \text{ gm}}$$

Problem 4.19: *Calculate the thickness of*

(i)   Quarter wave plate.

(ii) Half wave plate.

Given: μ_e = 1.553, μ_0 = 1.544, λ = 5000 A°.   **(04) (May 09)**

Solution: See problem 4.8 on page 4.26.

Problem 4.20: *At what angle of incidence should a beam of sodium light be directed upon the surface of diamond crystal to produce complete polarized light*

(Data Given: Critical angle for diamond = 24.5°)   **(03)**

Data: i_c = 24.5°

Formula: i) $$\mu = \frac{1}{\sin i_c}$$

ii) $\mu = \tan i_p$

Solution i) $$\mu = \frac{1}{\sin 24.5}$$

                         μ = 2.41

ii) $i_p = \tan^{-1}(2.41)$

                         $i_p = 67°28'$

SUMMARY

- Light from a natural source like the sun is unpolarized.
- Unpolarized light has the electric vector vibrating along all possible directions at right angles to the direction of propagation of light.
- There are three types of polarization (plane, circular and elliptical).
- Mixture of plane polarized light and unpolarized light is partially polarized light.
- If the vibrations of the electric vector in a light wave are confined to a single plane, then the light wave is plane polarized or linearly polarized.
- The phenomenon of confining vibrations of the light beam to a particular plane is called as polarization.
- Plane of vibration is that plane which contains the direction of vibration.
- Plane of polarization is that plane which contains no vibration. It is perpendicular to the plane of vibration.
- Plane polarized light can be produced from unpolarized light by reflection, refraction, scattering, selective absorption and double refraction.
- Brewster's law states that, tangent of the angle of polarization is proportional to the refractive index of the medium i.e. $\mu = \tan i_p$.
- Polarizing angle is that angle of incidence for which the reflected light is completely plane polarized.
- Law of Malus states that the intensity of the transmitted light is proportional to the square of the cosine of the angle between the plane of transmission of the analyzer and that of the polarizer i.e. $I = I_0 \cos^2 \theta$.
- When light passes through anisotropic crystals, it splits up into two rays, O-ray and E-ray. This phenomenon is known as double refraction or birefringence.
- Birefringence of the crystal is given by, $\Delta\mu = \mu_e - \mu_o$.
- If the velocity of ordinary ray is greater than that of the extraordinary ray ($\mu_e > \mu_o$) then the crystals are positive.
- If the velocity of extraordinary ray is greater than that of the ordinary ray ($\mu_o > \mu_e$) then the crystals are negative.
- Along the optic axis, O-ray and E-ray travel with the same velocity.
- A polaroid is a device that uses selective absorption for obtaining plane polarized light.
- Nicol prism is an optical device used for producing and analyzing plane polarized light.

- QWP and HWP are plates of doubly refracting uniaxial crystals of calcite or quartz of suitable thickness, whose refracting surface is cut parallel to the direction of optic axis.

- QWP introduces a path difference of $\dfrac{\lambda}{4}$ between the O-ray and E-ray.

$$\frac{\lambda}{4} = (\mu_O - \mu_e) \, t \text{ for negative crystals}$$

$$\frac{\lambda}{4} = (\mu_e - \mu_O) \, t \text{ for positive crystals}$$

- HWP introduces a path difference of $\dfrac{\lambda}{2}$ between the O-ray and E-ray.

$$\frac{\lambda}{2} = (\mu_O - \mu_e) \, t \text{ for negative crystals}$$

$$\frac{\lambda}{2} = (\mu_e - \mu_O) \, t \text{ for positive crystals}$$

- Using QWP and an analyzer, the state of polarization of any light can be determined.

IMPORTANT FORMULAE

- $\mu = \tan i_p$

- $i_p + r = \dfrac{\pi}{2}$

- $I = I_0 \cos^2 \theta$

- $\mu = \dfrac{1}{\sin c}$

- $\mu_O = \dfrac{\sin i}{\sin r_o} = \dfrac{c}{v_o}$

- $\mu_e = \dfrac{\sin i}{\sin r_e} = \dfrac{c}{v_e}$

- $t_{QWP} = \dfrac{\lambda}{4 \, (\mu_O - \mu_e)}$

- $t_{HWP} = \dfrac{\lambda}{2 \, (\mu_O - \mu_e)}$

EXERCISE

1. Explain the term polarization of light.

2. Define plane of polarization and plane of vibration. Explain a method to show that light waves are transverse.

3. Distinguish between polarized and unpolarized light.

4.   State Brewster's law and use it to prove that when light is incident on a transparent substance at the polarizing angle, the reflected and refracted rays are at right angles to each other.

5.   Explain how you would obtain plane polarized light by reflection.

6.   What is pile of plates ? Explain how it can be used for producing plane polarized light.

7.   What is polarizing angle ? Explain.

8.   State and explain the law of Malus.

9.   Explain the phenomenon of double refraction in calcite.

10. Describe the construction and working of a Nicol prism.

11. What is a Nicol prism ? Explain how a Nicol prism can be used as an analyzer and polarizer.

12. Explain giving diagrams the nature of refraction observed in the case of calcite crystal when:

     (a) optic axis is parallel to the refractive surface and lying in the plane of incidence (normal incidence).

     (b) optic axis is perpendicular to the refracting surface and lying in the plane of incidence (normal incidence).

13. Give Huygen's construction for ordinary and extraordinary wavefronts when the beam of light is refracted through a doubly refracting crystal when the optic axis is inclined to the crystal surface and lying in the plane of incidence (normal incidence).

14. What do you mean by selective absorption ? Explain.

15. What are polaroids ? Describe its construction and mention its uses.

16. What do you understand by retardation plates ? Give a short note on quarter wave plate and half wave plate.

17. How can elliptically polarized light and circularly polarized light be produced ?

18. How can you detect an elliptically and circularly polarized light ?

19. How will you distinguish circularly polarized light from unpolarized light and elliptically polarized light from partially plane polarized light ?

20. Mention the different methods of producing plane polarized light. Describe any one of them.

21. What is the basic principle of LCD ? Explain the working of LCD displays.

UNSOLVED PROBLEMS

1. If the plane of vibrations of the incident beam makes an angle of 30° with the optic axis, compare the intensities of extraordinary and ordinary light. $\left[\textbf{Ans.} \ \dfrac{I_e}{I_O} = 3 \right]$

2. Calculate the thickness of (i) quarter wave plate, (ii) half wave plate, given that $\mu_e = 1.553$, $\mu_o = 1.544$ and $\lambda = 5000$ A$^\circ$. [**Ans.** 1.39×10^{-3} cm, 2.78×10^{-3} cm]

3. A beam of light travelling in water strikes a glass plate which is also immersed in water. When the angle of incidence is 51°, the reflected beam is found to be polarized. Calculate the refractive index of glass. [**Ans.** 1.235]

4. A glass plate is used as a polarizer. Find the angle of polarization for it. Also find the angle of refraction, given μ for glass = 1.54. **Ans.** $57^\circ, 33^\circ$]

5. Two polarizing sheets have their polarizing directions parallel so that the intensity of the transmitted light is maximum. Through what angle must either sheet be turned so that the intensity becomes one half the initial value ? [**Ans.** $45^\circ, 135^\circ$]

6. The refractive index for plastic is 1.25. Calculate the angle of refraction for a ray of light inclined at polarizing angle. [**Ans.** 38.6°]

7. Plane polarized light of $\lambda = 6000$ A$^\circ$ is incident on a thin quartz plate cut with face parallel to the optic axis. Calculate,

   (i) the minimum thickness of the plate which introduces phase difference of 60° between O and E rays,

   (ii) the minimum thickness of the plate for which the O and E rays will combine to produce plane polarized light.

   Given $\mu_o = 1.544$ and $\mu_e = 1.553$ [**Ans.** 0.011 cm, 0.00333 cm]

8. A beam of light is passed through two Nicol prisms in series. In a particular setting, maximum light is passed by the system and it is 500 units. If one of the Nicols is now rotated by 20°, calculate the intensity of transmitted light. [**Ans.** 441.5 units]

9. Two Nicol prisms are oriented with their principal planes making an angle of 30°. What percentage of incident unpolarized light will pass through the system ?   [**Ans.** 37.5 %]

10. A polarizer and an analyzer are oriented so that the amount of light transmitted is maximum. To what fraction of its maximum value is the intensity of the transmitted light reduced when the analyzer is rotated through (i) 45°, (ii) 90° ?   [**Ans.** 0.5, 0]

SOLVED UNIVERSITY QUESTIONS

DECEMBER 2012

1. State the Phenomena of Double Refraction. Hence, explain Huygen's Wave Theory of Double Refraction.   **[6]**

Ans. Please Refer to Article 4.5.3 on Page No. 4.8 and Article 4.7 on Page No. 4.14.

2. How should the Polarizer and Analyzer be oriented to reduce intensity of beam to (i) 50%, (ii) 0.25 of its original intensity?   **[6]**

Ans. Please Refer to Problem 4.13 on Page No. 4.27.

MAY 2013

1. Define Double refraction. Explain Huygen's Theory of Double refracting crystal with diagram.   **[6]**

Ans. Please Refer to Articles No 4.5.3 on Page No 4.8 and Article No. 4.7 on Page No. 4.14

2. At what angle of incidence should a beam of sodium light be directed upon the surface of diamond crystal to produce complete polarized light.

(Data Given: Critical angle for diamond = 24.5°)   **[3]**

Ans. Data: $i_c = 24.5°$

Formula: (i) $\mu = \dfrac{1}{Sin\, i_c}$

(ii) $\mu = tan\, i_p$

Solution: (i) $\mu = \dfrac{1}{Sin\, 24.5}$

$\mu = 2.41$

(ii) $i_p = tan^{-1}(2.41)$

$i_p = 67°28'$

NOVEMBER 2013

1. Explain the propagation of light through a quartz crystal plate for normal incidence. When   **[6]**

   (i) Optic axis is parallel to the crystal surface and lying in the plane of incidence.

   (ii) Optic axis is perpendicular to the crystal surface and lying in the plane of incidence.

   (iii) Optic axis is inclined to the crystal surface and lying in the plane of incidence.

Ans. Please Refer to Article 4.8 on Page No. 4.16.

Note: In book explanation has been given of Calcite (negative) crystal. Therefore in current case i.e. quartz (positive) crystal, the sphere will be outside the ellipse. Please refer Fig. 4.16 (a).

MAY 2014

1. Explain double refraction and hence give Huygen's theory of double refraction.   **[6]**

Ans. Please Refer to Article 4.5.3 and 4.7 (Only the definition of double refraction) on Page No. 4.8 and 4.14.

DECEMBER 2014

2. Explain propagation of light in a doubly refracting crystal when the optic axis is parallel to the crystal surface, with the help of neat diagram.   **[3]**

Ans. Please Refer to Article 4.8.1 on Page No. 4.16.

3. How should the polarizer and analyzer be oriented to reduce the beam of light to (i) 50% (ii) 25% of its original intensity.   **[3]**

Ans. Please Refer to Article 4.6 on Page No. 4.13.

MAY 2015

1. State and prove Law of Malus.   **[3]**

Ans. Please Refer to Article 4.6, Page No. 4.13 to 4.14.

2. A retardation plate of thickness 2.275×10^{-3} cm is cut with its faces parallel to optic axis. If the emergent beam of light is elliptically polarized. Find the wavelength of monochromatic light made incident normally on the plate. Given that, $\mu_0 = 1.586$, $\mu_e = 1.592$.   **[3]**

Ans. Please Refer to Problem No. 4.6, Page No. 4.25.

NOVEMBER 2015

1. Plane polarized light of wavelength 5×10^{-5} cm is incident on a piece of quarter cut parallel to the optic axis. Find the least thickness of quarter for which the O-ray and E-ray combine to form plane polarized light. **[3]**

Ans. Please Refer to Problem 4.10 Page No. 4.26.

2. State and prove Malus law. **[3]**

Ans. Please Refer to Article 4.6, Page No. 4.25.

MAY 2016

1. What is double refraction? Explain this phenomenon on the basis of Huygen's theory. **[6]**

Ans. Please Refer to Article 4.5.3 and 4.7 on Page No. 4.8 and 4.14.

REFERENCE

Better understanding of polarization with some animations:

http://www.colorado.edu/physics/2000/polarization/index.html

Animation of double refraction:

http://www.olympusmicro.com/primer/java/polarizedlight/icelandspar/index.html

Three dimensional diagram showing different types of polarization:

http://hyperphysics.phy-astr.gsu.edu/hbase/phyopt/polclas.html.

✠ ✠ ✠

CHAPTER 5
LASER

5.1 INTRODUCTION

- The term laser stands for *'light amplification by stimulated emission of radiation'*.

- Laser is a light source which is highly coherent i.e. radiation emitted by all the emitters (atoms or molecules) in source agree in phase, direction of emission, polarisation and are essentially of one wavelength or colour (monochromatic).

- Due to coherence, a beam of laser light can travel many miles with only a negligible divergence. This makes it different from the conventional light sources which emit many wavelengths with phase and direction widely varying.

- Around 1917, Einstein first predicted the existence of two different kinds of processes by which an atom can emit radiation by (i) spontaneous emission, (ii) stimulated emission.

- In a laser, the process of stimulated emission is used for amplifying the light waves. The fact that stimulated emission process could be used in the construction of coherent optical sources was first put forward by Townes and Schawlow.

- The energy of an atom in any atomic system can change by

    (i) absorption   (ii) spontaneous emission   (iii) stimulated emission.

5.2 ABSORPTION

- When a photon of energy $h\upsilon$ is incident on an atomic system, the atom gets excited from a lower energy E_1 to a higher energy E_2, if the energy of photon equals the difference in the energy levels i.e. $h\upsilon = E_2 - E_1$. In this process, the photon gets absorbed and the atom is said to be excited.

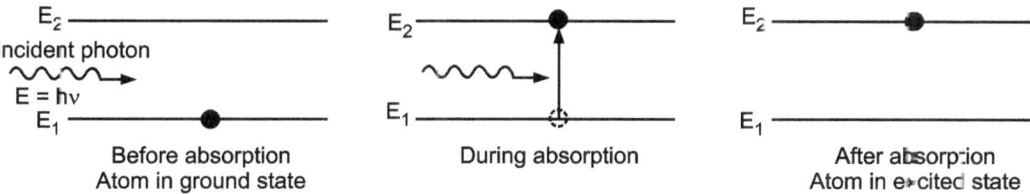

| Before absorption | During absorption | After absorption |
| Atom in ground state | | Atom in excited state |

Fig. 5.1: Absorption

5.3 SPONTANEOUS EMISSION

- When a photon of energy $E = h\upsilon$ is incident on an atom, the atom absorbs the energy to rise to an excited state. The difference of the energy levels should be equal to the absorbed energy ($E_2 - E_1 = h\upsilon$). Though the electron stays in the ground state for an infinite amount of time (being a stable state), but it remains in the excited state for a short time called the **'life time'** of the excited state ($\approx 10^{-8}$ sec). Energy levels for which the life time is greater than 10^{-8} sec are called as **'metastable states'**.

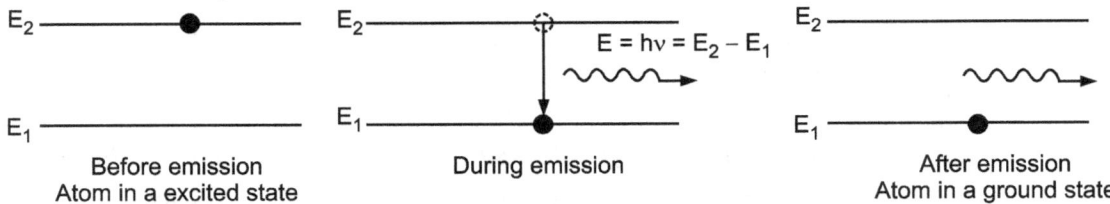

Fig. 5.2: Spontaneous emission

- The electron which is in an excited state E_2, spontaneously decays back to the lower energy level and radiates an energy equal to $E_2 - E_1$ in the form of photon of energy $h\upsilon$. Such an emission which is random in behaviour, depending only on the type of atom and the type of transition is known as **'spontaneous emission'**.

- The emitted radiations are not coherent and have a large range of wavelengths. Only those transitions occur which are permitted by selection rules.

5.4 REQUIREMENT FOR LASING ACTION

5.4.1 Stimulated Emission   [Nov. 13, May 16]

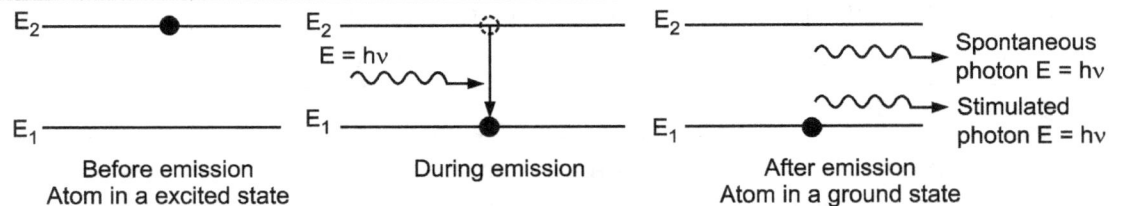

Fig. 5.3: Stimulated emission

- Consider Fig. 5.3 where the electrons are initially in the excited energy level and emission is stimulated before the spontaneous emission occurs. The excited atom is stimulated by a photon of exactly the same energy as the photon to be emitted. In such a case, two photons are emitted, one by the stimulated emission and the other stimulating photon.

- Both the photons travel in the same direction, have the same frequency and are in phase i.e. they are coherent.

- The emission of two photons with an input of only one photon implies amplification. The occurrence of spontaneous emission is directly proportional to the number of atoms in the specified energy level, whereas in stimulated emission, the rate of occurrence is proportional not only to the number of atoms in the excited state but also to the number of incident stimulating photons.

5.4.2 Population Inversion   [Nov. 13]

- The process of getting a large percentage of atoms into an excited state is called as *'population inversion'*. If a large number of atoms can be excited to upper energy levels, then the probability of stimulated emission and hence light amplification becomes greater.

- The states of the system, in which the population of the higher energy state is more than the population of the lower energy state, are called as *'negative temperature states'* (negative indicates a non-equilibrium state, not the physical state of the system).

- In any atomic system, the number of particles in a higher energy state is normally less than the number of particles in a lower energy state. If N_2 denotes the number of particles in higher energy level E_2, and N_1 denotes the number of particles in lower energy level E_1, then $N_2 < N_1$ i.e. the population of higher energy level is less than the population of lower energy level. This means that under normal conditions, the ground state E_1 is heavily populated than the excited state E_2.

- If photons of energy $h\upsilon = E_2 - E_1$ are incident on the atoms, a few of the incident photons get absorbed and some of the atoms get excited to the state E_2. This process of stimulated absorption depopulates level E_1. The rate at which this process occurs is expressed as

$$R_{12} = P_a N_1 \qquad\qquad \dots (1)$$

where P_a is the probability of stimulated absorption and N_1 is the population of state E_1.

- Similarly, the stimulated emission depopulates energy level E_2 resulting in the emission of photons. The rate at which this process occurs is expressed as

$$R_{21} = P_e N_2 \qquad\qquad \dots (2)$$

where P_e is the probability of the process of stimulated emission and N_2 is the population of state E_2.

- At thermal equilibrium, these probabilities are equal i.e. $P_a = P_e$. Then, on comparing the two rates, it is observed that more energy is absorbed than emitted.

  i.e. from (1) and (2),

$$P_a N_1 > P_e N_2 \text{ because } N_1 > N_2.$$

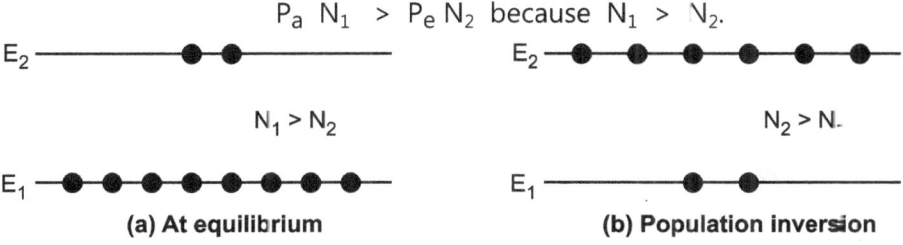

(a) At equilibrium   (b) Population inversion

Fig. 5.4

- To produce more emission, it is essential to have $N_2 > N_1$ i.e. the number of particles in higher energy level must be made more than the number of particles in lower energy level. This is called as **'population inversion'**.

- If this inversion is achieved, there can be more emission and incoming light will be amplified coherently. A system in which population inversion is achieved is called an **'active system'**.

- The method of raising atoms from lower energy levels to higher energy levels is called as **'pumping'**. It can be done by subjecting the atoms to a non-uniform electric field, flooding the gas with high intensity light, etc. A more common method of pumping is **'optical pumping'**.

5.4.3 Metastable State   [Nov. 15]

- The electron in an excited state has certain probability to decay or jump to a lower energy level. Generally, these probabilities are such that the jump occurs within 10^{-8} sec of excitation.

- However, there are some excited states, called **'metastable states'**, which have a very low probability of decay i.e. electrons stay for longer time.

- Electrons may stay in the metastable excited states for seconds, minutes or even hours. In stimulated emission, the electrons must remain in excited level and wait for stimulating photon.

- Therefore, the active medium must have a metastable state. The population inversion can be obtained by using metastable states as the electrons rest in metastable state for long time.

5.4.4 Active Medium

- A medium in which the population inversion takes place is called the **active medium**. The active medium is responsible for the light amplification and hence LASER. The active medium may be a solid, liquid or gas and accordingly the lasers are classified as solid state or gas lasers.

- Out of the total active medium, only small number of atoms are responsible for lasing action and remaining atoms help only in hosting active atoms or in population inversion. The atoms which particulate in stimulated emission are called **active centres**.

5.4.5 Resonant Cavity

- A cavity can be constructed using mirrors such that the light rays return to their original position after travelling through the cavity for a certain number of times. Such cavities are known as **resonant cavities**.

- Fig. 5.5 shows cavity formed by two parallel mirrors M_1 and M_2. One of the mirrors is completely silvered (M_1) and the other is partially silvered (M_2). The laser beam emerges from the resonant cavity through the partially silvered mirror M_2.

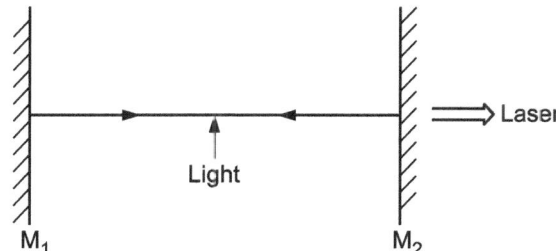

Fig. 5.5: Resonant cavity

- The active system is placed in the resonant cavity, the photon emitted will keep on reflecting back and forth within the cavity. The light which is incident parallel to the axis of optical cavity will only leak out as a laser. That is why, laser is highly directional.

5.4.6 Pumping   [May 14]

The method of raising atoms from lower energy levels to higher energy levels is called as *'pumping'*. The pumping is used for achieving population inversion which is necessary for optical amplification to take place. There are several methods for pumping electrons. They are as follows:

1. **Optical Pumping**

   - In optical pumping, an external light source (flash lamp) is used to produce a high population in some particular energy level E_2 (say) by selective absorption as shown in Fig. 5.6.

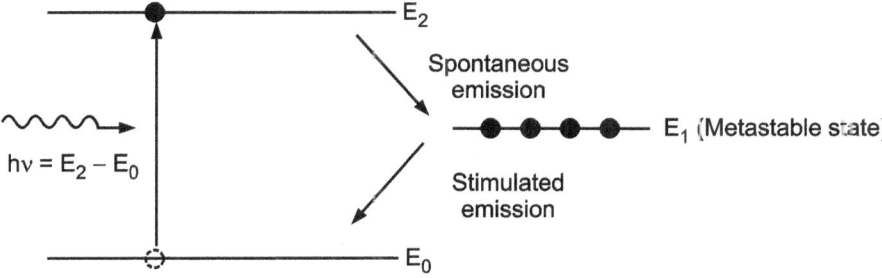

Fig. 5.6: Optical pumping

- When a flash of light falls on electrons in ground state, they absorb incident photons and get excited. After staying there for some time, some of the atoms make spontaneous transition to metastable state E_1. As the probability of spontaneous decay is less in metastable state, a large population accumulates in this level. This results in a population inversion between E_0 and E_1.

- Generally, this method is used in solid-state lasers, such as ruby laser.

2. **Inelastic Atom-Atom Collisions**

   - Here suitable mixtures of gases are used. The gases are selected in such a way that their excited states are almost same. This makes the energy exchange possible between the atoms of the gases. If two gases A and B have same excited state, A^* and B^* then,

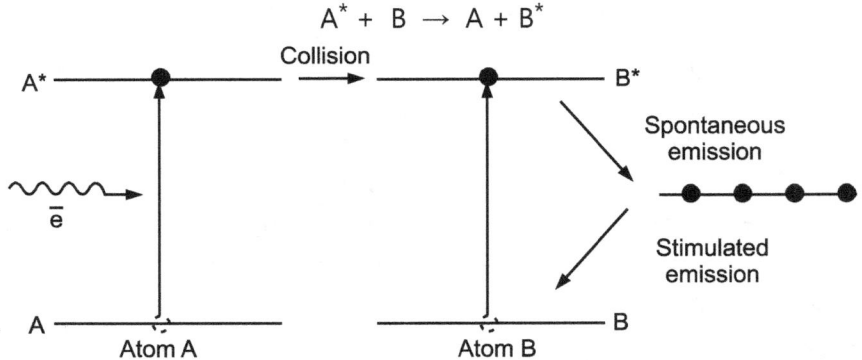

Fig. 5.7: Inelastic atom-atom collision

- The atom of gas A is excited by electric discharge. In collision with B, the energy is transferred to B. As a result, the excited level of atom B becomes more populated than lower level to which B can decay, as shown in Fig. 5.7.
- The best example is the He-Ne gas laser.

3. **Forward Biasing of a p-n Junction**

- If a p-n junction is formed with degenerate (heavily doped) semiconductors, the bands under forward bias appear as shown in Fig. 5.8.

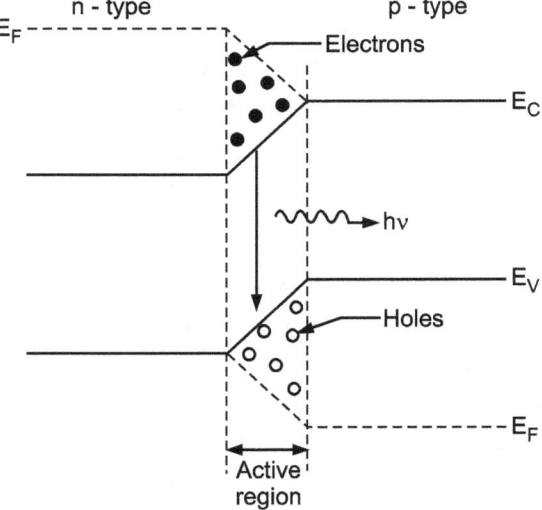

Fig. 5.8: Forward biasing of a p-n junction diode

- If the bias voltage is large enough, electrons and holes are injected into the active region. As a result, the depletion layer now contains a large number of electrons in conduction band and holes in valence band. If the population density is high enough, it gives population inversion. For a population inversion, the applied voltage should be selected in such a way that $eV > h\upsilon$ (= E_g).

- The other methods of pumping are electron excitation, chemical reactions etc. These methods will not be discussed in detail as they are beyond the scope of the text.

5.5 CHARACTERISTICS OF LASER

- Laser is basically a light source, but many of its properties are special or extreme. These properties make it different from ordinary sources.
- The basic properties of lasers which make different from ordinary light source are:

(a) Monochromaticity

➢ When the laser produces only one wavelength then it is fully monochromatic. This is impossible, in principle and in practice also.

➢ If $\Delta\lambda$ is the range of wavelengths included in a laser beam of wavelength λ, then $\Delta\upsilon$ is the corresponding frequency. This frequency band $\Delta\upsilon$ is called the **'line width'**.

➢ For white light consisting of all visible frequencies, the line width is ~10^{14} Hz, while for a good laser it is about 10^2 Hz.

(b) Coherence

➢ The light emerging from a laser is coherent both in space and time. The existence of finite bandwidth $\Delta\upsilon$ means that the different frequencies present in laser can get out of phase width each other.

➢ If two waves differ by frequency $\Delta\upsilon$, the time required to get out of phase by a full cycle is $1/\Delta\upsilon$. This is called as **'coherence time'** of a beam and is denoted by $\Delta\tau$.

i.e.
$$\Delta\tau = \frac{1}{\Delta\upsilon}$$
... (1)

➢ For a laser with $\Delta\upsilon = 1$ MHz, $\Delta\tau = 1$ μs. On the other hand, sunlight has a bandwidth $\Delta\upsilon = 10^{14}$ Hz, therefore, $\Delta\tau = 10^{-14}$ s which is much smaller than laser.

➢ The speed of light is so large that it travels a very large distance for a short coherence time. The distance $\Delta L = c\Delta\tau$ is called **'coherence length'** of the beam. For a laser beam with $\Delta\upsilon = 1$ MHz, the coherence length $\Delta L = 300$ m.

➢ Only the portions of the same beam, separated by a distance less than coherence length are capable of producing stable interference pattern.

(c) Directionality

➢ A laser has high degree of directionality and can travel very large distances without deviation. For a typical laser, the divergence is about 10^{-3} radians. This means that the laser beam diverges by ~1 mm for every meter that it travels.

➢ The reason is that the active material is placed in a resonant cavity. The light is reflected back and forth in the cavity and light travelling parallel to the axis gets emitted as the laser beam. The light travelling in the other direction is reflected back in the cavity.

(d) Brightness
> A laser radiates light into a narrow beam and its energy is concentrated in a small region. This is due to the fact that the divergence is very less. This results into extremely high intensity.

> Even a 1 W laser appears more intense than a ordinary 100 W lamp. This high concentration is used in many applications such as drilling, welding and cutting.

5.6 VARIOUS LEVELS OF LASER SYSTEMS

- The various levels of laser systems are:
  (a) Two level.
  (b) Three level.
  (c) Four level.

(a) Two Level Laser System
- A two-level laser system consists of only two energy levels, E_1 and E_2, ground state and excited state. The electrons from E_1 are pumped to E_2 as shown in Fig. 5.9.

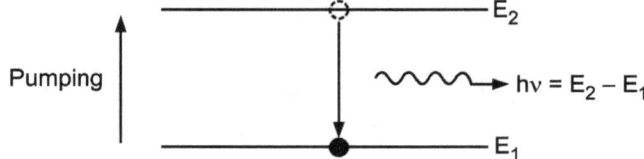

Fig. 5.9: Two-level laser system

- The electron from E_2 decays to E_1 radiating a photon of energy $h\upsilon$. The best example of two-level laser system is a diode laser.

(b) Three Level Laser System
- In a three-level laser system, three energy levels E_1, E_2 and E_3 are involved as shown in Fig. 5.10. Here one of the transitions is non-radiative. The transition between E_3 to E_2 is very fast and non-radiative.
- Here the electron is pumped to E_3 directly. As decay from E_3 to E_2 is very fast, hence E_2 will be more populated and decay from E_2 to E_1 gives a photon of energy $h\upsilon$. The best example of this category is ruby laser.

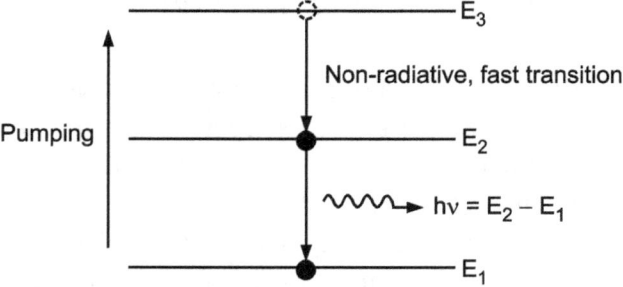

Fig. 5.10: Three-level laser system

(c) Four Level Laser System

- In a four-level laser system, the electrons are pumped to E_4 directly. The transitions will take place between E_4 to E_3, E_3 to E_2 and E_2 to E_1. Out of these three transitions, only one will be radiative and two will be non-radiative.

- Fig. 5.11 shows a four-level laser system. The best example is He-Ne laser. In a four level laser system, lasing action is always observed between E_3 and E_2.

- The life time of E_4 is very short. The transition between E_2 to E_1 is non-radiative and spontaneous. Moment electron reaches to E_1, it is pumped to level E_4, but due to short life time of energy level E_4, electron immediately jumps to E_3. Hence the levels E_1 and E_4 are free to accommodate electrons and the population of E_3 is always higher which favours for lasing action. Therefore, four level laser system works effectively.

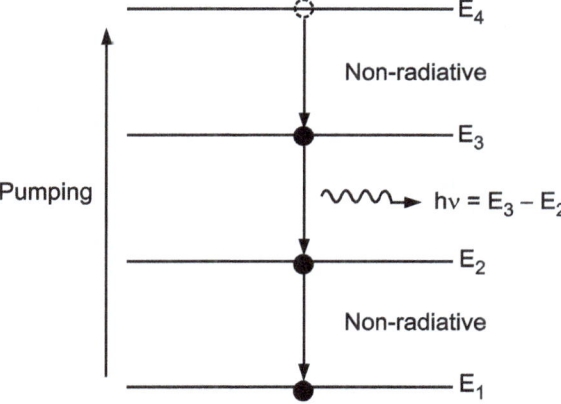

Fig. 5.11: Four-level laser system

Need of Three/Four-Level System

- If there are only two states, ground state and metastable state. When a photon is incident on it, it will be absorbed and electron will jump from ground state to metastable state. At the same time, due to stimulated emission, electron will jump to the ground state.

- During the process a situation will arise when half of the atoms are in the ground state (N_1) and half in the metastable state (N_2). i.e. $N_1 = N_2$. This will make the rate of stimulated emission and absorption equal. But to achieve population inversion, rate of absorption should be higher than stimulated emission.

- Thus if there are only two states the population inversion could not be achieved. And, therefore, laser action will not be possible.

5.7 SEMICONDUCTOR LASER – TWO LEVEL LASER SYSTEM

- A semiconductor diode laser is a p-n junction device that emits coherent light when forward biased. A p-n junction laser is also called **'injection laser'** as the charge carriers are injected into depletion region.

- The diode lasers are preferred over other lasers as they are compact, reliable and low cost.

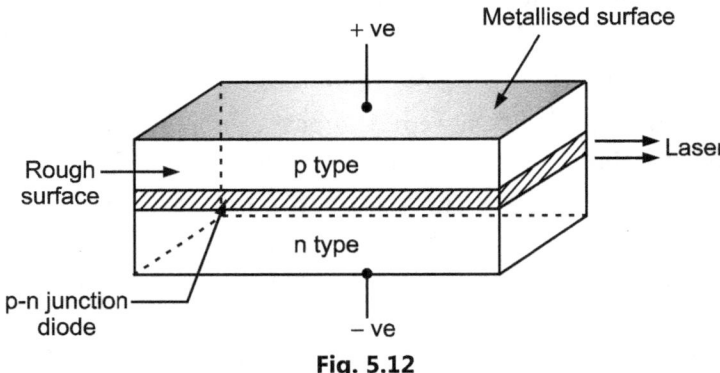

Fig. 5.12

Construction

- A laser diode is extremely small in size with sides of the order of 1 mm. The p-n junction of the diode lies in the horizontal plane. The top and bottom faces are metallised for making electrical contacts.
- Two plane mirrors are placed at front and back surface to form optical cavity. Sometimes the faces itself are polished to form optical cavity. The other two faces are roughened to prevent lasing action in that direction.

Working

(a) Under Equilibrium

- In semiconductor diode laser, the p-n semiconductor is heavily doped (degenerate semiconductor). Fig. 5.13 shows the energy band of highly doped p-region and n-region.

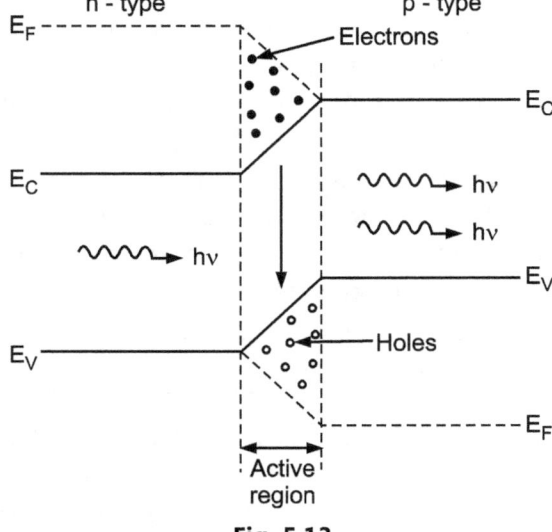

Fig. 5.13

- Due to very high doping on n-side, the donor level as well as a portion of conduction band is occupied by electrons. Hence, the Fermi level lies within the conduction band. Similarly, on the heavily doped p-side, holes exist in the valence band and hence the Fermi level lies in the valence band.

(b) Forward Bias, Pumping and Recombination

- At low forward current, the electron-hole recombinations cause spontaneous emission of photons and the junction acts as an LED. As the current is increased, the intensity of light increases.
- When the current reaches a threshold value, the carrier concentration in the depletion region reaches a very high value i.e. a large concentration of electrons in the conduction band and a large concentration of holes in the valence band.
- As a result, the higher energy levels in the depletion region are having high population density of electrons while the lower levels are vacant. This is a state of population inversion. The region where the population inversion is achieved is called as *active region*. The forward bias acts as the pumping agent.

(c) Built-Up of Laser

- Due to forward bias, the band gap is very small and therefore electrons in the conduction band can recombine with holes in the valence band. During this process of recombination of electrons and holes, electrons loose their energy emitting a photon of energy equal to band gap.
- Some of the photons emitted during the process of recombination are reflected back from the polished ends and stimulate the electrons initiating the laser process. The highly polished ends continuously reflect the light back and forth. The photons parallel to the axis of resonator will leak out as laser beam.
- The frequency of radiated photon is $\upsilon = E_g/h$, where E_g is band gap and h is Planck's constant. The wavelength of laser beam depends upon the material used for GaAs laser wavelength is 9000 A° in IR region and GaAsP it is 6500 A° in visible region at room temperature.

Advantage of Semiconductor Laser

- Very less power required, simple, compact, highly efficient, more divergent, less monochromatic and highly temperature sensitive.

5.8 RUBY LASER – THREE LEVEL LASER SYSTEM
[Dec. 14, May 15, Nov. 15]

- A ruby laser is a solid-state laser that uses a synthetic ruby crystal. Typical ruby laser is a pulsed laser of intense red colour.

Construction

- The laser consists of a ruby rod surrounded by a flash tube. One end of the rod is highly silvered while the other end is semi-silvered. The flash tube surrounds the ruby rod in the form of a spiral.

- Synthetic ruby consists of a crystal of aluminium oxide (Al_2O_3) in which a few of the aluminium atoms (Al^{3+}) are replaced by chromium atoms (Cr^{3+}). These atoms have the property of absorbing green light.

- The chromium impurity is the active atom of the laser. Doping of chromium gives ruby its characteristic red colour.

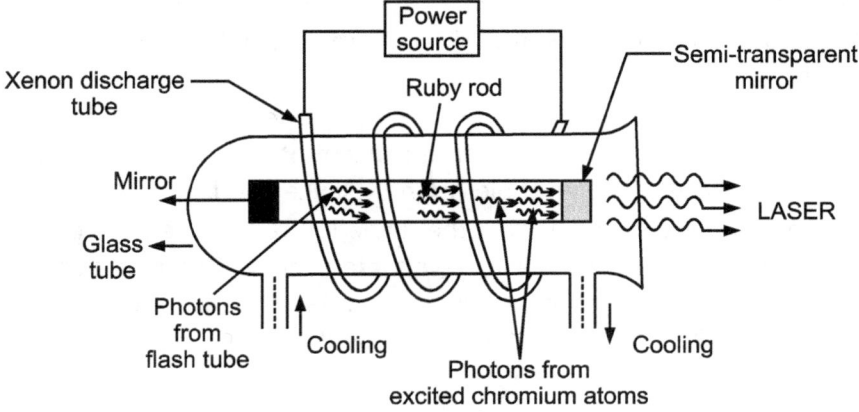

Fig. 5.14

(a) Pumping and Energy Levels of Chromium

- When ruby is in a steady magnetic field, chromium acquires energy states, of which three are represented schematically as shown in Fig. 5.15 (a).

- As is clear from the figure, this is a three-level laser system. Level M actually consists of a pair of levels corresponding to wavelengths of 6943 A° and 6929 A°. However, laser action takes place only on 6943 A° line due to higher population inversion.

- The pumping of chromium atoms is performed with a Xenon or Krypton flash lamp. The chromium atoms in the ground state absorb radiation around wavelengths 5500 A° and 4000 A° and are excited to the levels marked E_1 and E_2.

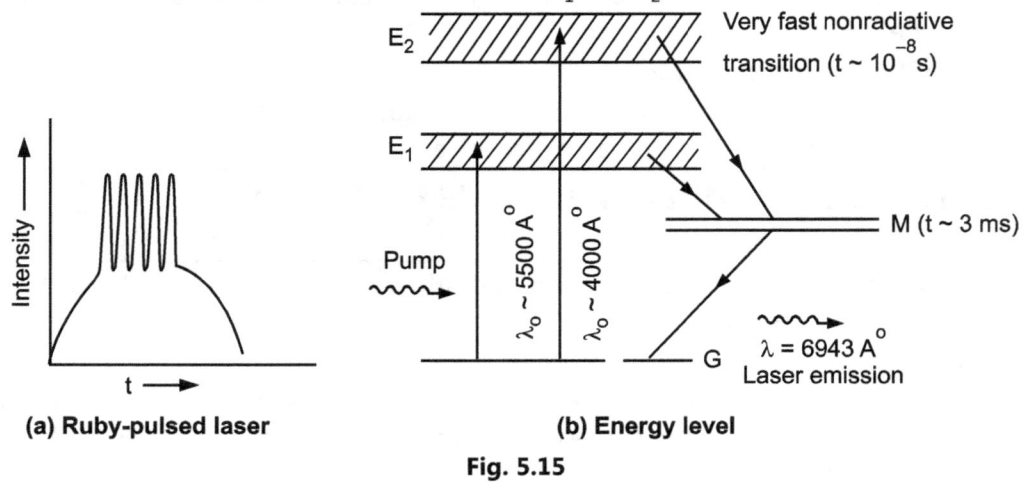

(a) Ruby-pulsed laser   **(b) Energy level**

Fig. 5.15

(b) Assembly of Chromium Atoms to Metastable State

- The chromium atoms excited to these levels, relax rapidly through a non-radiative transition (in a time 10^{-8} to 10^{-9} sec) to the metastable state M, which has a life time of ~3 m secs. Laser emission occurs between level M and the ground state G at an output wavelength of 6943 A°.

(c) Operation

- The operational sequence starts with the ignition of the Xenon flash tube. Chromium atoms in the ruby rod are energized by absorption of the energetic photons from the flash tube.

- When the excited electrons in the chromium atoms fall back to their normal states, photons are given off by spontaneous emission emitting red light (hence ruby has a natural red colour). Some of these photons escape from the rod but many oscillate or bounce back and forth along the length of the rod with the help of the mirror at the two ends.

- When the electrons in the excited state are exposed to these radiations of the same frequency which they are about to emit, the emission process is triggered. Radiation s now emitted, which is exactly in phase with the exposed radiation.

- This cumulative process of flash tube photons exciting chromium atoms which in turn emit photons in the same direction and phase, continues until the coherent laser beam penetrates through the partially reflecting mirror on one end of the rod to give a powerful beam of red light.

(d) Pulsed Output

- A certain stage is reached when the population inversion caused by one flash of Xenon tube is used up. As soon as the flash lamp stops operating, the population of the upper level is depleted very rapidly and laser action ceases until the arrival of the next flash. Refer Fig. 5.15 (b).

- Thus, ruby is a *'pulsed laser'*. The output beam has a principal wavelength of 6943 A° equal to 4.3×10^{14} Hz frequency (lies in the visible spectrum). The duration of the output flash is about 300 μsec.

- During the operation of a ruby laser, a very high temperature is produced. To prevent any damage to the ruby rod, it is surrounded by a liquid nitrogen container and is operated to give out the beam only in pulses.

- This laser is used in many applications as its output lies in the visible region where photographic emulsions and photo detectors are more sensitive than they are in the infrared region. Ruby lasers also find application in laser holography, laser ranging, etc.

5.9 HELIUM-NEON LASER – FOUR LEVEL LASER SYSTEM

- This is a *'continuous laser'* unlike the ruby laser. In this laser, the vapours of metal are used as the media.
- It is an extremely popular form of laser as it is simple, inexpensive and has an extremely broad range of emission wavelengths (0.6 to 100 μm depending on the type of gas used). The first gas laser to be operated successfully was the He - Ne laser.
- In solid-state lasers, pumping is usually done by using a flash lamp or a continuous high power lamp. Such a technique is efficient if the laser system has broad absorption bands. In gas lasers, as the atoms are characterized by sharp energy levels, an electrical discharge is generally used to pump the atoms.

Construction

- It consists of a quartz tube with a diameter of about 2-8 mm and a length of 10-100 cm. It is filled with helium and neon. The pressure of helium is approximately 10 times that of neon.
- The neon atoms provide energy states for the transitions while helium provides a mechanism for efficiently exciting neon atoms to upper metastable states i.e. helium serves merely as an energy transfer agent.
- At one end of the tube is a total reflector while at the other is a partial reflector. The gas is excited by means of a high frequency generator.

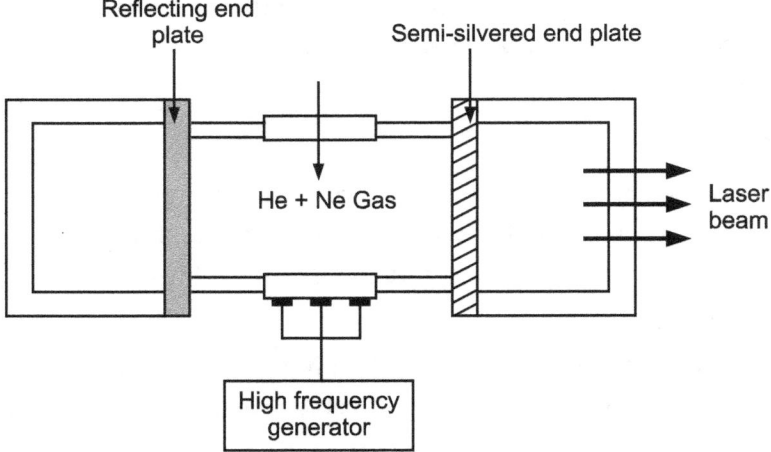

Fig. 5.16: He-ne laser

Principle

- In He-Ne laser, population inversion is produced through inelastic collisions between excited He atoms and Ne atoms in the ground state. The process can be expressed as

$$He^* + Ne \rightarrow He + Ne^*   (* \text{ shows an excited state})$$

- This is possible, because the levels Ne_4 and Ne_6 of neon atoms have almost the same energy as the levels He_2 and He_3 of helium atoms as shown in the energy level diagram.

Working

(a) Electric Discharge and Excitation of Helium

- When an electrical discharge is passed through the gas, the electrons which are accelerated down the tube collide with helium and neon atoms and excite them to higher energy levels. The helium atoms tend to accumulate at the levels He_2 and He_3 due to their long life times of $\approx 10^{-4}$ secs and 10^{-6} secs respectively.

(b) Transfer of Energy from Helium to Neon and Pumping

- As the levels Ne_4 and Ne_6 of neon atoms have almost the same energy as He_2 and He_3, excited helium atoms colliding with neon atoms in the ground state can excite the neon atoms to Ne_4 and Ne_6 states. As the pressure of helium is ten times that of neon, the levels Ne_4 and Ne_6 of neon are selectively populated as compared to other levels of neon.

i.e. $He^* + Ne \rightarrow He + Ne^*$ (* indicates excited state)

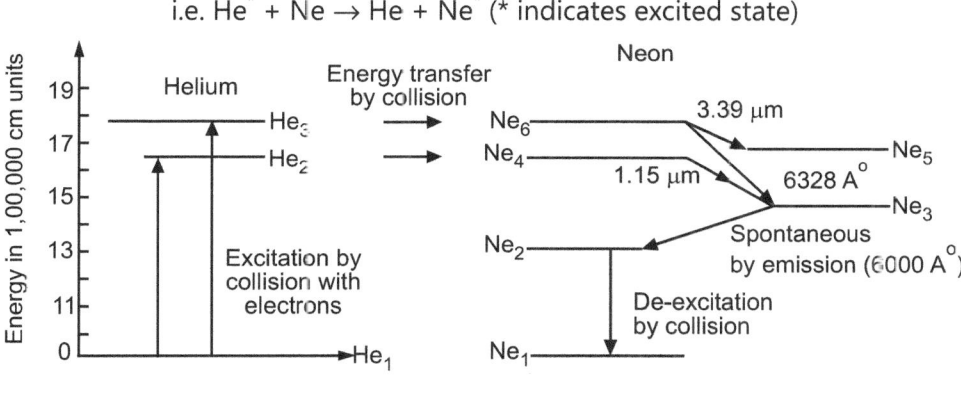

Fig. 5.17

(c) Population Inversion for Neon

- Transition between Ne_6 and Ne_3 produces the popular 6328 A° (632.8 nm) line of He - Ne laser. Neon atoms de-excite through spontaneous emission from Ne_3 to Ne_2 (life time $\sim 10^{-8}$ sec.). As this time is shorter than the life time of level Ne_6 ($\sim 10^{-7}$ sec.), steady state population inversion can be achieved between Ne_6 and Ne_3. Level Ne_2 is metastable and thus tends to collect atoms.

- The atoms from this level fall back to the ground level mainly through collisions with the walls of the tube. As Ne_2 is metastable, it is possible for the atoms in this level to absorb the spontaneously emitted radiation in $Ne_3 \rightarrow Ne_2$ transition to be re-excited to Ne_3. This tends to reduce the effect of inversion.

- It is for this reason that the gain in this laser transition is found to increase with decreasing tube diameter.

(d) Transition within Neon and Continuous Output

- The other two important wavelengths from the He - Ne laser correspond to the $Ne_4 \rightarrow Ne_3$ (1.15 µm) and $Ne_6 \rightarrow Ne_5$ (3.39 µm) transitions. The laser can be made to oscillate at 6328 A° by using optical elements (multilayer coated mirrors) in the path. These lasers are continuous, because the collision process maintains the energy states Ne_6 and Ne_4 at larger population densities than the lower states. This continued population inversion gives a continuous lasing action.

- A typical He - Ne laser operates with a current of 10 mA at a D.C. voltage of 2500 V and gives an optical output of 5 mW. It's efficiency is then $\dfrac{5 \times 10^{-3}}{2500 \times 10^{-2}}$ = 0.02 %.

- This is the only laser radiating in far infrared region. Hence, mostly used in laser **'Raman spectroscopy'**.

5.10 APPLICATION OF LASER IN INDUSTRY   [Dec. 12, May 16]

Laser can be focussed to a very high energy density into a small image (≈ 1 micron in diameter) with the help of suitable lenses. Due to the small size of the image and the control over the energy, lasers are used extensively for cutting, welding and drilling circuits.

1. **Drilling:** A laser beam is also used to drill holes of micron dimensions on printed circuit boards (PCBs). It is also used in resistance trimming in electric components industries. One can drill holes of the diameter of 10 µm through very hard substances like diamond. YAG laser is found to be very useful in such applications.

2. **Welding:** Lasers are used as a heat source in welding the joints of the metals. This type of precise welding is extremely important in micro-electronics in which thin films are used. Thermocouple wires can easily be welded with the help of high power laser beam.

3. **Micromachining:** Lasers are used for machining a surface in a slow and accurate manner to achieve an extraordinarily smooth finish.

4. **Cutting:** Another important industrial application is metal or fabric cutting. A finely focussed laser beam can cut thick and hard metal sheets with high precision and accuracy. It is also used in tailoring industries to cut thousands of layers of cloth at one instant.

5. Due to its intensity and directionality, laser is used in surveying. When tunnels are to be constructed, engineers use the laser beam as a reference, to check that it is being constructed along a straight line. Similarly, it can be used to dig a ditch to a certain prescribed depth. Its most interesting use in surveying has been in measuring the distance from the earth to the moon. This distance was measured to an accuracy of 600 ft, and with the aid of reflectors to within six inches. This accuracy will allow to determine the location of the north pole to within six inches. It is further believed that a laser could be used to check whether the gravitational constant is actually a constant.

6. A laser beam can determine precisely the distance, velocity and direction as well as the size and form of distant objects by means of the reflected signal as in radar. A Lidar (Laser radar), which sends out beams of laser light and detects echoes even from atmospheric layers has been developed.

5.11 APPLICATION OF LASER IN MEDICINE   [Dec. 12]

- Bloodless cancer surgeries can be performed as the beam can be focussed on a small area, so that only the harmful tissue can be destroyed without damaging the surrounding region.

- Laser has been successfully used in ophthalmology, in the treatment of detached retinas, in welding cornea, etc. At the command of the physician, laser produces a beam of light which is directed onto the eye under treatment, to produce a minute coagulation. A series of these lesions weld the detached retina.

- Laser is used as a tool in the study of genetics. Lasers have been built into or are devised to be attached to microscopes. As a high density energy is achieved, it can be used in micro-surgery, micro-burning, etc. Such a microscopic laser can concentrate millions of watts of power per square millimeter into a selected area. For example, a focussed microscope laser can be used to make tiny openings (of 25 μ in diameter) in the cell walls, of say the nervous system, heart, retina, etc. without causing irreversible damage.

- Laser microprobes can be used as dental drills giving an advantage of no heating, no anaesthetic and no pain to the patient. They have also been successfully used for localized treatment of skin growths and blemishes in human beings. A large amount of energy can be transmitted through the skin to interact with deeper different biological materials or structures which are damaged.

5.12 APPLICATION OF LASER IN COMMUNICATION   [Dec. 12]

- In this technology, optical energy is transferred through a guided media, called the **'glass fibre'**. When a beam of light enters at one end of a transparent rod (glass rod say), the light beam is totally internally reflected and gets trapped within the rod.

- A similar behaviour is exhibited by a bundle of fine fibres. A beam enters at one end and is transmitted through the wire to the other end, even when the fibre is curved.

- A bundle may consist of thousands of individual fibres with diameters in the range of 2×10^{-4} cm to 1×10^{-3} cm.

- The study of the properties of such a bundle is known as **'fibre optics'**. One of the most important areas of application of fibre optics is in telecommunication.

- Optical frequencies are extremely large ($\sim 10^{15}$ Hz) as compared to conventional radio waves ($\sim 10^6$ Hz) and microwaves ($\sim 10^{10}$ Hz). Due to the high optical frequency, a light beam acting as a carrier wave is capable of carrying far more information in comparison to radiowaves and microwaves.

- In addition to the capability of carrying a huge amount of information, recently developed fibres are characterized by extremely low losses. Today fibre optic cable is the most promising signal transmitting media.

5.12.1 Optical Fibre

- Optical fibre is a very thin and flexible medium having a cylindrical shape consisting of three sections: (i) the core, (ii) the cladding and (iii) the outer jacket.

Principle of Light Transmission

- The principle of light transmission through optical fibre is total internal reflection. For total internal reflection to take place at the fibre wall, the following conditions should be satisfied:

  ➢ The refractive index of the core material (μ_1) must be greater than that of the cladding (μ_2).

  ➢ At the core-cladding interface, the angle of incidence θ must be greater than the critical angle, where $\theta_C = \sin^{-1}\left(\dfrac{\mu_2}{\mu_1}\right)$.

- When a light ray travels from a denser to a rarer medium, the angle of refraction is greater than the angle of incidence. As the angle of incidence increases, the angle of refraction also increases and for a particular angle of incidence, the refracted ray grazes the interface between the core and the cladding. This angle of incidence is called as the **'critical angle θ_c'**.

- If angle of incidence is greater than θ_C, the ray will be reflected back into the core, i.e. it suffers **'total internal reflection'**. For angles equal to or greater than the critical angle the light will be totally reflected and no light will be refracted. Fig. 5.19 shows total internal reflection.

- When light is incident on core of the fibre optics, it will be refracted and will travel in the core. After some time it will strike one of the core-cladding interface say upper surface. If the angle of incidene is greater than critical angle, it will be totally reflected and remain in the core.

- Now, the reflected light will travel to the lower surface. It is then incident on the lower surface where the same process is repeated and light gets transmitted from one end to the other end as shown in Fig. 5.18.

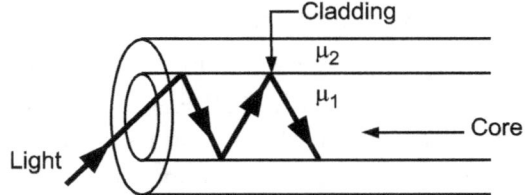

Fig. 5.18: Propagation of light in fibre optics

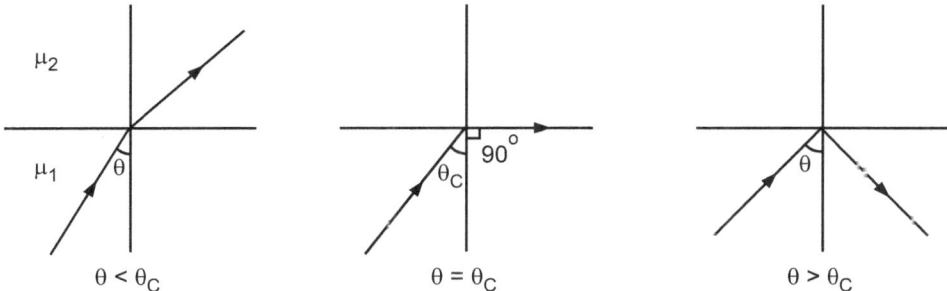

Fig. 5.19: Total internal reflection

5.12.2 Communication Kit

- One of the most important areas of application of fibre optics is in telecommunication. The communication kit consists of a transmitter, optical fibre and the receiver. The block diagram is as shown in Fig. 5.20.

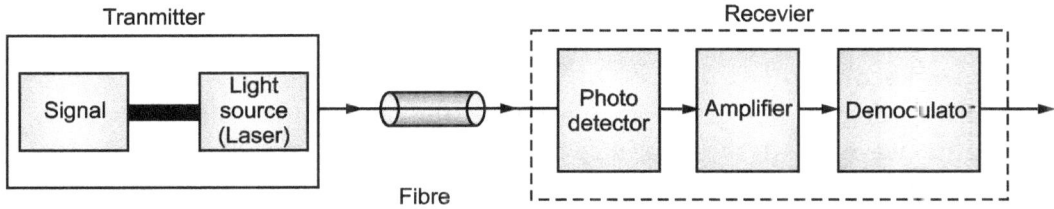

Fig. 5.20: Communication kit

- The transmitter consists of a light source, either LED or laser diode, with a signal. The light beam from the source is connected to the fibre, through optical connections.

- The carrier and signal frequency propagate through the fibre.

- At the other end, it is detected with the help of a photodetector. The received signal is demodulated and the information is stored or displayed by electronic circuits.

5.12.3 Advantages of Optical Fibre

- The optical frequencies are extremely high, of the order of 10^{14} Hz, the information carrying capacity is much higher than radio waves.

- The optical fibres are made of dielectric material, which offers electrical isolation between the transmitting and receiving circuits.

- The material used in fibres is silica glass (SiO_2), which is easily available and its cost is less.

- The fibres are very thin (few μm), light and occupy less space.

- As the transmission is due to total internal reflection, therefore losses are less.

- Does not form standing waves when the impedance of transmitter and receiver do not match.

5.13 APPLICATION IN INFORMATION TECHNOLOGY (HOLOGRAPHY)   [May 13, 14]

Holography

- This is a technique of producing an interference pattern between a direct laser beam and a laser beam reflected from an object on a photographic plate. This pattern on the developed photographic plate, when illuminated with laser in a proper manner, produces a three-dimensional image of the object called a **'hologram'**.

- Holography deals with three-dimensional image of the object whereas photography is a two-dimensional effect. In photography, the photographic plate records only the intensity of light due to the image formed on it. In holography, both the intensity and phase distribution are recorded simultaneously using interference technique. Due to this the image produced by the technique of holography has a true three-dimensional form and is as true as the object itself.

Basic Technique

The basic technique in holography is as follows:

(i) Hologram Recording

➤ The recording of hologram is achieved by superposition of **'the object wave'** with another wave called **'the reference wave'**.

➤ The reference wave is usually a plane wave.

➤ The resulting interference pattern is recorded on a photographic plate. As the shape of the object is very irregular, it results in complicated fringe pattern. Thus a hologram is a record of complicated interference fringe pattern.

➤ Fig. 5.21 shows a typical configuration used for recording a hologram. A portion of a coherent beam (e.g. laser) is allowed to be scattered by the object and the other portion is reflected by a mirror. The former corresponds to the object wave and the latter to the reference wave.

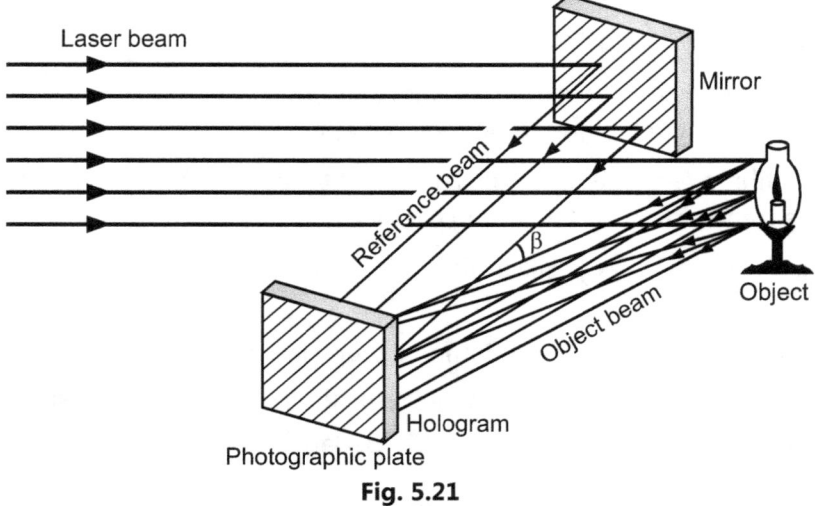

Fig. 5.21

➤ The object wave and the reference wave interfere and the resultant interference pattern is recorded on a photographic plate.

➤ When the photographic plate which has recorded the intensity variation is developed, one obtains a hologram of the object.

➤ The recorded interference pattern forms the hologram and contains information not only about the amplitude but also about the phase of the object wave. Unlike a photograph, the hologram bears little resemblance to the object.

(ii) Hologram Reconstruction

➤ To see the reconstructed image, the hologram is illuminated by the reference beam alone, maintaining the original alignment and orientation. This process is called as **'reconstruction'**.

➤ The developed photographic film (hologram) will have alternate transparent and opaque part of very irregular shape. Thus, it will serve as a diffraction grating when illuminated by the light source.

➤ The light from the hologram will be diffracted inward and outward. One set of diffracted rays will converge to form real image while one set will diverge to form virtual image as shown in Fig. 5.22.

➤ Thus, the hologram can form real as well as virtual images. The geometry of construction can be changed, so as to give more emphasis on real or virtual image.

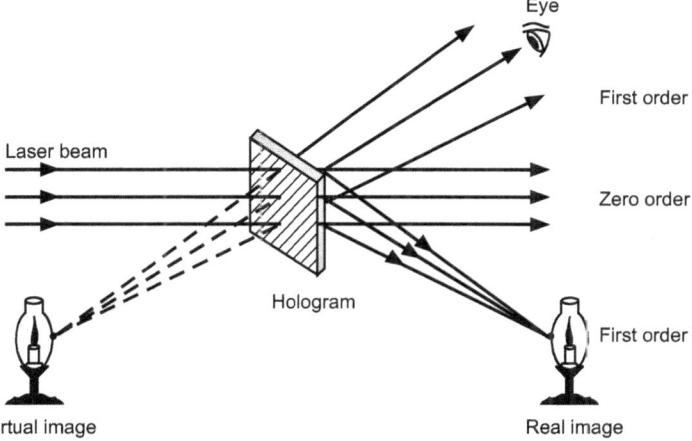

Fig. 5.22

SUMMARY

- The term LASER stands for light amplification by stimulated emission of radiation. It is an intense, coherent, monochromatic beam.

- **Absorption:** Absorption is a process in which a photon, of energy $h\upsilon$, gets absorbed by an atom and it goes from a lower energy state E_1 to a higher energy state E_2.

- **Emission: (i) Spontaneous Emission:** An electron which is raised to an excited state E_2 (due to absorption), spontaneously decays back to a lower energy level E_1

and radiates an energy equal to $E_2 - E_1$. Such an emission is called as spontaneous emission. This emission is random in nature and depends only on the type of atom and type of transition.

(ii) Stimulated Emission: A photon of energy $h\upsilon = E_2 - E_1$ triggers an excited atom to drop to the lower energy state giving up a photon. This phenomenon of forced emission of photons is called as stimulated emission.

- **Population Inversion:** The process of getting a large percentage of atoms into an excited state is called as population inversion.
- **Active System:** A system in which population inversion is achieved is called an active system.
- **Pumping:** A method of raising atoms from lower energy levels to higher energy levels is called as pumping. It can be done by subjecting the atoms to a non-uniform electric field, flooding the gas with high intensity light (optical pumping) etc.
- **Metastable States:** Ordinary energy levels have a life time of 10^{-8} to 10^{-9} secs. Energy levels having a life time greater than ordinary energy levels ($\sim 10^{-6}$ to 10^{-3} secs) are called as metastable states.
- **Types of Lasers:** Lasers are mainly divided into the following categories:
  (i) solid state laser, (ii) gas laser, (iii) semiconductor laser.
  They can be operated in two modes: (a) continuous, (b) pulsed.
- **Solid-State Laser:** Ruby laser is an example of solid-state laser. It produces an intense red beam using a three-level system with a wavelength of 6943 A°. It is a pulsed laser.
- **Gas Laser:** He-Ne laser is an example of a gas laser. It employs a four-level pumping scheme and operates in continuous mode. It produces a beam of wavelength 6328 A°.
- **Semiconductor Laser:** A semiconductor laser is a specially fabricated pn junction that emits coherent light when it is forward biased. The basic mechanism of producing laser in a semiconductor diode laser, is the electron-hole recombination at the pn junction when a current is passed through the diode.
- Light from a laser is different from light from other sources in four basic ways:
  (i) directionality, (ii) monochromaticity, (iii) coherence, (iv) polarizability.
- Due to its unique properties, lasers are used in a variety of fields like welding, machining, surveying, communication, holography, cutting, drilling, information processing, surgery and related medical fields, in CD players, printers, etc.

IMPORTANT FORMULAE

- Rate of absorption, $R_{12} = P_a N_1$.
- Rate of stimulated emission, $R_{21} = P_e N_2$.
- At equilibrium, $P_a = P_e$.
- Population inversion, $N_2 > N_1$.

- Frequency of photons emitted, $\upsilon = \dfrac{E_2 - E_1}{h}$.

- For light transmission in fibre optics, $\theta_c = \sin^{-1}\dfrac{n_2}{n_1}$.

EXERCISE

1. Explain the operation of Ruby laser with a neat labelled diagram.
2. Explain the following terms:
   (i) Spontaneous emission (ii) Stimulated emission (iii) Population inversion.
3. Explain action of gas laser. How does stimulated emission take place with exchange of energy between Helium and Neon atoms ?
4. What is population inversion ? Explain the operation of He - Ne laser.
5. Define and explain the terms:
   (i) pumping   (ii) active systems.
6. What are the different uses to which laser beams are put in industry, medicine ?
7. What are the properties of laser ?
8. Write a note on use of lasers in fibre communication systems and information technology.
9. Write a note on semiconductor laser.

SOLVED UNIVERSITY QUESTIONS

DECEMBER 2012

1. Explain any one application of Laser in brief.   [3]
Ans. Please Refer to Article 5.10, 5.11 and 5.12 on Pages 5.16, 5.17.

MAY 2013

2. Explain the process of recording Holdgram with the help of LASER.   [3]
Ans. Please Refer to Article No 5.13 on Page No 5.20.

NOVEMBER 2013

1. Explain the following:
   (i) Stimulated emission.
Ans. Please Refer to Article 5.4.1 on Page No. 5.2.
   (ii) Metastable state   **Ans.** Please Refer to Article 5.4.3 on Page No. 5.4.
   (iii) Population inversion.   **Ans.** Please Refer to Article 5.4.2 on Page No. 5.3.

MAY 2014

1. What is difference between normal photography and holography? Why lasers are used to record hologram ?   [3]
Ans. Please Refer to Article 5.13 (First two paragraphs) Laser have longer coherence length (of the order of $10''$ λ) hence it is easier to form visible interference and for stable fringes. This frienges when recorded on photographic film, they give high quality hologram. Due to higher coherence length it is also possible to have off-axis hologram Page No. 5.20.

2. Explain only the pumping process in Ruby laser and He-Ne laser.   **[3]**

Ans. Please Refer to Article 5.4.6 (1) and 5.4.6 (2) on Page No. 5.5.

DECEMBER 2014

1. Explain the construction and working of Ruby laser with the help of energy level diagram.   **[6]**

Ans. Please Refer to Article 5.8 on Page No. 5.11.

MAY 2015

1. A laser light of wavelength 6328 A.U. falls normally on a grating which is 2 cm long. The first order spectrum is observed at an angle of 20°. Find the total number of slits on grating.   **[3]**

Ans.

Data:
$$\lambda = 6328 \, A°$$
$$\text{Length of grating} = 2 \text{ cm}$$
$$n = 1$$
$$Q = 20°$$

Formula: (i)
$$(a + b) \sin \theta = n \lambda$$

(ii)
$$N = \frac{1}{a + b}$$

Solution:
$$(a + b) = \frac{1 \times 6328 \times 10^{-8}}{\sin 20} = 1.850 \times 10^{-4} \text{ cm}$$

$$\therefore \quad N = \frac{1}{1.850 \times 10^{-4}} = 5404 \text{ lines/cm}$$

Therefore, total lines on grating of length 2 cm = 5404 × 2 = 10808 lines.

2. Explain with neat labeled diagram construction and working of Ruby laser.   **[6]**

Ans. Please Refer to Article 5.8, Page No. 5.11 to 5.13.

NOVEMBER 2015

1. Explain construction and working of Ruby Laser with the help of energy level diagram.   **[6]**

Ans. Please Refer to Article 5.8, Page No. 5.11.

MAY 2016

1. What is stimulated emission of radiations? Explain its significance in production of laser.   **[3]**

Ans. Please Refer to Article 5.4.1 on Page No. 5.2.

2. Explain any one engineering application of laser.   **[3]**

Ans. Please Refer to Article 5.10 on Page No. 5.16.

✠ ✠ ✠

CHAPTER 6
SOLID STATE PHYSICS

6.1 INTRODUCTION

- From the engineering point of view, knowledge of electric, magnetic and dielectric properties of materials is very essential.

- Basically, solids can be class fied into different categories such as conductors, insulators and semiconductors. The classification of materials from electrical poir: of view into conductors, semiconductors and insulators is based according to their resistivity range.

- For conductors the resistivity ranges from 1.6×10^{-8} to 1.4×10^{-6} ohm-m. The resistivity range of semiconductors and insulators is respectively from 10^{-4} to 10^6 ohm-m and from 10^7 to 10^{16} ohm-m.

- Considering the rapid development of semiconductor electronics, stress has been given to discuss the semiconductor devices in this chapter. Semiconductor devices are high y compact, low power consuming and efficient. They have replaced vacuum tubes to a great extent.

- For a better knowledge of semiconductors, one should understand the properties of semiconductors on the basis of band theory of solids. For this, elementary knowledge of electronic configuration of atoms and quantum numbers is quite essential.

6.1.1 Electron Configuration of Atoms

- Different physical and chemical properties of various elements are attributed to different configuration of electrons in their atoms. The four quantum numbers that specify the electron state in an atom are n, l, m_l and m_s.

- As per **'Pauli's exclusion principle'**, no two electrons in an atom can have the same set of quantum numbers n, l, m_l and m_s. This principle gives the arrangement of electrons in different orbits.

- The various subshells are filled in the following manner:

  ➤ As we go from one atom to the next in the order of increasing atomic numbers, the electrons are added one by one to various shells.

  ➤ Electrons enter different subshells in the order of increasing energy. The subshell of lower energy is filled up first while the higher energy subshell is filled up later.

The sequence of filling different subshells can be remembered from Fig. 6.1.

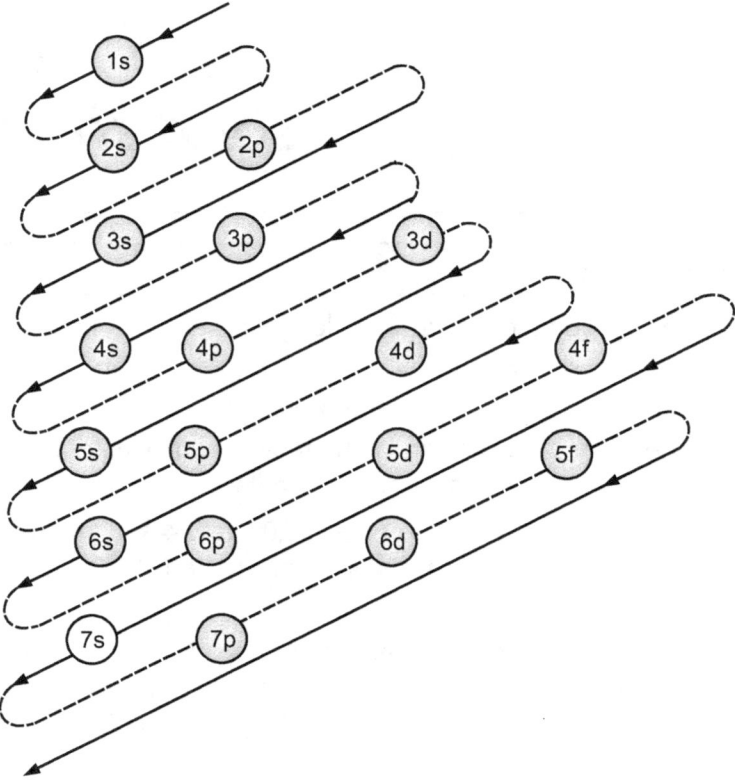

Fig. 6.1

➤ As per Pauli's principle, an orbital cannot have more than two electrons.

➤ According to Hund's rule, electron pairing does not take place in p, d, f orbitals until all the orbitals of the given subshell contain one electron each with parallel spin.

For example, the filling of various orbitals of nitrogen (Z = 7) can be

$1s^2\ 2s^2\ 2p_x^1\ 2p_y^1\ 2p_z^1$

↑	↓

↑	↓

↑	↑	↑

       1s   2s   2p

6.1.2 Electron Energy States of an Isolated Atom

• An isolated atom of an element with atomic number Z and mass number A consists of a positively charged nucleus, with Z protons and (A − Z) neutrons around which Z electrons revolve in different orbitals. The orbits are characterized by a set of four quantum numbers n, l, m_l, and m_s.

- The distribution of electrons in an atom i.e., energy states decide the properties of the element to which the atom belongs. The energy of an electron in an atom depends on n as well as l i.e. energy of the electron is a function of n, l, or $E = E (n, l)$.

- As n and l can have only discrete values, the energy E will have discrete values. The energy states characterized by n, l numbers are generally degenerate i.e electrons with different set of quantum numbers will have the same energy, due to different m_l values for a given l. The state with same n and l will be $(2l + 1)$ degenerate.

- The number of electrons that can have the same energy E (n, l) with given r and l is 2 $(2l + 1)$, the factor 2 is due to two possible values of m_s for each m_l. The state s is non-degenerate and has two electrons. But p, d, f states are respectively 3-fold, 5-fold, 7-fold degenerate and the number of electrons in those states are 6, 10, 14 respectively.

- As such the energy states of an isolated atom will be quite discrete. The energy states of an isolated lithium atom are shown in Fig. 6.2.

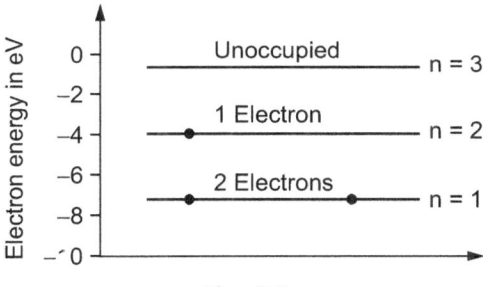

Fig. 6.2

6.2 BAND THEORY OF SOLIDS

- A solid is an aggregate of atoms in very close proximity. For example a crystal is a periodic arrangement of atoms in which the structure is built up by a regular repetition of a small unit called a **'unit cell'**.

- The energy states of an isolated atom consist of discrete energy levels. But when the atoms are brought into close proximity as in a crystal, the outermost or valence electrons of adjacent atoms interact with each other. The inner or non-valence electrons do not interact significantly at any realizable interatomic distance because they are too closely associated with the nuclei.

- As per Pauli's exclusion principle, since not more than two interacting electrons may have the same energy level, new levels must be established which are discrete but only infinitesimally different. The separation between split energy sublevel is of the order of 10^{-28} eV. This group of related levels in a polyatomic material is called an **'energy band'**.

- In short, in crystals or solids, the allowed energy levels of an atom are modified by the proximity of other atoms in such a way that the discrete energy levels of the individual atoms become bands in solids.

- Each band contains as many discrete levels as there are atoms in the material. In a solid containing N atoms, there are N possible energy levels in each band such that, only two electrons of opposite spin may occupy the same energy level. Thus, the N levels will accommodate a maximum of 2N electrons. In other words, a band formed from N atoms contains 2N energy states.

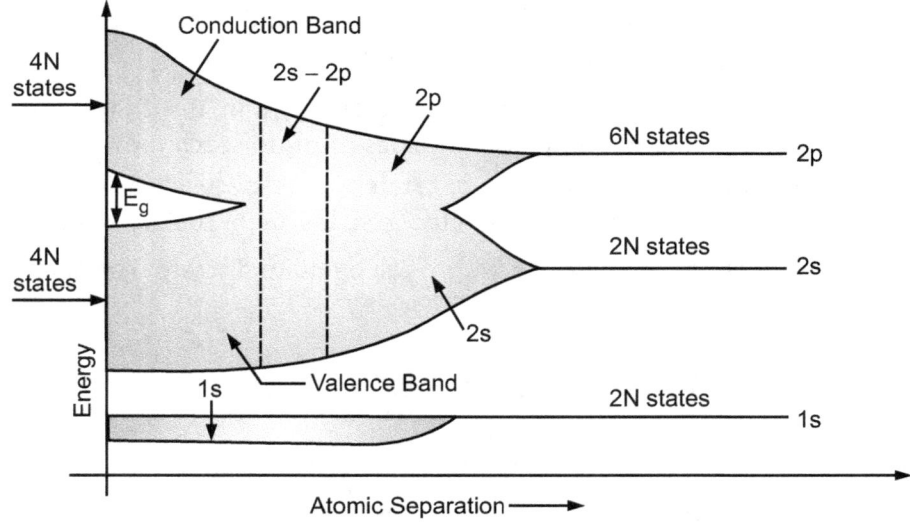

Fig. 6.3: Formation of energy bands in a diamond crystal

- The imaginary formation of a diamond crystal from isolated carbon atoms is shown in Fig. 6.3. Each isolated carbon atom has an electron structure $1s^2 \ 2s^2 \ 2p^2$. Each atom has available two 1s states, two 2s states and six 2p states and higher states.

- If we consider N atoms, there will be 2N states of 1s type, 2N states of 2s type and 6N states of 2p type. As the interatomic spacing decreases, these energy levels split into bands beginning with the outer (n = 2) shell. As the 2s and 2p bands grow, they merge into a single band composed of a mixture of energy levels.

- This band of '2s–2p' levels contains 8N available states. As the distance between atoms approaches the equilibrium interatomic spacing of diamond, this band splits into two bands separated by an energy gap or band gap E_g. The upper band is known as the **'conduction band'** while the lower one is known as the **'valence band'**. Thus, the conduction band contains 4N states and the valence band also contains 4N states.

- So, apart from the low lying and tightly bound 1s levels, the diamond crystal has two bands of available energy levels separated by energy gap E_g. The energy gap E_g does not contain allowed energy levels for electrons to occupy. This gap is also called as **'forbidden band'**.

- The lower 1s band is filled with 2N electrons which originally resided in the collective 1s states of the isolated atoms. However, there were 4N electrons in the original isolated n = 2 shell. (2N in 2s states and 2N in 2p states). These 4N electrons must occupy states in the valence band or the conduction band in the crystal.

- At 0 K, the electrons will occupy the lowest energy states available to them. In the case of the diamond crystal, there are exactly 4N states in the valence band available to the 4N electrons. So at 0 K every state in the valence band will be filled while the conduction band will be completely empty of electrons.

- This arrangement of completely filled and empty energy bands has an important effect on the electrical conductivity of the material. As conduction band is completely empty, the diamond will serve as an insulator.

6.2.1 Valence Band, Conduction Band and Forbidden Energy Gap

Energy Band

- In solids or crystals, allowed energy levels are modified by the proximity of other atoms in such a way that discrete energy levels of individual atoms are converted into series of energy levels. The difference in the energy sublevels is of the order of 10^{-28} eV. This series of energy levels is called *'energy band'*.

Valence Band

- The electrons in the inner shells are strongly bonded to their nuclei while the electrons in the outermost shells are not strongly bonded to their nuclei. It is these electrons which are most affected, when a number of atoms are brought very close together during the formation of a solid. The electrons in the outermost shell are called *'valence electrons'*. The band formed by a series of energy levels containing the valence electrons is known as **'valence band'**.

- The valence band may be defined as a band which is occupied by valence electrons or highest occupied energy band. The valence band is completely filled with electrons at 0 K.

Conduction Band

- The next higher permitted energy band is called the **'conduction band'**. This band may be either empty or partially filled with electrons. Conduction band may be defined as the lowest unfilled permitted energy band. It lies just above the valence band.

- The electrons occupying conduction band are known as *'conduction electrons'* and these electrons move freely in the conduction band.

Forbidden Gap

- The conduction band and valence band are separated by a region or a gap known as *'forbidden band'* or *'forbidden gap'*. This band is collectively formed by a series of nonpermitted energy levels above the top of the valence band to the bottom of the conduction band and is a measure of E_g.

- Thus, E_g is the amount of energy that should be imparted to the electron in the valence band for its migration to the conduction band. These bands are shown in Fig. 6.4.

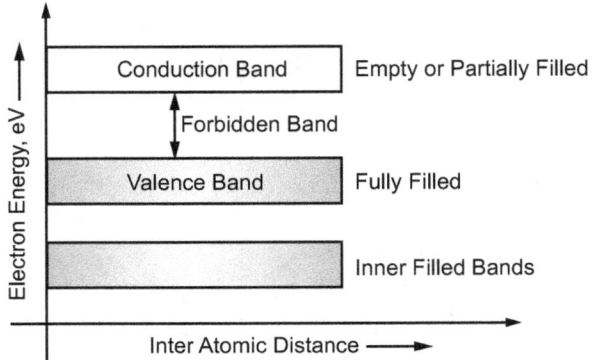

Fig. 6.4: Valence band, conduction band and forbidden gap at T = 0 K

- If a valence electron happens to absorb enough energy, it jumps across the forbidden energy gap and enters the conduction band. Also, if a conduction electron happens to radiate too much energy, it will suddenly reappear in the valence band once again.

6.3 CONCEPT OF ELECTRICAL CONDUCTIVITY

- The electrons in a partially filled conduction band are relatively free to move in the specimen as they are not bound to any atom but are in a band which is shared by the entire crystal. These electrons are called as **'free electrons'**.
- The electrons well inside the specimen are surrounded by positive ion cores from all the sides, hence net force exerted by the iron cores (or lattice points) on electrons is zero. Due to the thermal energy, the electrons are in constant motion with average velocity of 10^5 m/s at room temperature. But the direction of motion of electron is totally random and take a very complex path. This results in net zero current.
- On the way electrons collide with the lattice points which are in vibration motion due to thermal energy. This reduces the velocity of electrons and comes to almost rest. This results in small amount of resistivity and the loss of energy is converted into thermal energy.
- The average time between collisions is called the **'mean free time'** and the length of the path during this free time is called the **'mean free path'**. The mean free paths have different lengths. Fig. 6.5 (a) shows motion of electrons under equilibrium conditions.

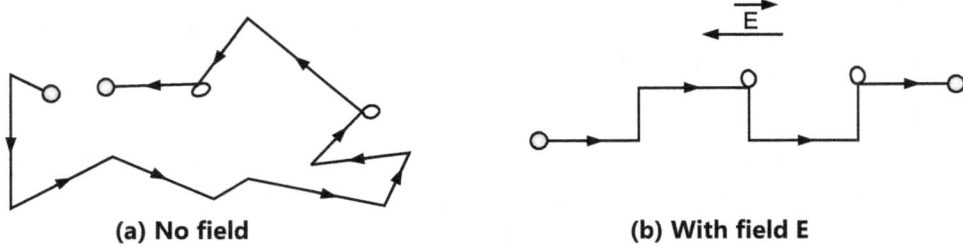

(a) No field   **(b) With field E**

Fig. 6.5: Motion of free electrons

- In presence of field $\vec{E}$, the direction of motion will be directed along the electric field. This results into net current flowing in a particular direction.
- As the electron tries to move in the field, the number of collisions increases. In fact, the external field simply bends the path of the electron between two collisions. In general, the conductivity depends on number of charge carriers and their freedom to move.

6.3.1 Free Electron Theory of Metals

- The free electron theory of metals was first proposed by Drude and later improved by Lorentz and hence the theory is called the Drude-Lorentz theory. Following are the basic assumptions made in the theory.

  ➢ All metals contain a fixed number of valence electrons forming an **electron gas**, which are free to move throughout the volume of the metal like molecules of a gas.

  ➢ The electron velocities in metals obey the classical **Maxwell-Boltzmann distribution** of velocities.

  ➢ The positive ions which can vibrate about their mean position, cannot move from one lattice site to another. The repulsive force between the negatively **charged electron** is ignored and the electric field due to the positive ions is assumed to be uniform.

  ➢ The electrons move from one point to another randomly with **random velocity** which is temperature dependent. At room temperature, this velocity is about 4×10^5 m/s.

  ➢ The **kinetic energy** of the electron is given by 3 kT/2, where k is Boltzmann's constant and T is absolute temperature.

  ➢ In absence of external electric field, the electrons move in **random directions**, making collisions from time to time with positive ions, which are fixed in lattice. This makes net current zero.

  ➢ When an electric field is applied, free electrons move towards positive terminal of the supply. Thus, the electrons will experience two motions – random motion due to temperature and drift motion due to applied voltage. As a result the electron will move in **opposite direction to the electric field** while maintaining their random motion.

  ➢ While drifting towards positive of the supply, the electrons colloid with positive ions. During each collision the electron loses all its drift velocity and starts from rest once again. The average distance covered by an electron between collisions is known as **mean free path** 'λ' and time taken to cover this distance is termed as relaxation time 'τ'.

  ➢ As the temperature increases, the vibration of the ion core increases this increases the probability of electron-core collision. As a result, **resistivity increases with increase in temperature**.

6.3.2 Free Electron Theory - Quantum Mechanical Treatment

- Quantum mechanical behaviour of electron gas was first investigated by Sommerfeld.
- The main failure of the classical theory was that it was developed on the basis of Boltzmann statistics. The quantum theory was developed on the basis of Fermi-Dirac statistics and is successful in explaining the behaviour of electron cloud.
- In Sommerfeld's model, it is assumed that the free electrons are the valence electrons of the atoms of the metals. The alkali metals contribute one electron per atom. These electrons are free to move within the metal but cannot come out of the metal surface due to presence of high potential barrier at the surface.
- The potential inside the conductor is zero. Thus, the metal acts as a potential well for the free electrons.

6.3.3 Drawbacks of Classical Free Electron Theory

- The free electron theory, successfully established Ohm's law, showed that the resistivity is directly proportional to the temperature and the Wiedemann-Franz relation was proved. However, the theory has many drawbacks.

The main drawbacks are:

- ➤ The specific heat capacity value based on classical theory shows that it is independent of temperature. But as per quantum theory, it directly depends on temperature i.e. it increases with the increase in temperature.
- ➤ As per classical theory, the paramagnetic susceptibility is inversely proportional to the temperature. But experimental results show that it is almost independent of temperature.
- ➤ The classical theory failed to explain occurrence of long mean free paths (10^8 or 10^9 times interatomic spacing).
- ➤ Classification of solids on band theory i.e. metals, semimetals, semiconductors and insulators cannot be done by classical theory.
- ➤ The positive values of Hall coefficient of metals could not be explained by classical theory.
- ➤ Classical theory also failed to explain photoelectric effect, Compton effect and black body radiation.

6.4 ELECTRICAL CONDUCTIVITY OF CONDUCTORS AND SEMICONDUCTORS

6.4.1 Conductivity of Conductors

- According to the free electron model of an atom, the valence electrons are not attached to individual atoms. They move about freely along all directions among the atoms. These free electrons are called as conduction electrons and they form the *'free electron cloud'* or *'free electron gas'* or *'Fermi gas'*.

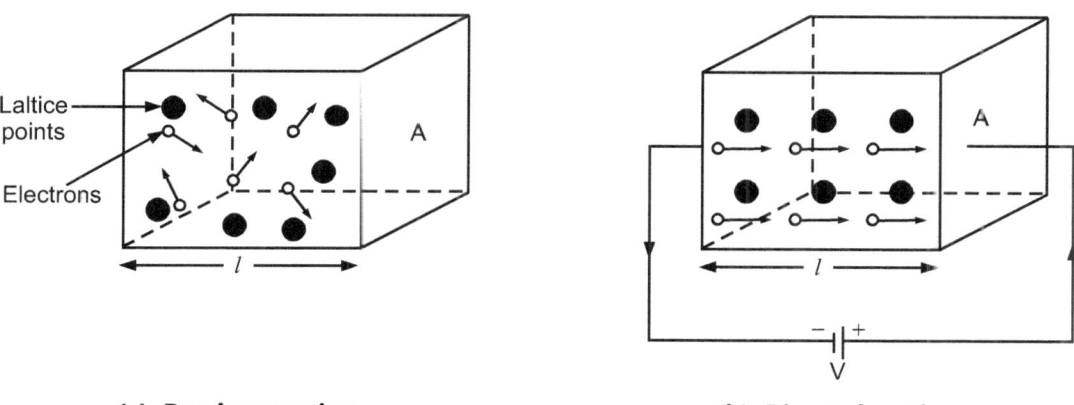

(a) **Random motion**   (b) **Directed motion**

Fig. 6.6: Current flow in conductors

- In the absence of an external electrical field, the electrons move randomly in all directions [See Fig. 6.6 (a)]. When an electric field is applied to the metal, the random motion becomes directed [See Fig. 6.6 (b)]. This type of directed motion is known as **'drift'**. The drift velocity v of the electrons depends upon the electron mobility μ_e and the applied electric field E.

- The drift velocity v is given by

$$v = \mu_e E \qquad \qquad \text{... (1)}$$

Let   A = conductor cross-section area

n = electron density (i.e. number of free electrons per unit volume of the conductor)

l = length of the conductor

V = voltage applied across the two ends of the conductor

E = electric field applied.

- Then the charge crossing the cross-section 'A' of the conductor in unit time is equal to n × (v × A) e. This rate of flow of charge constitutes the current.

i.e. $$I = n v A e \qquad \qquad \text{... (2)}$$

Substituting for v from equation (1), we get

$$I = n \mu_e E A e \qquad \qquad \text{... (3)}$$

Now, substituting for $E = \dfrac{V}{l}$ in equation (3), we get

$$I = n \mu_e \frac{V}{l} A e \qquad \qquad \text{... (4)}$$

$$\therefore \qquad \frac{V}{I} = \frac{l}{A} \cdot \frac{1}{n\mu_e\, e} \qquad \qquad \ldots (5)$$

By Ohm's law, we have, $\qquad R = \frac{V}{I} \qquad \qquad \ldots (6)$

$$\therefore \qquad R = \frac{l}{A} \cdot \frac{1}{n\,\mu_e\, e} \qquad \qquad \ldots (7)$$

But $\qquad \qquad R = \rho\, \frac{l}{A} \qquad \qquad \ldots (8)$

where ρ is the resistivity of the conductor. Comparing equations (7) and (8), we get,

$$\rho = \frac{1}{n\,\mu_e\, e} \qquad \qquad \ldots (9)$$

The unit of ρ is ohm-m.

- Conductivity 'σ' is defined as the reciprocal of resistivity.

$$\therefore \qquad \text{Conductivity,} \quad \sigma = \frac{1}{\rho} = n\, e\, \mu \ \text{mho/m} \qquad \qquad \ldots (10)$$

- Now, current density J is defined as the current flowing across the unit cross section.

From (3), we have, $\qquad J = \frac{I}{A} = n\, e\, \mu_e\, E \qquad \qquad \ldots (11)$

From (10) and (11), we have $\quad J = \sigma E \quad$ or $\quad \sigma = \frac{J}{E}$

6.4.2 Conductivity in a Semiconductor

Fig. 6.7 shows the total current flow in a semiconductor. This current is a sum of current flow due to electron flow and hole flow.

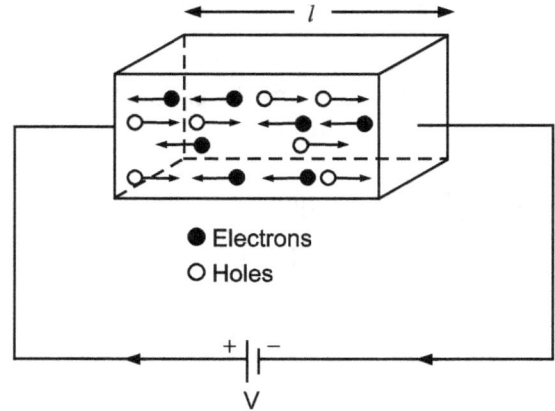

● Electrons
○ Holes

Fig. 6.7: Current flow in a semiconductor

In a semiconductor, let

n_e = electron density in the conduction band

n_p = hole density in valence band

μ_e = electron mobility

μ_p = hole mobility

v_e = drift velocity of electrons

v_p = drift velocity of holes

A = cross section of the semiconductor

V = voltage applied across the semiconductor of length l

The current due to electrons is given by

$$I_e = n_e v_e Ae \quad \dots (1)$$

and the current due to holes is given by

$$I_p = n_p v_p Ae \quad \dots (2)$$

Therefore, total current flowing through the semiconductor will be,

Total current, $I = I_e + I_p$

$$I = n_e v_e Ae + n_p v_p Ae$$

∴
$$I = Ae(n_e v_e + n_p v_p) \quad \dots (3)$$

The drift velocity of a charged particle in electric field E is,

$$v = \mu E$$

∴ For electrons,
$$v_e = \mu_e E$$

and for holes,
$$v_p = \mu_p E$$

But
$$E = \frac{V}{l}$$

∴
$$v_e = \mu_e \frac{V}{l} \quad \dots (4)$$

$$v_p = \mu_p \frac{V}{l} \quad \dots (5)$$

Substituting equations (4) and (5) in equation (3), we get

$$I = Ae\left(n_e \mu_e \frac{V}{l} + n_p \mu_p \frac{V}{l}\right)$$

$$I = \frac{AeV}{l}(n_e \mu_e + n_p \mu_p) \quad \dots (6)$$

$$\therefore \qquad R = \frac{V}{I} = \frac{l}{Ae\,(n_e\,\mu_e + n_p\,\mu_p)} \qquad \text{... (7)}$$

But
$$R = \rho\,\frac{l}{A} \qquad \text{... (8)}$$

$\therefore$ Resistivity of the given semiconductor is given by [comparing equations (7) and (8)],

$$\rho = \frac{1}{e\,(n_e\mu_e + n_p\,\mu_p)} \ \text{ohm-m} \qquad \text{... (9)}$$

The conductivity is reciprocal of resistivity.

$\therefore$ Conductivity
$$\sigma = \frac{1}{\rho} = e\,(n_e\,\mu_e + n_p\,\mu_p) \ \text{mho/m} \qquad \text{... (10)}$$

Hence, conductivity in a semiconductor is a sum of conductivity due to both electrons and holes.

Or
$$\sigma_{sc} = \sigma_e + \sigma_p$$

From equation (3),
$$\frac{I}{A} = e\,(n_e\,\mu_e + n_p\,\mu_p)\ E$$

$\therefore$ The current density
$$J = \frac{I}{A} = e\,(n_e\,\mu_e + n_p\,\mu_p)\ E \qquad \text{... (11)}$$

From (10) and (11),
$$J = \sigma E$$

Case (i): Intrinsic Semiconductor

•   For intrinsic semi conductors, number of electrons and holes are exactly same,

$$n_e = n_p = n_i$$

$\therefore$ Conductivity of an intrinsic semiconductor is

$$\sigma_i = e\,n_i\,(\mu_e + \mu_p)$$

Case (ii): N-type Extrinsic Semiconductor

•   For N-type semiconductors, electron concentration is much greater than the hole concentration.

$\therefore$
$$n_e \gg n_p \quad \text{or} \quad n_e\,\mu_e \gg n_p\,\mu_p$$

Hence
$$\sigma_N \approx e\,n_e\,\mu_e$$

•   If n_a is electron concentration or concentration of donor atoms,

then,
$$\sigma_N \approx e\,n_d\,\mu_e \quad (\text{as } n_e \approx n_d)$$

Case (iii): P-type Extrinsic Semiconductor

- In P-type semiconductor, electron concentration is negligibly small in comparison to hole concentration.

    Then $n_p >> n_e$ or $n_p \mu_p >> n_e \mu_e$

    $\therefore$ $\sigma_p \approx e\, n_p\, \mu_p$

- If n_a is acceptor atom concentration then $\sigma_p \approx e\, n_a\, \mu_p$ (as $n_p \approx n_a$)

6.4.3 Influence of External Factors on Conductivity   [Nov. 13]

- The conductivity of a solid depends basically on the charge concentration or charge density present in the sample. Different factors such as presence of impurity, temperature and light affect the concentration of charge carriers and therefore the conductivity.

1. **Temperature**

   ➤ In case of metals, the increase in temperature increases the vibrations of lattice points. As the amplitude of vibrations is greater, changes of collision with electrons increase. This decreases the drift velocity of the free electrons. Thus the conductivity decreases and resistivity increases with temperature in metals.

   ➤ In case of semiconductors as the energy gap between valence band and conduction band is small, a rise in temperature excites an electron from valence to conduction band. This creates electron-hole pair and both will participate in conduction.

   ➤ As the conduction charge density increases with temperature, the conductivity also increases. Therefore, in semiconductors the resistivity decreases with increase in temperature. Fig. 6.8 shows the variation of resistivity with temperature.

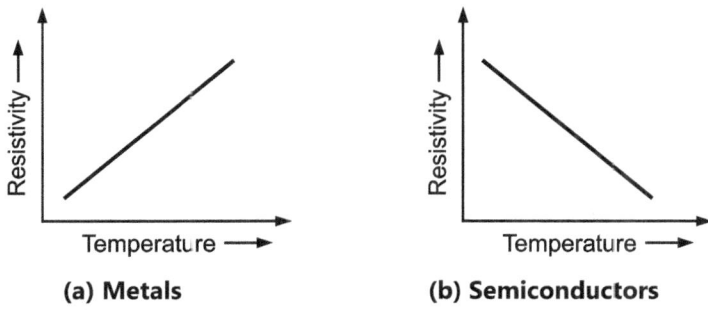

(a) Metals   (b) Semiconductors

Fig. 6.8: Variation of resistivity with temperature

2. **Light**

   ➤ In metals, whenever a light is incident and energy of photon is more than a critical value, an electron is ejected from a metal surface. But this does not affect the overall resistivity of the metal. Therefore, the resistivity of metals do not depend on light.

➤ Just like temperature affects the resistivity of semiconductors, light also affects the resistivity. When photon of energy equal to the band gap is incident on the semiconductor, the photon will be absorbed and an electron will be excited to the conduction band leaving a hole in the valence band.

➤ This increase in the number of conduction charge carriers increases the conductivity and decreases the resistivity. Fig. 6.9 shows the variation of resistivity with light intensity.

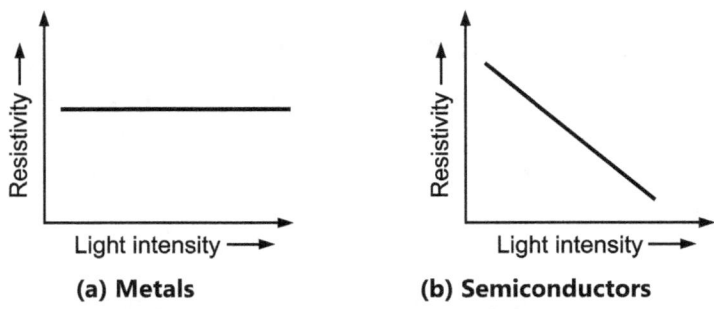

(a) Metals   (b) Semiconductors

Fig. 6.9: Variation of resistivity with light intensity

3. Impurity

➤ In metals, the presence of impurity increases the scattering of conduction electrons at impurity atoms, thereby decreasing the drift velocity. The fall in drift velocity results in increase in resistivity and decrease in conductivity. As the changes of collision increases with impurity concentration, the resistivity also increases with impurity concentration.

➤ On the other hand, in semiconductors the addition of proper impurity (doping) increases the concentration of charge carriers (electrons or hole). This increases the conductivity and decreases the resistivity with the impurity concentration. Fig. 6.10 shows the variation of resistivity with impurity concentration.

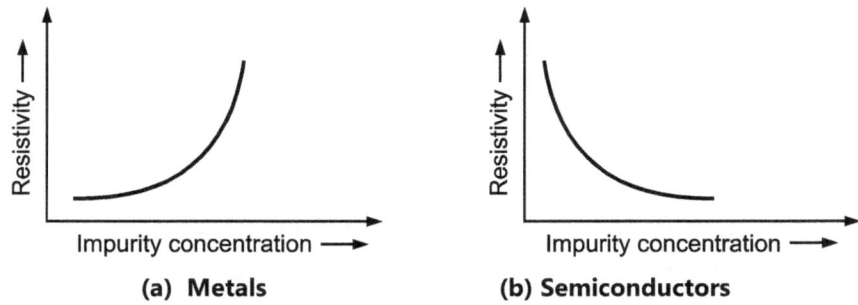

(a) Metals   (b) Semiconductors

Fig. 6.10: Variation of resistivity with impurity concentration

➤ The above features cannot be explained be classical physics. They can be completely explained only on the basis of quantum physics of solids, which is popularly called as the **band theory of solids**.

SOLVED PROBLEMS

Problem 6.1: *Calculate the current produced in a small Germanium plate of area 1 cm² and of thickness 0.3 mm when a P.D. of 2 V is applied across the faces.*

Given:	$n_i = 2 \times 10^{19} /m^3$
	$e = 1.6 \times 10^{-19} C$
	$\mu_e = 0.36 \ m^2/volt\text{-}sec$
	$\mu_h = 0.17 \ m^2/volt\text{-}sec$
Solution: Data:	$A = 1 \times 10^{-4} \ m^3$
	$V = 2 \ volts$
	$l = 0.3 \ mm = 0.3 \times 10^{-3} \ m$

Formula:

$$I = n_i \ e \ (\mu_e + \mu_h) \ \frac{V}{l} \cdot A$$

Solution:

$$I = 2 \times 10^{19} \times 1.6 \times 10^{-19} (0.36 + 0.17) \frac{2 \times 10^{-4}}{0.3 \times 10^{-3}}$$

$$= \boxed{1.13 \ amp.}$$

Problem 6.2: *Calculate the conductivity of pure silicon at room temperature when the concentration of carriers is 1.5 × 10¹⁶ / m³ and the mobilities of electrons and holes are 0.12 and 0.05 m²/V - sec respectively at room temperature.*

Data: $n_i = 1.5 \times 10^{16} /m^3$, $\mu_e = 0.12 \ m^2/V\text{-}sec$, $\mu_h = 0.05 \ m^2/V\text{-}sec$.

Formula:

$$\sigma_{in} = \sigma_n + \sigma_p$$

$$\sigma_{in} = n_i \ e(\mu_e + \mu_h)$$

Solution:

$$\sigma_{in} = 1.5 \times 10^{16} \times 1.6 \times 10^{-19} (0.12 + 0.05)$$

$$= \boxed{4.1 \times 10^{-4} \ mho/m}$$

Problem 6.3: *Calculate the conductivity of the Germanium specimen if a donor impurity is added to the extent of one part in 10⁸ Germanium atoms in room temperature.*

Given:	Avogadro number $= 6.02 \times 10^{23}$ atoms/moles
	At. wt. of Ge $= 72.6$
	Density of Ge $= 5.32 \ g/cm^3$
	Mobility $\mu_e = 3800 \ cm^2/ V\text{-}sec$
Formula:	$\sigma \approx e \ n_d \ \mu_e$

Solution: Concentration of Ge atoms

$$= \frac{6.02 \times 10^{23}}{72.6} \times 5.32$$

$$= 4.41 \times 10^{22} \text{ /cm}^3$$

Since there is one donor atom per 10^8 Germanium atoms then

$$n_d = \frac{4.41 \times 10^{22}}{10^8} = 4.41 \times 10^{14} \text{ / cm}^3$$

In N-type semiconductor, $n > p$

then $\sigma = e \, n_d \, \mu_e$

$$= 1.6 \times 10^{-19} \times 4.41 \times 10^{14} \times 3800$$

$$= \boxed{0.268 \text{ mho/cm.}}$$

Problem 6.4: *The resistivity of an n-type semiconductor is 10^{-6} Ω cm. Calculate the number of donor atoms which must be added to obtain the resistivity.*

Given: $\mu_e = 1000$ cm²/V-sec.

Data: $\rho = 10^{-6}$ Ω cm

$$\mu_e = 1000 \text{ cm}^2/\text{V-sec}$$

Formula: **Resistivity** $\rho \approx \dfrac{1}{n_d \, e \, \mu_e}$

Solution: $n_d = \dfrac{1}{\rho \, e \, \mu_e}$

$\therefore$ $n_d = \dfrac{1}{10^{-6} \times 1.6 \times 10^{-19} \times 1000}$

$$= \boxed{6.25 \times 10^{21} \text{ atoms.}}$$

Problem 6.5: *Calculate the conductivity of extrinsic silicon at room temperature if the donor impurity added is 1 in 10^8 silicon atoms.*

Given: At room temperature,

$$n_i = 1.5 \times 10^{10} \text{ per cm}^3$$

$$\mu_e = 1300 \text{ cm}^2 \text{ / volt-sec}$$

and number of silicon atoms per unit volume = 5×10^{22}.

Formula: $\sigma_n \approx n e \, \mu_e$

Solution: If there is 1 donor atom per 10 silicon atoms, then the number of donor atoms per cm³

$$n_d = \frac{\text{number of silicon atoms/unit volume}}{10^8}$$

$$= \frac{5 \times 10^{22}}{10^8} = 5 \times 10^{14}$$

Assuming all the donors are ionised and n >> p, hole conduction can be neglected.

$$\therefore \qquad \sigma_n = n\, e\, \mu_e$$

$$\sigma_n = n_d\, e\, \mu_e$$

$$= 5 \times 10^{14} \times 1.6 \times 10^{-19} \times 1300$$

$$= \boxed{0.104 \text{ mho/cm.}}$$

Problem 6.6: *In Germanium, the energy gap is 0.75 eV. What is the wavelength at which Germanium starts to absorb light ?*

Data: $\qquad\qquad\qquad\qquad E_g = 0.75$ eV

Formula: $\qquad\qquad\qquad \mathbf{E_g = h\upsilon = \dfrac{hc}{\lambda}}$

Solution: Energy gap in a semiconductor is the minimum energy required to shift an electron from the top of valence band to the bottom of the conduction band. If photons of minimum energy $h\upsilon$ are absorbed by a material to enable electrons to cross the energy gap, then

$$h\upsilon = E_g$$

$$\therefore \qquad E_g = h\upsilon = h\frac{c}{\lambda} = \frac{6.625 \times 10^{-34} \times 3 \times 10^8}{\lambda}\, J$$

$$= \frac{6.625 \times 10^{-34} \times 3 \times 10^8}{1.6 \times 10^{-19} \times \lambda}\, eV$$

i.e. $\qquad\qquad E_g = \dfrac{12400}{\lambda}\, eV$, if λ is in A.

$$\therefore \qquad \lambda \cong \frac{12400}{E_g} = \frac{12400}{0.75}$$

$$\therefore \qquad \boxed{\lambda = 1653 \text{ A}^\circ}$$

Problem 6.7: *Calculate the average thermal velocity, the drift velocity and the mobility of electrons in copper in an electric field of 100 V/cm. Calculate also the density of the electric currents. The resistivity of copper is 1.72×10^{-8} ohm-m at 25°C. Boltzmann constant is 1.38×10^{-23} J/K, density of copper is 8.9×10^3 kg/m³ and At. wt. is 63.54.*

Data: $\quad E = 100$ V/cm, $\quad \rho = 1.72 \times 10^{-8}\, \Omega$-m,

$\qquad\quad k = 1.38 \times 10^{-23}$ J/K, $\quad$ density $= 8.9 \times 10^3$ kg/m³, At. wt. = 63.54.

Formulae: (i) $v = \sqrt{\dfrac{3kT}{m}}$, (ii) $v_d = \mu E$, (iii) $\sigma = ne\mu = \dfrac{1}{\rho}$.

Solution: At equilibrium, the electrons follow the Maxwell-Boltzmann distribution. So their average K.E. for each degree of freedom is $\dfrac{1}{2}kT$. For particles moving in three dimensions, we can write,

$$\frac{1}{2}mv^2 = \frac{3}{2}kT$$

$$\therefore \qquad v = \left(\frac{3\,kT}{m}\right)^{1/2} = \left(\frac{3 \times 1.38 \times 10^{-23} \times 298}{9.1 \times 10^{-31}}\right)^{1/2}$$

$$v = 1.16 \times 10^5 \text{ m/sec.}$$

Since each copper atom contributes one valence electron to the conduction band, the number of electrons/m³ will be equal to the number of copper atoms/m³.

$$\therefore \qquad \text{No. of electrons/m}^3 = n = \frac{6.02 \times 10^{26} \times 8.9 \times 10^3}{63.54}$$

$$= 0.84 \times 10^{29} \text{ atoms/m}^3$$

$$\text{Mobility } \mu = \frac{1}{\rho \cdot n \cdot e}$$

$$\mu = \frac{1}{1.72 \times 10^{-8} \times 0.84 \times 10^{29} \times 1.6 \times 10^{-19}}$$

$$= 4.33 \times 10^{-3} \text{ m}^2/\text{volt-sec}$$

$$\text{Drift velocity } v_d = \mu \cdot E$$

$$= 4.33 \times 10^{-3} \times 100$$

$$\therefore \qquad \boxed{v_d = 0.433 \text{ m/sec.}}$$

Problem 6.8: *Calculate the conductivity of pure silicon at room temperature when the concentration of carriers is 1.6×10^{10} /cm³.* **(May 04, Dec. 14)**

$$\mu_e = 1500 \text{ cm}^2/\text{volt-sec}$$

$$\mu_h = 500 \text{ cm}^2/\text{volt-sec at room temperature}$$

Data:

$$n_i = 1.6 \times 10^{10}/\text{cm}^3$$

$$\mu_e = 1500 \text{ cm}^3/\text{V-sec}$$

$$\mu_n = 500 \text{ cm}^3/\text{V-sec}$$

Formula:

$$\sigma_{in} = \sigma_n + \sigma_p$$

Solution:

$$\sigma_{in} = n_i \, e \, (\mu_e + \mu_n)$$

$$= 1.6 \times 10^{10} \times 1.6 \times 10^{-19} \, (1500 + 500)$$

$$= \boxed{5.12 \times 10^{-6} \, \text{mho/cm}}$$

6.5 FERMI ENERGY   [May 13, 15, 16, Nov. 15]

(a) Fermi Level in Conductors or Metals

- The statement that a solid is composed of N atoms implies that each atomic level split into N-energy levels and bands of energy are formed. The filling of the bands follows a simple rule. States of lowest energy are filled first, then the next lowest and so on, till all the electrons are accommodated.

- The highest filled state is called the **Fermi level** and its corresponding energy is called the '**Fermi energy**' E_F. The magnitude of E_F depends on the number of electrons per unit volume in the solid because the electron density determines how many electrons must go into the bands.

- At 0 K, all states upto E_F are full and all states above E_F are empty.

- At higher temperatures, the random thermal energy will empty a few states below E_F by elevating a few electrons to yet higher energy states. No transitions to states below E_F occur as they are full. Thus, an electron cannot change its state unless enough energy is provided to take it above E_F

- **The highest filled state in the highest energy band which contains electrons in a metal, at 0 K, is called the Fermi level and its corresponding energy is called the Fermi energy E_F.**

(b) Fermi Level in Semiconductors

- In semiconductors, the Fermi level is a reference level that gives the probability of occupancy of states in conduction band as well as in valence band.

- In case of intrinsic semiconductors, the band picture consists of a band of completely filled states called as the '**valence band**' separated from a band of unoccupied states called as the '**conduction band**', by an energy gap E_g. For an intrinsic semiconductor, the Fermi level lies at the centre of the forbidden band, indicating that the states occupied in conduction band are equal to the states unoccupied in valence band. In other words, for every electron in the conduction band, there is a hole in the valence band.

- **So Fermi level in the semiconductors may be defined as the energy which corresponds to the centre of gravity of conduction electrons and holes when 'weighted' according to their energies.**

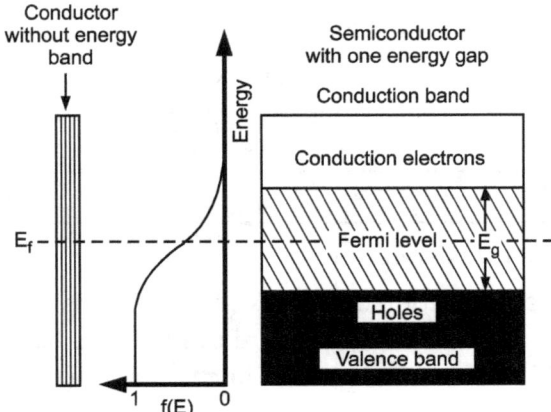

Fig. 6.11

- However, it is to be noted that Fermi level is only an abstraction. A hollow body can have a centre of gravity at the centre where there is no matter. Similarly, a material can have a Fermi level at an energy which is forbidden to all electrons. For example, in an intrinsic semiconductor, the Fermi level is at the centre of the forbidden band.

6.6 DENSITY STATE

- The energy band in a solid can accommodate a large number of electrons in the energy levels. Every energy level in a energy band consists of two states and each state can accommodate only one electron. Thus, an electron can have only two states with opposite spins.

- For understanding the properties of solids it is important how energy levels are distributed in a band and how electrons are distributed in the energy levels.

- It is also important to know the energy states available for accommodating the electrons. The number of states lying in the range of energies between E and E + dE is given by

$$g(E) \, dE \; = \; \frac{4\pi}{h^3} \, (2m)^{3/2} \, E^{1/2} \, dE \qquad \qquad \dots \text{(I)}$$

The function g(E) is known as **density of states function**.

- The **density of states** is defined as the number of available states per unit volume per unit energy interval centered around E. The variation of density of states with energy is shown in Fig. 6.12.

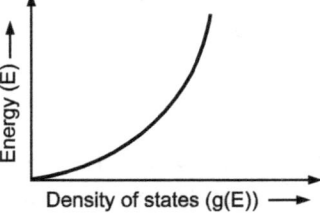

Fig. 6.12: Density of states

- It is seen from the graph that the number of available states decreases with energy and becomes zero at the bottom edge of the band.

- Although the density of states give the number of states that could be occupied by the charge carrier, but at the energy states may not be filled in an energy band.

- A particular energy level E is occupied or not is determined by the probability P(E) that a carrier can have the energy E. Therefore, the number of carriers per unit volume within a given energy range depends both on the number of available states within the range and probability that the carrier can occupy the states.

- The carrier concentration in energy range dE will be the product of the density states and probability of their occupation.

  Therefore, the carrier concentration is given by

  $$N(E) \, dE = P(E) \, g(E) \, dE$$

  where N(E) is the carrier distribution function.

6.7 CONCEPT OF EFFECTIVE MASS OF ELECTRONS AND HOLES

- An isolated electron or free electron moving in vacuum has a well defined mass and obeys Newtonian mechanics when accelerated by an electric field. But inside the crystal an electron is not free to move.

- Consider an electron inside a material moving under the external electric or magnetic field. The electron will experience periodic variation of potential due to ons while moving in the material. Now the electron moving through this changing potential under the action of external electric or magnetic field, the mass of electron is different than free electron in vacuum and is referred as **effective mass of electron**. The effective mass of an electron is denoted by m*.

- The effective mass of an electron is given by the relation.

$$m^* = \left(\frac{h}{2\pi}\right)\left(\frac{d^2E}{dk^2}\right)^{-1} \qquad \ldots \text{(I)}$$

where,   h = Planck's constant

               k = Wave number

               k = Number of complete wave cycles in one meter of linear space

               $k = \dfrac{2\pi}{\lambda}$

- When electron moves inside the lattice, its position in terms of k varies and therefore the effective mass. The effective mass cannot be only greater than m but also less than m. Sometimes, it can be negative also.

- Fig. 6.13 shows the variation of effective mass with wave number. When k = 0, the effective mass of electron approaches the mass of free electron ($m^* = m$). As the value of k increases m^* increases reaching a maximum value at the point of inflection.

- Above the point of inflection, m* is negative and at k → π/a, it decreases to a small negative value, where 'a' is lattice constant.

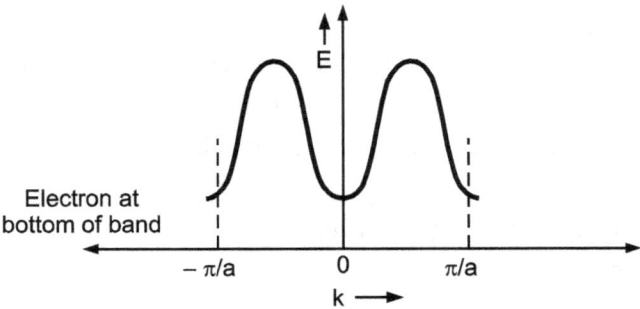

Fig. 6.13: Variation of effective mass with wave number

- The effective mass of an electron depends on its location. The electrons near the bottom of the conduction band have an effective mass equal to mass of the free electron while the electrons near the top of the valence band have negative effective mass.

- Near the bottom of the band, the effective mass m^* has a constant, value which is positive. But as k increases, m^* varies as it is a function of k. Beyond the inflection point, the mass m^* becomes negative, the region is close to the top of the band.

- The velocity of electron decreases for k > k_o, thus acceleration is negative. Therefore, the velocity will be opposite to the applied force, implying a negative mass.

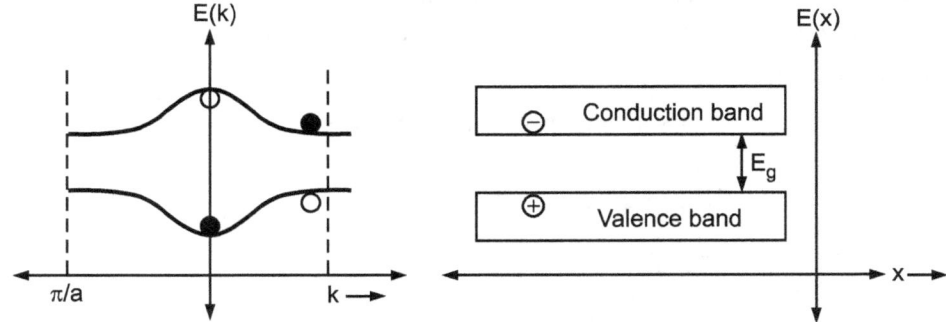

Fig. 6.14: Concept of electron and hole

- In this region of k-space, the lattice exerts such a large retarding force on the electron that it overcomes the applied force and produces a negative acceleration. Thus, in upper half of the band, the removal of a electron with a negative effective mass is identical to creating in its place a particle of positive effective mass. This is termed as **hole** and a hole is considered to have an effective mass m_h^*.

6.8 CONCEPT OF HOLES

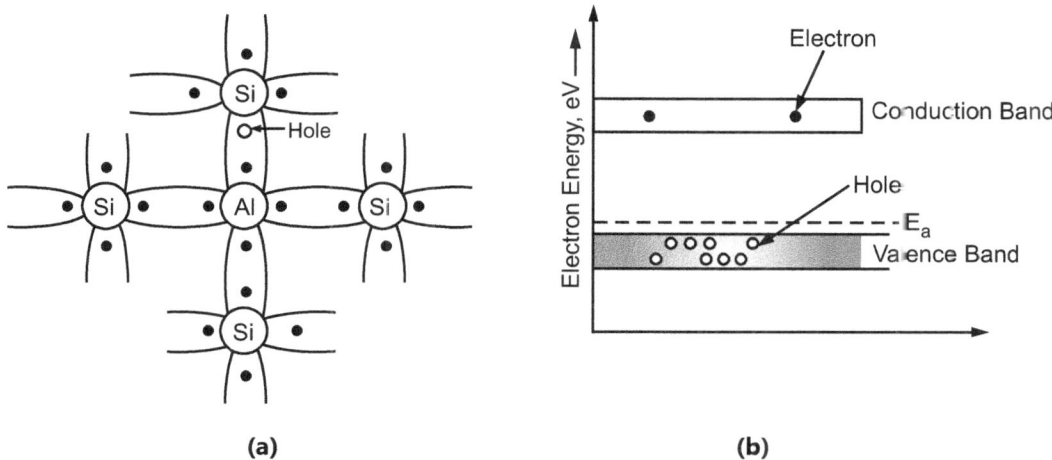

(a)   **(b)**

Fig. 6.15: P-Type semiconductor

• A P-type of semiconductor can be obtained by adding small amount of group III element in the pure germanium or silicon. Indium, gallium, aluinimum etc. are group III elements and they have three valence electrons. The concentration of impurity is very low, hence impurity atom is surrounded by the semiconductor atoms.

• The semiconducting element forms four covalent bonds for stability but impurity has only three electrons, so one bond is left incomplete and gives rise to a **hole** as shown in Fig. 6.15 (a).

• A hole in the cloud of electrons in the valence band is analogous to a bubble in a liquid. A bubble has a shape, size and also velocity and acceleration. In reality a bubble is the absence of liquid. The bubble move by moving the surrounding liquid.

• Similarly, a hole is absence of electron. Instead of considering the complicated motion of surrounding electrons, the motion of absence of electron is referred to as a hole and it is considered as an entity.

6.9 FERMI-DIRAC PROBABILITY DISTRIBUTION FUNCTION

[May 14, Dec. 14]

• An electrons in solids obey Fermi-Dirac statistics. In the development of this type of statistics, the wave nature of electrons and the Pauli's exclusion principle will have to be taken into consideration.

• The result of the statistical arrangement gives the distribution of electrons over a range of allowed energy levels at thermal equilibrium.

i.e. $$P(E) = \frac{1}{1 + e^{(E - E_F)/kT}}$$ ...(1)

where k is Boltzmann's constant.

- The Fermi-Dirac distribution function P(E) gives the probability that an energy state of energy E will be occupied by an electron at absolute temperature T. The quantity E_F is the Fermi energy.

  ➢ For an energy E equal to the Fermi level E_F, the probability of occupation is given by

$$P\,(E_F)\ =\ [1 + e^{(E_F - E_F)/kT}]^{-1} \qquad \qquad ...\,(2)$$

$$P\,(E_F)\ =\ \frac{1}{2}$$

   Thus, an energy state at the Fermi level has a probability $\frac{1}{2}$ of being occupied by an electron for a temperature T > 0 K.

  ➢ At T = 0 K for E < E_F, the term $e^{(E - E_F)/kT}$ = 0 so that P (E) = 1; i.e. the probability of finding an electron with energy less than Fermi energy is unity. Or it can be said that at T = 0 K all energy states below E_F, have a probability of occupancy of unity i.e. they are certainly occupied.

  ➢ At T = 0 K for E > E_F, the term $e^{(E - E_F)/kT}$ = ∞ so that P (E) = 0; i.e. the energy states above E_F have zero probability of occupancy and they are therefore empty. The probability function plotted for different temperatures is shown in Fig. 6.16.

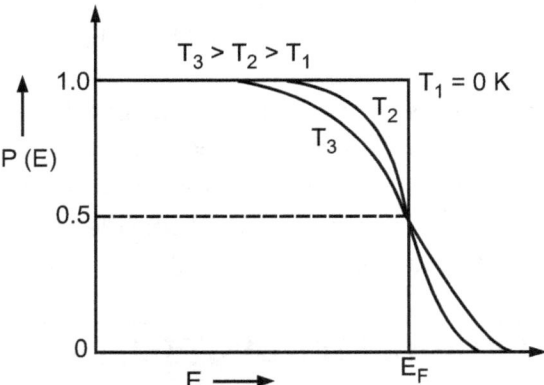

Fig. 6.16: The fermi-dirac distribution function

- The rectangular distribution implies that at 0 K every available energy state upto E_F is filled with electrons and all the states above E_F are empty.

- At temperatures higher than 0 K, some probability exists for states above Fermi level to be filled. When the temperature is raised, there is a greater possibility of electrons being found above the Fermi level with an equal probability of finding a hole below the Fermi level.

6.10 POSITION OF FERMI LEVEL IN INTRINSIC SEMICONDUCTORS

- The Fermi-Dirac probability function is

$$P(E) = \frac{1}{1 + e^{(E - E_F)/kT}} \qquad \qquad \dots (1)$$

and it gives the probability of an electron occupying a state of energy E.

- The derivation of the position of Fermi level in intrinsic semiconductors is based on the following assumptions:

  ➤ The widths of the valence band and conduction band are small when compared to the forbidden gap E_g.

  ➤ As band widths are small, all levels in the band have the same energy. The levels in the conduction band have energy E_c while levels in valence band have energy E_v.

  ➤ At 0 K, the solid is like an insulator i.e. no conduction is possible as valence band is completely filled and conduction band is completely empty.

- At any other temperature say T,

  Let n_c = number of electrons in the conduction band.

  n_v = number of electrons in the valence band.

  $N = n_c + n_v$ = number of electrons in both the bands

  From the probability theory, we have

$$P(E_c) = \frac{n_c}{N}$$

i.e. $\qquad \qquad n_c = N\,P(E_c) \qquad \qquad \dots (2)$

where $P(E_c)$ is the probability of an electron having an energy E_c in the conduction band.

- So, according to Fermi-Dirac probability distribution function defined in equation (1), we have,

$$P(E_c) = \frac{1}{1 + e^{(E_c - E_F)/kT}} \qquad \qquad \dots (3)$$

From equations (2) and (3), $\qquad n_c = \frac{N}{1 + e^{(E_c - E_F)/kT}} \qquad \qquad \dots (4)$

Similarly, $\qquad \qquad n_v = \frac{N}{1 + e^{(E_v - E_F)/kT}} \qquad \qquad \dots (5)$

Substituting (4) and (5) in $\quad N = n_c + n_v,$

$\therefore \qquad \qquad N = \frac{N}{1 + e^{(E_c - E_F)/kT}} + \frac{N}{1 + e^{(E_v - E_F)/kT}}$

Or $[1 + e^{(E_C - E_F)/kT}] [1 + e^{(E_V - E_F)/kT}] = 1 + e^{(E_C - E_F)/kT} + 1 + e^{(E_V - E_F)/kT}$

This gives $\qquad e^{(E_C + E_V - 2E_F)/kT} = 1$

i.e. $\qquad \dfrac{E_C + E_V - 2E_F}{kT} = 0$

or $\qquad E_C + E_V - 2E_F = 0$

$\therefore \qquad\qquad\qquad E_F = \dfrac{E_C + E_V}{2}$

- Thus, Fermi level in intrinsic semiconductors is exactly in the middle of the forbidden gap as shown in Fig. 6.17.

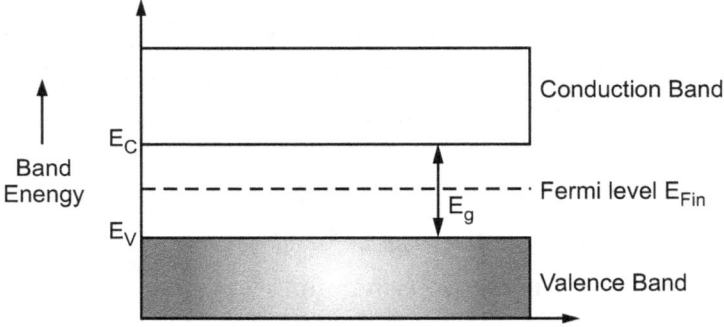

Fig. 6.17: Position of fermi level in intrinsic semiconductor

6.11 POSITION OF FERMI LEVEL IN EXTRINSIC SEMICONDUCTORS   [May 15]

(a) Position of Fermi Level in N-type Semiconductor

- The N-type or pentavalent impurity semiconductor has more conduction electrons than holes. This moves the 'centre of gravity' up so that the Fermi level is above the middle of the forbidden band.

- Donors represent isolated energy levels located very close to the bottom of the unfilled conduction band. (Normally for Ge, 0.01 eV below the lower edge of conduction band). Hence, very little energy is required to raise an electron from the donor level into the conduction band where it is free for conduction of electricity.

- In Fig. 6.18, the energy levels of the impurity atom (donor) are shown as isolated circles not as a band because here atoms are isolated from each other. E_{Fin} represents the position of Fermi level in the case of intrinsic semiconductors.

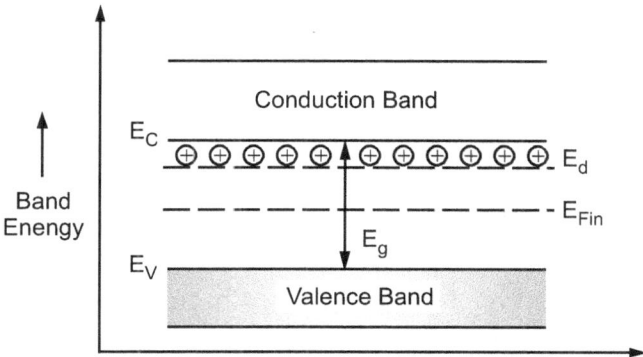

Fig. 6.18: Indicates donor level

- The position of Fermi level in the case of extrinsic semiconductor depends both on the doping and on the temperature. At 0 K all the donor levels are occupied and there are no electrons in the conduction band. Since P (E) = 1 upto the donor levels and P(E) = 0 at the conduction band, Fermi level E_F must be somewhere in the range $E_d \le E_F \le E_C$. (See Fig. 6.19).

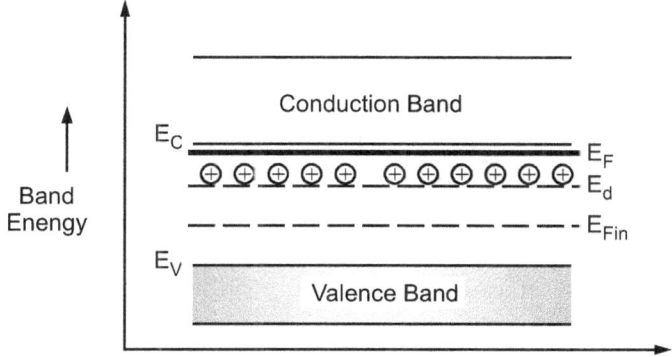

Fig. 6.19: Position of E_F at T = 0 K

(b) Position of Fermi Level in P-type Semiconductor

- In P-type semiconductor, the concentration of holes is greater than that of electrons.

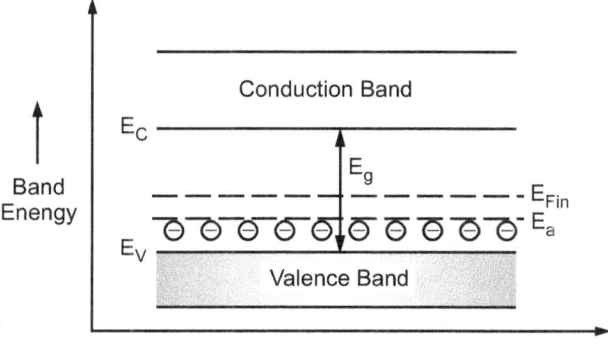

Fig. 6.20: Indicates acceptor level

- This makes the **'centre of gravity'** move down, so that Fermi level is below the middle of the forbidden band. Acceptors represent isolated energy levels, and lie close to the top of filled valence band.

- In Ge, this discrete energy level is only 0.01 eV above the valence band. Hence, a very small amount of energy is required for an electron to leave the valence band and occupy the acceptor energy level. Thus, holes are created in the valence band. Fig. 6.20 indicates the acceptor level in a P-type semiconductor.

- At T = 0 K the Fermi level lies somewhere in the range between $E_V \leq E_F \leq E_a$ (See Fig. 6.21). At this temperature, the conduction band is empty.

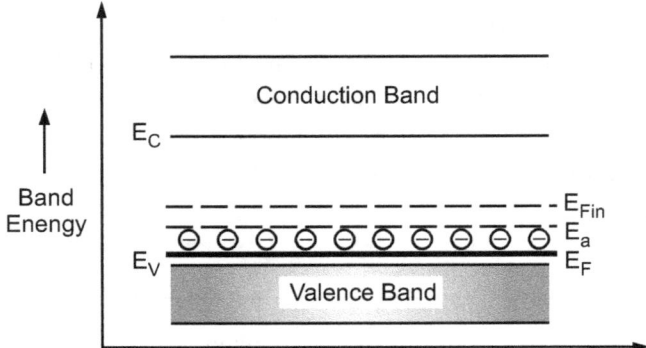

Fig. 6.21: Indicates position of E_F at T = 0 K

6.12 DEPENDENCE OF FERMI LEVEL ON TEMPERATURE AND DOPING CONCENTRATION

- In semiconductors as discussed earlier, the position of Fermi level is not fixed but changes depending upon the type of semiconductor, temperature and doping concentration. Here, we will be discussing the effect of temperature and doping concentration on Fermi level.

6.12.1 Temperature   [May 13, 15]

1. N-type Semiconductor

In N-type semiconductor, the energy levels of donor atoms are very close to the bottom of unfilled conduction band and the Fermi level is above the energy level of donor atoms and close to the bottom of the conduction band.

At Very Low Temperature

- A large number of atoms stay in unionised state for a certain temperature range known as **freeze out range**. Only few donors are ionised and will contribute electron to the conduction band.

- At this temperature, the electrons in the conduction band are just due to donor atoms. As the electron concentration is large in comparison with holes in the valence band, the Fermi level lies above the energy level of donor and bottom edge of the conduction band.

With Increase in Temperature

- As temperature increases, large number of donor atoms ionise and donor level gradually decreases and Fermi level also decreases. At certain temperature, Fermi level coincides with the donor energy level.

- As the temperature is increased further the electron density in conduction band will reach maximum. This is known as **saturation range**.

At Moderately High Temperature

- A further increase in temperature results in generation of electron-hole pair due to the breaking of covalent bond of intrinsic semiconductor atoms.

- As temperature increases, the contribution of electrons due to electron-hole pair creation will become very high, therefore the Fermi level approaches to intrinsic value i.e. at the centre of conduction band and valence band.

- At still higher temperature, the extrinsic semiconductor transforms to intrinsic semiconductor with the Fermi level at the centre. Fig. 6.22 shows the variation of the Fermi level with temperature.

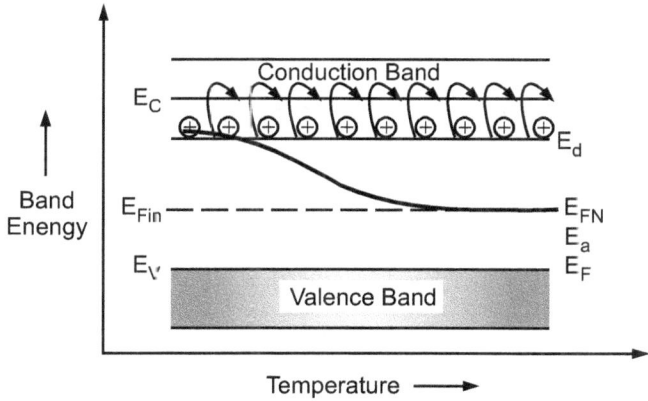

Fig. 6.22: Variation of fermi level with temperature

2. P-type Semiconductor

In P-type of semiconductor, the energy levels of acceptor atoms are very close to top of the valence band and the Fermi level is below the energy level of acceptor atoms and close to the top of the valence band.

At Very Low Temperature

- At very low temperature, all the acceptor levels are empty and only few electrons from valence band are excited to the acceptor level. The Fermi level lies just at the top of the valence band and below the acceptor level.

With Increase in Temperature
- With rise in temperature, the intrinsic semiconductor atoms start ionising. The electrons from valence band will jump to acceptor level leaving holes in the valence band.
- Therefore, the Fermi level starts rising with increase in temperature. The Fermi level will shift from the top of valence band (below acceptor level) to above the acceptor level. At a particular temperature all the acceptor atoms are full and the hole density will reach a maximum.

At Moderately High Temperature
- A further increase in temperature, the valence electrons will gain enough energy to migrate to the conduction band, creates an electron-hole pair.
- At high temperature the contribution of charge carrier by intrinsic process becomes significant and the Fermi level reaches to the intrinsic value $E_{F_i} = E_g/2$. At this temperature the behaviour of extrinsic semiconductor transforms into intrinsic semiconductor type. Fig. 6.23 shows the behaviour of the Fermi level with temperature.

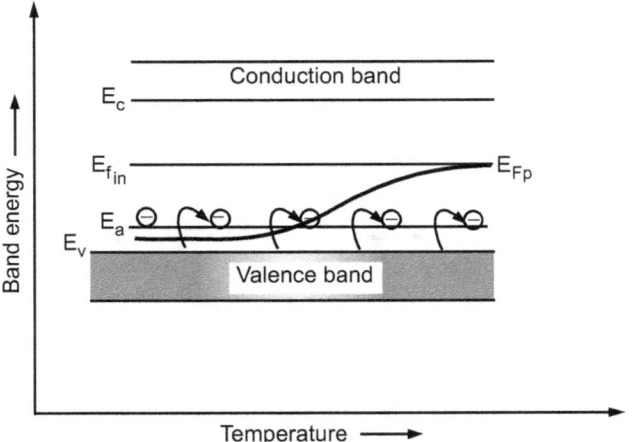

Fig. 6.23: Variation of fermi level with temperature

6.12.2 Doping Concentration

- The impurity atom energy levels are selected in such a way that the energy level of impurity atom is very close to the conduction band (in n-type for donor atom) or the valence band (in p-type for acceptor atom).
- When donor atoms are added to the intrinsic, they form discrete energy level just below the bottom edge of the conduction band as shown in Fig. 6.24 (a). At low impurity concentration, the impurity atoms are placed far apart and they do not interact with each other. Therefore, they show discrete energy levels.
- With an increase in the impurity concentration, the impurity atom separation in the crystal decreases and the interaction between them increases. As a result, the donor

levels split and form an energy band below the conduction band as shown in Fig. 6.24 (b).
- At still larger concentration of the donor atoms the energy band corresponding to the donor level will broaden and will overlap with the conduction band as shown in Fig. 6.24 (c). Thus the donor electrons start occupying upper vacant levels in the conduction band.
- The broadening of the donor energy band decreases the width of the forbidden gap and the Fermi level is displaced upward closer to the conduction band.
- The Fermi level moves closer and closer to the conduction band with increasing impurity concentration and finally moves into the conduction band as the donor band overlaps the conduction band.

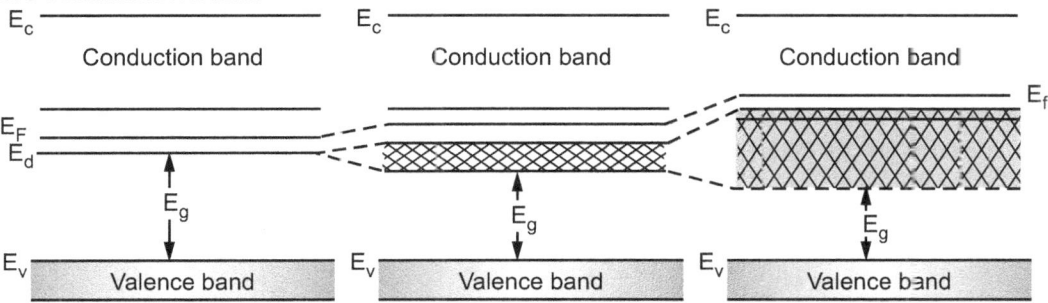

(a) Low concentration (b) Mid concentration (c) High concentration

Fig. 6.24: Variation of fermi level with impurity concentration

- Similarly, in P-type semiconductor, the acceptor levels split and form a band with increasing impurity concentration, which overlap with the valence band at high concentration. The Fermi level moves down closer to the valence band and finally shifts into the valence band.

6.13 DIFFUSION AND DRIFT CURRENT

The flow of current through a semiconductor material is one of the following types:
- Drift current due to motion of charged carrier in presence of an electric field.
- Diffusion current due to redistribution or spreading of charge carriers from areas of higher concentration to lower concentration.

Drift Current
- When an electron is subjected to an electric field in free space it will be accelerated in a straight line from the negative terminal to the positive terminal of the applied voltage.
- The electrons under the influence of electric field will move towards the positive terminal of the applied voltage by continuously colliding with ion cores or lattice points. After every collision, the electron is redirected in the direction of electric field. This produces a drift current which is usual kind of current flow that occurs in conductors or semiconductors.

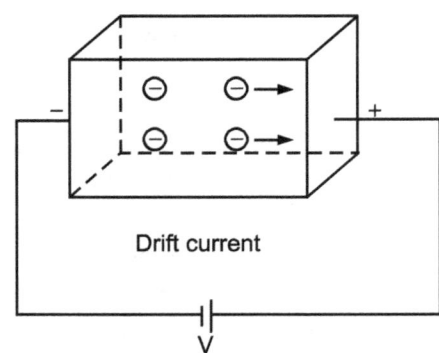

Fig. 6.25: Drift current

Diffusion Current

- In semiconductors in the absence of an external electric field, when there is uneven distribution of charge carriers (either holes or electrons) i.e. the number of electrons or holes is greater in one region as compared to the other region. This is called as *carrier concentration gradient*.

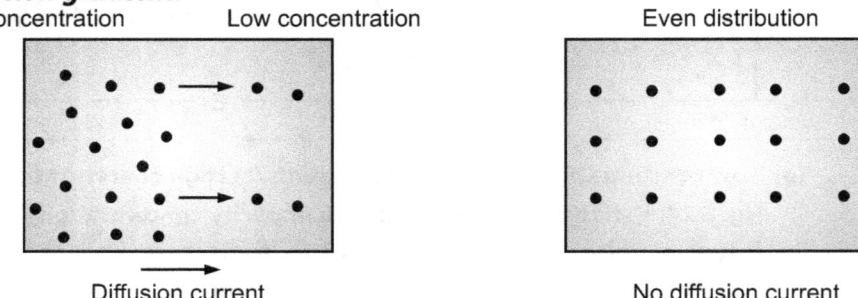

Fig. 6.26: Diffusion current

- As a result of uneven distribution of charge carriers, they tend to move gradually from the region of high concentration to the region of low concentration. The process is called *diffusion*. This directional movement of charge carriers produces a current known as *diffusion current*.

- The process continues until the charge carriers are evenly distributed. After even distribution of charge is achieved, without external electric field, there will no diffusion current.

6.14 P-N JUNCTION DIODE

- When a crystal of a pure semiconductor is doped so that one half of it is P-type and the other half is N-type, then the border between P-type and N-type is called **'P-N junction'**. The P-N junction have non-linear resistance which is the basis for all solid state electronic devices.

- A junction diode is a two terminal device having one P-N junction. The junction diode passes a large current in one direction and almost no current in the other direction. Therefore, such a diode can be used as a rectifier.

- The Fermi level in P-type material is located close to the top of the valence band, whereas in N-type material Fermi level lies close to the bottom of the conduction band.
- The P-type material has more holes than free electrons and the N-type material has more free electrons than holes. When the junction is made between these materials, the holes would tend to move from P-type material into the N-type material and electrons would tend to move from the N-type material into the P-type material, due to the difference in the concentration of holes and electrons on either side of a P-N junction. This process is called as **'diffusion'**.
- The diffused charge carriers combine at the junction to neutralize each other. Due to this neutralisation, a charge free space called **'depletion layer'**, of width of the order of a few microns, is formed near the junction.

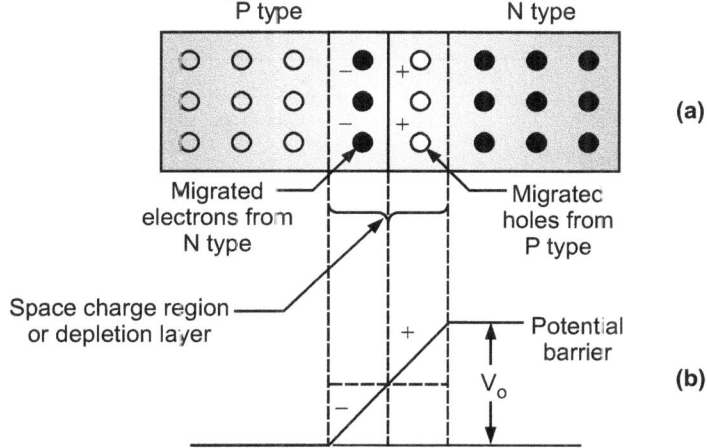

Fig. 6.27: (a) p-n Junction (After joining), (b) Potential barrier

- Due to the diffusion of holes from P to N region, negative ions are produced in P region. Similarly, due to the diffusion of electrons from N into P region, positive ions are produced in N-region. Both these negative and positive ions are immobile and form parallel rows of opposite charges facing each other across the depletion layer.
- Because of this charge separation, an electric potential V_O develops across the junction under an equilibrium condition, i.e. with the junction externally isolated. This potential is called as the **'junction potential'**, or **'barrier potential'** and it can be represented by a battery called as the **'space charge equivalent battery'**. Once the potential barrier is established, further diffusion of majority charge carriers across the junction is prevented.

6.15 ENERGY BAND PICTURE OF A P-N JUNCTION DIODE
[Dec. 12, May 16]

(a) Zero Bias
- Consider a P-N junction formed by fusing a P-type and an N-type semiconductor under unbiased condition. Under this condition, the Fermi level will have to realign such that it exists as a single energy level for the entire specimen.

- This Fermi level in P-type is located close to the top of the valence band whereas in N-type it is close to the bottom of the conduction band. Because the Fermi level is lower on the P-side relative to the N-side, electrons move across the boundary to the P-side and thereby equalize the Fermi levels.

- The band edges in the two specimen shift themselves to make the alignment of Fermi levels possible and the energy band diagram remains no more the same (See Fig. 6.28) but assumes a shape as shown in Fig. 6.29.

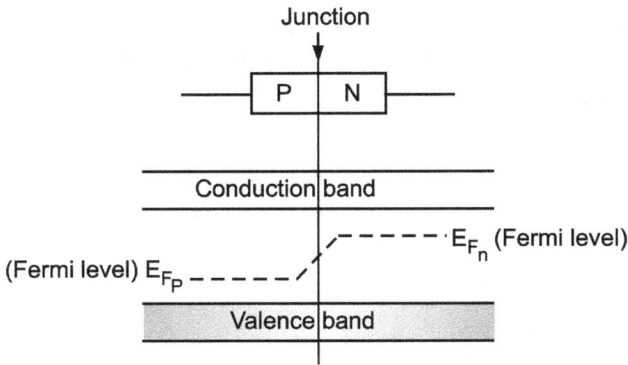

Fig. 6.28: Non-equilibrium energy band picture of a p-n junction

- The conduction band of P-type is shifted upwards by eV_B over the conduction band of N-type where V_B is the **'potential barrier'** across the junction.

- The minority electrons in the conduction band of P-type are at a higher energy than the majority electrons in the conduction band of N-type. Hence, the electrons crossing the junction from P-region will not encounter the potential barrier while the electrons crossing the junction from N-region side will face the potential barrier. The band picture for a zero bias diode at equilibrium is shown in Fig. 6.29.

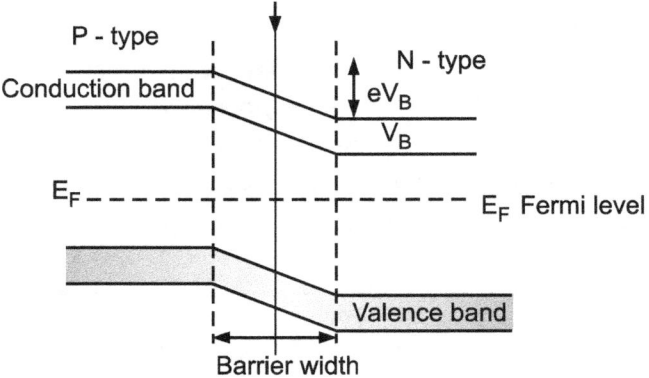

Fig. 6.29: Shifting of the band in P and N-type semiconductors

(b) Forward Bias

- Under forward biasing the P-side is connected to the positive terminal and N-side to the negative terminal of the battery.

- Due to the forward bias, equilibrium conditions are disturbed and therefore energy bands and the Fermi levels are altered. Since in forward bias, negative terminal of the battery is connected to N-type side, the energy of the electrons in the N-side increases by an amount eV, where V is the externally applied voltage.

- Consequently, Fermi level raises by eV and the energy bands adjust their positions so as to suit the elevation of Fermi level.

- Due to the increase in energy in N-type side, the potential barrier is reduced to $e(V_B - V)$ and the barrier width is reduced. Hence the electrons crossing the junction from N-side will now face a low potential barrier and they can easily cross the junction

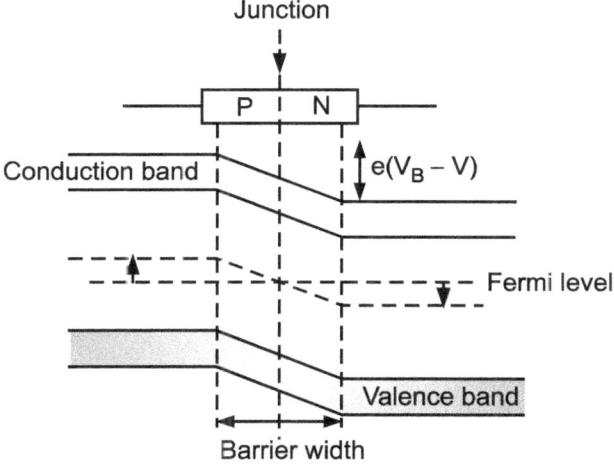

Fig. 6.30: Forward bias

- For conduction to take place in a P-N diode, the forward bias potential should be greater than the barrier potential. Band picture of P-N junction diode in forward bias condition is shown in Fig. 6.30.

(c) Reverse Bias

- In this case, N-side is connected to the positive terminal and P-side to the negative terminal of the battery.

- This lowers the Fermi level on N-side by an amount eV raising the barrier height to $e(V_B + V)$ and thereby increasing the width of the depletion layer. See Fig. 6.31.

- The electrons which are the majority carriers in the N-side will now face a greater potential barrier in crossing the junction. Therefore the number of electrons crossing from N-side to P-side decreases and hence the current is very much reduced.

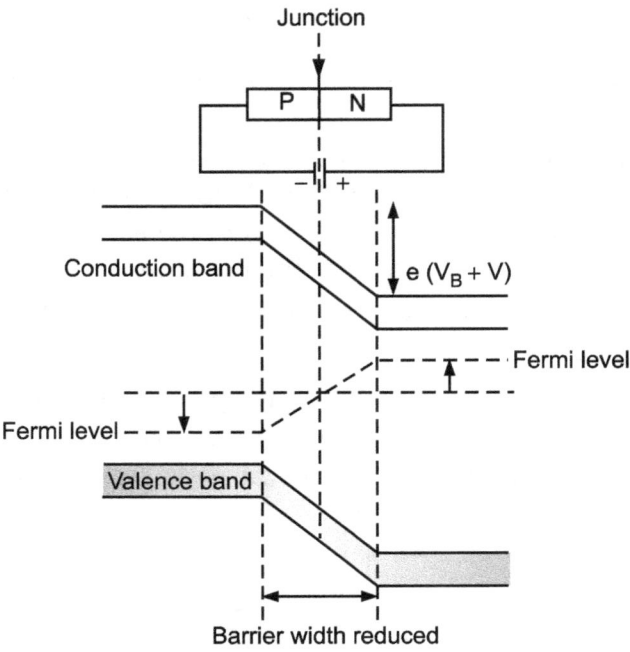

Fig. 6.31: Reverse bias

6.16 THE JUNCTION TRANSISTOR

- The word transistor is derived from **'transfer + resistor'**. Transistors are designed to transform the resistance i.e. electrical magnitudes i.e. voltage and current.

- In electronic circuits the transistor can be used as a solid state **'switch'** or an **'amplifier'**. A transistor consists of two P-N junctions and three layers of semiconductor with different types of doping i.e. P-type and N-type.

- The current flowing through the transistor is because of electrons as well as holes, hence it is also termed as **'bipolar transistor'**.

- The three layers of transistor are emitter, base and collector. The middle part is base and the extreme ends are emitter and collector. These three parts are doped with different types of impurity and different concentration.

- If base is of N-type then emitter and collector will be of P-type. The junction between base and emitter is called **'emitter junction'** or **'emitter diode'** and the junction between collector and base is called **'collector junction'** or **'collector diode'**.

(i) Emitter

> The part on one extremity is called **'emitter'** and depending on the type of transistor, either it will be of N-type or P-type. The size of emitter is very large in comparison with base and it is very heavily doped.

➤ The main function of emitter is to supply majority charge carrier to the transistor and it injects the charge carrier in the base.

➤ For normal transistor operation, emitter diode is always kept forward biased. In symbol, Fig. 6.32 (b), there is an arrow at emitter indicating direction of flow of conventional current.

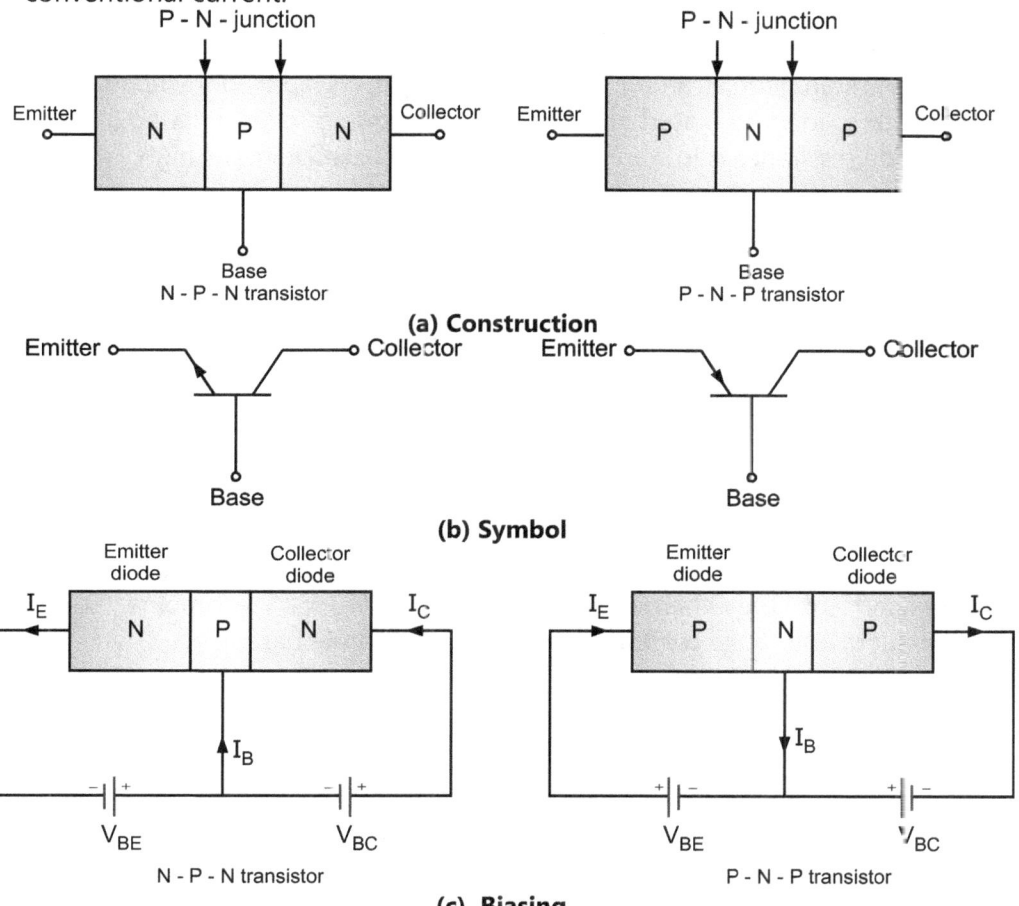

(a) Construction

(b) Symbol

(c) Biasing

Fig. 6.32: Transistor

(ii) Base

➤ The middle part of the transistor is termed as **'base'**. In comparison with emitter and collector, base is thinnest one and the very lightly doped.

➤ The type of impurity in the base is opposite to one used in the emitter. If the emitter is of P-type, then the base will be of N-type.

➤ The function of the base is to control the current flow in a transistor.

(iii) Collector

➤ The part on other extremity is called **'collector'**. The size of the collector is very large in comparison with base and is lightly doped.

➤ The type of semiconductor of the collector is same as that for the emitter. The function of the collector is to collect the majority carriers injected by the emitter.

➤ For normal transistor operation, collector diode is always kept reverse biased.

➤ On the basis of sandwitching, the transistors are classified as (i) P-N-P transistor, (ii) N-P-N transistor.

6.17 TRANSISTOR WORKING

• For using the transistor as an amplifier, the voltages are applied in such a way that the emitter diode is forward biased and the collector diode is reverse biased. As a result, the emitter diode resistance is low and the collector diode resistance is high.

• The emitter junction current-voltage characteristics is the forward current-voltage characteristics of a diode while the collector junction current-voltage characteristics is similar to the reverse current-voltage section of diode characteristics.

• Fig. 6.33 shows biasing of NPN and PNP transistors. As the voltage V_{BE} increases, the height of potential barrier decreases at emitter junction as it is forward biased. This increases the current through this junction. The current flowing through emitter is called **'emitter current'** I_E.

• The charge carriers (electrons in N-type and holes in P-type) forming this current are injected in the base, which contain opposite type of charge carriers. As base region is very thin with low concentration of charge carrier; the most of the charges injected by emitter will pass through it without recombination and will reach collector junction. Only a small part of the charge carrier (about 1%) will recombine (electron-hole recombination) and **'base current'** I_B will flow through the base.

• The charge carriers which have reached collector junction will be attracted by collector base voltage V_{BC} as it has opposite polarity. This increases **'collector current'** I_C.

• Remember working of P-N-P and N-P-N transistors is same except for the type of majority charge carrier. In P-N-P transistor, holes are majority charge carriers, supplied by the emitter and in N-P-N transistor, electrons are majority charge carriers.

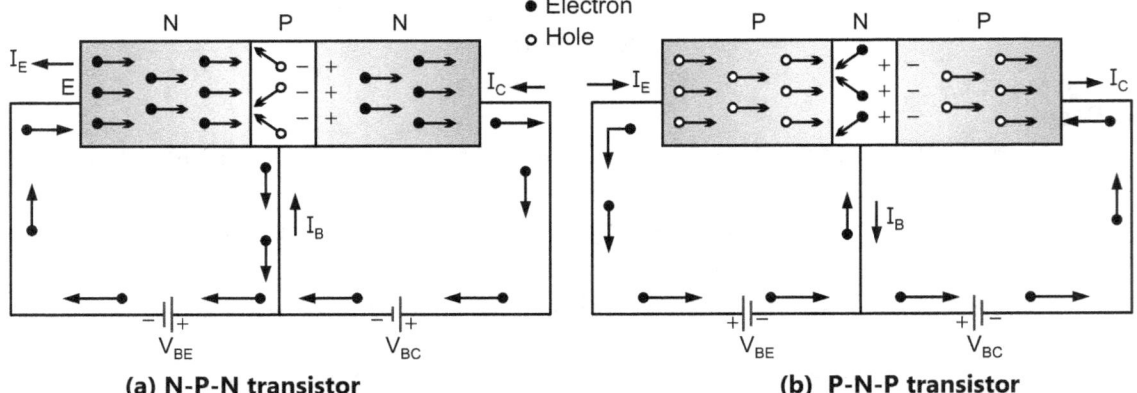

(a) N-P-N transistor   (b) P-N-P transistor

Fig. 6.33: Working of a Transistor

6.17.1 Energy Band Diagram of a N-P-N Transistor

- The schematic non-equilibrium energy band diagram is shown in Fig. 6.34 for an unbiased transistor. Initially, diffusion of minority charge carriers takes place across the junctions. The Fermi level in the emitter and collector regions lie close to the conduction band and in the base region lies close to the valence band for an N-P-N transistor.

- As emitter is heavily doped, the Fermi level will be closer to conduction band in comparison to collector. As the Fermi level is lower on the P-side relative to the N-side, electrons move across the boundary trying to equalize the Fermi levels.

- The Fermi level will have to realign such that it exists as a single energy level for the entire crystal. The band edges in the P and N-regions shift themselves to make the alignment of the Fermi level possible and energy band diagram is no longer the same but assumes the shape as shown in Fig. 6.34.

(a) **Non-Equilibrium Energy Band Picture of an Unbiased N-P-N Transistor**

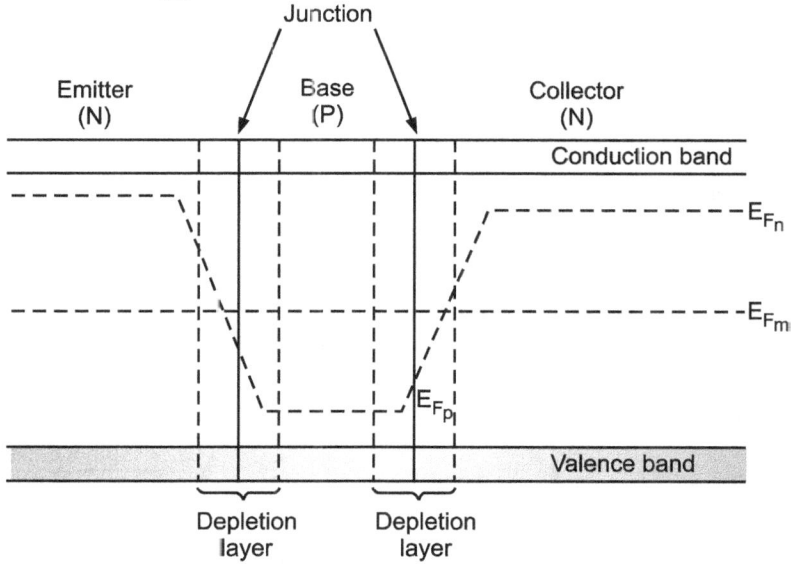

Fig. 6.34: Unbiased N-P-N transistor (Non-equilibrium)

(b) **Equilibrium Energy Band Diagram of an Unbiased N-P-N Transistor**

- The conduction band of P-type (base) is shifted upwards by eV_B over the conduction band of N-type (emitter and collector). The slope of bending of band at emitter-base junction is larger than that base-collector junction as emitter is heavily doped.

- The minority electrons in the conduction band of P-type (base) are at a higher energy than the majority electrons in the conduction bands of N-type (emitter) and N-type (collector). Hence, the electrons crossing the junction from P-region into N-regions will not encounter the potential barrier while the electrons crossing the junctions from N-regions will face the barrier.

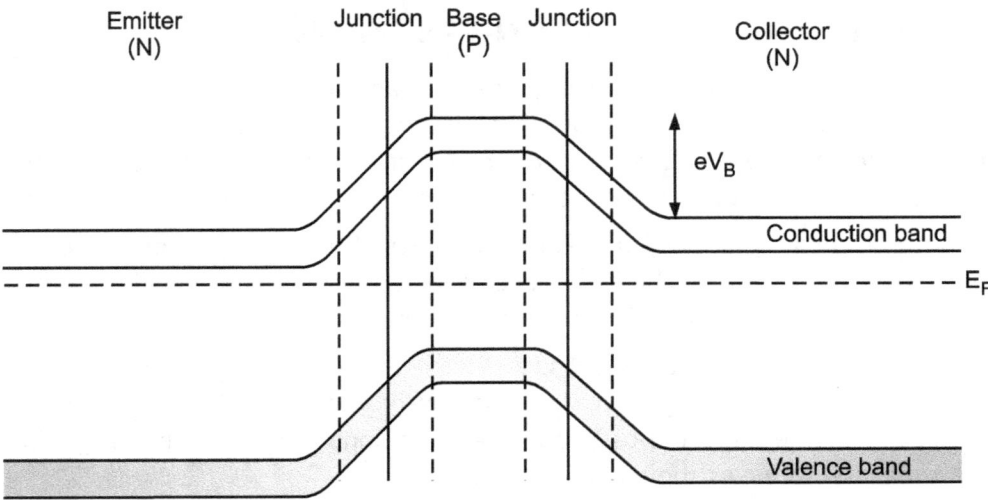

Fig. 6.35: Unbiased N-P-N transistor (At equilibrium)

(c) Biased N-P-N Transistor

*   The energy band diagram of a biased N-P-N transistor is shown in Fig. 6.36. The transistor is connected in common base configuration. In the circuit diagram shown, the collector-base junction has a strong reverse bias (upto 50 volts) V_{CB} and the emitter-base junction has a small bias of (say 0.5 volts) V_{BE}.

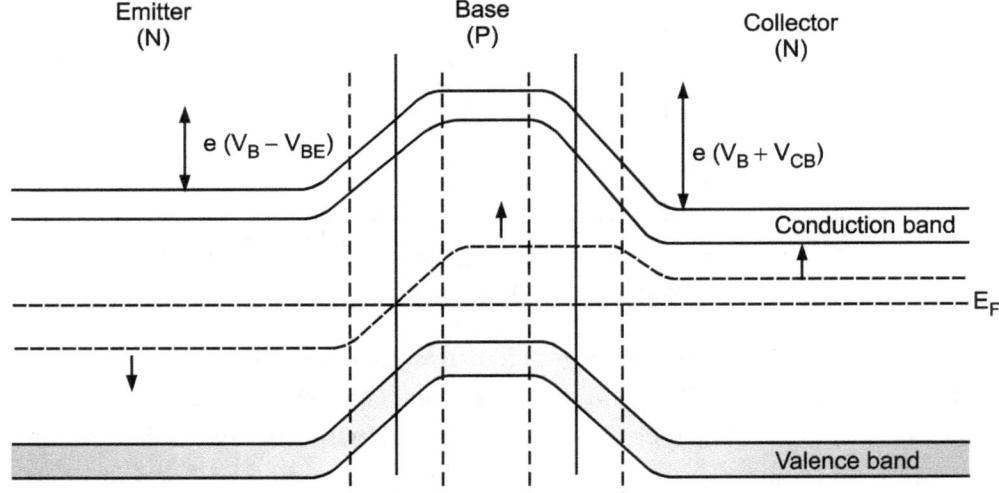

Fig. 6.36: Biased N-P-N transistor

*   On forward biasing the emitter-base junction, the Fermi levels in the emitter region (N-region) and base (P-region) undergo displacement as equilibrium conditions are disturbed. As the negative terminal of V_{BE} is connected to N-region, the energy of the electrons in the emitter region increases by an amount eV_{BE}, where V_{BE} is the emitter

base voltage. Consequently, Fermi level in N-region rises by eV_{BE} and the energy bands adjust their positions to suit the elevation. Due to this increase in energy, the potential barrier is reduced to $e(V_B - V_{BE})$ and barrier width is reduced.

- Though the energy bands in N-region are pushed up, those in the P-region are pulled downward due to the addition of energy from the bias.

- The reverse bias at the collector-base junction of V_{CB} causes the Fermi level in collector region to be lowered by eV_{CB} raising the barrier height to $e(V_B + V_{CB})$.

- As emitter base junction is forward biased, large number of electrons from the emitter can overcome the potential barrier to enter into the base causing a current to flow. Similarly, holes from base region can move into the emitter causing a hole current density. As the emitter is heavily doped and larger than the base, the electron current density is greater than the hole current density.

- Almost all the electrons leaving the emitter and entering the base pass into the collector. In fact, the collector current is less than the emitter current by an amount which is equal to the base current which is very small.

- Out of the electrons injected into the base, about 2 % undergo recombination by falling from the conduction band into the valence band. It is this recombination that causes the base current.

- The energy band diagrams of an N-P-N transistor in CE or CC configurations are essentially the same or are very much similar to that shown in Figs. 6.35 and 6.36.

6.18 HALL EFFECT AND HALL COEFFICIENT   [May 13, Nov. 15]

6.18.1 Hall Effect   [Dec. 14, May 15]

- It often becomes necessary to determine whether a material is an N-type or a P-type semiconductor. Measurement of conductivity alone does not give this information as no distinction can be made between hole and electron conduction.

- Hall effect is used to differentiate between the two types of carriers. It provides a means of determining the density and mobility of charge carriers and gives information about the sign of the predominant charge carrier.

- If a piece of conductor (metal or semiconductor) carrying a current is placed in a transverse magnetic field, an electric field is produced inside the conductor in a direction normal to both the current and the magnetic field. This phenomenon is known as **'Hall effect'** and the voltage so generated is called as **'Hall voltage'**.

Explanation of the Effect

- Assume that the sample material is an N-type semiconductor. The current flow consists, almost entirely, of electrons moving from right to left. This movement corresponds to the direction of conventional current from left to right as shown in Fig. 6.37 (a).

- If v is the drift velocity of the electrons moving perpendicular to the magnetic field B, there is a downward force Bev acting on each electron. This causes the electrons to be deflected in the downward direction. This makes negative charges to accumulate on the bottom face of the slab [See Fig. 6.37 (b)] leaving positive ions on the top surface.
- This gives rise to a potential difference along the top and bottom faces of the specimen across points M and N with the bottom face being negative. This potential difference causes a field E_H in the negative y-direction and so a force eE_H acts on the electrons in the upward direction.
- Under equilibrium, the upward force due to the electric field just balances the downward force due to the magnetic field.

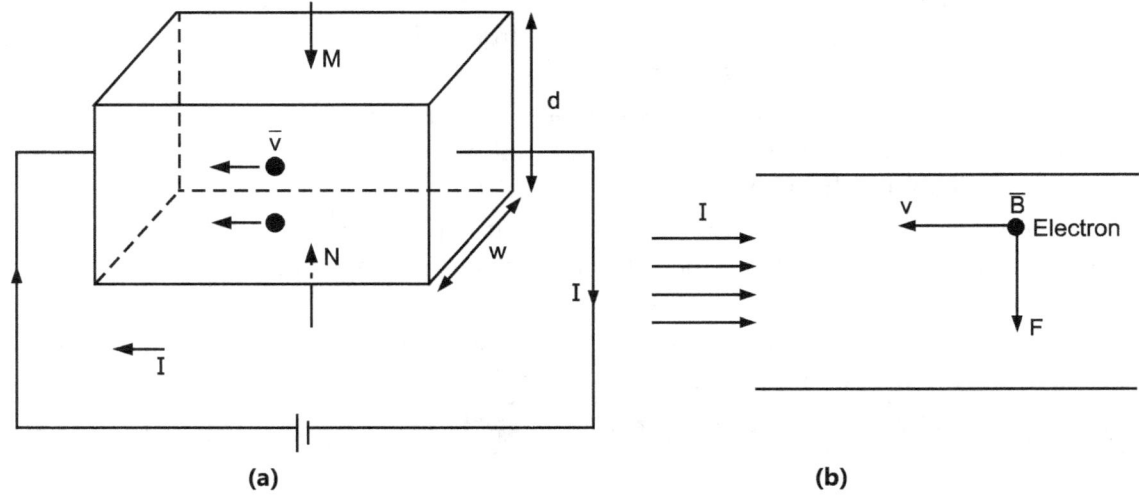

(a)   (b)

Fig. 6.37: Hall effect

Thus, $e E_H = e B v$

∴ $E_H = v B$ ... (1)

- If I is the current in the x-direction then,

                $I = n v A e$

or $v = \dfrac{I}{neA}$ ...(2)

where n is the concentration of charge carriers.

∴ $E_H = \dfrac{B I}{neA}$ ... (3)

Also $E_H = \dfrac{V_H}{d}$

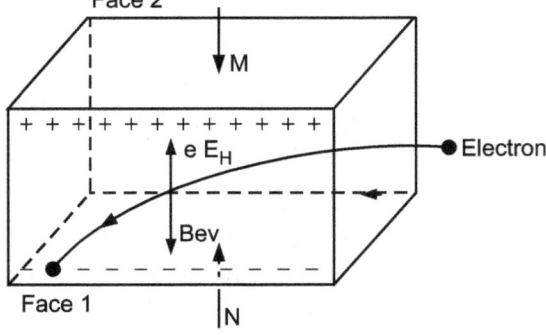

Fig. 6.38: Motion of electrons in an n-type semiconductor

where V_H is the Hall voltage named after the scientist Hall who first predicted and measured the Hall voltage.

$\therefore$ $\qquad\qquad V_H = E_H d$ $\qquad\qquad\qquad\qquad$ ... (4)

Substituting this in expression (3),

$$V_H = \frac{1}{ne} \cdot \frac{BId}{A} \qquad\qquad ...\,(5)$$

or $\qquad\qquad V_H = R_H \frac{BId}{A}$ $\qquad\qquad\qquad\qquad$ ... (6)

where $\qquad\qquad R_H = \frac{1}{ne}$ is the Hall coefficient for any charge e. $\qquad$ ... (7)

- If J_x is the current density of charge carriers in x-direction then,

$$V_H = \frac{1}{ne} \cdot B\,J\,d \quad \left(as\ J = \frac{I}{A}\right) \qquad ...\,(8)$$

In this specimen, as the dominant charge carriers are electrons,

$\therefore$ $\qquad\qquad V_H = -\frac{1}{ne} B\,J\,d$ $\qquad\qquad\qquad\qquad$ ... (9)

- In expression (8), all three quantities V_H, B and J can be measured. Hence, Hall coefficient and current density can be found.

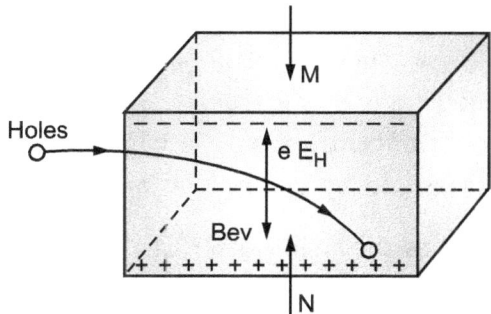

Fig. 6.39: Motion of holes in p-type semiconductor

- Similarly, formulae can be derived for P-type semiconductors. All the formulae are same except that the Hall coefficient will be positive.

- The sign of the Hall voltage gives the sign of the charge carrier and this provides one of the few methods by which the sign of the charge carrier can be ascertained.

$\therefore$ $\qquad$ Hall voltage, $V_H = R_H \cdot \frac{BId}{A} = R_H\,B\,J\,d$ $\qquad\qquad$ ... (10)

6.18.2 Hall Coefficient (R_H)

- The Hall coefficient R_H is determined by measuring the Hall voltage that generates the Hall field. If V_H is the Hall voltage across the sample of thickness d then

$$V_H = E_H\,d \qquad\qquad ...\,(1)$$

Also, the Hall voltage is given by,

$$V_H = R_H \frac{BId}{A} \qquad \qquad \cdots (2)$$

If w is the width of the sample, then its cross-section will be d × w.

$$\therefore \qquad V_H = R_H \frac{BId}{dw} \doteq R_H \frac{BI}{w} \qquad \qquad \cdots (3)$$

$$\text{or} \qquad R_H = \frac{w}{BI} V_H = \frac{1}{nq} \qquad \qquad \cdots (4)$$

- As all quantities in relation (4) are measurable except for n, this relation is used to find the number of charge carriers per unit volume. For metals such as Na, Cu, Ag and Au, the value of n given by this equation is close to the number of valence electrons per unit volume.

- In the case of semiconductors, the interpretation becomes more complex. However, it should be noted that the Hall voltage varies inversely as n, so one would expect it to be larger for semiconductors than for metals.

6.18.3 Applications of Hall Effect

Determination of Type of Semiconductor

- For an N-type semiconductor, the Hall coefficient is negative whereas for a P-type semiconductor, it is positive. Thus, the sign of Hall coefficient is used to determine whether a given semiconductor is N or P-type.

Calculation of Charge Carrier Concentration

- The Hall voltage V_H is measured by placing two probes at the centres of the top and bottom faces of the sample as shown in Fig. 6.38. If $\vec{B}$ is the magnetic flux density, then

$$n = \frac{1}{e} \cdot \frac{BId}{A} \cdot \frac{1}{V_H}$$

- Current I is measured using a current measuring device. Therefore, R_H and hence n can be calculated.

Determination of Mobility

- If conduction is due to one type of charge carriers, for example electrons, then

$$\sigma = ne\,\mu_e$$

$$\mu_e = \frac{\sigma}{ne} = \sigma R_H$$

$$\mu_e = \sigma \cdot \left(\frac{V_H A}{B I d} \right)$$

Knowing σ, and measuring other parameters as in the above applications, the mobility of electrons μ_e can be determined.

SOLVED PROBLEMS

Problem 6.9: *Find the drift velocity for the electron in silver wire of radius 1.00 mm and carrying a current of 2 amperes. Density of silver is 10.5 g/cm³.*

Data: r = 1.00 mm,   I = 2 amp,   density = 10.5 g/cc.

Formula: $v = \dfrac{I}{q \cdot n \cdot A}$

Solution: I = q n v A

Silver is monovalent. So each atom may be assumed to contribute one electron. One gram atomic weight of silver, 108 g, has 6×10^{23} atoms (Avogadro's number).

The density of silver is 10.5 g/cm³. So 108 g will occupy 108/10.5 ≈ 10.3 cm³.

∴   Number of electrons per unit volume, $n = \dfrac{6 \times 10^{23}}{10.3} \approx 6 \times 10^{22}$

or $n = 6 \times 10^{28}$ per m³

The cross-sectional area of wire, $A = \pi r^2 = \pi (10^{-3})^2 \approx 3 \times 10^{-6}$ m²

Now, $v = \dfrac{I}{q \times n \times A}$

$$= \dfrac{2}{(1.6 \times 10^{-19}) \times (6 \times 10^{28}) \times (3 \times 10^{-6})}$$

$$\boxed{v = 7 \times 10^{-5} \text{ m/sec.}}$$

Problem 6.10: *Find the current density in the wire of the preceding example.*

Solution: Current density $J = \dfrac{I}{A} = \dfrac{2.0 \text{ amperes}}{3.0 \times 10^{-6} \text{ m}^2}$

∴ $\boxed{J = 6.7 \times 10^5 \text{ A/m}^2}$

Problem 6.11: *A silver wire is in the form of a ribbon 0.50 cm wide and 0.10 mm thick. When a current of 2A passes through the ribbon perpendicular to a 0.80 T magnetic field, how large a hall voltage is produced along the width ? The density of silver is 10.5 g/cm³.* **(Dec. 12)**

Data: d = 0.50 cm, t = 0.10 mm, I = 2 amp, B = 0.80 T, density = 10.5 g/cc.

Formula: $V_H = \dfrac{1}{nq} \cdot \dfrac{BId}{A}$

Solution: The atomic weight of silver is 108, so the number of atoms in 1 cm³ is

$$n = (6 \times 10^{23}) \left(\dfrac{10.5}{108}\right) \approx 6 \times 10^{22} \text{ per cm}^3$$

Silver is monovalent and we can assume that each atom contributes one electron.

∴   Number of electrons per m³ = 6×10^{28}

$$A = 0.05 \times 0.001 = 5 \times 10^{-5} \text{ m}^2$$

Hall voltage, $V_H = \dfrac{1}{nq} \cdot \dfrac{B I \cdot d}{A}$

$$= \dfrac{1}{6 \times 10^{28} \times 1.6 \times 10^{-19}} \times \dfrac{0.80 \times 2.0 \times 0.05}{5 \times 10^{-5}}$$

$$\approx \boxed{1.67 \times 10^{-7} \text{ volt.}}$$

Problem 6.12: *A copper specimen having length 1 metre, width 1 cm and thickness 1 mm is conducting 1 amp current along its length and is applied with a magnetic field of 1 Tesla along its thickness. It experiences a Hall effect and a Hall voltage of 0.074 microvolts appears along its width. Calculate the Hall coefficient and the mobility of electrons in copper. Conductivity of copper is σ = 5.8 ×10⁷ (Ωm)⁻¹.*

Data: $l = 1$ m, d = 1 cm = 10^{-2} m, t = 1 mm = 10^{-3} m, B = 1 Tesla, I = amp.

$V_H = 0.074 \times 10^{-6}$ volts, σ = 5.8×10^7 (Ωm)⁻¹

Formulae: (i) $V_H = R_H \cdot \dfrac{BId}{A}$, **(ii)** $\sigma = \dfrac{\mu}{R_H}$.

Solution: (i) $R_H = \dfrac{V_H \cdot A}{BId} = \dfrac{0.074 \times 10^{-6} \times 10^{-2}}{1 \times 1 \times 10^{-2}} = \boxed{0.074 \times 10^{-6} \text{ m}^3/\text{coulomb}}$

(ii) $\mu = \sigma R_H = 5.8 \times 10^7 \times 0.074 \times 10^{-6} = \boxed{4.292 \text{ m}^2/\text{volt-sec.}}$

6.19 SOLAR CELLS

- Solar cell is a type of photo-voltaic cell. Photo-electric cells are of three types:

  1. Photo-emissive cell.   2. Photo-voltaic cell.   3. Photo-conductive cell

- All these are based on the principle of photo-electric effect i.e. photon energy is being converted into electrical energy.

- The photo-voltaic cells are based on the photo-voltaic effect which is the conversion of light into an electric current without the aid of an external battery. In this case, voltage is developed in the cell. Solar cells are the best example of this type.

6.19.1 Action of a Solar Cell

- When a P-N junction is exposed to sunlight, photons of energy hv are absorbed, if hv is greater than the band gap E_g. Electron-hole pairs are then generated in both the P-side and N-side of the junction. The electrons and holes that are produced within a small distance of the junction reach the space charge region by diffusion.

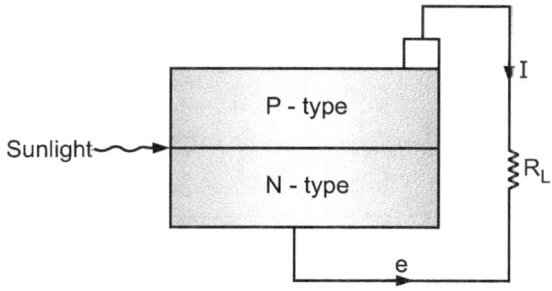

Fig. 6.40: Solar cell p-n junction with load resistance R_L

• The electron-hole pairs are separated by the strong barrier field existing across the space charge region. Electrons in the P-side slide down the barrier potential to move to the N-side while holes in N-side move towards the P-side. [See Fig. 6.41 (b)]

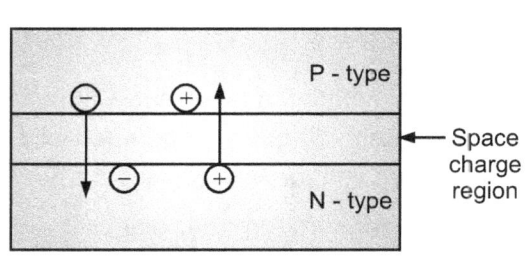

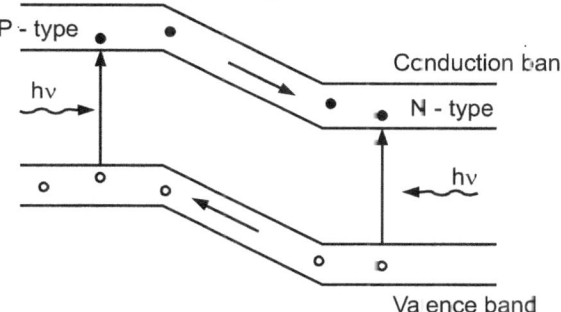

(a) Diffusion of electrons and holes

(b) Energy band diagram corresponding to diffusion of electrons and holes

Fig. 6.41

• When the P-N junction is open circuited, the accumulation of electrons and holes on the two sides of the junction gives rise to an **'open-circuited voltage'** V_{OC}. When a load resistance is connected across the diode, current flows in the circuit. This effect is known as **'photovoltaic effect'**.

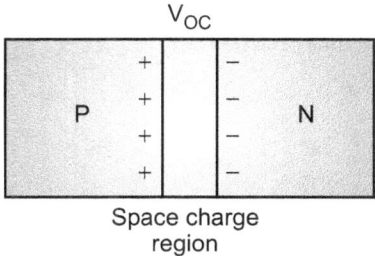

Fig. 6.42

• When the diode terminals are short circuited, the maximum current obtained is called the short **'circuit current'** I_{SC}.

- The current flows as long as the diode is illuminated by sunlight. The magnitude of current flowing is proportional to the light intensity. The electrical energy generated in the solar cell is in the form of dc voltage of approximately 0.5 V. The current varies with the surface area of photo-voltaic cell and with the intensity of the incident light falling on it. The efficiency of the solar cell is given by,

$$\eta = \frac{\text{Power output}}{\text{Incident solar power}}$$

6.19.2 I-V Characteristics of a Solar Cell

- Fig. 6.43 shows I-V characteristics of a solar cell. The I-V characteristics of solar cell is studied by changing the load resistance R_L and measuring current flowing through and voltage appearing across it. When load R_L is zero maximum current flows through it but voltage will be zero, this current is called the **'short-circuit current I_{SC}'**. As voltage is zero it will come on current axis.

- As load increase at a particular stage when R_L becomes infinity, the current will be zero and voltage will reach the maximum value. This maximum voltage is called **open-circuit voltage V_{OC}** and is plotted on voltage axis. For maximum voltage V_{OC}, current is zero.

- So the product $V_{OC} I_{SC}$ will not give the maximum power drawn from the solar cell.

- For getting maximum power from the solar cell, draw a line at 45° passing from origin, the point (V_m, I_m) where the line will cut the curve will give maximum usable power. The ratio of maximum usable power to ideal power is called as **fill factor**.

$$\text{Fill factor 'f'} = \frac{\text{Usable power}}{\text{Ideal power}}$$

i.e. $\text{fill factor 'f'} = \dfrac{V_m \cdot I_m}{V_{OC} \cdot I_{SC}}$

where,

I_m and V_m are the maximum usable current and voltage obtained experimentally.

I_{SC} = short-circuit current

V_{OC} = open-circuit voltage

$V_{OC} \cdot I_{SC}$ = theoretically obtained maximum
power of the solar cell.

$V_m \cdot I_m$ = experimentally obtained maximum
power of the cell.

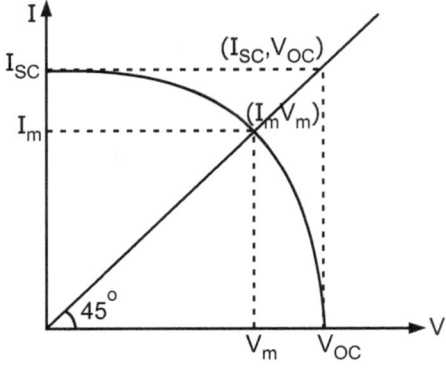

Fig. 6.43

- As the potential difference increases, the recombination of electrons and holes also increases and hence potential difference cannot be increased beyond certain limits. To reduce the recombination, the upper region is of smaller width so that carriers can reach the junction before they recombine.
- When photovoltaic cells are connected in series or parallel, they form a solar battery.

6.19.3 Advantages

- It is an environmentally clean source of energy.
- It is free and available in adequate quantities.
- It is used in satellite communication.
- It is used as power source in artificial satellites.
- It can be used to supply power to places in remote areas and in fuel starved areas.

6.19.4 Disadvantages

- *Dilute source:* Even in the hottest region on earth, radiation flux rarely exceeds 1 kW/m^2 which is the value for technological utilization. It requires large collecting areas in moving application, which results in excessive cost. Thus, use is restricted because of its high price.
- Solar energy varies with time because of day-night cycle.

6.20 SOLAR CELL APPLICATIONS

- Solar cells are used extensively in satellites and space vehicles for long duration power supply. Their first application was in 1958 to power Vangaurd I, a space satellite. Since then solar cells have remained as an important source of power in space applications due to their low weight, reliability and durability.
- Success of solar cells in space led to their terrestrial applications. For terrestrial use, there are three broad categories, namely: industrial, social and consumer applications.

I. **Industrial Applications**

   ➢ **Navigational Aids:** Marine beacons, remote light beacons near the airport and navigational lights around the world were earlier powered by kerosene/batteries having several maintenance problems. Now-a-days, they are powered by simple solar cells which are reliable and cost effective.

   ➢ **Alarm Systems:** Railway signals, alarm systems for fire, flood warnings, traffic lights, highway telephones, etc. are all being powered by solar cells.

   ➢ **Defence Equipments:** Many defence equipments for example, mobiles, telephones, remote radar, large instruments used in remote areas, etc. are now being effectively powered by solar cell.

➤ **Telecommunications:** Telecommunication equipments are often located in remote and inaccessible areas, for example, islands, deserts, etc. They now consume reduced power due to the use of solid-state devices. This has facilitated the use of solar cell as an economical and reliable power source.

➤ **Emergency Equipment:** Charging of batteries on rafts, boats and for providing essential services after natural disasters like earthquakes, floods, etc. can be done efficiently by a solar cell.

➤ **Automatic Meteorological Stations:** A meteorological station collects meteorological data at fixed time intervals at several locations and analyses them to predict weather forecasting accurately. A solar powered meteorological weather station is reliable, economical and is relatively free of maintenance problems.

II. Social Applications

➤ Providing electric power to remote villages and islands, specially in developing countries, by solar cell. These villages are unconnected to the main grid. A small stand-alone type solar cell can provide a rural house enough power for lighting tubes, TV and a small refrigerator.

➤ Solar cell powered pumps are being installed to provide potable water and for irrigation purposes.

➤ Special solar cell powered portable refrigerators are being used for the transportation and storage of vaccines. These vaccines are used for mass immunisation programmes for improving rural standards and reducing infant mortality rate.

➤ Providing electricity to TV, for schools, for educational and recreational purposes.

III. Consumer Applications

➤ A large number of consumer items which are low powered are now being powered by solar cells. Some of these products are pocket calculators, clocks, torches, watches, radios, lights, electric fans, toys, battery chargers, etc.

UNIVERSITY SOLVED PROBLEMS

Problem 6.13: *Calculate the conductivity of pure silicon at room temperature when the concentration of carriers is 1.6×10^{10} per cm^3.*

> *Take μ_e = 1500 cm^3/V-sec and*
>
> *μ_h = 500 cm^3/V-sec at room temperature*   **(04) (May 04, 05)**

Solution: See Example 6.8.

Problem 6.14: *A copper specimen having length 1 meter, width 1 cm and thickness 1 m is conducting 1 ampere current along its length and is applied with a magnetic field of 1 tesla along its thickness. It experiences Hall effect and a Hall voltage of 0.074 micro volts appearing along its width. Calculate the Hall coefficient and the mobility of electrons in copper. Conductivity of copper is $\sigma = 5.8 \times 10^7$ $(\Omega m)^{-1}$.* **(04) (Dec. 05)**

Solution: See Example 6.12.

Problem 6.15: *Calculate the conductivity of a Germanium sample if a donor impurity is added to the extent of one part in 10^7 Ge atoms at room temperature.* **(04) (May 06)**

Given: Avogadro number N_a = 6.02×10^{23} atoms/gm-mole

Atomic weight of Ge = 72.6

Density of Ge = 5.32 gm/cc

Mobility μ_e = 3800 cm^2/V-sec

Formula: $\sigma = e\, n_d\, \mu_e$

Solution: Concentration of Ge atoms

$$= \frac{6.02 \times 10^{23}}{72.6} \times 5.32$$

$$= 4.41 \times 10^{22} \text{ /cm}^3$$

Since there is one donor atom per 10^7 Ge atoms then

$$n_d = \frac{4.41 \times 10^{22}}{10^7} = 4.41 \times 10^{15} \text{ /cm}^3$$

$\therefore$ $\sigma = 1.6 \times 10^{-19} \times 4.41 \times 10^{15} \times 3800$

$$\boxed{\sigma = 2.68 \text{ mho/cm}}$$

Problem 6.16: *A silver wire is in the form of a ribbon 0.50 cm wide and 0.10 mm thick. When a current of 2 amp. passes through the ribbon, perpendicular to 0.80 tesla magnetic field, calculate the Hall voltage produced. The density of silver is 10.5 gm/cc and atomic weight of Ag is 108.* **(04) (May 07)**

Solution: See example 6.11.

Problem 6.17: *Calculate the energy gap of silicon, given that it is transparent to radiation of wavelength greater than 11000 A°.* **(04) (May 07)**

Given: λ = 11000 A°

Formula: $E_g = h\upsilon = \dfrac{hc}{\lambda}$

Solution: $E_g = \dfrac{hc}{\lambda}$

$$E_g = \frac{6.63 \times 10^{-34} \times 3 \times 10^8}{11000 \times 10^{-10}}$$

$$E_g = 1.808 \times 10^{-19} \text{ J}$$

$$\boxed{E_g = 1.13 \text{ eV}}$$

Problem 6.18: *Calculate the number of donor atoms which must be added to an intrinsic semiconductor to obtain resistivity as 10^{-6} Ωm.*

Given: $\mu_e = 1000$ cm²/V-sec   **(04) (Nov. 07)**

Solution: See example 6.4.

Problem 6.19: *Calculate the number of acceptors to be added to a Germanium sample to obtain the resistivity of 10 Ω-cm.*   **(04) (May 08)**

Given: $\mu = 1700$ cm²/volt-sec

Data: $\rho = 10$ cm

                                      $\mu = 1700$ cm² /V-sec

Formula: $\rho = \dfrac{1}{n_a \, \mu_a \, e}$

Solution: $n_a = \dfrac{1}{\rho \, \mu_a \, e}$

                                      $n_a = \dfrac{1}{10 \times 1700 \times 1.6 \times 10^{-19}}$

                                      $\boxed{n_a = 3.6 \times 10^{14} / \text{cm}^3}$

Problem 6.20: *Calculate the mobility of charge carriers in a doped silicon whose conductivity is 100 per Ω-m and the Hall coefficient is 3.6×10^{-4} m³/Coulomb.*   **(04) (May 09)**

Data: $\sigma = 100$ per Ω-m

                                      $R_H = 3.6 \times 10^{-4}$ m³/Coulomb

Formula: $\mu = 6\,R_H$

Solution: $\mu = 6\,R_H$

                                      $\mu = 100 \times 3.6 \times 10^{-4}$

                                      $\boxed{\mu = 0.036 \text{ m}^2/\text{V-sec}}$

Problem 6.21: *Calculate the conductivity of Ge specimen if donor is added to the extent of one part in 10^8 Ge atoms at room temperature.*

*(**Given:** Atomic weight of Ge = 72.6, Density of Ge = 5.32 gm/cm³, Mobility of electrons = 3800 cm²V-sec, Avogadro number = 6.02×10^{23} atoms/mole.*   **(04) (Dec. 09)**

Solution: See example 6.1.

Problem 6.22: *In an N-type semiconductor the Fermi level lies 0.3 eV below the conduction band at room temperature. if the temperature is raised to 330 K, find the position of Fermi level.* **(04) (Dec. 09)**

Data: $\qquad\qquad E_C - E_F = 0.3$ eV at room temperature T = 27°C

Formula: $\qquad\qquad E_F = E_C - kT \ln\left(\dfrac{N_d}{N_c}\right)$

Solution: At $\qquad\qquad T = 300$ K

$$E_C - E_F = kT \ln\left(\frac{N_d}{N_c}\right)$$

$$0.3 = k \times 300 \ln\left(\frac{N_d}{N_c}\right)$$

$\therefore\qquad\qquad k \ln\left(\dfrac{N_d}{N_c}\right) = \dfrac{0.3}{300}$

At $\qquad\qquad T = 330$ K

$$E_C - E_F = 330 \times \frac{0.3}{300}$$

$\therefore\qquad\qquad \boxed{E_C - E_F = 0.33 \text{ eV}}$

Fermi level lies 0.33 eV below the conduction band.

Problem 6.23: *Calculate the band gap energy in Germanium. Given that it is transparent to radiation of wavelength greater than 17760 A°.* **(04) (May 10)**

Data: $\qquad\qquad \lambda = 17760$ A°

Formula: $\qquad\qquad E_g = h\upsilon = \dfrac{hc}{\lambda}$

Solution: $\qquad\qquad E_g = \dfrac{6.63 \times 10^{-34} \times 3 \times 10^8}{17760 \times 10^{-10}}$

$\qquad\qquad\qquad E_g = 1.12 \times 10^{-19}$ J

$\qquad\qquad\qquad E_g = \dfrac{1.12 \times 10^{-19}}{1.6 \times 10^{-19}}$

$\qquad\qquad\qquad \boxed{E_g = 0.7 \text{ eV}}$

Problem 6.24: *Calculate the mobility of charge carriers in a doped silicon of which conductivity is 100 mho/m and Hall coefficient is 3.6 $\times 10^{-4}$ m^3/C.* **(04) (May 11)**

Data: $\qquad\qquad \sigma = 100$ mho/m

$\qquad\qquad\qquad R_H = 3.6 \times 10^{-4}$ m^3/C

Solution: See example 6.8.

Problem 6.25: *Intrinsic silicon is doped with phosphorus, with the atomic ratio of 10^8 (Si): 1 (P). Calculate the conductivity of N type of silicon thus formed. Given mobility of electrons in silicon μ_e = 1400 cm^2 Vs^{-1}. Atomic weight of intrinsic silicon = 28.085, Avogadro's number = 6.022 $\times 10^{23}$ atoms per mole, Density of silicon = 2.33 gm/cm^3.* **(04) (Dec. 11)**

Data: Avogadro number = 6.022×10^{23} atoms/moles

At. wt. of Si = 28.085

Density of Si = 5.32 gm/cm^3

Mobility μ_e = 1400 cm^2 Vs^{-1}

Formula: $\sigma \approx e\, n_d\, \mu_e$

Solution: Concentration of Si atoms

$$= \frac{6.022 \times 10^{23}}{28.085} \times 2.33 = 4.996 \times 10^{22} \text{ / cm}^3$$

Since there is one donor atom per 10^8 Si atoms,

then, $n_d = \dfrac{4.996 \times 10^{22}}{10^8} = 4.996 \times 10^{14}$ / cm^3

The conductivity is, $\sigma = e\, n_d\, \mu_e$

$$= 1.6 \times 10^{-19} \times 4.996 \times 10^{14} \times 1400$$

$$= 1.119 \times 10^{-1} \text{ mho/cm} = 0.1119 \text{ mho/cm}$$

Problem 6.26: *A specimen having length 1.00 cm, width 1.00 mm and thickness 0.1 mm is made to conduct with 1.00 mA current and is placed in a magnetic field of 1.0 Wb/m^2, acting along the thickness. Calculate the Hall voltage in case of (i) N type semiconductor with Hall coefficient of -3.44×10^{-8} m^3/C and (ii) Aluminium with Hall coefficient of -0.3×10^{-10} m^3/C. Which of these materials is more sensitive to Hall effect ? Why ?* **(05) (Dec. 11)**

Data: l = 1.00 cm, d = 1.00 mm, t = 0.1 mm, I = 1.00 mA, B = 1.0 Wb/m^2.   For semiconductor, $R_H = -3.44 \times 10^{-8}$ m^3/C.

For aluminium, $R_H = -0.3 \times 10^{-10}$ m^3/C

Formula: $V_H = R_H \cdot \dfrac{BId}{A}$

Solution: (1) For N-type semiconductor,

$$V_H = -3.44 \times 10^{-8} \times \frac{1 \times 1 \times 10^{-3} \times 1 \times 10^{-3}}{0.1 \times 10^{-3} \times 1 \times 10^{-3}}$$

$\therefore$ $\boxed{V_H = -3.44 \times 10^{-7} \text{ V}}$

(2) For aluminium, $V_H = -0.3 \times 10^{-10} \times \dfrac{1 \times 1 \times 10^{-3} \times 1 \times 10^{-3}}{0.1 \times 10^{-3} \times 1 \times 10^{-3}}$

$$\boxed{V_H = -0.3 \times 10^{-9} \text{ V}}$$

N-type semiconductor is more sensitive to Hall effect than aluminium. Because for same experimental setup, it gives more Hall voltage.

Problem 6.27: *A slab of silicon 2 cm in length 1.5 cm wide and 2mm thick is applied with magnetic field of 0.4 T along its thickness. When a current of 75 A flows along the length, the voltage measured across the width is 0.81 mV. Calculate the concentration of mobile electrons in silicon.* **(03) (May 14)**

Data: h = 2 cm, d = 1.5 cm, t = 2mm, I = 75 A, B = 0.4 T, V = 0.81 mV

Formula: $V_H = \dfrac{1}{nq} \cdot \dfrac{\beta I d}{A}$

$n = \dfrac{1}{0.81 \times 10^{-3} \times 1.6 \times 10^{-19}} \cdot \dfrac{0.4 \times 75 \times 2 \times 10^{-2}}{2 \times 10^{-2} \times 2 \times 10^{-3}}$

$$n = 1.157 \times 10^{26} \text{ / m}^3$$

Problem 6.28: *The hall coefficient of a specimen of a doped Silicon is found to be 3.66×10^4 m^3/C. The resistivity of the specimen is 8.93×10^{-3} Ωm. Determine the mobility of the charge carriers.* **(03) (Nov 13)**

Data: $R_H = 3.66 \times 10^4$ m³/C

$\rho = 8.93 \times 10^{-3}$ Ωm

Formula: $R_H = \dfrac{1}{n_e}$ and $\sigma = n_e \mu$

$\therefore \quad \rho = \dfrac{1}{n_e \mu} = \dfrac{R_H}{\mu}$

or $\mu = \dfrac{R_H}{\rho} = \dfrac{3.66 \times 10^{-4}}{8.93 \times 10^{-3}}$

$\mu = 4.098 \times 10^{-2}$ m²/V-sec

Problem 6.29: *Calculate the specific rotation of the sugar solution of 4.5% concentration, if the plane of polarization is rotated through 6.8° in passing through a length of 1.8 decimeter of the solution.* **(Nov. 13)**

Data: $\theta = 6.8°$

$l = 1.8$ dm

$C = 0.45\% = 0.045$ gm/cc

Formula: $S = \dfrac{\theta}{l \cdot C}$

$S = \dfrac{6.8}{1.8 \times 0.045}$

$S = 83.95°$

SUMMARY

- The energy levels of an isolated atom are discrete.
- In crystals or solids, the allowed energy levels of an atom are modified by the proximity of other atoms in such a way that the discrete energy levels of the individual atoms become bands. Each band contains as many discrete levels as there are atoms in the material.
- Elements are classified as (i) conductors, (ii) semiconductors and (iii) insulators.
- The band formed by a series of energy levels containing the valence electrons is known as valence band.
- The lowest unfilled permitted energy band is called the conduction band.
- The energy required for an electron to jump from the valence band to the conduction band is called the 'band gap' or forbidden gap of the semiconductor.
- Materials having properties intermediate between those of conductors and insulators are known as semiconductors.
- Semiconductors are of two types: (i) intrinsic and (ii) extrinsic.
- Intrinsic semiconductors are those which are pure (free from electroactive and crystalline defects).
- Doping is the process of adding an impurity to intrinsic semiconductors to increase its conductivity.
- Extrinsic semiconductors are obtained by doping an intrinsic semiconductor. They are of two types: (i) p-type extrinsic semiconductor, (ii) n-type extrinsic semiconductor.
- An extrinsic semiconductor formed by doping a trivalent impurity is called a p-type semiconductor. In this type, holes are the majority charge carriers and electrons are the minority charge carriers.
- An extrinsic semiconductor formed by doping a pentavalent impurity is called as n-type semiconductor. In this type, electrons are the majority charge carriers and holes are the minority charge carriers.
- For a metal, electrical conductivity,

$$\sigma = n_e\, e\, \mu_e$$

- For a semiconductor,

$$\sigma_{sc} = e\, (n_e\, \mu_e + n_p\, \mu_p)$$

- For an intrinsic semiconductor,

$$\sigma_{in} = e\, n_i\, (\mu_e + \mu_p)$$

- For a p-type extrinsic semiconductor,

$$\sigma_p \approx e\, n_p\, \mu_p \approx e\, n_a\, \mu_p$$

- For an n-type extrinsic semiconductor,

$$\sigma_n \approx e\, n_e\, \mu_e \approx e\, n_d\, \mu_e$$

- When a current carrying specimen (I) is placed in a transverse magnetic field (B), an electric field 'E' is induced in the specimen perpendicular to both I and B. This phenomenon is called as Hall effect and the voltage hence developed is called as Hall voltage.

- Hall voltage, $V_H = R_H \cdot \dfrac{BId}{A}$

- Hall coefficient, $R_H = \dfrac{1}{nq}$.

- The highest filled state in the highest occupied energy band at 0 K is called the Fermi level for a metal. The corresponding energy is called the Fermi energy (E_F).

- Fermi level in semiconductors is defined as the energy which corresponds to the centre of gravity of conduction electrons and holes when weighted according to their energies. It is a reference level that gives the probability of occupancy of states in conduction band as well as in valence band.

- The Fermi-Dirac probability distribution function P(E) gives the probability that an energy state of energy E is occupied by an electron at T K.

$$P(E) = \dfrac{1}{1 + e^{(E - E_F)/kT}}$$

- The Fermi level in intrinsic semiconductors is exactly in the middle of the forbidden gap.

$$E_F = \dfrac{E_c + E_v}{2}$$

- The position of the Fermi level in a p-type extrinsic semiconductor is close to the valence band as holes are the majority charge carriers.

- The Fermi level in an n-type extrinsic semiconductor is close to the conduction band as electrons are the majority charge carriers.

- When a pn junction is illuminated with light, it has the property of producing an e.m.f. This effect is called as photovoltaic effect.

- Solar cell is a semiconducting device that converts sunlight into electricity. It works on the principle of photovoltaic effect.

- Due to their low weight, reliability and durability, solar cells are used widely in industrial, social and consumer applications.

IMPORTANT FORMULAE

- $v = \mu_e E$

- $I = n \, \mu_e \, \dfrac{V}{l} \cdot A \cdot l$ (for metals)

- $\rho = \dfrac{1}{n \, e \, \mu_e}$

- $\sigma = \dfrac{1}{\rho} = n \cdot e \, \mu_e$ (for conductors/metals)

- $I = l \cdot A \cdot \dfrac{V}{\rho} \, (n \, \mu_e + \, p \, \mu_h)$ (for semiconductors)

- $\rho = \dfrac{1}{e \, (n \, \mu_e + p \, \mu_h)}$ (for semiconductors)

- $\sigma = \dfrac{1}{\rho} = e \, (n \, \mu_e + p \cdot \mu_h)$ (for semiconductors)

- $\sigma_i = e \, n_i \, (\mu_e + \mu_h)$ (for intrinsic semiconductors)

- $\sigma_n = n_e \, e \, \mu_e \approx n_d \, e \, \mu_e$ (for n-type semiconductors)

- $\sigma_p = n_h e \mu_h \approx n_a e \mu_h$ (for p-type semiconductors)

- $V_H = R_H \cdot \dfrac{BId}{A}$

- $R_H = \dfrac{1}{nq}$

- $\mu = \sigma \, R_H.$

EXERCISE

1. Describe in brief the formation of energy bands in solids.
2. Explain the terms valence band, conduction band and forbidden energy gap.
3. Classify the elements into conductors, insulators and semiconductors on the basis of band theory of solids.
4. Give the energy band picture of lithium, beryllium, sodium, diamond and silicon.
5. Derive an expression for conductivity in a metal.
6. Derive an expression for conductivity in an intrinsic and extrinsic semiconductor.
7. Discuss dependence of conductivity on temperature.
8. Explain Hall effect and Hall coefficient.

9. What is Fermi energy ? Show the location of Fermi energy levels in intrinsic and extrinsic semiconductors.

10. What is Fermi function ? Show that the Fermi level lies at the centre of the energy gap in an intrinsic semiconductor.

11. Explain why a potential difference develops across an open circuited P-N junction.

12. Give the energy band picture of a P-N junction diode and explain the effect of biasing on the band picture.

13. "P-N junction is a unidirectional device". Explain.

14. Explain the working of a P - N junction diode under forward and reverse bias.

15. Explain the process that takes place in and around the depletion layer.

16. What are transistors ? Explain the working of PNP / NPN transistor.

17. Discuss the working of an NPN transistor with respect to the energy band diagram.

18. Write a note on construction and characteristics of a solar cell.

19. Explain the working of a solar cell. Give the significance of the cell parameters I_{SC}, V_{OC} and fill factor.

20. Discuss applications of a solar cell.

21. Explain effect of temperature and impurity atoms on the position of Fermi level.

22. Write a short note on drift current and diffusion current.

23. Explain free electron theory in short. Give its short comings.

UNSOLVED PROBLEMS

1. The mobilities of carriers in intrinsic germanium sample at room temperature are μ_e = 3600 cm²/volt-sec and μ_p = 1700 cm²/volt-sec. If the density of electrons is same as holes and is equal to 2.5×10^{13} per cm³, calculate the conductivity.

   (Ans. 2.12 mho/m)

2. Calculate the number of acceptors to be added to a Germanium sample to obtain the resistivity ρ = 10 ohm. cm. Given μ = 1700 cm²/volt-sec.

   (Ans. 3.676×10^{14} per cm³)

3. At room temperature the conductivity of a silicon crystal is 5×10^{-4} mho/cm. If the electron and hole mobilities are 0.14 m²/volt-sec and 0.05 m²/volt-sec determine the density of carriers. **(Ans.** 1.54×10^{16} / m³)

4. The specific density of tungsten is 18.8 g/cm³ and its atomic wt. is 184.0. Assume that there are two free electrons per atom. Calculate the concentration of free electrons. Av. No. = 6.025×10^{23} / gmole. **(Ans.** 2.5×10^{23}/cm³)

5. Compute the conductivity of copper for which μ_e = 34.8 cm²/volt-sec and d = 8.9 gm/cm³. Assume that there is one free electron per atom.

Av. No. = 6.025×10^{23} / g mole, at. wt. of Cu = 63.5.

If an electric field is applied across such a copper bar with an intensity of 10 V/cm, find the average velocity of free electrons.   (**Ans.** 47.02×10^{-4} mho/cm, 348 cm/sec.)

6. The resistivity of copper wire of diameter 1.03 mm is 6.51 ohm per 300 m. The concentration of free electrons in copper is 8.4×10^{28} / m^3. If the current is 2 A, find (a) mobility, (b) drift velocity, (c) conductivity.

(**Ans.** 0.413 m^2/volt-sec, 0.286×10^{-20} m/sec, 55.5×10^8 mho/m)

7. Calculate the energy gap in silicon if it is given that it is transparent to radiation of wavelength greater than 11000 A°.   (**Ans.** 1.13 eV)

8. An N-type semiconductor is to have a resistivity of 10 ohm-cm. Calculate the number of donor atoms which must be added to achieve this.   (**Ans.** 12.5×10^{23})

Assume μ_e = 500 cm^2/volt-sec.

SOLVED UNIVERSITY QUESTIONS

DECEMBER 2012

1. Draw energy band picture for P-N junction in case of (i) Zero Bias, (ii) Forward Bias, (iii) Reverse Bias.   **[3]**

Ans. Please Refer to Article 6.15 on Page No. 6.33.

2. A silver wire is in form of a ribbon 0.5 cm wide and 0.1 mm thick. When a current of 2 amp passes through the ribbon perpendicular to 0.8 Tesla magnetic field. Calculate the Hall voltage produced.

(Given : Density of Silver = 10.5 gm/cc, Atomic weight of Silver = 108, Avogadros Number 6.02×10^{23} gm/mole)   **[3]**

Ans. Please Refer to Problem 6.11 on Page No. 6.45.

3. Derive an expression for Conductivity in Semiconductor.   **[6]**

Ans. Please Refer to Article 6.4.2 on Page No. 6.10.

MAY 2013

1. Define Fermi level. Plot the variation of Fermi level with the increase of temperature for n-type and p-type semiconductor.   **[3]**

Ans. Please Refer to Article 6.5 on Page No .6.19 and 6.12.1 on Page No 6.28.

2. Calculate the conductivity of Ge sample it the donor impurity is added to an extent of one part in 10^8 Ge atoms at room termperature (Data Given: N_a = 6.023×10^{23} atoms/gn-mole. At. Wt. of Ge = 72.6).

(Density of Ge = 5.32gm/cc. μ = 3800 cm^2/v-s.)   **[3]**

Ans. Data :   At. Wt. Of Ge = 72.6

Density of Ge = 5.32 gm/cc

μ = 3800 cm^2/V.S.

Formula: $\sigma = nd\mu e$

Solution:

Number of Ge atoms/unit volume $= \dfrac{6.023'10^{23}'5.32}{72.6}$ $= 4.41 \times 10^{22}$/cm^3

As ratio of donor to pure semiconductor for is $1: 10^8$

$\therefore$ $n_d = \dfrac{4.41'10^{22}}{10^8}$ $= 4.41 \times 10^{14}$/cm^3

Conductivity $\sigma = 4.41 \times 10^{14} \times 1.6 \times 10^{-19} \times 3800$

$\therefore$ $\sigma = 0.268$ mho/cm.

3. Define Hall effect. Derive the expression of Hall coefficient, Hall Voltage and discuss their applications. **[6]**

Ans. Please Refer to Article 6.18 on Page No 6.41.

NOVEMBER 2013

1. What is the effect of following factors on the conductivity of semiconductors ? **[3]**

(i) Increase in impurity of concentration.

(ii) Increase in temperature.

(iii) Increase in intensity of light.

Ans. Please Refer to Article 6.4.3 on Page No. 6.13.

2. The hall coefficient of a specimen of a doped Silicon is found to be 3.66×10^4 m^3/C. The resistivity of the specimen is 8.93×10^{-3} Ωm. Determine the mobility of the charge carriers. **[3]**

Ans. Data: $R_H = 3.66 \times 10^4$ m^3/C

$\rho = 8.93 \times 10^{-3}$ Ωm

Formula: $R_H = \dfrac{1}{n_e}$ and $\sigma = n_e\mu$

$\therefore$ $\rho = \dfrac{1}{n_e\mu} = \dfrac{R_H}{\mu}$

or $\mu = \dfrac{R_H}{\rho} = \dfrac{3.66 \times 10^{-4}}{8.93 \times 10^{-3}}$

$\mu = 4.098 \times 10^{-2}$ m^2/V-sec

Note: As there are misprints in the paper received by colleges. The value of answer may be different for different data pointed in paper.

3. Explain the classification of solids into conductors, semiconductors and insulators on the basis of band theory of solids. **[6]**

Ans. Depending upon the difference between conduction and valence band i.e. width of forbidden energy gap, solids can be classified into three categories.

    (i) Insulators (ii) Semiconductors (iii) Conductors.

(i) Insulators: In an insulator the valence electrons are tightly bound with the nucleus and free electrons are totally absent. As valence electrons are very tightly bound, they need very high energy to separate them from the nucleus. The resistivity of insulators are very high and is of the order of 10^{12} Ω-cm.

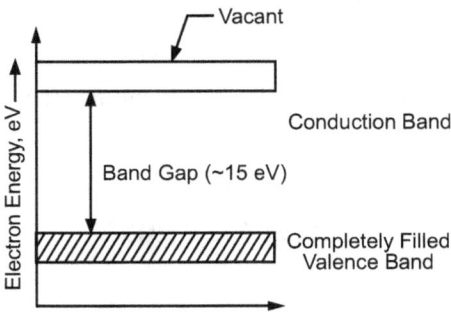

Fig. 1: Energy bands in an insulator

In terms of energy band, insulators have completely filled valence band and conduction band is completely empty. The energy gap is very large (upto 15 eV). Under ordinary circumstances, no electron can jump to conduction band. But when very high temperature or electric field is applied, some of the electrons can jump to conduction band and become poor conductors e.g. mica, diamond, quartz etc.

(ii) Semiconductors: In semiconductors, electron is loosely bound to the nucleus, hence requires less energy for separating them from the nucleus. Semiconductors are materials whose electrical resistivity lies between insulator and conductor. Pure semiconductor is similar to insulators except that they have lower electrical resistivity and is of the order of 10^{6} Ω-cm. The main feature of semiconductor is that the resistivity decrease with increase in temperature that is they have negative temperature coefficient. Semiconductors are group of IV element. e.g. silicon (Si) and germanium. Compounds formed between element of groups III and V or groups II and VI of periodic table can also be semiconductors. e.g. Gallium arsenide (GaAs) and cadmium sulphide (CdS).

In terms of energy band, they are similar to insulators i.e. valence band is completely filled and conduction band is completely empty. The only difference is that the band gap is comparatively smaller (upto 2 eV). Therefore, smaller energy is required to push the electrons from the valence band to conduction band. The migration of electron to conduction band creates a **'hole'** in the valence band.

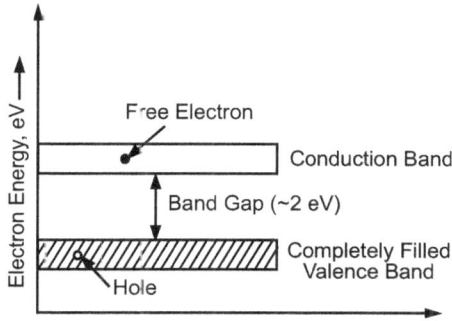

Fig. 2: Semiconductors

(iii)   Conductors: The conductors have free or conduction electrons at room temperature. These electrons take part in conduction and they are free to move within specimen, hence electrical resistivity of conductor is very low and is of the order of 10^{-6} Ω-cm.

In terms of energy band they have overlapping valence band and conduction band and they do not have band gap at all, hence large number of free electrons are available. Or conductors can have partial y filled conduction band. The free electrons from conduction band contribute in the current and therefore holes are not created in valence band.

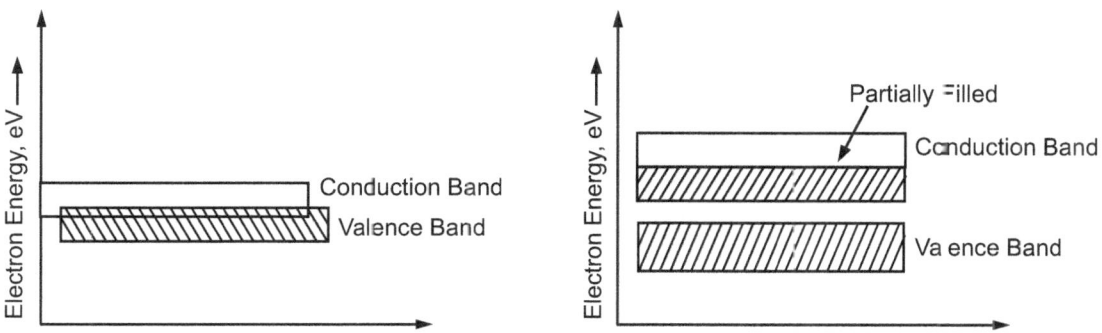

Fig. 3: Conductors

4. Calculate the specific rotation of the sugar solution of 4.5% concentration, if the plane of polarization is rotated through 6.8° in passing through a length of 1.8 decimeter of the solution.

Ans. Data: $\theta = 6.8°$

$l = 1.8$ dm

$C = 0.45\% = 0.045$ gm/cc

Formula:

$$S = \frac{\theta}{l \cdot C}$$

$$S = \frac{6.8}{1.8 \times 0.045}$$

$$S = 83.95°$$

MAY 2014

5. Explain Fermi-Dirac distribution function specifying the meaning of each term in it.**[3]**

Ans. Please Refer to Article 6.9 on Page No. 6.23.

6. A slab of silicon 2 cm in length 1.5 cm wide and 2mm thick is applied with magnetic field of 0.4 T along its thickness. When a current of 75 A flows along the length, the voltage measured across the width is 0.81 mV. Calculate the concentration of mobile electrons in silicon. **[3]**

Ans. Data: h = 2 cm, d = 1.5 cm, t = 2mm, I = 75 A, B = 0.4 T, V = 0.81 mV

Formula:

$$V_H = \frac{1}{nq} \cdot \frac{\beta I d}{A}$$

$$n = \frac{1}{0.81 \times 10^{-3} \times 1.6 \times 10^{-19}} \cdot \frac{0.4 \times 75 \times 2 \times 10^{-2}}{2 \times 10^{-2} \times 2 \times 10^{-3}}$$

$$n = 1.157 \times 10^{26} / m^3$$

7. Derive the expression for the conductivity of intrinsic and extrinsic semiconductor.**[6]**

Ans. Please Refer to Article 6.4.2 on Page No. 6.10.

DECEMBER 2014

1. Explain Fermi dirac probability distribution function with the meaning of each symbol in it. **[3]**

Ans. Please Refer to Article 6.9 on Page No. 6.23.

2. Calculate the conductivity of pure silicon at room temperature when the concentration of charge carriers is $1.6 \times 10^{10}/cm^3$. Given that, μ_e = 1500 cm^2/V.Sec. μ_n = 500 cm^2/V.sec. **[3]**

Ans. Please Refer to Problem 6.8 on Page No. 6.18.

3. Explain Hall effect. Derive the equation of Hall voltage and Hall coefficient. **[6]**

Ans. Please Refer to Article 6.18.1 and 6.18.2 on Page No. 6.41 and 6.43.

MAY 2015

1. What is Fermi level ? Show the position of Fermi level in P-type semiconductor at temperature $T = 0$ K and $T > 0$ K. **[3]**

Ans. Please Refer to Article 6.5, 6.11 (b), 6.12.1 (2), Page No. 6.19 to 6.20, 6.27 to 6.28 and 6.28 to 6.29.

2. Calculate the number of acceptors to be added to a germanium sample to obtain the resistivity of 10 Ω cm. **[3]**

   ($\mu = 1700$ cm^2/V.sec.)

Ans. Data: $\rho = 10$ Ω.cm, $\mu = 1700$ cm^2/V.sec.

Formula: $$\rho = \frac{1}{n_a \, e \, \mu}$$

Solution: $$n_a = \frac{1}{10 \times 1.6 \times 10^{-19} \times 1700}$$

$$n_a = 3.676 \times 10^{14} \text{ /cm}^3$$

3. What is Hall effect ? Derive the equation of Hall voltage. **[6]**

Ans. Please Refer to Article 6.18.1, Page No. 6.44 to 6.47.

NOVEMBER 2015

1. What is Fermi level ? Explain Fermi-Dirac probability distribution function. **[3]**

Ans. Please Refer to Article 6.5 and 6.9, Page No. 6.19 and 6.23.

2. Explain Hall effect. Derive the equation of Hall voltage and Hall coefficient. **[6]**

Ans. Please Refer to Article 6.18, Page No. 6.41.

3. Calculate the number of acceptors to be added to a germanium sample to obtain the resistivity of 20 Ω cm. **[3]**

Given: $\mu = 1700$ cm^2/V.sec.

Ans.

Given: $\mu = 1700$ cm^2/ V.sec

Data: $\rho = 20$ Ω cm

$\mu_p = 1700$ cm^2/ V.sec

Formula: Resistivity $\rho = \dfrac{1}{n_a \mu_p e}$

Solution: No. of acceptor N_a = $\dfrac{1}{20 \times 1700 \times 1.6 \times 10^{-19}}$

N_a = 1.838×10^{14} atoms

MAY 2016

1. What is Fermi energy in semiconductor? With the help of labelled diagram show the position of Fermi level in the case of a diode that is connected in forward bias.   **[3]**

Ans. Please Refer to Article 6.5 and 6.15 (b) (Fig. only) on Page No. 6.19 and 6.35.

2. Calculate the number of acceptor atoms that need to be doped in germanium sample to obtain the resistivity of 8 Ω cm. [Given: mobility μ = 1600 cm^2/V.s]   **[3]**

Ans. Data : S = 8 Ω cm, μ_a = 1600 cm^2/V-sec, **Formula :** S = $\dfrac{1}{\lambda_a \mu_a e}$

Solution : n_a = $\dfrac{1}{8 \times 1600 \times 1.6 \times 10^{-19}}$ = 4.88×10^{14}/cm^3

3. Derive an expression for conductivity in case of intrinsic and extrinsic semiconductors.   **[6]**

Ans. Please Refer to Article 6.4.2 on Page No. 6.10.

✠ ✠ ✠

CHAPTER 7
WAVE MECHANICS

7.1 INTRODUCTION

- The most outstanding development in modern science is the conception of quantum mechanics. The quantum mechanics is better than Newtonian classical mechanics in explaining the fundamental physics. There was big development in physics between the time of Newton and the time of quantum mechanics.

- Newton showed that the motion of planets and the free fall of an object on earth is governed by the same law. Thus, he unified terrestrial and celestial mechanics. This was in contrast to ancient belief that the world of the earth and heaven is governed by different laws.

- It was earlier believed that the heat is some peculiar substance called 'caloric', which flows from a hot object to a cold object. But latter it was proved that the heat is the random motion or vibration of constituents of matter. Thus, thermodynamics and mechanics were unified.

- For a long time, the phenomena of electricity, magnetism and light were treated as independent branches and were unconnected. But in nineteenth century, Faraday and Maxwell along with others unified these independent branches of physics. They proved that all three phenomena are manifestations of electromagnetic field.

- The simplest example is the electric field of an electric charge that exerts a force an another charge when it comes in the range. An electric current produces a magnetic field that exerts a force on magnetic materials.

- Such fields can travel through space, independent of charge and magnet, in the form of electromagnetic wave. The best example of electromagnetic wave is light. Finally, Einstein unified space, time and gravity in his theory of relativity.

- Quantum mechanics also unified two branches of science: physics and chemistry.

- In previous developments in physics, fundamental concepts were not different from those of everyday experience, such as particle, position, speed, mass, force, energy and even field. These concepts are referred as 'classical'.

- The world of atoms cannot be described and understood with these concepts. For atoms and molecules, the ideas and concepts used in dealing with objects in day to day life is not sufficient. Thus, it needed new concepts to understand the properties of atoms.

- A group of scientists W. Heisenberg, E. Schroedinger, P.A.M. Dirac, W. Pauli, M. Born and Neils Bohr, conceived and formulated these new ideas in the beginning of 20th century. This new formulation, a branch of physics, was named as **quantum mechanics**.

7.1.1 Limitations of Classical Mechanics

- The classical physics is complete and beautiful in explaining daily experiences where big bodies are involved. But it breaks down severely at subatomic level and failed to explain some of the phenomenon totally.

- The phenomenas which classical physics failed to explain are black body radiation, photoelectric effect, emission of X-rays, etc.

- In classical physics, a body which is very small in comparison with other body is termed as *'particle'*. Whereas in quantum mechanics, the body which cannot be divided further is termed as *'particle'*.

- The other main difference is the quantized energy state. In classical physics, an oscillating body can assume any possible energy. On the contrary, quantum mechanics says that it can have only descrete non-zero energy.

7.1.2 Need of Quantum Mechanics

- Classical mechanics successfully explained the motions of object which are observable directly or by instruments like microscope. But when classical mechanics is applied to the particles of atomic levels, it fails to explain actual behaviour. Therefore, the classical mechanics cannot be applied to atomic level, e.g. motion of an electron in an atom.

- Other phenomenas which classical mechanics failed to explain are black body radiation, photoelectric effect, emission of X-rays, etc.

- The above problems were solved by Max Planck in 1900 by the introduction of the formula

$$E = nh\upsilon \qquad \qquad \dots (1)$$

where, $n = 0, 1, 2, \dots ,$

                $h = $ Planck's constant $= 6.63 \times 10^{-34}$ J/s

- This is known as *'quantum hypothesis'* and marked the beginning of modern physics. The whole microscopic world obeys the above formula.

7.2 WAVE PARTICLE DUALITY OF RADIATION AND MATTER

The wave and particle duality of radiation can be easily understood by knowing what is a wave and what is a particle.

Wave

- A *wave* originates due to vibrations, and it is spread out over a large region of space. A wave cannot be located at a particular place and mass cannot be attached to a wave.

- Actually, a wave is a spread out disturbance specified by its amplitude a, frequency υ, wavelength λ, phase δ and intensity I.

Particle

- A ***particle*** is located at some definite point and it has mass. It can move from place to place. A particle gains energy when it is accelerated and it loses energy when it is slowed down.

- A particle is characterized by mass m, velocity v, momentum p, and energy E.

- Looking at the above facts, it might appear difficult to accept wave particle duality of radiation, i.e. radiation is a wave which is spread out over all space and that it is also a particle which is localised at a point in space.

- But this wave particle duality of radiation has to be accepted because, sometimes radiation has to be assigned the behaviour of a wave and at other times radiation is to be assigned particle nature as discussed below.

- The phenomena of interference, diffraction and polarisation require the presence of two or more waves at the same time and at the same position. It is very clear that two or more particles cannot occupy the same position at the same time. So one has to conclude that radiation behaves like waves.

- Spectra of black body radiation, production and scattering of X-rays, Compton effect, photoelectric effect, etc. could not be explained on wave nature of radiation. These phenomena established that radiant energy interacts with matter in the form of photons or quanta. With this, Planck's quantum theory came into being to conclude that radiation behaves like particles.

- Thus, radiation sometimes behaves as a wave and at some other times as a particle. It is to be noted that radiation cannot simultaneously exhibit its wave and particle properties. Now, wave-particle duality of radiation is universally accepted.

7.3 DE BROGLIE'S CONCEPT OF MATTER WAVES   [Dec. 12]

- Discrete particle nature of matter is very well established and now it is known that matter is composed of atoms and that electrons, protons and neutrons are the building blocks of all types of atoms.

- The electromagnetic wave theory explained the phenomena of interference, diffraction and polarisation. The quantum theory provided both qualitative and quantitative explanation of spectra of black body radiation, scattering of X-rays and Compton effect, emission of line spectra, photoelectric effect, etc.

- These two theories coupled together established wave-particle duality of radiation. But inspite of the success of this duality of radiation, the two fundamental postulates of Bohr's theory of atomic structure remained unexplained for a long time.

- In the mean time Einstein's mass-energy relation, $E = mc^2$, had been verified, establishing that radiation and mass are mutually convertible.

- On this background, in 1924 De Broglie extended the idea of dual nature of radiation to matter and proposed that matter possesses particle as well as wave characteristics. *He believed that motion of electron within an atom is guided by a peculiar kind of waves called 'Pilot waves'.*

- While adverting the concept of matter waves, De Broglie was guided by wave - particle duality of radiation and the way in which nature manifests herself.

- ***De Broglie put forth following arguments:***

  ➢ Nature manifests herself mainly as matter and radiation, and nature loves symmetry. So wave particle duality of radiation points to similar duality of matter.

  ➢ The principle of least action in mechanics and the principle of least time in optics imply similar conditions. This close analogy of these two principles from two different branches of physics, shows the probability of the behaviour of matter as a wave like entity under suitable circumstances. This close parallelism between mechanics and optics also indicates similarity between matter and radiation, i.e. if radiation has dual nature then matter must also have similar wave-particle duality.

  ➢ Bohr orbits are of definite size and are selected by quantum rules. The radii of these quantum orbits are proportional to the square of integral numbers $\left[r_n = \dfrac{h^2 \in_0}{\pi \, me^2} , n^2 \right]$ and electrons stay in these orbits for a considerable time without radiating energy. Thus, the stable non-radiating orbits of electrons in an atom are governed by integer rules. Now the only phenomena involving integers in physics are those of interference and modes of vibration of a stretched string, and both of them imply wave motion. So there must be a latent relationship between Bohr orbits and integers associated with them. This latent relationship can be understood by considering the length of a Bohr orbit as consisting of integral number of wavelengths (equal to the principal quantum number of the orbit) of the waves associated with electrons moving in that orbit (See Fig. 7.1).

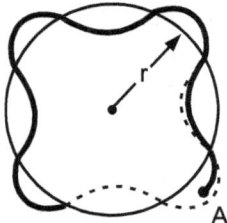

Fig. 7.1: If the orbit length 2πr is an integral number of wavelengths, the wave will reinforce itself when it returns to the starting point A. In the case shown, 2πr = 4λ

- Now, the quantum condition for Bohr orbits is $mvr = n\dfrac{h}{2\pi}$. So the principal quantum number $n = \dfrac{2\pi mvr}{h}$, and *'De Broglie wavelength'* can be obtained by dividing the circumference $2\pi r$ of the nth permissible orbit by its principal quantum number n.

So,

$$\lambda = \frac{2\pi r}{n}$$

$$\lambda = \frac{2\pi r}{(2\pi mvr/h)}$$

$$\lambda = \frac{h}{mv}$$

- This expression for De Broglie wavelength, agrees with the one he postulated, namely $\lambda = \dfrac{\text{Planck's constant}}{\text{momentum of the particle}}$, on the basis of his hypothesis of matter waves.

- According to wave mechanics, electrons move around the nucleus as wave-packets which are formed in a somewhat similar manner as standing waves are formed.

7.3.1 Wavelength of Matter Waves or De Broglie Wavelength   [Nov. 13]

- By De Broglie's hypothesis, a moving material particle is associated with a wave whose wavelength is called *De Broglie wavelength* and it is given by the ratio of Planck's constant to the momentum of the particle.

$$\lambda = \frac{h}{p} = \frac{h}{mv}$$

where p is the momentum of the particle, m its mass, and v the velocity.

- We can arrive at this expression for De Broglie wavelength, (1) by analogy with radiation and (2) by relativistic considerations.

7.3.2 De Broglie Wavelength by Analogy with Radiation

- By Einstein's mass-energy relation, we have

$$E = mc^2 \qquad \qquad \text{... (1)}$$

where E is the energy equivalent of mass m, and c is the velocity of light.

- By Planck's quantum theory of radiation, the energy of a photon is given by

$$E = h\upsilon \qquad \qquad \text{... (2)}$$

where h is Planck's constant and υ is the frequency of oscillations.

From equations (1) and (2), we get

$$h\upsilon = mc^2$$

But $\qquad \qquad \qquad \qquad \upsilon = \dfrac{c}{\lambda},\qquad$ (Since velocity = frequency × wavelength)

$\therefore \qquad \qquad \qquad \qquad h \cdot \dfrac{c}{\lambda} = mc^2$

or $\qquad \qquad \qquad \qquad \lambda = \dfrac{h}{mc} = \dfrac{h}{p}$ ... (3)

where p = mc is the momentum associated with the photon and λ is its wavelength.

7.3.3 De Broglie Wavelength in terms of K.E. of the Particle

[Dec. 12, 14, May 14]

- The momentum of a particle of mass m moving with velocity v is given by p = mv; and the De Broglie wavelength associated with the particle is given by

$$\lambda = \dfrac{h}{mv} = \dfrac{h}{p} \qquad \qquad ... (1)$$

- The K.E. of the particle is given by

$$E = \dfrac{1}{2} mv^2$$

$$E = \dfrac{m^2 v^2}{2\,m} = \dfrac{p^2}{2\,m}$$

$\therefore \qquad \qquad \qquad \qquad p = \sqrt{2\,m\,E}$ ... (2)

From equations (1) and (2), we have

$$\lambda = \dfrac{h}{p} = \dfrac{h}{\sqrt{2\,m\,E}} \qquad \qquad ... (3)$$

In equation (3), De Broglie wavelength λ of a moving particle has been expressed in terms of K.E. of the particle.

7.3.4 De Broglie Wavelength for an Electron in terms of Potential Difference

If an electron acquires velocity v on accelerating it through a potential difference of V volts, then the work done on the electron is eV, e being charge of the electron. This work is converted into kinetic energy of the electron,

i.e. $\qquad \qquad \qquad \qquad E = \dfrac{1}{2} mv^2 = eV$ ... (1)

If e is in coulombs, m in kg, V in volts, then velocity v will be in m/s.

But $\lambda = \dfrac{h}{\sqrt{2mE}}$

From equation (1), $\lambda = \dfrac{h}{\sqrt{2meV}}$ ... (2)

Ignoring relativistic correction, we can take $m = m_o$

∴ $\lambda = \dfrac{h}{\sqrt{2\,m_o\,eV}}$ ... (3)

Now,   h, m_o and e are universal constants with values

$$h = 6.625 \times 10^{-34} \text{ J - s}$$
$$e = 1.6 \times 10^{-19} \text{ C}$$
$$m_o = 9.1 \times 10^{-31} \text{ kg.}$$

Substituting these values in equation (3), we get

$$\lambda = \dfrac{6.625 \times 10^{-34}}{\sqrt{2 \times 9.1 \times 10^{-31} \times 1.6 \times 10^{-19} \times V}} \text{ metres}$$

$$= \dfrac{12.27 \times 10^{-10}}{\sqrt{V}} \text{ metres}$$

∴ $\lambda = \dfrac{12.27}{\sqrt{V}} \text{ A}°$ ... (4)

7.4 CONCEPT OF GROUP VELOCITY AND PHASE VELOCITY
[Dec. 12, Nov. 15, May 16]

7.4.1 Phase Velocity   **[May 13, 14, 15]**

- As we know, with every material particle, a wave called De Broglie wave is associated, which becomes important at microscopic levels.

- The speed with which a crest or trough of a wave travels, is called the *'phase velocity'* of De Broglie waves. It is also called as *'wave velocity'* (u). For wave velocity, the phase remains constant.

- For a particle of mass m, moving with a velocity v, the De Broglie wavelength λ is given by

$$\lambda = \dfrac{h}{mv}$$ ... (1)

and energy, $E = h\upsilon = mc^2$

∴ $\upsilon = \dfrac{mc^2}{h}$ ... (2)

- The equation of motion of a plane wave of frequency υ and wavelength λ moving in x direction is, $\qquad y = a \sin(\omega t - kx)$

  where $\qquad\qquad\qquad \omega = 2\pi\upsilon$, the angular frequency $\qquad\qquad$ ... (3)

  and $\qquad\qquad\qquad k = \dfrac{2\pi}{\lambda}$, the propagation constant of the wave.

- For wave velocity, the phase remains constant i.e.

  $$\omega t - kx = \text{constant} \qquad\qquad\qquad ...(4)$$

- The wave velocity, $\qquad u = \dfrac{dx}{dt} = \dfrac{\omega}{k}$ $\qquad\qquad$ (by differentiating equation 4)

  $\therefore \qquad\qquad\qquad u = 2\pi\upsilon \times \dfrac{\lambda}{2\pi} = \upsilon\lambda \qquad\qquad ...(5)$

  where υ is the frequency of the matter waves.

  Substitution of equations (1) and (2) in (5) gives

  $$u = \frac{mc^2}{h} \times \frac{h}{mv}$$

  $$u = \frac{c^2}{v}$$

  i.e. $\qquad\qquad$ Wave velocity, $u = \dfrac{c^2}{v}$ $\qquad\qquad\qquad ...(6)$

- For any particle, as v is always less than c, the speed of light, we see that the phase velocity u comes to be greater than c, which is an unexpected result. The difficulty raised above can be overcome by understanding the wave group and group velocity v_g.

7.4.2 Group Velocity $\qquad\qquad\qquad\qquad\qquad\qquad$ [May 13, Dec. 14]

- A material particle can be represented by a wave packet or the group of waves and the velocity of wave group is called as **'group velocity'**. The individual waves travel inside the group with their phase velocities or wave velocities.

- Wave group (wave packet) can be obtained by interference of many waves of different frequencies and amplitudes so that resultant has a high value of amplitude near the vicinity of the particle and gets attenuated outside this region as shown in Fig. 7.2.

- We can say that the particle is somewhere in the wave packet and that wave packet moves with velocity of the particle carrying that particle in it. It can be shown that the group velocity v_g is the same as that of the particle velocity v.

Fig. 7.2: Group of waves

- Consider the superposition of two waves of equal amplitude a, different angular frequencies ω_1 and ω_2, and propagation constants k_1 and k_2.

Let y_1 = a sin $(\omega_1 t - k_1 x)$

and y_2 = a sin $(\omega_2 t - k_2 x)$

- The resultant will be

$$y = y_1 + y_2$$

$$y = a \left[\sin (\omega_1 t - k_1 x) + \sin (\omega_2 t - k_2 x) \right]$$

$$y = 2a \cos \left[\frac{(\omega_1 - \omega_2) t}{2} - \frac{(k_1 - k_2) x}{2} \right] \sin \left[\frac{(\omega_1 + \omega_2) t}{2} - \frac{(k_1 + k_2) x}{2} \right]$$

$$\left[\because \sin A + \sin B = 2 \sin \frac{A + B}{2} \cos \frac{A - B}{2} \right]$$

The resultant wave has the angular frequency $\dfrac{(\omega_1 + \omega_2)}{2}$ and its amplitude is

$$A = 2a \cos \left[\frac{(\omega_1 - \omega_2) t}{2} - \frac{(k_1 - k_2) x}{2} \right]$$

- Thus, the amplitude of the wave group is modulated both in space and time. The velocity with which this envelope moves is given by

$$v_g = \frac{\omega_1 - \omega_2}{k_1 - k_2} = \frac{d\omega}{dk} \qquad \qquad \text{... (1)}$$

This is the general formula for a group velocity.

7.4.3 To Show that, Group Velocity v_g is Equal to Particle Velocity v

[Dec. 14]

Consider a particle whose kinetic energy is

$$E = \frac{1}{2} mv^2 = \frac{p^2}{2m} \qquad \qquad \text{... (1)}$$

where p = mv = momentum

We have,   E = hυ

$\therefore$ $E = \hbar \omega$,   where $\hbar = \dfrac{h}{2\pi}$ and $\omega = 2\pi\upsilon$ ... (2)

The De Broglie wavelength is $\lambda = \dfrac{h}{p}$

$\therefore$ $p = \dfrac{h}{\lambda} = \dfrac{h}{2\pi} \times \dfrac{2\pi}{\lambda}$

                                    $p = \hbar k$ ... (3)

Using equations (2) and (3), the energy equation (1) becomes

$$\hbar\omega = \frac{\hbar^2 k^2}{2m}$$

$$\omega = \frac{\hbar k^2}{2m}$$

which gives

$$d\omega = \frac{\hbar k \, dk}{m}$$

∴

$$\frac{d\omega}{dk} = \frac{\hbar k}{m}$$

i.e.

$$v_g = \frac{\hbar k}{m} \qquad \left(\because v_g = \frac{d\omega}{dk}\right)$$

$$v_g = \frac{p}{m} \quad \text{(from equation (3))}$$

$$v_g = \frac{mv}{m} = v$$

∴

$$v_g = v \qquad \qquad \dots (4)$$

Thus, group velocity v_g is equal to particle velocity v.

Hence the packet can guide the motion of the particle. A wave group or wave packet is associated with a moving body and that the phase velocity (or wave velocity u) has no physical significance.

Thus, De Broglie wave associated with a moving body is a wave group which travels with the same speed as that of the body.

7.4.4 Phase Velocity in Terms of Wavelength

Consider a particle of mass m and velocity v which is accelerated through a p.d. of V volts. Then

$$E = \frac{1}{2}mv^2 = eV \qquad \qquad \dots (1)$$

Also, we have,

$$E = h\upsilon$$

∴

$$\upsilon = \frac{E}{h} \qquad \qquad \dots (2)$$

From equations (1) and (2), we get

$$\upsilon = \frac{E}{h} = \frac{1/2 \, mv^2}{h} = \frac{eV}{h}$$

Multiplying and dividing by $\dfrac{h}{2m}$,

$$\upsilon = \frac{h}{2m} \cdot \frac{eV}{h} \frac{2m}{h} = \frac{h}{2m} \frac{1}{\lambda^2} \qquad \qquad \dots (3)$$

$$\left[as \ \lambda = \frac{h}{\sqrt{2\,mE}} = \frac{h}{\sqrt{2\,meV}} \right]$$

Using $\qquad\qquad\qquad u = \upsilon\lambda$

$$= \frac{h}{2m\lambda^2} \cdot \lambda = \frac{h}{2m\lambda}$$

∴ The phase velocity, $\qquad u = \dfrac{h}{2m\lambda}$

Hence, the wave velocity of matter wave depends inversely on the wavelength λ. This is the basic difference between matter waves and light waves.

7.5 PROPERTIES OF MATTER WAVES   [Nov. 13]

Matter waves are generated by a moving matter particle. If a particle of mass m moves with velocity v, then the wavelength of matter waves associated with it is given by $\lambda = \dfrac{h}{mv}$ and these waves travel with velocity $u = \dfrac{c^2}{v}$.

From this, properties of matter waves can be stated as:

➢ Lighter the particle, greater would be the wavelength of the matter waves associated with it. $\left(\lambda \propto \dfrac{1}{m}, \text{ for v constant} \right)$.

➢ Smaller the velocity of the particle, greater would be the wavelength of the matter waves. $\left(\lambda \propto \dfrac{1}{v}, \text{ for m constant} \right)$.

➢ For $v = \infty$, λ becomes zero and for $v = 0$, λ becomes infinity i.e. the wave becomes indeterminate when $v = 0$. This simply means that matter waves are produced by particles moving with finite velocities.

➢ Matter waves are different from electromagnetic waves, because matter waves can be produced by a moving particle which may be charged or uncharged, whereas electromagnetic waves are produced only by a moving charged particle. As the De Broglie wavelength $\lambda = \dfrac{h}{mv}$ is independent of charge, it is evident that matter waves are not electromagnetic waves.

➤ The velocity of matter waves depends on the velocity of the particle generating them $\left(u = \dfrac{c^2}{v}\right)$ and it is not constant.

➤ Matter waves travel faster than light, because the particle velocity v cannot exceed the velocity of light c. So the velocity of matter waves $u = \dfrac{c^2}{v}$ is greater than c.

➤ A wave is spread out in space and it cannot be localised at any point. So the wave nature of matter introduces a certain uncertainty in the position of the particle.

SOLVED PROBLEMS

Problem 7.1: *What is the De Broglie wavelength of an electron when accelerated through a p.d. of 10,000 volts ?*

Data: $V = 10,000$ volts

Formula: $\lambda = \dfrac{12.27}{\sqrt{V}}$ A°

Solution: $\lambda = \dfrac{12.27}{\sqrt{10,000}}$

              $= \boxed{0.1227 \text{ A°}}$

Problem 7.2: *Compute the wavelength of the De Broglie waves associated with a proton moving with 5 % of the velocity of light. Proton has 1836 times the mass of one electron.*

Data: $m = 1836 \times 9.1 \times 10^{-31}$ kg, $h = 6.63 \times 10^{-34}$ Joule-sec.,

$v = \dfrac{5}{100} \times 3 \times 10^8$ m/sec.

Formula: $\lambda = h/mv$

Solution: $\lambda = \dfrac{6.63 \times 10^{-34}}{1836 \times 9.1 \times 10^{-31} \times \dfrac{5}{100} \times 3 \times 10^8}$

              $= \boxed{2.65 \times 10^{-14} \text{ m}}$

Problem 7.3: *Compute the kinetic energy and velocity of an electron in terms of those of a neutron, when their De Broglie wavelengths are equal to 1 A°. Take neutron mass as 1835 times the mass of electron.*

Data: $\lambda_n = \lambda_e = 1$ A°; $m_n = 1835\, m_e$

Formula: $\lambda = \dfrac{h}{mv} = \dfrac{h}{\sqrt{2\,mE}}$

Solution: For electron, $\lambda_e = \dfrac{h}{m_e\, v_e} = \dfrac{h}{\sqrt{2\, m_e\, E_e}}$

For neutron, $\lambda_n = \dfrac{h}{m_n\, v_n} = \dfrac{h}{\sqrt{2\, m_n\, E_n}}$

Taking ratios $\dfrac{\lambda_n}{\lambda_e} = \dfrac{m_n\, v_n}{m_e\, v_e} = 1$ (given)

We have, $\dfrac{v_n}{v_e} = \dfrac{m_e}{m_n} = \dfrac{1}{1835}$

or $v_e = 1835\, v_n$

and $\sqrt{\dfrac{2\, m_n\, E_n}{2\, m_e\, E_e}} = 1$

$\therefore$ $\dfrac{E_n}{E_e} = \dfrac{m_e}{m_n} = \dfrac{1}{1835}$

or $\boxed{E_e = 1835\, E_n}$

Problem 7.4: De Broglie wavelength of electrons in a monoenergetic beam is 7.2×10^{-11} metres. Calculate the momentum and energy of electrons in the beam in electron volts.

Data: $\lambda = 7.2 \times 10^{-11}$ m; $h = 6.6 \times 10^{-34}$ J - s

Formulae: $p = \dfrac{h}{\lambda}, \quad E = \dfrac{p^2}{2\,m}$

Solution: $p = \dfrac{6.6 \times 10^{-34}}{7.2 \times 10^{-11}}$

$= \boxed{0.916 \times 10^{-23} \text{ kg - m/sec}}$

$E = \dfrac{(0.916 \times 10^{-23})^2}{2 \times 9.1 \times 10^{-31}} \text{ J}$

$= 0.0461 \times 10^{-15} \text{ J}$

$= \dfrac{0.0461 \times 10^{-15}}{1.6 \times 10^{-19}} \text{ eV}$

$= 0.0289 \times 10^4 \text{ eV} = \boxed{289 \text{ eV}}$

Problem 7.5: *What is the De Broglie wavelength associated with a 5000 kg car having a constant speed of 20 m/sec. ?*

Data: m = 5000 kg, h = 6.6×10^{-34} J - sec, v = 20 m /sec.

Formula: $\lambda = \dfrac{h}{mv}$

Solution: $\lambda = \dfrac{6.6 \times 10^{-34}}{5000 \times 20} = \boxed{6.6 \times 10^{-39} \text{ m}}$

As can be seen, the De Broglie wave associated with a macroscopic body is too small to be significant.

Problem 7.6: *A beam of 10 kV electrons is passed through a thin metallic sheet whose interplanar spacing is 0.55 A°. Calculate the angle of deviation of the first-order diffraction maximum.*

Data: V = 10 kV = 10×10^3 volts, d = 0.55 A° = 0.55×10^{-10} m, n = 1

Formulae: $\lambda = \dfrac{12.27}{\sqrt{V}}$ A° and $2d \sin \theta = n\lambda$

Solution: $\lambda = \dfrac{12.27}{\sqrt{V}}$ A° $= \dfrac{12.27}{\sqrt{10^4}} = 0.1227$ A°

$$2 \, d \sin \theta = n \, \lambda$$

Substituting for n, λ and d,

$$\sin \theta = \dfrac{0.1227 \times 10^{-10}}{2 \times 0.55 \times 10^{-10}} = 0.111545$$

$$\theta = \sin^{-1}(0.111545) = \boxed{6.40° = 6°24'}$$

Problem 7.7: *The spacing between the atoms of a certain crystal is 1.2 A°. At what angle will the first-order Bragg reflection occur for thermal neutrons ?*

Kinetic energy = 0.025 eV, Mass of neutron is 1.67×10^{-27} kg

Data: d = 1.2 A°, n = 1, E = 0.025 eV = $0.025 \times 1.6 \times 10^{-19}$ J

Formulae: $\lambda = \dfrac{h}{\sqrt{2mE}}$ and $2d \sin \theta = n\lambda$

$$\lambda = \dfrac{6.6 \times 10^{-34}}{\sqrt{2 \times 1.67 \times 10^{-27} \times 0.025 \times 1.6 \times 10^{-19}}}$$

$$= 18.057 \times 10^{-11} \text{ m} = 1.8057 \text{ A°}$$

$$\sin \theta = \dfrac{\lambda}{2d} = \dfrac{1.8057 \times 10^{-11}}{2 \times 1.2 \times 10^{-11}} = 0.7524$$

$$\theta = \sin^{-1}(0.7524) = \boxed{48.79° = 48°48'}$$

Ch. 7 | 7.14

Problem 7.8: *Find the K.E. of a neutron which has a wavelength of 3 A°. At what angle will such a neutron undergo first-order Bragg reflection from a calcite crystal for which the grating space is 3.036 A° ? Mass of neutron is 1.67×10^{-27} kg.*

Data: $\lambda = 3$ A° $= 3 \times 10^{-10}$ m, n = 1, d = 3.036 A° = 3.036×10^{-10} m, m = 1.67×10^{-27} kg

Formulae: (i) $\lambda = \dfrac{h}{\sqrt{2\,mE}}$

(ii) $2\,d \sin \theta = n\lambda$

Solution:

(i) $E = \dfrac{h^2}{2\,m\,\lambda^2} = \dfrac{(6.6 \times 10^{-34})^2}{2 \times 1.67 \times 10^{-27} \times (3 \times 10^{-10})^2}$

$= \boxed{1.449 \times 10^{-21} \text{ J}}$

(ii) $\sin \theta = \dfrac{\lambda}{2d} = \dfrac{3 \times 10^{-10}}{2 \times 3.036 \times 10^{-10}} = 0.49407$

$\theta = \sin^{-1}(0.49407)$

$= \boxed{29.6085° = 29° \ 36'}$

Problem 7.9: *An electron initially at rest is accelerated through a p.d. of 5000 V. Compute (i) the momentum, (ii) the De Broglie wavelength and (iii) the wave number of the electron. Also calculate the Bragg angle for its first-order reflection from (111) planes of nickel which are 2.04 A° apart.*

Data: V = 5000 V, n = 1, d = 2.04 A° = 2.04×10^{-11} m

Formulae: (i) $p = \sqrt{2\,meV}$, (ii) $\lambda = \dfrac{12.27}{\sqrt{V}}$ A°, (iii) $\bar{\upsilon} = \dfrac{1}{\lambda}$, (iv) $2\,d \sin \theta = n\lambda$

Solution: (i) $p = \sqrt{2 \times 9.1 \times 10^{-31} \times 1.6 \times 10^{-19} \times 5000}$

$= \boxed{3.815 \times 10^{-23} \text{ kg - m/sec}}$

(ii) $\lambda = \dfrac{12.27}{\sqrt{5000}}$ A°

$= 0.17352$ A° $= \boxed{0.17352 \times 10^{-10} \text{ m}}$

(iii)   Wave number, $\bar{\upsilon} = \dfrac{1}{\lambda} = \boxed{5.76 \times 10^{10} \text{ m}}$

(iv) $2\,d \sin \theta = n\lambda$

$\sin \theta = \dfrac{\lambda}{2\,d} = \dfrac{0.17352 \times 10^{-10}}{2 \times 2.04 \times 10^{-10}} = 0.0425$

$\theta = \sin^{-1}(0.0425) = \boxed{2.43° = 2°26'}$

Problem 7.10: *Electrons from a heated filament accelerated by a p.d. of 10 kV are passed through a thin film of a metal for which the atomic spacing is 0.55 A. What is the angle of deviation of the first-order maximum ?*

Solution: We have the relation

$$\lambda = \frac{h}{mv} = \frac{h}{\sqrt{2meV}} = \frac{12.27}{\sqrt{V}} \ A°$$

$\therefore$
$$\lambda = \frac{12.27}{\sqrt{10 \times 10^3}} = \boxed{0.122 \ A°}$$

Now, from Bragg's law, $2d \sin \theta = n\lambda$

Here, n = 1
$$\sin \theta = \frac{n\lambda}{2d} = \frac{1 \times 0.122}{2 \times 0.55} = 0.111$$

$$\boxed{\theta = 6° \ 22'}$$

Hence, required angle of deviation for the first-order maximum is 6° 22'.

7.6 HEISENBERG'S UNCERTAINTY PRINCIPLE

[May 13, 14, 15, 16 Nov. 13, 15]

- One of the tacit assumptions of classical physics, that the position of a mechanical system can be uniquely determined without disturbing its motion, is valid only for the motion of a body of ordinary size, like a cricket ball.

- But if one is considering the motion of an atomic particle, like an electron, a certain uncertainty is unavoidably introduced into the experimental measurement of its position and momentum.

- This uncertainty is not due to the imperfection of the measuring instruments but is something inherent in the nature of a moving body.

- The fact that a moving body must be regarded as a De Broglie wave group (packet) rather than as a localised entity suggests that, there is a fundamental limit to the accuracy with which we can measure its particle properties.

- A De Broglie wave group is shown in Fig. 7.3 (a). The particle may be anywhere within the group. For a very narrow wave group, as in Fig. 7.3 (b), the position of the particle can be readily found, but the wavelength λ, and hence the momentum $p = \frac{h}{\lambda}$, is impossible to establish.

- For a wide wave group, as in Fig. 7.3 (c), the wavelength and hence momentum estimate is satisfactory, but then the location of the position of the particle becomes uncertain.

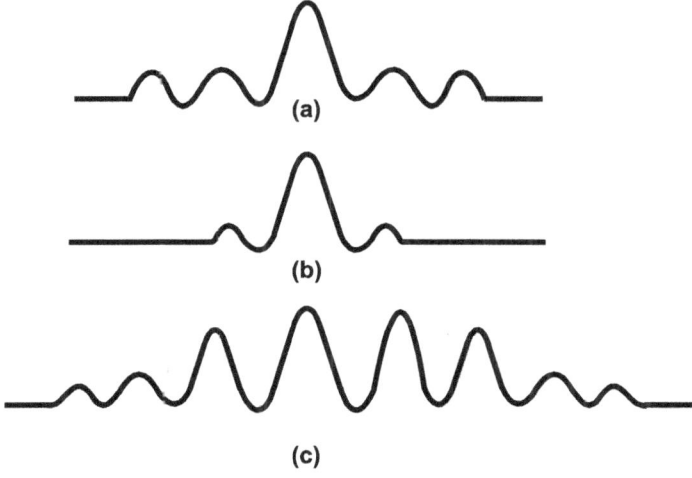

Fig. 7.3

- The answer to this question was given by Heisenberg in 1927, when he put forth the uncertainty principle.

Statement:

- Heisenberg's uncertainty principle states that, ***it is impossible to determine accurately and simultaneously the values of both the members of a pair of physical variables which describe the motion of an atomic system.*** Such pairs of variables like position x and momentum p; or energy E and time t, are called ***canonically conjugate variables.***

- To examine the uncertainty principle, consider an electron of mass m associated with matter waves of wavelength λ. This electron can be found somewhere within this wave and therefore, the uncertainty in its position measurement Δx is equal to its wavelength λ.

$\therefore$ $$\Delta x = \lambda \qquad \qquad \qquad \dots (1)$$

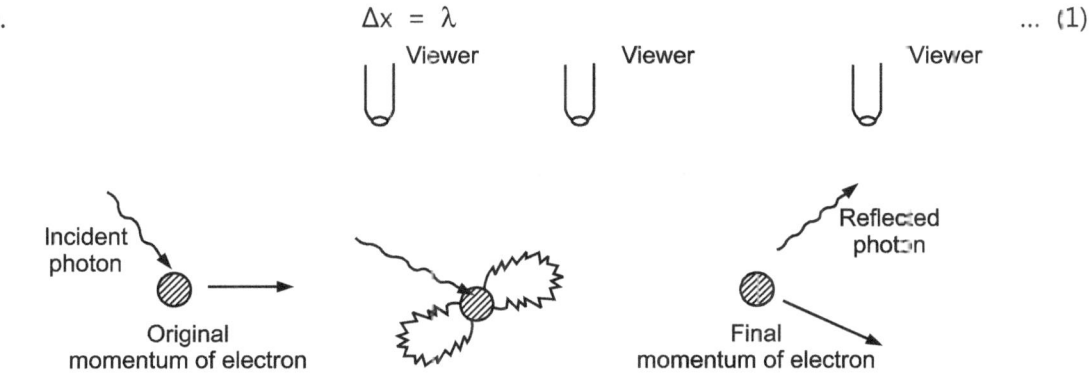

Fig. 7.4: An electron cannot be observed without changing its momentum by an indeterminate amount

- To observe the electron we have to illuminate it with light, say of wavelength λ, as in Fig. 7.4. In this process, photons of light strike the electron and bounce off it. Each photon possesses the momentum $\frac{h}{\lambda}$ and when it collides with the electron, original momentum p of the electron is changed.

- The precise change of the momentum of the electron cannot be predicted, but it is likely to be of the same order of magnitude as the photon momentum $\frac{h}{\lambda}$. Thus, the electron cannot be observed without changing its momentum by an indeterminate amount.

- The act of measurement of its position introduces an uncertainty in its momentum Δp and this uncertainty in the momentum is at least equal to the momentum of incident photon.

$$\therefore \qquad \Delta p = \frac{h}{\lambda} \qquad\qquad\qquad ... (2)$$

From equations (1) and (2),

$$\Delta x \cdot \Delta p = \lambda \cdot \frac{h}{\lambda} = h \qquad\qquad\qquad ... (3)$$

- It is clear from equation (3) that if the position of the electron is known exactly at any given instant, i.e. if Δx = 0, then the momentum becomes indeterminate and vice-versa. Thus, both the position and the momentum cannot be determined accurately and simultaneously.

- The product of uncertainty in position measurement Δx of a body at some instant and the uncertainty in its momentum measurement Δp at the same instant is at best equal to the Planck's constant h (more correctly $\frac{h}{4\pi}$).

i.e.

$$\Delta x \cdot \Delta p \geq \frac{h}{4\pi}$$

This is Heisenberg's uncertainty principle.

7.6.1 Uncertainty Principle Applied to the Pair of Variables   [May 14]

Energy and Time

- Kinetic energy and time form another pair of canonically conjugate variables. Consider again the Problem of an electron of mass m moving with velocity v. We can write the K.E. of the electron as

$$E = \frac{1}{2}mv^2 \qquad\qquad\qquad ... (1)$$

- The uncertainty in the energy measurement ΔE can be found by differentiating equation (1), assuming mass to be constant.

$$\therefore \quad \Delta E = \frac{1}{2} m \cdot 2 v \Delta v$$

$$\Delta E = v (m \cdot \Delta v)$$

$$\Delta E = v \cdot \Delta p$$

$$\Delta E = \frac{\Delta x}{\Delta t} \cdot \Delta p \qquad\qquad (\because v = \frac{\Delta x}{\Delta t})$$

Hence $\quad \Delta E \cdot \Delta t = \Delta x \cdot \Delta p$

- But by Heisenberg's uncertainty principle,

$$\Delta x \cdot \Delta p \geq \frac{h}{4\pi}$$

$$\therefore \quad\quad \Delta E \cdot \Delta t \geq \frac{h}{4\pi}$$

- This means that the product of uncertainties in energy and time measurements is of the order of Planck's constant.

7.6.2 Illustration of Uncertainty Principle   [May 13, 15, Nov. 13, Dec. 14]

(1) Diffraction at a Single Slit

- Consider a narrow beam of electrons passing normally through a single vertical narrow slit of width Δy and producing a diffraction pattern on the screen. (See Fig. 7.5)

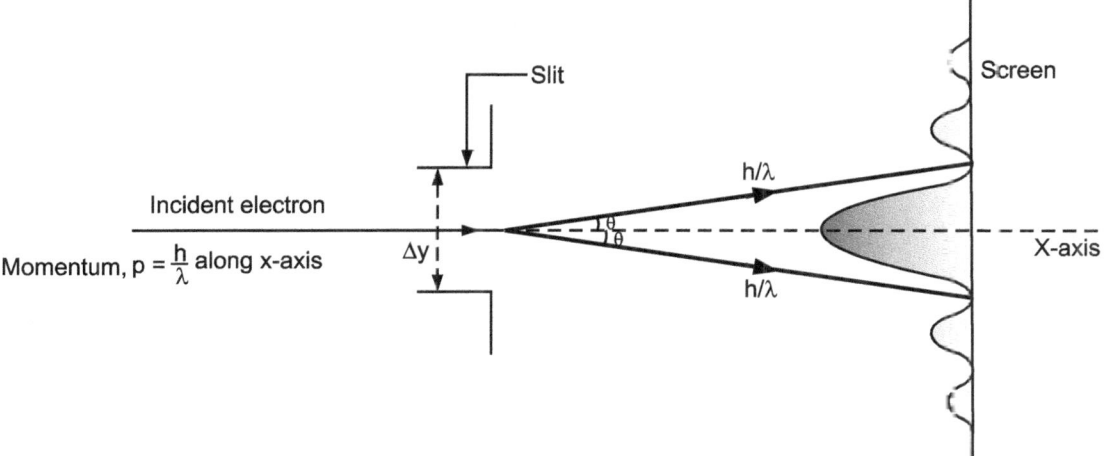

Fig. 7.5: Diffraction of electrons at a single slit

- We know that the positions of minima in the diffraction pattern due to a slit of width a formed by incident light of wavelength λ are given by

$$a \sin \theta = n \lambda \qquad\qquad \dots (1)$$

where θ is the angle of deviation of nth order minimum in the diffraction pattern.

- So if the first order minimum in the diffraction pattern due to a slit of width Δy is formed for an angle θ, when electron waves of wavelength λ are diffracted by it, we shall have

$$\Delta y \sin \theta = 1 \cdot \lambda \qquad \dots (2)$$

- All the electrons producing the diffraction pattern on the screen have passed through the slit, but we cannot say definitely at what position of the slit. So the uncertainty in position determination of electrons is equal to the width Δy of the slit, and from equation (2), we have

$$\Delta y = \frac{\lambda}{\sin \theta} \qquad \dots (3)$$

- Electrons are initially moving along positive x-axis. Their momentum along x-axis is $\frac{h}{\lambda}$ and they do not have any component of momentum along y-axis.

- But after diffraction at the slit, electrons are deviated from their initial path to form the diffraction pattern, and the y-component of their momentum may be between $\frac{h}{\lambda} \sin \theta$ and $-\frac{h}{\lambda} \sin \theta$ (See Fig. 7.5).

- So the uncertainty in momentum measurement along y - direction is given by

$$\Delta p_y = \frac{h}{\lambda} \sin \theta - \left(-\frac{h}{\lambda} \sin \theta\right)$$

$$\Delta p_y = \frac{2h}{\lambda} \sin \theta \qquad \dots (4)$$

From equations (2) and (3), we have

$$\Delta y \cdot \Delta p_y = \frac{\lambda}{\sin \theta} \cdot \frac{2h}{\lambda} \sin \theta = 2h$$

i.e. $\qquad \Delta y \cdot \Delta p_y \geq h$

- Thus, the product of uncertainties in position and momentum measurements of the electron is of the order of Planck's constant, which is Heisenberg's uncertainty principle.

(2) Why an Electron cannot Exist in the Nucleus

- If the electrons had to exist inside the nucleus then its De-Broglie wavelength should be roughly of the order of nucleus diameter i.e. 10^{-14} m. Therefore, the corresponding momentum will be

$$p = \frac{h}{\lambda} = \frac{6.63 \times 10^{-34}}{10^{-14}} = 6.63 \times 10^{-20} \text{ kg-m/sec}$$

$$\therefore \qquad E = \frac{p^2}{2m} = \frac{(6.63 \times 10^{-34})^2}{2 \times 9.1 \times 10^{-31}} = 2.42 \times 10^{-9} \text{ J}$$

$$= \frac{2.42 \times 10^{-9}}{1.6 \times 10^{-19}} \text{ eV } = 15095 \text{ MeV}$$

- If the electron had to exist in the nucleus then its energy should be 15095 MeV. However, this is greater than the maximum binding energy of the nucleus. Thus, the electron cannot exist inside the nucleus.

SOLVED PROBLEMS

Problem 7.11: *In an experiment, the wavelength of a photon is measured to an accuracy of one part per million. What is the uncertainty Δx in a simultaneous measurement of the position of the photon having a wavelength of 6000 A° ?*

Data: $\lambda = 6000$ A° $= 6000 \times 10^{-10}$ m, $h = 6.6 \times 10^{-34}$ J-sec

$$\frac{\Delta\lambda}{\lambda} = \frac{1}{10^6}$$

Formulae: $\qquad \Delta p = \dfrac{h}{\Delta\lambda}, \qquad \Delta x \cdot \Delta p \approx h$

Solution: $\qquad \Delta p = \dfrac{6.6 \times 10^{-34}}{6000 \times 10^{-16}}$

$$= 1.1 \times 10^{-21} \text{ kg-m/sec}$$

$$\Delta x = \frac{h}{\Delta p} = \frac{6.6 \times 10^{-34}}{1.1 \times 10^{-21}} = \boxed{6 \times 10^{-13} \text{ m}}$$

Problem 7.12: *In order to locate the electron in an atom within a distance of 5×10^{-12} m using electromagnetic waves, the wavelength must be of the same order. Calculate the energy and momentum of the photon. What is the corresponding uncertainty in its momentum ?*

Data: $\qquad\qquad\qquad \lambda = \Delta x = 5 \times 10^{-12}$ m

Formulae: $p = \dfrac{h}{\lambda}, \quad E = \dfrac{hc}{\lambda}, \quad \Delta p_x = \dfrac{h}{\Delta x}$

Solution: $\qquad\qquad p = \dfrac{6.6 \times 10^{-34}}{5 \times 10^{-12}} = 1.32 \times 10^{-22} \text{ kg-m/sec}$

$$E = \frac{6.6 \times 10^{-34} \times 3 \times 10^8}{5 \times 10^{-12}}$$

$$= 3.96 \times 10^{-14} \text{ J}$$

$$\Delta p_x = \frac{6.6 \times 10^{-34}}{5 \times 10^{-12}}$$

$$= \boxed{1.32 \times 10^{-22} \text{ kg-m/sec}}$$

Problem 7.13: *Compute the uncertainty in the location of a 2 gram mass moving with a speed of 1.5 m/sec. and the minimum uncertainty in the location of an electron moving with a speed of 0.5×10^8 m/sec. Given, $\Delta p = 10^{-3}$ p.*

Data: $v_e = 0.5 \times 10^8$ m/sec, $\Delta p = 10^{-3}$ p, m = 2 grams = 2×10^{-3} kg,

$$v \text{ for the body } = 1.5 \text{ m/sec}$$

Formula: $$\Delta x \, \Delta p = h$$

Solution:

(i) For the body, $\quad\quad\quad\quad\quad \Delta p = 10^{-3} \, p = 10^{-3} \, (mv)$

$$\Delta x \cdot \Delta p = h$$

$$\Delta x = \frac{h}{\Delta p} = \frac{6.6 \times 10^{-34}}{10^{-3} \times 2 \times 1.5 \times 10^{-3}}$$

$$= \boxed{2.2 \times 10^{-28} \text{ m}}$$

(ii) For the electron, $\quad\quad \Delta x = \frac{6.6 \times 10^{-34}}{10^{-3} \times 9.1 \times 10^{-31} \times 0.5 \times 10^8}$

$$= \boxed{1.45 \times 10^{-8} \text{ m}}$$

It can be seen that the uncertainty associated with a microscopic body is very large and therefore, it plays a significant role in measurements.

Problem 7.14: *Assume that the uncertainty in the location of a particle is equal to its De Broglie wavelength. Show that the uncertainty in its velocity is equal to its velocity.*

(03) (Nov. 13)

Data: $\quad\quad\quad\quad\quad\quad\quad\quad \Delta x = \lambda$

Formula: $\quad\quad\quad\quad\quad\quad \Delta x \cdot \Delta p = h$

Solution: $\quad\quad\quad\quad\quad \Delta x \cdot m \, \Delta v_x = h$

$$\Delta v_x = \frac{h}{\Delta x \cdot m} = \frac{h}{m \, \lambda}$$

Using $\quad\quad\quad\quad\quad\quad\quad \lambda = \frac{h}{mv}$

we have $\quad\quad\quad\quad\quad\quad \Delta v_x = \frac{h \, m \, v}{mh} = v$

Problem 7.15: *An electron is confined to a box of length 1 A°. Calculate the minimum uncertainty in its velocity, given mass of electron = 9.1×10^{-31} kg, $h = 6.6 \times 10^{-34}$ J-sec.*

Data: $\Delta x = 1$ A° = 10^{-10} m, h = 6.6×10^{-34} J-sec, m = 9.1×10^{-31} kg

Formula: $\quad\quad\quad\quad\quad\quad \Delta x \, \Delta p_x = h$

Solution: $(\Delta x)_{max} (\Delta p_x)_{min} = h$

$(\Delta x)_{max} (\Delta v)_{min} = h$

$(\Delta v)_{min} = \dfrac{h}{m \, \Delta x} = \dfrac{6.6 \times 10^{-34}}{9.1 \times 10^{-31} \times 10^{-10}}$

$= \boxed{0.725 \times 10^7 \text{ m/sec.}}$

This is comparable to the speed of the electron and is therefore very large

Problem 7.16: *What accelerating potential would be required for a proton with zero velocity to acquire a velocity corresponding to De Broglie wavelength of 10^{-14} m ?*

Data: $h = 6.62 \times 10^{-34}$ J-sec, $m = 1.67 \times 10^{-27}$ kg, $e = 1.6 \times 10^{-19}$ C

Formula: $V = \dfrac{h^2}{2 \, me\lambda^2}$

Solution: $V = \dfrac{(6.62 \times 10^{-34})^2}{2 \times 1.67 \times 10^{-27} \times 1.6 \times 10^{-19} \times (10^{-14})^2}$

$= 8.2 \times 10^6 \text{ volts} = \boxed{8.2 \text{ M volts}}$

Problem 7.17: *Find De Broglie wavelength of 10 keV electrons.*

Data: $E = 10 \text{ keV} = 10 \times 10^3 \times 1.6 \times 10^{-19}$ J

Formula: $\lambda = \dfrac{h}{\sqrt{2mE}}$

Solution: $\lambda = \dfrac{6.6 \times 10^{-34}}{\sqrt{2 \times 9.1 \times 10^{-31} \times 10^4 \times 1.6 \times 10^{-19}}}$

$= 1.22 \times 10^{-11} \text{ m} = \boxed{0.122 \text{ A}^\circ}$

Problem 7.18: *Calculate the minimum uncertainty in the velocity of an electron confined to a box of length 10 A°.*

Data: $L = 10 \text{ A}^\circ = 10 \times 10^{-10}$ m

Formula: $\Delta x \cdot \Delta p_x = h$

Solution: $(\Delta x)_{max} (\Delta p_x)_{min} = h$

i.e. $(\Delta x)_{max} \, m(\Delta v_x)_{min} = h$

$\Delta v_x = \dfrac{h}{m \cdot (\Delta x)_{max}} = \dfrac{6.6 \times 10^{-34}}{9.1 \times 10^{-31} \times 10^{-9}}$

$= \boxed{0.725 \times 10^6 \text{ m/sec.}}$

Problem 7.19: *Electrons moving with a speed of 7.3 $\times 10^7$ m/sec have a wavelength of 0.1 A°. Calculate the Planck's constant.*

Data: λ = 0.1 A° = 0.1 $\times 10^{-10}$ m

                             v = 7.3 $\times 10^7$ m/sec.

Formula: **h = $\lambda \cdot$ m v**

Solution: h = 0.1 $\times 10^{-10} \times$ 9.1 $\times 10^{-31} \times$ 7.3 $\times 10^7$

                             = $\boxed{6.643 \times 10^{-34} \text{ J-sec.}}$

Problem 7.20: *Calculate the wavelength of an electron of energy 291 eV.*

Data: E = 291 eV = 291 $\times$ 1.6 $\times 10^{-19}$ J

Formula: $\lambda = \dfrac{h}{\sqrt{2 \text{ m E}}}$

Solution: $\lambda = \dfrac{6.6 \times 10^{-34}}{\sqrt{2 \times 9.1 \times 10^{-31} \times 291 \times 1.6 \times 10^{-19}}}$

                             = $\boxed{0.717 \text{ A°}}$

Problem 7.21: *An electron has a speed of 600 m/sec with an accuracy of 0.005 %. Calculate the uncertainty with which we can locate the position of the electron.*

Data: v = 600 m/sec

                             Δv = 0.005 % of v

                             = $\dfrac{0.005}{100} \times$ 600 m/sec

Formula: **$\Delta x \cdot \Delta p$ = h**

                       $\Delta x = \dfrac{h}{\Delta p} = \dfrac{h}{m \, \Delta v} = \dfrac{6.6 \times 10^{-34}}{9.1 \times 10^{-31}} \times \dfrac{0.005}{100} \times 600$

                       = $\boxed{0.024 \text{ m}}$

Problem 7.22: *Proton and deuteron are accelerated by the same potential. Compare their De Broglie wavelengths. Assume mass of deuterium to be twice the mass of a proton.*

Data: m_d = 2 m_p

Formula: $\lambda = \dfrac{h}{\sqrt{2 \text{ meV}}}$

Solution: For proton, $\lambda_p = \dfrac{h}{\sqrt{2 \, m_p \, eV}}$

For deuteron, $\lambda_d = \dfrac{h}{\sqrt{2\ m_d eV}} = \dfrac{h}{\sqrt{4\ m_p eV}}$

$$\dfrac{\lambda_p}{\lambda_d} = \dfrac{h/\sqrt{2\ m_p\ eV}}{h/\sqrt{4\ m_p\ eV}} = \sqrt{2}$$

∴ $\boxed{\lambda_p : \lambda_d = \sqrt{2} : 1}$

Problem 7.23: *Find the kinetic energy of a neutron in eV, whose De-Broglie wavelength is 1 A° ($M_n = 1.67 \times 10^{-27}$ kg).*

Solution: Given:

$\lambda_n = 1\ A° = 1 \times 10^{-10}$ m

$M_n = 1.67 \times 10^{-27}$ kg

$h = 6.63 \times 10^{-34}$ J.sec

$\lambda = \dfrac{h}{\sqrt{2mE}}$

∴ $E = \dfrac{h^2}{2m\lambda^2} = \dfrac{(6.63 \times 10^{-34})^2}{2 \times 1.67 \times 10^{-27} \times (1 \times 10^{-10})^2}$

∴ $E = 1.3160 \times 10^{-20}$ J

$\boxed{E = 8.225 \times 10^{-2}\ eV}$

Problem 7.24: *Find the De-Broglie wavelength of an electron accelerated through a potential difference of 100 volts.*

Data: $V = 100$ volts

Formula: $\lambda = \dfrac{12.27}{\sqrt{V}}\ A°$

Solution: $\lambda = \dfrac{12.27}{\sqrt{100}} = \boxed{1.227\ A°}$

7.7 CONCEPT OF WAVE FUNCTION ψ AND PROBABILITY INTERPRETATION OF $|\psi|^2$ [Nov. 13, 15, May 15, 16]

- A wave motion appears in almost all branches of physics. A wave motion is defined as a *periodic disturbance travelling with finite velocity through a medium or space.*

- The simplest form of vibration is simple harmonic motion (S.H.M.) and a particle executing S.H.M. acts as a source which radiates waves.

- The wave motion provides a way for energy and momentum to move from one place to another without material particles making that journey.

- The waves can be classified according to their broad physical properties into mainly three categories:
  - ➤ Electromagnetic waves which need not require any medium to propagate.
  - ➤ Matter waves which give the probability amplitude of finding a particle at a given position and time.
  - ➤ **Mechanical Waves:** The mechanical waves are simplest one to understand because they are produced by some sort of mechanical vibrations which we can see.

- When a mechanical wave passes through a medium, the medium particles perform an S.H.M. given by equation

$$y = A \cos \omega t \qquad \qquad ...(1)$$

where A is the amplitude of the oscillation and $\omega = 2\pi\upsilon$, where υ is the frequency.

- This equation is applicable to all individual particles affected by the wave. Suppose the wave is progressing forward with velocity v. If P is the origin of the wave, then a particle at Q at a distance x from P will receive the wave x/v sec later than P did.

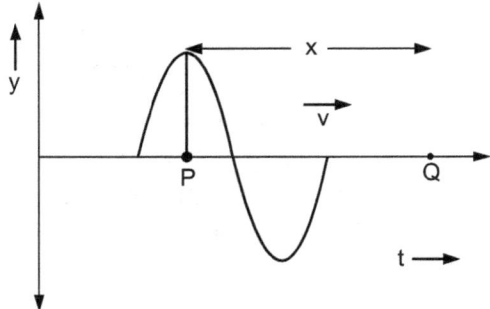

Fig. 7.6: Progressive wave moving with velocity v

- Hence, its displacement at time t and distance x from the origin will be

$$y = A \cos \omega \left(t - \frac{x}{v} \right) \qquad \qquad ...(2)$$

The wave equation of such a wave is

$$\frac{d^2y}{dt^2} = v^2 \frac{d^2y}{dx^2} \qquad \qquad ...(3)$$

The solution of equation (3) is given by

$$y = Ae^{-i\omega (t - x/v)} \qquad \qquad ...(4)$$

- In a string we can represent the wave disturbance by the transverse displacement of y. Similarly, for light waves the field vectors E and B vary in space and time, for sound waves, pressure P varies in space and time. In the same way, for matter waves, the wave function ψ varies in space and time.

- So ψ in wave mechanics is analogous to electric field E in electromagnetic waves or to pressure P in the sound waves. However, ψ itself unlike E and P has no direct physical significance, but gives a measure of the probability of finding a particle at a particular position. Hence, it is called ***probability amplitude***.

- However, a probability is always real and positive, whereas ψ can be positive or negative. Therefore, ψ^2 is taken which is always positive. In general, ψ is complex, therefore, one takes $|\psi|^2$ instead of ψ^2, where $|\psi|^2 = \psi^* \psi$, ψ^* denoting the complex conjugate of ψ. In any case, $\psi^* \psi$ is always real and positive.

- If dv is a volume element located at a point, then the probability of finding the particle in the volume element at time t is proportional to ψ*ψdv. By analogy with ordinary mass density, the square of the wave function $\psi^*\psi$ is called the ***probability density*** i.e. ***probability per unit volume***.

7.7.1 Physical Significance of the Wave Function ψ

[Dec. 12, Nov. 13, May 15]

- Schroedinger interpreted ψ in terms of charge density. If A is the amplitude of an electromagnetic wave, then the energy per unit volume, i.e. energy density is equal to A^2. Also, the photon energy hυ is constant. So the number of photons per unit volume, i.e. the photon density is equal to $\dfrac{A^2}{h\upsilon}$, and it is proportional to the amplitude square.

- Similarly, if ψ is the amplitude of matter waves at any point in space, the particle density at that point may be taken as proportional to $|\psi|^2$. So $|\psi|^2$ is a measure of particle density and on multiplying this by the charge of the particle, we shall get the charge density. Thus, $|\psi|^2$ is a measure of **'*charge density*'**.

- According to Max Born, the value of $|\psi|^2$ at a point at a given time is related to the probability of finding the body described by its wave function ψ at that point at that instant. A large value of $|\psi|^2$ means a strong possibility of the presence of the body, while a small value of $|\psi|^2$ means a slight possibility of its presence. As long as $|\psi|^2$ is not actually zero somewhere, there is a definite chance, however small, of detecting the body there.

- Although the wave function ψ of a particle is spread out in space, this does not mean that the particle itself is also thus spread out. When an experiment is performed to detect a particle, an electron for instance, a whole electron is either found at a certain place and time, or it is not. There is nothing like 20 % of an electron. However, it s certainly possible that there is 20 % chance that the electron be found at that place and time, and it's likelihood that is specified by $|\psi|^2$ or ψψ*, ψ* being the complex conjugate of ψ.

- $|\psi|^2$ or $\psi\psi^*$ is taken as the probability density, i.e. the probability of finding the particle in unit volume. So the probability of the particle being present in a volume element dx·dy·dz is $|\psi|^2$ dx dy dz. Then, the wave function ψ is called the **'probability density amplitude'**.

- Since the particle is certainly to be found somewhere in space, we must have,

$$\iiint \; |\psi|^2 \, dx \, dy \, dz \;=\; 1 \qquad\qquad\qquad \dots (1)$$

   the triple integral extending over all possible values of x, y, z.

- A function ψ satisfying this relation is called a **'normalised wave function'** and equation (1) is known as the **'normalisation condition'**. Thus, ψ has to be a normalisable function.

   Besides being normalisable, ψ must also satisfy the following conditions:

   ➤ ψ must be a single valued function, because ψ is related to the probability of finding the particle at a given place and time, and the probability can have only one value at a given point and time.

   ➤ ψ must be finite, because the particle exists somewhere in space, and so integral over all space must be finite.

   ➤ ψ and its derivatives $\dfrac{\partial\psi}{\partial x}$, $\dfrac{\partial\psi}{\partial y}$, $\dfrac{\partial\psi}{\partial z}$ must be continuous everywhere in the region where ψ is defined.

7.8 SCHROEDINGER'S WAVE EQUATION   [May 15, 16]

- Schroedinger started with De Broglie's idea of matter waves and developed it into a mathematical theory known as **'wave mechanics'**. Schroedinger's wave equation is the mathematical representation of matter waves associated with a moving particle. There are two types of Schroedinger's wave equations:

   ➤ Schroedinger's time independent wave equation

   ➤ Schroedinger's time dependent wave equation.

7.8.1 Schroedinger's Time Independent Wave Equation

[Dec. 12, 14, Nov. 15, May 13, 14, 15]

- According to De Broglie's theory, a particle of mass m moving with a velocity v has a wave system of some kind associated with it, and its wavelength is given by $\lambda = \dfrac{h}{mv}$. The waves are produced only when something oscillates. Though we do not know the quantity that vibrates to produce the matter waves, but we can indicate that quantity by ψ.

- The periodic changes in ψ produce the wave system associated with the particle, just as the periodic changes in the displacement y of a string produce a wave system along the string.

- In quantum mechanics, ψ corresponds to the displacement y of wave motion in a string. However, ψ, unlike y, is not itself a measurable quantity and it may be complex.

- Consider a system of stationary waves associated with a particle. Let (x, y, z) be the coordinates of the particle and let ψ denote the wave displacement of matter waves at time t.

- By analogy with the wave equation

$$\frac{d^2 y}{dt^2} = v^2 \frac{d^2 y}{dx^2}$$ of a two-dimensional wave (in xy plane), the

wave equation for a three-dimensional wave with wave velocity u can be written as

$$\frac{\partial^2 \psi}{\partial t^2} = u^2 \left(\frac{\partial^2 \psi}{\partial x^2} + \frac{\partial^2 \psi}{\partial y^2} + \frac{\partial^2 \psi}{\partial z^2} \right)$$

$$\frac{\partial^2 \psi}{\partial t^2} = u^2 \nabla^2 \psi \qquad \text{... (1)}$$

where $\nabla^2 = \frac{\partial^2}{\partial x^2} + \frac{\partial^2}{\partial y^2} + \frac{\partial^2}{\partial z^2}$ is the '**Laplacian operator**'.

The solution of equation (1) is

$$\psi (x, y, z, t) = \psi_0 (x, y, z) e^{-i \omega t} \qquad \text{... (2)}$$

where $\psi_0 (x, y, z)$ represents the amplitude of the wave at the point considered.

- The position vector of a point whose Cartesian coordinates are (x, y, z) is given by

$$\vec{r} = x \hat{i} + y \hat{j} + z \hat{k}$$

$\hat{i}, \hat{j}, \hat{k}$ being unit vectors along the axes. So equation (2) can be written as

$$\psi (\vec{r}, t) = \psi_0 (\vec{r}) e^{-i \omega t} \qquad \text{... (3)}$$

Differentiating equation (3) twice with respect to time t, we get

$$\frac{\partial \psi}{\partial t} = -i \omega \psi_0 (r) e^{-i \omega t}$$

and

$$\frac{\partial^2 \psi}{\partial t^2} = (-i\omega)^2 \psi_0 (\vec{r}) e^{-i \omega t} = -\omega^2 \psi \qquad \text{... (4)}$$

From equations (1) and (4), we get

$$u^2 \nabla^2 \psi = -\omega^2 \psi$$

$$\therefore \qquad \nabla^2 \psi + \frac{\omega^2}{u^2} \psi = 0 \qquad \qquad \dots (5)$$

But $\omega = 2\pi \upsilon$, and $u = \upsilon \lambda$

$\therefore$ Equation (5) becomes

$$\nabla^2 \psi + \frac{4\pi^2}{\lambda^2} \psi = 0 \qquad \qquad \dots (6)$$

- The De Broglie wavelength of the waves associated with the particle is given by

$$\lambda = \frac{h}{mv} = \frac{h}{p} \qquad \qquad \dots (7)$$

Substituting equation (7) in (6), we get

$$\nabla^2 \psi + \frac{4\pi^2 p^2}{h^2} \psi = 0 \qquad \qquad \dots (8)$$

- The total energy E of the particle is the sum of it's K.E. $= \frac{1}{2} mv^2$ and potential energy V.

$$\therefore \qquad E = \frac{1}{2} mv^2 + V$$

$$E = \frac{p^2}{2m} + V$$

This gives $\qquad p^2 = 2m(E - V) \qquad \qquad \dots (9)$

Substituting equation (9) in (8), we get

$$\nabla^2 \psi + \frac{8\pi^2 m(E - V)}{h^2} \psi = 0 \qquad \qquad \dots (10)$$

- Equation (10) is called **'Schroedinger's time independent wave equation'**.

Taking $\qquad \hbar = \frac{h}{2\pi}$, equation (10) becomes

$$\nabla^2 \psi + \frac{2m(E - V)}{\hbar^2} \psi = 0 \qquad \qquad \dots (11)$$

7.8.2 Schroedinger's Time Dependent Wave Equation

- Schroedinger's time independent wave equation is

$$\nabla^2 \psi + \frac{8\pi^2 m}{h^2} (E - V) \psi = 0 \qquad \qquad \dots (1)$$

- The time dependent wave equation is obtained by eliminating E from the time independent equation.

Consider a system of stationary waves associated with a particle. Let (x, y, z) be the coordinates of the particle and let ψ denote the wave displacement of the matter waves at time t. If u be the wave velocity. then the equation for a three-dimensional wave motion can be written as,

$$\frac{\partial^2 \psi}{\partial t^2} = u^2 \left(\frac{\partial^2 \psi}{\partial x^2} + \frac{\partial^2 \psi}{\partial y^2} + \frac{\partial^2 \psi}{\partial z^2} \right) = u^2 \nabla^2 \psi \qquad \ldots (2)$$

where $\qquad \nabla^2 = \frac{\partial^2}{\partial x^2} + \frac{\partial^2}{\partial y^2} + \frac{\partial^2}{\partial z^2}$ is the **'Laplacian operator'**

The solution of equation (2) is

$$\psi (x, y, z, t) = \psi_0 (x, y, z) e^{-i\omega t} = \psi_0 (\vec{r}) e^{-i\omega t} \qquad \ldots (3)$$

where $\psi_0 (x, y, z)$ is the amplitude of the wave at the point considered.

- Differentiating equation (3) with respect to time t, we get

$$\frac{\partial \psi}{\partial t} = (-i\omega) \psi_0 (\vec{r}) e^{-i\omega t} = -i\omega \psi \qquad \ldots (4)$$

Now, $\omega = 2\pi\upsilon$ and $E = h\upsilon$ or $\upsilon = \dfrac{E}{h}$

$$\therefore \qquad \omega = \frac{2\pi E}{h}$$

Putting this value of ω in equation (4), we get

$$\frac{\partial \psi}{\partial t} = -i \frac{2\pi E}{h} \psi \qquad \ldots (5)$$

Multiplying both sides of equation (5) by i,

$$i \frac{\partial \psi}{\partial t} = i^2 \frac{2\pi}{h} E\psi$$

$$\therefore \qquad E\psi = i \frac{h}{2\pi} \frac{\partial \psi}{\partial t} = i\hbar \frac{\partial \psi}{\partial t} \qquad \ldots (6)$$

From equations (1) and (6), we get

$$\nabla^2 \psi + \frac{8\pi^2 m}{h^2} \left(\frac{ih}{2\pi} \frac{\partial \psi}{\partial t} - V\psi \right) = 0$$

Multiplying both sides of this equation by $\dfrac{-h^2}{8\pi^2 m}$, we get

$$-\frac{h^2}{8\pi^2 m} \nabla^2 \psi - \frac{ih}{2\pi} \frac{\partial \psi}{\partial t} + V\psi = 0$$

$$\left(-\frac{h^2}{8\pi^2 m} \nabla^2 + V \right) \psi = \frac{ih}{2\pi} \frac{\partial \psi}{\partial t} \qquad \ldots (7)$$

or
$$\left(\frac{-h^2}{2m}\nabla^2 + V\right)\psi = i\hbar\frac{\partial\psi}{\partial t}$$
... (8)

Equation (8) is called **'Schroedinger's time dependent wave equation'**.

Taking
$$H = \left(-\frac{h^2}{8\pi^2 m}\nabla^2 + V\right) = \left(\frac{-\hbar^2}{2m}\nabla^2 + V\right)$$
as **'Hamiltonian operator'**

and
$$E = \frac{ih}{2\pi}\frac{\partial}{\partial t} = i\hbar\frac{\partial}{\partial t}$$
as **'Eigen operator'**,

equation (8) becomes

$$H\psi = E\psi$$
... (9)

7.9 APPLICATIONS OF SCHROEDINGER'S TIME INDEPENDENT WAVE EQUATION

* In quantum mechanics, the wave function of a system gives the description of that system. We apply Schroedinger's wave equation to a system, and then solve it to find the wave function of the system. We shall study how Schroedinger's time independent wave equation can be applied to a system and then solved to find the energy and wave function of the system under given conditions.

* We also aim at learning characteristic properties of solutions of this equation and comparing the predictions of quantum mechanics with those of Newtonian mechanics.

* As simple applications of Schroedinger's time independent wave equation, here we shall discuss the problems of:

  ➢ Particle in a rigid box

  ➢ Particle in a non-rigid box

  ➢ Tunneling effect.

7.10 PARTICLE IN A RIGID BOX   [Nov. 13]

* Consider a particle confined to a rigid box and restricted to travelling along x-axis between x = 0 and x = L (See Fig. 7.7). Such a box has infinitely hard walls, and a particle does not lose energy when it collides with such walls. So the total energy E of the particle remains constant. The case under discussion is also called **'infinite potential well'**.

* As shown in Fig. 7.7, the potential energy V of the particle is infinite on both sides of the box, while V is constant (say V = 0 for convenience) inside the box. This means that V (x) = 0 in the region 0 < x < L; and V (x) = ∞ for x ≤ 0 and x ≥ L.

* The particle cannot have an infinite amount of energy. So it cannot exist outside the box and hence particle wave function ψ is zero for x ≤ 0 and x ≥ L. We now find the wave

function ψ of the particle within the box, i.e. in the region $0 < x < L$. We use Schroedinger's time independent wave equation and solve it for this purpose.

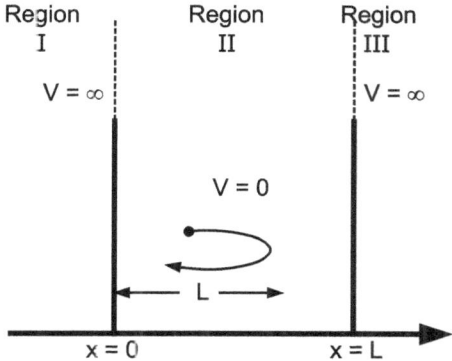

Fig. 7.7: Infinite potential well

- Schroedinger's time independent wave equation is

$$\nabla^2 \psi + \frac{8\pi^2 m}{h^2} (E - V) \psi = 0 \qquad \ldots (1)$$

- Now, the motion of the particle is along x-axis. So $\nabla^2\psi$ can be replaced by the total derivative $\frac{d^2\psi}{dx^2}$. Also $V(x) = 0$ inside the box. So for this problem, Schroedinger's equation (1) becomes

$$\frac{d^2\psi}{dx^2} + \frac{8\pi^2 m E}{h^2} \psi = 0$$

i.e.

$$\frac{d^2\psi}{dx^2} + k^2 \psi = 0 \qquad \ldots (2)$$

where

$$k^2 = \frac{8\pi^2 m E}{h^2} \qquad \ldots (3)$$

- Equation (2) is a total differential equation of second order with imaginary roots, and its general solution will involve two arbitrary constants. So the solution of equation (2) can be taken as

$$\psi(x) = A e^{ikx} + B e^{-ikx} \qquad \ldots (4)$$

- We now apply boundary conditions, namely $\psi(0) = 0$ and $\psi(L) = 0$. So from equation (4), we get

From first boundary condition, $\psi(0) = 0$.

$$\psi(0) = A + B = 0 \quad \text{i.e. } B = -A$$

and from second boundary condition, $\psi(L) = 0$.

$$\psi(L) = A e^{ikL} + B e^{-ikL} = 0$$

Taking $B = -A$, we get

$$A e^{ikL} - A e^{-ikL} = 0$$

Multiplying and dividing by 2i.

$$\therefore \quad 2i \cdot A \frac{(e^{ikL} - e^{-ikL})}{2i} = 0$$

or $\qquad\qquad 2iA \sin kL = 0 \qquad\qquad$ ... (5)

As $A \neq 0$, we infer from equation (5) that

$$\sin kL = 0$$

i.e. $\qquad kL = n\pi, \text{ where } n = 1, 2, 3, \ldots\ldots$

$$\therefore \qquad\qquad k = \frac{n\pi}{L} \qquad\qquad \text{... (6)}$$

From equations (3) and (6), we have

$$k^2 = \frac{8\pi^2 m E}{h^2} = \frac{n^2 \pi^2}{L^2}$$

or $\qquad E_n = \frac{n^2 \cdot h^2}{8 mL^2} \qquad\qquad$ ... (7)

- Equation (7) gives the energy values of the particle and it is evident that the energy of the particle can have only certain specific values as specified by equation (7). These energy values are called **'Eigen values'**.

- Thus, the energy of a particle confined to a rigid box is quantized. It cannot have an arbitrary energy; the fact of its confinement leads to restrictions on its wave function that permit it to have only those energies as specified by equation (7).

- The integer n corresponding to the energy level E_n is called its **'quantum number'**. n = 0 is not possible because the particle cannot have zero energy; and if it did, the particle wave function ψ would have to be zero everywhere in the box, and this means that the particle cannot be present there.

- The exclusion of E = 0 as a possible value for the energy of a trapped particle, like the limitation of E to a discrete set of definite values, is a quantum mechanical result. Classically, all energies, including zero, are presumed possible.

Putting $m = 9.1 \times 10^{-31}$ kg, $h = 6.63 \times 10^{-34}$ J-s and $L = 10^{-10}$ m in equation (7), we get

$$E_n = 6 \times 10^{-18} n^2 \text{ joules}$$

$$= \frac{6 \times 10^{-18}}{1.6 \times 10^{-19}} n^2 \text{ eV}$$

$$\cong 38 n^2 \text{ eV}$$

- The energy levels of such electron trapped in a potential well of width 1 A° s shown in Fig. 7.8.

Fig. 7.8: Energy levels of electron in a rigid box of width 1 A°

7.10.1 Wave Function of a Particle in a Rigid Box

- The wave function $\psi(x)$ of a particle inside a rigid box of width L is given by

$$\psi(x) = 2iA \sin kx \qquad \dots (1)$$

where

$$k = \sqrt{\frac{8\pi^2 m E}{h^2}} = \frac{n\pi}{L} \qquad \dots (2)$$

From equations (1) and (2),

$$\psi(x) = 2iA \sin \frac{n\pi}{L} x \qquad \dots (3)$$

Equation (3) gives Eigen functions corresponding to energy Eigen values

$$E_n = \frac{n^2 h^2}{8 m L^2} \qquad \dots (4)$$

The complex conjugate of $\psi(x)$ is

$$\psi(x) = -2iA \sin \frac{n\pi}{L} x$$

To evaluate the constant A, we use the normalization condition.

i.e.

$$\int_0^L \psi\psi^* \, dx = 1$$

$$\int_0^L 4A^2 \sin^2 \frac{n\pi}{L} x \, dx = 1$$

This gives $2A^2 L = 1$ or $A = \dfrac{1}{\sqrt{2L}}$

- Putting this value of A in equation (3), we get the normalized wave function of the particle as

$$\psi_n = \frac{2i}{\sqrt{2L}} \sin \frac{n\pi}{L} x = i \sqrt{\frac{2}{L}} \cdot \sin \cdot \frac{n\pi}{L} x \qquad \text{... (5)}$$

- The normalized wave functions ψ_1, ψ_2 and ψ_3 together with the corresponding probability densities $|\psi_1|^2$, $|\psi_2|^2$ and $|\psi_3|^2$ are shown in Fig. 7.9 (a) and (b) respectively.

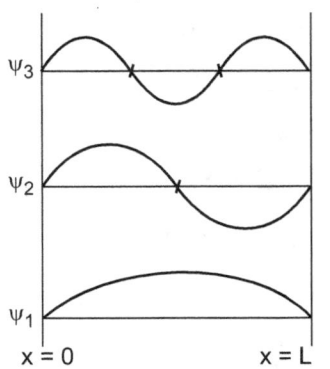

Fig. 7.9 (a): Wave function   **Fig. 7.9 (b): Probability densities**

- While ψ_n may be negative as well as positive, $|\psi_n|^2$ is always positive. It is seen from Fig. 7.9 (b) that
  - In every case $|\psi_n|^2 = 0$ at $x = 0$ and $x = L$, the boundaries of the box.
  - The probability of the particle being present at a particular point in the box may be different for different quantum numbers. e.g. For $n = 1$, the probability is maximum at $x = \frac{L}{2}$. For $n = 2$ there is zero probability of the particle being present at $x = \frac{L}{2}$ and there are two maxima at $x = \frac{L}{4}$ and $x = \frac{3L}{4}$. Classical physics predicts the same probability for the particle to be present anywhere in the box.
- The wave function shown in Fig. 7.9 (a) resembles the possible vibrations of a string fixed at both ends. This is so because the waves in a stretched string and the waves representing a particle obey wave equation of the same form, and when similar restrictions are placed upon each kind of wave, the solutions are identical.

7.10.2 Comparison of Quantum Mechanical and Classical Mechanical Predictions

Quantum Mechanical	Classical Mechanical
1. The energy of the particle confined is quantized i.e. can have only discrete energy levels.	1. The energy of the particle has continuous values i.e. can have all possible values from 0 to ∞.

Quantum Mechanical	Classical Mechanical
2. Energy E = 0 is not possible as the result of Heisenberg's uncertainty principle.	2. Can have energy E = 0.
3. Probability of finding the particle is different at different position.	3. Probability of finding the particle is same energy where.
4. Probability of finding the particle depends on the principle number and hence on energy state.	4. Probability of finding the particle is independent of energy level.
5. Probability is zero at the walls of the potential well.	5. Probability is maximum at the walls of the potential well i.e. at the boundaries.

7.11 PARTICLE IN A NON-RIGID BOX

- Consider a particle trapped in a non-rigid box and restricted to travelling along x-axis between x = 0 and x = L (See Fig. 7.10). The walls of the box are non-rigid. The potential outside the box is finite, say V_0. The potential V_0 is greater than the energy E of the particle inside the box. The potential energy of the particle inside the box is considered to be zero, i.e. V = 0. The case under discussion is also called *'finite potential well'*.

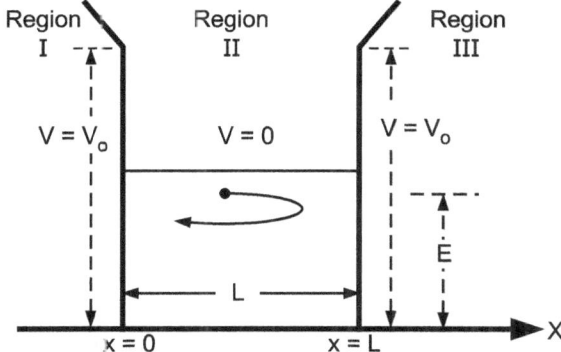

Fig. 7.10: Finite potential well

- As shown in Fig. 7.10, the potential outside the box is finite, say V_0, and inside the box V = 0. This means that V (x) = 0 in the region 0 < x < L and V (x) = V_0 for x ≤ 0 and x ≥ L.

- Now, it is possible for the particle to have energy E that exceeds V_0. So the particle can exist outside the box and wave function ψ of the particle will not be zero at the boundaries of the box. We use Schroedinger's time independent wave equation to find wave function of the particle inside and on the two sides of the box.

- The Schroedinger's time independent wave equation is

$$\nabla^2 \psi + \frac{8\pi^2 m}{h^2} (E - V) \psi = 0 \qquad \qquad \dots (1)$$

- Now, the motion of the particle is only along x-axis. So $\nabla^2\psi$ can be replaced by $\dfrac{d^2\psi}{dx^2}$. Also $V(x) = V_0$ outside the box. So the Schroedinger's equation (1) becomes

$$\frac{d^2\psi}{dx^2} + \frac{8\pi^2 m}{h^2}(E - V_0)\,\psi = 0$$

i.e.
$$\frac{d^2\psi}{dx^2} - k'^2\,\psi = 0 \qquad\qquad \text{... (2)}$$

where
$$k'^2 = \frac{8\pi^2 m}{h^2}(V_0 - E) \qquad\qquad \text{... (3)}$$

- Let the wave functions be denoted by ψ_I, ψ_{II} and ψ_{III} respectively in regions I, II and III. Equation (2) is a total differential equation of second order with real roots, and its general solution will involve two arbitrary constants. So the solutions of equation (2) can be written as:

For region I, i.e. for x < 0,
$$\psi_I(x) = A\,e^{k'x} + B\,e^{-k'x} \qquad\qquad \text{... (4)}$$

and for region III, i.e. for x > L,
$$\psi_{III}(x) = C\,e^{k'x} + D\,e^{-k'x} \qquad\qquad \text{... (5)}$$

- If the wave function of the particle is not to be infinite as we go away from the boundaries of the box, the negative exponential term in equation (4) and the positive exponential term in equation (5) should be absent. i.e. B = 0 and C = 0.

$\therefore$
$$\psi_I(x) = A\,e^{k'x} \qquad\qquad \text{... (6)}$$

and
$$\psi_{III}(x) = D\,e^{-k'x} \qquad\qquad \text{... (7)}$$

- Equations (6) and (7) give wave functions of the particle on the two sides of the non-rigid box.

- Now, to find the wave function inside the box, we take $V(x) = 0$ inside the box. So the equation (1) becomes,

$$\frac{d^2\psi}{dx^2} + \frac{8\pi^2 mE}{h^2}\,\psi = 0$$

i.e.
$$\frac{d^2\psi}{dx^2} + k^2\,\psi = 0 \qquad\qquad \text{... (8)}$$

where
$$k^2 = \frac{8\pi^2 mE}{h^2} \qquad\qquad \text{... (9)}$$

- Equation (8) is a total differential equation of second order with imaginary roots. So its solution can be taken as

$$\psi_{II}(x) = P\,e^{ikx} + Q\,e^{-ikx} \qquad\qquad \text{... (10)}$$

- Equation (10) gives the wave function inside the box.
- The wave function of the particle will be known completely, both outside and inside the box, if we can evaluate the four constants A, D, P and Q of equations (6), (7) and (10).
- For this we need four independent equations among these constants, and they can be obtained by using the property of the wave function that ψ and $\dfrac{\partial \psi}{\partial x}$ must be continuous everywhere in the region where ψ is defined.

So, $\psi_I (0) = \psi_{II} (0)$

i.e. $A = P + Q$ ... (11)

and $\psi_{II} (L) = \psi_{III} (L)$

i.e. $P\, e^{ikL} + Q\, e^{-ikL} = D\, e^{-k'L}$ ... (12)

Similarly, $\left| \dfrac{\partial \psi_I}{\partial x} \right|_{x=0} = \left| \dfrac{\partial \psi_{II}}{\partial x} \right|_{x=0}$

i.e. $Ak' = iPk - iQk$ ... (13)

and $\left| \dfrac{\partial \psi_{II}}{\partial x} \right|_{x=L} = \left| \dfrac{\partial \psi_{III}}{\partial x} \right|_{x=L}$

i.e. $P\, i k\, e^{ikL} - Q\, i k\, e^{-ikL} = -D k'\, e^{-k'L}$ ... (14)

- The constants A, D, P and Q can be evaluated by solving equations (11), (12), (13) and (14). Thus, the wave function of the particle in a non-rigid box is known completely.
- The first few wave functions of a particle in a non-rigid box and the corresponding probability densities are shown in Fig. 7.11 (a) and (b).

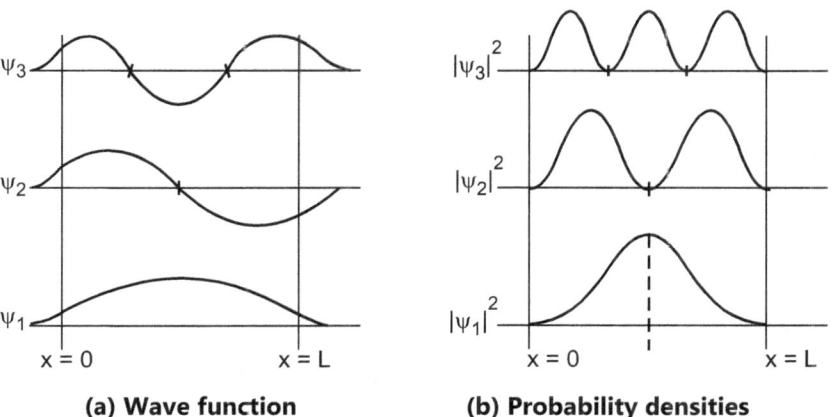

(a) Wave function   (b) Probability densities

Fig. 7.11

- It can be seen from Fig. 7.11 (a) that the wave functions ψ_n are not equal to zero outside the box. This means that even though the particle energy E is smaller than the value of potential outside the box, there is still a definite probability that the particle be found outside the box.
- In other words, even though the particle does not have sufficient energy to break through the walls of the box, it may nevertheless somehow penetrate them and leak out.
- The wave functions of a particle in a box, with rigid walls are zero at the walls. [See Fig. 7.11 (a)]. But when the confining box has non-rigid walls, the wave functions of the particle are not equal to zero at the walls. This means that the particle wave functions are somewhat longer in the case of a non-rigid box than the wave functions in the case of rigid box. i.e. wavelengths of the particle are larger when it is in a non-rigid box than the wavelengths when it is in a rigid box.
- A larger wavelength means a smaller frequency and hence smaller energy. Hence energy levels of a particle in a non-rigid box are lower than the corresponding energy levels of a particle in a rigid box. This is shown in Fig. 7.12 where full lines show energy levels of a particle in a rigid box and dotted lines show energy levels of a particle in a non-rigid box.

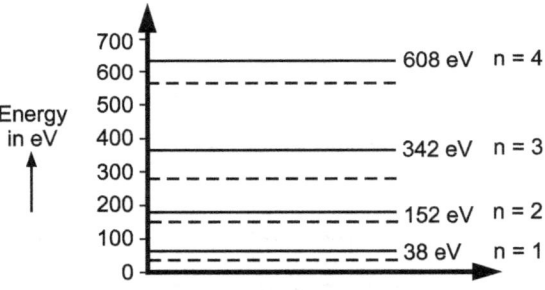

Fig. 7.12: Energy levels

- When the potential energy outside the box is finite, say V_0, it will be possible for a particle to have energy E that exceeds V_0. Such a particle is not trapped inside the box, for it always has sufficient energy to penetrate the walls of the box. Energy of the particle is not quantized but it may have any value above V_0. However, the K.E. of the particle outside the box is $(E - V_0)$ and it is always less than its K.E. inside the box.
- This is because whole energy E of the particle inside the box is K.E. as V = 0 there. Less energy means longer wavelength. So wave function ψ has a longer wavelength outside the box than inside.

7.12 TUNNELING EFFECT

- The phenomenon of the particles penetrating the potential barrier is called the **'tunnel effect'** or **'tunneling'**. The examples of tunneling are tunnel diode, alfa decay, tunneling microscope, etc. The kinetic energy of α-particle is only few MeV but still it can escape from a nucleus whose potential wall is 25 MeV due to tunneling.

- Consider a particle approaching the potential barrier from the left i.e. from Ist region. If the particle has energy less than height of potential barrier V_0 i.e. $E < V_0$, classically, the particle will be always reflected back and hence will not penetrate the barrier. However, by quantum mechanics, there is some probability of penetrating to region III. The probability of penetration increases if $(V_0 - E)$ and L i.e. height and width of potential barrier are smaller.

- On the other hand, if $E > V_0$ classical mechanics predicts that the particle will always be transmitted. But quantum mechanics says that there is a finite probability of transmission and hence it is not certain that the particle will penetrate the barrier.

- Let us consider the one-dimensional potential barrier, where the height of the barrier is V_0 and width is L. The potential function is defined as $V(x) = 0$ for $x \le 0$ and $x \ge L$ and $V(x) = V_0$ for $0 < x < L$ as shown in Fig. 7.13.

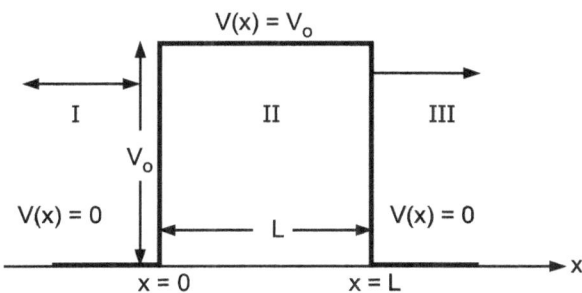

Fig. 7.13

- The Schroedinger's time independent equation is

$$\nabla^2 \psi + \frac{8\pi^2 m}{h^2}(E - V)\psi = 0 \qquad \text{... (1)}$$

- As the motion of the particle is in x-direction, so $\nabla^2 \psi$ can be replaced by $\frac{d^2 \psi}{dx^2}$. For regions I and III, $V(x) = 0$, therefore equation (1) becomes

$$\frac{d^2 \psi}{dx^2} + \frac{8\pi^2 m}{h^2}E\psi = 0$$

Let
$$k^2 = \frac{8\pi^2 m}{h^2}E \qquad \text{... (2)}$$

$\therefore$
$$\frac{d^2 \psi}{dx^2} + k^2 \psi = 0 \qquad \text{... (3)}$$

- The equation (3) is a total differential equation of second order with imaginary roots and its general solution will involve two arbitrary constants. So the solution can be written as, For region I, i.e. $x \le 0$,

$$\psi_I(x) = A e^{ikx} + B e^{-ikx} \qquad \text{... (4)}$$

For region III, i.e. $x \geq L$

$$\psi_{III\,(x)} = C\,e^{ikx} + D\,e^{-ikx} \qquad \ldots (5)$$

- In equation (5), the first term represents the wave travelling along positive X-axis in region III i.e. the wave transmitted at $x = L$. The second term represents the wave travelling along negative X-axis in region III, but no wave travels back from infinity in region III. Therefore, taking $D = 0$ in equation (5),

$$\psi_{III}(x) = C\,e^{ikx} \qquad \ldots (6)$$

For region II i.e. $0 < x < L$ the $V(x) = V_0$, so the equation (1) becomes

$$\frac{d^2\psi}{dx^2} + \frac{8\pi^2 m}{h^2}(E - V_0)\,\psi = 0$$

Let

$$\frac{8\pi^2 m}{h^2}(E - V_0) = k'^2 \qquad \ldots (7)$$

$\therefore$

$$\frac{d^2\psi}{dx^2} + k'^2\psi = 0 \qquad \ldots (8)$$

The solution of above differential equation is given by

$$\psi_{II}(x) = P\,e^{ik'x} + Q\,e^{-ik'x} \qquad \ldots (9)$$

- The first term of the solution represents the wave travelling along positive X-axis in region II i.e. the wave transmitted at $x = 0$ and second term represents the wave travelling along negative X-axis in region II i.e. the wave reflected at $x = L$.

- For determining the constants A, B, C, P and Q, the boundary conditions are applied at $x = 0$ and $x = L$.

i.e.

$$\psi_I = \psi_{II}$$

$$\frac{\partial \psi_I}{\partial x} = \frac{\partial \psi_{II}}{\partial x} \quad \text{at} \ \ x = 0$$

and

$$\psi_{II} = \psi_{III}$$

$$\frac{\partial \psi_{II}}{\partial x} = \frac{\partial \psi_{III}}{\partial x} \quad \text{at} \ \ x = L$$

- The property of the barrier penetration is due to the wave nature of matter and is similar to the total internal reflection of light. If two glass plates are placed close to each other with a thin layer of air trapped between them, then the light coming from one plate will be transmitted by the second plate even if the angle is greater than the critical angle. But the intensity of the transmitted light will decrease exponentially with the thickness of the barrier.

- If a particle incidenting on the potential barrier with energy less than the height of the potential barrier, there is always some probability of transmission through the barrier. This phenomenon of crossing the barrier is called the **'tunneling effect'**.

7.12.1 Examples of Tunneling Effect

1. **Tunnel Diode**

   - A **'tunnel diode'** is a semiconductor device that uses the phenomenon of tunneling. The current flowing in the tunnel diode is produced by electrons tunneling through the potential barrier developed by depletion layer.

   - A tunnel diode is constructed in the same way as ordinary diode but the concentration of impurity is very high. This results in high conductivity or low resistivity than ordinary diode. The semiconductors with low resistivity, approaching conductors are termed as **'degenerate semiconductors'**. A p-n junction in a degenerate semiconductor is very thin ($\sim 10^{-6}$ cm) and potential barrier is about twice as high in case of ordinary diode.

   - The potential barrier height in an ordinary diode is about one half of the forbidden bandwidth, while in tunnel diode it is wider than the forbidden band. As a result of the barrier layer being extremely thin, the electric field is very high ($\sim 10^6$ V/m) even in absence of an external voltage.

   - In a tunnel diode, the charge carriers cross the junction by diffusion due to an electric field along with tunneling effect. In tunneling effect, there is certain probability of electron penetration through the barrier without a change in electron energy levels when the barrier is thin enough.

   - The tunnel electron transfer takes place when the energies of electrons are less than the potential barrier height provided that on other side of the barrier unoccupied energy levels are available for the tunneling electrons. This electron transfer can take place in both directions.

   - The tunnel currents originating in a p-n junction of a tunnel diode are shown in Fig. 7.14. Here diffusion and conduction currents are omitted to simplify the presentation of tunnel effect.

   - Fig. 7.14 (a) shows energy level diagram of unbiased diode. The energy levels in valence and conduction bands occupied by electrons are represented by horizontal lines and the spacing between them indicate the energy levels unoccupied by electrons. As shown in the figure, the conduction band of n-type semiconductor and the valence band of p-type semiconductor show occupied energy levels corresponding to the same electron energies. Thus, tunnel transfer from the n-region to p-region (forward tunnel current i_f) and from the p-region to n-region (reverse tunnel current i_r) is possible. These currents are equal in magnitude and completely cancel each other, reducing the total current to zero.

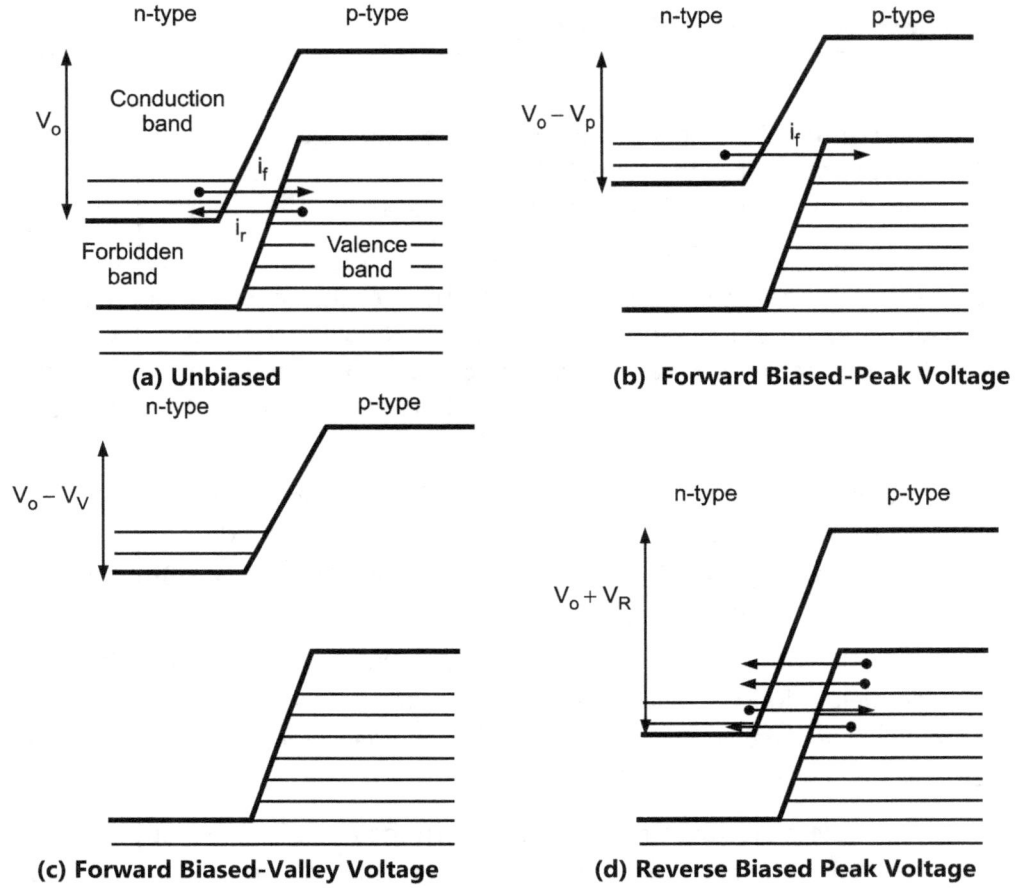

(a) **Unbiased**

(b) **Forward Biased-Peak Voltage**

(c) **Forward Biased-Valley Voltage**

(d) **Reverse Biased Peak Voltage**

Fig. 7.14: Tunnel diode

- When forward peak voltage V_p is applied, the potential barrier height is lowered to $(V_o - V_p)$ as shown in Fig. 7.14 (b). This increases tunnel transfer of electrons for the n-region into the p-region as there are free energy levels in the valence band in the p-region corresponding to occupied energy levels in the conduction band of the n-region.

- At the same time, electron transfer in the opposite direction is impossible, since the occupied energy levels of the p-region valence band correspond to the forbidden band of the n-region. Thus, reverse current is absent and forward current is maximum. The maximum current is called **'peak current'** and corresponding forward voltage is called **'peak voltage'** (V_p).

- In case of a higher forward voltage (V_v) as shown in Fig. 7.14 (c), the potential barrier height decreases to $(V_o - V_v)$. Under this condition, tunnel electron transfer becomes impossible, since occupied energy levels of one region correspond to the forbidden band of the other. This makes the tunnel current zero, but small current may be present due to other effects i.e. diffusion and leakage. This current is called "**valley current**" and voltage '**valley voltage**' V_V.

- A further rise in forward voltage results in an increase of the usual forward diffusion current as in ordinary diode. For forward voltages less than valley voltage, the diffusion current is negligible in comparison to the tunnel current. While for forward voltages more than valley voltage, diffusion current increases and attains characteristic of ordinary diode.

- In case of reverse biasing, the potential barrier height is increased to $(V_O + V_R)$ as shown in Fig. 7.14 (d). The number of occupied energy levels in the valence band of the p-region corresponding to free levels in the n-region conduction band increases considerably. This results in a significant rise in the reverse tunnel current, which can attain the same magnitude as forward tunnel current under forward voltage conditions.

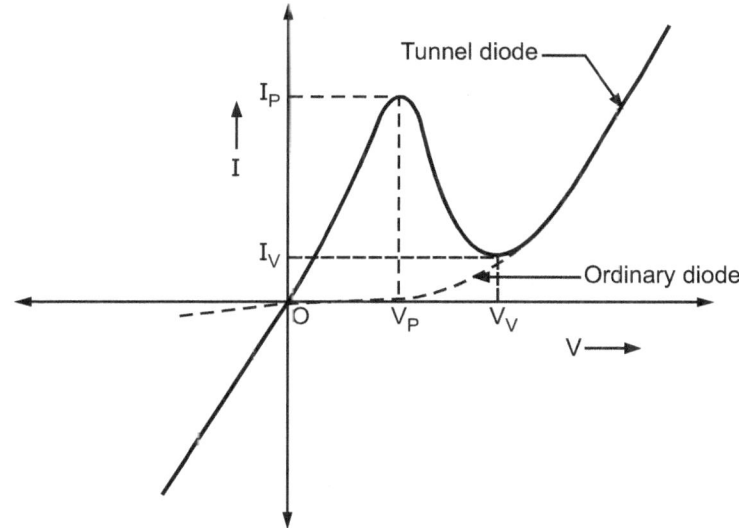

Fig. 7.15: I-V Characteristics of a tunnel diode

- The I-V characteristics of a tunnel diode has been shown in Fig. 7.15. It can be seen that the current is absent at V = 0. A rise in forward voltage results in an increase in tunnel current and is maximum at a voltage V_p. A further increase in forward voltage reduces the tunnel current until it reaches a maximum current at V_V. This results in a negative resistance. If the voltage is increased further, the current increases due to usual diffusion current. The reverse current is of the same order i.e. many times higher than ordinary diode.

- The tunnel electron transfer can take place at very short interval i.e. 10^{-14} sec to 10^{-12} sec, therefore they can be used at microwave frequencies ($\sim 10^9$ Hz).

2. **Scanning Tunneling Microscope (STM)**

- A scanning tunneling microscope (STM) is an instrument for imaging surfaces at the atomic level by using the principle of tunneling effect. The resolution of an STM is 0.1

nm lateral and 0.0 nm depth measurement. With such high resolution, individual atoms of material can be imagined.

- The STM is based on the concept of quantum tunneling. When a conducting tip is brought close to the surface to be examined, the bias voltage applied between them will allow electrons to tunnel through the vacuum between them. The tunneling current between them will depend on the width of the barrier i.e. the distance between the probe and the surface if bias voltage between them is constant.

- This voltage can be recorded and displayed simulating the surface of the sample. The probe is moved vertically so that the distance between the probe and the surface remains constant as the probe scans laterally. Fig. 7.16 shows the basic mechanism of STM.

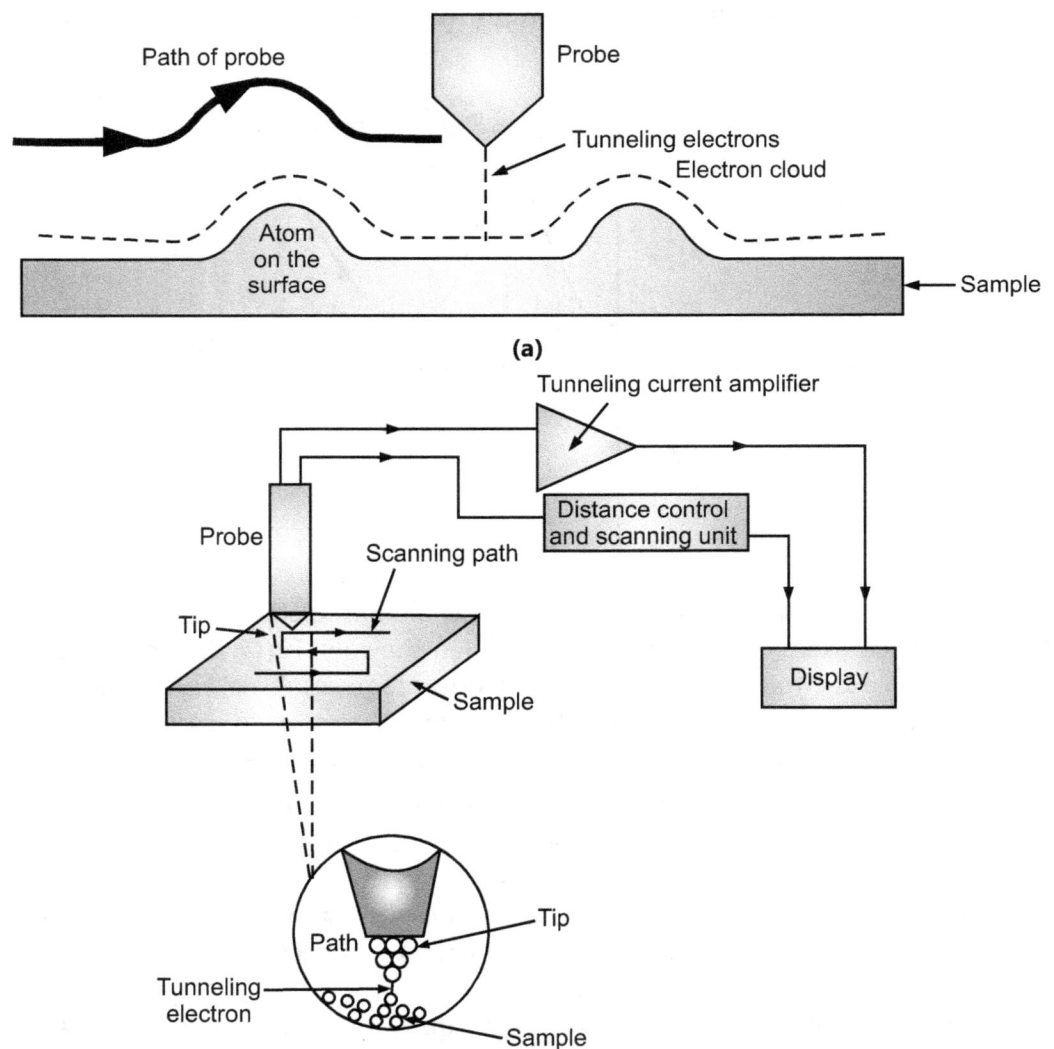

(b)

Fig. 7.16: Schematic diagram of STM

SOLVED PROBLEMS

Problem 7.25: *Compute the permitted energy levels of an electron in an infinite potential well of width 1 A°.*

Data: $m = 9.1 \times 10^{-31}$ kg, $L = 1$ A° $= 10^{-10}$ m

Formula:
$$E_n = \frac{n^2 h^2}{8 mL^2}$$

Solution:
$$E_n = \frac{n^2 (6.6 \times 10^{-34})^2}{8 \times 9.1 \times 10^{-31} \times (10^{-10})^2}$$

$$\approx 6 \times 10^{-18} n^2 \text{ J}$$

$$E_n \approx 38 n^2 \text{ eV}$$

For $n = 1$, $\boxed{E_1 = 38 \text{ eV}}$

$n = 2$, $\boxed{E_2 = 152 \text{ eV}}$

$n = 3$, $\boxed{E_3 = 342 \text{ eV}}$ etc.

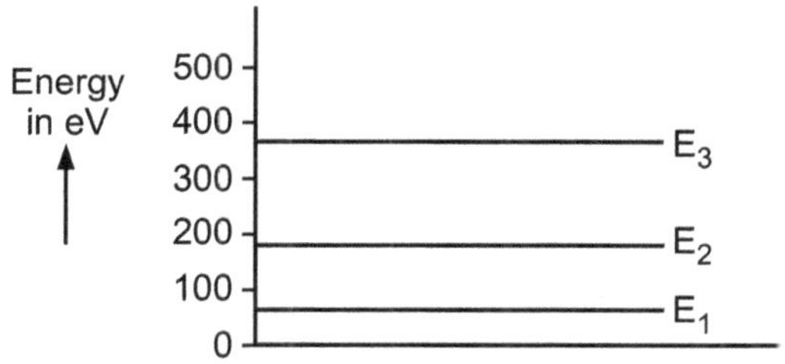

Fig. 7.17

Problem 7.26: *An infinite square well has a width of 1 A°. What is the fractional change in the lowest two permissible energies of one electron in this well if the width is increased to 2 A°?*

Data: $L = 1$ A° $= 10^{-10}$ m, $L' = 2 \times 10^{-10}$ m

Formula:
$$E_n = \frac{n^2 h^2}{8 mL^2}$$

Solution: From previous numerical,

For $L = 1$, $E_n \approx 38 n^2$ eV

i.e. $E_1 = 38$ eV   and $E_2 = 152$ eV

For $L = 2$ the energies reduce by a factor of 4

$\therefore \quad E_1' = 9.5 \text{ eV} \quad$ and $\quad E_2' = 38 \text{ eV}$

Fractional change, $\quad \Delta E_1 = E_1 - E_1'$

$$\Delta E_2 = E_2 - E_2'$$

$$\Delta E_1 = 38 - 9.5 = \boxed{28.5 \text{ eV}}$$

$$\Delta E_2 = 152 - 38 = \boxed{114 \text{ eV}}$$

Problem 7.27: *Lowest energy level of an electron trapped in a potential well is 38 eV. Find the width of the well.*

Data: $\quad E = 38 \text{ eV}, \ n = 1.$

Formula: $\qquad\qquad E = \dfrac{n^2 h^2}{8 \, mL^2}$

Solution: $\qquad\qquad L^2 = \dfrac{n^2 h^2}{8 \, mE}$

$$L = \sqrt{\dfrac{(6.6 \times 10^{-34})^2}{8 \times 9.1 \times 10^{-31} \times 38 \times 1.6 \times 10^{-19}}}$$

$$= \boxed{10^{-10} \text{ m} = 1 \text{ A}^\circ}$$

Problem 7.28: *An electron is trapped in a rigid box of width 1 A°. Find its lowest energy level and momentum. Hence find energy of 5th level.* **(Dec. 14)**

Data: $\qquad\qquad L = 1 \text{ A}^\circ = 10^{-10} \text{ m}$

Formula: $\qquad\qquad E_n = \dfrac{n^2 h^2}{8 \, mL^2} \approx 38 \, n^2$

Solution: $\qquad\qquad E_1 = 38 \text{ eV}$

$$E_1 = \dfrac{p_1^2}{2m}$$

$\therefore \qquad\qquad p_1^2 = 2 \, m \, E_1$

$$= 2 \times 9.1 \times 10^{-31} \times 38 \times 1.6 \times 10^{-19}$$

$$= 1106.56 \times 10^{-50}$$

$$\boxed{p_1 = 33.26 \times 10^{-25} \text{ kg - m/sec}}$$

$$E_5 \approx 25 \times 38 \text{ eV} \approx \boxed{950 \text{ eV}}$$

UNIVERSITY SOLVED PROBLEMS

Problem 7.29: *Find the kinetic energy of a neutron in eV, whose De-Broglie wavelength is 1 A°($M_n = 1.67 \times 10^{-27}$ kg).* **(03) (May 04, Dec. 09)**

Solution: See Problem 7.24 on page 7.28.

Problem 7.30: *If the uncertainty in the location of a particle is equal to it's De-Broglie wavelength then show that the uncertainty in its velocity is equal to it's velocity* **(03) (May 04)**

Solution: See Problem 7.14 on page 7.25.

Problem 7.31: *An electron is accelerated through a potential difference of 10 kV. Calculate the De-Broglie wavelength and momentum of the electron.* **(04) (Dec. 04)**

Data: $V = 10,000$ volts

Formulae: (i) $\lambda = \dfrac{12.27}{\sqrt{V}}$ A°,   (ii) $p = \dfrac{h}{\lambda}$

Solution: (i) $\lambda = \dfrac{12.27}{\sqrt{10000}}$

$$\boxed{\lambda = 0.1227 \text{ A°}}$$

(ii) $p = \dfrac{6.6 \times 10^{-34}}{0.1227 \times 10^{-10}}$

$$\boxed{p = 5.378 \times 10^{-23} \text{ kg-m/sec}}$$

Problem 7.32: *Proton and alpha particles are accelerated through same potential difference. Compute the ratio of their De-Broglie wavelengths.* **(04) (May 05)**

Data: $M_\alpha = 4 M_p$, $e_\alpha = 2 e_p$

Formula: $\lambda = \dfrac{L}{\sqrt{2meV}}$

Solution: For proton, $\lambda_p = \dfrac{h}{2m_p e_p V}$

For alpha particle, $\lambda_\alpha = \dfrac{h}{\sqrt{2m_\alpha e_\alpha V}}$

But, $m_\alpha = 4m_p$ and $e_\alpha = 2e_p$

$\therefore$ $\lambda_\alpha = \dfrac{h}{\sqrt{16m_p e_p V}}$

$$\therefore \quad \frac{\lambda_\alpha}{\lambda_p} = \frac{h}{\sqrt{16m_p\, e_p V}} \cdot \frac{\sqrt{2m_p\, e_p V}}{h} = \boxed{\frac{1}{\sqrt{8}}}$$

Problem 7.33: *Find the De-Broglie wavelength of an electron accelerated through a potential difference of 100 volts.* **(02) (Dec. 05)**

Data: $V = 100$ volts

Formula: $\lambda = \dfrac{12.27}{\sqrt{V}}\ A^\circ$

Solution: $\lambda = \dfrac{12.27}{\sqrt{100}}$

$$\boxed{\lambda = 1.227\ A^\circ}$$

Problem 7.34: *What potential difference must be applied to an electron microscope to obtain electrons of wavelength 0.3 A° ?* **(04) (May 06)**

Data: $\lambda = 0.3\ A^\circ$

Formula: $\lambda = \dfrac{12.27}{\sqrt{V}}\ A^\circ$

Solution: $0.3 = \dfrac{12.27}{\sqrt{V}}$

$$\sqrt{V} = 40.9$$

$$\therefore \quad \boxed{V = 1672.8\ \text{volts}}$$

Problem 7.35: *Calculate the velocity and De-Broglie wavelength of an α-particle of energy 1 keV.* **(04) (May 07)**

Data: $E = 1\ keV,\quad m_\alpha = 4\,m_p$

Formula: $\lambda = \dfrac{h}{\sqrt{2mE}}$

Solution: $\lambda = \dfrac{6.6 \times 10^{-34}}{\sqrt{2 \times 4 \times 1.67 \times 10^{-27} \times 1 \times 10^3 \times 1.6 \times 10^{-19}}}$

$$\lambda = 4.514 \times 10^{-13}\ m$$

$$\boxed{\lambda = 0.00451\ A^\circ}$$

Problem 7.36: *Which has a shorter wavelength of 1 eV photon or 1 eV electron ? Calculate the value and explain.* **(04) (May 07)**

Data: $E_p = 1\ eV$

                                  $E_e = 1\ eV$

Formula: $\lambda = \dfrac{h}{\sqrt{2mE}}$

Solution: $\lambda_p = \dfrac{h}{\sqrt{2m_p\,E_p}}$

$\lambda_p = \dfrac{6.6 \times 10^{-34}}{\sqrt{2 \times 1.67 \times 10^{-27} \times 1 \times 1.6 \times 10^{-19}}}$

$\lambda_p = 2.855 \times 10^{-11}$ m = $\boxed{0.2855\ A^\circ}$

$\lambda_e = \dfrac{h}{\sqrt{2m_e\,E_e}}$

$\lambda_e = \dfrac{6.6 \times 10^{-34}}{\sqrt{2 \times 9.1 \times 10^{-31} \times 1 \times 1.6 \times 10^{-19}}}$

$\lambda_e = 1.223 \times 10^{-9}$ m = $\boxed{12.23\ A^\circ}$

$\lambda_e > \lambda_p$

Because lighter the particle, greater will be the wavelength of the matter waves $\left(\lambda \propto \dfrac{1}{m}\right)$.

Problem 7.37: *An electron has kinetic energy equal to its rest mass energy. Calculate De-Broglie's wavelength associated with it.* **(04) (Nov. 07)**

Data: E = m

Formula: $\lambda = \dfrac{h}{\sqrt{2mE}}$

Solution: $\lambda = \dfrac{h}{\sqrt{2m^2}}$

$\lambda = \dfrac{6.6 \times 10^{-34}}{9.1 \times 10^{-31}\sqrt{2}}$

$\boxed{\lambda = 5.129 \times 10^{-4}\ m}$

Problem 7.38: *In a T.V. set, electrons are accelerated by a p.d. of 10 kV. What is the wavelength associated with these electrons ?* **(04) (May 08)**

Solution: See Problem 7.10 (part 1) on page 7.17.

Problem 7.39: *Calculate De-Broglie wavelength of 10 keV electron.* **(03) (Dec. 08)**

Solution: See Problem 7.17 on page 7.26.

Problem 7.40: *Find the De Broglie's wavelength associated with monoenergetic electron beam having momentum 10^{-23} kg m/s.* **(04) (May 09)**

Data: p = 10^{-23} kg m/s

Formula: $\lambda = \dfrac{h}{p}$

Solution: $\lambda = \dfrac{h}{p}$

$\lambda = \dfrac{6.63 \times 10^{-34}}{10^{-23}}$

$\lambda = 6.63 \times 10^{-11}$ m

or $\boxed{\lambda = 0.663 \ A^\circ}$

Problem 7.41: *Find the energy of neutron in unit of electron volt whose De-Broglie wavelength is 1 A°. (**Given:** $M_n = 1.674 \times 10^{-27}$ kg).*   **(04) (Dec. 09)**

Data: $M_n = 1.674 \times 10^{-27}, \ \lambda = 1 \ A^\circ$

Formula: $\lambda = \dfrac{h}{\sqrt{2mE}}$

Solution: $E = \dfrac{h^2}{2m\lambda^2}$

$E = \dfrac{(6.63 \times 10^{-34})^2}{2 \times 1.67 \times 10^{-27} \times (1 \times 10^{-10})^2}$

$E = 1.316 \times 10^{-20}$ J

$\boxed{E = 8.225 \times 10^{-2} \ eV}$

Problem 7.42: *Calculate the De-Broglie wavelength of 10 keV protons in eV.*

(04) (May 10)

Data: $E = 10 \ keV, \ m = 1.67 \times 10^{-27}$ kg

Formula: $\lambda = \dfrac{h}{\sqrt{2mE}}$

Solution: $\lambda = \dfrac{6.63 \times 10^{-34}}{\sqrt{2 \times 1.67 \times 10^{-27} \times 10 \times 10^3 \times 1.6 \times 10^{-19}}}$

$\lambda = 2.868 \times 10^{-13}$ m

$\boxed{\lambda = 2.868 \times 10^{-3} \ A^\circ}$

Problem 7.43: *At what kinetic energy an electron will have a wavelength of 5000 A°?*

(04) (Dec. 10)

Data: $\lambda = 5000 \ A^\circ$

Formula: $\lambda = \dfrac{h}{\sqrt{2mE}}$

Solution: $\lambda^2 = \dfrac{h^2}{2mE}$

$\therefore$ $E = \dfrac{(6.63 \times 10^{-34})^2}{2\,(9.1 \times 10^{-31})\,(5000 \times 10^{-10})^2}$

$E = 9.66 \times 10^{-25}$ J

$\boxed{E = 6.038 \times 10^{-6} \text{ eV}}$

Problem 7.44: *Calculate De-Broglie wavelength of 10 keV protons in angstrom.*

(04) (May 11)

Solution: See Problem 7.13 on page 7.24.

Problem 7.45: *Calculate the wavelength of a photon and an electron both having an energy 1.0 eV. (**Given:** Planck's constant h = 6.63 $\times 10^{-34}$ J-s, Mass of electron = 9.1 $\times 10^{-31}$ kg).*

(04) (Dec. 11)

Data: $E = 1.0$ eV

Formulae: (i) For electron, $\lambda = \dfrac{h}{\sqrt{2mE}}$ (ii) For photon, $E = h\upsilon$ i.e. $\lambda = \dfrac{hc}{E}$

Solution: (i) For electron, $\lambda = \dfrac{6.63 \times 10^{-34}}{\sqrt{2 \times 9.1 \times 10^{-31} \times 1 \times 1.6 \times 10^{-19}}}$

$\lambda = 1.228 \times 10^{-9}$ m $= \boxed{12.28 \text{ A}^\circ}$

(ii) For photon, $\lambda = \dfrac{6.63 \times 10^{-34} \times 3 \times 10^8}{1 \times 1.6 \times 10^{-19}}$

$\lambda = 1.243 \times 10^{-6}$ m

$= \boxed{12430 \text{ A}^\circ}$

Problem 7.46: *Assuming atomic nucleus to be a rigid box (infinite potential well), calculate the ground state energy of an electron if it existed inside the nucleus.*

*(**Given:** Planck's constant = 6.63 $\times 10^{-34}$ J-s, Mass of the electron = 9.1 $\times 10^{-31}$ kg and size of the nucleus ~ 10^{-15} m. Using this result, argue that electron cannot exist inside the nucleus. Given maximum binding energy per nucleon = 8.8 MeV).* **(05) (Dec. 11)**

Data: $d = 10^{-15}$ m, $m = 9.1 \times 10^{-31}$ kg, $\dfrac{\text{B.E.}}{\text{N}} = 8.8$ MeV

Formulae: $\quad$ (i) $E_n = \dfrac{n^2 h^2}{8mL^2}$ $\quad$ (ii) $\Delta x \Delta p = h$

Solution: $\quad$ (i) $E_n = \dfrac{(1)^2 (6.63 \times 10^{-34})^2}{8 \times 9.1 \times 10^{-31} \times (10^{-15})^2}$

$\qquad\qquad\qquad E_n = 6.038 \times 10^{-10} \text{ J}$

$\qquad\qquad\qquad \boxed{E_n = 3.774 \times 10^9 \text{ eV}}$

$\quad$ (ii) $\Delta x \Delta p = h$

$\qquad\qquad\qquad \Delta p = \dfrac{6.63 \times 10^{-34}}{10^{-15}}$

$\qquad\qquad\qquad \boxed{\Delta p = 6.63 \times 10^{-19} \text{ kg m/s}}$

If this is the uncertainty in the momentum of electron in the nucleus, the momentum itself must be at least comparable to Δp i.e. $p \sim \Delta p$.

$\therefore \qquad\qquad\qquad E = \dfrac{p^2}{2m} = \dfrac{(6.63 \times 10^{-19})^2}{2 \times 9.1 \times 10^{-31}}$

$\qquad\qquad\qquad E = 2.415 \times 10^{-7} \text{ J}$

$\qquad\qquad\qquad \boxed{E = 1.510 \times 10^{12} \text{ eV}}$

This shows that if the electron exist in the nucleus, the energy must be at least 1.51×10^{12} eV, which is much more than B.E. per nucleon. Therefore, it cannot exist in the nucleus.

Problem 7.47: *Lowest energy of an electron trapped in a potential well is 38 eV. Calculate the width of the well.* **(4) (Dec. 04, May 05)**

Solution: [See Problem 7.3]

Problem 7.48: *An electron is bound by a potential which closely approaches an infinite square well of width 1 A°. Calculate the lowest three permissible energies (in electron volts) the electron can have.* **(4) (Dec. 05)**

Solution: [See Problem 7.1]

Problem 7.49: *An electron is trapped in a rigid box of width 2 A°. Find its lowest energy level and momentum. Hence, find energy of the 3rd energy level.* **(4) (May 06, 15)**

Data: $L = 2$ A°.

Formulae: $\qquad E_n = \dfrac{n^2 h^2}{8mL^2}$, $\quad P_n = \sqrt{2mE_n}$

Solution: For lowest energy level, $n = 1$

$\qquad\qquad E_1 = \dfrac{1^2 \times (6.6 \times 10^{-34})^2}{8 \times 9.1 \times 10^{-31} \times (2 \times 10^{-10})^2}$

$\qquad\qquad E_1 = 1.50 \times 10^{-18} \text{ J}$

---

or $E_1 = 9.37$ eV

$\therefore$ $P_1 = \sqrt{2 \times 9.1 \times 10^{-31} \times 1.51 \times 10^{-18}}$

                            $P_1 = 1.66 \times 10^{-24}$ kg-m/sec

For third energy level, n = 3.

$\therefore$ $E_3 = \dfrac{3^2 \times (6.6 \times 10^{-34})^2}{8 \times 9.1 \times 10^{-31} \times (2 \times 10^{-10})}$

$\boxed{E_3 = 13.5 \times 10^{-18} \text{ J}}$

or $\boxed{E_3 = 84.33 \text{ eV}}$

Problem 7.50: *Calculate first two energy eigen values of an electron in eV which is confined to a box of length 2 A°.*   **(04) (Dec. 08)**

Solution: See Problem 7.2.

Problem 7.51: *Compare the lowest three energy states for an electron confined in an infinite potential well of width 10 A°.*   **(04) (May 09)**

Data: $L = 10$ A°

Formula: $E_n = \dfrac{n^2 h^2}{8mL^2}$

Solution: $E_n = \dfrac{n^2 h^2}{8mL^2}$

                            $E_n = \dfrac{n^2 (6.63 \times 10^{-34})^2}{8 \times 9.1 \times 10^{-31} \times (10 \times 10^{-10})^2}$

                            $E_n = 0.603 \times 10^{-19} n^2$ J

or $E_n = 0.38 n^2$ eV

For first energy level, $n = 1$

$\therefore$ $\boxed{E_1 = 0.38 \text{ eV}}$

For second energy level, $n = 2$

$\therefore$ $\boxed{E_2 = 1.52 \text{ eV}}$

For third energy level, $n = 3$

$\therefore$ $\boxed{E_3 = 3.42 \text{ eV}}$

Problem 7.52: *Calculate first two energy eigen values of an electron trapped in an infinite potential well of length 1 A°.* **(04) (May 10)**

Solution: See Problem 7.1.

Problem 7.53: *Compute energy difference between the ground state and first excited state for an electron in a one-dimensional rigid box of length 10^{-8} cm.* **(04) (Dec. 10, Nov 13)**

Data: $L = 10^{-8}$ cm

Formula: $E_n = \dfrac{n^2 h^2}{8mL^2}$

Solution: $E_1 = \dfrac{(1)^2 h^2}{8mL^2}$

and $E_2 = \dfrac{(2)^2 h^2}{8mL^2}$

$\therefore$ $E_2 - E_1 = \dfrac{4h^2}{8mL^2} - \dfrac{h^2}{8mL^2}$

$= \dfrac{3 \times (6.63 \times 10^{-34})^2}{8 \times (9.1 \times 10^{-31})\,(10^{-10})^2}$

$= 1.8114 \times 10^{-17}$ J

$\boxed{E_2 - E_1 = 113.21 \text{ eV}}$

Problem 7.54: *Calculate the first energy eigen value of electron in eV trapped in a rigid box of length 1 A.U.* **(04) (May 11)**

Solution: See Problem 7.1.

Problem 7.55: *Calculate the De-Broglie wavelength associated with 1 Mev proton $(m_p = 1.67 \times 10^{-27} kg)$* **[03] (May 13)**

Data: $E = 1$MeV

$m_p = 1.67 \times 10^{-27}$ kg

Formula: $\lambda = \dfrac{1}{\sqrt{2m_p E}}$

Solution: $\lambda = \dfrac{6.63 \times 10^{-34}}{\sqrt{2 \times 1.67 \times 10^{-27} \times 1 \times 10^6 \times 1.6 \times 10^{-19}}}$

$\lambda = 2.86 \times 10^{-14}$m

$\lambda = 2.86 \times 10^{-4}$A°

Problem 7.55: *The position and momentum of 1 keV electron are simultaneously measured. If its position is located with 1 A°. Find the percentage of uncertainty in its momentum. Dec 12*

(Given: $h = 6.64 \times 10^{-34}$ J-sec., $m = 9.1 \times 10^{-31}$ kg)   **(03)**

Data: $h = 6.64 \times 10^{-34}$ J-sec., $m = 9.1 \times 10^{-31}$ kg, $\Delta x = 1A° = 1 \times 10^{-10}$ m.

Formulae: $\lambda = \dfrac{12.27}{\sqrt{V}}$ A°, $p = \dfrac{h}{\lambda}$ and $\Delta p_x = \dfrac{h}{\Delta x}$

$\therefore$ Wavelength, $\lambda = \dfrac{12.27}{\sqrt{V}}$ A°

$= \dfrac{12.27}{\sqrt{10^3}} = 0.388$ A°

For electron, Momentum, $p = \dfrac{h}{\lambda} = \dfrac{6.64 \times 10^{-34}}{0.388 \times 10^{-10}}$

$= 17.11 \times 10^{-24}$

$= 1.71 \times 10^{-23}$ kg-m/sec.

Now, $\Delta p_x = \dfrac{h}{\Delta x}$

$= \dfrac{6.64 \times 10^{-34}}{1 \times 10^{-10}}$

$= 6.64 \times 10^{-24}$ kg-m/sec.

$= 0.664 \times 10^{-23}$ kg-m/sec.

Per cent change in momentum $= \dfrac{1.71 \times 10^{-23} - 0.664 \times 10^{-23}}{1.71 \times 10^{-23}} \times 100$

$= \dfrac{1.71 - 0.664}{1.71} \times 100$

$= 61\%$

$\therefore$ Percentage of uncertainty in momentum of electron = **39%**.

Problem 7.56: *An electron is bounded by an infinite potential well of width 2×10^{-8} cm. Calculate the lowest two permissible energies of an electron.   Dec 12*

(Given: $h = 6.64 \times 10^{-34}$ J-sec., $m = 9.1 \times 10^{-31}$ kg)   **(03)**

Data: $h = 6.64 \times 10^{-34}$ J-sec., $m = 9.1 \times 10^{-31}$ kg, $n = 1$, $L = 2 \times 10^{-10}$ m

Formula: $E_n = \dfrac{n^2 h^2}{8 \, mL^2}$

$$\therefore \quad E_n = \frac{n^2 (6.64 \times 10^{-34})^2}{8 \times 9.1 \times 10^{-31} \times (2 \times 10^{-10})^2}$$

$$\therefore \quad E_n = 1.5 \times 10^{-18} \, n^2 \, J$$

$$\therefore \quad E_n = 9.44 \, n^2 \, eV \approx 9.5 \, n^2 \, eV$$

For n = 1, E_1 = **9.5 eV**

For n = 2, E_2 = 9.5 (2^2) eV

$$\therefore \quad E_2 = \textbf{38 eV}$$

Problem 7.57: *Calculate the energy and momentum of an electron confined in a rigid box of width 2A^{0}for lowest energy state.* **(04) (May 13)**

Data: L = $2A^0$

Formula: i) $E_n = \dfrac{n^2 h^2}{8mL^2}$

ii) $P = \sqrt{2mE}$

Solution: i) $E_1 = \dfrac{1^2 (6.63 \times 10^{-34})^2}{8 \times 9.1 \times 10^{-31} \times (2 \times 10^{-10})^2}$

$$E_1 = 1.509 \times 10^{-18} J$$

$$E_1 = 9.44 e^{-V}$$

ii) $P_1 = \sqrt{2 \times 9/1 \times 10^{-31} \times 1.509 \times 10^{-18}}$

$$P_1 = 1.663 \times 10^{-24} \, kg\text{-}m/sec$$

Problem 7.58: *What accelerating potential would be required for a proton with zero initial velocity to acquire a velocity corresponding to its de-Broglie wavelength of 10^{-10} m. [Given: m_p = 1.67 $\times 10^{-27}$ kg]* **(03) (May 14)**

Data: m = 1.67 $\times 10^{-27}$ kg, λ = 10^{-10} m

Formula: $\lambda = \dfrac{h}{\sqrt{2mev}}$

Solution: $V = \dfrac{(6.63 \times 10^{-34})^2}{2 \times 1.67 \times 10^{-27} \times 1.6 \times 10^{-19} \times (10^{-10})^2}$

$$V = 0.082 \, V$$

SUMMARY

- De Broglie's hypothesis states that a material particle of mass 'm' moving with a velocity v has a wave associated with it. This wave is called as a De Broglie wave and its wavelength is given by, $\lambda = h/mv$.

- De Broglie wavelength in terms of kinetic energy of a particle is $\lambda = \dfrac{h}{\sqrt{2mE}}$.

- For a charged particle accelerated through a potential difference of V, the De Broglie wavelength, $\lambda = \dfrac{h}{\sqrt{2mqV}}$.

  For an electron, the De Broglie wavelength is $\lambda = \dfrac{12.27}{\sqrt{V}}$ A°.

- The speed with which the De Broglie wave travels is called the phase velocity v_p. It is also called as the wave velocity (u).

- The phase velocity of matter waves is given by $v_p = u = \dfrac{c^2}{v}$, which s greater than the speed of light.

- The material can be represented by a wave packet or a group of waves. The velocity of the wave group is called as the group velocity (v_g). The group velocity v_g is equal to the particle velocity v.

- Phase velocity in terms of wavelength λ : $v_p = u = \dfrac{h}{2m\lambda}$.

- Heisenberg's uncertainty principle states that it is impossible to determine precisely and simultaneously the values of both the members of a pair of physical variables which describe the motion of an atomic system. Such pairs of variables are called as canonically conjugate variables.

$$\Delta x \cdot \Delta p \geq h$$

(Heisenberg's uncertainty principle for position and momentum.)

$$\Delta E \cdot \Delta t \geq h$$

(Heisenberg's uncertainty principle for energy and time.)

- Schroedinger's wave equation is the mathematical representation of matter waves associated with a moving particle. They are of two types:

(i) Schroedinger's time independent wave equation:

$$\nabla^2 \psi + \frac{8\pi^2 m}{h^2} (E - V) \psi = 0$$

(ii)   Schroedinger's time dependent wave equation:

$$\left(\frac{-h^2}{8\pi^2 m}\nabla^2 + V\right)\psi = \frac{ih}{2\pi}\frac{\partial\psi}{\partial t}$$

i.e. $H\psi = E\psi$

- The variable quantity characterizing De Broglie waves is denoted by ψ and it is called the wave function of the particle. This wave function contains all the information about the particle.

- The quantity $|\psi(x, y, z, t)|^2$, called the probability density or probability distribution function, determines the probability in unit volume of finding a particle at a given position at a given time.

- The probability of a particle being present in a volume element $dx \cdot dy \cdot dz$ is $|\psi|^2 \cdot dx\,dy\,dz$.

  The probability of finding the particle in all space is $\displaystyle\iiint\limits_{\text{all space}} |\psi|^2\,dx\,dy\,dz = 1$.

  This is the normalization condition. A wave function ψ satisfying this relation is called a normalized wave function.

- The wave function should satisfy the following conditions:

  (i)   It should be a normalized function.

  (ii) It should be a well behaved function i.e., single valued, finite and continuous.

- For a particle in a rigid box, the wave function is given by

  $$\psi_n(x, t) = i \cdot \sqrt{\frac{2}{L}} \cdot \sin\left(\frac{n\pi}{L}\right)x$$

  The energy level of the particle is given by

  $$E_n = \frac{n^2 h^2}{8mL^2} \text{ and is quantized. } n = 1, 2, 3.$$

- For a non-rigid box, the particle wave functions are longer than the wave functions in the case of rigid box.

- Particles trapped in a box, despite having insufficient energy ($E < V_0$) to penetrate the walls some how leak out. This is a tunneling effect which is a behaviour unique to Quantum Mechanics.

IMPORTANT FORMULAE

- $\lambda = \dfrac{h}{mv} = \dfrac{h}{p}$

- $E = h\upsilon, \quad E = \dfrac{p^2}{2m}$

- $E = mc^2$

- $\lambda = \dfrac{h}{\sqrt{2mE}}$

- $\lambda = \dfrac{h}{\sqrt{2meV}} \quad$ and $\quad \lambda \cong \dfrac{12.27}{\sqrt{v}} A°$

- $u = \dfrac{h}{2m\lambda}$

- $\Delta x \cdot \Delta p \geq h$

- $\Delta E \cdot \Delta t \geq h$

- $\nabla^2 \psi + \dfrac{8\pi^2 m}{h^2} (E - V) \psi = 0$

- $\left(-\dfrac{h^2}{8\pi^2 m} \nabla^2 + V \right) \psi = \dfrac{ih}{2\pi} \dfrac{\partial \psi}{\partial t} ; \quad H\psi = E\psi$

- $E_n = \dfrac{n^2 h^2}{8mL^2} ;$ where $n = 1, 2. \ldots$

- Normalization condition $\displaystyle\int\limits_{-\infty}^{+\infty}\int\int + \psi^* \, dx \, dy \, dz = 1.$

EXERCISE

1. Explain briefly the wave nature of matter and obtain an expression for the De-Broglie wavelength.

2. Starting from the De-Broglie concept, obtain Heisenberg's uncertainty principle. Give an illustration of the principle.

3. Show that De-Broglie wavelength of a charged particle is inversely proportional to the square root of the accelerating potential.

4. Write a short note on duality of matter and radiation.

5. Write a note on properties of matter waves. How are they different from electromagnetic and mechanical waves ?

6. What are group and phase velocities ? Explain them.

7. Discuss the properties of matter waves.

8. What are matter waves ? Show that the wavelength λ associated with an electron of mass m and kinetic energy E is given by $\lambda = \dfrac{h}{\sqrt{2\,mE}}$.

9. Write a short note on Heisenberg's uncertainty principle.

10. State Heisenberg's uncertainty principle and explain it using the concept of De-Broglie wave groups.

11. Derive Schroedinger's time dependent and time independent wave equation.

12. Derive an expression for the energy levels and wave function of a particle enclosed in an infinite potential well.

13. Explain Harmonic oscillator classically and quantum mechanically. Compare between the two.

14. Explain the physical significance of ψ, ψ^2.

15. Explain particle in a non-rigid box. How is this situation different from a rigid box ?

16. Write a note on a particle in a potential well with infinite sides.

17. Write a short note on eigen values of particle in a rigid box.

18. Starting with the wave function for a particle moving in a one-dimensional potential well, show that the probability of existence within the well changes with quantum number.

19. Using Schroedinger's wave equation, find energy and wave function of a particle in a rigid box.

20. Explain De-Broglie's concept of matter waves. Show that the wavelength associated with electrons accelerated by a potential difference of V volts is given by $\dfrac{h}{\sqrt{2\,meV}}$.

21. Explaining De-Broglie's hypothesis of matter waves, describe an experiment in support of it.

22. State and explain the principle of uncertainty and illustrate it by an experiment on diffraction at a single slit.

23. State and explain Heisenberg's uncertainty principle. Illustrate it by the experiment for location of a particle by microscope.

24. Discuss properties of matter waves.

25. What is tunneling ? Explain working of tunneling diode.

26. Write a short note on STM.

UNSOLVED PROBLEMS

1. Calculate the De-Broglie wavelength of a 10 keV neutron.

   Given: Mass of the neutron = 1.67×10^{-27} kg.   (**Ans.** λ = 0.285 A°)

2. The De-Broglie wavelength of electrons in a monoenergetic beam is 7.2×10^{-11} m. Calculate the momentum and energy of electrons in the beam in electron volts.

   (**Ans.** 0.92×10^{-23} kg-m/sec., E = 288 eV)

3. An electron is bound by a potential box of infinite height having a width 2.5 A°. Calculate the minimum uncertainty in its velocity.   (**Ans.** 0.725×10^7 m/sec.)

4. Calculate the wavelength associated with a particle of mass 1 g and moving with a velocity of 2×10^5 cm/sec. Describe the possibility of performing a successful diffraction experiment with a beam of such particles.

   (**Ans.** 3.312×10^{-34} m, experiment not successful)

5. A bullet of mass 25 gm is moving with a speed of 400 m/sec. The speed is measured accurately upto 0.02 %. Calculate the certainty with which the position of the bullet can be located. Given h = 6.6×10^{-34} J.s.   (**Ans.** 5.25×10^{-32} m)

6. Assume that a particle cannot be confined to a spherical volume of diameter less than the De-Broglie wavelength of the particle. Estimate the minimum K.E. a proton confined to a nucleus of diameter 10^{-14} m may have. What K.E. would an electron have to possess if it were confined to this nucleus ?   (**Ans.** 8.2 MeV, 124 MeV)

7. What potential difference must be applied to an electron microscope to produce electrons of wavelength 0.4 A° ?   (**Ans.** 937.9 volts)

8. The average time that an atom retains excess excitation energy before emitting it as electromagnetic radiation is 10^{-8} sec. Calculate the limit of accuracy with which the excitation energy of the emitted radiation can be determined.   (**Ans.** 6.63×10^{-26} J)

9. Find the lowest K.E. permissible for an electron in (i) a cubical box of side 1 cm. (ii) same box of side 3 A°.   (**Ans.** 1.13×10^{-14} eV, 12.6 eV)

10. An electron is bounded by a potential that is approximated by an infinite square well of width 2×10^{-8} cm. Calculate the lowest two permissible energies of the electron.

    (**Ans.** 19 eV, 38 eV)

SOLVED UNIVERSITY QUESTIONS

DECEMBER 2012

1. Define Phase Velocity and Group Velocity. Hence obtain the relation between V_p and V_g for DeBroglie Wave.   **[6]**

Ans. Please Refer to Article 7.4 on Page No. 7.7.

2. State DeBroglie's Hypothesis. Hence obtain the relation for DeBroglie's Wavelength in terms of Energy. **[4]**

Ans. Please Refer to Article 7.3 and 7.3.3 on Page No. 7.3 and 7.6.

3. The position and momentum of 1 keV electron are simultaneously measured. If its position is located with 1 A°. Find the percentage of uncertainty in its momentum.

(Given : h = 6.64×10^{-34} J-sec., m = 9.1×10^{-31} kg) **[3]**

Ans. Data: h = 6.64×10^{-34} J-sec., m = 9.1×10^{-31} kg, Δx = 1A° = 1×10^{-10} m.

Formulae : $\lambda = \dfrac{12.27}{\sqrt{V}}$ A°, $p = \dfrac{h}{\lambda}$ and $\Delta p_x = \dfrac{h}{\Delta x}$

∴ Wavelength, $\lambda = \dfrac{12.27}{\sqrt{V}}$ A° $= \dfrac{12.27}{\sqrt{10^3}} = 0.388$ A°

For electron, Momentum, $p = \dfrac{h}{\lambda} = \dfrac{6.64 \times 10^{-34}}{0.388 \times 10^{-10}}$

$= 17.11 \times 10^{-24}$

$= 1.71 \times 10^{-23}$ kg-m/sec.

Now, $\Delta p_x = \dfrac{h}{\Delta x} = \dfrac{6.64 \times 10^{-34}}{1 \times 10^{-10}}$

$= 6.64 \times 10^{-24}$ kg-m/sec.

$= 0.664 \times 10^{-23}$ kg-m/sec.

∴ Per cent change in momentum $= \dfrac{1.71 \times 10^{-23} - 0.664 \times 10^{-23}}{1.71 \times 10^{-23}} \times 100$

$= \dfrac{1.71 - 0.664}{1.71} \times 100$

$= 61\%$

∴ Percentage of uncertainty in momentum of electron = **39%**.

4. Explain the physical significance of ψ and $|\psi|^2$. **[4]**

Ans. Please Refer to Article 7.7.1 on Page No. 7.29.

5. An electron is bounded by an infinite potential well of width 2×10^{-8} cm. Calculate the lowest two permissible energies of an electron.

(Given : h = 6.64×10^{-34} J-sec., m = 9.1×10^{-31} kg) **[3]**

Ans. Data: h = 6.64×10^{-34} J-sec., m = 9.1×10^{-31} kg, n = 1, L = 2×10^{-10} m

Formula : $E_n = \dfrac{n^2 h^2}{8 mL^2}$

$$\therefore \qquad E_n = \frac{n^2 (6.64 \times 10^{-34})^2}{8 \times 9.1 \times 10^{-31} \times (2 \times 10^{-10})^2}$$

$$\therefore \qquad E_n = 1.5 \times 10^{-18} n^2 \, J$$

$$\therefore \qquad E_n = 9.44 \, n^2 \, eV \approx 9.5 \, n^2 \, eV$$

For n = 1, $\qquad E_1 = $ **9.5 eV**

For n = 2, $\qquad E_2 = 9.5 \, (2^2) \, eV$

$$\therefore \qquad E_2 = \textbf{38 eV}$$

6. Derive Schrodinger's Time Independent Wave Equation.   [6]

Ans. Please Refer to Article 7.8.1 or Page No. 7.28.

MAY 2013

1. Derive Schroedinger time independent wave equation.   [6]

Ans. Please Refer to Article No 7.8.1 on Page No 7.28.

2. Define phase velocity, Group velocity and Derive their expressions   [4]

Ans. Please Refer to Article No 7.4.1 and Article No 7.4.2 on Page No 7.7 and 7.8.

3. Calculate the De-Broglie wavelength associated with 1 Mev proton ($m_p = 1.67 \times 10^{-27}$ kg)   [3]

Ans. **Data:** $\qquad E = 1MeV$

$$m_p = 1.67 \times 10^{-27} \, kg$$

Formula: $\qquad \lambda = \frac{1}{\sqrt{2m_pE}}$

Solution: $\qquad \lambda = \frac{6.63 \times 10^{-34}}{\sqrt{2 \times 1.67 \times 10^{-27} \times 1 \times 10^6 \times 1.6 \times 10^{-19}}}$

$$\lambda = 2.86 \times 10^{-14} m$$

$$\lambda = 2.86 \times 10^{-4} A^\circ$$

4. Explain Heisenberg Uncertainty Principle and prove this principle using single slit Diffraction experiment   [6]

Ans. Please Refer to Article No 7.6 and 7.6.2 on Page No 7.16 and 7.19.

5. Calculate the energy and momentum of an electron confined in a rigid box of width $2A^\circ$ for lowest energy state.   [4]

Ans. **Data:** $\qquad L = 2A^0$

Formula: (i) $\qquad E_n = \frac{n^2 h^2}{8mL^2}$

(ii) $$P = \sqrt{2mE}$$

Solution: (i) $$E_1 = \frac{1^2(6.63 \times 10^{-34})^2}{8 \times 9.1 \times 10^{-31} \times (2 \times 10^{-10})^2}$$

$$E_1 = 1.509 \times 10^{-18} J$$

$$E_1 = 9.44 e^{-V}$$

(ii) $$P_1 = \sqrt{2´9/1´10^{-31} \times 1.509 \times 10^{-18}}$$

$$P_1 = 1.663 \times 10^{-24} \text{ kg-m/sec}$$

6. Does the matter waves are electromagnetic waves? Explain.   **[3]**

Ans. No, Matter waves are not electromagnetic waves because

(1) The matter waves are generated by charged as well as uncharged particles where as electromagnetic waves are generated only by charged particle.

(2) The velocity of matter waves is not constant but depends on velocity of particles generating them I.e. $u = \dfrac{C^2}{V}$. Where as electromagnetic waves travel with uniform velocity C in a given medium.

NOVEMBER 2013

1. Derive an expression for energy of a particle trapped in an infinite potential wall.   **[6]**
Ans. Please Refer to Article 7.10 on Page No. 7.32.

2. State and explain De Broglie's hypothesis of matter waves. State any two properties of matter waves.
Ans. Please Refer to Articles 7.3.1 and 7.5 on Page No. 7.5 and 7.11.

3. The uncertainty in the location of the particle is equal to its De Brogile wavelength. Show that the uncertainty in the velocity of a particle is equal to the particle velocity itself.   **[3]**
Ans. Please Refer to Problem 7.14 on Page No. 7.22.

4. State and explain Heisenberg's uncertainty principle. Illustrate it by an experiment of electron diffraction at a single slit.   **[6]**
Ans. Please Refer to Articles 7.6 and 7.6.2 on Page No. 7.16 and 7.19.

5. What is wave function ψ ? Write down the conditions satisfied by wave function ψ. **[4]**
Ans. Please Refer to Articles 7.7 and 7.7.1 on Page No. 7.25 and 7.27.

6. Calculate the energy difference between the ground state and first excited state of an electron in the rigid box of length 1 A°.   **[3]**
Ans. Please Refer to Problem 7.53 on Page No. 7.56.

MAY 2014

1. State and explain Heisenberg's uncertainty principle. Prove the same for pair of variables energy and time. **[6]**

Ans. Please Refer to Article 7.6 and 7.6.1 on Page No. 7.16 and 7.18.

2. Explain in brief, working of Scanning Tunneling Microscope (STM). **[4]**

Ans. Please Refer to Article 7.12.1 (2) on Page No. 7.45.

3. What accelerating potential would be required for a proton with zero initial velocity to acquire a velocity corresponding to its de-Broglie wavelength of 10^{-10} m. [Given: $m_p = 1.67 \times 10^{-27}$ kg] **[3]**

Ans. Data: m = 1.67×10^{-27} kg, $\lambda = 10^{-10}$ m

Formula: $\lambda = \dfrac{h}{\sqrt{2mev}}$

Solution: $V = \dfrac{(6.63 \times 10^{-34})^2}{2 \times 1.67 \times 10^{-27} \times 1.6 \times 10^{-19} \times (10^{-10})^2}$

$V = 0.082$ V

4. Deduce Schrodinger's time independent wave equation. **[6]**

Ans. Please Refer to Article 7.8.1 on Page No. 7.28.

5. Define phase velocity of a matter wave. Show that phase velocity of matter wave is greater than velocity of light. **[4]**

Ans. Please Refer to Article 7.4.1 on Page No. 7.7.

6. Starting from $\lambda = \dfrac{h}{mv}$, obtain $\lambda = \dfrac{h}{\sqrt{2mE}}$, where E is KE of the particle. **[3]**

Ans. Please Refer to Article 7.3.3 on Page No. 7.6.

DECEMBER 2014

1. Deduce Schrodinger time independent wave equation. **[6]**

Ans. Please Refer to Article 7.8.1 on Page No. 7.28.

2. Define group velocity. Show that the group velocity of matter wave is equal to particle velocity. **[4]**

Ans. Please Refer to Article 7.4.2 and 7.4.3 on Page No. 7.8 and 7.9.

3. Calculate the de Broglie wavelength of electron having kinetic energy 1 KeV. **[3]**

Ans. Please Refer to Article 7.3.3 on Page No. 7.6.

4. State Heisenberg's uncertainty principle and prove it by thought experiment of electron diffraction at a single slit. **[6]**

Ans. Please Refer to Article 7.6.2 on Page No. 7.19.

5. What is wave function ? Explain what is normalization of wave function. **[4]**

Ans. Please Refer to Article 7.10.1 on Page No. 7.35.

6. An electron is trapped in a rigid box of width 2 A°. Find its lowest energy level. **[3]**

Ans. Please Refer to Problem 7.28 on Page No. 7.48.

MAY 2015

1. State and explain Heisenberg's Uncertainty principle. Illustrate the same with electron diffraction at a single slit. **[6]**

Ans. Please Refer to Article 7.6 and 7.6.2 on Page No. 7.16 to 7.19.

2. What is wave function ψ ? Give the physical significance of it. **[4]**

Ans. Please Refer to Article 7.7 and 7.7.1 on Page No. 7.25 to 7.27.

3. An electron is trapped in a rigid box of width 2 A.U. Find its lowest energy in eV. **[3]**

Ans. Please Refer to Problem No. 7.49 on Page No. 7.54.

4. Deduce Schrödinger's time independent wave equation. **[6]**

Ans. Please Refer to Article 7.8 and 7.8.1 on Page No. 7.28 to 7.30.

5. Define phase velocity and prove that it is always greater than velocity of light. **[4]**

Ans. Please Refer to Article 7.4.1 on Page No. 7.7 to 7.8.

6. Calculate the de Broglie wavelength of proton when it is accelerated by potential difference of 10 kV. **[3]**

Ans.

Data: V = 10 kV, m_p = 1.67 × 10^{-27} kg.

Formula:
$$\lambda = \frac{h}{\sqrt{2meV}}$$

Solution:
$$\lambda = \frac{6.63 \times 10^{-34}}{\sqrt{2 \times 1.67 \times 10^{-27} \times 1.6 \times 10^{-19} \times 10000}}$$

$$\lambda = 2.868 \times 10^{-13} \text{ m}$$

$$\lambda = 2.868 \times 10^{-3} \text{ A}°$$

NOVEMBER 2015

1. Deduce Schrodinger's time independent wave equation. **[6]**

Ans. Please Refer to Article 7.8.1 on Page No. 7.28.

2. Define phase (wave) velocity. Show that the phase velocity of matter wave is greater than the velocity of light. **[4]**

Ans. Please Refer to Article 7.4.1 on Page No. 7.7.

3. Calculate the de Broglie wavelength of electron of energy 1 keV.   **[3]**

Ans.

Data: $E = 1 \text{ KeV}$

Formula: $\lambda = \dfrac{h}{r(2mE)}$

Solution: $\lambda = \dfrac{6.6 \times 10^{-34}}{\sqrt{2 \times 9.1 \times 10^{-31} \times 10^{3} \times 1.6 \times 10^{-19}}}$

$\lambda = 3.87 \times 10^{-11} \text{ m}$

$\lambda = 0.387 \text{ A}°$

4. State Heisenberg's Uncertainty principle and prove it by thought experiment of electron diffraction at a single slit.   **[6]**

Ans. Please Refer to Article 7.6 and 7.6.2 (1) on Page No. 7.16 and 7.18.

5. What is wave function ? Explain what is normalization of wave function.   **[4]**

Ans. Please Refer to Article 7.7 on Page No. 7.25.

6. The lowest energy of an electron trapped in a rigid box is 4.19 eV. Find the width of the box in A.U.   **[3]**

Ans.

Data: $n = 1, E = 4.19 \text{ eV}$

Formula: $E = \dfrac{n^{2}h^{2}}{8mL^{2}}$

Solution: $L = \sqrt{\dfrac{n^{2}h^{2}}{8mE}}$

$L = \sqrt{\dfrac{(1)^{2}\,(6.6 \times 10^{-34})^{2}}{8 \times 9.1 \times 10^{-31} \times 4.19 \times 1.6 \times 10^{-19}}}$

$L = 2.987 \times 10^{-10} \text{ m}$

$L = 2.987 \text{ A}°$

MAY 2016

1. Deduce Schr0dinger's t me independent wave equation.   **[6]**

Ans. Please Refer to Article 7.8.1 on Page No. 7.28.

2. State and explain Heisenberg's uncertainty principle.   **[4]**

Ans. Please Refer to Article 7.6 on Page No. 7.16.

3. Calculate the de Broglie wavelength for a proton moving with velocity 1 percent of velocity of light. **[3]**

Ans. Data : $m_p = 1.673 \times 10^{-27}$ kg, $V = \dfrac{1}{100} \times 3 \times 10^8$ m/sec.

Formula : $\lambda = \dfrac{h}{mv}$ **Solution :** $\lambda = \dfrac{6.63 \times 10^{-34}}{1.673 \times 10^{-27} \times \dfrac{1}{100} \times 3 \times 10^8} = 1.32 \times 10^{-13}$ m

4. Define phase velocity and group velocity. Show that group velocity is equal to particle velocity. **[6]**

Ans. Please Refer to Article 7.4 on Page No. 7.7.

5. Explain why probability of finding of a particle cannot be predicted by the interpretation of wave function ψ. Explain physical significance of $|\psi|^2$. **[4]**

Ans. Please Refer to Article 7.7 on Page No. 7.25.

6. A neutron is trapped in an infinite potential well of width 10^{-14} m. Calculate its first energy eigenvalue in eV. **[3]**

Ans. Data : $m_n = 1.675 \times 10^{-27}$, $L = 10^{-14}$ m, n = 1, **Formula :** $En = \dfrac{n^2 h^2}{8mL^2}$

Solution : $En = \dfrac{(1)^2 (6.63 \times 10^{-34})^2}{8 \times 1.675 \times 10^{-27} \times (10^{-14})^2}$

$En = 3.28 \times 10^{-13}$ J

$En = 2.05$ MeV.

✠ ✠ ✠

CHAPTER 8
SUPERCONDUCTIVITY

8.1 INTRODUCTION

- Superconductivity is one of the most exciting phenomena because of its special feature when compared to conductors and has wide range of applications in industry. Experimentally, superconductivity was discovered by Dutch physicist, Heike Kamerlingh Onnes in 1911. While studying the temperature dependence of resistance of metals, he discovered that the electrical resistance in certain metals such as lead and mercury suddenly disappears at around 4 K.

- In 1933, W. Hans Meissner revealed that the superconductors repel the magnetic lines of force when it is placed in an external magnetic field.

- The theoretical explanation of superconductivity was given by John Bardeen, Leon N. Cooper and J. Robert Schreiffer in 1957. The theory is famous as **BCS theory** which explained superconductivity based on pairing of electrons called **'Cooper pair'**.

- Some important features of superconductivity are as follows:

  ➤ The electrical resistance drops to zero at critical temperature.

  ➤ The magnetic flux lines are excluded from the bulk of superconductor.

8.2 INTRODUCTION TO SUPERCONDUCTIVITY

[Dec. 12, Nov. 13, May 14]

- It is a known fact that the resistivity of pure metals decreases with decreasing temperature. When the temperature falls below a certain value (the exact value depending on the substance), the resistivity vanishes entirely.

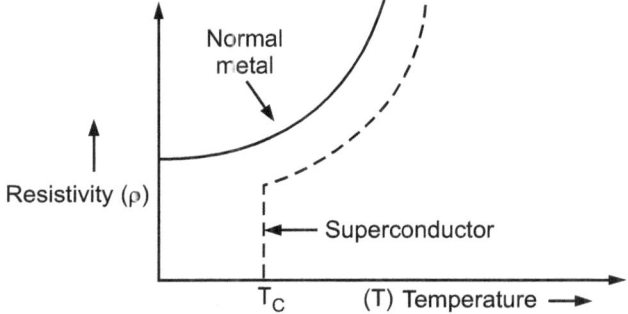

Fig. 8.1: Variation of resistance with temperature

- In metals, both the thermal vibrations of atoms and the presence of impurities or imperfections scatter the moving conduction electrons. This gives rise to electrical resistivity. The variation of resistivity for a pure metal and superconductor is shown in Fig. 8.1.

- At the beginning of the twentieth century, in 1908, H. Kamerling Onnes, a Dutch Physicist, successfully liquified helium. As helium boils at 8.2 K, it therefore became possible to study the properties of materials at low temperature.

- In 1911, he observed that the electrical resistivity of pure mercury dropped suddenly to zero at about the boiling point of helium. He concluded that mercury had passed into a new state, which he called the **superconducting state** due to its remarkable electrical properties.

- The temperature at which the material changes its state from a state of normal resistivity to a superconducting state, is called the **transition or critical temperature T_c.**

- A conductor having zero (or almost zero) electrical resistance is called a **superconductor** and this phenomenon is called as **superconductivity**.

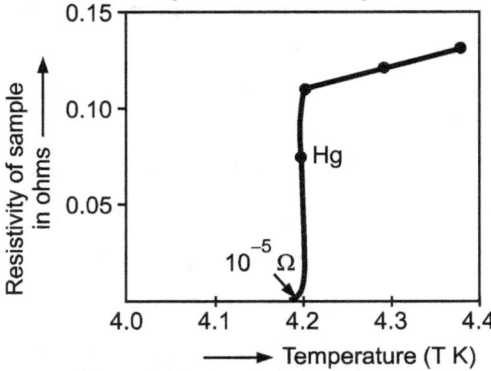

Fig. 8.2: Resistance of mercury as a function of temperature showing a transition from normal state to superconducting state at a critical temperature of 4.2 K

- The superconducting transition is found to be very sharp for a pure metal and it is broad for an impure metal. The zero magnetic induction in a superconductor is responsible for levitation effects.

- In a famous levitation experiment, a horizontal bar magnet was suspended from a chain. It was lowered over a sheet of lead, which had been cooled to the superconducting state. As the magnet came nearer to the superconducting state, the magnet remained floating horizontally over the lead sheet.

- The field of the approaching magnet induces a current on the surface of the superconductor. As the resistance is zero in the superconductor, the current persisted and the field due to the current repelled the bar magnet.

- This persistence of currents is found uniquely in superconductors. Certain experiments on the study of decay of these supercurrents in a solenoid found decay time to be greater than 10^5 years.

8.3 PROPERTIES OF SUPERCONDUCTORS

Following are the properties of superconductors:

8.3.1 Zero Electrical Resistance

*   A superconductor is characterized by zero electrical resistance. The temperature below which the resistance of the material vanishes is called as the **'transition temperature'** or **'critical temperature'**. It is referred as T_C.

*   As it is not possible to test experimentally whether the resistance is zero, the specimen is connected in a circuit as shown in Fig. 8.3.

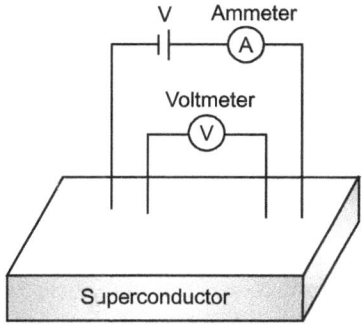

Fig. 8.3

*   When the material is in normal conducting state, a voltage drop is measured across its ends. As the material is cooled below its transition temperature T_C, the voltage drop disappears as its resistance drops to zero ($R = V/I$).

*   A more sensitive method devised by K. Onnes consists in measuring the decrease of current in a closed ring of superconducting wire.

Table 8.1: A List of Some Superconductors Alongwith their Critical Temperature

Sr. No.	Material	T_C in K
1.	Copper, silver, gold	Non-superconducting
2.	Rhodium	240×10^{-6}
3.	Aluminium	1.1
4.	Tin	3.72
5.	Mercury	4.15
6.	Lead	7.2
7.	Niobium	9.3
8.	Niobium-titanium alloys	9-11
9.	Lead molybdenum sulphide	14
10.	Niobium-tin	18.3
11.	Vanadium-gallium	15.4
12.	Niobium-germanium	23.3

*   It has been observed that traces of paramagnetic elements in the specimen can lower the transition temperature. Hence, it becomes necessary to remove these traces completely. Non-magnetic impurities have no marked effect on the transition temperature.

8.3.2 Meissner Effect   [Dec. 12, 14, Nov. 15, May 13, 14, 15, 16]

- Meissner and Ochsenfeld discovered in 1933 that a superconductor completely expels any magnetic field lines that were initially penetrating it in its normal state. This property is independent of the path by which the superconducting state is reached.

Path 1

- The sample is in superconducting state and is brought to the magnetic field. It is found that the magnetic flux is totally expelled from the sample.

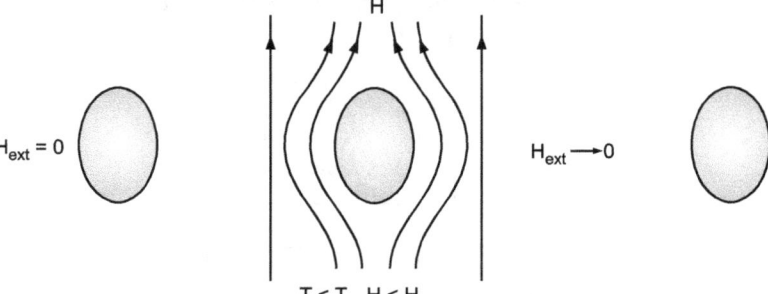

$T < T_c$, $H < H_c$

(a) Superconductor is initially outside the magnetic field	(b) When the superconductor is transported into the magnetic field, it pushes the field lines aside	(c) When the magnetic field is switched off

Fig. 8.4

Path 2

The magnetic field is applied first to the sample in the normal state. Then the material be cooled to below T_C in the presence of the magnetic field. Meissner and Ochsenfeld found that the magnetic flux is totally expelled from the sample as it becomes superconducting. This expulsion of magnetic flux during the transition from normal to superconducting state is called as **'Meissner effect'**.

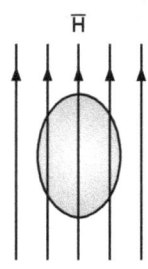
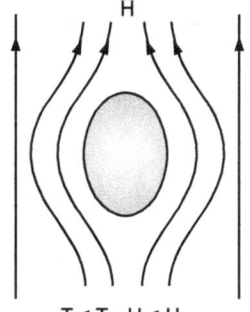
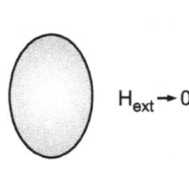

$T > T_c$, $H > H_c$ $T < T_c$, $H < H_c$

(a) Superconductor in a magnetic field at $T > T_c$, magnetic field penetrates the body in normal state	(b) On cooling the superconductor in the presence of magnetic field, it expels the flux lines within the specimen at $T = T_c$. This is Meissner effect	(c) When the field is switched off, field is not trapped within the superconductor. Superconductivity is thus characterized by perfect diamagnetism

Fig. 8.5

Ch. 8 | 8.4

Explanation of Meissner Effect

- When a superconducting sample is placed in a magnetic field, it induces currents which circulate on the surface of the specimen in a manner that it creates a magnetic field everywhere equal and opposite to the applied magnetic field.

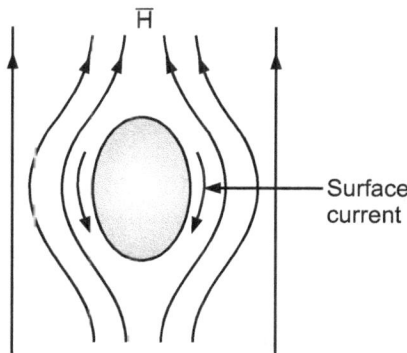

Fig. 8.6: Meissner effect

- Meissner effect cannot be explained by the assumption that a superconductor is a resistanceless conductor. A superconductor is not just a perfect conductor but has an additional property. A material in the superconducting state does not permit any magnetic flux to exist within the body of the material.

- When a perfect conductor is cooled in a magnetic field until its resistance becomes zero, the magnetic field in the material is frozen or trapped in the material. It cannot change subsequently, irrespective of the applied field. Therefore, a conductor does not exhibit diamagnetic behaviour even slightly.

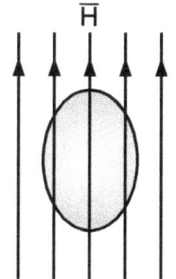
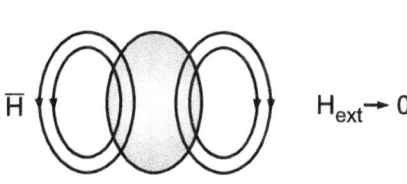

| (a) Conductor held in magnetic field is cooled to the state of zero electrical resistance | (b) When magnetic field H_{ext} is switched off, magnetic field is trapped in the ideal conductor |

Fig. 8.7

- The magnetic induction inside the specimen is given by,

$$B = \mu_0 (H + M) \qquad \text{(Normal state } T > T_c)$$

where,   H — external applied field

M – magnetisation produced within the specimen

For T < T_C,   B = 0

∴ μ_0 (H + M) = 0   (Superconducting state)

⇒   H = −M

The susceptibility of the material,

$$\chi = \frac{M}{H} = -1 \qquad \text{(Perfect diamagnetism)}$$

- Thus, the superconducting state is characterized by perfect diamagnetism. Meissner effect conclusively proves whether a particular material has become a superconductor or not. Because of Meissner effect, superconducting materials strongly repel external magnets, it leads to both **'levitation effect'** and **'suspension effect'**.

8.3.3 Critical Field: Effect of External Magnetic Field   [May 13, 16, Nov. 15]

- K. Onnes discovered in 1913 that, when a superconductor is placed in an increasing magnetic field, it loses superconductivity at a certain value H_C of the field. The magnetic field strength at which superconductivity gets destroyed is called the **'critical magnetic field'** H_C. This value is a characteristic of the metal and depends on its orientation in the magnetic field and the temperature.
- The relation between superconductivity and magnetic field plays an important role in the study of properties of superconductors. Obviously, the value of H_C varies with temperature. Fig. 8.8 shows the variation of H_C with temperature for a typical superconductor.

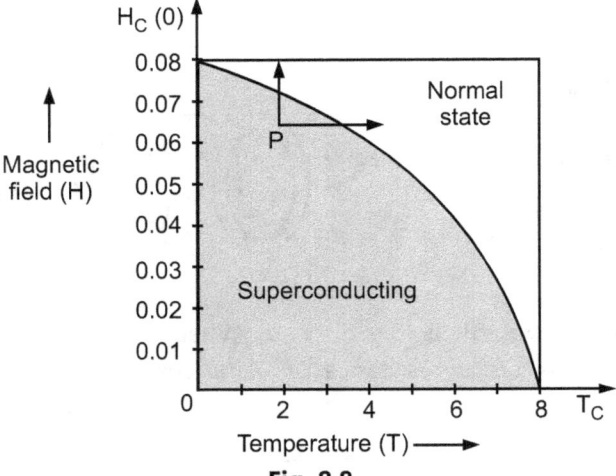

Fig. 8.8

- From Fig. 8.8, consider point P, where the temperature and the magnetic field are within the shaded region, the metal is in the superconducting state. On increasing either the temperature or the field, it can be driven into the normal state. Hence, it can be seen that a superconductor has two possible states: (i) the superconducting one which is resistanceless and perfectly diamagnetic and (ii) a normal state which is the same as a normal metal.

- At any temperature $T < T_c$, the material remains superconducting until a corresponding critical magnetic field is applied. When the magnetic field exceeds the critical value, the material goes into the normal state. The critical field required to destroy the superconducting state decreases progressively with increase in temperature.

- For example, a magnetic field of 0.04 T will destroy the superconductivity of mercury at $T \approx 0$ K, whereas a field of 0.02 T is sufficient to destroy its superconductivity at $T \approx 3$ K. The variation of critical field with temperature is given by the relation

$$H_c(T) = H_c(0) \left[1 - \left(\frac{T}{T_c}\right)\right]^2$$

where $H_c(0)$ is the critical magnetic field at 0 K.

8.3.4 Persistent Currents   [Dec. 12]

- Consider a superconducting ring placed in a magnetic field. When cooled to below the critical temperature, it becomes superconducting. The external field induces a current in the ring. When switched off, the current will continue to keep flowing, on its own accord, around the loop, as long as the loop is held below the critical temperature.

- Such a steady current flowing with undiminished strength is called **persistent current**. This current does not need external power to maintain it as there does not exist I^2R losses. If the superconducting ring has a finite resistance R, the current circulating in the ring would decrease according to the relation,

$$I(t) = I(0) \ e^{-Rt/L}$$

where L is the inductance of the ring.

- Calculations show that once the current flow is initiated, it persists for more than 10^5 years. Persistent current is one of the most important properties of a superconductor.

- Superconductor coils with persistent currents produce magnetic fields. They can therefore be used as magnets which do not require a power supply to maintain its magnetic field.

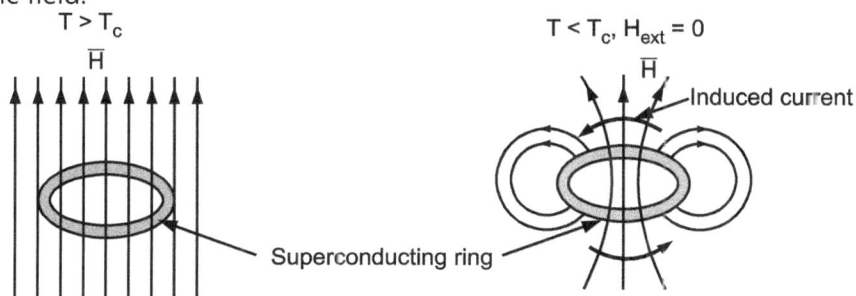

(a) **Superconducting ring is cooled in the presence of a magnetic field**

(b) **At $T < T_c$, the magnetic field is switched off. Persistent current is induced in the ring**

Fig. 8.9

8.3.5 Isotope Effect

- Maxwell and Reynolds found independently that the critical temperature of superconductors varies with isotopic mass. It is found to decrease with increasing isotopic mass M.

- Since a heavier isotopic mass lowers the lattice vibrations, this indicates that superconductivity is due to an interaction between electrons and lattice vibrations. To get an idea of the magnitude of the effect for mercury, T_c varies from 4.185 K to 4.146 K as the isotopic mass M varies from 199.5 to 203.4. The transition temperature changes smoothly when different isotopes of the same element are mixed. The experimental results within each series of isotopes can be given by the relation:

$$T_c \propto \frac{1}{\sqrt{M}}$$

i.e.
$$T_c \propto M^{-1/2}$$

or
$$M^{1/2} \cdot T_c = \text{constant.}$$

8.3.6 Critical Current Density (J_C)

- The magnetic field which destroys superconductivity, need not be due to an externally applied field, but it may be the field produced as a result of current flow in the superconductor ring itself. If the field produced by itself exceeds H_c, the superconductivity of the ring is destroyed.

- Thus, if a superconducting material carries a current and if the magnetic field produced by it is equal to H_c, then superconductivity disappears. The maximum current density J at which superconductivity vanishes is called the **'critical current density'** J_c. For $J < J_c$, the current can sustain itself while for $J > J_c$, the current cannot sustain itself. A superconducting ring of radius R loses its superconductivity when the current is,

$$I_c = 2\pi R H_c$$

∴   The critical current density,

$$J_c = \frac{\text{Critical current}}{\text{Area of the ring}}$$

$$J_c = \frac{2\pi R H_c}{\pi R^2} = \frac{2H_c}{R}$$

This sets a limit to the maximum current a superconductor can carry without disturbing its superconducting state.

- As the temperature is raised, the maximum current that a superconductor can carry decreases as the temperature is raised and falls to zero at the transition temperature T_c. This maximum current leads to a maximum applied magnetic field. As critical current falls with the temperature, the critical magnetic field will also decrease as the transition temperature is approached. The variation of critical current density J_c and critical magnetic field H_c with temperature is shown in Fig. 8.10.

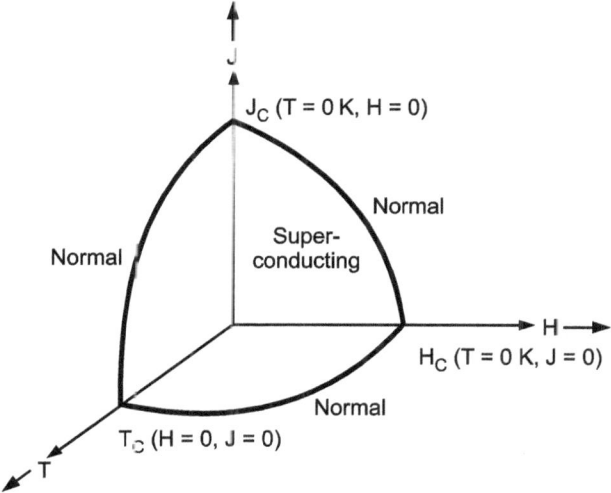

Fig. 8.10

- Fig. 8.10 shows the combined effects of temperature, current density and magnetic field on a superconductor. The boundary separates superconducting and normal states. Within the boundary, the state is superconducting.

In the superconduction state,

$$T < T_c$$
$$H < H_c$$
and $$J < J_c$$

8.4 BCS THEORY   [Dec. 12, Nov. 13, 15, May 14, 16]

- Two theories were advanced to explain the phenomenon of superconductivity
  (i) The London theory, (ii) Gorter and Casimi theory.
- However, none of them were experimentally proved. Then, in the year 1957 came the BCS (named after the American physicists, John Bardeen, Leon N. Cooper and John Robert Schrieffer) quantum theory of superconductivity, which was successful in giving an explanation.
- The superconducting state is known to be an ordered state of the conducting electrons of the metal. The order lies below the transition temperature. Above it, they are disordered. The BCS theory explained the nature and origin of the electron ordering.
- According to this theory, there is an electron - lattice - electron interaction resulting from the interactions of the electrons with the vibrations of the atoms in the lattice. This results in an overall attraction between two electrons. At low temperatures, this attraction overcomes the coulomb repulsion.

(a) Base of the Theory
- This theory is based on the concept of electron-lattice-electron interaction.

(b) Approach of Electron and Lattice Distortion
- When an electron approaches an ion in the lattice, there is coulomb attraction between the electron and the lattice ion. This produces a distortion in the lattice. The distortion causes an increase in the density of ions in the region of distortion.
- The higher density of ions in the distorted region will attract, in turn, a nearby electron. The interaction between the lattice and the electron can be thought of as the constant emission and reabsorption of phonons by the lattice.
- Thus, a free electron exerts a small attractive force on another electron through phonons, which are quanta of lattice vibrations.

(c) Formation of Cooper Pair
- An electron of wave factor k as shown in Fig. 8.11 emits a phonon q which is absorbed by an electron of wave vector k'. This scatters k into k–q and k' into k' + q. This process is virtual and energy need not be conserved. Hence, the phonons are called as *'virtual phonons'*.
- The nature of the resulting interaction depends on the relative magnitudes of electronic energy change and phonon energy ($h\omega_q$). If this phonon energy exceeds the electronic energy, the interaction is attractive.
- As a result of this interaction, electrons form together bound pairs. A pair of free electrons thus coupled through a phonon is called a **Cooper pair**. The energy of pairing i.e., the net attraction is very weak. Only a tiny temperature is needed to throw apart the electrons by thermal agitation and convert them back to normal electrons.

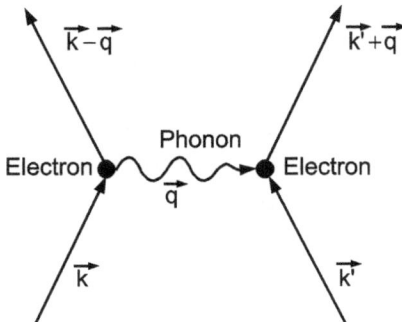

Fig. 8.11: Electron-phonon-electron interaction

(d) Almost Zero Resistance below Critical Temperature
- When the temperature is sufficiently low, the electrons try to get into the lowest state by forming Cooper pairs. Several pairs occupy the same state at the same time. This state is the ground state. Thus, the superconducting state is an ordered state of the **'conduction electrons'**.

- The motion of all Cooper pairs is the same. Either they are at rest, or if the superconductor carries a current, they drift with the same velocity. As the density of Cooper pairs is very high, even large currents require a small velocity. The small velocity of Cooper pairs combined with their precise ordering minimizes collisions and it leads to vanishing resistivity. Once particles get into the ordered state, it would be very difficult to change the state of any one of them.

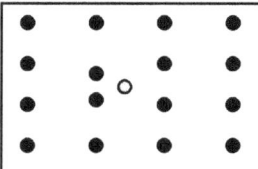

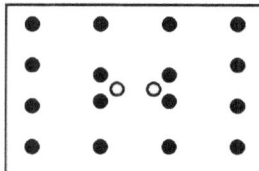

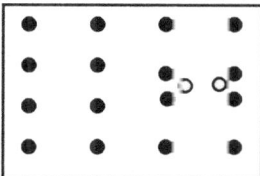

| (a) Electron approaches lattice and lattice ions are attracted towards electrons resulting development of positive charge on the electron | (b) Another electron is attracted towards the positive regions surrounding to the first electron | (c) As first electron moves ahead, second electron follows it and both move together as "Cooper Pair" |

Fig. 8.12

Conclusions from BCS Theory

➢ The electron-lattice-electron interaction is attractive at low temperature and can overcome the coulomb repulsion between the electrons.

➢ The electrons of a Cooper pair have a lower energy than two unpaired electrons. Hence, the energy spectrum shows an energy gap. The Cooper pairs occupy the lower state. The energy gap prevents the pairs from breaking apart.

➢ The theory explains Isotope effect and Meissner effect in a natural manner. The London penetration depth, etc. are natural consequences of the BCS ground state.

➢ The BCS theory predicts a relation for T_c (critical temperature) which is also found to be satisfied qualitatively by experimental results.

➢ Magnetic flux through a superconducting ring is quantized and the effective unit of charge is 2e rather than e. This can be understood when one considers the BCS ground state involving pairs of electrons.

8.5 TYPES OF SUPERCONDUCTORS   [May 13, 15, Nov. 15]

- There are two types of superconductors: type I and type II. There is no difference in the mechanism of superconductivity in both the types. Both have similar thermal properties at the transition temperature in zero magnetic field.
- The difference lies in their behaviour in a magnetic field, particularly in Meissner effect.

8.5.1 Type-I Superconductors

- In a type-I superconductor, the transition from a superconducting state to normal state, in the presence of a magnetic field, occurs sharply at the critical value H_c. At this point, the field penetrates completely.
- Below H_c, type-I superconductors are perfectly diamagnetic. They completely expel the magnetic field from the interior of the specimen. Upto the critical field strength, magnetization of the material grows in proportion to the external field. At the transition temperature, it suddenly drops to zero to the normal conducting state.
- The magnetic field penetrates only the surface layer and current flows only in this layer. Aluminium and lead are examples of type-I superconductors.
- As superconductivity gets destroyed at low values of critical field, type-I superconductors cannot be used in solenoids for producing large magnetic fields. Such superconductors are also called as **'soft superconductors'**.

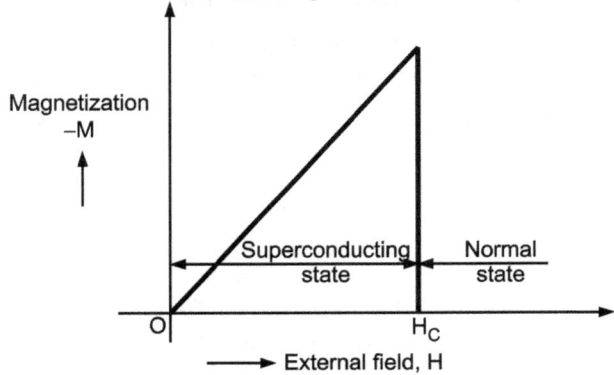

Fig. 8.13: Magnetization curve for a type-I superconductor

8.5.2 Type-II Superconductors   [Dec. 14]

- Type-II superconductor, also known as **'hard superconductor'** is characterized by two critical fields H_{c1} and H_{c2}. ($H_{c1} < H_c < H_{c2}$). It exists in three states: superconducting, mixed and normal.

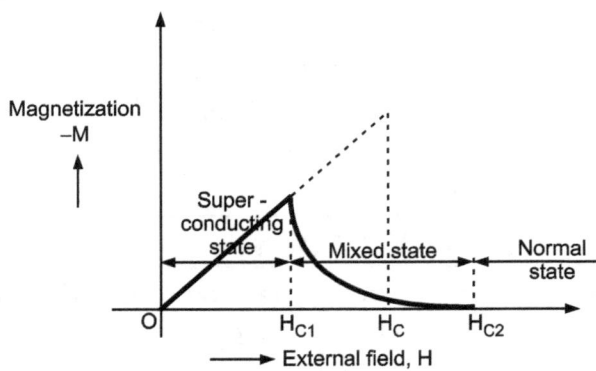

Fig. 8.14: Magnetization curve in type-II superconductor

Superconducting State

- This occurs upto a critical field H_{c_1}. The magnetization increases with the applied magnetic field and the external magnetic flux is completely expelled from the interior of the material.

Mixed State

- This region extends from H_{c_1} to H_{c_2}. At H_{c_1}, the magnetic flux penetrates the material. Between H_{c_1} and H_{c_2}, the material is in a mixed state magnetically but electrically it is a superconductor. Meissner effect is incomplete. In this region, the superconductor s threaded by flux lines and is said to be in a **_vortex state_**. Value of H_{c_2} may be 100 times higher than H_c (~20 to 50 Wb/m^2).

- As superconductivity is retained upto high values of magnetic fields, type-II superconductors are found useful in applications where high magnetic fields are created. Commercial solenoids wound with type-II superconductors produce high, steady magnetic fields above 10 T.

- Once the magnetic field is created by a superconductor solenoid, it does not require electrical power to maintain it. But the solenoid must be kept below critical transition temperature.

Normal State

- When the magnetic field exceeds critical field strength H_{c_2}, magnetization vanishes completely. The sample is penetrated by the external field and superconductivity s destroyed. The specimen reverts from superconducting state to normal state.

- Type-II superconductors have a distinguishing feature. The supercurrents arising in an external magnetic field can flow not only on the surface but also in its bulk. The magnitude of the currents carried is also large when the magnetic field is between H_{c_1} and H_{c_2}.

Table 8.2: Types of superconductor - Differences

Sr.	Property	Type-I Superconductor	Type-II Superconductor
1.	Variation of magnetic field with temperature		
2.	Critical magnetic field	Has one critical magnetic field H_c.	Has two critical magnetic fields H_{c1} and H_{c2}.

Sr.	Property	Type-I Superconductor	Type-II Superconductor
3.	Transition from superconducting to normal state	Transition from superconducting state to normal state in the presence of a magnetic field occurs sharply at the critical value H_c.	If external magnetic field is less than H_{c1}, material remains superconductor. When external magnetic field increases above H_{c2}, their superconductivity is destroyed.
4.	Magnetization below and above critical magnetic field	They are perfectly diamagnetic below H_c and completely expel magnetic field from interior of the superconducting phase.	For $H_{c1} < H < H_{c2}$ they exist in magnetically mixed and electronically superconducting state.
5.	Change in magnetization with external magnetic field	Upto H_c magnetization of the material grows in proportion to the external field and then abruptly drops to zero at the transition to the normally conducting state.	The magnetization of Type-II superconductors grows in proportion to the external field upto H_{c1}. The external magnetic flux is expelled from the interior of the material till then. At H_{c1}, magnetic field lines begin penetrating the material. As magnetic field increases further, the magnetic flux through the material increases. At H_{c2}, magnetization vanishes completely. External magnetic field penetrates completely and superconductivity is destroyed.
6.	Current carrying capacity	They are poor carriers of electrical current.	They are good carriers of electrical current.
7.	Magnetic field generation capacity	About 0.01 to 0.2 Wb/m^2 (value of H_c).	About 20 to 50 Wb/m^2 (Value of H_{c2}).
8.	Applications as magnets	Not much useful due to low H_c.	Useful due to high H_{c2}.
9.	Examples	Aluminium, lead, indium	Transition metals and alloys consisting of niobium, silicon and vanadium, Nb-Ti alloys, Nb$_3$Sn, etc.

8.6 APPLICATIONS OF SUPERCONDUCTIVITY

[Nov. 15, May 13, Dec. 14]

- The phenomenon of superconductivity finds numerous applications which can be broadly classified into two types.

   1. Large-Scale Applications

   These are applications requiring large currents, long lengths of superconductors in environments where the magnetic field may be several tesla (1 tesla = 10^4 Oersted).

Examples include magnets and power transmission lines, transformers and generators, where current densities of atleast 10^5 amps/cm^2 are required. Superconductors are more advantageous than normal conductors because of their lower resistance and hence smaller power loss.

2.   Small-Scale Applications

These are applications involving minute amounts of current or fields. Examples are detection systems like SQUIDS.

8.7 LARGE-SCALE APPLICATIONS

- The cost of energy consumption in the world and the electrical energy in particular are staggering. It is said that about one-fifth the power generated is lost due to I^2R losses. The elimination of even a small fraction of the resistive load will have a staggering impact.
- Another important area of application is the use of high temperature superconductors in the production of strong magnetic fields above the 2 Tesla level. This will eliminate the use of iron cores in motors, generators and transformers resulting in reduced size, weight and losses from iron cores.

Wires and Superconducting Magnets

- As R = 0 for a superconductor, there are no I^2R losses. There is no energy dissipation associated with the flow of a current through a superconductor. A current set up in a closed loop of a superconductor persists, almost forever, without decay.
- Superconducting wires could be used for very economical long distance power transmission, as energy dissipation is low and electrical power transmission can be done at a lower voltage level. Electric generators made with superconducting wire are more efficient than conventional generators wound with copper wire.

Magnetic levitation (Maglev)

- The zero magnetic induction in a superconductor is responsible for levitation effects.
- This phenomenon has led to one of the most spectacular applications, maglev or magnetically levitated train. Superconducting magnetic coils produce the magnetic repulsion required to levitate the train. Maglev trains will not slide over the rails but will float on an air cushion over a magnetised track. As there is no mechanical friction, speeds upto 500 km/hr can be achieved easily. As these trains are capable of very high speeds, they can compete with short hop plane flights in crowded air corridors.
- There are several maglev train test strips and there is talk about a 13 mile commercial line in the Orlando-Florida area and a longer one between Los Angeles and Las Vegas. One proposal is to use an on-board electromagnet to levitate the train above the laminated iron rail in the guide with ~1 cm air gap.
- A second proposal is to use superconducting wire coils in the vehicle to produce a magnetic field of the same polarity as coils in the guides, the repulsive force lifts the vehicle above the track (about 10-15 cm). As iron is not required for the magnetic field, the vehicle could be much lighter.

Electronics Industry

- Superconductors will change the face of the electronics industry, particularly IC fabrication. Currently, due to large amounts of heat generated (I^2R losses) there is a limit to the number of components that can be placed on a single chip. With the use of superconductors, more densely packed chips may be used.

- With the use of superconducting chips in digital electronics, logic delays of 13 pico seconds and switching times of 9 pico seconds have been achieved. By using basic Josephson junctions (refer small-scale applications), sensitive microwave detectors, magnetometers and stable voltage sources have been manufactured.

Computer Industry

- Currently, logic elements operate at speeds of nanoseconds. By using Josephson junctions, information can be transmitted more rapidly and by several orders of magnitude. Research is being conducted on 'petaflop' computers. A petaflop is a thousand-trillion floating point operations per second. Today's fastest computer has only achieved 'teraflop' speeds - trillions of operations per second.

Superconducting Magnets

- The most important use of superconductivity has been in the production of high magnetic fields (> 10^5 Gauss or 10 Tesla) over large volumes without a large consumption of electrical power.

- As superconductors are capable of carrying, without energy loss, about 100 times larger current densities as compared to normal conductors like copper, they can be used for building light weight, high intensity, compact magnets useful in various applications. Relatively small superconducting magnets have very economically replaced gigantic water-cooled copper conductor magnets which dissipate several megawatts of electrical power. Superconducting magnets (SCM) find application in many areas in technology, including energy storage devices for electrical power industry, electric motor windings, electromagnetic pumps, etc.

- Superconducting magnets are also used in the field of medicine for NMR (Nuclear Magnetic Resonance) imaging particularly for producing NMR tomography. This is of particular importance for investigating pathological changes in the brain. By applying a strong magnetic field from a superconducting magnet across the body, hydrogen atoms inside the body are forced to take up energy from the magnetic field. This energy is then released at a frequency that can be detected and displayed on a computer. This method is called as Magnet Resonance Imaging (MRI) and is widely used in hospitals.

- Superconducting magnets are also used in high energy physics experiments. Large particle accelerators employ magnets producing high fields for bending and guiding the accelerated particles. Controlled nuclear fusion requires confining high temperature plasma within a closed region. This is done by using superconducting magnets. Superconducting magnets have also been employed for magnetically separating refining ores, isotopes and chemicals.

Military Applications

- Superconductors have found a wide variety of applications in the military. HTSC (high temperature superconductors) are being used to detect mines and submarines.

- Smaller motors are being built by Navy ships using superconducting wires.

- 'E-bombs' have been used by the US army in March 2003 when US forces attacked Iraq. These are devices that use strong superconducting magnets to create a fast, high intensity electromagnetic pulse to disable an enemy's electronic equipment.

8.8 SMALL-SCALE APPLICATIONS OF SUPERCONDUCTIVITY

- Brian D. Josephson, a graduate student at Cambridge University, in 1962, predicted that electrical current would flow between two superconducting materials even when they are separated by a non-superconductor or insulator. This tunneling phenomenon is called as the **'Josephson Effect'**.

- It has been applied to electronic devices such as the SQUID, an instrument capable of detecting and measuring extremely weak magnetic fields.

8.9 JOSEPHSON EFFECT

Josephson Junction

- Two superconductors connected by a thin layer of insulating material (~ 1-2 nm) is called a **'Josephson junction'**. Under suitable conditions, Josephson found that remarkable effects were associated with the tunneling of superconducting electron pairs from a superconductor, through a layer of an insulator, into another superconductor. This junction is called a **weak link**. The effect found to be associated with the pair tunneling is called **Josephson effect**.

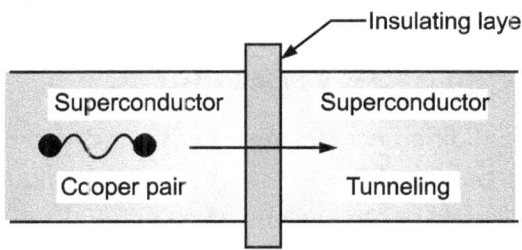

Fig. 8.15: Josephson junction

8.9.1 DC Josephson Effect   [Nov. 13]

- When two superconductors are separated by a thin insulating layer, Cooper pairs tunnel through the junction and current flows across the junction without any external applied voltage. If this current does not exceed critical current I_c, voltage across the junction is zero. This effect is known as **dc Josephson effect**.

- The Cooper pairs on each side of the junction can be represented by a wave function. The dc current obtained due to the tunneling of Cooper pairs through the insulating layer is given by $I_J = I_C \sin \phi$, where ϕ is the phase difference between wave functions of Cooper pairs on either side.

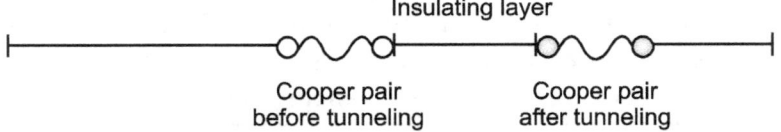

Fig. 8.16: DC effect

8.9.2 AC Josephson Effect   [Nov. 13]

- When a dc voltage is applied to the Josephson junction and the current I_J through the junction exceeds a critical value I_c, a potential difference V appears across the Josephson junction and the junction current I_J varies sinusoidally with time. This effect is known as ac **Josephson effect**.

- In such a case, the energies of the Cooper pair on both the sides of the barrier differ by 2 eV. The alternating supercurrents are accompanied by the emission or absorption of electromagnetic radiation.

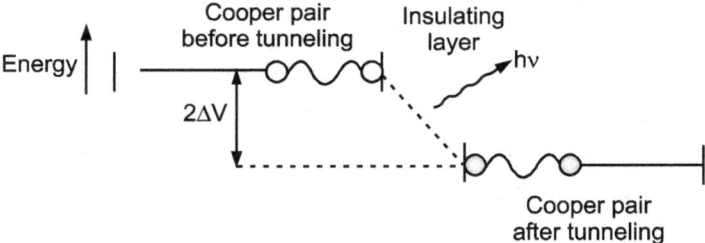

Fig. 8.17: AC effect

- If ΔV is the finite potential difference between the superconductors, the electron pairs on opposite sides of the barrier differ in energy by an amount $2\Delta V = 2$ eV. Hence, frequency υ of the associated photon will be given by,

$$h\upsilon = 2\,eV \quad \text{or} \quad \upsilon = 2\left(\frac{e}{h}\right)V.$$

- Josephson suggested the determination of h/e from this relation after measuring applied voltage and frequency of emitted radiation. This experiment was carried out between 1967 and 1968. It is one of the simplest methods available to measure the fundamental constant.

UNIVERSITY SOLVED PROBLEMS

Problem 8.1: *The critical temperature of a superconductor with isotopic mass 200 is 5 K. Calculate the critical temperature of the superconductor when isotopic mass is 196.*

(May 2004)

Data: $\quad\quad\quad\quad$ M = 200, $\quad T_{200}$ = 5 K

Formula: $\quad\quad\quad$ $T_C \propto M^{-1/2}$

Solution: $\quad\quad\quad$ $\dfrac{T_{200}}{T_{196}} = \dfrac{200^{-1/2}}{196^{-1/2}}$

$$T_{196} = \dfrac{196^{-1/2}}{200^{-1/2}} \cdot 5$$

$$T_{196} = \sqrt{\dfrac{200}{196}} \cdot 5$$

$$\boxed{T_{196} = 5.05 \text{ K}}$$

The critical temperature for M = 196 is 5.05 K.

Problem 8.2 : *Calculate the conductivity of Ge sample it the donor impurity is added to an extent of one part in 10^8 Ge atoms at room termperature (Data Given: N_a = 6.023 $\times 10^{23}$ atoms/gn-mole. At. Wt. of Ge = 72.6). may 13 (Density of Ge = 5.32gm/cc. μ = 3800 cm^2/v-s.)* $\quad\quad$ *(03)*

Ans. $\quad\quad$ Data $\quad\quad\quad\quad\quad$ At. Wt. of Ge = 72.6

$\quad\quad\quad\quad\quad\quad\quad\quad\quad\quad\quad$ Density of Ge = 5.32 gm/cc

$\quad\quad\quad\quad\quad\quad\quad\quad\quad\quad\quad\quad\quad$ μ = 3800 cm^2/V.S.

Formula: $\quad\quad\quad\quad\quad\quad\quad\quad\quad\quad\quad$ σ = ndμe

Solution:

Number of Ge atoms/unit volume $\quad = \dfrac{6.023 \times 10^{23} \times 5.32}{72.6}$ = 4.41 $\times 10^{22}$/cm^3

As ratio of donor to pure semiconductor for is 1: 10^8

$\therefore \quad\quad\quad\quad\quad\quad n_d = \dfrac{4.41 \times 10^{22}}{10^8}$ = 4.41 $\times 10^{14}$/cm^3

Conductivity $\quad\quad\quad\quad\quad\quad\quad\quad\quad$ σ = 4.41 $\times 10^{14} \times$ 1.6 $\times 10^{-19} \times$ 3800

$\therefore \quad\quad\quad\quad\quad\quad\quad\quad\quad\quad\quad\quad\quad$ σ = 0.268 mho/cm.

SUMMARY

- A conductor having zero electrical resistance is called a superconductor and this phenomenon is called as superconductivity.
- The temperature below which superconductivity is exhibited is called as critical transition temperature (T_C).
- Superconductivity vanishes if temperature, magnetic field and current density exceed the critical value. For superconducting state, T < T_c, H < H_c and J < J_c.

- BCS theory states that the superconducting state is an ordered state of a pair of conduction electrons coupled through a phonon called a Cooper pair.
- The expulsion of magnetic field/flux from the interior of the specimen, when cooled below the critical temperature is called as Meissner effect.
- Critical temperature for different isotopes varies with the mass.

$$M^{1/2} T_c = \text{constant.}$$

- Variation of critical magnetic field with temperature is given by

$$H_c(T) = H_c(0) \left[1 - \frac{T}{T_c} \right]^2$$

where $H_c(0)$ is the critical magnetic field at 0 K.

- Persistent currents: When a current is induced in a superconducting ring or loop held below the critical temperature, it persists undiminished as long as the temperature remains below the critical temperature T_c.
- Type-I superconductors are pure specimens which expel completely magnetic field lines. They exhibit perfect diamagnetism. They are also called as soft superconductors.
- Type-II superconductors are characterized by two critical fields. Between the two critical fields, the magnetic flux partially penetrates the material. Above the upper critical field flux, penetration is total. They are also called as hard superconductors.
- Tunneling of current between two superconductors separated by an insulator is known as Josephson effect.
- The flow of a dc current across the Josephson junction, in the absence of any electric or magnetic field is known as dc Josephson effect.
- When a dc voltage is applied across the Josephson junction, RF current oscillations are setup across the junction along with the emission or absorption of electromagnetic radiation. This is known as ac Josephson effect.

IMPORTANT FORMULAE

- Isotope effect, $M^{1/2} T_c = \text{constant.}$

- $\lambda = \dfrac{\lambda_o}{\left[1 - \left(\dfrac{T}{T_c} \right)^4 \right]}$.

- $H_c = H_o \left[1 - \left(\dfrac{T}{T_c} \right)^2 \right]$.

EXERCISE

1. Explain BCS theory to explain superconductivity.
2. What is superconductivity ? What are the characteristics of superconductors ?

3. Explain Meissner effect, isotope effect, critical temperature and critical field.

4. What are the types of superconductors ? Where do they find application ?

5. Enumerate the different applications of superconductors. How are they advantageous as compared to normal conductors ?

6. Explain some properties of type-I and type-II superconductors.

SOLVED UNIVERSITY QUESTIONS

DECEMBER 2012

1. Explain the Phenomena of Super-conductivity. Explain Type - I and Type - II Super-conductors. **[6]**

Ans. Please Refer to Article 8.2 on Page No. 8.1.

2. Explain BCS Theory of Super-conductivity. **[4]**

Ans. Please Refer to Article 8.4 on Page No. 8.9.

3. State and explain : **[3]**

(a) Meissner Effect.

Ans. Please Refer to Article 8.3.2 on Page No. 8.4.

(b) Persistent Current.

Ans. Please Refer to Article 8.3.4 on Page No. 8.7.

MAY 2013

1. Differentiate between Type-I and Type-II Superconductor with diagram **[4]**

Ans. Please Refer to Article No 8.5 on Page No 8.11.

2. Explain two applications of Superconductivity. **[3]**

Ans. Please Refer to Article No 8.6 on Page No 8.14.

3. Explain Meissner effect and Critical magnetic field for Superconductivity. **[6]**

Ans. Please Refer to Articles No 8.3.2 and 8.3.3 on Page No 8.4 and 8.6.

NOVEMBER 2013

1. What is superconductivity ? Explain the BCS theory of superconductors. **[6]**

Ans. Please Refer to Articles 8.2 and 8.4 on Page No. 8.1 and 8.9.

2. Explain D.C. and A.C. Josephson effect. **[4]**

Ans. Please Refer to Articles 8.9.1 and 8.9.2 on Page No. 8.17 and 8.18.

3. Distinguish between Type-I and Type-II superconductors. (Any 3 points) **[3]**

Ans. Please Refer to Article 8.5 on Page No. 8.11

MAY 2014

1. State Meissner effect. Why materials in superconducting state exhibit diamagnetism. **[4]**

Ans. Please Refer to Article 8.3.2 on Page No. 8.4.

2. State any six applications of superconductors. [3]
Ans. Please Refer to Article 8.7 on Page No. 8.15.
3. What is superconductivity ? Explain BCS theory of superconductors. [6]
Ans. Please Refer to Article 8.2 and 8.4 on Page No. 8.1 and 8.9.

DECEMBER 2014

1. Explain critical field of a superconductor and give any three points to differentiate type – I and type – II superconductors. [6]
Ans. Please Refer to Article 8.5.2 on Page No. 8.12.
2. Explain the Meissner effect. What important property of superconductor it explain.[4]
Ans. Please Refer to Article 8.3.2 on Page No. 8.4.
3. Explain two applications of superconductivity. [3]
Ans. Please Refer to Article 8.6 on Page No. 8.14.

MAY 2015

1. State and explain Meissner effect and hence show that superconductivity is influenced by perfect diamagnetism. [6]
Ans. Please Refer to Article 8.3.2 on Page No. 8.4 to 8.6.
2. Distinguish between type-I and type-II superconductors. [4]
Ans. Please Refer to Article 8.5 (Table 8.2) on Page No. 8.15.
3. State any six applications of superconductivity. [3]
Ans. Please Refer to Article 8.7 on Page No. 8.15.

NOVEMBER 2015

1. Explain: [6]
   (i) Critical field   (ii) Meissner effect.
Ans. Please Refer to Article 8.3.3 and 8.3.2 on Page No. 8.6 and 8.4
2. Explain in brief the BCS theory of superconductivity. [4]
Ans. Please Refer to Article 8.4 on Page No. 8.9.
3. Give any six applications of superconductivity. [3]
Ans. Please Refer to Article 8.7 on Page No. 8.15.

MAY 2016

1. Explain BCS theory of superconductivity. Mention why superconductivity is observed below critical temperature. [6]
Ans. Please Refer to Article 8.4 on Page No. 8.9.
2. Explain in brief: [4]
   (i) Meissner effect   (ii) Critical magnetic field.
Ans. Please Refer to Article 8.3.2 and 8.3.3 on Page No. 8.4 and 8.6.
3. Explain the applications of superconductors in the field of electronics. [3]
Ans. Please Refer to Article 8.7 (3) on Page No. 8.16.

✠ ✠ ✠

CHAPTER 9
PHYSICS OF NANOPARTICLES

9.1 INTRODUCTION

- Nano, Greek for **'dwarf'**, means one billionth. The measurement at this level is in nanometer (abbreviated "nm") – billionth of a meter.

- To get a sense of nanoscale, a human hair measures roughly 75,000 nm, a bacterial cell measures a few hundred nanometers. On the other side, ten hydrogen atoms lined up end-to-end make up 1 nm. The smallest thing which can be seen with naked human eye is of the order of 10,000 nm.

- **'Nanoscience'** is the study of the fundamental principles of molecules and structures with at least one dimension is in the size range of 1 to 100 nm. These structures are known as **'nanostructures'**. The research and application of the nanostructures into nanoscale devices is called **'nanotechnology'**.

9.2 NANOPARTICLES

- An atom or small molecule in the form of vapour is smaller than a nanometer in size. But as they are in gaseous form and their molecules are not in arranged manner, hence do not fall in category of nanoscience.

- The nanostructures are the smallest solid things that is possible to make At nanoscale, most of the physical properties like conductivity, hardness or melting point are totally different than when they are in gaseous or crystal form. At nanoscale these properties depend on not only on the material but also the size of the nanostructure.

- At such a size, the classical Newtonian mechanics or thermodynamics is not able to explain the observed properties. So one has to apply quantum mechanics to explain the properties of nanoscale materials.

- The basic nanoscience is not new, the chemist have been doing nanoscience for hundreds of years.

- The stained glass windows in medieval charges contain different size gold nano particles. The different size gold particles created different colours as orange, purple, red or greenish in the glass. The new about current nanoscience is aggressive focus on developing applied technology and the right tools for doing it.

- Here, we will be studying different properties, methods of synthesis and applications of nanotechnology.

9.3 PROPERTIES OF NANOPARTICLES   [Dec. 12, Nov. 15, May 15, 16]

- The properties of nanoparticles are different from the properties when they are in bulk form (crystal) or in vapour form (gas). The nanoparticles are the smallest solid things possible to make. The properties of the materials are size dependent when it is below critical size (usually less than 100 nm).

- At such a small size, the shape of the nanostructure also decides the property of the material. By making nanomaterials of different size and shape, one can obtain desired property. These properties can be used in many applications in the fields of science, engineering, medicine and environment. Some of the major properties are as follows.

9.3.1 Optical   [May 13, 16, Nov. 13]

- The stained glasses are made by mixing small amount of metal particles like gold, cobalt, nickel, etc. Basically, glass is transparent and the colour appearing on the glass is due to nanoparticles of metals of different sizes.

- The colour of nanoparticles are different from the colour of bulk material. When nanoparticles of gold are formed, they give bright red colour instead of yellow as it appears in bulk form.

    In 1908, G. Mie explained the phenomenon by using classical electromagnetic theory. When a beam of light of intensity I_0 and wavelength λ passes through a medium, the transmitted intensity is given by,

$$I = I_0 \, e^{-\mu x} \qquad\qquad \text{... (I)}$$

    where μ is the **_extinction coefficient_** and depends on number of particles in medium, volume of colloidal particles and extinction cross-section of a particle.

- When the light is passed through a medium, a fraction is absorbed and a part is scattered, hence the extinction cross-section is the sum of **_absorption extinction_** and **_scattered extinction cross-section_**. The scattering coefficient of the light depends on wavelength λ and the absorption coefficient depends inversely on the volume of the colloidal particles i.e. $1/V$ or $1/R^3$ and dielectric constant.

- Thus, the absorption is independent of particle size. This theory explained the observation of absorption of light for metal nanoparticle in visible range. But for particles of size less than ~10 nm failed to explain the size dependency of the optical properties.

- The Drude model explained the particle size dependency of optical properties. For explaining it he assumed that the dielectric constant not only depends on frequency but also on particle size. According to the Drude model, the electrons can be considered as plasma.

9.3.2 Electrical   [May 13, 14, 16, Nov. 13, Dec. 14]

* The ease with which the material can conduct electricity is called **'conductivity'**. The conductivity of any material depends on the number of charge carriers, charge, mass of charge carrier and the relaxation time (time between two collisions with on core). The inverse of conductivity is called **'resistivity'**.

* When a voltage V is applied across the conductor, current flowing through it is given by Ohm's law and gives a linear graph as shown in Fig. 9.1 (a). But for nanoparticles, the variation of current with changing voltage is as shown in Fig. 9.1 (b).

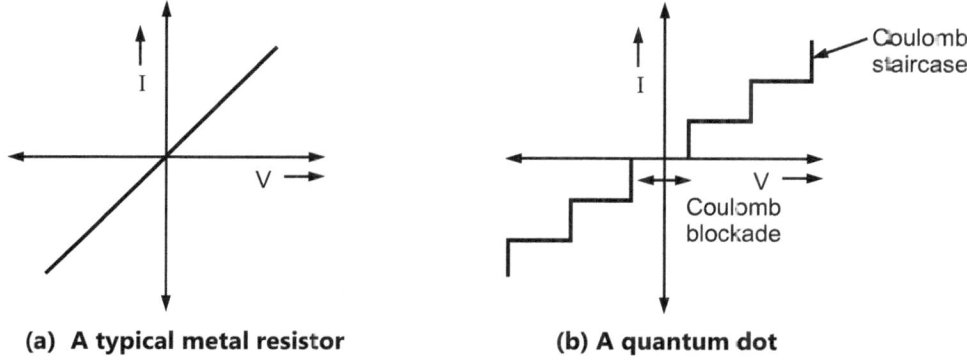

(a) A typical metal resistor   **(b) A quantum dot**

Fig. 9.1: Voltage versus current

* If the dimensions of metal piece is reduced to 100 nm or less, there appears a region around zero voltage for which there is no current.

* The electrons are transferred when the voltage is $\pm e/2C$. A single electron is transferred by tunneling when the voltage is $\pm e/2C$. Therefore, when the voltage is less than this, electrons cannot be transferred. This gives a region of zero current at low bias voltage and is known as **'Coulomb blockade region'**. The repeated tunneling of single electron produces **'Coulomb staircase'**.

* In general, electrical resistivity of materials having nanosized grain is larger than the polycrystalline materials. When electrons are moving, they get scattered at grain boundaries. This results in higher resistivity. The materials having nanosized grains have larger number of grain boundaries than polycrystalline materials. This results in higher resistivity in materials having nanosized grains.

9.3.3 Magnetic

* Basically, magnetism in bulk material is due to orbital and spin motion of the electrons around the nucleus. The magnetic materials have magnetic domains. Depending upon orientation of domains, magnetic materials are classified as paramagnetic or ferromagnetic materials.

* The magnetic materials have these domains to minimize the total magnetostatic energy of the system. Bulk of ferromagnetic materials have spontaneously magnetized domains.

When the particle size is less than a critical size, domain formation is not favoured and material prefers to be single domain.

- The single domain particles do not show coercivity or hysteresis. These type of particles are known as **'superparamagnetic particles'**. Fig. 9.2 shows magnetization of superpara-magnetic material on the application of external magnetic field.

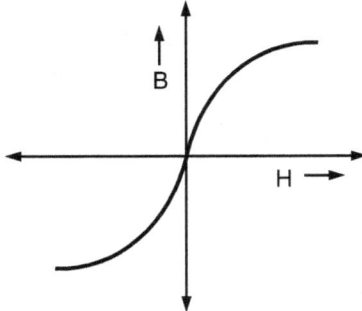

Fig. 9.2: Magnetization of superparamagnetic particles

- In superparamagnetic particles, spins are oriented in one direction and switches coherently in the opposite direction on the application of external magnetic field. Thus, we will get a curve as shown in Fig. 9.2 with no coercive field.

- The nanoparticles have large surface to volume ratio. At the surfaces, the symmetry and lattice constant change. Due to this, some materials show ferromagnetic behaviour which are not ferromagnetic in the bulk form.

9.3.4 Structural   [May 14]

- Starting with an individual atom, one can make bulk material by putting atoms in some particular manner. In nanostructures, small number of atoms are placed in the manner which is different from the arrangement of atoms in the bulk form. Thus, the nanoparticles are not just the fragments of bulk materials and have different structures.

- The structure formed is mainly affected by temperature and pressure. Starting from few atoms, nanoparticles undergo structural changes till they reach the bulk material. Fig. 9.3 (a) shows structural formation in silicon. The formation is not as the fragment of unit cell as shown in Fig. 9.3 (b) but is totally different as shown in Fig. 9.3 (c).

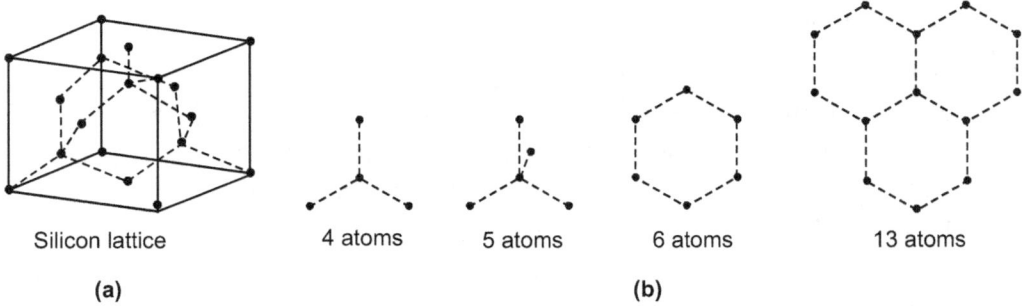

Silicon lattice   4 atoms   5 atoms   6 atoms   13 atoms

        (a)   (b)

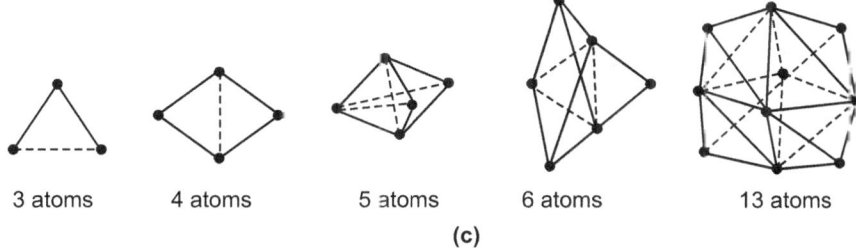

| 3 atoms | 4 atoms | 5 atoms | 6 atoms | 13 atoms |

(c)

Fig. 9.3: (a) Silicon atoms forming a unit cell, (b) Fragments of silicon unit cell and (c) Experimentally observed stable clusters of silicon

9.3.5 Mechanical

- The mechanical properties of a material depend upon the composition and bonds between the atoms. The mechanical properties like elasticity, hardness, ductility, etc. are result of this.

- The presence of impurities and imperfections in crystalline forms change these properties. For a nanoscale material, the material tends to form a single crystal. The nanocrystals are highly pure and free of imperfections.

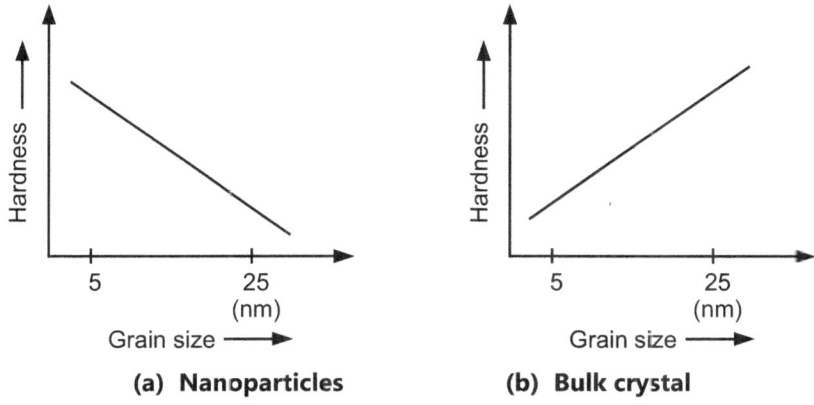

(a) Nanoparticles   (b) Bulk crystal

Fig. 9.4: Hardness variation with grain size

- It has been observed that in metallic nanocrystals, Young's modulus reduces drammatically. For example, magnesium nanocrystal has Young's modulus equal to 3900 N/mm^2 against 4100 N/mm^2 for polycrystalline form.

- For bulk material, the hardness increases linearly with the grain size. But in nanomaterials, the hardness increases linearly with decrease of the particle size as shown in Fig. 9.4.

- But the density of nanocrystalline pellet is often low as some pores are left when the powder is compressed to form pellets. When the deposition is done at high temperature, the densities approach the density of polycrystalline materials.

9.4 BRIEF INTRODUCTION TO DIFFERENT METHODS OF SYNTHESIS OF NANOPARTICLES   [May 16]

- As it has been discussed earlier, the physical properties of material change drammatically when they are reduced to nanoscale. The process by which the nanoscale particles are obtained is termed as *'nano-fabrication'* or *'nanoscale manufacturing'* or *'synthesis'*.

- For getting nanoparticles one can start from a bulk material and can cut down to the nanoscale. This particular type of nanofabrication is called *'top-down nanofabrication'*, because it starts with a large structure and proceeded to make it smaller.

- Conversely, starting with individual atoms and building up a nanomaterial is called *'bottom-up nanofabrication'*.

- Large number of techniques are available to manufacture (synthesis) different types of nanomaterials in different forms i.e. colloids, cluster, powder, thin films etc. There are various physical, chemical, biological and hybrid techniques to synthesize nanomaterials.

- The chart shows different commonly used techniques. The technique selected is decided by the material of interest, type of nanostructure, size, quality and quantity.

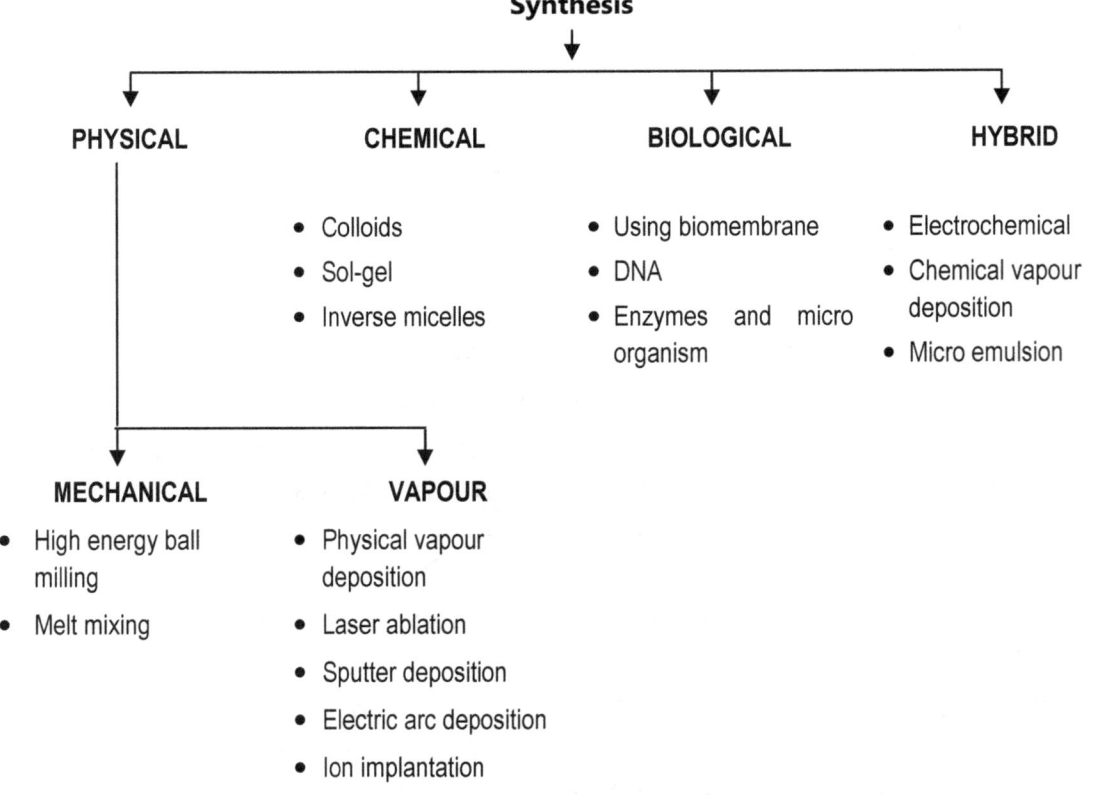

9.4.1 Physical Methods: Mechanical Method   [May 14]

High Energy Ball Milling:

- This is one of the simplest methods of making nanoparticles of some metals and alloys. This gives nanoparticles in powder form. This is top-down nanofabrication where the material in powder or flakes of dimensions less than 50 µm are reduced to nanoparticles in powder form. The different types of mills used are planetary, vibratory, rod etc. Usually one or more containers are used and the container size depends on the quantity of nanoparticles to be fabricated.

- Hardened steel or tungsten carbide balls are put in container along with powder or flakes of the bulk material. The initial material is in bulk form and is of arbitrary size and shape. The ratio of the balls and material is 2: 1 and container should be less than half filled as shown in Fig. 9.5.

- If the container is more than half filled, the efficiency of milling reduces. Use of large balls increases the impact energy on collision and hence gives smaller grain size but produces larger defects in the particles. In the process, some impurities may be added from balls.

- The air present in the container may also contaminate the nanoparticles. The whole process is carried out in a tight lid container. The containers are rotated at high speed around own axis.

- In addition to this, they may be rotated around some central axis and are called as **'planetary ball mill'**. Due to collisions, the temperature may rise from 100 to 1100°C, but a lower temperature is favoured. Generally, liquid nitrogen is used to dissipate the heat generated.

- When the containers are rotating around the central axis, the material is forced to the walls and is pressed against the walls due to centrifugal force. But due to the motion of containers around their own axis, the material is forced to other region of the container as shown in Fig. 9.6.

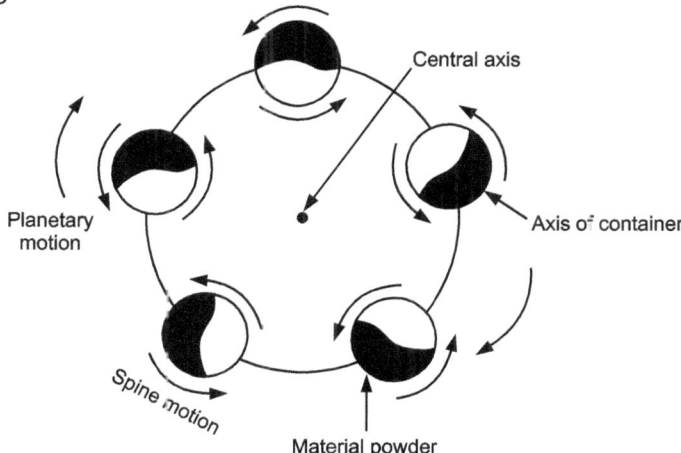

Fig. 9.5: Planetary ball mill

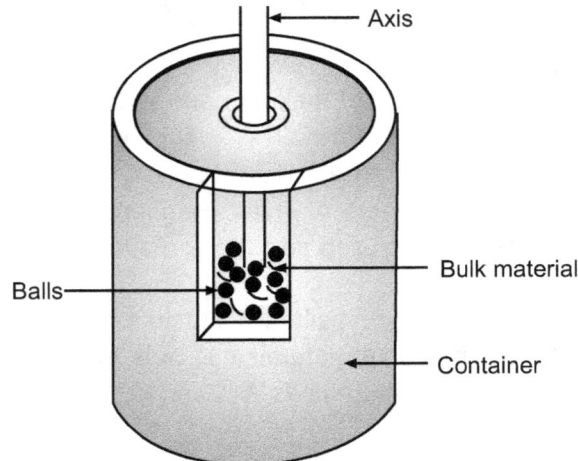

Fig. 9.6: Ball mill container

- Controlling the speed of rotation, planetary as well as axial, a fine powder of uniform size (few nm to few tens of nm) can be obtained. The nanoparticles of Co, Cr, Al-Fe, Ag-Fe etc. can be synthesized in short time. The amount obtained is few 'milligrams' to few 'kilograms'.

9.4.2 Chemical Method

- In chemical method, the nanoparticles are obtained in colloidal form, which can be filtered or centrifuged and dried to obtain powder. A thin film can be obtained by electrodeposition, etching etc.

  The advantages of chemical synthesis are:

  ➢ Less expensive.

  ➢ Requires low temperature.

  ➢ Doping is possible during synthesis.

  ➢ Variety of shapes and sizes can be obtained.

  ➢ Large quantity can be obtained.

  ➢ Particles are in colloidal form and can be converted to powder easily.

  In most of the cases, the nanoparticles obtained are in the colloidal form.

Colloids

- Colloids are class of materials in which two or more phases (solid, liquid or gas) of same or different materials co-exist with at least one dimension less than a micrometer. The nanomaterials are a sub-class of colloids, in which one of the dimensions are in nano range (< 100 nm).

- More generally, it is defined as very small particles (within 1 nm to 1000 nm range) that remain dispersed in a liquid for a long time. Their small size prevents them from being filtered easily or settled rapidly. Some examples of colloids are fog (liquid in gas), tinted glass (solid in solid) and foam (gas in liquid).

- The colloids can be used for self-assembly of nanoparticles on a neutral base. In colloidal self-assembly, colloids assemble themselves into useful alignments. Fig. 9.7 shows self-assembly of nanoparticles dissolved in ethanol.

- As the temperature rises and the ethanol evaporates, the surface of the liquid moves down the plate, making it easier for nanoparticle spheres floating nearby to stick to the plate. As ethanol level goes down, more and more particles deposit themselves on the plate, forming an orderly pattern. When all the ethanol is evaporated, the first layer is completed.

- The number of layers can be added by repeating the process. The process is called **colloidal self-assembly**. Fig. 9.7 illustrates the process.

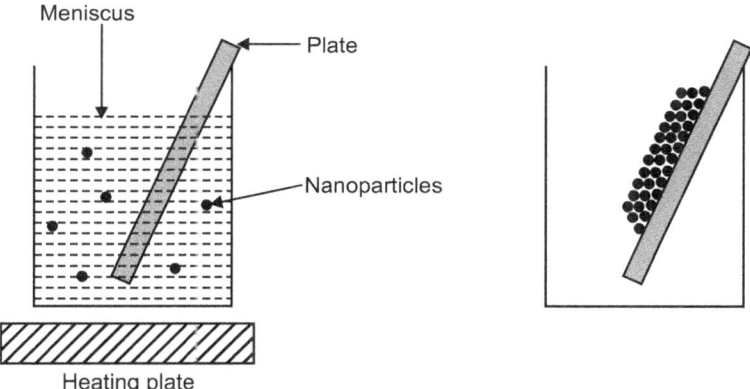

Fig. 9.7: Self-assembly process

The synthesis of colloids will be discussed in later part of the chapter.

9.4.3 Biological Methods

- In biological system we have leaves, roots, cells, tissues etc. which are organic. But biological system also has inorganic material such as bones, shells and nanomagnets. Inorganic materials inside the organic matter or organisms are known as **'biocomposites'**.

- These biocomposites are synthesized by microorganisms, animals and plants in nature. Now scientists have started using the methods by which inorganic materials are synthesized by using biomaterials like enzymes, DNA, membrane etc. A variety of metals, semiconductors and insulator nanoparticles or their assemblies have been made. The biological methods are eco-friendly and so-called **'green synthesis'**.

- The biological methods are:

  ➢ Use of microorganisms like fungi, yeast or bacteria.

  ➢ Use of plant extracts or enzymes.

  ➢ Use of templates like DNA, membranes, viruses and diatoms.

9.4.4 Synthesis using Microorganisms

- The microorganisms are capable of interacting with metals coming in contact with, them through their cells and form nanoparticles. Fig. 9.8 shows bacteria (eukaryotic) cell. The interaction of cell-metal is very complex due to complexity of cells themselves. Some microorganisms are capable of separating metal ions and is widely used to recover precious metals or detoxify water.

- Some microorganisms produce hydrogen sulfide (H_2S) gas, which can oxidize organic matter forming sulphate. This acts like an electron acceptor for metabolism. This H_2S can convert metal ions into metal sulphide which deposits extracellularly.

- In some cases, metal ions from a metal salt enter the cell body. The metal ions are then converted into a nontoxic form. Then it is covered with certain proteins to protect the remaining part of the cell from toxic environment.

Fig. 9.8 shows metal-microorganism interaction.

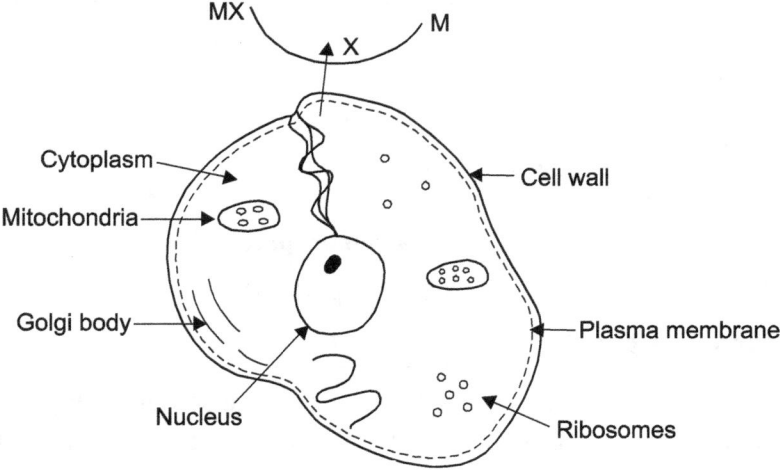

Fig. 9.8: Metal-microorganism interaction

- Pseudomonas Stutzeri Ag 259 bacteria found in silver mines are capable of accumulating silver inside or outside of the cell walls. Many silver nanoparticles of different shapes can be used to produce having size < 200 nm intracellularly.

- Fungi can be used to obtain large quantities of metal nanoparticles. For example, fusarium oxysporum challenged with gold or silver, produces gold or silver nanoparticles extracellularly.

- Low concentration of metal ions can be converted to metal nanoparticles by Lactobacillus present in butter milk. By exposing the mixture of two different metal salts to bacteria, it is possible to obtain alloys under certain conditions.

9.5 SYNTHESIS OF COLLOIDS   [May 13, 15, Nov. 13, Dec. 14]

- *'Colloids'* are phase separated nanoparticles suspended in some host matrix in various shapes such as spheres, rods, tubes, fibres, plates etc. Colloids of metals, semiconductors and insulators of various shapes can be synthesized in aqueous (water) or non-aqueous media. The particles acquire surface charge in the media. The coulomb force acting on them stabilizes and stops the further growth.

- In general, the colloids in liquid can have positive, negative charges or may be neutral. But in most of the cases, they are charged. The various sources by which colloids acquire charge through composition of colloidal material, properties of dispersing medium and concentration of colloids.

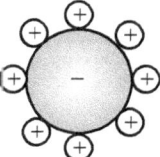

Fig. 9.9: Charges on colloids

- Soon charges develop on particles, ions of opposite charges accumulate around them. The oppositely charged ions are known as *'counter ions'*. Fig. 9.9 shows accumulation of counter ions on a particle. This accumulation of counter ions leads to formation of an electric double layer.

- When two charged colloidal particles come closer, they start repelling each other. This stabilizes the colloids. Nanoparticles are special class of colloidals where colloids have one dimension in the range of nanoparticles.

- Making nanoparticles using colloidal route goes back to 19th century when M. Faraday synthesized gold nanoparticle by chemistry method. The particles developed are still stable.

- Fig. 9.10 illustrates a simple arrangement for synthesis of nanoparticles by colloical method.

- The chemical reaction in which colloids are obtained is carried out at very slow rate by keeping concentration and temperature low. The whole reaction is carried out in a glass reactor of suitable size. The reactor has provision to introduce some precursors, gases and measure temperature, pH etc. Usually a trineck flask is used as a reactor.

- The reaction is carried out in an inert atmosphere (argon or nitrogen gas) to avoid unwanted oxidation of the nanoparticles. The reaction temperature can be controlled by a thermostatic heater. Magnetic stirrer is used during the reaction for proper mixing of the reactants.

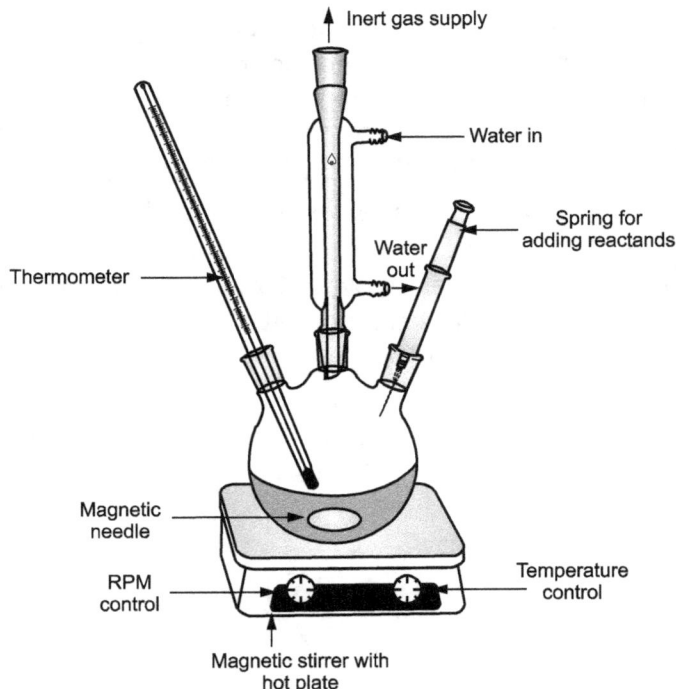

Fig. 9.10: Chemical reactor to synthesize nanoparticles

9.6 GROWTH OF NANOPARTICLES   [May 13]

- Chemical method is a **'bottom-up fabrication'**, where the particle size grows. Monodispersed nanoparticles i.e. particles of nearly same size can be obtained by controlling various steps involved. The **'nucleation'** and **'growth'** of particles can be understood by LaMer diagram as shown in Fig. 9.11.

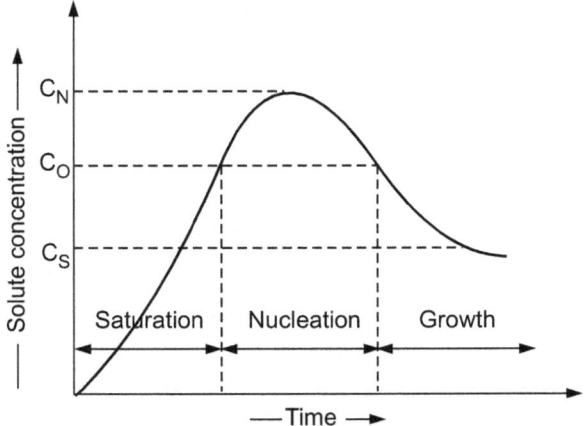

Fig. 9.11: LaMer diagram

- As the concentration increases, at certain concentration C_O, the formation of nuclei begins. A further increase in the concentration increases the nuclei formation. The nucleation (formation of nucleus) increases upto a concentration C_N above which there is **'supersaturation'**. The concentration C_N denotes the maximum rate of nucleation.

- After saturation, no new nuclei can be formed and crystal growth reduces the concentration. Thus, again at C_O the minimum concentration of nucleation is reached.

- This gives an equilibrium at concentration C_S. If new nuclei are formed during the growth, the growth will be in different stages i.e. growth of nuclei formed earlier and growth of new nuclei formed. This results in various sized nanoparticles. Thus, the concentration is to be properly adjusted so that no fresh nuclei are formed once the concentration reaches C_N.

- The larger particles have lower surface free energy, hence the larger particles are more stable and grow at the expense of smaller particles. This growth is known as **'Ostwald ripening'**.

- Aggregation of particles also reduces surface free energy. Therefore, experimentally, it has been found that there is aggregation of particles in some cases. Thus, for reducing the surface free energy, Ostwald ripening and aggregation are competing processes. Fig. 9.12 shows Ostwald ripening and aggregation.

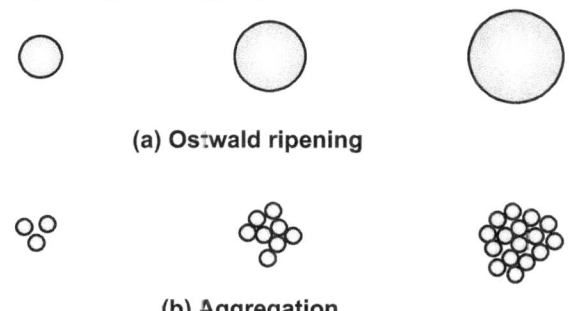

(a) Ostwald ripening

(b) Aggregation

Fig. 9.12: Growth of nanoparticles

9.7 SYNTHESIS OF METAL NANOPARTICLES BY COLLOIDAL ROUTE   [Dec. 12, May 13, Nov. 13, 15]

- The colloidal metal nanoparticles are synthesized by reduction of metal salt or acid. Highly stable gold particles can be obtained by reducing chloroauric acid ($HAuCl_4$) with trisodium citrate ($Na_3C_6H_5C_7$).

$$HAuCl_4 + Na_3C_6H_5O_7 \longrightarrow Au^+ + C_6H_5O_7^- + HCl + 3\ NaCl$$

- The gold nanoparticles are formed by nucleation and condensation. The growth is bigger in size by reduction of more Au^+ ions on the surface. These atoms are stabilized by oppositely charged citrate ions. Fig. 9.13 shows formation of gold nanoparticles.

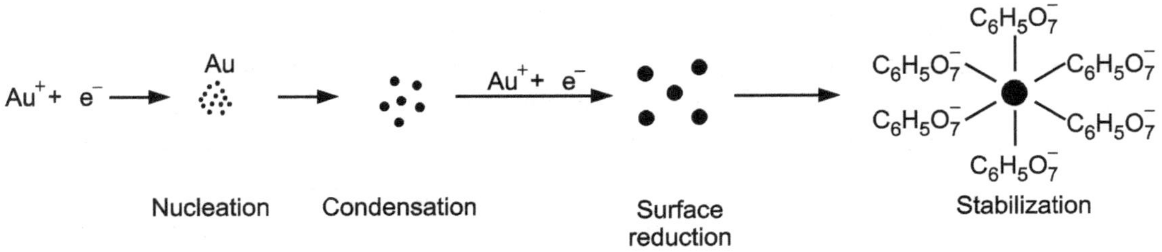

Fig. 9.13: Growth of gold nanoparticles

- The reaction is carried out in aqueous (water) solution as explained earlier. The gold nanoparticles fabricated in above manner are stable by Coulomb force. It is also possible to use capping such as thiol to stabilize them.

- In the same way, nanoparticles of metals such as copper, silver etc. can be fabricated by using proper precursors, temperature, pH, duration of synthesis, etc. Also by controlling above parameters, particle parameters such as size, shape, distribution can be controlled.

- The gold nanoparticles in colloidal form show different colours depending upon the size of nanoparticles.

9.8 APPLICATIONS OF NANOTECHNOLOGY [Dec. 12, May 14, Nov. 15]

- At nanoscale the materials change their physical properties such as colour, resistance, strength etc. drammatically. These special properties can be used in many fields for making new devices, instruments and consumer goods. These nanoscale devices are extremely small in dimensions and have unique features. Some of the applications are as mentioned below.

9.8.1 Electronics　　　　　　　　　　　　　　　　[May 13, Nov. 13, Dec. 14]

- The discovery of semiconductor transistor replaced the heavy and power consuming vacuum tubes. The transistors are power saving, small and light weight. The Integrated Circuits (ICs) made the instruments still smaller by fabricating a number of large components on a small chip. But the size of components cannot be reduced to atomic level, because after some level the properties of materials become size dependent. At this level, the *'nanoscience'* or *'nanotechnology'* comes into the picture.

- Single Electron Transistor (SET). Spin Valves and Magnetic Tunnel Junctions (MTJ) are the new devices based on nanotechnology. These devices are small, faster and relatively cheaper. The spin valve type devices are used in personal computers to read disk, which have enabled to increase data storage capacity of hard disks. These are the devices based on charge and spin. Earlier, devices were based on charge only and spin was neglected. The spin-based electronics is called as *'spintronic'* or *'magnetoelectronics'*.

- Using an external magnetic field, spin transport can be controlled. The advantage with spin is that it cannot be easily destroyed by scattering from collisions with other charges, impurities or imperfections. Some of the spin-based devices are Spin FET, Spin LED, Spin RTD etc.

- Nanotechnology can also be used in computers for designing *'nonvolatile memory'*, smaller and faster microprocessor and better quality monitors. The nanoparticle coating on screen of TV or monitors will improve quality and resolution.

9.8.2 Energy

- Currently used energy sources are firewood, coal, oil and gas. These sources are limited in nature and large-scale use of these sources is damaging environment. So scientists have started searching some alternatives which will solve problems with conventional sources of energies. Some of the non-conventional sources of energies are solar energy, hydel energy, tidal energy, biomass energy etc.

- The disadvantage of solar cells is that their efficiency is less (~ 30%) and hence require large surface area. Research is going on to use nanomaterials for making solar cells, which will reduce the size of the cells and increase the efficiency. Other source of energy is hydrogen fuel, which can be obtained by splitting water (H_2O) using sunlight in presence of nanomaterials. The nanomaterial will work as *'photocatalyst'*. The main problem with hydrogen is storage as it can catch fire easily. Materials like carbon nanotubes can be used as storage material without risk.

- Portable electronic appliances such as mobile phones, laptops, calculators etc. require rechargeable, light-weight batteries. Such batteries require frequent replacement or recharging as their energy density is low. Attempts are being made to increase their energy density by replacing the electrode materials.

9.8.3 Automobiles   [Dec. 14, May 16]

- The body of a car is made up of steel and some alloys. The body structure should be strong and non-deformable. The nanotube composites have mechanical strength better than steel and attempts are made to make composites that can replace steel.

- Currently, manufacturing of nanotubes is expensive but scientists are trying to make it economical. Nanoparticle paints provide smooth, thin and attractive coating. Research is going on to change the colour of car by applying a small voltage.

- Self-cleaning glass can be made by mixing small amount of titania (TiO_2) nanoparticles while manufacturing it. The titania is capable of dissociating organic dust in presence of UV light present in sunlight. Once dissociated it may fall down or evaporate. Water droplets on glass give hazy look, but titania glass can spread the water evenly giving clear sight. Such special glass can be used to make window glass of a car.

- By using nanoparticles light weight and less rubber consuming, thinner tyres can be made. This will reduce the weight, price of the car and will increase the mileage as a result of reduced weight. Nanoparticles can be used as catalysts to convert harmful emissions into less harmful gases. With the help of nanocarbon tubes, hydrogen fuel can be stored safely and can be used for running a car. The hydrogen fuel is eco-friendly and ever lasting.

9.8.4 Space and Defence

- In space and defence also, scientists are trying to replace the conventional materials by nanomaterials. A nanoporous material called **'aerogels'** have extremely low density ranging between 0.01 to 0.8 gm/cm^3. Aerogels have small nanosized pores in them and can be of various materials. Basically, aerogels are poor conductors of heat. Therefore, aerogels can be used in spacecrafts to reduce the weight. Even special light-weight suits and jackets can be made using aerogels.

- In satellites or spacecrafts, we use solar energy. But solar cells have low efficiency resulting in large surface area and heavy weight. Nanoparticles can be used to reduce the size and weight of solar cells. Space vehicles also need materials which can withstand harsh and extreme conditions during launching and in space. Polymer composites using silica fibres and nanoparticles have larger Young's modulus, low temperature coefficient of expansion and high impact strength. The nanoparticles in polymer composites are better radiation protectors in comparison to microparticle-based composites.

9.8.5 Medical　　　　　　　　　　　　　　　　　　[May 13, Nov. 13, May 15]

- The nanoparticles can be used for drug delivery, detection of cancer or tumor and treating them. As nanoparticles are very small in size, they can be injected easily and can be guided towards specific part in the body. Recently, gold nanorods which have strong scattering and absorption property in the infrared are used to detect and destroy cancer cells in rats. The infrared laser beam can be used to detect and destroy cancer cells without affecting the healthy cells. This is possible because healthy cells require twice the laser power as compared to cancer cell for destruction and infrared light can get easily transmitted through cells and muscles. Thus, by using low power infrared laser, only cancer cells can be killed without affecting the healthy cells.

- Drugs can be encapsulated in nanocapsules and can be guided towards desired part of the body. Then drug can be delivered in controlled manner, fastly and slowly, by opening the capsule in desired way. The opening of capsule can be controlled externally by magnetic field, infrared light or physiologically. This will help in treating diabetic or HIV affected patients.

- The scientists are also working to develop better body implants. The body implants should be strong and biocompatible. The body implant should be strong enough so that it does not get deformed easily. Also, it should be biocompatible so that once implanted body cells should be able to grow.

- Some nanotechnology-based tests are developed which are simple and fast. These tests can be used for detection of viruses, DNA, proteins and antibodies. Porous silicon and carbon nanotubes-based sensors can also be used in medical field.

9.8.6 Environmental

- Whenever a new technology emerges, there is always concern about its impact on social life, health and environment. Technology brings comfort in life but it also creates problems such as global climatic changes, pollution, new deceases, depletion of natural resources, etc. Therefore, the question arises whether the nanotechnology will solve or increase these problems. Although ill effects of nanoparticles are possible but they are not studied yet.

- On the other hand, it is believed that nanomaterials themselves will reduce the pollution and environment related problems. Efficient production of nanomaterial by low temperature synthesis routes will help to reduce industrial pollution. Use of nanomaterials as hydrogen fuel storage and oil filters may reduce emission by vehicles. The nanomaterials are light weight and require only small quantity. This will bring down the prices of products making them affordable. Thus likely to solve problems of poor people.

- The nanoparticle-based sensors are much sensitive than conventional sensors being used. These nanoparticle-based sensors will be capable to detect and rectify problems. Such sensors will be useful in water purification systems, detection of toxic ions, metal ions, pesticides etc. and their remediation on large scale.

9.8.7 Textile

- The special threads and dyes used in textile industry are products of nanotechnology. Clothes produced with such technology will give pleasant look of synthetic fiber but comfort of cotton. These clothes will not require ironing or frequent cleaning. Some of the washing machine companies are trying to use silver nanoparticles in washing machines which will make the clothes germ-free.

9.8.8 Cosmetics

- Nanoparticles are widely used in cosmetic industry. Due to their small size nanoparticle-based creams are better option as they can be used in small amount and do not leave any gaps between them. This gives a smooth appearance. Zinc oxide and titanium oxide nanoparticles of uniform size are able to absorb ultraviolet light and protect the skin from ultraviolet radiations.

- The small nanoparticles in some of the creams scatter light in such a way that the appearance of wrinkles is suppressed. Nanoparticle-based dyes and colours are harmless to skin and can be used in hair creams or gels. Some creams using nanoparticles are already in market and becoming quite popular.

SUMMARY

- The Greek word nano means one billionth.
- Nanoscience is the study of the fundamental principles of molecules and structures with at least one dimension of nanosize.
- The research and application of the nanostructures into nanoscale devices is called nanotechnology.
- Most of the physical properties of nanomaterials are different than when they are in bulk form.
- The colour of nanoparticles are different from the colour of bulk material.
- The resistivity of materials having nanosized grain is larger than polycrystalline materials.
- The nanoparticles having single domain do not show coercivity or hysteresis.
- The nanoparticles are not just the fragments of bulk material and have different structures.
- The nanocrystalline pellet have low density as some pores are left when the powder is compressed.
- The process by which the nanoparticles are obtained is called as nano-fabrication or nano-scale manufacturing or synthesis.
- In top-down nanofabrication, we start with large structure and is made smaller.
- In bottom-up nanofabrication, we start with individual atom and make nanostructures.
- In physical method, high energy ball milling or vapour deposition method is used to get nanostructures.
- In chemical method, the nanoparticles are obtained in colloidal form.
- In biological method, microorganisms are used for nanoparticle synthesis.
- Colloids are phase separated nanoparticles suspended in some host matrix.
- The growth of nanoparticles takes place either by Ostwald ripening or aggregation.
- The colloidal metal nanoparticles are synthesized by reduction of metal salt or acid.
- The nanoparticles have vast applications in almost all the fields.
- Most of the applications are still in trial stage and very few are commercially available.

EXERCISE

1. What is nanoscience ? Why classical mechanics cannot be applied to nanoparticles ?
2. Why properties of nanoparticles are different from what they are in bulk form ? Explain optical and electrical properties of nanoparticles.
3. State and explain any three properties of nanoparticles.

4. Explain the following properties of nanoparticles:
   (i) Magnetic properties.   (ii) Mechanical properties.
5. What are different types of nano-fabrications ? Explain physical method for getting nanoparticles.
6. Write short notes on:
   (i) High energy ball milling.   (ii) Physical vapour deposition.
7. What are colloids ? Give advantages of chemical method.
8. Write a short note on biological methods for nanoparticle synthesis.
9. What are colloids ? How colloids can be synthesized ?
10. Explain different methods of nanoparticle growth with LaMer diagram.
11. Explain synthesis of metal nanoparticles by colloidal route.
12. Explain the applications of nanoparticles in the field of (a) automobile, (b) medical.
13. Give advantages of nanoparticles over bulk material in the field of (a) environment, (b) space and defence.
14. Nanoparticles will reduce environmental pollution. Justify.

SOLVED UNIVERSITY QUESTIONS

DECEMBER 2012

1. Explain any two applications of Nano-technology.   [4]
Ans. Please Refer to Article 9.8 on Page No. 9.14.
2. Explain any two properties of Nano-particle.   [3]
Ans. Please Refer to Article 9.3 on Page No. 9.2.
3. Explain Synthesis of Metal Nano-particle by Colloidal Route Method.   [3]
Ans. Please Refer to Article 9.7 on Page No. 9.13.

MAY 2013

1. Explain the synthesis of nanoparticles through colloidal route with diagram   [6]
Ans. Please Refer to Articles 9.5, 9.6 and 9.7 on Pages No 9.11, 9.12, 9.13.
2. Explain the optical and electrical properties of nanoparticles   [4]
Ans. Please Refer to Articles 9.3.1 and 9.3.2 on Page No 9.2 and 9.3.
3. Explain the applications of nanoparticles in medical and electronic Industry.   [3]
Ans. Please Refer to Articles 9.8.5 and 9.8.1 on Page No 9.16 and 9.14.

NOVEMBER 2013

1. Explain following properties of nano-particles: [4]
   (i) Optical property.
Ans. Please Refer to Article 9.3.1 on Page No. 9.2.
   (ii) Electrical property.
Ans. Please Refer to Article 9.3.2 on Page No. 9.3.
2. Explain the applications of nanoparticles in medical and electronic field.   [3]
Ans. Please Refer to Articles 9.8.5 and 9.8.1 on Page No. 9.16 and 9.14.
3. Explain the synthesis of gold nanoparticles by colloidal route method.   [6]
Ans. Please Refer to Articles 9.5 and 9.7 on Page No. 9.11 and 9.13.

MAY 2014

1. Discuss the electrical and structural properties of nano-materials. **[6]**
Ans. Please Refer to Article 9.3.2 and 9.3.4 on Page No. 9.3 and 9.4.

2. Explain any one physical method of synthesis of nano-particles. **[4]**
Ans. Please Refer to Article 9.4.1 on Page No. 9.7.

3. Explain any one application of nanotechnology. **[3]**
Ans. Please Refer to Article 9.8 (Any one application) on Page No. 9.14.

DECEMBER 2014

1. Explain the applications of nanoparticles in automobile and electronic industry. **[4]**
Ans. Please Refer to Articles 9.8.1 and 9.8.3 on Page No. 9.14 and 9.15.

2. Explain electrical properties of nano-particles. **[3]**
Ans. Please Refer to Article 9.3.2 on Page No. 9.3.

3. Explain the synthesis of nanoparticles in automobile and electronic by colloidal route with diagram. **[6]**
Ans. Please Refer to Article 9.5 on Page No. 9.11.

MAY 2015

1. Explain how colloids are synthesized by the chemical route. **[4]**
Ans. Please Refer to Article 9.5, Page No. 9.11 to 9.12.

2. Discuss applications of nanotechnology in medical field. **[3]**
Ans. Please Refer to Article 9.8.5, Page No. 9.16.

3. Explain any two properties of nanoparticle. (Note: Discuss any two). **[6]**
Ans. Please Refer to Article 9.3, Page No. 9.2 to 9.5.

NOVEMBER 2015

1. Explain any two properties of nano-particles in brief. **[4]**
Ans. Please refer Articles 9.3.1 and 9.3.2, Page No. 9.2 and 9.3

2. Explain the applications of nano-particles in electronic industry. **[3]**
Ans. Please refer Article 9.8.1, Page No. 9.14.

3. Explain the synthesis of nano-particles by chemical method in colloidal form with diagram and example. **[6]**
Ans. Please refer Articles 9.5, 9.6 and 9.7, Page No. 9.11, 9.12 and 9.13.

MAY 2016

1. Explain any one method for synthesis of nano-particles. **[4]**
Ans. Please Refer to Article 9.4 (any one) on Page No. 9.6.

2. Explain the applications of nano-particles in the field of automobiles. **[3]**
Ans. Please Refer to Article 9.8.3 on Page No. 9.15.

3. Why are the properties of nano-particles different from that of the bulk materials? Explain any two properties of non-particles. **[6]**
Ans. Please Refer to Articles 9.3, 9.3.1 and 9.3.2 on Page No. 9.2 and 9.3.

✠ ✠ ✠

Sample Question Papers

Paper – I

End-Sem. (Theory) Examination

Time : 2 Hours   **Max. Marks : 50**

1. (a) Explain the formation of Newton's rings. Prove that in Newton's rings by reflected light, the diameter of bright ring is proportional to the square root of odd natural numbers. **[6]**

OR

(a) Discuss the Fraunhoffer's diffraction at a single slit and obtain the conditions for principal maxima and minima. **[6]**

(b) Solve any two of the following: **[6]**

   (i) Define echo. Which precautions are to be taken to avoid echo while constructing the building ?

   (ii) Explain the term 'Piezoelectric effect' with diagram.

   (iii) What are the limitations over the production of ultrasonics by using magnetostriction oscillator?

   (iv) A hall of volume 1000 m^3 has a seating capacity of 100 people. If the sound absorbed by per person is 5, calculate the reverberation time when it is with full capacity.

2. (a) Explain the phenomenon of double refraction on the basis of Huygen's wave theory. **[6]**

OR

(a) Explain principle, construction and working of He-Ne low power gas laser with neat labelled diagram. **[6]**

(b) Solve any two of the following: **[6]**

   (i) If the conductivity of the semiconductor is $\sigma_{sc} = e\,(n_e\mu_e + n_p\mu_p)$, what will be the equation for conductivity of pure extrinsic type semiconductors ?

   (ii) Write down the equation for the Fermi-Dirac probability distribution of electrons at given temperature T K. What will be the probability of electrons when the temperature is $T = 0$ K and $E > E_F$?

   (iii) Draw the Fermi energy level diagram for the pn junction diode when it is before and after forward biased.

   (iv) Calculate the mobility of charge carriers in a doped silicon whose conductivity is 100 per Ω-m and the Hall coefficient is 3.6×10^{-4} m^3/C.

3. (a) State Heisenberg's uncertainty principle. Give its proof with the evidence of electron diffraction through a single slit. **[6]**

OR

(a) Deduce Schroedinger's time independent wave equation. **[6]**

(b) Solve any one of the following: **[4]**

    (i) Derive an expression for the de Broglie's wavelength in terms of energy.

    (ii) De Broglie wavelength of electrons in a monoenergetic beam is 7.2×10^{-11} m. Calculate the momentum and energy of electrons in the beam in eV.

(c) Solve any one of the following: **[3]**

    (i) Explain the dependence of de Broglie's wavelength on mass and velocity of moving particle.

    (ii) Derive the wave function of the particle confined in 1-D rigid box of infinite height and of width L A° when it is $\psi(x) = 2iA \sin kx$.

4. (a) What is superconductivity? Explain Meissner's effect. **[6]**

OR

(a) What is superconductivity? Explain BCS theory. **[6]**

(b) Solve any one of the following: **[4]**

    (i) Explain how the optical properties of nano particles are changing with its size.

    (ii) Explain how the mechanical properties of nano particles are changing with its size.

(c) Solve any one of the following: **[3]**

    (i) Give in brief any three applications of nano particles to the engineering.

    (ii) Draw the hysteresis curve for the magnetic material when it is in bulk and nano size.

Paper – II
End-Sem. (Theory) Examination

Time : 2 Hours   **Max. Marks : 50**

1. (a) Explain the method of production of ultrasonics by using Piezo-electric oscillator.
   [6]

OR

   (a) Explain the term 'Reverberation'. Give Sabine's formula, explain each term involved in it. **[6]**

   (b) Solve any two of the following: **[6]**

   (i) Assuming the equation for the diameter of dark ring, show that the area between the two consecutive Newton's dark rings is constant.

   (ii) Explain the effect of slit width 'a' on intensity distribution in diffraction pattern for the given light of wavelength λ.

   (iii) For the film of uniform thickness, write down the conditions of maximum and minimum intensity for the interference of light in reflected system. How does it vary if the film is wedge shaped?

   (iv) A thin film of refractive index 1.4 is coated on glass plate in order to reduce the reflection from the glass surface using interference. Determine the thickness of the film for its effectiveness to the wavelength 5880 A°.

2. (a) What is Hall effect ? Obtain an expression for Hall voltage and Hall coefficient. **[6]**

OR

   (a) Explain with neat labelled diagram the working of NPN transistor on the basis of Fermi energy level. **[6]**

   (b) Solve any two of the following: **[6]**

   (i) Explain the term 'Population inversion' in brief.

   (ii) Draw neat energy level diagram of Ruby laser.

   (iii) What are the retardation plates? Give their types and write down the equation for their working thickness.

   (iv) If the plane of vibration of incident beam makes an angle of 30° with the optic axis, compare the intensities of the extra-ordinary and ordinary light.

3. (a) What is group velocity and phase velocity ? Show that group velocity is equal to particle velocity. **[6]**

OR

(a) Derive an expression for the energy levels of the particle enclosed within an infinite deep potential well. **[6]**

(b) Solve any one of the following: **[4]**

   (i)   Give the physical significance of the wave function ψ.

   (ii) Discuss the properties of matter waves.

(c) Solve any one of the following: **[3]**

   (i)   Compute the wavelength of de Broglie's wave associated with a proton moving with 5% of the velocity of light. Proton has 1836 times the mass of one electron.
         $M_e = 9.1 \times 10^{-31}$ kg, $h = 6.63 \times 10^{-34}$ Js

   (ii) Derive de Broglie's wavelength of matter waves in different form.

4. (a) Explain the synthesis of nano particles by colloidal route. **[6]**

OR

(a) Explain the structural and mechanical properties of nano particles. **[6]**

(b) Solve any one of the following: **[4]**

   (i)   Give the manifestation of Meissner's effect.

   (ii) Explain the behavioral difference of type I and type II superconductors to the externally applied magnetic field.

(c) Solve any one of the following: **[3]**

   (i)   State and explain isotope effect in superconductivity.

   (ii) Explain in brief the term 'Critical field' and its temperature dependence in superconductivity.

✠ ✠ ✠

University Question Papers

DECEMBER 2012

Time: 2 Hours   **Max. Marks: 50**

Instructions :

    (1)   Assume suitable data, if necessary.

    (2)   Neat diagrams must be drawn wherever necessary.

---

1. (a) Prove that in Newton's Rings by reflected light the diameter of bright ring are proportional to the square root of the odd natural number. **[6]**

    (b) Explain any one application of Ultrasonic Waves. **[3]**

    (c) The average reverberation time of a hall is 1.5 sec. and the area of the interior surface is 3340 m^2. If the volume of the hall is 13000 m^3. Find the absorption coefficient. **[3]**

OR

2. (a) Explain how piezoelectric effect can be used for generating Ultrasonic Waves? **[6]**

    (b) Define fringe width for wedge shaped film, obtain an expression for it. **[3]**

    (c) Find the half angular width of the central maxima in the fraunhofer diffraction pattern of slit having width 10×10^{-5} cm. When illuminated by light having wave length 5000 A°. **[3]**

3. (a) State the Phenomena of Double Refraction. Hence, explain Huygen's Wave Theory of Double Refraction. **[6]**

    (b) Draw energy band picture for P-N junction in case of (i) Zero Bias, (ii) Forward Bias, (iii) Reverse Bias. **[3]**

    (c) A silver wire is in form of a ribbon 0.5 cm wide and 0.1 mm thick. When a current of 2 amp passes through the ribbon perpendicular to 0.8 Tesla magnetic field. Calculate the Hall voltage produced.

    (Given : Density of Silver = 10.5 gm/cc, Atomic weight of Silver = 108, Avogadros Number 6.02×10^{23} gm/mole) **[3]**

OR

4. (a) Derive an expression for Conductivity in Semiconductor. **[6]**

    (b) Explain any one application of Laser in brief. **[3]**

    (c) How should the Polarizer and Analyzer be oriented to reduce intensity of beam to (i) 50%, (ii) 0.25 of its original intensity? **[3]**

5. (a) Define Phase Velocity and Group Velocity. Hence obtain the relation between V_p and V_g for DeBroglie Wave. **[6]**

(b) Explain the physical significance of ψ and $|\psi|^2$.   **[4]**

(c) An electron is bounded by an infinite potential well of width 2×10^{-8} cm. Calculate the lowest two permissible energies of an electron.

(Given : $h = 6.64 \times 10^{-34}$ J-sec., $m = 9.1 \times 10^{-31}$ kg)   **[3]**

OR

6. (a) Derive Schrodinger's Time Independent Wave Equation.   **[6]**

(b) State DeBroglie's Hypothesis. Hence obtain the relation for DeBroglie's Wavelength in terms of Energy.   **[4]**

(c) The position and momentum of 1 keV electron are simultaneously measured. If its position is located with 1 A°. Find the percentage of uncertainty in its momentum.

(Given : $h = 6.64 \times 10^{-34}$ J-sec., $m = 9.1 \times 10^{-31}$ kg)   **[3]**

7. (a) Explain the Phenomena of Super-conductivity. Explain Type - I and Type - II Super-conductors.   **[6]**

(b) Explain any two applications of Nano-technology.   **[4]**

(c) Explain any two properties of Nano-particle.   **[3]**

OR

8. (a) Explain Synthesis of Metal Nano-particle by Colloidal Route Method.   **[3]**

(b) Explain BCS Theory of Super-conductivity.   **[4]**

(c) State and explain :   **[6]**

    (a) Meissner Effect.

    (b) Persistent Current.

MAY 2013

Time: 2 Hours   **Max. Marks: 50**

Instructions:

    (1) Answer all the questions.

    (2) Black figures to the right indicate full marks.

    (3) Neat Diagram must be drawn wherever necessary.

    (4) Electronic Pocket calculator is allowed

    (5) Assume suitable data, if necessary

Constants: $h = 6.63 \times 10^{-34}$ J-s $e = 1.6 \times 10^{-19}$

                 $m_e = 9.31 \times 10^{-31}$ kg $c = 3 \times 10^8$ m/s

1. (a) Explain the formation Newton's ring with diagram and drive the diameter of bright ring.   **[6]**

(b) Discuss the use of ultrasonic's for flaw Detection.   **[3]**

(c) A auditorium of volume $5500m^3$ is found to have reverberation time 2.5 secs. The sound absorbing surface of the auditorium has an area of $750m^2$. Calculate the average absorption coefficient of the auditorium.   **[3]**

OR

2. (a) Define magnetostriction effect. Explain how magnetostriction oscillator is used to produce ultrasonic waves with the help of neat circuit diagram.   **[6]**

    (b) Explain with diagram how interference Principle is used to design anti reflection coating.   **[3]**

    (c) Monochromatic light from He-Ne laser source ($\lambda=6328A^0$) is incident normally on a diffraction grating having 6000 lines/cm. find the angle at which one would observe second order maximum.   **[3]**

3. (a) Define Double refraction. Explain Huygen's Theory of Double refracting crystal with diagram.   **[6]**

    (b) Define Fermi level. Plot the variation of Fermi level with the increase of temperature for n-type and p-type semiconductor.   **[3]**

    (c) Calculate the conductivity of Ge sample it the donor impurity is added to an extent of one part in 10^8 Ge atoms at room termperature
    (Data Given: N_a = 6.023 $\times 10^{23}$ atoms/gn-mole. At. Wt. of Ge = 72.6).
    (Density of Ge = 5.32gm/cc. μ = 3800 cm^2/v-s.)   **[3]**

OR

4. (a) Define Hall effect. Derive the expression of Hall coefficient, Hall Voltage and discuss their applications.   **[6]**

    (b) Explain the process of recording Holdgram with the help of LASER.   **[3]**

    (c) At what angle of incidence should a beam of sodium light be directed upon the surface of diamond crystal to produce complete polarized light
    (Data Given: Critical angle for diamond = 24.5°)   **[3]**

5. (a) Derive Schroedinger time independent wave equation.   **[6]**

    (b) Define phase velocity, Group velocity and Derive their expressions   **[4]**

    (c) Calculate the De-Broglie wavelength associated with 1 Mev proton (m_p = 1.67 $\times 10^{-27}$ kg)   **[3]**

OR

6. (a) Explain Heisenberg Uncertainty Principle and prove this principle using single slit Diffraction experiment   **[6]**

    (b) Calculate the energy and momentum of an electron confined in a rigid box of width 2A° for lowest energy state.   **[4]**

    (c) Does the matter waves are electromagnetic waves? Explain.   **[3]**

7. (a) Explain the synthesis of nanoparticles through colloidal route with diagram.   **[6]**

   (b) Differentiate between Type-I and Type-II Superconductor with diagram   **[4]**

   (c) Explain two applications of Superconductivity.   **[3]**

OR

8. (a) Explain Meissner effect and Critical magnetic field for Superconductivity.   **[6]**

   (b) Explain the optical and electrical properties of nanoparticles   **[4]**

   (c) Explain the applications of nanoparticles in medical and electronic Industry.   **[3]**

NOVEMBER 2013

Time: 2 Hours   **Max. Marks: 50**

Physical Constants:

Avogadro's number = 6.023×10^{23} gms/mole.

Charge on electron (e) = 1.6×10^{-19} C

Plank's constant (h) = 6.63×10^{-34} J-sec

Mass of electron (me) = 9.1×10^{-31} Kg

Velocity of light (c) = 3×10^{8} m/sec.

1. (a) What are Newton's rings ? Draw the experimental set-up to obtain Newton's rings in the laboratory. Show that diameters of Newton's dark rings are proportional to the square root of natural numbers.   **[6]**

   (b) Define the following terms: **[3]**

      (i) Reverberation.

      (ii) Intensity of sound.

      (iii) Timbre of sound.

   (c) Calculate the natural frequency of vibration for X-cut quartz plate of thickness 5.5 mm.   **[3]**

OR

2. (a) What is piezoelectric effect ? Explain the method to produce ultrasonic waves by using piezoelectric oscillator.   **[6]**

   (b) What is diffraction ? Distinguish between Fresnel and Fraunhofer diffraction (2 points).   **[3]**

   (c) Interference fringes are produced with monochromatic light falling normally on a wedge shaped film of refractive index 1.4. The angle of wedge is 10 sec of an arc and the distance between successive fringes is 0.5 cm. What is the wavelength of light used ?   **[3]**

3. (a) Explain the propagation of light through a quartz crystal plate for normal incidence. When **[6]**

  (i) Optic axis is parallel to the crystal surface and lying in the plane of incidence.

  (ii) Optic axis is perpendicular to the crystal surface and lying in the plane of incidence.

  (iii) Optic axis is inclined to the crystal surface and lying in the plane of incidence.

 (b) What is the effect of following factors on the conductivity of semiconductors ? **[3]**

  (i) Increase in impurity of concentration.

  (ii) Increase in temperature.

  (iii) Increase in intensity of light.

 (c) The hall coefficient of a specimen of a doped Silicon is found to be 3.66×10^4 m^3/C. The resistivity of the specimen is 8.93×10^{-3} Ωm. Determine the mobility of the charge carriers. **[3]**

OR

4. (a) Explain the classification of solids into conductors, semiconductors and insulators on the basis of band theory of solids. **[6]**

 (b) Explain the following: **[3]**

  (i) Stimulated emission.

  (ii) Metastable state.

  (iii) Population inversion.

 (c) Calculate the specific rotation of the sugar solution of 4.5% concentration, if the plane of polarization is rotated through 6.8° in passing through a length of 1.8 decimeter of the solution. **[3]**

5. (a) Derive an expression for energy of a particle trapped in an infinite potential wall. **[6]**

 (b) State and explain De Broglie's hypothesis of matter waves. State any two properties of matter waves. **[3]**

 (c) The uncertainty in the location of the particle is equal to its De Brogile wavelength. Show that the uncertainty in the velocity of a particle is equal to the particle velocity itself. **[3]**

OR

6. (a) State and explain Heisenberg's uncertainty principle. Illustrate it by an experiment of electron diffraction at a single slit. **[6]**

 (b) What is wave function ψ ? Write down the conditions satisfied by wave function ψ.**[4]**

(c) Calculate the energy difference between the ground state and first excited state of an electron in the rigid box of length 1 A°. **[3]**

7. (a) What is superconductivity ? Explain the BCS theory of superconductors. **[6]**

   (b) Explain following properties of nano-particles: **[4]**

      (i) Optical property.

      (ii) Electrical property.

   (c) Explain the applications of nanoparticles in medical and electronic field. **[3]**

OR

8. (a) Explain the synthesis of gold nanoparticles by colloidal route method. **[6]**

   (b) Explain D.C. and A.C. Josephson effect. **[4]**

   (c) Distinguish between Type-I and Type-II superconductors. (Any 3 points) **[3]**

MAY 2014

Time: 2 Hours   **Max. Marks: 50**

Constants:

   1. $h = 6.63 \times 10^{-34}$ J.s

   2. $m_e = 9.1 \times 10^{-31}$ kg

   3. $e = 1.6 \times 10^{-19}$ C

   4. $c = 3 \times 10^{8}$ m/s

1. (a) Derive the equation of path difference between reflected rays when monochromatic light of wavelength 'λ' falls with angle of incidence 'I' on the uniform thickness film of refractive index 'μ'. Write the conditions of maxima and minima. **[6]**

   (b) Explain how cavitation technique can be used for cleaning purpose. **[3]**

   (c) Calculate the intensity level of a fighter plane just leaving the runway having a sound intensity of about 100 W/m². Given that threshold intensity $= 10^{-12}$ W/m². **[3]**

OR

2. (a) What is magnetostriction effect? With the help of neat circuit diagram, explain the working of magnetostriction oscillator to obtain the ultrasonic waves. **[6]**

   (b) Define diffraction of light. Draw intensity distribution pattern obtained because of diffraction of light at a single slit and label the significant points in the same. **[3]**

   (c) In a grating, the angle of diffraction for the second order principal maximum for the light of wavelength 5×10^{-5} cm is 30°. Calculate the number of lines per centimetre of the grating surface. **[3]**

3. (a) Explain double refraction and hence give Huygen's theory of double refraction.   **[6]**

   (b) Explain Fermi-Dirac distribution function specifying the meaning of each term in it. **[3]**

   (c) A slab of silicon 2 cm in length 1.5 cm wide and 2mm thick is applied with magnetic field of 0.4 T along its thickness. When a current of 75 A flows along the length, the voltage measured across the width is 0.81 mV. Calculate the concentration of mobile electrons in silicon.   **[3]**

OR

4. (a) Derive the expression for the conductivity of intrinsic and extrinsic semiconductor. **[6]**

   (b) What is difference between normal photography and holography? Why lasers are used to record hologram ?   **[3]**

   (c) Explain only the pumping process in Ruby laser and He-Ne laser.   **[3]**

5. (a) State and explain Heisenberg's uncertainty principle. Prove the same for pair of variables energy and time.   **[6]**

   (b) Explain in brief, working of Scanning Tunneling Microscope (STM).   **[4]**

   (c) What accelerating potential would be required for a proton with zero initial velocity to acquire a velocity corresponding to its de-Broglie wavelength of 10^{-10} m. [Given: $m_p = 1.67 \times 10^{-27}$ kg]   **[3]**

OR

6. (a) Deduce Schrodinger's time independent wave equation.   **[6]**

   (b) Define phase velocity of a matter wave. Show that phase velocity of matter wave is greater than velocity of light.   **[4]**

   (c) Starting from $\lambda = \dfrac{h}{mv}$, obtain $\lambda = \dfrac{h}{\sqrt{2mE}}$, where E is KE of the particle.   **[3]**

7. (a) Discuss the electrical and structural properties of nano-materials.   **[6]**

   (b) State Meissner effect. Why materials in superconducting state exhibit diamagnetism.   **[4]**

   (c) State any six applications of superconductors.   **[3]**

OR

8. (a) What is superconductivity ? Explain BCS theory of superconductors.   **[6]**

   (b) Explain any one physical method of synthesis of nano-particles.   **[4]**

   (c) Explain any one application of nanotechnology.   **[3]**

DECEMBER 2014

Time: 2 Hours   **Max. Marks: 50**

Physical Constants:

    1. $h = 6.63 \times 10^{-34}$ J.sec.

    2. $e = 1.6 \times 10^{-19}$ C

    3. $m_e = 9.1 \times 10^{-31}$ Kg

    4. $C = 3 \times 10^8$ m/s

1. (a) Prove that in Newton's ring by reflected light the diameter of bright ring is proportional to square root of the odd natural numbers. **[6]**

    (b) Distinguish between musical sound and noise. **[3]**

    (c) A monochromatic beam of light of wavelength 5893 A° is incident normally on the top of a glass which is coated by transparent material MgF_2 having R.I. 1.38. Calculate smallest thickness of the MgF_2 layer which will act as a non reflecting surface. **[3]**

OR

2. (a) Define magnetostriction effect. Explain how magnetostriction oscillator is used to produce ultrasonic waves, with the help of neat ckt. diagram. **[6]**

    (b) What is diffraction ? What are the types of diffraction ? Distinguish between them (any two point). **[3]**

    (c) The average reverberation time of a hall is 1.5 sec. and the area of interior surface is 3340 m^2. If the volume of the hall is 13000 m^3. Find the absorption coefficient. **[3]**

3. (a) Explain the construction and working of Ruby laser with the help of energy level diagram. **[6]**

    (b) Explain Fermi dirac probability distribution function with the meaning of each symbol in it. **[3]**

    (c) Calculate the conductivity of pure silicon at room temperature when the concentration of charge carriers is $1.6 \times 10^{10}/cm^3$. Given that, $\mu_e = 1500$ cm^2/V.Sec. $\mu_n = 500$ cm^2/V.sec. **[3]**

OR

4. (a) Explain Hall effect. Derive the equation of Hall voltage and Hall coefficient. **[6]**

    (b) Explain propagation of light in a doubly refracting crystal when the optic axis is parallel to the crystal surface, with the help of neat diagram. **[3]**

    (c) How should the polarizer and analyzer be oriented to reduce the beam of light to (i) 50% (ii) 25% of its original intensity. **[3]**

5. (a) Deduce Schrodinger time independent wave equation.   **[6]**

    (b) Define group velocity. Show that the group velocity of matter wave is equal to particle velocity.   **[4]**

    (c) Calculate the de Broglie wavelength of electron having kinetic energy 1 KeV.   **[3]**

OR

6. (a) State Heisenberg's uncertainty principle and prove it by thought experiment of electron diffraction at a single slit.   **[6]**

    (b) What is wave function ? Explain what is normalization of wave function.   **[4]**

    (c) An electron is trapped in a rigid box of width 2 A°. Find its lowest energy level.   **[3]**

7. (a) Explain critical field of a superconductor and give any three points to differentiate type – I and type – II superconductors.   **[6]**

    (b) Explain the applications of nanoparticles in automobile and electronic industry.   **[4]**

    (c) Explain electrical properties of nano-particles.   **[3]**

OR

8. (a) Explain the synthesis of nanoparticles in automobile and electronic by colloidal route with diagram.   **[6]**

    (b) Explain the Meissner effect. What important property of superconductor it explain.**[4]**

    (c) Explain two applications of superconductivity.   **[3]**

MAY 2015

[Time: 2 Hours   Max. Marks: 50

Physical Constants:

1. $h = 6.63 \times 10^{-34}$ J.Sec.

2. $c = 3 \times 10^8$ m/s

3. $e = 1.6 \times 10^{-19}$ C

4. $m_e = 9.1 \times 10^{-31}$ kg.

5. $m_p = 1.67 \times 10^{-27}$ kg.

1. (a) Derive an equation for path difference in reflected light when monochromatic light falls on the uniform thickness film and hence state the conditions for maxima and minima.   **[6]**

    (b) State any two factors affecting the acoustics of a hall and explain in brief remedies on that.   **[3]**

    (c) Calculate the reverberation time of hall with volume of 1500 m^3 and total absorption is equivalent to 100 m^2 Sabine.   **[3]**

OR

2. (a) What is Piezoelectric effect ? Draw a neat circuit diagram and explain Piezoelectric generator for the production of ultrasonic waves. **[6]**

(b) Explain the formation of Newton's rings in the laboratory. **[3]**

(Note: Derivation is not expected).

(c) A laser light of wavelength 6328 A.U. falls normally on a grating which is 2 cm long. The first order spectrum is observed at an angle of 20°. Find the total number of slits on grating. **[3]**

3. (a) Explain with neat labeled diagram construction and working of Ruby laser. **[6]**

(b) What is Fermi level ? Show the position of Fermi level in P-type semiconductor at temperature T = 0 K and T > 0 K. **[3]**

(c) Calculate the number of acceptors to be added to a germanium sample to obtain the resistivity of 10 Ω cm. **[3]**

(μ = 1700 cm^2/V.sec.)

OR

4. (a) What is Hall effect ? Derive the equation of Hall voltage. **[6]**

(b) State and prove Law of Malus. **[3]**

(c) A retardation plate of thickness 2.275×10^{-3} cm is cut with its faces parallel to optic axis. If the emergent beam of light is elliptically polarized. Find the wavelength of monochromatic light made incident normally on the plate. Given that, μ_0 = 1.586, μ_e = 1.592. **[3]**

5. (a) State and explain Heisenberg's Uncertainty principle. Illustrate the same with electron diffraction at a single slit. **[6]**

(b) What is wave function ψ ? Give the physical significance of it. **[4]**

(c) An electron is trapped in a rigid box of width 2 A.U. Find its lowest energy in eV. **[3]**

OR

6. (a) Deduce Schrödinger's time independent wave equation. **[6]**

(b) Define phase velocity and prove that it is always greater than velocity of light. **[4]**

(c) Calculate the de Broglie wavelength of proton when it is accelerated by potential difference of 10 kV. **[3]**

7. (a) State and explain Meissner effect and hence show that superconductivity is influenced by perfect diamagnetism. **[6]**

(b) Explain how colloids are synthesized by the chemical route. **[4]**

(c) Discuss applications of nanotechnology in medical field. **[3]**

OR

8. (a) Explain any two properties of nanoparticle.   **[6]**

(b) Distinguish between type-I and type-II superconductors.   **[4]**

(c) State any six applications of superconductivity.   **[3]**

NOVEMBER 2015

Time: 2 Hours   **Max. Marks: 50**

Constants:

1.   h $= 6.63 \times 10^{-34}$ J.sec

2.   e $= 1.6 \times 10^{-19}$ C

3. $m_e = 9.1 \times 10^{-31}$ kg.

4.   c $= 3 \times 10^8$ m/s

---

1. (a) Prove that in Newton's rings by reflected light the diameter of dark ring is proportional to square root of a natural number.   **[6]**

(b) Explain any two factors affecting the acoustics of a hall and remedies on that.   **[3]**

(c) The classroom has dimension, $20 \times 15 \times 5$ m^3. The reverberation time is 3.5 sec. Calculate the total absorption of its surface and the average absorption   **[3]**

OR

2. (a) Explain piezoelectric effect. Explain how piezoelectric oscillator is used to produce ultrasonic waves, with the help of a neat circuit diagram.   **[6]**

(b) The resultant amplitude of a wave when monochromatic light is diffracted from a single slit is $E_\theta = E_m \dfrac{\text{Sin } \alpha}{\alpha}$. Then derive the condition of minima.   **[3]**

(c) A soap film having refractive index 1.33, and thickness 5×10^{-5} cm is viewed at an angle of 35° to the normal. Find the wavelengths of light in the visible spectrum which will be absent from the reflected light.   **[3]**

3. (a) Explain construction and working of Ruby Laser with the help of energy level diagram.   **[6]**

(b) What is Fermi level ? Explain Fermi-Dirac probability distribution function.   **[3]**

(c) Plane polarized light of wavelength 5×10^{-5} cm is incident on a piece of quarter cut parallel to the optic axis. Find the least thickness of quarter for which the O-ray and E-ray combine to form plane polarized light.   **[3]**

OR

4. (a) Explain Hall effect. Derive the equation of Hall voltage and Hall coefficient. **[6]**

   (b) State and prove Malus law. **[3]**

   (c) Calculate the number of acceptors to be added to a germanium sample to obtain the resistivity of 20 Ω cm. **[3]**

      Given:

      $$\mu = 1700 \text{ cm}^2/\text{V.sec.}$$

5. (a) Deduce Schrödinger's time independent wave equation. **[6]**

   (b) Define phase (wave) velocity. Show that the phase velocity of matter wave is greater than the velocity of light. **[4]**

   (c) Calculate the de Broglie wavelength of electron of energy 1 keV. **[3]**

OR

6. (a) State Heisenberg's Uncertainty principle and prove it by thought experiment of electron diffraction at a single slit. **[6]**

   (b) What is wave function ? Explain what is normalization of wave function. **[4]**

   (c) The lowest energy of an electron trapped in a rigid box is 4.19 eV. Find the width of the box in A.U. **[3]**

7. (a) Explain: **[6]**

      (i) Critical field

      (ii) Meissner effect.

   (b) Explain any two properties of nano-particles in brief. **[4]**

   (c) Explain the applications of nano-particles in electronic industry. **[3]**

OR

8. (a) Explain the synthesis of nano-particles by chemical method in colloidal form with diagram and example. **[6]**

   (b) Explain in brief the BCS theory of superconductivity. **[4]**

   (c) Give any six applications of superconductivity. **[3]**

MAY 2016

Time: 2 Hours   **Max. Marks: 50**

Physical Constants:

1. Mass of electron = m_e = 9.1×10^{-31} Kg

2. Charge on electron = e = 1.9×10^{-19} C

3. Mass of proton = m_p = 1.673×10^{-27} kg

4. Mass of neutron = m_n = 1.675×10^{-27} kg

5. Plank's constant = h = 6.63×10^{-34} J.sec.

6. Velocity of light = C = 3×10^8 m/s

1. (a) For a plane diffraction grating, starting from the equations of resultant amplitude and intensity, derive conditions for maxima and minima of the diffraction pattern. **[6]**

   The resultant amplitude is $E_Q = E_m \dfrac{\sin \alpha}{\alpha} \cdot \dfrac{\sin N\beta}{\sin \beta}$

   (b) Explain how ultrasonic waves are used for detection of flaws in metal. **[3]**

   (c) A hall of dimensions 20 m $\times$ 20 m $\times$ 20 m has a reverberation time c 1.2 sec. Find average absorption coefficient. **[3]**

OR

2. (a) What is magnetostriction effect? Explain construction and working of magnetostriction oscillator. **[6]**

   (b) Explain with suitable diagram how interference is used to design anti-reflection coating. **[3]**

   (c) A parallel beam of light 622 nm incident on a glass plate of refractive index 1.5 such that angle of refraction into the plate is 60°. Calculate the smallest thickness of the plate which will appear dark by reflection. **[3]**

3. (a) What is double refraction? Explain this phenomenon on the basis of Huygen's theory. **[6]**

   (b) What is Fermi energy in semiconductor? With the help of labelled diagram show the position of Fermi level in the case of a diode that is connected in forward bias. **[3]**

   (c) Calculate the number of acceptor atoms that need to be doped in germanium sample to obtain the resistivity of 8 Ω cm. [Given: mobility $\mu = 1600$ cm^2/V.s] **[3]**

OR

4. (a) Derive an expression for conductivity in case of intrinsic and extrinsic semiconductors. **[6]**

   (b) What is stimulated emission of radiations? Explain its significance in production of laser. **[3]**

   (c) Explain any one engineering application of laser. **[3]**

5. (a) Deduce Schrödinger's time independent wave equation. **[6]**

   (b) State and explain Heisenberg's uncertainty principle. **[4]**

   (c) Calculate the de Broglie wavelength for a proton moving with velocity 1 percent of velocity of light. **[3]**

OR

6. (a) Define phase velocity and group velocity. Show that group velocity is equal to particle velocity. **[6]**

   (b) Explain why probability of finding of a particle cannot be predicted by the interpretation of wave function ψ. Explain physical significance of $|\psi|^2$. **[4]**

   (c) A neutron is trapped in an infinite potential well of width 10^{-14} m. Calculate its first energy eigenvalue in eV. **[3]**

7. (a) Explain BCS theory of superconductivity. Mention why superconductivity is observed below critical temperature. **[6]**

   (b) Explain any one method for synthesis of nano-particles. **[4]**

   (c) Explain the applications of nano-particles in the field of automobiles. **[3]**

OR

8. (a) Why are the properties of nano-particles different from that of the bulk materials? Explain any two properties of non-particles. **[6]**

   (b) Explain in brief: **[4]**

      (i)   Meissner effect

      (ii) Critical magnetic field.

   (c) Explain the applications of superconductors in the field of electronics. **[3]**

NOVEMBER 2016

Time : 2 Hours   **Max. Marks : 50**

N.B. :—

(1) Figures to the right indicate full marks.

(2) Assume suitable data, if necessary.

(3) Neat diagrams must be drawn wherever necessary.

(4) Use of Non-Programmable calculator is allowed.

Physical Constants :

Avogadro's number = 6.023×10^{23} gms/mole

Charge on electron (e) = 1.6×10^{-19} C

Planck's constant (h) = 6.63×10^{-34} J-sec.

Mass of electron (me)) = 9.1×10^{-31} kg.

Velocity of light (c) = 3×10^8 m/sec.

1. (a) Derive expression for path difference in reflected light and derive the conditions for constructive and destructive interference for a film of uniform thickness   **[6]**

    (b) Explain any one application of ultrasonic waves.   **[3]**

    (c) The average reverberation time of a hall is 1.5 sec and the area of the interior surface is 3340 m^2. If the volume of the hall is 13000 m^3, find the absorption coefficient.   **[3]**

OR

2. (a) Explain magneto-striction effect Explain how magneto-striction oscillator is used to produce ultrasonic waves with the help of neat circuit diagram.   **[6]**

    (b) Explain an application of interference Antireflection coating.   **[3]**

    (c) A plane transmission grating has 5000 lines/cm. Find out the highest order spectrum observed if incident light has X = 6000 $\overset{\circ}{A}$.   **[3]**

3. (a) What is Double refraction ? Explain Huygens's theory of double refraction.   **[6]**

    (b) What is Holography ? Explain the process of hologram recording.   **[3]**

    (c) Calculate the mobility of charge carriers in doped silicon whose conductivity is 100/ Ω-m and the Hall coefficient is 3.6×10^{-4} m^3/C.   **[3]**

OR

4. **(a)** Derive an expression for conductivity in intrinsic and extrinsic Semiconductors. **[6]**

   (b) Define the following **[3]**

   (i) Stimulated Emission (ii) Meta-stable state (iii) Pumping.

   (c) Plane polarized light passes through a positive double refracting crystal of thickness 40 μm and emerges out as circularly polarized light. If the birefringence of the crystal is 4×10^{-5}, find the wavelength of the incident light. **[3]**

5. **(a)** Derive an expression for energy of a particle trapped in an infinite potential well. **[6]**

   (b) Define phase velocity and group velocity. Derive the relation between them. **[4]**

   (c) An electron beam is accelerated from rest through a potential difference of 200 V. Calculate the associated wavelength. **[3]**

OR

6. **(a)** What is De-Broglie's hypothesis of matter waves. Show that the De-Broglie's wavelength of a charged particle is inversely proportional to the square root of the accelerating potential. **[6]**

   (b) Write down the conditions which are to be satisfied by well behaved wave function. **[4]**

   (c) Calculate the energy required to excite the electron from its ground state to fourth excited state in a rigid box of length 0.1 nm. **[3]**

7. **(a)** What is superconductivity ? Explain the Meissner effect in superconductors. **[6]**

   (b) Explain the following properties of Nano-particles **[4]**

   (i) Magnetic property

   (ii) Mechanical property.

   (c) Explain the applications of nano particles in medical and automobile field. **[3]**

OR

8. **(a)** Explain the synthesis of Nano particles by using mechanical method. **[6]**

   (b) Explain zero electrical resistance property and isotope effect in superconductor. **[4]**

   (c) Explain any one application of superconductors in brief. **[3]**

✠ ✠ ✠

MAY 2017

Time : 2 Hours   **Max. Marks : 50**

Instructions to the candidates :

(1) Neat diagrams must be drawn wherever necessary.

(2) Figures to the right indicate full marks.

(3) Use of logarithmic tables, slide rule, Mollier charts, electronic pocket calculator and steam tables is allowed.

(4) Assume suitable data, if necessary.

Constants :

(1) Mass of electron = 9.1×10^{-31} kg

(2) Charge on electron, e = $1.6 \times 10^{-1}k^9$

(3) Mass of proton, M_p = 1.673×10^{-27} g

(4) Mass of Nutron, M_n = 1.673×10^{-27} kg

(5) Planck's constant, h = 6.63×10^{-34} J.s

(6) Velocity of light in vacuum, c = 3×10^8 m/s

1. **(a)** A thin film of uniform thickness is illuminated by a monochromatic light. Derive an expression for path difference for the reflected rays system. Hence obtain the conditions for constructive and destructive interference. **[6]**

   (b) What is reverberation time? Explain any two measures to control reverberation time in an auditorium. **[3]**

   (c) Calculate the reverberation time for an empty hall of volume 1200 m^3 that has total sound absorption of 450 m^2 sabine. When the hall is completely occupied, total sound absorption is further increased by 450 m^2 sabine. Hence calculate the reverberation time. **[3]**

OR

2. **(a)** What is piezoelectric effect ? Draw neat and labeled diagram for piezoelectric oscillator and hence explain its construction and working. **[6]**

   (b) What is diffraction of light ? Differentiate between Fresnel and Fraunhoffer diffraction (two points). **[3]**

   (c) A monochromatic light of wavelength 5500 $\overset{\circ}{A}$ incident normally on a slit of width 2×10^{-4} cm. Calculate the angular position of first and second minimum. **[3]**

3. **(a)** Why is the combination of Helium and Neon gases chosen in He-Ne laser system? Explain construction and working of He-Ne laser system with the help of energy level diagram. **[6]**

   (b) Define Fermi level for a semiconductor. Draw a neat and labeled diagram showing position of Fermi level in intrinsic semiconductor and in N-type semiconductor. **[3]**

(c) A sample of intrinsic germanimum at room temperature has a carrier concentration 4.41×10^{22} cm^3. Donor impurity is added in the ratio 1 donor atom per 10^8 atoms/cm^3 of germanium. Determine the resistivity of the material thus formed. (Given : m$_e$ 3800 cm^2/V.s) **[3]**

OR

4. **(a)** What is hall effect ? Derive the expression for Hall voltage and Hall coefficient. State applications of Hall effect. **[6]**

(b) What is double refraction ? Draw neat and labelled diagram (either for positive or negative crystal) showing propagation of light within a doubly refracting crystal when optic axis is : **[3]**
  (i) parallel to crystal surface
  (ii) perpendicular to crystal surface

(c) Sugar solution is kept in a 20 cm long tube. When plane polarized light is passed trhough this solution, its plane of polarization is rotated by 10°. If the concentration of sugar is 0.07575, calculate the specific rotation of sugar. **[3]**

5. **(a)** Deduce Schrodinger's time independent wave equation. **[6]**

(b) What is de-Broglie hypothesis. Derive an expression for de-Broglie wavelength for an electron when it is accelerated by potential difference 'V' **[4]**

(c) Calculate the energy (in eV) with which a proton has to acquire de-Broglie wavelength of 0.1Å **[3]**

OR

6. **(a)** State and explain Heisenberg's uncertainty principle. Illustrate the principle by electron diffraction at a single slit. **[6]**

(b) Explain physical significance of wave function ψ and (ψ)^2. State the mathematical conditions that wave function ψ should satisfy. **[4]**

(c) A neutron is trapped in an infinite potential well of width 1 Å Calculate the values of energy and momentum in its ground state. **[3]**

7. **(a)** Explain critical magnetic field of superconductor. Differentiate between type-I and type-II superconductors (four points). **[6]**

(b) With necessary diagram, explain physical method for synthesis of nanoparticles. **[4]**

(c) State applications of nano-particles. Explain any one applications. **[3]**

OR

8. **(a)** What is nanotechnology ? Explain optical and electrical properties of nano-particles. **[6]**

(b) Explain Meissner effect and show that superconductors exhibit perfect diamagnetism. **[4]**

(c) State applications of superconductors. Explain any one application. **[3]**

✠ ✠ ✠

Notes

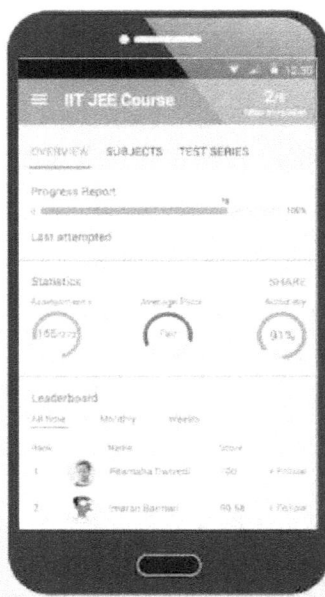

www.ingramcontent.com/pod-product-compliance
Lightning Source LLC
Chambersburg PA
CBHW081326090726
47907CB00010B/2385